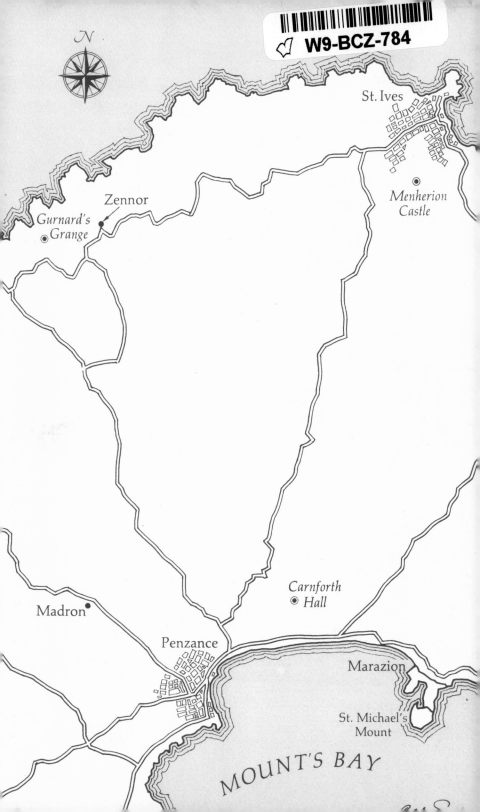

N

St. Ives

Menherion
Castle

Zennor

Gurnard's
Grange

Carnforth
Hall

Madron

Penzance

Marazion

St. Michael's
Mount

MOUNT'S BAY

PENMARRIC

by SUSAN HOWATCH

SIMON AND SCHUSTER

NEW YORK

To Joseph

CONTENTS

THE NARRATORS
AND THEIR STANDARDS

I   MARK: 1890
    Honor and Dishonor   9

II JANNA: 1890–1904
    Love and Hate   107

III ADRIAN: 1904–1914
    Good and Evil   241

IV PHILIP: 1914–1930
    Truth and Falsehood   373

V   JAN-IVES: 1930–1945
    Justice and Injustice   543

I

MARK: 1890
Honor and Dishonor

He was a young man of twenty, always travelling about on intolerable daily journeys which seemed twice the normal length. . . . He worked far into the night. Those about him ascribed his perpetual labours to fear of getting too fat.
—English Society in the Early Middle Ages,
Doris Mary Stenton

Of medium height and stocky build, with a tendency to corpulence, he gave the impression of a figure molded for strength. Essentially a man of action he was never idle. His restless energy is perhaps his most marked characteristic . . . he had the taste for literature of a well-educated man, and he enjoyed the society of wits and scholars.
—Oxford History of England:
From Domesday Book to Magna Carta,
A. L. Poole

Despite the looseness of his personal morals he commanded affection and respect . . .
—"Henry II,"
Encyclopaedia Britannica

1

[1]

I was ten years old when I first saw the Inheritance and twenty
years old when I first saw Janna Roslyn, but my reaction to both
was identical. I wanted them.

I wanted the Inheritance because the Gothic style of that architectural nightmare of a house captivated my child's imagination,
because my mother's fight to secure the place for me seemed to
my child's eyes not shabby and degrading but shining with nobility and courage, because the estate had been denied me and
there is nothing a child wants so much as something he cannot
have. And I wanted Janna Roslyn because I was twenty years
old and fancied women, particularly beautiful women, and particularly women who were beautiful yet had no place among the
class into which I had been born.

We met by chance. I had no good reason for being in Zillan churchyard at two o'clock on that hot July afternoon in 1890; I had no good reason even for being in Zillan. I was a stranger in that part of Cornwall, for I had been born and bred near the Helford River, and the gentle mildness of South Cornwall with its trees and estuaries and rolling hills is a world away from the stark mining coast of the North with its windswept moors, precipitous cliffs and treacherous surf.

Zillan was a moorland parish of the North.

I had walked there that afternoon after quarreling with my father at his temporary residence in the nearby parish, and, being greatly upset at the time, I paid no attention to my surroundings until I found myself wandering up the village street toward the church. Zillan was a prettier village than the usual austere huddle of cottages that passes for a village in North Cornwall. The gardens of the graystone cottages were filled with flowers, the pub called The Tinners' Luck had been freshly painted, and even the local stray dog looked well fed. Evidently the poverty that was following the steady decline of the Cornish mining industry had so far left this corner of the Duchy untouched. With a glance at the smoke belching from the cluster of mines on the horizon, I opened the lych-gate into the churchyard and strolled aimlessly beneath the shadow of the Norman tower toward the main door.

In the porch I paused, uncertain what to do next. I was trying not to think of my recent quarrel with my father, trying not to think of my interminable battles with my mother, trying not to think of the Inheritance which I had wanted so much for so long. I dimly realized that I was more alone than I had ever been in my life, but I was too lost and confused to be fully aware of the extent of my unhappiness. I simply remained in the porch of Zillan church as if I were taking sanctuary from some oppressive pursuing force, and as I stood there a breeze blew across the moors and the afternoon sun shone on that moorland parish from that cloudless summer sky. It was peaceful in the churchyard. I was aware of the tranquillity suddenly, of an overwhelming calmness. Everywhere was so still. The very landscape seemed poised as if it were mysteriously waiting, and as I remained motionless, mesmerized by that air of expectancy, I looked through the lych-gate to the end of the village street and saw the solitary figure of a woman walking slowly toward me across the moors.

[2]

She wore black and carried a spray of red roses.

I went on watching her from the shadow of the porch, and somewhere far above me in the church tower a bell began to toll the hour.

She passed the first cottage on the outskirts of the village, and so smooth and effortless were her movements that she seemed to glide noiselessly down the narrow street. She looked neither to right nor to left. The light breeze from the moors lifted the veil of her hat for a second, and she raised a black-gloved hand to touch the veil back into place.

She reached the lych-gate. The flowers were only simple wild roses such as the ones that grew on the walls of the cottages nearby, and yet their very simplicity made the hothouse roses of London seem vulgar and ostentatious. She walked through the churchyard toward the porch, and I was on the point of moving out of the shadows into the light when she saw me.

She must have been surprised to see a stranger in that remote moorland village, but not even a nuance of her surprise showed itself in her face. She went on walking as if I did not exist, and I saw she intended to walk past the porch and down the path to the other side of the churchyard.

I moved involuntarily. I was hatless, but my hand moved upward before I remembered I was bareheaded.

"Good afternoon," I said.

She allowed herself to look at me. Her eyes were blue, wide-set, black-lashed behind her veil. The next moment she had inclined her head slightly in acknowledgment of my greeting and walked past me without a word.

I stared after her. Presently I strolled to the churchyard wall and stole a glance at the graves behind the church. She was there. The red roses were laid beside a new tombstone and she was standing motionless beside it, her head bent forward, her hands clasped before her. She did not see me.

I decided to sit on the wall and survey the architecture of a nearby house which I assumed to be the rectory. I inspected it for some time. I was just deciding that it was a most unprepossessing building when I heard the click of the lych-gate and saw her walk away down the street. At the end of the village she took the path again across the moors and I went on watching her until she had vanished from sight.

As soon as she was gone my mind was made up; I was no longer so dejected that I knew not where to turn next. Soon afterward I was hurrying back to my father's house to seek permission to stay longer with him in that part of Cornwall, and throughout the entire journey across the moors to Morvah I could think of nothing but red roses glowing in a quiet country church-yard and a black veil blowing in the wind.

[3]

Until that moment I suppose—reluctantly—that my mother had been the most important woman in my life. This may seem a very obvious statement since most mothers are expected to hold a special place in their sons' affections, but my mother was not like other mothers and my affection for her was so distorted by dislike and resentment that our relationship could hardly be con-sidered typical.

"The first thing you must understand," said my mother when I renewed my acquaintance with her at the age of ten after a separation that had lasted six years, "is that in regard to Our Inheritance I consider it a matter of Honor that Justice should be done."

My mother, I discovered, always spoke of honor and justice as if the initial letters were written in capitals.

"You see," she added in explanation, "Penmarric should have been mine." We were sitting in the large and dreary drawing room of that townhouse in London, I a small boy in a stiff black suit and stiffer collar, she very handsome in violet silk, black lace and an ugly string of pearls. "The entire estate and all the Penmar fortune would have been mine if my father—like the majority of men—had not possessed this ingrained prejudice against women. He was fond of me in his own way, but it was my brother Arthur who was the apple of his eye. It made no difference to him that Arthur was feckless, foolish and irrespon-sible while I was intelligent, able and devoted to every brick of Penmarric and every inch of the estate. As far as my father was concerned, Arthur was the boy, the son and heir, and I was a mere daughter, little better than a vegetable, someone who must be married off as well and as early as possible. . . . Even after

Arthur was drowned in the sailing accident my father's attitude toward me never wavered. For a time I did hope that he might change his views and realize I was deserving of all he might wish to bestow upon me, but then . . ." She paused. Her mouth narrowed into a hard line; her black eyes were colder than a midwinter sea. "Then," said my mother, "Giles came."

"Do not under any circumstances mention the name of Giles Penmar to your mother," her devoted slave and first cousin Robert Yorke had begged me when we had met for the first time earlier that afternoon. He had been ordered by my mother to meet me at the station and escort me to the townhouse, and throughout the journey he had regaled me with so many worried warnings and anxious instructions that I had nearly run away in sheer fright. But he had not meant to frighten me, of course; he was merely eager that my confrontation with my mother should be as painless as possible. He was a small, mild, kindly man with an air that reminded me of my father's cocker spaniel. The townhouse in Park Lane where my mother lived belonged to him; so subjugated was he by the force of her personality, so enthralled by a nature so different from his own, that he gave her whatever she wanted, did whatever he was told, expected—and received—nothing but a peremptory affection in return.

"Dear Robert," said my mother to me later. "He would have married me if I had been free to become his wife, but fortunately my marital ties with your father have prevented him from making such a foolish mistake. Really, men are extraordinarily foolish sometimes! Even my father, who was exceptionally intelligent, made a complete fool of himself where Giles was concerned . . ."

"Do not speak to your mother of Giles," Cousin Robert Yorke had begged me in the carriage on the way from the station. "Maud is very sensitive on the subject of Giles Penmar."

". . . of course his name wasn't really Giles Penmar at all," my mother was saying. I can see her now, pouring tea from a silver teapot, rings flashing on her fingers, arrogance coruscating from the straight line of her back, the carriage of her head and the tilt of her elbow. "It was Giles Baker. Baker was the family name, you know, before my grandfather won Penmarric from the Prince Regent in a game of dice and then proceeded to change his name to suit his change of fortune. Giles was a distant cousin. An adventurer, of course. All the Penmars were adventurers with an eye for making money. My father, for instance, more than doubled the family fortune when he was in India as a young man. . . . So it was not unnatural that Giles, the poor relation, should have had an eye for family fortunes. My brother Arthur's death was his golden chance. He arrived at Penmarric, inveigled himself into my ailing father's affections, changed his name to Penmar, even made himself agreeable to me—oh yes, he knew how to be charming! All successful adventurers do, no doubt, and Giles was certainly successful. By a combination of trickery, knavery and malign influence he arranged matters so that when my father finally died . . ."

"The entire family estate was left to Giles," Cousin Robert Yorke had whispered to me while I had been receiving my frenzied briefing for the meeting with my mother. "It was monstrously unjust and the most crushing blow to poor Maud. Her father at least had the decency to leave her a moderate annuity, but Penmarric and the rest of the Penmar fortune fell into that blackguard's hands. However, if Giles thought that Maud would accept the situation and let the matter rest he was very gravely mistaken . . ."

". . . so naturally," said my mother, setting down the teapot with a bang, "I considered it my moral duty to take the matter to court. It was a point of Honor. Justice had to be done. I trust, child, that your father has brought you up with a proper respect for Honorable Conduct, if for nothing else . . ."

". . . Under no circumstances mention your father to Maud," Cousin Robert Yorke had pleaded with me earlier. "Maud is very sensitive on the subject of her unfortunate marriage to your father."

". . . Your father told you nothing about the Inheritance, I presume," said my mother in contempt as she reached for a hot buttered crumpet. "How typical! He told you nothing, I suppose, about the legal battles I've been fighting—and am continuing to fight—since I left his roof six years ago? Nothing about my ceaseless quest for Justice—nothing about my continuing efforts to ensure that the Inheritance will one day be yours? Well, perhaps I should hardly be surprised. No doubt he's been poisoning your mind with untruths about me during the past six years!"

I managed to speak. I opened my mouth and heard a quavering treble that sounded most unlike my voice say: "He never speaks of you, ma'am."

"You may call me Mama. There's no need to address me as if I were the Queen. So Laurence never speaks of me! How remarkable! And do you and Nigel never speak of me to him?"

"No, Mama. Nanny said we weren't to."

"Dear me, what a disagreeable woman! Well, since I am considered so unspeakable, why did your father permit you to visit me for a week in this fashion?"

And suddenly I was back in Cornwall, back at my home in Gweek by the Helford River, back in that mellow beautiful manor house where my father's family had lived for hundreds of years before an upstart named Baker had gambled his way into a fortune and changed his name to Penmar. I was in my father's study and my father was holding my mother's letter in his hands and saying in that quiet voice I loved so much: "But of course you must go, Mark. You have a filial obligation to visit her if she wishes it."

And all I could say was a mutinous "But why does she want to see me? She's never wanted to see me before! And why doesn't she want to see Nigel? He's her son, too!"

"Perhaps Nigel will see her later."

And later in the nursery Nigel had said placidly to me, "I don't mind her not wishing to see me. I don't suppose she's nearly so nice as Nanny." Nigel was Nanny's favorite. He had golden curls, blue eyes and the virtuous expression of an insufferable cherub. "In fact the more I think about it," said Nigel, "the nicer I think it would be if Mama preferred you to me. Sometimes I don't think it's very fair that everyone prefers me to you."

He seemed surprised when I started fighting him, although he should have known by that time that I always seized every excuse he gave me to use my fists. Some children are incorrigibly slow learners.

"Mark," my father was always saying to me wearily, "you must make more effort to control your unfortunate temper."

My mother had possessed an unfortunate temper. Even though she had left Gweekellis Manor more than six years ago, the memory of her temper lingered on among the servants.

"You take after your mama," Nanny was in the habit of saying to me, and each time she would add darkly to the nursemaid, "More's the pity."

"Well!" said my mother, pouring herself a second cup of tea in the gloomy drawing room of Cousin Robert Yorke's house in Park Lane and pausing to regard me with a critical eye. "You're a little short, a trifle stout and undeniably plain, but you'll do. I recognize that look in your eyes. You're tough. You're like me. Don't look so horrified! That's a compliment. I need a tough strong son. Now help yourself to another crumpet and listen to what I propose to do. I have a feeling you and I are going to get on exceedingly well together."

She was wrong. We did not get on well at all. Looking back, I can see that she wrongly estimated her own needs and wrongly assumed she required a tough strong son. She did not. She wanted a son who would echo her, a weak shadow, a masculine complement to her dominant personality. When I was a child not yet eleven years old she subjugated me as she subjugated Robert Yorke—by sheer force of character—but once I was no longer a child I was no longer so easily held in subjugation. But a relationship had sprung into existence between us that day at the townhouse, and throughout the ten years that followed before I finally broke her will and reversed our roles, we were never indifferent to each other.

"You are ten years old," said my mother to me during that first confrontation in London, "and you have never seen your Inheritance. I intend to remedy that immediately. We leave for Penzance tomorrow."

Evidently this was the sole reason for her request to see me. Ten was judged to be an age when I could clap my hands in delight when I saw my Inheritance for the first time.

Naturally I was excited at the prospect of seeing Penmarric; I thought I would be able to explore the grounds, ride around the estate and tour the house from top to bottom. This, however, was not what my mother had in mind. After an arduous journey to Penzance, three hundred miles away from London in the southwest, we stayed at a hotel on the esplanade called the Metropole and next morning hired a carriage to begin another wearisome journey north over the moors to the parish of St. Just. I was too young to appreciate the scenery; all I knew was that it was a world away from my home at Gweek, from the peaceful estuary and fishing boats. I looked at the landscape of this alien strip of Cornwall and my child's mind thought: The devil would feel quite at home here. For the scenery was bleak and powerful, dominated by stretches of arid moors without trace of a tree or house, and the moors snarled into towering hills crowned with outcrops of black rock. The emptiness of the landscape combined with the steep gradient of the road produced sweeping views; I remember looking back toward Penzance and glimpsing the castle of St. Michael's Mount shimmering far off in the blue of the bay.

For a moment I wished that St. Michael's Mount were my Inheritance, although naturally I did not dare admit as much to my mother.

As we moved inland the mines began to dot the harsh landscape and I had my first glimpse of the copper and tin industry for which Cornwall had been famous for centuries, the stone towers of the engine houses, the black belches of smoke, the eerie piles of slag. There were two mines on the Penmarric estate, my mother told me, but only one, Sennen Garth, was still operating. The other, King Walloe, had been closed for decades.

"Can I go down the mine?" I inquired hopefully.

"Good gracious, no, child, you're not an artisan. . . . Now, look out of the window and you can see the coast of the North. There! Is it not a magnificent view here from the top of the ridge? There are three parishes side by side which border the sea. St. Just is the one to the west, Morvah is straight ahead of us, and Zennor is to the east of Morvah. Penmarric, of course, is in the parish of St. Just."

"Which parish are we in now?"

"Zillan. It's an inland moorland parish lying behind Morvah. . . . Robert, tell the coachman to hurry!"

We continued westward, through the gray mining village of St. Just and out along the road to Land's End, but presently we turned off the Land's End road and headed north to the sea.

"Now," said my mother at last. "Tell the coachman to stop, Robert."

The carriage rolled to a halt.

"Get out, child."

I did as I was told. The spring breeze blew lightly against my cheek and the sun was warm as it shone from the spring skies. There were wildflowers already by the roadside, and beyond the wildflowers the banks of gorse were poised to burst into a blaze of yellow blooms.

My mother grabbed my arm. "Look."

I looked. Across a shallow valley, beyond a spinney of trees unusual in that barren landscape, stood a castle built on cliffs facing the sea. I gasped and then saw on a second examination that the building was not a castle at all but an immense house built of gray-black stone and endowed with turrets and towers and fanciful architectural fripperies which captivated my childish imagination. Later I was to dismiss the whole preposterous design as a contortion of modern taste, but to me, as I saw the house for the first time through my child's eyes, it was beautiful.

"I want that house," said my mother, echoing my thoughts, and the bond was forged that was to chain us to each other throughout all the quarrelsome years ahead. "I want that house, and I'm going to get it—if not for myself, then at least for you."

And I said, "Can we go on? Why are we stopped here? Can we not drive to the house and call on Cousin Giles?"

She looked at me as if I had gone mad. "Call on Giles? My dear child! Do you really think that after six years of incessant litigation I would be received as a guest under the roof which he illegally claims as his own? What an extraordinarily unintelligent remark! I hope you're not going to grow up to be a fool." She turned to our driver, a Cornish yokel who was gaping at our conversation as he struggled to understand our English accents. "Home to Penzance at once, my man. The purpose of our drive is accomplished."

I allowed myself one last look at Penmarric before I followed her into the carriage. It was four years before I was to see my Inheritance again.

[4]

I was fourteen when my mother won her lawsuit and demanded to see me once more. Again we journeyed down to Penmarric, this time with the intention of crossing the threshold since Giles was no longer the legal owner of the house, but Giles had lodged an appeal against the decision and the matter was no longer resolved but *sub judice*. The front door was closed and bolted in our faces; my mother, trembling with rage, battered the panels with her fists, but her gesture was worse than useless. Penmarric still belonged to Giles.

Two more long years of litigation passed, and then came the disaster. The Court of Appeal decided in favor of Giles and the decision of the court below was reversed.

"I shall appeal to the House of Lords!" cried my mother, wild-eyed with grief. "I shall never give up, never!"

But the House of Lords rejected her suit. Years of futile litigation and endless expense had ended in the annihilation of her cause.

Yet still she refused to give up. Something, she decided, must be salvaged from the wreck of her hopes. She would travel down to Penmarric, make her peace with Giles and at least coax him to allow her to visit the house now and then. In vain Cousin Robert Yorke and I pointed out that there was no reason why Giles should pursue a policy of forgiving and forgetting the past twelve years of extreme animosity; in vain we told her she would be wasting her time. She remained—as always when her will was opposed—high-handed, domineering and incorrigibly inflexible.

"Very well," I said with all the aggressive defiance of a sixteen-year-old youth who wished to show some independence. "Go alone, if you wish. But don't expect me to waste my time by coming with you."

"You're coming with me whether you like it or not!" My mother was more than a match for any sixteen-year-old youth anxious to rebel. "Robert, remind the boy of his filial duty!"

"Mark, you really do owe it to your mother, you know," said Cousin Robert obediently. "Maud's worked so hard on your behalf."

I gave in with a great show of sulkiness and my mother somehow managed to refrain from boxing my ears.

It was on this, my third visit to Penmarric, that I first met Giles's children, my three cousins, Raymond, Harry and Clarissa Penmar. In actual fact Giles had only the one child, my cousin Raymond, who was the same age as I was, but Giles's wife, who was now dead, had taken pity on an orphaned nephew and niece of hers, and Giles had assumed the responsibilities of guardianship when he had allowed her to bring them to live at his house. Harry, the adopted son, was by this time eighteen; his sister Clarissa was a year or two younger than Raymond and myself. I knew nothing about them beyond these sparse facts, and later, particularly where Clarissa was concerned, I was to wish I had remained in ignorance. Why was it that I disliked Clarissa so much? At sixteen when I first saw her I was certainly old enough to appreciate her looks, but dark girls have never attracted me, perhaps because they remind me of my mother and her domineering attitudes, and besides, my dislike of Clarissa went further than a mere antipathy to her good looks. On reflection I suspect that my dislike sprang into existence on our first meeting on the steps of Penmarric, when she insulted me with the cattiness of a fifteen-year-old schoolgirl and gave me forewarning of the spitefulness which I was to encounter with such disastrous results when we were older. Perhaps even when I first saw her I sensed that her influence on my life was not destined to be benign.

The trouble began when—to no one's surprise but my mother's —we were refused admittance to the house by the butler. My mother at once demanded to see Giles in person, but the butler, who was by this time very white around the gills, said that Mr. Penmar was indisposed and could see no one. It was at this moment that I had the unfortunate idea of parleying with my cousin Raymond; I suppose I thought that two sixteen-year-old youths were more likely to reach a friendly agreement than our parents were, but that was my mistake. When Raymond emerged cautiously from the hall the first thing he did was to order me off the porch as if I had yellow fever.

"You get away from here!" he yelled with the sort of charm that I at once realized was characteristic of him. He was a tall youth with a spoiled mouth, soft hands and a petulant expression. Pitching his voice loud enough to reach my mother, who was waiting with Cousin Robert in the carriage, he added, "Penmarric will never be yours now, so you can go back to London and rot for all I care!"

"Well, ——— you, old chap," I said politely, in the language I had learned from my years at Eton, and gave in to my overwhelming urge to punch him on the nose.

He fell like a stone.

I was just savoring the effectiveness of my handiwork when the front door flew open and I was face to face with a protagonist far more dangerous than my ineffectual cousin Raymond. His adopted brother Harry was tall and tough, with a strong pair of shoulders and a pair of fists that made me decide that the time had come to beat a quick but graceful retreat.

"Damn you, you bastard," said Harry Penmar through his teeth. "Damn you, get out of here before you wish you'd never come."

And before I could think of a reply his sister appeared, pushing past him and kneeling by Raymond's inert body, her breast rising and falling rapidly in her agitation. I would have looked at her closely if I had had the chance, but by then I was too busy jeering at Harry Penmar as my feet concentrated on the task of widening the gap between us. "And who do you think you are?" I drawled at him insolently, anxious to disguise the fact that I was in full retreat. "The Light Brigade before the Charge?"

But it was the girl who answered me. She looked down at me from the top of the steps as my feet crunched on the gravel of the drive, and suddenly I was aware only of dark eyes blazing and a wild passionate mouth.

"You ugly little brute!" she spat at me. "You fat repulsive cretin, go away and take your abominable mother with you and never—*never*—come near us again!"

Despite my natural aggressiveness and the self-confidence infused by a public school education. I was still more vulnerable than I cared to acknowledge. Sixteen is a sensitive age. I knew I was still a trifle stout. I knew that despite sharing a strong family resemblance with my mother I did not share her good looks. I knew too by this time that I would never be tall. But nevertheless I did not like to hear a young woman, particularly a girl of my own age, tell me to my face that I was short, fat and plain.

I was still staring at her, my cheeks starting to burn with a helpless rage, when my mother called from the carriage in a voice that stopped even Harry Penmar dead in his tracks: "Mark! We leave at once, if you please!"

My third visit to Penmarric was at an end, as much a failure as my mother's attempts to retrieve the Inheritance in the courts of law. Our cause was lost; Giles was beyond appeasement; Penmarric was forever beyond my reach.

It was the first time that I saw my mother cry. She watched Penmarric disappear from sight and shed two large tears, but when Cousin Robert anxiously offered her his handkerchief she pushed it aside.

"Put that away, you silly man," she said, autocratic even in grief, and tilted her head a fraction higher. "Well, that's that, I suppose. I shall return to London and occupy my future time with worthy causes instead of with lawsuits. Women's suffrage, perhaps. That's a worthy cause. Or the propagation of birth control."

Cousin Robert and I exchanged horrified glances but had enough sympathy for her to remain silent and not risk upsetting her further. We ought to have known that despite everything she would never give up hope of recovering Penmarric, even when all hope was seemingly gone. Where Penmarric was concerned she was too much of a fanatic to accept the idea of a total and permanent defeat, and her resilience was such that by the time we arrived at the Metropole Hotel in Penzance she had recovered her composure sufficiently to consider plans for the future. For the time being at least Penmarric could no longer be discussed, but I was judged to be a worthy substitute.

"Well, Mark," she said, having dispatched Cousin Robert on some errand in order that she could speak to me alone, "I have enjoyed seeing you during our struggles for the Inheritance, and I hope that I shall continue to see you even now our struggles are at an end. Why don't you come to London and live with me at the townhouse? You could have your own suite of rooms, a generous allowance and the freedom to sample the cultural delights of the greatest city on earth."

"No, thank you, Mama."

"Why on earth not?" She was affronted by such an abrupt refusal. "How ungrateful!"

"My home is at Gweek with my father."

"Your father! Your dull provincial country squire of a father who always has his nose buried in those dry-as-dust history books! My dear boy, you can't convince me that you have anything in common with him! Now, listen to me. I—"

"No," I said, suddenly losing my temper, "you listen to me! You abandoned me when I was four, dragged me along for a week to Penzance when I was old enough to be interested in your schemes, pulled me away from my home when I was fourteen, kept me with you for a few weeks longer, wrote to me—a big concession, that one!—once a term, and now you have the insufferable insolence to suggest I should abandon everything and become one of your satellites, like poor Cousin Robert!"

It was her turn now to lose her temper. We must have hurled insults at each other for at least ten minutes before she screamed, scarlet with rage, "Go back to your decaying manor house in Gweek, in that case! Go back to your dull, dreary father, and good riddance, and don't come crawling back to me later when you realize your mistake and want to live as a young man about town in London!"

"And don't come crawling back to me," I yelled at her, "when you find yourself face to face with a lonely old age!"

And as I returned to Gweek and to my father I firmly resolved never to set eyes on her again.

[5]

I thought my father would be pleased that I had finally removed myself from my mother's influence, but he said nothing.

Although he had allowed and even encouraged me to see my mother whenever she demanded it, he never questioned me afterward about my visits, and even at the age of ten I sensed he had no more wish to discuss my mother's schemes to regain Penmarric than he had to discuss my mother herself. The unspoken subjects became a barrier between us, and as I grew older it seemed to me that although he always treated me with kindness and interest his conventional parental attitude, so faithfully produced for my benefit, masked a wall of estrangement which hurt as much as it baffled me. I knew I must often remind him of my mother. I could see that Nigel's facile good-naturedness was easier for him to respond to than my own more complex behavior. But I was his elder son, the son who shared his love of history—how hard I had worked at my history!—and it seemed unjust that he should unwittingly be prejudiced against me on account of my mother and all the more unjust since I was the one who yearned to be like him, to live as he lived and to share his standards and beliefs.

He was a quiet man. I could understand why my mother thought he was dull and provincial, for he loathed city life and was always happiest in the tranquil Cornish backwater of Gweek where he could ride a little, mingle occasionally with his friends among the local gentry whom he had known all his life, and, most important of all, write his historical articles and monographs in peace and seclusion. My father did not talk much about honor and justice, the concepts which my mother so dearly loved to brandish, but there was no need for him to talk of them; he gave neither Nigel nor myself long lectures about moral conduct but merely took it for granted that we would follow in his footsteps. For my father was a good man and he was chaste, and the example he set us was so clear that there was no need for it to be defined in words.

So strong was my desire to be like him that I managed to suppress my Penmar inclinations until I was nearly seventeen, but the Penmars were adventurers; whatever virtues they possessed, chastity was not one of them.

Curiously enough it was the quarrel with my mother that proved to be my undoing. It was illogical and incomprehensible to me, but I missed her and would have written to mend the breach between us if my pride had permitted it. But my pride did not permit it, so I reached out instead for the sex my mother represented, and in a fit of depression I turned my back on my father's standards during a casual visit I paid one day to Mullion Cove.

The woman was a fisherman's wife. Her husband was away at sea and she needed money as well as companionship, so I gave her five shillings. She was grateful—and so was I at first, but as soon as the episode was over I found my guilt made me feel even unhappier than I had felt before. To make matters worse I found it impossible to behave as if the incident had never happened and return to a life of abstinence. Finally in a muddled effort to make amends both to my conscience, which was making me miserable, and to my father, who remained unaware of my weakness, I flung myself into my work more energetically than ever before and vowed I would not rest until I had become as fine a scholar as he himself was.

I went early to Oxford. It will sound immodest if I write that there was no more they could teach me at Eton, but I yearned for deeper studies and was anxious to escape from the restrictions of school life to the freedom of the Varsity. I took my final examinations in the summer before my twenty-first birthday and was awarded a first, a great rarity for a young man only twenty years old. My tutor wanted me to stay on and devote myself to an academic life, but I was weary of studies at last after so much concentrated effort and told him I wanted to rest for a time before coming to any firm decision about my future.

A friend invited me to stay at his family's house in London to sample the remainder of the Season, and I accepted. It was a peaceful summer that year, the summer of 1890. England was marking time; the Irish question had been manipulated into abeyance by the conservative government of Lord Salisbury; the labor strikes of the early Nineties were still to come. The world was between international crises; nobody was rattling their sabers at one another and even the spirit of Jingoism had temporarily abated. In London after my toils at Oxford I too began to feel as lulled into false security as the world around me, but then suddenly without any warning my mother entered my life again and I became shackled to the chain of events which was to lead me to that country churchyard in Zillan and to Janna Roslyn's eyes wide-set and black-lashed behind her widow's veil.

2 Stephen's heir was his elder son Eustace, and he had tried to ensure Eustace's succession. . . . In 1153 Eustace suddenly died.

—The Saxon and Norman Kings,
CHRISTOPHER BROOKE

In despair Stephen gave up the interminable struggle. He had not long to live and he knew it; now that his destined heir was dead his sole remaining wish was to die still King of England . . . he acknowledged as his heir Henry fitzEmpress, Duke of Normandy. . . .

—The Devil's Brood,
ALFRED DUGGAN

[1]

I was about to rent chambers in Bruton Street when I met my mother again. I had no wish to outstay my welcome at my Oxonian friend's house, and although I had earlier planned to return to Gweek after sampling the delights of the Season for two or three weeks, I now discovered that this course of action was no longer open to me. My father had temporarily closed Gweekellis Manor in a gesture I found surprising to say the least and had retreated to a small property he owned in the parish of Morvah on the Cornish North Coast about five miles from Penmarric. He had inherited the property, Deveral Farm, long ago from his mother, who had belonged to a land-owning family in a neighboring parish, but the land had been leased to tenants for decades and I think he had almost forgotten he had property there until in the spring of 1890 the tenant died, the long lease expired simultaneously and certain legal problems connected with the estate required a visit from the landlord. While I was still up at Oxford I had received a letter from him saying he was considering staying on at Morvah for two or three weeks; Nigel was by that time abroad on a Grand Tour of Europe, I was to be staying in London and Gweekellis Manor had suddenly seemed lonelier than usual; besides, his thesis on the subject of Henry II's coinage reforms was not going well and he thought a change of scenery might improve matters.

Evidently it did; I was in London by the time his second letter reached me and I learned that he had closed Gweekellis for the summer after deciding to remain at Deveral Farm until the autumn.

"After so many years spent in South Cornwall," he had written, "I had quite forgotten how beautiful it is here on the starker, more spectacular North Coast, and I find I have a craving for solitude which my circle of friends would not permit me to assuage at Gweek. Perhaps I shall end my days as a recluse! Let me know when you wish to return to Gweek and I shall make arrangements to open the house for you, but no doubt you will stay in London until the end of the Season and then I dare say you will have invitations to a variety of country houses. . . ."

This was true; I had indeed planned originally to remain in London until the end of the Season and I had no doubt there would be invitations to the country, just as he had foreseen, but I had been quickly disillusioned by the Season and had found my opportunities to meet so many young girls of my own age and class unrewarding. I might be the elder son of a country gentleman, but I had no title, no wealth apart from my modest quarterly allowance and, as Clarissa Penmar had pointed out so painstakingly, no good looks. To the married seamstress and unwed chambermaid at Oxford I might have seemed rich and aristocratic enough to be attractive, but to young girls of my own class and their aspiring mamas I was a nonentity.

However, it was exciting to be in London even if the Season did not measure up to my expectations, so after receiving my father's letter I resolved to stay on in town and make the best of the situation. I did toy with the idea of joining him at Morvah, but he had not asked me to stay, and I was too proud to arrive on his doorstep uninvited as if I were a wayward puppy running up to his master for a pat on the head.

I was just walking down Piccadilly one morning on my way to Bruton Street to inspect some chambers which were for rent when I met my mother face to face outside the Royal Academy.

"Mark!" She greeted me as if it were four days, not four years, since we had last met. "You're just the person I wanted to see! Have you heard the news?"

"What news?"

"Good heavens, don't you read the obituary column of *The Times*? Your cousin Raymond Penmar is dead! He was abroad apparently—Egypt—and caught cholera. Dead in two days, of course. Terribly sad for Giles. Now listen, Mark. Think what this means. All Giles has now are those two adopted children of his, Harry and Clarissa, and they're not really Penmars at all, not even his own flesh and blood. And I hear young Harry is very wild and so Giles is probably disappointed in him . . ."

I listened, too disgusted by her attitude to speak, yet too overcome by the force of her personality to turn my back and walk away. The next moment, before I could protest, she was propelling me into Green Park and forcing me to sit down beside her on the nearest bench. ". . . I wrote to you at Gweek—didn't you get my letters? How fortunate that I should meet you like this! God moves in Mysterious Ways sometimes, but he does nonetheless move."

"Mama—"

"Now don't be disagreeable, Mark. It's absolutely imperative that we discuss this together . . ."

There was no escape. Once we were seated on the bench I crossed my arms and glowered at the lush grass at our feet, but she was too excited to take any notice.

". . . so I wrote to Giles—a letter of sympathy, naturally—and said . . ."

She had had the truly amazing insolence to write to this man who had just lost his only son and suggest that now that I was his only surviving male relative (she had, as usual, forgotten Nigel's existence) he might agree to devise Penmarric to me in his will.

"I pointed out," she said, "that it was a point of Honor that the estate should remain in the family."

I was speechless, but at last at the moment when I had summoned the words to tell her what I thought of her she said triumphantly, "I know what you're thinking, but you're wrong! You thought Giles would be too offended to reply, didn't you? Well, he wasn't! I had a reply to my letter within the week and the letter was everything I could have wished for."

"Are you attempting to tell me—"

"Yes," she said. "I am. Giles wants to see you. We are invited to Penmarric."

I was speechless again. But suddenly I found myself remembering Penmarric, the huge rolling moors of North Cornwall, the tors capped with granite, the graystone walls and square church towers of a strange and distant land. And I thought of that house with its turrets and battlements rising from the cliffs, a shining dream which I longed to cloak with reality but which I had thought would forever lie beyond my reach.

"Is it really so surprising to you?" my mother was saying abruptly. "Blood usually does run thicker than water, you know."

I said nothing. I was still thinking of Penmarric.

"Mark, there is something I feel I should discuss with you. I had no intention of mentioning it before, but now that your Inheritance has reached such a crucial stage and so much depends on this interview with Giles . . ." She stopped. "Mark, you're not listening to me."

I roused myself with an effort. "I'm sorry."

"You see, I described you to Giles. I said that you looked and thought and behaved like a Penmar . . ."

This infuriated me. I had spent too much time trying to be like my father to welcome any statement from her that I bore no resemblance to him. Before I could stop myself I said in my sharpest tone of voice, "I'm just as much a Castallack as I am a Penmar!"

"Really?" said my mother. "I wish I could be as certain of that as you are."

For a moment nothing happened.

I went on looking at her. She was wearing a voluminous purple gown that was fastened at the throat with a diamond clasp, and presently that clasp was all I could see. I can remember it still. I can close my eyes and see all those diamonds, shoulder to shoulder, a row of jagged predatory teeth that glittered brilliantly in the hard midday light.

"Well, I never meant to tell you because I wasn't entirely

certain, but you see, I told Giles . . ." She was talking again, talking rapidly, not looking at me, and her voice seemed alien and remote, the voice of a stranger who spoke of things I did not want to understand.

". . . unhappy when I was young, I had no wish to marry, all I wanted was to keep house for my father, to stay at Penmarric . . . My father was horrified, he said unless I married within the year he would cut me out of his will . . . so I married the next man who asked me. Well, I mean, how could your father and I be happy under those circumstances? How could we? I didn't love him, refused to behave as a wife should . . . he asked me to leave in the end. My father had to take me back then because there was nowhere else I could go. It was summer. Giles was there. The rhododendrons were in bloom, you should have seen the rhododendrons, they were so beautiful, it was such a beautiful summer . . . I wanted to annul my marriage to Laurence and marry Giles, but my father wouldn't have it. He approved of Laurence. The Penmars were still considered upstarts, you see, still *nouveaux riches,* and the Castallacks of Gweek were such an old and well-respected family . . . And my father did not approve of marriages between cousins and he had other plans for Giles, an heiress from Launceston. I would have defied my father even then, but Giles . . . Defiance didn't come easily to Giles. After it was all over I went back to Laurence at Gweek. I wanted to show Giles that I too could turn my back on someone I loved and live with someone else . . . God knows why Laurence took me back. I suppose he felt it was his duty. For five years we lived as husband and wife, five pregnancies, you, Nigel, two miscarriages and—but you wouldn't remember the baby who died soon after he was born. And then at last my father died and I had the means to escape to London . . . I never saw Giles again after my father's funeral, you know. Sixteen years . . . He never once came to London to see the way his case was being conducted in the law courts. Everything was done through his lawyers. Apart from the occasion of my father's funeral—when he all but ignored me—I haven't seen Giles since I left Penmarric just before the Christmas of 1868 . . . Nine months before you were born."

She stopped. There was a long pause before she said in a more normal voice, "So when I heard Raymond was dead and I knew I must write to Giles, I suddenly realized that if Giles knew—if he thought . . . I never told anyone, you see, because I wasn't certain. But since you show no resemblance at all to Laurence Castallack . . ."

I stood up.

"But surely you can understand, Mark! If Giles thinks you're his son he won't even consider making Harry his heir! Mark, I acted in your best interests! If one day you can inherit Penmarric—"

"Damn Penmarric."

"Mark!"

"And damn you," I said carefully and began to run. I ran through the park, raced across those smooth lawns, beneath trees tired with the summer heat, past nursemaids with perambulators and children with hoops. I ran until my breath was sobbing in my throat—and yet still she refused to let me escape. She came after me, and finally I stopped running, sank down on another bench and waited for the inevitable quarrel to begin.

"Mark . . ." She was at my elbow at last, scarlet-faced, out of breath but very far from speechless. "Mark, please! Listen to me! I—"

"No," I said, "no, you're going to listen to me. I've listened to you long enough. I'm never going to Penmarric. I'm never going to see Giles Penmar. And I never want to set eyes on you again as long as I live."

We quarreled for some time. She shouted, bullied, pleaded, cajoled and even cried. And then finally she used the one argument that could persuade me to change my mind.

"But, Mark," she said, shedding a despairing tear, "how am I ever to live at Penmarric unless Giles makes you his heir? You know it's the dearest wish of my life to spend my declining years there! If you don't want to live at Penmarric yourself, then of course you need not, but . . . please, Mark, for my sake . . ."

I saw it all then as clearly as if it had been set down before me in black and white. I saw the exact pattern of my revenge and of the course I must steer to achieve it. When she paused for breath at last I heard myself say shortly, "Very well, Mama, I'll do as you wish. I do so against my will and better judgment, but if you wish to see Giles I suppose I shall have to accompany you."

She was overjoyed; tears of relief shone in her eyes, but if she had anticipated my revenge I doubt that she would have felt so satisfied with her hard-won and odious victory.

[2]

I was still two months short of my twenty-first birthday when I first crossed the threshold of Penmarric. It no longer seemed an enchanted castle to me, only an old house that had been remodeled with pseudo-Gothic clumsiness by my grandfather Mark Penmar. The hall was gloomy and ill-kept, the servants were slovenly and the wainscoting bore the marks of mice. We were ushered into a dreary morning room with dark wallpaper, cumbersome furniture and a threadbare Indian carpet. Windows led out onto the terrace that overlooked the sea, but the terrace was overgrown with weeds and rust had corroded the absurd cannon that had been placed long ago on the flagstones to decorate the battlements.

It was no better than a neglected tomb, a desolate epitaph to decay.

"It's not as I remember it," said my mother, very white around the lips. "Can Giles have exhausted his financial resources? Surely not! Yet how could he have let the place become like this? Giles was so gay, so fastidious! I think you will be impressed by Giles. He was a tall man with a brilliant smile and a splendid manner. He was handsome."

But people change. When the door opened at last I understood why he had never gone to London to champion his cause in person, why he had confined himself so rigorously to Penmarric. A nurse brought in an invalid in a wheelchair, a shriveled, hunched invalid with a lined face and lifeless eyes. I had never before seen a man so close to death yet still, improbably, alive.

After the nurse had gone I waited for my mother to speak, but she could not. There was a long silence. He was looking at her, not at me. I think he hardly noticed that there was another person present. He looked only at her with his tired dark eyes, and after a long while he said slowly, "How well you look, Maud," as if he felt in some remote degree surprised by her obvious health and untarnished good looks.

"Giles," she said. She did not say any more. She went on looking at him, but presently I saw her glance wander to the shabby surroundings shrouded by that oppressive pall of neglect.

"I lost interest," he said. "I lost interest long ago when I first became ill. I continued the fight for Raymond, but now that Raymond's dead it doesn't matter."

"Yes," she said. She seemed incapable of speech. She turned as if she could not bear to face him any longer, and as she turned she saw me standing in the shadows. "Mark."

I stepped forward. The man in the wheelchair looked at me without expression.

"Giles, this is Mark."

He said nothing.

"How do you do, sir," my voice said stiffly.

He still was silent. All his energies were channeled toward the effort of visual concentration, but although I nerved myself for his comment that I looked like a Penmar, the comment did not come.

"I hear," he said politely at last, a knife-edged sharpness to his voice, "that you're a talented historian. Allow me to congratulate you."

"I . . . thank you, sir."

"Of course your father is a historian of some repute, is he not? How nice for him, is it not, Maud, that he has a son to follow so successfully in his footsteps."

My mother went crimson. I had never seen her embarrassed before. I had always assumed she was beyond embarrassment.

"It's many years since I've seen your father," he said to me, "but I remember him well. He was one of the few honest gentlemen who have crossed the threshold of this house. A fine man. I was pleased to hear that in your tastes and in your intellectual inclinations you resemble him and not your mother's family. I would not have cared to leave my property to a man who had inherited the worst faults of the Penmars."

Even my mother's neck was now stained with her ugly blush. I would not have thought it possible for her to have remained silent for so long.

"Well, Maud," he said to her coldly, "since I tire easily I suggest we come straight to the point. My fortune is diminished, thanks to the enormous sums I have had to pay in legal fees, but it is still substantial. I propose to leave a third of it to my adopted children Harry and Clarissa and two-thirds to your son. The two-thirds will include the house. I see no reason why I should leave him more than two-thirds of my money since he will inherit a fortune from both you and his father one day, and in fact I consider two-thirds to be an extravagantly generous sum. The only reason why I am prompted to such generosity is because

Harry and I are on bad terms at the moment and I don't feel inclined to leave him a penny. I trust that such an arrangement is satisfactory to you."

"Yes, sir," I said as my mother was still speechless. "Thank you."

He stared at me. "I would invite you to stay here to become acquainted with the place," he said, "but I fear you would have an unpleasant reception from Harry and Clarissa and would soon want to leave. Naturally they resent you very much. It was a pity I ever formally adopted them, but they were orphans and my wife was insistent, so I complied. Clarissa I am fond of, but Harry is a great trial to me and always has been." He tried to reach for the bell, but he was too weak. "Ring it for me, would you, boy? . . . Thank you. Now, Maud, before I return to my room to rest is there anything more you wish to say?"

She shook her head.

"Then it's settled," he said bleakly. "I shall summon my lawyers and make a new will. As soon as it's drawn up I shall request them to send you a copy so that you can see I keep my word a little better now than I did twenty-two years ago."

Bright tears shone in her eyes. She looked old suddenly, ravaged by a grief too deep to conceal. "Giles . . ."

"You were right," he said. "I should have married you. But I was weak and avaricious and wanted only to please your father so that I might inherit his money and live in his house. You had good reason to pester me with those lawsuits, the best reason in the world for any woman. It wasn't love of justice, was it, Maud? It wasn't love of truth—or honor—or any other high-flown principle, was it? It was vengeance. Did you ever tell your lawyers that? Or your admiring cousin Robert Yorke? Or even your son here? No, of course you didn't! You liked to appear noble and long-suffering, motivated by splendid principles, not a disappointed lover engaged in perpetuating a sordid episode of hole-in-the-corner adultery! But never mind. You won in the end. How does it feel to win, Maud? Do you feel that justice has prevailed over injustice? Do you? Or can you at last admit to yourself that your cause had nothing to do with justice at all but only with the monumental pursuit of a singularly petty revenge?"

"Oh, Giles, Giles . . ."

"In the end you even called your son a bastard in an attempt to ensure your victory, did you not? You deliberately perverted the truth for your own ends."

"No! I never lie!"

"You have lived a lie, Maud. For nearly seventeen years, ever since your father died and you began the litigation, you have lived with your lies. Don't attempt to tell me now that you never lie."

"But Mark is your son! I am certain—convinced—"

"How can you be either certain or convinced when you have no proof?"

"But—"

"The plain truth of the matter is that you're not certain who his father is, so why twist the truth by assuming a certainty you don't possess?"

"But, Giles, I thought if I were to tell you—"

"Indeed why should you not tell me when you knew you had nothing to lose by such an admission? Yes, I can see why you told me. But why did you have to tell the boy? I could see at once that he had been told. That was a cruel, wicked thing to do, Maud. You had no right to use the boy as a pawn in our own private and personal feud."

There was a knock on the door and the nurse entered the room. "You rang, Mr. Penmar?"

"Yes, take me back to my room. And tell Medlyn to show the visitors to the door."

"Giles . . ."

"There is nothing more to be said, Maud. I bear you no grudge. I simply have nothing else to say. Goodbye, young man. I wish you well and only regret I shall not have the chance to know you better."

"Thank you, sir," I said. "Goodbye."

"Goodbye, Maud."

But my mother could not answer. As the wheels of the invalid carriage trickled into the distance across the hall, she covered her face with her hands and sank down upon the nearest chair.

I closed the door. We were alone.

At last she said, not looking at me, "I must be sensible. Naturally I feel upset, Giles ill, so obviously dying, the house . . . not as I remember it. But . . ." She hesitated before adding with her old arrogant determination, "But we can transform the house, can't we? A few repairs, a little redecoration here and there, new furniture . . . It could soon be as splendid as it was in my father's day. I could have the Tower Room, that magnificent Tower Room which overlooks the sea . . ."

The moment of revenge had arrived. I stood motionless on that worn Indian carpet and looked her straight in the eyes and said, "No, Mama."

She stared at me. She did not understand. "But surely I can at least choose my own rooms! I must insist, Mark, that when I'm living here—"

"You won't be living here, Mama."

She continued to stare at me. And as I saw the comprehension creep into her eyes, the understanding of the enormity of my revenge, I wondered why it was I felt no satisfaction in my hour of triumph but only a bleak emotional emptiness that no amount of revenge could ever fill.

"You always said you wanted the house for me," I heard myself say, and my voice was as calm as if I neither loved nor hated her but was merely indifferent to her presence beside me in that dark depressing house. "Before long I shall have it and your dearest wish will be realized. But if you think we could ever live together in amity beneath one roof, I fear you're very much mistaken. I intend to be my own master, not a pale echo of your wishes like poor Cousin Robert. I've been at your beck and call for too long already."

She was so angry by this time that she could not speak but merely stood trembling with rage. Then without warning her rage dissolved into sobs and she began to plead with me. "Mark, please . . . I can't bear you to be unkind too . . . Please . . . I love you . . . Let me stay . . . don't turn me away . . ."

And suddenly I longed for her to stay, longed to give her all she wanted, longed for her gratitude and pride and affection. I was almost afraid to speak for fear I would betray how close I was to an irrational and sentimental *volte-face*. But I spoke. I said, giving her a dose of her own callousness, "My mind's made up and nothing can change it. I'm sorry."

She started to shout at me but I took no notice. I merely suggested we should leave the house without further delay, and when we reached the carriage I told the coachman to return to Penzance via Morvah.

"Morvah?" said my mother. "Morvah? Why Morvah?"

"My father is there visiting property of his and I intend to stay with him for a few days. Cousin Robert will look after you when you reach Penzance; there's no need for me to escort you back to London."

"But—"

"I want to see my father."

"But why choose this time to see him?" She was half furious, half despairing. "I need you more than he does!"

"Perhaps," I said. "But I need him more than I need you."

She did not answer. Perhaps she had at last realized that she possessed no answer to offer me. She cried all the way to Morvah, but when the carriage halted by the hamlet's little church her pride returned to her and she averted her face when I tried to kiss her goodbye.

"I'll call on you when I'm next in London, Mama," I said after a moment. "I wish you a safe journey."

"Pray don't bother to call," she said icily, and then suddenly she was crying again, clinging to me and begging me to stay with her because after all I was her son, was I not, and I did owe her something.

"I'm not your only son," I said. "There's Nigel."

"Oh yes," she said emptily. "Nigel. I was very ill when he was born. I nearly died. I'm afraid I never cared for him greatly after I recovered."

"He would visit you if you were to invite him." I jumped down from the carriage and told the coachman to drive on. "Goodbye, Mama."

She did not answer. The carriage rolled slowly away along the road which led south on to the moors, and I watched it until it had slowly surmounted the ridge and crawled out of sight. After that, still feeling numb with the emotional exhaustion of the scene at Penmarric, I asked directions from a passing yokel and five minutes later I was half running, half walking down the track to Deveral Farm.

[3]

I was shocked to see the house my father had decided to use as a summer residence. I had, it was true, known that the property was described as a farm, but I had thought that the word must be an obsolete description and that the house would be a small country mansion with perhaps a humble farm nearby to furnish it with essential food supplies. When I left the Penzance road and turned down the lane toward the cluster of graystone buildings visible quarter of a mile away I was puzzled by their rustic aspect, but I merely thought that the outbuildings of the farm hid the mansion from view. It was not until I reached the farmyard that I made the discovery.

There was no mansion.

There was not even a farm, for the outbuildings were disused and the barn was in a bad state of repair. All the estate consisted of was an old farmhouse, four-square and ugly, which could not possibly have contained more than ten rooms. I cast a sharp glance over the exterior for pipes which would hint at interior sanitation, but there was none; a water butt caught rainwater from the gutters but that was all. Crossing the overgrown, weed-strewn patch of garden at the side of the house, I reached the front door and, hardly believing that my father could have chosen to live in such a place, rapped on the panels.

I was admitted by a gray-haired Cornish woman, humbly dressed but respectable, who showed me into the "parlor," a dingy room that possessed plain furniture and an air of being permanently unused. I began to wonder if my father had taken leave of his senses. I thought of Gweekellis Manor, aged and beautiful, its mellow façade, its spendidly vaulted hall, its sunken garden still recognizable as a medieval moat; I thought of the woods which stretched from the lawns to the estuary, the peace and tranquillity of the South Cornish countryside. My father had belonged there so absolutely that I could not imagine him living anywhere else, least of all amidst this savage landscape of the Cornish Tin Coast in a humble working-class farmhouse. I was just wondering if I should be bold enough to inquire directly into his motives when the door opened and he came into the room.

"Mark!" he exclaimed. "What a pleasant surprise! How are you?" And he took me in his arms and embraced me. He must have been surprised when he tried to disentangle himself and found me still clinging to him, but he smiled and patted my shoulder and said kindly, "Come into my study and I'll ask my housekeeper Mrs. Mannack, to bring us some tea."

I looked at him, at his familiar face that I knew and loved so well, and suddenly I saw him as if through the eyes of a stranger, saw his candid blue eyes and his sensitive mouth and the fine bone structure of his face, saw his thin, immensely tall frame and his gray-brown receding hair and his long-fingered scholar's hands. I thought of my mother's rapid, uneven words in that park in London, but even as grief gripped me like a vise my voice said clear and untroubled, "It seems strange to see you in such humble surroundings, sir! I hadn't realized your property here was so modest. Surely by this time you must be missing Gweekellis Manor and feeling anxious to return?"

"I can understand your surprise . . ." He led the way into his study. As I followed him inside I recognized his favorite books, his inkstand, even his favorite pipe; a copy of *The Times* lay tossed upon the window seat, and beyond the window was a spectacular view of Carn Kenidjack and the sea. "The change of scenery has helped my writing," he was saying apologetically, as if he knew his decision to spend time at the farm was eccentric, but the next moment the note of apology was replaced by enthusiasm. "And what scenery it is! I've become fascinated by the views across the moors to the sea on the one hand and across the moors to the ridge on the other—the stark ugliness of the mines somehow only emphasizes the austere beauty of the parishes. . . . Yes, Mrs. Mannack, we will have tea, if you please, and some of those excellent wine biscuits, if you have any left. . . . Sit down, Mark. Where was I? Ah yes, the parishes. Historically this is a most interesting area. There's an ancient hill fort on the summit of the ridge behind the house—at least two thousand years old, I should think—Chûn Castle, it's called, Chûn after the Cornish 'Chy-An-Woon,' meaning 'House on the Down,' and nearby is a quoit of the same name. . . ."

It was not until the housekeeper had brought tea to us that he remembered to ask me why I should be in Cornwall when I was supposed to be relaxing in London after my hard work at Oxford.

"I was visiting Penmarric with my mother," I said.

"I see." He looked away. "Let me show you the postcard I received from Nigel this morning from Florence—"

"Papa . . ."

"Yes?"

"I went to Penmarric because Giles Penmar asked to see me. Now that his only son is dead he has decided to make me his heir. Penmarric will be mine when he dies."

There was a silence. He did not answer but I saw his hand tremble as he pushed the tobacco into his pipe. I said unsteadily, "I'll refuse it, if you prefer. Your wishes mean more to me than my mother's."

"My dear Mark, don't be so foolish!" he said at once. "Of course you must accept the situation. You have every right to inherit Penmarric by virtue of your mother's claims, and if I've always seemed reluctant to discuss either your mother or her inheritance with you it's only because I find it painful to speak of your mother, who brought me so much unhappiness, and repugnant to speak of her sordid quarrels with Giles Penmar. I also felt guilty because I felt I was failing in my parental duty by allowing you to see her and become involved in her quarrels, but what else could I have done? It takes a hard man to keep a son from his mother, and besides, I was afraid Maud would make all manner of distressing scenes if I refused to let you see her, and I think I would have hated that more than anything else on earth." He laid his pipe on the table absent-mindedly and glanced out of the window. "However, if your mother's quarrel with Giles Penmar is now at an end I suppose I should feel glad for her sake—and for yours—that the matter is finally settled. Penmarric will make a fine inheritance for you one day."

There was a pause. He picked up his pipe again. "It makes a certain decision easier for me too," he said at last, and I could hear the relief in his voice. "Now that you're so well provided for I need have no qualms about leaving Gweekellis Manor to Nigel."

I was on my feet before I realized it. I saw his startled expression and I believe he spoke, but I heard nothing he said because by then I was already shouting at him in a harsh voice that did not sound like my own, shouting that Gweekellis was mine—mine—mine because I was the elder son, and how dare he give it to Nigel and how dare he favor Nigel and how dare he treat me as if—

The harsh shouting suddenly ceased. Panic made me feel as if I were suffocating. I began to back away toward the door.

"Mark," he said, much distressed, "Mark, please. I think you forget yourself."

I reached the door. My fingers groped blindly for the handle.

"Your mother has been trying to turn you against me," he said. "What has she been saying? You'd better tell me at once."

I was in the narrow hall and stumbling past the stairs to the front door.

"Mark . . ."

But I had escaped. I could not hear or speak or see, but suddenly I knew I was outside, for the air was fresh against my aching throat and the sea breeze ran light fingers over my hot cheeks and burning eyes. I began to run. Heather, coarse and tough, tugged at my trousers and scratched my shoes. I was on the moors, the desolate silent moors where there was nothing except my choking gasps for breath and my single-minded determination to run until there was no more strength left in my body. So I went on running, stumbling across the summit of the ridge, groping my way downhill into the valley of Zillan parish, and it was there in the porch of the parish church that I first saw Janna Roslyn and decided that despite everything that had happened I would stay on in Cornwall and postpone my return to London.

3

It was Count Geoffrey's intention that at his death Henry should be content with the Kingdom of England, if he could secure it, and that the ancestral fiefs of the Angevin house should pass to his second son.

—King John,
W. L. WARREN

Henry was a young man, eleven years Eleanor's junior. . . .

—Henry II,
JOHN T. APPLEBY

[1]

After Janna Roslyn had left the churchyard and I had watched her until she disappeared from sight I walked slowly over to the grave where the red roses bloomed on the quiet grass.

"Here lyeth JOHN HENRY ROSLYN," ran the inscription on the tombstone, "who died on the 15th day of May, 1890, aged 66 years. Also his wife REBECCA MARY, who died on the 12th day of April, 1885, aged 58 years. May their souls rest in peace. This stone was erected to their memory by their devoted sons, JARED JOHN ROSLYN AND JONAS HENRY ROSLYN, in the Year of Our Lord 1890."

I was still staring at the inscription and trying to deduce the identity of the woman who had brought the flowers to the grave when a resonant voice remarked behind me, "So Mrs. Roslyn has brought some more beautiful roses! How fortunate she is to have such a plentiful supply at Roslyn Farm."

I swung round to find myself face to face with the rector of Zillan. He was a slender man in his middle forties with prematurely white hair and odd dark eyes. I write "odd" because the only time I had seen such eyes before had been during a variety act in London; a man with similarly odd eyes had read people's thoughts and printed them neatly on a blackboard to the accompaniment of admiring applause from his audience. It occurred to me in alarm that it might be most embarrassing to be ministered to by a parson who practiced telepathy. One might make all manner of unwanted admissions.

"Good afternoon," he said pleasantly in response to my uneasy greeting. "Welcome to Zillan. We very seldom have visitors from England. Or are you perhaps a Cornishman after all? You have a Cornish look about you. . . . Allow me to introduce myself. My name is Edward Barnwell and I am, as you have no doubt gathered from my clerical appearance, the rector of this parish."

When I told him who I was he seemed startled and then explained that he knew my father well; they had been at school together long ago, and my father had been attending church at Zillan since he had taken up residence at Deveral Farm. I learned too that my father lunched regularly at the rectory with Mr. Barnwell and his family after matins every Sunday before returning over the moors in the ponytrap to his solitary existence at Morvah.

"If you are to be staying with your father for a few days," said Mr. Barnwell, "I hope you will accompany him when he lunches with us at the rectory next Sunday. My wife will be delighted to see you and my daughter Miriam will be pleased to see a new face for a change. I fear we are very isolated here at Zillan. . . . Miriam is eighteen now and quite accomplished, although naturally I speak as a prejudiced parent. Well, I mustn't delay you any longer. Pray give my regards to your father and I hope I shall have the chance to see you again soon."

"Yes, sir. Thank you," I said politely, and then before I could stop myself I heard myself add, "Sir, did you say that it was a Mrs. Roslyn who had brought these flowers? Would she be the wife of one of the sons who erected this tombstone?"

He looked at me, his odd eyes betraying nothing, but just as

I was cursing myself for asking such a question he said as casually as if we had been discussing the weather, "No, Mrs. Roslyn was the second wife of Mr. John Henry Roslyn, who died in May, and the stepmother of the sons mentioned in the inscription. She still lives at Roslyn Farm, which is situated across the moors toward Chûn. Have you visited Chûn Castle yet? My wife says it's merely a heap of old stones and hardly worth a visit, but it would be of interest to you, I think, if you share your father's dedication to history."

"I must look for the castle on my way back to Morvah," I said hurriedly and escaped at last, but I could feel his dark eyes watching me all the way down the street, just as my eyes had watched Mrs. Roslyn earlier.

When I arrived once more at Deveral Farm I went immediately to my father's study and apologized fully for my earlier behavior. "I can only conclude that it was the strain of the interview with Giles Penmar which made me so unlike myself," I added, and my voice, calm and controlled, betrayed nothing. "I'm afraid I behaved very foolishly."

"I understand," he said at once. "We'll say no more about it." But he still looked profoundly uncomfortable.

"And of course Nigel should have Gweekellis if I'm to have Penmarric," I said. "That's only fair. I can see that now. Please forgive me for what I said earlier."

"Yes . . . of course." But he looked unhappier than ever.

To change the subject before he could begin to question me again about my mother, I said rapidly, "Would it inconvenience you if I stayed here at Deveral Farm for a while? I have a thesis which I want to write about King John. . . . If the atmosphere here is so conducive to writing—"

"Of course!" he said at once, seizing the opportunity to be kind to me. "Stay as long as you wish! A thesis on King John? But what attracts you to such a disagreeable character? Surely of all the Plantagenets . . . But we can discuss that later at our leisure. I'll tell Mrs. Mannack to prepare one of the spare rooms for you."

"I wouldn't want to interfere with your work—"

"I'm certain you would not—on the contrary, it will be good for me to have some congenial companionship after living like a recluse for the past few months. . . . I prefer to work in the mornings, and two or three afternoons a week I like to take solitary walks along the cliffs, but that still leaves us plenty of time together."

"The countryside does indeed seem interesting . . ." I began to talk about my walk to Zillan and my meeting with Mr. Barnwell. So self-possessed was I, so confident that I was in control of myself that it gave me a shock when I found I could not resist saying carelessly to him, "Papa, do you know any of the parishioners of Zillan?"

"Well, by sight, I suppose," he said doubtfully. "Having attended matins there every week, their faces have become familiar. But there's no one of my own class there save Barnwell himself. The only substantial landowner in Zillan parish, an old bachelor named Meredith, is too crippled with arthritis to leave his home to attend matins, so I've yet to meet him."

"I see." I could not stop myself. I had to go on. "I was wondering if you knew anything about a Mrs. Roslyn, a very beautiful woman of perhaps thirty or less." And as he looked at me in astonishment I said glibly, "I saw her this afternoon and the rector spoke of her. I wondered if you knew her too."

"I might know her by sight." He smiled a little. "Surely a woman of 'perhaps thirty or less' would seem somewhat old to a boy of your age?"

"I was merely struck by her good looks," I mumbled and tried to think of some plausible way to excuse myself from his presence, but he spoke before any attempt at escape was possible.

"There's no need to look embarrassed," he said gently, touched by what he supposed to be my naïve admiration. "I realize that you have reached an age when the opposite sex seems attractive to you. Perhaps while we're mentioning the subject I should say . . ."

The long-awaited discourse on matters pertinent to a gentleman's private life. I wished I were three hundred miles away in London.

". . . how pleased I was," he was saying, "that you conducted yourself so well at Oxford. Of course I was confident that you would always behave honorably, but you were young and had a great deal of unaccustomed freedom, and I know that it's often far from easy for a young man to maintain high standards in such circumstances . . ."

I thought of the women I had known at Oxford, the lower-class women who were willing to oblige a young gentleman in search of discreet amusement, the women who had belonged to a part of my life so private that even my closest friends had failed to suspect its existence. Shame washed through me in a hot tide; I could feel my cheeks burning with my guilt.

". . . but I knew my trust in you would be justified," said my father and turned aside tactfully to ignore what might have been my innocent blushes. "Now let me speak to Mrs. Mannack about preparing a room for you."

I slept badly that night. I kept waking up and vowing I would turn over a new leaf without delay, but when morning came at last I could think only of Janna Roslyn, and after breakfasting early I left the house and began my walk across the moors to Roslyn Farm.

[2]

Chûn Castle was no doubt of considerable archaeological interest, but I had other matters on my mind besides archaeology that morning, so I did not linger by the double ring of old walls that stood atop the ridge but merely admired the splendor of the views to the sea beyond Penzance in the south and the sea beyond the cliffs of Morvah to the north, before I descended into the valley of Zillan parish. I saw the farms soon afterward; there were two below the ridge where Chûn Castle stood, one a substantial farmhouse with a variety of outbuildings and the other a mere cottage with a small barn. I decided that Mr. John Henry Roslyn, deceased, would have resided at the farmhouse and leased the cottage to tenants—if indeed he had even owned the land in the first place. The Penmars owned much land in Zillan parish and it was possible that Roslyn had been a tenant instead of a yeoman farmer with his own land.

I drew nearer the farmhouse. It was old, older than my father's ugly house at Morvah, and although built of the usual somber Cornish stone, it had a mellow air which reminded me of my home at Gweek. Around the porch grew the wild roses, entwined with clusters of honeysuckle. There was a little garden in front of the house and someone, presumably the mistress, had tended it carefully and used the soil to grow herbs. I smelled thyme and lavender, and for a moment I stood by the front gate and savored the mingling scents and the peace of the old stone house. Presently when I moved into the farmyard the smell of manure contrasted sharply with the scents of the herb garden, and I wrinkled my nose with distaste as I picked my way through the mud and the hens to the back door.

The door was ajar. I was just wondering why the place was so quiet and deserted when the voice rang out to meet me, a harsh voice that jabbed furiously through the still morning air.

"You lying tinker's bitch," said a man in the ugly accents of an uneducated Cornishman. "It was an ill day for us when Father brought you home from St. Ives."

I stopped dead. And then as my heart missed a beat I heard the woman say coolly, "It was an ill day for your father when he begot you." Her voice bore a note of disdain. It was a low, self-possessed voice and she spoke with a soft Cornish lilt. "Fine sons you were to him! You've only yourself to blame that you didn't inherit this farm when he died."

"It was *you* who was to blame!" shouted a second man. "If it hadn't been for you—"

"Hold your tongue, Joss," said the first man grimly. "Now listen to me, Janna. I don't know how you get the money to keep this place in order and to be blunt I don't care. But I'll make you one last offer for this land and this house—a good offer in good coin—and you can take it or leave it. But think twice before you turn it down. I want this place and I intend to have it. If you won't give it to me in a proper legal way I swear I'll drive you out by every means I know of and you'll be sorry the day ever dawned when you crossed Jared Roslyn."

I had already moved swiftly and noiselessly across the yard, and now as soon as the man finished speaking I pushed the back door wide and said clearly from the threshold, "You'd best be careful, Mr. Roslyn. Extortion is a criminal offense. I'm sure you'd be averse to being brought before the bench and spending the next few years in prison."

And as the silence fell upon the room like a pall I crossed the threshold and walked into the large farm kitchen beyond.

She had her back to the window so that the light was behind her and I could not see her expression. She was very still. By the range stood a small but well-knit youth of about my own age whom I guessed to be Joss, the younger brother, and close to me by the door stood a dark, powerfully built farmer of thirty with hard eyes and a narrow mouth.

I looked at him, I a boy of twenty face to face with a man ten years my senior, and as I looked at him I measured him as one might measure an opponent in the ring. And when I had measured him I raised the massive barrier of my class, which was the only weapon I had, and prepared to use it to annihilate him.

"I don't know you, sir," I said with the studied insolence I had acquired from the titled young aristocrats of Eton. "Nor do I wish to. I'm not accustomed to meeting louts who abuse a widow still in mourning and trespass on her property in order to threaten her and cause her distress. Giles Penmar, who I am sure is known to you, is my cousin and Harry Penmar is a personal friend of mine. Unless you want to find yourself in trouble of the most serious kind I would advise you to remove yourself and your brother immediately from this property, where I believe you have no right to be in the first place, and if I hear that Mrs. Roslyn has been bothered again by either of you, then—to quote your own singularly pertinent phrase—you'll be 'sorry the day ever dawned' when you failed to observe my advice."

The man turned a dull deep red. I stood my ground, but finally all he said when he could control his voice was "You're lucky with your friends, Janna."

The woman's face was still in shadow. She said nothing, and after a moment Roslyn motioned his brother and with the boy at his heels walked past me into the farmyard.

I stepped into the kitchen, closed the door and found her before me. For a second we stood inches apart facing each other. It was the first time I had seen her without her veil, and I had not realized before how fair she was. I had seen the blue black-lashed eyes and the white skin, but not the color of her hair. It was golden, a deep pure shade of gold, rich and exciting. I knew instinctively that the hair would be long and thick when it was loosened, smooth and heavy to the touch.

"Thank you, sir," she said coolly, shunning any hint of effusive gratitude. "It was kind of you to save me from such an embarrassing scene. May I have the honor of knowing whom I am addressing?"

I had noticed the improvement in her speech since she had begun to talk to me and I found her correctness of manner surprising. The Cornish lilt was still much in evidence, but she had an odd veneer of education and quality which was unexpected in a woman of her position. I tried to place her in some convenient category of class against an appropriate background, but could not.

"My name is Castallack," I said slowly. "Mark Castallack. I come from Gweek, near Helston."

There was a slight pause before she said, "Castallack? There's a village of that name between Mousehole and Lamorna. . . . Well, how do you do, Mr. Castallack. May I offer you a glass of elderberry wine?"

"That would be delightful, Mrs. Roslyn. Thank you. I was on my way to Zillan from my father's house at Morvah, and somehow I managed to lose my way, so I decided to stop at your farm to ask directions. . . ." The lies slipped smoothly from my tongue as I followed her out of the kitchen down a passage to the front of the house. She was tall for a woman, but slender, very graceful. As I followed her down the passage to the stairs and hall I noticed how her plain drab black dress clung to her waist and lingered in clinging folds about her hips. At the front of the house she opened a door and led the way into a neat parlor, scrupulously clean and well dusted. There were even flowers on the mantelshelf above the fireplace, a fact that surprised me, for I had thought the working classes seldom used the "front room" of their homes. By the window which faced the herb garden and the moors stood a small oak table, and Mrs. Roslyn asked me to be seated while she fetched the wine.

When she returned she sat down opposite me. Her drab black dress was buttoned up to her throat, and my glance traveled instinctively from her waist to her neck and back to her waist again before I remembered my manners and stared out of the window to regain my composure.

"Will you be long in this part of Cornwall, Mr. Castallack?" she asked effortlessly while I struggled with an unexpected wave of self-consciousness. I was suddenly much too aware of my youth, my lack of inches, my plain features and my thickset frame.

"For a few weeks, perhaps." I made a great effort, determined to overcome my reserve. She was, after all, only a working-class woman, despite her airs and graces. There was no need for me to feel so paralytically shy. I took a sip of the home-made wine and began to explain that I had just finished my studies at Oxford and had decided to visit my father, who was spending the summer at Deveral Farm. The wine, powerful as only home-made wine can be, soon enabled me to summon the boldness to question her about herself. Had she always lived in Cornwall? Were her stepsons in the habit of persecuting her in such a distasteful fashion? Had it been hard for her since her husband died? I learned that, yes, she had always lived in Cornwall and in fact had never been east of the Tamar, and that, yes, her stepsons entertained nothing but ill-will toward her since her husband had left the house to her in his will, but she was not afraid of her stepsons since there was nothing they could do to evict her from her home. She managed well enough; she had had to work harder since her husband's death, but she had help; the young servant girl Annie was half-witted but very biddable, and there was always Griselda.

"Griselda?" I said.

"Griselda came with me from St. Ives when I married," said Mrs. Roslyn, and some small edge to her voice told me that she did not wish to pursue the subject.

"I hear St. Ives is a very picturesque town," I said after a slight pause. "I've long wanted to visit it some day."

She smiled but said nothing, and I realized then that the distasteful subject was not the unknown Griselda at all but the town where she had lived until her marriage.

"I have friends there," I said rapidly. "The St. Enedocs—or at least Russell St. Enedoc was a friend of mine at school although I haven't seen him for a year or two now . . ." And I went on talking of matters of no particular importance, the parts of Cornwall I knew best, the local gentry with whom I happened to be acquainted, my impressions of Morvah and Zillan, until at last her polite silence hinted that she was waiting for me to leave.

I rose to my feet so clumsily that I almost upset my empty wineglass. "If you'll excuse me, Mrs. Roslyn, I think I should be on my way."

"Ah yes," she said, "you told me you were on your way to Zillan when you became lost and decided to stop at the farm to seek directions." Her clear eyes looked straight into mine and I thought I saw a flicker of irony in her expression as she repeated the lie I had told her. "Take the lane down to the road, then cross the road and you will see Zillan before you across the moors."

"Thank you." We were in the hall by this time and she was opening the front door. As she turned to face me again I held out my hand and after a slight hesitation she put her hand in mine. Her fingers were long and sinuous. I could imagine how they might feel under different circumstances, and because my imagination was unusually vivid I held her hand too long and she was obliged to withdraw it to preserve the proprieties.

I said clumsily, "May I call again?"

"Please do," she said, "if you happen to be in this neighborhood." But her voice was merely civil. It was not an encouraging invitation. "The mornings are the best time," she added, just as I was beginning to feel unpleasantly rebuffed, "because in the afternoons I try to rest or at least to do some sewing or ironing before I cook the evening meal. But don't call on Thursday. Thursday is the big market day in Penzance and I spend all day there selling the farm produce."

I felt appeased. After we had parted I walked down the path to the lane before I looked back over my shoulder, but she had already gone back into the house and the front door was closed. When I reached the lane I glanced back a second time as if unable to believe that she was no longer watching me, and strangely enough my instinct was correct. The curtain on one side of the parlor window moved slightly; she had been watching me all the time.

[3]

I was so disturbed by the meeting and so restless that I was quite unable to sleep that night and arose the next morning feeling that the last thing I desired was to accompany my father to church at Zillan and lunch afterward with Mr., Mrs. and Miss Barnwell at the rectory. But I could hardly explain to my father that I would have preferred to ease my intolerable restlessness by walking to Penzance and buying a discreet list of female names and addresses from the head porter of the Metropole Hotel. Controlling myself with an effort, I accompanied him meekly in the ponytrap to church and spent the entire service, I regret to say, imagining what might happen if Mrs. Roslyn and I were alone together behind the locked door of a darkened room. It was not that I was irreligious; on the contrary, I was then much more religious than I am now, for my father had instilled churchgoing habits into both Nigel and myself at an early age, and this religious background was so closely interwoven with my father's standards which I admired so deeply that my acceptance of it was complete.

Despite the post-Darwin tides of atheism I had encountered at Oxford and the independence of thought fostered by the academic climate, it had never occurred to me not to believe in God and worship Him dutifully every Sunday, and even later in life when I moved toward agnosticism I still derived a sense of security from regular attendance at church. Hypocritical perhaps, but when I was twenty I was not aware of any hypocrisy. My father believed, and if he believed, then I believed too.

During the first hymn I glanced over my shoulder and nearly dropped my hymnbook when I saw Mrs. Roslyn in one of the back pews. I had not seen her enter the church and had assumed she was not attending matins that week. When I managed to look at her a second time I noticed the ugly hunched old crone who was standing next to her and realized with a shock that this must be the mysterious Griselda who had accompanied Mrs. Roslyn to Zillan on her marriage. The old crone looked little better than a fishwife. I wondered what her connection was with Mrs. Roslyn, and not for the first time I began to speculate about Mrs. Roslyn's early life in St. Ives.

The service ended at last, but there was no chance for a word with Mrs. Roslyn, for she and the crone left immediately and I was detained in the aisle to be introduced to the rector's wife and daughter before we all retreated to the rectory for luncheon. As I had suspected, the meal turned out to be dinner, served early to spare the servants undue labor on the Sabbath, and I ate hungrily as I observed my host and his family. Mrs. Barnwell was a gossipy woman with a long nose that clearly enjoyed poking its way into other people's business; I was surprised that the rector, who was an interesting man, should have selected such an uninteresting woman to be his life-long companion. Their daughter Miriam at first appeared to be as dreary as her mother, although where Mrs. Barnwell was garrulous Miriam was quiet and where Miriam was sedate Mrs. Barnwell was effusive, but after lunch when Mrs. Barnwell suggested coyly that her daughter might take me on a "grand tour of the garden," I found that Miss Miriam Barnwell was not nearly so negative as I had supposed. I had felt sorry for her, knowing how hard it was for daughters of clergymen to meet suitable young men, and reflecting how isolated her existence must be at Zillan rectory, but I soon realized that not only was she uninterested in my sympathy but she was also uninterested in me as a possible suitor. At first I felt affronted since as far as she was concerned I was eligible enough and could expect to be treated as such, but presently my sense of humor enabled me to see the funny side of the situation and I began to wonder idly where her interests lay. Looking at her more closely, I saw to my surprise that she was not unattractive. She had her father's fine dark eyes, a quantity of soft brown hair and one of those small delicate figures that some men with a penchant for porcelain find irresistible.

"I am very well acquainted with your cousins," she said casually as we toured the hydrangea bushes at the far edge of the lawn. "Did Papa tell you? I used to do my lessons with them at Penmarric."

"No, he didn't mention it."

"I haven't seen much of them recently. Poor Raymond had been abroad for some time before he died in Cairo, and Clarissa was too busy with her London debut last year to be much at Penmarric. I was invited to her ball, but did not go." Dislike, polite but deadly, tinged her voice and was gone. "Harry I still see occasionally, but he is often in London nowadays. . . . Will you be calling regularly now at Penmarric, Mr. Castallack? After all, now that Mr. Penmar has made you his heir . . ." She stopped abruptly and gazed for one long angry moment at the nearest hydrangea bush as she bit her lip.

"How you intrigue me, Miss Barnwell!" I said dryly after my initial surprise had worn off. "How could you possibly know I'm Giles Penmar's heir? It's no secret, I grant you, but it's hardly common knowledge either at present! Are you a mind reader by any chance?"

She laughed and blushed very prettily. I was already feeling much less sorry for her. It occurred to me that she was a young woman who could be most adept at fending for herself, and I decided that if she were a governess she would have the unattached master of the house proposing to her in less time than it took Mr. Rochester to say good morning to Jane Eyre.

"Miss Barnwell," I persisted, amused, "before I expire with curiosity, do, I entreat you, enlighten me. How did you hear the news so fast?"

"Well, you see . . ." She began to explain. She had recently become acquainted with a Mr. Michael Vincent, a young man from Launceston whose family was known to her father. He had come to Penzance earlier that year to join the firm of Holmes, Holmes, Trebarvah and Holmes—

"The Penmar solicitors," I said. "I think I'm beginning to understand." It occurred to me that a young lawyer would be a very seemly match for her, and I thought I could now understand her lack of interest in me as a possible suitor.

"Mr. Vincent dined with us yesterday—he dines with us quite often—and he happened to mention—in a most oblique way, of course, I'm sure he did nothing improper—"

"Of course," I murmured soothingly.

"Mr. Vincent is often at Penmarric. On business." But her voice implied that his business provided him with a convenient excuse for calling there.

"Oh?" I said. "Is he a friend of Harry's?"

"No," said Miriam, spiteful as a cat with unsheathed claws, "but he is infatuated with Clarissa. She considers it a great joke."

So that, I thought, was how the land lay. Miriam was in love with the young solicitor, who was infatuated with my unusually striking cousin-by-adoption. No wonder I had heard the dislike in Miriam's voice when she had spoken of Clarissa earlier! And I thought of the one time I had seen Clarissa, those brief minutes four years before at Penmarric, and remembered her brilliant dark eyes and wide passionate mouth. I had not been in London the previous summer when Clarissa had made her debut in society, but word of her success had still managed to reach me. One of my friends at Oxford had met her and sent her a sonnet a day until his inspiration was exhausted; she was reported to be on the verge of marrying either a duke or an earl or a rich American; her own sex, particularly her fellow-debutantes, were reported to be stupefied by such undeserved success—undeserved because Clarissa did not conform to the conventional standards of feminine beauty— and were delighted when for some unaccountable reason she married none of her ardent suitors and merely returned to Cornwall when the Season had reached its end. The scandal began soon afterward. After all, there had to be some reason why her suitors' ardor had cooled; it was said she returned to Cornwall in disgrace. How true all this gossip was I had no idea, but it was true that Clarissa now had a "reputation" and that this young solicitor Michael Vincent was only one of a long line of men who had found her unconventional looks irresistible.

In the ponytrap on the way home from Zillan that afternoon I said to my father, "I fancy Miss Barnwell has an unrequited passion for that young man Michael Vincent whom Mr. Barnwell mentioned just before we left."

"Really?" said my father, who was exhausted by his weekly concession to social intercourse but not so exhausted that he could not look astonished by my remark. "I think you must be mistaken. I dislike gossip, but I had heard that little Miss Barnwell had set her cap a good deal higher than a mere country solicitor. I had heard that Raymond Penmar was interested in her and that she in fact was the reason he was sent abroad to Rome, Athens and Cairo. Giles Penmar not unnaturally wanted his son to marry well and not to become involved with a clergyman's daughter."

I gaped at him. "Did Mr. Barnwell tell you that?"

"No, it was Mrs. Barnwell who dropped the hints, but Barnwell was present and did not deny the implications of his wife's remarks. He later said he deeply regretted allowing his daughter to associate with the Penmars. Young Harry has a bad reputation and as for Clarissa—but that's gossip I have no intention of repeating. Let it suffice to say that I hope you won't become acquainted with either Harry or Clarissa while you're staying with me at Morvah."

"There's little likelihood of that happening," I said frankly. "If I even tried to bid Harry good day I think he'd try and knock me down."

He was silent, evidently satisfied by my assurance. His housekeeper's husband, Walter Mannack, drove us out of Zillan parish and across the hills to Morvah, and presently I forgot the Penmars and the rector's daughter and began to think once more of Mrs. Janna Roslyn.

[4]

I called at Roslyn Farm on Monday morning, but the old crone Griselda told me Mrs. Roslyn was "tired" and "resting" and could not receive visitors. On Tuesday I was informed she had gone to Penzance to spend an extra day marketing produce; the market was held three times a week in Penzance, and although the largest market was held on Thursdays, I was told that since her husband's death Mrs. Roslyn had often been obliged to go to market on Tuesdays and Saturdays as well—presumably on account of trying financial circumstances. On Wednesday I again tried to see her, but she was away visiting a neighboring farm, and on Thursday, of course, she went to Penzance again. By Friday I had received the distinct impression that she wanted to administer a rebuff, but so anxious was I to see her that a rebuff was a mere inconvenience which I was prepared to tolerate. What I could not endure was another day without the prospect of exchanging a few words with her, so on Friday morning I saddled my father's horse again and rode over the hills past Chûn Castle to the farm.

She was at home. She consented to see me. We drank another glass of wine together in her front parlor and I spoke of London and a dozen other matters, but she said little and I was forced to carry the burden of the conversation. She did not appear to be bored. She did not appear to be especially interested, but she was always faultlessly polite. I think it was then, on that second meeting, that I began to realize I was wasting my time, but by then it was already too late. It was useless to try to tell myself I had best forget her attraction for me and move to fresher woods and greener pastures. I could not turn my back on her, could not continue through life as if she had never crossed my path. I had to go on seeing her. My obsession was utterly irrational but I could not rid myself of it. I knew I was making a fool of myself, and I knew that every visit I paid to the farm was yet another step down a blind alley, but I simply could not stop calling on her. Visits to other women, a useful panacea in the past to ease the raw ache of frustration, now made little difference to my peace of mind. I remained obsessed.

In love, I called it, but it was not love. An infatuation others might have judged it, but it was not merely an infatuation. It was a painful combination of lust, greed, admiration and longing, and above all the desire to possess. My favorite daydream was concerned solely with images of completed possession. I dreamt of her surrendering—but not willingly. That somehow would be less satisfactory. But I dreamt of an unwilling surrender which I had forced upon her yet was not a form of rape. I dreamt of her taking off her clothes, one by one, each article torn from her body by those long sinuous fingers and folded neatly before being placed upon a chair. She would be cool, stony-faced, contemptuous. Since she was a respectable woman she would not undress to the point of complete nudity but would keep on her last petticoat, and when she sat down on the bed with her back to me and lifted her white arms to her head to undo her hair I would lean forward and unfasten the hooks of her bodice and slip my hands around her body to her breasts. . . . Her hair would fall silently down her back and I would bury my face in it and pull her down on the pillows and then . . .

Nothing else mattered. All I wanted was to possess.

And I went on daydreaming, wiling away hour after hour, and so young was I, so ingenuous in my desires, that it never once occurred to me as I cherished my fantasies that in possessing her I would become myself possessed.

[5]

Meanwhile I had quickly adjusted myself to my new surroundings. Walter Mannack, the housekeeper's husband who acted as gardener and handyman at Deveral Farm, had collected the luggage I had left at the Metropole Hotel in Penzance, and presently in response to a request sent to the housekeeper remaining in charge of Gweekellis Manor I received some more clothes as well as the box in which I kept my writing materials and my notes for the thesis on King John. However, having no desire to resume my historical labors at that point and being anxious to discover some way of passing the time in between my visits to Roslyn Farm, I rode into Penzance and explored the town thoroughly—an excursion which I had never before had time to make during previous fleeting visits with my mother. I found it a curious mixture of a place, the new gentility of the seaside town mellowing the ancient coarseness of the fishing port. The Metropole Hotel was part of the new gentility, a modern building that faced the sea and catered to visitors anxious to breathe the sea air in refined surroundings, but the town's high street was far older than the esplanade and stood farther inland to remind the stranger that a sea view had not always been considered desirable by the inhabitants. The mixture of old and new was again emphasized, however, by the new market house at the top of the historic Market Jew Street and by the new public gardens with their semitropical vegetation a stone's throw from the narrow streets and cobbled alleys around the harbor. And beyond the harbor, reducing both the old and the new to insignificance, rose the fairy-tale castle of St. Michael's Mount, which as a child I had once wished could be included in my Penmar inheritance.

I did not know the St. Aubyns who lived at the Mount, but I

did meet the heir of Carnforth Hall, a large, wealthy estate which stood a mile or two from the sea east of Penzance. Justin Carnforth was three years my senior and a dreadful bore who could talk of nothing but horses, but he was friendly and hospitable and I did not consider myself above joining the card parties he gave from time to time whenever his parents were away from home. He had a sister, Judith Carnforth, but she was a plain, priggish girl and I was unable to find her congenial company; however, since her fortune was as large as her sense of humor was small, I supposed she would have no trouble finding a husband eventually.

It was through the card parties that I met several other contemporaries of mine, including my kinsman Roger Waymark, whose family owned Gurnards Grange at Zennor, the parish adjoining Morvah to the east; my father's mother had been a Waymark of Zennor and it had been through her that my father had inherited Deveral Farm. Waymark was a pleasant fellow, but unfortunately he shared Carnforth's obsession with horses, and since I have always regarded these animals merely as a convenient form of transport I soon found I had little to say to him. Harry Penmar had formerly been a member of the card-party set but had found it difficult to honor his debts; while he remained welcome at Carnforth Hall he was no longer invited there to play cards. I heard he had his eye on Judith Carnforth, but I did not believe that even Harry Penmar, who was notorious for his debts, could be desperate enough to consider Miss Carnforth as a matrimonial prospect.

I was first introduced to Justin Carnforth—and thus to the card parties at Carnforth Hall—by the young man whose name I had first heard mentioned at Zillan rectory, the solicitor Michael Vincent of Holmes, Holmes, Trebarvah and Holmes. I met him on my second visit to the rectory for lunch, and although he too had little in common with me, I soon decided that he was the only one of my new acquaintances whom I could truly consider a friend.

Being the youngest of four sons, he had been obliged to earn his living, but his education and background made him acceptable at Carnforth Hall even if his lack of money and abundance of moral scruples excluded him from the gambling circle there. When I first met him the disparity in our ages was then at its widest; I was still not yet twenty-one, while he was less than three years on the right side of thirty, a qualified lawyer making his own way in the world. Yet he was not sophisticated. When he was not working at his office he liked simple pleasures such as fishing or playing cricket, and although he enjoyed reading he had no taste for historical biography but preferred historical novels. But I found it easy to talk to him of casual matters, of the walks along the cliffs from Penzance to Lamorna, of expeditions to Logan's Rock, of summer sailing in Mount's Bay, and easier still to appreciate his good-naturedness and enjoy his company. I needed a friend and I sensed he needed one too; he had not been long in Penzance, and although he was well acquainted with the young men in the Carnforth Hall set I suspected they bored him as frequently as they bored me. Roger Waymark was too immature for him, Justin Carnforth too limited, and although Vincent never said so I was sure he disliked Harry Penmar as much as he worshiped Harry's sister Clarissa.

"How beautiful she is!" he would sigh, quite besotted, and would repeat for the hundredth time how hard it was that he had no money behind him and was not in a position to pursue his admiration to its logical conclusion.

But I was still immune to Clarissa. By this time I had seen her once or twice in Penzance, but nevertheless I could only feel cynical about the looks Vincent admired so much. I had seen women before with that full-lipped red mouth and that figure curving lushly to the point of vulgarity, and those women did not usually travel in carriages.

"She may be more like her brother than you think," I warned him one day.

But he would not hear of it. "I hesitate to say this about your cousin, Castallack, but I wouldn't trust Harry Penmar an inch. I don't know why they tolerate him at Carnforth Hall; it's obvious he only wants to marry Judith because he needs to ally himself with an heiress to please his creditors."

"Is it definite that he wants to marry her?"

"There's talk of an engagement. Judith is eager for it, and although Sir James and Lady Carnforth are not so enthusiastic as she is, I think they will eventually give their consent."

"Well, Miss Carnforth hardly has the face that launched a thousand ships," I said practically. "She could do much worse than marry a Penmar."

"Oh, I'm not implying anything against the Penmars as a family! God knows if I had the chance to further my suit with Clarissa—"

60

I sighed. Vincent was apt to become tedious on the subject of Clarissa and I often wondered what he would say if I were to tell him that I too knew what it was to be obsessed with a woman— a farmer's widow ten years older than I was. He would probably be profoundly shocked; he was, I was beginning to discover, a very conventional person. I had never realized how unconventional I was until I became friends with Michael Vincent.

"I'm glad you've made friends with young Vincent," said my father to me at breakfast one morning in August. "He seems a steady fellow, not the kind who would lead you into debt or wild ways. . . . By the way, while on the subject of money, are you managing well enough on your present allowance? You seem to spend a great deal of time in Penzance, and I know how easy it can be to spend money when visiting a town."

I felt both guilty and embarrassed, but I could not tell him I had been supplementing my income by winning money from a set of young men I had met through Michael Vincent. In the end all I said was "I manage well enough, thank you, sir."

"Good, I'm glad. But you won't get into debt, will you, Mark? You will come to me, won't you, if you get into financial difficulties? I don't want you trying to borrow from everyone and ending with a reputation as bad as Harry Penmar's."

"No, sir, I won't get into debt." My guilty conscience made me add, "I shan't be going to Penzance so much anyway in future. I want to start writing my thesis on King John. In fact I think I shall make a start on it this morning."

And I did indeed try to make a start. I went to the morning room with paper and ink, with my notes on the writings of medieval chroniclers, with Kate Norgate's *England Under the Angevin Kings* and other works which purported to deal with my subject; I even phrased an opening statement: "The purpose of this thesis," I wrote boldly, "is to refute the implications of the statement made by Mr. J. R. Green (quoting Matthew Paris): 'Foul as it is, Hell is itself defiled by the fouler presence of King John.'"

I had extremely bold views for a man of my age. "Radical" my tutor had called them coldly when I had tried to argue that the traditional public image of King John was based on the gossipy reminiscences of a couple of chroniclers writing long after John's death. But I was convinced there was a large scope for any historian in a study of John's reign. During my closing months at Oxford I had become determined to remove some of the notoriety from John's reputation, and the idea of a thesis exploding some of the famous myths about him had long been on my mind.

I sat and thought about John for some time.

Beyond the window lay the fields and beyond the fields lay the hamlet of Morvah and beyond Morvah lay the cliffs falling sheer to the sea. It was a hot sunny morning. I could go out, I thought, and walk along the cliffs to Zennor and perhaps call on Roger Waymark at Gurnards Grange.

So I went out, but I did not walk east along the cliffs to Zennor. My feet took me up onto the moors toward Zillan until at last I was passing Chûn Castle and scrambling down the steep hillside to Roslyn Farm.

[6]

At the farm I discovered that Mrs. Roslyn had walked over to Zillan to lay more roses on her husband's grave. It took me at least five minutes to wheedle the information from that hostile old crone Griselda, who had for some unknown reason taken a firm dislike to me.

"Thee's awasting yurr time!" she screeched after me in her heavy Cornish accent as I walked away from the front door through the herb garden. "She don't holden with boys yurr age!"

"That's an extraordinarily insolent remark from a servant in your position!" I retorted, spinning around angrily to face her, but she only replied with a shrill "I ain't no servant!" before retreating to the hall and banging the front door behind her.

I wondered again about the exact nature of her relationship with Mrs. Roslyn.

When I was halfway to Zillan I saw her coming toward me across the moors. She saw me soon afterward; she hesitated slightly, then walked on along the path. It was five minutes before we were finally face to face.

"Good morning, Mr. Castallack," she said politely.

"Good morning, Mrs. Roslyn."

She still wore black since she was still in mourning. All through that summer I saw her wearing only black. I can remember how it accentuated the whiteness of her skin and the gold of her hair and the clearness of her eyes.

I offered to carry her basket. She accepted with a smile and I made some remark about the weather. After we had agreed that it had been unusually clement lately I suggested that as the weather was so encouraging she might wish to venture into Penzance one evening to have dinner with me.

"Thank you," she said, "but I must refuse. I haven't a suitable gown for such an occasion."

"If you would prefer to lunch rather than dine—"

"Thank you, but no, I must ask you to excuse me. I apologize if I seem rude."

Much against my better judgment I found myself compelled to interrogate her about her decision. Was it because she was still in mourning? Was it because I was too young? Was there some other man who—

"Please, Mr. Castallack," she said, and her eyes were so cold that they were no longer blue but gray, "I think you must be forgetting yourself. I am grateful for your offer to take me to Penzance but I do not wish to accept because I do not wish to become associated with you in that particular way. I enjoy your society, and should you wish to call at the farm occasionally I trust you will always have a hospitable reception, but I see no purpose in furthering our association on a more intimate basis. There is no 'other man' in my life. If there were I would have told you about him long ago since I am not and never have been the sort of woman who enjoys a hole-in-the-corner intrigue. I'm a respectable woman, Mr. Castallack, and it's because any more intimate association with you could not have a respectable end that I am obliged to refuse your attentions. Good day."

She reached to take the basket from me, but when I held it away from her she quickened her pace and moved in front of me as if the basket were of no consequence. I caught up with her, my cheeks burning, my heart hammering in my lungs.

"I apologize," I said rapidly. "Please forgive me, Mrs. Roslyn."

She turned to face me again and held out her hand for the basket. "I think I would prefer to return home alone. Excuse me, if you please."

"No, I insist—"

"If you please, Mr. Castallack."

I gave her the basket. "May I at least know," I said unevenly, "if my apologies are accepted? I had no intention of implying by my attentions to you that I thought you to be other than a respectable woman—"

"Really, sir? Then what did you hope to achieve by such attentions?"

"I wished merely to show that I admired you by inviting you to dine with me—"

"And what would have been your next invitation?"

"Mrs. Roslyn, you do yourself an injustice by asking such a question—"

"Perhaps," she said, "but that still shouldn't prevent you from answering it."

"I can only repeat that I have never doubted your respectability."

"I'm glad to hear it. That's not a conclusion I would have reached by judging the way you look at me sometimes."

"I apologize if I've ever given you offense—"

"And besides," she said, not allowing me to finish, "young gentlemen of your breeding and background usually pursue a woman of lower rank for one purpose and one purpose only. You may be very young, but you have that certain degree of arrogance which tells me you fully expect to get your own way. Well, you have miscalculated, Mr. Castallack. I'm not that kind of woman and even if I were I would hardly wish to commit myself to a boy scarce out of his teens."

After a moment I said, "I see."

I slowed my pace; she quickened hers, and we parted. I stood staring after her but presently I stepped aside and slumped down in the heather. A warm wind, slewing across my face, blew my hair into my eyes. I tried to think, to collect my wits, but the encounter had left me so numb that it was not for some minutes that I realized I was furiously angry.

"Bitch!" I said softly to the warm breeze from the hills. "Bitch!"

Her stepson Jared Roslyn had called her that. I could remember how shocked I had been to hear him address her in that fashion when I had first called at Roslyn Farm.

Tears pricked my eyes. I dashed them aside, stood up, shoved my fists into my pockets. Walking uphill, I went over the entire conversation word for word and decided what I should have said. She had had the upper hand from beginning to end. I should have taken a much firmer line, been less meek, less ready to stammer apologies. No wonder she had thought me too young to consider seriously! I had behaved like a schoolboy, allowed her to dictate to me and turn the conversation whichever way she chose. Very well, I thought fiercely, she was a respectable woman. But that did not mean she couldn't be won. Just because I had tried to win her did not give her the right to adopt such haughty airs and behave in such an icily contemptuous manner. I tried to remember if I had ever given her serious cause to take offense and came to the conclusion that I had not. Finally I was driven to conclude that she was weary of my continual calls at the farm and had deliberately effected a quarrel with me to sever the tenuous relationship that existed between us.

Tears pricked my eyes again. My anger had ebbed and only the misery of rejection was left. I walked on blindly to the summit of the ridge, and at last on reaching Chûn I stumbled into the peaceful shelter of the castle walls.

"Bitch!" I said aloud for the third time and began to cry quietly to myself amidst the piles of ancient stones.

My emotions seemed to run in a cycle. Presently I began to feel angry again, and soon I was so angry that I could no longer keep still. Leaving the castle, I passed Chûn Quoit on my way downhill into Morvah parish, and as I walked I could hear her say the offensive word "boy" again and her disdainful comment: "Young gentlemen of your breeding and background usually pursue a woman of lower rank for one purpose and one purpose only." The comment incensed me for some reason. It was not until I was within quarter of a mile of my father's house that I realized why. It incensed me because it was true and because she—a mere uneducated woman, a farmer's widow—had used the truth in order to outwit me.

I seethed with rage.

When I reached Deveral Farm I shut myself in my room, wept again, fumed again and finally began to pace up and down in an agony of restlessness. In the end I could no longer contain myself. Seeking my father, I told him I intended to ride into St. Ives to spend a day or two with my former school friend Russell St. Enedoc, and although he was startled by my sudden decision he raised no objection to it. Afterward, without even waiting to have lunch, I set off east along the road to Zennor, and late in the afternoon I began my ride down from the hills into St. Ives.

4

Henry consoled himself by taking as his mistress one Rosamund Clifford, the "Fair Rosamund" of later ballads and legends.

—Henry II,
JOHN T. APPLEBY

Rosamund Clifford was a lady of good family.

—The Devil's Brood,
ALFRED DUGGAN

[1]

I had no intention of riding at once to Menherion Castle, the home of the St. Enedocs, and asking for Russell. Instead I left my horse at an inn, reserved a room for the night and set off on foot to explore the town. At the back of my mind lurked the thought that if I searched hard enough I might encounter some acceptable working-class girl on her afternoon off, and presently I moved away from the twisted alleys around the harbor and wandered around the bay toward the beach and the better residential section of the town.

I had often heard it said that St. Ives was as unique as it was picturesque, and now I saw for myself that the reports had not been exaggerated. As I walked through its streets late on that August afternoon I thought it a strange foreign town with its medieval streets and cobbled alleys, its white walls dazzling beneath those warm southern skies. Here at least one could remember that not many centuries ago Cornwall had been another country instead of a remote appendage of England, but I soon realized that St. Ives, far from looking back yearningly toward the past, was beginning to look to the future; there were already signs that it might one day rival Penzance as a seaside resort, and since the coming of the railway the inhabitants of the town, I was told, had become accustomed to the idea that visitors would stay at the boarding houses during August and September while artists would linger in the town to savor the special quality of the light.

The more modern section of St. Ives on the other side of the bay was hardly as quaint as the jumbled collection of fishermen's cottages on the peninsula, but at least it was free from the reek of fish and the odor of medieval sanitation. Regretting that such scenery should be so picturesque from a distance yet so squalid when explored more carefully, I took the path that led down to the sandy beach and glanced around for some promise of a welcome feminine diversion among the bathing tents, the groups of preposterously garbed swimmers and the children playing with their buckets and spades.

I should have returned to my inn when it became clear to me that this was not the day when most working-class girls had their afternoon off. Or I should have walked up to Menherion Castle and called at once on the St. Enedocs. I should have done so many things instead of remaining on that beach, but of course everyone knows how easy it is to be wise after the event, and for me at that moment the event had not even begun.

Unaware of my own foolishness, I lingered by the sea.

I was still wandering aimlessly along the sands when a red beach ball bounced up to strike me on the thigh, and as I swung around in surprise a pugnacious infant elbowed his way past my knees and chased the ball to the water's edge.

"James!" cried a girl's light musical voice behind me on a note of great distress. "How naughty! Apologize to the gentleman at once!" And then as her charge ignored her she called, distraught, "I'm terribly sorry—he's rather naughty today, I'm afraid. I do apologize!"

"Not at all," I said courteously. "Please don't worry."

She looked about eighteen years old. I was amazed when I discovered later that she was a year older than I was. She had pretty fair hair which, being fine, had partially escaped from its fastenings and now fell in curling strands about her face and neck. She had blue eyes and a gentle mouth and an exquisite pink and white skin. If I had not had Janna's memory nailed so forcibly to the forefront of my mind I might have considered this girl reasonably fetching, but as it was I merely thought her a pale reflection of a woman I wanted but could not have.

Of course I knew at once that she was hardly the kind of girl with whom I could amuse myself in the manner I had had in mind, but before I was fully aware of what I was doing I found myself striking up a conversation with her. Her name, I learned, was Rose Parrish. With naïve pleasure I thought how well the name Rose suited her. Her employers, a Mr. and Mrs. Treen of St. Ives, had engaged her as a nursemaid three months previously after her father, a country doctor in Devon, had died penniless and obliged her to earn her own living.

"At first they said I should be a governess," explained Rose, "but my head aches when I begin to think of sums and arithmetic and things like that. Papa tried to teach me, but I was never any good at lessons."

"That's as it should be," I said firmly. "Women were never meant to spend their time doing sums."

Encouraged by my approbation, she lost some of her shyness. "Yes . . . well, I decided I would much prefer to look after children rather than instruct them, so I was very pleased to obtain this post with the Treens. James is a good little boy really." She saw my expression as I looked after the pugnacious infant. "Well, all children are a little willful sometimes, but—"

"Do you bring him down to the beach every afternoon, Miss Parrish?"

"If it's fine, yes."

"Will you be here tomorrow?"

"Oh, tomorrow is my afternoon off."

"It is? How fortunate! Perhaps you would care to have tea with me tomorrow in St. Ives?"

"You're—you're *most* kind, but . . . well, I couldn't possibly . . . Mrs. Treen wouldn't approve at all. You see . . . well, it's hard to explain, but she feels that she is in a way *responsible* for me, so I —well, I would love to, but—"

"I'll call on her and introduce myself," I said "Perhaps if she were to meet me and learn that I'm in St. Ives to visit the St. Enedocs at Menherion Castle—"

"The St. Enedocs!" I might have been referring to a connection with royalty. "Oh, then I'm sure Mrs. Treen wouldn't object! She often engages in charity work with Lady St. Enedoc, and occasionally she and Mr. Treen dine at the castle . . ."

And so it was settled. Nothing could have been easier.

"I'm so sorry," said Rose when at last it was time for her to collect James and leave the beach, "I feel shy of asking again after we've been talking for so long, but what did you say your surname was, sir?"

"Castallack," I responded, and seeing the blank expression with which the English customarily greet Cornish names, I added with an ease born of long practice, " 'Cast' as in 'castigate,' 'allack' as in the abbreviation of Alexander, and the emphasis on the second of the three syllables."

"Mr. Mark Castallack," said Rose, sighing, and the sigh was the sigh of one who is alone in the world and has longed in her loneliness to be befriended by a well-intentioned gentleman. "Oh, I shall be so looking forward to seeing you for tea tomorrow, Mr. Castallack!"

After we had parted I rationalized my foolish behavior by telling myself that tea was the most innocuous social convention ever invented and that as soon as it was over I could continue on my way without seeing her again.

So much for my good intentions.

At three-thirty the following afternoon I presented myself to Mrs. Roderick Treen and was duly scrutinzed by her with meticulous care for some minutes. Finally, having satisfied herself that I was indeed who I said I was and that I appeared to be an honorable gentleman, she summoned Rose to the drawing room, gave us both her blessing and told me she expected Rose to be home by six.

Over a cream tea in a tea shop near the High Street I found conversation was far from difficult. I told her about Oxford and London and she listened breathlessly, hanging on my every word; I told her of my taste for historical scholarship and she drank in everything I said, the sincerity of her admiration shining in her eyes; I told her of my father and brother and home at Gweek, and she, who had neither home nor relatives, sighed and was wistful and said how she wished she could be as fortunate as I was.

"Mr. and Mrs. Treen are very kind and considerate," she was quick to add, "but, after all, I'm only the nursemaid and can't expect too much."

My heart went out to her. I thought of the girls I had met in London that Season, rich, spoiled heiresses who threw tantrums unless they had the exact shade of material they wanted for their ball gowns, who went into a decline if they could not capture a title for themselves in the marriage market. Yet here was this doctor's daughter, worth ten of any female paraded for the London Season only not one tenth as fortunate in terms of affluence and position.

Naturally I saw her the next day. She did not have the afternoon off, but I met her by arrangement on the sands and hired one of the bathing tents in order that we could have greater privacy. The bathing tents, which had been erected by some daring local entrepreneur to cater to the most modern of the summer visitors, were attended by an old man who made a great fuss when I took Rose to the tent I had hired in the gentlemen's section, but a guinea soon silenced him and he made no further effort to disturb us.

After we had eaten the picnic tea Rose had brought, Master James was set to work digging sand castles and Rose and I remained in the tent out of the wind. Presently I leaned forward, closed the flap and secured it tightly against the world outside.

"Please," said Rose anxiously at once, "I must be able to see James. If anything should happen to him . . ."

I kissed her. I thought: One kiss won't make any difference. What's one kiss? It needn't go any further. So I kissed her until all I could see was the sheen of fair hair, the shimmer of white skin, the blur of blue eyes, and suddenly it was as if I were kissing not her at all but Janna and I was in the parlor of Roslyn Farm.

"Please," said Rose's soft, well-bred English voice, so different from Janna's. "Please, Mark . . . no . . ."

Sanity returned with a rush. I released her. "I'm sorry," I said rapidly. "Please forgive me. I've behaved very badly, particularly since I have to leave St. Ives soon and have no idea when I shall be able to return. Our . . . friendship can have no future and it would be utterly wrong of me to pretend otherwise."

She nodded, not looking at me, dumb with disappointment, and suddenly pity destroyed all my good sense and I was leaning forward, taking her in my arms again and holding her in a long and intimate embrace.

"Oh no . . . no, please . . ."

Her lips were soft and warm and very feminine. Her lashes flickered against my cheek and were still.

"Mark . . . no, Mark . . ."

I could feel her breasts straining against her blouse. I undid one button. And another.

"No, you mustn't . . ."

"I won't do anything."

"Then . . ."

"Let me just . . ."

"No!"

"Please, Rose, please." I felt her hesitate at my tone of voice. She no longer stiffened or tried to draw away from me. "Please . . . please . . ."

"You mustn't. I . . ."

"I must. You're so pretty. I must just see . . ."

"I . . ."

"I won't hurt you."

But I did. I was more careful than I had ever been with a woman before, but I still hurt her. Afterward she cried and clung to me and would not let go.

"I didn't mean to . . . What a low opinion you must have of me . . ." She wept, overcome with horrified remorse. "If Mrs. Treen were to find out . . ."

I started reassuring her, consoling her, swearing that I had a higher opinion of her than ever, and all the time I was thinking: This must never happen again. Presently when her tears stopped she gazed at me with such adoration that I looked away in embarrassment. "You're so kind," she said tremulously, "and so good. I knew from the beginning that I would fall in love with you."

I cleared my throat. "I can't offer you anything, Rose. In fact, I—"

"But you can!" she said with shining eyes. "You have!"

I laughed uneasily. "I can hardly expect you to be content with meetings in a tent!"

"I don't mind," she said truthfully. "I think it's romantic. And I did so long for romance when I was alone with no one to talk to."

I was touched again by her simplicity, confused by her unexpected willingness.

"Could you meet me again tomorrow—here—like this?"

"Oh yes—please, yes."

"Rose . . ." I kissed her again. Somewhere far away in the back of my mind common sense stirred and was still. "I suppose," I said idly as an afterthought, "I suppose it's . . . convenient? I mean, you're sure, of course, that it's the right time of the month?"

She blushed scarlet at such an indelicate inquiry and looked away at once. "Yes," I heard her whisper.

It did not occur to me until it was too late that she had completely misunderstood the question.

[2]

I stayed seven days in St. Ives. After the third day I wrote to my father to tell him my intention of prolonging the visit, and on the seventh day, so that I would not be obliged to lie to him later, I called at Menherion Castle to see my friend Russell St. Enedoc and his family. I was penniless. I had just enough money to pay my bill at the inn and I knew I would not be able to return to St. Ives again until I received my next quarter's allowance on the thirtieth of September, a date still more than a month away. However, I left Rose with the promise that I would write and set off at last along the road to Morvah.

I did mean to write. But when I returned to my father's house sanity reclaimed me, and I began to be appalled by what I had done. To treat a whore like a whore was one thing; to treat a well-bred innocent girl like a whore was quite another. The memory of Rose became an embarrassment to me. I knew it would be the height of stupidity to continue the relationship and hoped that she would not be too unhappy if I did not write, but, I told myself firmly, I had to be cruel in order to be kind. It would be better for her as well as for me if she never saw me again.

In an effort to turn my back on such a disgraceful episode I tried to pick up the threads of my old life and spent time seeing Michael Vincent, lunching at the rectory and making sporadic, largely unsuccessful efforts to work on my thesis. I would have tried my hand at gambling again to recoup the money I had spent in St. Ives, but I was already living on borrowed money from my father and I was too afraid of losing it and having to ask him for more. Besides, perhaps fortunately, my card-playing companions were all otherwise engaged at that time; three or four of them, including Roger Waymark, were away in London, and Justin Carnforth was busy entertaining my cousin Harry Penmar, who had become formally engaged to Carnforth's plain but wealthy sister. Soon I was deprived even of Michael Vincent's company, for Clarissa had decided to amuse herself by taking an interest in him and the poor fool was forever rushing over to Penmarric to dance attendance on her. No doubt Miriam Barnwell was full of scorn for him in consequence, but she had become unwell at the time that Harry had announced his engagement to Miss Carnforth, and I had not seen her either for several days despite my weekly visits with my father to the rectory at Zillan.

At first I was glad to have no diversions and thought that at last I might steel myself to do some serious writing, but the will to tackle the thesis still eluded me, and instead, in order to pass the time, I began to write my autobiography (the original draft of this later manuscript). However, this frivolous literary venture was hardly the practice I needed for my intellectual excursions as a historian, and to make matters worse I could not concentrate on the task for more than half an hour at a time. I was continually thinking of Janna, and as the weeks passed I found I was also, much against my will, thinking of Rose.

The scene which haunted me most was the one in which I had carelessly inquired, "You're sure, of course, that it's the right time of the month?" and had accepted unquestioningly her embarrassed murmur of assent. An unpleasant chill tiptoed down my spine whenever I recalled the conversation. What did girls such as Rose know of counting days and making sordid calculations? Supposing she had misunderstood? I now saw it was more likely that she had misinterpreted my question and had thought I was referring to that other time of the month, the unmentionable time that no lady would ever discuss with a member of the opposite sex.

Her letter appealing to me for help came on the day after my twenty-first birthday in late September. I had celebrated my coming of age quietly, drinking champagne with my father, who had given me a handsome gold watch and Gibbon's *Decline and Fall of the Roman Empire*, and having decided to mark the occasion with greater festivities once we had both returned to Gweek for the winter, I was well content to spend an uneventful day at Morvah in my father's company. We discussed my thesis at length, and after he had confessed that he was much impressed by my approach I went to bed with his praises ringing in my ears.

It was a pity my happiness was so short-lived. Within twenty-four hours I was again facing Rose in St. Ives.

[3]

She came to the inn to see me. I had already called at the house where she lived and had been informed by Mrs. Treen that Rose was then indisposed but would be pleased to take tea with me on the morrow, and afterward, trying not to remember Mrs. Treen's pleasure at the apparent revival of Rose's flagging romance, I spent at least two hours walking around the town and dwelling on my predicament.

At last when I finally dragged myself back to the inn I found Rose waiting for me in the hall.

I braced myself, expecting her to burst into tears and dash into my arms in an embarrassing manner, but she did not. I think it was then that I first glimpsed her unexpected strength of character. A spark of admiration flared in my mind briefly and was gone.

"Rose!" I exclaimed. "How did you manage to come here at this hour?"

"Mrs. Treen thinks I'm taking an early night. I asked not to be disturbed and then slipped out by the back stairs when everyone was at dinner. I remembered that you stayed here last time." We stood facing each other. Her face was white and there were violet circles beneath her eyes. She looked fragile, delicate and unhappy. "It was good of you to come," she said at last.

"I came as quickly as I could." I offered her dinner, but she was not hungry, so I suggested we withdraw to my room in order to gain some privacy. She shrank from the suggestion, looking around her desperately as if she were afraid someone was watching, but eventually she agreed to go upstairs with me. In my room we sat down together on the edge of the bed and presently I took her hand and held it.

"Now, Rose . . ." I knew exactly what I was going to say. I had rehearsed the interview twenty times throughout my long ride from Morvah and had made up my mind exactly what was to be done, so I started out by speaking with a confidence that was intended to reassure her. "The first thing we must do," I said briskly, "is see a doctor. There must be a proper diagnosis. Then if the worst is true you can leave all the arrangements to me. I'll take care of you. I'm not rich—in fact I have virtually no money at present—but I do have expectations and I believe I know how I can obtain the money I need. Once I have the money I'll write a letter to you on my mother's notepaper—by a stroke of luck I still have a sheet or two of her stationery in my writing case—and pretend that my mother is offering you a post in London. You can show the letter to Mrs. Treen and I don't think she'll question it. That'll give you the excuse to leave St. Ives. Now, while you're waiting I think it would be best if you lived in Penzance—at least so long as I'm at Morvah; if I have to return to Gweek I can arrange for you to move to Helston. However, Penzance is best at present since it's near enough to Morvah to enable me to visit you every week to see that all's well. I'll rent some rooms for you there, and I'll pay the doctor and the midwife and the rent and all the other expenses. There's no need for you to worry, you see. You can wear a wedding ring and be known as Mrs. Parrish, a widow, and no one will ever guess the truth. After it's all over, you can have the baby adopted. There are plenty of well-to-do childless couples—"

"No," she said.

There was a silence. As I caught my breath I saw a tear trickle silently down her cheek. "But, Rose—"

"No," she said and set her gentle mouth in a stubborn line. "I couldn't. I couldn't give away my own baby. It would break my heart."

I was silenced. I did not know what to do. I had not considered this possibility at all.

"I won't ask you for help after he's born," she said. "I'll manage somehow. But I won't give him away."

"But, Rose, I don't see how I can support—"

"I've said I won't ask you for help."

"But of course I must help you!" I felt trapped and angry. "But don't you think you're being selfish? Don't you think well-to-do foster-parents would give him more of a start in life than—"

"No," she said, "I'm his own mother and I shall love him and no child can have a better start in life than love. You're the one who's being selfish."

I stood up abruptly. "I'm merely trying to be practical and constructive and do what's best for us both! Da—" I checked the profanity just in time—"dash it, Rose, if you keep the child you may never get married! At least as an unattached woman you would have more chance to—"

"If I can't marry you I don't want to marry anyone."

I was silenced again. "But I . . ." Words failed me. At last I managed to stammer, "But I can't marry you, Rose! I can't!"

"Yes, you explained," she said. "You have no money." She hesitated before adding rapidly, not looking at me, "But if you have expectations . . . perhaps later . . ."

"It's not just the question of money." Guilt made me confess a truth which I had always intended to keep from her. "You see, there's this other woman . . ."

She put her hands over her ears. "I don't want to hear."

"But . . ."

She let her hands fall. "If there was someone else, why did you pay attention to me that week when you came to St. Ives?"

"It was wrong of me—"

"So you never cared. Not even then."

"Yes, I did—I did in a way . . . I *am* fond of you, Rose, but—"

"Are you and she—as we were in the bathing tent?"

"No."

She looked wretched. As I stared at her in misery she tried to speak but the words would not come. At last she managed to say unevenly, "I shouldn't have consented . . . in the bathing tent . . . but I loved you so much I scarcely knew what was happening until—oh, how foolish you must think me, how foolish and ignorant and contemptible!"

"It wasn't your fault, Rose. Of course any decent well-brought-up girl should be ignorant of such things. That goes without saying. The fault was mine, and why you should even want to marry me after I've treated you so shamefully—"

"I love you," she said simply.

"You can't possibly!"

"I do, I can't help it." Her eyes were bright with tears again. "I've never met anyone like you before. You're so different, Mark, from the young men I used to know in Devon. You're so clever, so full of energy and—and purpose . . . even to be with you is exciting and novel. You cannot conceive how much those few days we spent together meant to me. They were the most wonderful days of my whole life."

I was scarlet with embarrassment, speechless with remorse.

"Don't be angry with me, Mark. Please."

"I'm not angry with you, Rose," I said. "I'm not." I felt so consumed with shame that I could hardly bear to stay in the same room with her. "But I'm plain!" I said angrily, wanting her to hate me, wanting her contempt, wanting anything that would take the edge from my enormous sense of guilt. "I'm ugly! I'm too stout! I'm not even attractive! How can I seem exciting to you?"

She stared, her cheeks wet with tears, her lips trembling, but in spite of her grief I saw a faint smile hover at the corner of her mouth. "Oh?" she said. "I never noticed. I always thought your looks were so striking. I never thought you were plain."

I opened the window and leaned out over the sill. The fresh air cooled my face. Gulls wheeled over the harbor far below and soared effortlessly into the sky above the narrow alleys of the town.

Her hand touched my arm. "Mark, I should go before Mrs. Treen discovers I'm missing. Oh, Mark, forgive me for being sad and cross. I am so very grateful to you for coming to help me like this."

And after that there was nothing else I could do but say that I was sorry too if I had spoken harshly or been unkind.

When I had escorted her back to the Treens' house I stopped at the gates of the drive to kiss her good night. "Remember that there's no need for you to worry," I said for the last time that evening. "I promise I'll look after you. You mustn't worry any more."

She smiled as well as she could. Her face was by this time pinched with exhaustion, but even as I opened my mouth to express my concern she turned away from me without another word and walked on alone up the drive to the house.

[4]

The doctor eventually decided that she was pregnant. Moving ahead at once with the plans I had made earlier, I paved the way for Rose's withdrawal from St. Ives by forging the necessary letter from my mother and sent it to Rose with a suitably bland note to say that she might wish to show the letter to Mrs. Treen. After that I turned my attentions away from St. Ives and rode into Penzance to confide my troubles to Michael Vincent.

He looked pale, as if he had spent long hours working at some unrewarding task. His gray eyes were bloodshot, and I noticed for the first time that his hair was already thinning at the temples.

"How are you?" I said perfunctorily. "I haven't seen you for a long time. How's Clarissa?"

He shrugged. "I haven't been at Penmarric lately."

So that was it. Clarissa had become bored with toying with the affections of an impecunious provincial lawyer and had turned her attentions elsewhere. I felt sorry for him. After making arrangements to lunch with him I left him to his business and did not see him again until we met two hours later at the tavern we frequented.

Once we were seated I embarked on the difficult task of seeking his advice after providing him with the minimum of explanation. Knowing he was well acquainted with Penzance, I asked if he could advise me where to look to find respectable but reasonably priced rooms for Rose, and as I had anticipated he was able to make several helpful suggestions. However, his curiosity was finally aroused and I felt obliged to tell him that I required the rooms for a friend of mine who had had the misfortune to succumb to a certain feminine condition.

He stared at me round-eyed. "Good God," he muttered at last, "you Penmars are a fast crowd, I must say. We had to pay off one of Harry's mistresses the other day. She had heard of his engagement to Judith Carnforth and was trying to make trouble."

"My name is not Penmar," I said, much too sharply. "It's Castallack. And Harry isn't related to me by blood at all. He's the adopted son of Giles, his nephew by marriage."

"Yes, I know. I—"

"And frankly, Vincent, if you'll forgive me saying so, you had no business to tell me that story about paying off one of Harry's mistresses. I thought lawyers were supposed to hold that sort of thing in confidence."

"Yes—yes, I'm sorry. You're absolutely right." He looked haggard. "I'm afraid I'm rather embittered about the Penmars at the moment. You mustn't listen to me. But, Castallack, what kind of woman is this—this friend of yours? How did it happen? What the devil are you going to do if your father finds out?"

"He won't find out because you're the only person I intend to tell." The very thought that my father might discover my affair with Rose was enough to make me feel stiff with fright. I told Vincent as little as possible, but he was still shocked to the core. It was clear he thought I should marry Rose to put matters right and disapproved of the fact that I took the practical and not the gentlemanly point of view.

After lunch I walked back to his office with him. It was a gray day at the end of September and the smell of boats and fish floated up toward us from the harbor. Close at hand the clock of the church on the hill was pointing its hands to two o'clock, and

I was just about to bid Vincent goodbye when there was a stormy clatter of horse's hoofs behind us, and, swinging around, we saw Justin Carnforth rein to a halt as he shouted a greeting in our direction.

"Castallack! Vincent! Wait a moment!"

We tried not to groan. Conversations with Carnforth had an annoying habit of being one-sided and interminable, and the odds were that this one would be no exception.

"How are you, Carnforth?" called Vincent politely, and then, seeing his expression, added at once, "Is something wrong?"

"Wrong! By God!" His face was dark with rage. "Haven't you heard the news? I'm so angry I can scarcely contain myself! That blackguard Harry Penmar! By Jove, if I ever get my hands on him I'll—"

"What's he done?" I interrupted, suddenly becoming interested. "What's happened?"

Carnforth was spluttering with emotion. "My sister—Judith— his own wife-to-be—"

"He eloped with her?" said Vincent, amazed.

"No!" roared Carnforth. "No, damn it, sir, he jilted her! He's eloped with the rector of Zillan's daughter! He's eloped with little Miriam Barnwell! A clergyman's daughter, by heavens! When I think of my poor sister, humiliated, shamed—"

"Good God," said Vincent. "What a terrible shock for the rector!"

"Mrs. Barnwell will be pleased anyway," I said, amused. "Her daughter will be marrying into county circles even if the marriage is conducted in a rather unorthodox fashion."

"Damn the Barnwells!" spluttered Carnforth. "What about my sister? Jilted, by God! Now listen, Vincent—you're often at Penmarric nowadays, aren't you? When you next see Clarissa you tell her to tell her brother that if he ever sets foot in Penzance again, I'll—"

"Yes, yes," said Vincent hastily, a little white around the lips at this mention of Clarissa but anxious to quieten Carnforth as quickly as possible. His loud-voiced histrionics had already attracted the attention of the passers-by. "I'll tell her."

"And if you're ever at Penmarric, Castallack—"

"I never am," I said politely, and as soon as I had spoken I remembered my intention to go there the very next day in order to beg the money I needed from Giles Penmar.

79

"What a disgraceful situation," said my father to me at dinner. "To think that Miriam Barnwell, a clergyman's daughter, a well-brought-up, gentle young girl, should suddenly abandon all the moral principles instilled in her and run off with a rake like that! I can't understand it. It's always distressing when a girl of her background behaves in an unprincipled fashion, and this time it's doubly distressing because I feel so sorry for her parents. Poor Barnwell will be dreadfully upset."

"Yes, sir."

"I hesitate to say this, but I fear part of the blame must be put upon Mrs. Barnwell. She was always much too anxious for her daughter to marry well. I'm sure she engineered and encouraged Miriam's flirtation with young Raymond last summer before Giles sent him abroad, and it wouldn't surprise me if she had turned a blind eye to this latest business with Harry. Heavens, surely she must have known the two of them were having secret meetings somewhere even after Harry became engaged to Judith Carnforth! How could she have let such a thing happen right under her nose? I suppose Harry decided to marry Judith in order to please Giles and his creditors and then backed out at the last minute to run away with a girl he found more attractive."

"Yes, sir."

"How any young man could behave so despicably I can't imagine. It wouldn't surprise me if he didn't even marry poor little Miriam, and then what will happen to her? She'll be completely ruined. Much as I blame her for her deplorable moral lapse, I feel I must blame Harry more. I really think that any young man who uses a well-brought-up, respectable young girl for his own selfish and wanton purposes must be exceptionally wicked."

"Yes."

He looked at me closely. "I think you're as shocked by the news as I am," he observed. "You're very quiet tonight. Are you feeling well?"

"I'm a little tired," I said. "I think, if you'll excuse me, sir . . ."

"Yes, certainly. I hope you sleep well and have a good rest." He smiled at me, his eyes so blue and honest, and of course it never even occurred to him as he bade me good night that I might have behaved as despicably as Harry Penmar.

[6]

It was the following morning that I rode to Penmarric to see Giles.

After I had received Rose's letter begging my assistance and realized that I would soon need to borrow a large sum of money, I had wracked my brains for some time to decide whom I should approach. For a while I almost thought I might overcome my pride and attempt to borrow from my mother, but I was too afraid she might write to my father and—believing herself to be acting in my best interests—demand to know why he gave me such a meager allowance that I was obliged to approach her for financial support. No, I thought, better not to involve my mother in a situation that was already disastrous. But who else was there? Cousin Robert Yorke was wealthy and fond enough of me, I knew, to give me any sum I needed, but he was my mother's puppet and could not be expected to keep the secret from her. To approach my father, of course, was out of the question.

That left Giles Penmar.

But as soon as I had decided that he would be likely to help me I pushed all thought of him from my mind. Thinking of Giles was a dangerous pastime, a habit which I knew must be instantly suppressed. After the first onslaught of shock that had followed my mother's wild revelations some weeks ago I had built a wall around the memory to protect myself from it, and the wall had effectively repelled all speculation that might have caused me to lose control over my emotions and initiate scenes that could only end in disaster. So I refused to think of Giles, refused to think of those revelations that I would not and could not believe. I remembered only that I was his heir and that he would probably grant me a portion of the money he intended to leave me in his will, and then the door to my mind slammed shut and I did not think of him again until I realized I could no longer postpone the ordeal of a further interview at Penmarric.

When I arrived at the house that morning I found it lonely and deserted, its somber walls wreathed in an oppressive Cornish mist. For one long moment I stared at the place, not knowing why I loved it when it was so ugly, but aware that it was waiting for me to infuse it with life. I smiled, amused by my sentimentality, but the sentiment stayed, lodged irrevocably in my mind. It was my house, my land; and one day I would take possession.

Five minutes later, after a tousle-headed groom had taken my horse and a footman, anxious to please his future master, had ushered me speedily across the threshold, I was standing once more in the morning room with the threadbare Indian carpet and watching the cool mist blowing across the terrace from the sea.

I was just wondering in an agony of suspense how much longer I would have to wait for the master of the house to appear when the door opened and I saw not the dreaded spectacle of my cousin in his wheelchair but the far from unpleasant sight of his adopted daughter Clarissa.

"My dear Cousin Mark!" she said in a tone of voice designed to make my spine tingle with delight. "I come bearing the olive branch of peace at last!"

To give credit where credit is due, I must confess that my spine did tingle once or twice before I managed to recall my long-standing indifference to her looks. She was wearing a cream-colored gown shot with apple-green silk and it suited her very well. It was also too tight in some questionable places, and I fancied that if she had had a mother or an aunt or indeed any kind of female chaperone the dress would either have gone un-worn or else would have been sent to the seamstress to be altered.

"Good morning, Cousin Clarissa," I said guardedly. "I thank you for the olive branch and accept it with pleasure."

"I'm sure you're wondering why I've decided to sue for peace," she said, arranging herself cleverly on the chaise longue and mo-tioning me to sit down beside her. "After all, we've been enemies for such a long time, have we not?"

"I've never wished to be enemies with anyone here at Pen-marric, Clarissa," I said, sitting down on one of the armchairs. "The choice was yours, not mine."

"Oh, but surely you can understand how we felt! Harry and I were always just the two little poor relations who weren't really Penmars at all. Papa—my adopted Papa, I should say—cared only for Raymond, and once Raymond was gone he saw nothing odd about making his will in favor of a complete stranger. Surely you can understand how Harry and I felt."

"Perhaps . . . But why should you feel any differently toward me now?"

"You can thank that sly little fortune hunter Miriam Barnwell! Oh, how Harry could have been deceived by that girl simply

82

defies all explanation! Of course, this is the final straw—Papa will disinherit him now and I don't suppose I shall see him again for years and years and . . . well, it's very lonely here at Penmarric, Cousin Mark." She gave me a long lonely look from her dark lonely eyes. They were beautiful eyes, large, brilliant and long-lashed. "It's such a dreary, desolate house! I could not bear to think that with Harry gone I might be entombed here for weeks without anyone coming to see me."

"My dear Clarissa," I said pleasantly, "you're far too modest. You know as well as I do that you have only to raise your little finger and my friend Vincent will come racing over the moors to keep you company."

"Oh, I had forgotten dear Mr. Vincent was a friend of yours!" She smiled at me before adding carelessly, "But how could I have forgotten? It's true I had decided not to see him so frequently, but last night he came to Penmarric on some errand or other and I took pity on him—we drank a glass of port together and he told me—oh!—*so* many fascinating things about you, Cousin Mark!"

I looked at her. She went on smiling. I can remember thinking to myself very precisely: If that fool Vincent has breathed one word to this girl about my predicament with Rose I'll see he wishes he'd never set eyes on either me or Clarissa Penmar.

"He really seems to know an amazing amount about you. I hear you're very popular with the ladies, Cousin Mark. In fact that was one of the reasons why I decided to present you with the olive branch. I'm always intrigued by gentlemen who have a romantic reputation."

"Romantic?" said my voice, matching the languor of her meas-ured drawl. "I fear Vincent has been too generous in his appraisal of my achievements in that field. As you see, I'm hardly suffi-ciently endowed with romantic looks to follow your brother Harry's example."

"Who cares about romantic looks once the curtains are drawn and the candle's out?"

I rose to my feet as if I had been jerked upward by a violent hand. I think I even gasped. I had never heard such words from a girl of her age and background before.

She laughed. "Don't look so shocked! I've been Harry's confi-dante for years! I know what goes on in the world." She too rose to her feet, and as she strolled gracefully across the room toward me I realized with an even deeper shock that every shred of the lascivious gossip about her was true. "Would you like me to give you a tour of the house?" she said lightly. "I could show you—"

"No thanks," I said shortly.

I saw her dark eyebrows raise themselves slightly at my tone of voice. Her smile faded. "Come, Mark, that's hardly very civil, is it? I thought you'd accepted the olive branch."

I turned away from her and moved toward the bell with the intention of reminding the footman that I was still waiting to see Giles. But before I could touch the bell she said coolly in that warm, flexible voice of hers, "I really think you would find me more entertaining than a doctor's daughter. There's something so terribly dreary about the middle classes, don't you think?"

I spun around but found myself unable to speak.

She laughed at my expression. "You're angry because I know about your miserable little doctor's daughter!"

"Listen, Clarissa," I said in an exceptionally polite voice, "if you say one word more in that tone about a woman who is a thousand times more a lady than you'll ever be—"

"How boring to have a ladylike mistress!"

I struck her. I slapped her across the face with the palm of my hand and saw her eyes blaze as her hand flew to her cheek.

"You . . . bastard!" She spat at me as hard as she could, and the ugly word selected by her on an impulse without regard to its true meaning rang in my ears more viciously than any four-lettered obscenity from the gutter. "You . . . miserable . . . bastard . . ." She could hardly speak. She began to tremble with rage "How dare you strike me like that?" she said in a rush at last. "Get out! Get out this minute or you'll be sorry you ever came!"

I pulled out my handkerchief, wiped her spittle from my cheek and sat down deliberately on the chaise longue.

"Very well," she said, still shaking with rage. "I'll summon the footmen and have you thrown out."

I had been on the verge of losing my temper for several minutes and now I lost it completely. Leaping to my feet, I grabbed her before she could ring the bell and shook her till she was speechless. "You little . . . running around like a . . ." My white-hot temper had been the bane of my childhood, and although I had now reached an age when I could control it even under extreme provocation, once it was lost it was lost and I cared not what I said. "Do you think I can't guess why you're so angry? Do you imagine I don't realize that you can't endure to think yourself resistible? You were being vicious and spiteful to pay me back for my lack of interest in you! You think you can treat me like you treat that fool Vincent, but by God you've come to the wrong person this time! No woman dictates to me or tries to push me into doing what she wants. Besides, why should I be interested in you? You're not even beautiful with your brown cow's eyes and your thick-lipped mouth and your repulsive mass of black curls! Why, I wouldn't even go to bed with you if you paid me!"

And as I threw her aside so violently that she stumbled upon the chaise longue, the door of the room opened, someone coughed from the threshold and the next moment the butler was announcing in a voice filled with respectful trepidation that the master of the house was waiting to receive me.

[7]

"What's your name?" I demanded abruptly of the butler as I followed him across the vast gloomy hall to the wide staircase. I was straightening my tie as I spoke and wiping the sweat of rage from my forehead. My hand was still trembling.

"Medlyn, sir." I could see that I had already proved conclusively to him that I was as wild in my ways as any Penmar, and as we ascended the staircase to the gallery he drew my attention to the portraits of my upstart ancestors that lined the walls. The first Penmar, the gambler called Baker who had won Penmarric from the Prince Regent, had elected to be painted with the notorious dice in his hands; his air was one of cynicism and worldliness, and despite the effete costume of the Brummel era he looked indisputably tough. Beyond him were the portraits of his three sons, the older two who had come to uncertain ends and the youngest, my grandfather Mark Penmar, who had made a fortune by profiteering in India before he had become master of Penmarric. I stared at the father my mother had loved so much. As she had often said, I was much like him to look at; I recognized the dark slanting eyes, the ugly nose and the wide mouth, but not the cold expression which I disliked, nor the craftiness about the eyes which I distrusted. Last came the portraits of my mother and her brother Arthur, who had drowned in a sailing accident to

leave Penmarric without an heir; he was certainly the first Penmar who could be described as handsome, but he was also the
first who looked a complete fool. I turned to the portrait of my
mother, painted when she had been eighteen, and searched for
some likeness to the hard, embittered, overbearing woman I knew,
but there was none. Her dark eyes shone softly; her lips were
Sadness gripped me suddenly. I turned aside and followed Med-
slightly parted. She was radiant.
lyn away from the gallery into a long corridor which led to the
bedroom of the master of the house, the famous Tower Room of
Penmarric where my cousin was slowly dying in his bed which
faced the sea.

The stench of the sickroom met me as I crossed the threshold,
but I tried not to flinch. His dark eyes were sunk deep in their
sockets and his face was like a death mask as he greeted me and
bade me sit down. The elderly nurse withdrew in silence. We
were alone.

"So you came back," he said at last. "I wondered if you
would."

"Yes, sir." But I could no longer look at him. I was too much
aware that I felt nothing, no chord of response, no intangible
bond, no communication, understanding or love. He was merely
a stranger whom I would never know.

"But of course you had a strong reason for choosing to visit
me," he said dryly. "I'm not naïve." When I did not speak he said
abruptly, "You heard about Harry, of course. Well, don't think
it will mean you'll now get all my money. You won't. I've given
you quite enough to satisfy my conscience. I'm adding Harry's
share to Clarissa's dowry in the hope that some man will feel
inclined to marry her for her money. Lord knows no man will
feel inclined to marry her for her reputation."

I was embarrassed. I glanced around uneasily at the huge cir-
cular room with its windows facing the moors and the sea and
remained silent.

At last he said sardonically, "Well, you'd better tell me. How
much do you want?"

"If—if you could treat the sum as a portion, sir, and not as a
gift—"

"Naturally. How much?"

I mentioned a figure.

"Why do you need this money? Doesn't your father give you
an allowance?"

We were already on dangerous ground. The numbness was leaving me and I was beginning to feel the pain, but when I spoke my voice was cooler than ever, cold and crisp and self-possessed. "Sir, I don't like to ask him for such a sum since I can't ask him to treat it as a portion. He intends to leave most of his money to my younger brother."

"Does he indeed! And why's that, do you suppose?"

The pain was drenching me, soaking through every nerve in my body as my face flamed beneath his stare. "It would be unfair, sir . . . since I am to inherit Penmarric . . ." I hardly knew what I said. "Nigel should have Gweekellis Manor . . . only fair and just . . ."

"I can think of nothing more unjust than disinheriting an elder son in favor of a younger—unless, of course, Castallack believes he has only one son."

In the second after he spoke I thought the pain was too great to tolerate a second longer and rose to my feet to stumble from the room. But he stopped me. He mistook my misery for rage, and as I turned my back on him and groped for the door he called after me in a rapid, uneven voice, "Wait! I'll give you the money! There's no need to lose your temper. I apologize for speaking of such a painful subject, but ever since you came here with your mother I've been thinking about you and wondering if—however, that makes little difference now, I suppose. Now, go over to the secretaire and open the top drawer. . . . That's right. There's paper there and a pen. You'll have to write at my dictation. I shall ask Trebarvah, my lawyer, to make the necessary arrangements at the bank to transfer the money to you."

By a great effort of will I steadied my shaking fingers, picked up the pen and did as I was told.

After the letter was signed I heard him advise me to spend the money profitably instead of frittering it away in typical Penmar fashion on cards, horses and women, but by this time I had a new grip on my self-control and anger was elbowing the pain aside. When I retorted, "My name is Castallack, sir, not Penmar," my voice was as cold as the gray sea beyond the windows and as bleak as the moors beyond the grounds.

"Ah yes," he said, and as our glances met for one long moment I was aware of things I had no wish to be aware of—of a chord of response within me, a shaft of understanding, a shadow of compassion which I could not help but acknowledge. "Ah yes," said Giles Penmar, and I saw the loneliness in his sick, gaunt face and somehow managed to forgive him. "Your name is Castallack." His mouth curved in a small, polite sneer. "I beg your pardon."

I left soon after that. I half walked, half ran down the dark passage to the gallery, and all the past Penmars seemed to mock me from their frames as I stumbled down the stairs to the hall. No house had ever seemed as oppressive to me as Penmarric seemed at that moment, and as I rode off down the drive at the gallop I wished in a fit of misery that my great-grandfather had lost his notorious game of dice with the Prince Regent and had remained a nobody called Baker for the remainder of his adventurer's career.

5

In despair he sent messengers to King Stephen to beg him as his kinsman to help him. . . . [Stephen] immediately sent the boy who had tried to usurp his crown all the money he needed.

Geoffrey complained of not feeling well. . . . The Count developed a high fever and made his preparations for death.

—Henry II,
JOHN T. APPLEBY

[1]

Much to my annoyance I lay awake for some time that night and thought of Clarissa Penmar. No doubt if I had not thought of Clarissa I would have lain awake thinking of the interview with Giles, but I was making a great effort not to dwell upon that scene in the Tower Room, and in the attempt to suppress all thought of it from my mind it was a relief instead to turn to Clarissa and recall my quarrel with her word for word.

In the past I had met my share of disreputable women, but at least they had made no pretense to be better than they were, and it was easy to blame their lack of respectability on the lot of the lower classes and sundry other social circumstances. To have money and an aristocratic background and still choose to behave in an unprincipled fashion was a phenomenon I had not en-countered before. Discreet immorality, yes; I knew as well as anyone what went on in London circles, but flagrant promiscuity by an unmarried girl was rare; most—I had thought all—girls of my class were virgins until they married no matter what might happen to their sense of values in later life. Often this virginity might not have been due to chaste principles at all but more to lack of opportunity, for even when they made their debut in London society they would always be chaperoned. Even Cla-rissa must have had her chaperone when she had taken part in the London Season, but evidently her chaperone had been very far from omnipresent.

I could not help wondering how many men Clarissa had se-duced, and much to my disgust I found myself remembering her with an unwilling but prurient interest. I had told her in the height of my rage that she did not attract me and that was true, but most men have a sneaking interest in a woman they know to be promiscuous and it seemed to my annoyance that I was no exception.

In an effort to turn my mind to other matters I began to think of Michael Vincent. I was so angry with him for betraying my confidence that I found it difficult to think rationally on the sub-ject, but finally when morning came I rode into Penzance to see him.

"Castallack!" he exclaimed as the clerk showed me into his office. "What a pleasant surprise!"

"I think not," I said abruptly and waited for the clerk to close the door. Then: "Damn you," I said. My voice was trembling with anger although I had myself tightly in control. "Damn you. If we were not in your office where people would hear any noise we made I'd knock you down and, with luck, break your bloody nose."

"Castallack . . ." He was ashen. "I don't—"

"No, don't tell me you don't know what I'm talking about! You damned fool! How dare you tell your mistress about my private life!"

"Mistress!" He looked as if he were about to faint.

"Mistress!" I yelled at him. "Mistress! You told that whore at Penmarric about Rose Parrish!"

"Clarissa's not my mistress," he said. "She's not."

"You think you can convince me of that?" I could feel my

temper slipping away from me again. I tried to grab hold of it before it slipped out of my control. "Why, she'd give herself to any man who offered his services! Good God, she even offered herself to me! So don't attempt to tell me—"

He stood up. He was shaking in every limb. "You—you . . ." He could not speak. "You mean you and she—"

"God Almighty, Vincent, don't be such a bloody fool! Do you think I would have the inclination to fornicate on a threadbare Indian carpet in the morning room at Penmarric after I knew that you'd told her—"

"Oh God," he said and sat down again very suddenly. "Oh God." And he covered his face with his hands.

I stared at him. "Very well," I said bitterly at last. "Very well. She's not your mistress. Maybe she's sleeping with the head groom instead. But if she's not even your mistress you have even less excuse than I imagined for telling her about Rose Parrish! I told you about Rose in the strictest confidence—I relied on your ethical standards as a lawyer and as a gentleman, but you be-trayed that confidence and you betrayed those standards—"

"Don't talk to me about ethical standards," he said. "You don't possess any. If you'd behaved like a gentleman you would never have had to tell me about Rose Parrish in the first place."

"God damn it!" I shouted. "Don't you preach to me!"

"Then don't preach to me either!"

"Why, you—"

"Very well, I'm sorry. I'm sorry I told her! I'm sorry! I didn't mean to tell her, it was simply that we were talking of you and she was making some remark about—about you not sharing your cousin Raymond's good looks, and I said—without thinking—that other women found you good-looking enough—"

"You weak, spineless—"

"I didn't mean to tell her, I swear it! But I loved her, Castal-lack, I still love her—when I'm with her I forget everything, I'm clay in her hands—"

"Clay!" I stared at him in contempt. "Why, you poor devil, she'll break you. She'll snap you in two! You're wasting your time because she'll never love you. The most you can hope for is a few hours in her bedroom at Penmarric before she turns to someone else."

He hit me so quickly that I did not react fast enough to duck away from his fist. One moment he was slumped apathetically in his chair and the next he was on his feet, leaning forward and punching me across the room. I crashed into three deed boxes, knocked a sheaf of papers off a stool and collided with a wooden cupboard. The cupboard door flew open. Pens, nibs and blotting paper cascaded onto the floor.

"Castallack—are you all right?" He was so completely the gentleman that he even tried to help me to my feet after he had knocked me down.

I picked myself up unaided and turned my back on him.

"Castallack, I'm sorry. Look, I don't want to quarrel with you. Please forgive me and let's continue to be friends. I know I behaved abominably in betraying your confidence and I apologize from the bottom of my heart, but—"

"I'll never trust you again," I said between my teeth and walked out of the room.

The door slammed as I jerked the handle. In the outer office the three old clerks looked up at me curiously over the tops of their spectacles, but I did not stop. Hardly aware of where I was going, I strode out into the street and then, still speechless with rage, blazed downhill to the esplanade and the soothing serenity of the Metropole Hotel.

It was a long time before I returned to that office to make my peace with Michael Vincent; we were to remain estranged for many months to come.

[2]

That afternoon I found a suite of rooms for Rose which overlooked the sea and engaged the landlady's daughter, a pleasant, efficient woman, to look after Rose by doing the cooking, shopping and other household business.

"My cousin Mrs. Parrish is in a delicate state of health," I said to both the landlady and her daughter after the arrangements were completed. "Her husband died very tragically only a month ago in France."

They sighed in sympathy.

"Poor soul," said the landlady. "Poor young lady."

"He was experimenting there with a horseless carriage," I said. "The engine blew up and it went out of control. It was a great tragedy."

They were round-eyed. They had heard that such things went on in France but this was their first acquaintance with someone who was directly connected with this latest contribution to modern science.

"All those newfangled inventions" was the landlady's disapproving comment.

"No good will come of them," said her daughter. "No good at all."

They nodded in unison. I left them still pondering on the fate of the mythical Mr. Parrish and visited the writing room of the Metropole to draft a note to Rose. I told her I had taken the rooms and engaged a maid and promised to send a hired carriage over to St. Ives to fetch her the very next Monday.

"You can tell the Treens the carriage is taking you to the station to catch the train to London," I wrote. "If they want to come with you to see you off, tell them that the strain of a station parting would be too much for you. I'll try to be at your rooms when you arrive, but if I'm not there Mrs. Polgear and her daughter will be expecting you, so there is no need to worry. I'm leaving twenty pounds for you with the Manager of the Great Western Bank, 16, Market Jew Street, and if ever you are in great need and cannot communicate with me at once you can always go for help to Mr. Michael Vincent, a lawyer in the firm of Holmes, Holmes, Trebarvah and Holmes at 3, Bolitho Alley, off Market Jew Street near the statue of Sir Humphrey Davey. I will of course be in touch with you every week. . . ."

I thought that there was no harm in giving her Vincent's name. No matter what our current relationship happened to be he would always help a lady in distress if the need arose.

I sealed the letter, posted it, returned to my horse. It was early evening by that time and I knew I would have to hurry in order to be home in time for dinner. Accordingly, feeling satisfied that the arrangements for Rose were completed yet still bitter about my quarrel with Vincent, I left Penzance and rode up into the hills through Zillan to my father's house at Morvah.

[3]

I did not see my father when I arrived home. I presumed he was working in his study, and after I had rubbed down my horse and left him in the care of Mannack in the stables I went to my room and began to change for dinner. Presently Mrs. Mannack brought me hot water.

"Mr. Castallack says he would like to see you, sir," she said, setting down the ewer on the stand. "At your convenience."

"Very well. Thank you, Mrs. Mannack."

"Thank you, sir." She withdrew.

I washed and changed quickly; when I was ready I went downstairs and knocked on the door of my father's study.

"Come in," I heard him call.

I entered the room. He was standing by the window and watching the evening light cast long shadows over the moors. I was halfway across the floor toward him before I saw he had a letter in his hand.

I stopped. He turned. His eyes were shadowed and unhappy. He held out the letter.

"Please read this," he said. He did not say anything else, just "Please read this," so I took the letter and looked at it and there at the top of the page was the familiar Penmar crest and at the foot of the page the signature "Clarissa Penmar."

I looked up at him. Nothing happened. There was a clock ticking somewhere, and far away beyond the window the sun was sinking to a bloody death in that opaque Cornish sea.

"Read it," he said.

I looked back at the letter. "Dear Mr. Castallack," Clarissa had written in a childish, spiteful hand, "you might be interested to know that your son was here today to beg for money—or so my father told me. It seems Cousin Mark wishes to keep a woman in Penzance, a doctor's—"

The page drifted from my fingers and fell to the floor without a sound. There was a terrible tightness in my throat. I turned away.

After a long while he said, "Is it true?"

I did not answer. I was by his desk, touching his pen, his inkwell. My fingers trailed meaninglessly over his books. I could not see.

"Is it true, Mark?"

"No," I said. "No, it's all lies."

I was moving all the time. I could not keep still. When I turned away from the desk I saw the letter lying on the carpet like a white leaf and I picked it up and smoothed it with my fingers and tried to read it again. But I could not.

"All lies?" he said. "But you did go to Giles, surely. Why should Clarissa have lied about that? You did go to Penmarric."

"Yes." His chess set was arranged on a table near the door. I picked up a black knight and a black pawn and put them down again.

"You borrowed money from Giles."

"Yes."

"But for what purpose?"

"I . . . needed it."

"But why didn't you come to me? I asked you, Mark, if ever you were in debt to come to me for the money, not to go to other people—to strangers . . ."

"I did not want to ask you," I said. "I did not want to be a burden to you. The Penmar money is mine by right."

"But you should have come to me! I told you to! Why did you go to Giles?"

"Only because it was impossible for me to go to you." My fingers were still fumbling with the chess set, moving the little ivory figures into a disordered line. "I didn't want you to know."

"About this woman?"

"There's no woman," I said. "It's all lies."

"Then why did you want the money?"

"It was cards. I got into debt at cards. At Carnforth Hall."

"So this doctor's daughter doesn't exist."

"No," I said. "She doesn't. Clarissa was making it up."

There was a long silence. The white queen slipped between my fingers and fell to the board with a clatter.

"I'm afraid I don't believe you," he said.

There was another silence. I took the black knight again and squeezed it as if I could crush it to pulp. Tears pricked humiliatingly behind my eyelids.

"I think you'd better tell me about it."

I said nothing. My back was to him. All I could see was the board and the little ivory figures.

"If you please, Mark."

"There's no need for you to know," I said. "Everything is settled. It's all finished. I've made all the arrangements. There's absolutely no need for you to know about it. I don't want you to know about it."

"I don't understand, I'm afraid. How can it be 'all finished' when Clarissa writes that you plan—in the future—to keep this woman in Penzance?"

"It'll only be for the next few months," I said rapidly, "and then when she's had the baby . . ."

I stopped. There was a deep, appalled silence. I swung around to face him, saw his expression, scrabbled to look at the letter again. And then I knew.

Clarissa had not mentioned that Rose was pregnant. Vincent had not, after all, been totally indiscreet.

"Oh God." I sat down and leaned my elbows on the chess table and some of the ivory figures spilled onto the carpet. My cheeks seemed to burn the palms of my hands. "Oh no." Great hot tears sprang to my eyes. I was crying. "Oh no, no . . ."

"Please," he said. "Please, Mark."

I went on crying.

"I think you had best tell me the whole story."

"No," I said, "I don't want to tell you. I don't want you to know."

"But I do know. You had an affair with a doctor's daughter and she's going to have your child."

I could not endure to hear his voice. I tried to stop my ears and the tears fell upon the ivory chessmen and trickled onto the polished surface of the board.

"I'm giving you a chance to explain yourself."

"I can't explain." How could I explain that I had wanted Rose because she reminded me of Janna and that I had wanted Janna because it was necessary for me to have such a woman and that such a woman was necessary to me because . . . But I did not know. I had never understood why it was so impossible for me to be celibate. I had never understood why I should long so frequently for a woman who would go through the motions of loving me even though I knew no love existed between us. All I knew was that the unhappier I was the more impossible it became for me to stay celibate and that my obsession with Janna had begun at a time when I had never before felt so distressed and confused and alone.

But now was hardly the time to start thinking of my mother.

My father was speaking again. I had to struggle to listen to him and concentrate upon what he was saying.

"But who is this woman?" His voice was still grave and quiet but it was obvious he was becoming more upset. "How did you meet her?"

"It happened by chance in St. Ives. She was a nursemaid. She's penniless and without relations." My hand shook as I groped for a handkerchief. "We met every day for a week."

"You mean she came to your hotel? A doctor's daughter? A well-brought-up young woman?"

"No, I—I hired a bathing tent on the beach."

"Where you conducted an affair with her."

"Yes."

"For a week."

"Yes."

"Did you deceive her by saying at the time you would marry her later?"

"No, I made no promises."

"And now—have you offered to marry her?"

"No."

"I see. So you used her for a few days, ruined her and then offered to buy her off your conscience with money borrowed from Giles Penmar. Did you tell Giles—"

"No."

"But you went to Giles," he said. "You didn't come to me."

"I couldn't—I didn't want to distress you."

"You've distressed me even more by going to Giles. Of course you've behaved despicably and I'm ashamed of you and very deeply shocked, but no man is perfect; everyone has faults, makes mistakes. . . . I don't deny that I'm very angry with you, but I am trying hard to understand and forgive. Yet what I find hardest to forgive is not so much your immorality—although that's bad enough—but your duplicity. You deceived me, lied to me—"

"Only because—"

"—because you had not the courage to confess to such dishonorable behavior! However, I must try not to be too angry with you; the fault must not only be in you but in me as well. I've tried hard to be a good father to you and give you a decent upbringing and instill you with certain principles, but I see I've failed. I did my best, but obviously my best wasn't good enough."

"Don't say that. Please." I stood up, still holding Clarissa's letter. My face was wet with my tears. "Don't, don't, don't."

"It's true," he said. "I've never been able to understand you. I never understood your mother and I don't understand you. There's nothing of me in you, nothing at all. I've searched and searched for some spark I could recognize, some likeness I would know, but there's nothing—even your historical taste is a veneer cultivated by your desire to surpass Nigel in everything you undertake. You're like your mother. You're a Penmar. I suppose I've really known it in my heart ever since you were born."

"No!" I shouted. Some terrible all-consuming emotion was making me so weak I could hardly stand. "No, no, no—"

"And you went to Giles," he said. "You went to Giles. You didn't come to me. You went to him."

"Yes, I went to him!" I could hardly speak. I pushed my fists into my eyes like a child trying not to cry. "I went to him because you were the one who mattered and Giles didn't matter at all—"

"Giles," he said. "Giles Penmar. He was an unprincipled, dishonorable man. They all were, all those Penmars. They were a wicked, immoral, dissipated family."

"But I'm not . . . like them . . ." I tried to catch the cuff of his jacket, but he turned aside as if he could not endure to look at me. "I'm like you," I said. "I know it. I know I'm like you. You must believe it. Please say you believe it. Please. Please say it."

"I've tried to believe it," he said, "but all I know is that I've failed."

And after that there was a silence because there was nothing else to say. I backed away from him, too full of grief even to cry, and blundered out of the room into the hall. Opening the front door, I stumbled outside. It was twilight and a strong wind was blowing a massive formation of black clouds toward the land from the sea.

I began to run. I ran away from the house, across the fields, over the stone walls to the moors, and the wind howled around me as I reached the crest of the ridge. It was dark. The heather scratched my shoes and clawed my trousers, but I went on, my breath coming in sobbing gasps, and all at once, rising eerily into the darkness from the ancient ground, were the stone walls of Chûn Castle.

I stopped for breath. Pushing back my hair, I wiped my face for tears long since dried, and then, straightening my tie, I stumbled downhill into the valley, to the lighted windows of Roslyn Farm.

[4]

Lightning flared. The blast of thunder muffled the noise of my fist as I hammered on the back door. Lightning flared again and far away on the skyline to the east I saw the engine house of Ding Dong mine silhouetted for one ghostly moment against that stormy sky.

"Is anyone at home?" I shouted, and as I spoke the door opened an inch and the old crone Griselda poked her nose through the slit to see who I was.

"What do 'ee want?" She regarded me with profound suspicion. "What do 'ee want 'ere with us?"

"Let me in." I would have pushed her aside but the door was on a chain. "Where's your mistress?"

Somewhere far away in the lighted room beyond I heard her voice call softly. "Who is it, Griselda?"

The old witch turned her head. "Young Mr. Mark," she said. I can still hear her say that. She did not say "Mr. Castallack" or even "young Mr. Castallack." It was "young Mr. Mark."

"Well, let him in!" said Janna Roslyn, a hint of impatience in her smooth, even voice. "Really, Griselda, need we be so inhospitable?"

The old crone unhooked the chain grumpily and opened the door a few inches wider. I pushed past her into the room.

She was standing by the table. I had not seen her for some time and her poise and beauty struck me so forcibly that it was as if I had not seen her before. As always, she wore black, and at her throat was an old brooch, a cameo set in semi-precious stones. I remember being surprised to see that she was carrying a copy of the Penzance *Tidings* and that I had evidently interrupted her as she perused it. It seemed strange to see even a local newspaper in the possession of the female owner of a remote country farm.

"Good evening, Mr. Castallack," she said. "This is an unexpected surprise."

"Good evening, Mrs. Roslyn," I heard myself say.

It was beginning to rain. Lightning streaked across the landscape outside again and a second later the thunder crashed overhead.

"Griselda," said Janna, "are the upstairs windows all shut? Now, Annie—" the poor little simpleton of a servant girl was shivering like a dog—"there's no need to be frightened. The thunder can't hurt you." She turned to me. "We've just made some tea. Would you care for some?"

"Yes . . . please. If I may."

She went to the cupboard, took out an extra cup and saucer and set them on the table. Ink-black tea trickled from the spout of the teapot. "Milk?"

"Yes. A little."

"Sugar?"

"No, thank you."

She placed my cup and her own on a tray and took it over to the door. "Would you care to come to the parlor?"

I followed her down the passage to the front room. I felt less numb suddenly, less drained of all strength and energy.

"Please sit down." She drew the curtains. "Are you chilled? Would you like a fire?"

"No, thank you."

We sat down, facing each other across the little table. Outside the thunder rolled around the valley again and the rain hurled itself against the window.

"You look very tired, Mr. Castallack," she said. "Do you feel quite well?"

"Yes, I'm well."

She looked at me closely as if she half suspected I was drunk, but evidently I satisfied her scrutiny and was judged sober.

"May I ask why you have come to visit me at this hour?"

"Yes," I said. "You can ask. But I have no answer. I don't know why I came. Perhaps it was because I had nowhere else to go."

She sipped her tea. She asked no questions. She merely waited for me to explain myself, but there were no explanations I could offer her, so after a moment I merely asked for lack of anything else to say, "Why do you read the *Tidings?*"

There was a pause. She looked surprised. "Perhaps," she said at last, "because I am able to."

I knew then why the paper had looked so odd in her hands. Despite the social legislation of the Seventies most women of her class were still illiterate.

"You went to school?" I said awkwardly at last.

"No."

"Yet you read."

"I learned."

"You must be most gifted if you learned to read without proper instruction."

"I had some instruction. But not in a school."

"Oh . . . and did you receive instruction in other subjects too?"

"Yes, Mr. Castallack," she said. "I suppose you could put it in that fashion. Reading was only one of the many things I learned when I was younger."

"In St. Ives?"

"In St. Ives."

I tasted the tea. It was strong, like a drug. I took another sip. "Why don't you like St. Ives, Mrs. Roslyn?"

"Why?" she said. Her eyes were clear, faintly disdainful, faintly amused. "There's no special reason. I simply became tired of the smell of fish."

"I see." Outside the thunder sounded farther away but the rain still beat against the windows. "Yet it's pleasant to live by the sea," I said at last. "One day I shall live by the sea, at Penmarric. Did you know that?"

"I . . . had heard rumors."

"It's a big estate. I'm fortunate to have such—how shall I say? —such—"

"Great expectations," she said, smiling.

"Precisely." I looked her straight in the eyes. "I'm glad you know the facts; I wanted to make sure you were fully aware of my position."

"Oh? Why?"

"Because I wanted to ask you if you would marry me, Mrs. Roslyn."

She stared at me. Her clear eyes were filled with amazement. "Marry you, Mr. Castallack?"

"Marry me, Mrs. Roslyn. Will you?"

She pulled herself together abruptly. I saw her glance at the cup of tea on the table before her as she tried to remember another appropriate literary phrase glimpsed long ago in St. Ives. "Well, Mr. Castallack," she said carefully, choosing each word with extreme caution, "I am, of course, fully sensible of the honor you have bestowed upon me . . ."

I tried to remember whether that phrase was from Dickens too. It sounded more like Jane Austen.

". . . but unfortunately I fear I must decline your proposal.

I'm most grateful but regret that I cannot become your wife."
She smiled at me uneasily. Her eyes were wary.

At last I said, "Wouldn't you like time to think the matter
over? You've hardly had time to consider the decision."

"I'm afraid I need no further time to make up my mind on
this particular issue, Mr. Castallack. But thank you nonetheless."

"May I ask if you have any special reason for reaching your
decision?"

"I do not wish to marry again at present. It's too soon after my
husband's death."

"Then may I approach you again when—"

"No, Mr. Castallack. Thank you."

"Is it because I'm too young?"

She hesitated. "Perhaps."

"Then when I'm older—"

"No, Mr. Castallack. I'm sorry. There can be no question of
marriage."

I stared at her. My hands clasped themselves tightly and were
still. I had no thought in my mind except that I wanted to spend
the night in bed with her yet could not.

"I'm sorry," she said. "Please forgive me. But it can't be. I'm
sorry."

"It can be," I said, "and it shall be." I stood up. "I apologize for
intruding on your time in this fashion, Mrs. Roslyn. I must ask
you to excuse me." I moved toward the door.

She was startled. "You're going?"

"Yes. I've already outstayed my welcome."

"But it's still raining! Won't you at least stay until the storm
has passed?"

"No, I must leave. At once. Excuse me." I moved blindly out
into the hall and fumbled with the fastenings on the front door.

"Good night, Mr. Castallack." She sounded ill-at-ease still.
"Thank you for calling."

"Good night, Mrs. Roslyn," I said, unable to look at her, and
stepped into the wind and rain and darkness outside.

The door closed.

I stood still, breathing quickly, the useless tears pricking my
eyelids again, and as another flash of lightning illuminated the
valley I saw the engine house once more on the skyline, the stone
tower of Ding Dong mine. Thunder vibrated far away toward
Penzance and Marazion. Rain slewed across my face like the

lashes of a puny whip. Turning at last, I stumbled through the darkness to the back of the house and began my hard climb up the hillside to the windswept walls of Chûn.

[5]

When I arrived home my father was gone and there was no sign of him.

"He saddled his horse," said Mrs. Mannack, "and went off looking for you. Terrible worried he were. I told him there was a storm coming up but he took no notice. 'Never mind the storm,' he says. He looked in a terrible worried state."

I was stricken with horror and remorse. "But which way did he go?"

"Said he'd ride west to St. Just. Don't 'ee fret, Mr. Mark. Like as not he sheltered at the inn."

He would have ridden to Penmarric. He would have thought I had returned to Giles. I put on a coat and scarf and a pair of riding boots and ran outside into the lane that joined the road to Morvah. The rain had lessened but the wind was still strong and tried to force me backward as I pressed downhill to the church. I had just taken the turning to St. Just when I heard the faint sound of horse's hoofs.

"Papa!" I ran forward, my feet slipping in the mud, my teeth chattering with the cold and the damp. "Papa!" I shouted, and the wind whipped the word from my mouth and carried it far over the moors to Chûn. "Papa!"

The horse rounded the bend in the road. The night was so dark that I could not see the face of the rider.

"Papa—"

"Mark." He was beside me, dismounting from his horse. "Mark, I've been so worried about you. So worried." He held me in his arms and I pressed my face against his chest as if I were still a small child long ago at Gweek. "Where did you go?" he said. "I searched for you. I went all the way to Penmarric, but the butler said you hadn't been there. Where were you?"

"At Chûn."

"In the storm?"

"I sheltered—a nearby farm—"

"That was sensible of you. Poor boy, you're shivering from

head to foot! Here, take the horse and ride home as fast as you can and take a hot bath. I'll never forgive myself if you catch your death of cold."

"No, I shall be all right. . . . Isn't there room for us both? Couldn't we—"

"No, I'm too tall and too heavy and the horse is too old to carry us both. Do as I say and ride back at once to the house. Don't worry about me."

I protested but he was adamant, so finally I gave in and did as I was told. As soon as I reached the house I told Mrs. Mannack to heat as much water as possible and retired to my room to peel off my wet clothes. After wrapping myself in a blanket I had just returned to the kitchen to sit by the range when my father walked in.

"Is the water being heated?"

"Yes, sir," said Mrs. Mannack.

"Good. Are you still shivering, Mark?"

"No," I said. "No, I'm warm now."

"I hope to God you don't catch pneumonia."

"I'm sure I won't," I said. "I never catch anything."

I was right. I did not catch pneumonia. But the next morning my father confessed he felt unwell and by noon I was already riding into Penzance to fetch a doctor.

[6]

He was ill for ten days. Most of the time he had such a high fever that he did not know me, and toward the end he did not even speak but lay unconscious upon the pillows. On the eve of the tenth day I sent Mannack to fetch the doctor again and returned to sit by the bedside. After a while I took one of his hands and held it in mine, but there was no response and he remained unconscious, his eyes closed, his breathing shallow, his face drawn with sickness and shadowed with death. I went on sitting there, went on trying not to feel wretched and frightened and alone, but at last I released his hand and moved to the window. It was a cold, bleak day. The sea was as gray as the sky, and the long eeriness of twilight was falling over the moors to cast odd shadows upon that godforsaken scenery.

I tried to pray. "Let him speak," I thought. "Let him just

say . . ." The words formed yearningly in my mind. "I ask for nothing else. Please . . . let him speak."

And as if in answer to my prayers I heard the faint shifting sound of sheet grazing sheet, and I spun around once more to face him.

His eyes were open. He looked at me, knew who I was. "Mark."

I thought with that searing relief when hope is restored after all hope is gone: He's turned the corner. He's getting better. He'll live.

"Mark."

"Yes," I said, the words tumbling from my mouth, "yes, I'm here, Papa, I'm here." I stumbled to the bedside, knelt down beside him, clasped his hand. "Do you want anything? What can I fetch you? What can I do?"

He said evenly but with a great effort, "There is something I have left undone."

"Yes," I said, "but don't worry, Papa, you're going to get better. Everything will be well. You mustn't worry."

It was as if he did not hear me. His eyes, so large, so brilliantly blue, looked at me but could not seem to focus on my face. He said again, "There's something I have left undone."

"Tell me," I said. "I'll see to it. I'll do whatever you want. Tell me what you want me to do."

His lips moved. I strained my ears, leaned forward so that his mouth was against my ear.

"Yes," I said. "Tell me. Tell me, Papa. What is it?"

He drew a deep breath. It was the last breath he would ever take, although I did not know it then. And as I strained my whole being to catch the sound of the words I longed so much to hear, he said very slowly, in a distinct, precise voice: "Look after Janna, Mark. See that she wants for nothing."

II
JANNA: 1890-1904
Love and Hate

> *Richard thought her "an incomparable woman: beautiful yet gracious, strong-willed yet kind, unassuming yet sagacious (which is a rare combination in a woman)." Nonetheless, he could not resist insinuations about her scandalous youth: "Many knew what I wish none of us knew . . . let no one say more about it, though I know it well. Hush!"*
>
> —King John,
> W. L. WARREN

> *Many criticisms have been levelled at Eleanor, both as to what she was and what she did; she has been depicted as a common whore, a woman possessed of the devil, a termagant driven by hatred. . . .*
>
> —Eleanor of Aquitaine,
> REGINE PERNOUD

1

Eleanor was a famous beauty. . . . She was also notoriously flighty and said to be wanton.

—My Life for My Sheep,
ALFRED DUGGAN

[Eleanor was] probably perfectly virtuous but gossip said that she had more than flirted with Geoffrey of Anjou. . . .

—King John,
W. L. WARREN

[1]

He died in October when the roses were gone and the heather was dead on the moors. The rector of Zillan told me. I suppose it was best that I should hear the news from the rector rather than from some old gossip in Penzance, but it seemed horrible that I should hear the news from a clergyman in the course of a casual conversation. I was visiting my husband's grave; I visited it every week to thank him in my prayers for helping me escape from St. Ives, and even after Laurence began to call at the farm I never missed my weekly visits to the churchyard at Zillan.

The rector said, "I had a sad piece of news today. A very old friend of mine from Morvah—you have probably seen him in the congregation—such a nice fellow . . ."

The rector's eyes were watchful, as if he knew all there was to know and was telling me that dreadful news in the most compassionate way possible, and when it was over and I had understood what he had said he asked me if I would like to sit down for a while and offered to take me into the church.

"Thank you, sir," I said, "but no. I'm quite well."

I was ashamed that he knew, but then the moment of shame had passed because it did not matter, nothing mattered any more, and all I could do was to stare down at my husband's grave and watch the short grass blow in the cool autumn breeze, and I thought: Why, why, why does nothing ever go right for me, why do I have to struggle through life with luck always against me, have I not been punished enough for days long since past? Yet there was no answer, just as there never is any answer to unanswerable questions, and all I was left with was the knowledge that Laurence was dead and I was alone.

But I had always been alone. All I had ever wanted was not to be alone and not to be consumed by loneliness, all I had ever wanted was to be loved and to have security through love—how I longed for security!—but love never lasted and security was always just beyond my reach and it seemed to me then as I stumbled through the heather that I had spent all my life seeking the things that so many people took for granted and always, always without fail, I had ended my searches alone.

"Laurence!" I cried as I stumbled home across the moors, but he was gone, and the grief was a great darkness that dimmed my eyes so that I could not see. When I reached the farm I went to my room and tried to weep, but I was beyond tears. I sat there dry-eyed in the room where we had loved each other, but when I tried to remember him I could think only of my husband and fancied I heard him laughing at me from beyond the grave.

"Laurence!" I screamed. "Laurence!" And suddenly Griselda was there, my own dearest Griselda, who had seen me through so many hardships, and with her arms around me I wept as I had not wept since I was a child long ago in that godforsaken little fishing village called St. Ives.

[2]

I was born in St. Ives. I can still remember the one-room hovel where my earliest years were spent. Griselda lived with us then, and every day she would go down to the quay to gut fish. St. Ives was famous for its pilchards, which were cured, packed in hogsheads and exported to Italy, and for its mackerel, which were sent to London and other big cities. Griselda had worked with fish all her life, but my mother, who was her niece, held herself above such lowly employment and used to take in laundry. However, laundering is hard work and my mother was foolish enough to suppose that it is not necessary to work hard in order to improve one's position in the world.

Her inevitable end might have been otherwise if my father had not been the man he was, but his work as a fisherman kept him constantly away from home and he had an unfortunate inclination to spend his wages even before he reached the door of our cottage on his return from the sea. He was a Frenchman who loved to be gay and generous. He used to bring me home little toys from Brittany and, once, gingerbread from the Channel Islands. He did not start to bring home the gin until later, but once my mother had abandoned her laundering for the painted shutters of Shrimp Street he drank more and more until nobody wanted to give him a place on their fishing boats. I was nine when he died. He fell down in the gutter and was run over by a carriage. My mother did not attend his pauper's funeral because she was ill herself by that time and died two weeks later in a workhouse.

Women such as my mother, I learned later from the Evangelist Mission for the Redemption of Fallen Women, did not as a rule live to a ripe old age.

But I was not like my mother. I was willing to work hard, as hard as I could to escape from the stink of fish and the stench of the crooked alleys and the reek of the yellow-toothed harbor rats. The local ladies of quality who occupied themselves with Charity to the Poor were of the opinion that I must be consigned to an orphanage, but I knew better. I washed my hair and my underclothes and my smock and borrowed some shoes and then I walked up to Menherion Castle, the grandest house in all St. Ives.

By a most fortunate chance I found there was a vacancy for a scullery maid. Inexperienced girls with a clean, neat appearance were being considered for the post.

"You *are* rather young," said the housekeeper, who was a kind woman, "but you seem a bright little girl and if you promise to work hard . . ."

Oh, how I worked! I spent nearly nine years at Menherion Castle, and during the early years I managed to work my way up from the sculleries to the stillroom until finally I became one of the housemaids. Even Lady St. Enedoc, the mistress of the house, began to notice my efficiency, and the housekeeper told me that if I did not become swollen-headed with conceit I should go far.

At last when I was fifteen my greatest triumph came: I was appointed personal maid to the eldest daughter of the house, Miss Charlotte, who was only a year my senior, and this meant that I was able to look after all her lovely clothes and dress her hair and above all to have the opportunity of conversing with her. I had never conversed at length with a lady before and at first was very shy, but Miss Charlotte was sweet and unaffected so that I soon overcame my nervousness.

By that time I had learned to speak correctly—or at least as correctly as a girl of my station could have hoped to speak—and, what was even more valuable, I had learned how to behave and about the code of etiquette to which the upper classes conformed. Not long after my arrival at the castle I had been befriended by the butler and he had taught me a little arithmetic and the letters of the alphabet when he had heard that my most cherished ambition was to be housekeeper one day; no servant might aspire to such a position, of course, if she could not read or write or calculate.

Miss Charlotte also helped me to read by letting me look at her fashion magazines, which were sent to her from London, and later allowed me to borrow her novels and take them away to my room in the servants' wing. She also let me have her dresses which she no longer chose to wear, and ironically it was because of Miss Charlotte's generosity in this direction that my troubles began. I wore one of her old dresses to the servants' Christmas party in the servants' hall; I must have looked fetching in the dress, for I was never without a partner during the dancing, but afterward while I was on an errand in the main wing of the house a disaster occurred. I met the master of the house, Sir Bertram St. Enedoc, and he, inebriated with an overdose of Christmas spirit, made it clear he found the dress as charming on me as the footmen had done.

I escaped as adroitly as I could, but I was alarmed. I had no desire at all for any nonsense of that kind. I was ambitious but not stupid, and I was quite intelligent enough to understand that the road to success in life did not lie between the sheets of Sir Bertram's bed whenever Lady St. Enedoc chanced to be looking the other way. I wanted only to keep my position as Miss Charlotte's maid and perhaps be housekeeper one day. I was not like my mother, who thought there was an easier road to comfort and security. Besides, I thought Sir Bertram a repulsive old man and was not in the least stimulated by the idea of succumbing to his heavy-handed attempts at seduction.

Unfortunately Lady St. Enedoc was unable to believe her husband so easily resistible. Rumor of her husband's weakness reached her, and soon after my eighteenth birthday I was told to pack my bags and leave.

[3]

There is nothing more impossible to fight than rumor or that dreadful phrase "no smoke without a fire." No one believed I was innocent. Jealous tongues called me "scheming" and "fast" and "sly." Even my friend the butler looked at me as if I were a fallen woman. Furiously angry yet too proud to stage a dramatic scene protesting my innocence, I walked away from the castle with my head held high and told myself I was quite polished enough to obtain an excellent position elsewhere.

But I had reckoned without Lady St. Enedoc's malice. And I had reckoned without the fact that I had been summarily dismissed with no references.

No one would look at me.

At last when my savings were spent and I was at my wits' end to know what to do, I left the lodging house above the town and went back to the crooked alleys and Griselda.

"My, my," she said disapprovingly, "we're powerful high and mighty these days—far too high and mighty to take humble work. Thee's like yurr mother the way 'ee gives yurrself airs. What's wrong with a shop? Or one of they new hotels?"

I recoiled from the idea. Once one has ever worked in a grand household such as Menherion Castle, one feels that working in a shop is a waste of one's training and experience. But Griselda's remark about my mother made me think again and swallow my pride.

I worked for six months in a furniture shop, and then one of my employer's customers, a lawyer called William Pomeroy, having heard of my training, offered me a position as his house-keeper. I was overjoyed at the thought of returning to respect-ability at last, so I accepted eagerly. The house was out at Carbis Bay near St. Ives, a beautiful house overlooking the sea; I was in charge of a cook, a maid and a gardener—a small establishment after the St. Enedocs' perhaps, but I was naturally delighted to be a housekeeper with a house of my own to supervise.

It was a month before Mr. Pomeroy made his intentions clear, but it takes less than a month to fall in love with a house and a way of life. I was never foolish enough to suppose he would marry me, but I did believe that if we reached the agreement he suggested I would at least have a degree of security.

I spent an entire evening weighing up the situation. Mr. Pomeroy was a widower of thirty-five and not unattractive, al-though I personally felt no desire to swoon whenever he entered the room. He was witty and amusing and not unkind. I felt he would treat me well. Besides, it was not as if I were giving myself in return for money; I did an honest day's work and was paid an honest wage, for I wanted to work hard in a respectable environment, not to slip down into the gutter so that I was throwing open a pair of the painted shutters of Shrimp Street to beckon the passers-by.

I was not like my mother.

Another aspect of the situation was that I would be nineteen on my next birthday. Most girls of my class were by that time either wives or mothers or both. It would be foolish to hold back from Mr. Pomeroy on account of squeamishness, modesty was out of place in such a situation, and anyway Mr. Pomeroy had by this time probably heard the rumor that I had been Sir Bertram's mistress and would not believe any maidenly protesta-tions I might be foolish enough to make.

I decided it would be wrong to disappoint him of his high expectations.

I myself expected nothing. I was not in love with him although I liked him well enough. One did not expect rapture from some-one in those circumstances, and so because I expected nothing I was not disappointed. After a while I think I was vaguely sur-prised by how easy it was. His liberties meant nothing to me, although after a time I was grateful enough to try to please him as much as possible, and the benefits I received from our association continued to be more than adequate in compensation for any discomfort I suffered.

I had no regrets at all until I was pregnant. After that everything ended very quickly and I was back with Griselda again in that disgusting hovel while she mixed me an equally disgusting potion to cure my ills.

I became sick. For two days I did nothing but moan and pray to die, but at last it was over and I was alone on my back in that flea-ridden room with only the mice for company while Griselda gutted fish down by the quay. By the time she arrived home on the evening of the second day I felt that I had more than learned my lesson.

"I shall never, never go through that again," I said between my teeth. "Never. And no man lays one fingertip on me again until I'm wearing his wedding ring."

Griselda, nettled by my lack of appreciation of her potion, said that I need not have got myself into such a predicament. "There be ways and means," she added in a sour voice. "Ways and means."

"You can keep them," I retorted ungratefully. "I'm finished with all that. It never meant anything to me anyway."

I stood by my word. Throughout the next five years I moved from job to job, each post worse than the one before, and throughout the years I was constantly confronted with the menace of my past trying to repeat itself. It was only when I was thoroughly convinced that I was destined to work for a succession of foolish men and dismissed by a succession of jealous wives that I found an employer who was so happily married that he was not in the least interested in pestering me with illicit attentions. The work he offered me was the most menial I had yet encountered, but I was too desperate for employment to refuse him when he asked me to serve behind the bar of his little tavern.

I approached the prospect of being a barmaid with great dread, but curiously enough it was not as bad as I had feared it would be. My disdainful, high-handed air proved attractive; the bar became flooded with customers and the landlord, delighted with me, said I gave his establishment "class."

Three years passed; on the whole I was not too unhappy. I was just wondering in despair if I would spend all my life serving ale to rough fishermen when at last my luck turned. One light spring evening shortly before my twenty-seventh birthday the door of the taproom was flung open with a bang and in walked Jared Roslyn.

[4]

I found Jared attractive. By that time I was resigned to the fact that I was unlikely to fall wildly in love with anyone, but not even my disillusionment could prevent me from finding some men more attractive than others. Jared definitely interested me. He was a tall, solid man with dark hair and eyes and a tight-lipped mouth. I discovered that he was a bachelor, a fact that surprised me, for he was at least as old as I was and rural folk often marry young. I concluded that his good looks had enabled him to get his own way too often to necessitate the purchase of a wedding ring.

He was the elder of two sons, he told me, and his father, although a mere farmer, actually owned land in the moorland parish of Zillan several miles away to the west. My interest in him deepened, especially when he began to describe his home, "the most beautiful farmhouse between Penzance and St. Just," but I had no illusions about the likelihood of his asking me to marry him. It was a pity that by this time I was socially so far below him; if we had met directly after my dismissal from Menherion Castle I might have had more chance of becoming his wife, but men with expectations like Jared Roslyn do not marry barmaids.

"Why don't you ride with me to Zillan on your next free afternoon?" he proposed one hot August evening, but I knew what lay behind that proposition. He had reached the stage where he could barely contain his lust.

"Why, how delightful!" I said. "But how do I know I will end my journey at Roslyn Farm and not in some tavern along the way?"

For several days after that I thought I had lost him, but I was wrong. He reappeared a week later and with him was a small, wiry man of about sixty, very agile, with a merry laugh and alert, sparkling blue eyes.

It was Jared's father, John Henry Roslyn. He was a widower, Jared had told me, and had lost his wife the previous year after nearly thirty years of happy marriage.

"So this is what makes you take that long journey to St. Ives so often, you young rascal!" he said accusingly to Jared, and added to me: "I can't say I blame him. You're pretty as a picture, my dear. Treat yourself to a little glass of port or whatever you young ladies drink nowadays, and Jared and I'll have a pint of bitter apiece."

It seems, I know, quite absurd to admit it, but his words touched me and brought unexpected tears to my eyes. To hear him call me a "young lady" as I stood behind the bar of that common little tavern made me feel as if I were in the drawing room of Menherion Castle. But it was not only his kindness that impressed me; I decided that I had never before met anyone so cheerful or nimble-witted as he was. Beside him Jared seemed a ponderous oaf in contrast.

They came regularly to the tavern after that, but I soon lost interest in Jared. I looked forward to their visits, and afterward I would retire to my tiny bedroom in the attic and not even mind the cramped space, the stuffiness or the tapping of the mice in the wainscoting. And then one day at the end of summer old Mr. Roslyn came to the bar alone.

We had been talking for only a minute or two before he said suddenly, "This is no place for a young lady like you. You should have a house to manage like other young ladies. Could you keep house?"

I hesitated, not sure what he meant. "For you?"

"For me and Jared and my younger boy Joss. It's a full year now since my wife died and everything's in a pretty mess. We have two servants, a deaf old woman who's eighty if she's a day and her granddaughter, Annie, who's a sweet child but half-witted. There's nothing I'd like better than a good housekeeper."

"I . . ." I hesitated again. It was really most awkward. "Well, that's most kind of you and I'm very grateful for the opportunity, but I could only come on the understanding . . ."

"Well, of course you'd be Mrs. Roslyn," he said. "No nonsense about that part of it. I wouldn't ask a respectable young lady to come to be housekeeper for a widower and two bachelors unless I could offer her a way of keeping up her respectability."

I stared at him. Around us people laughed and shouted. Someone called for a drink but I did not move.

"Well?" said old Mr. Roslyn, suddenly brisk and businesslike. "Will you?"

There was another moment of silence. Then: "Yes," I said. "Yes. Thank you."

"Good!" he said with his wide, gap-toothed smile, his lined face wrinkling with pleasure. "Nothing could please me more."

"But—"

"Yes?"

"Your first wife . . . isn't it a little soon? I—"

"She's been dead over a year, my dear, and one can't grieve forever. She was a good woman and I miss her, but nothing's going to bring her back. Besides, isn't it a tribute to her that now she's gone I hate to live without a woman in the house?"

"Yes . . . yes, I had not thought of it like that."

"Tomorrow I'll see the rector of Zillan and have him call the banns, and before I leave here I'll call on the parson, whosoever he may be, and have him call the banns in this parish too. Would you prefer to be wed here in St. Ives?"

"I . . . have not been a churchgoer."

"In that case Zillan would be best." He drank deeply from his beer and smiled at me again. "I'll make the arrangements."

"I . . . I'm a little overwhelmed."

"Of course—only natural. Sure you wouldn't like time to think it over?"

"No," I said. "No, I've no doubts at all. It's just that . . . I had not expected, thought . . ." I broke off in confusion. Then: "Jared—"

"Never mind Jared. He could have had you but he let his chance slip by. I often told him he'd regret it one day if he went on expecting every woman he fancied to forget all thought of wedding rings so long as he talked to her sweetly enough, so this'll teach him a lesson." He laughed, finished his beer and stood up to go, but on his feet he hesitated. The laughter died from his eyes.

"Just one thing, my dear," he said. "Don't expect too much. I'm an old man past my prime. I can't offer you as much as Jared could. If you'd rather marry Jared, you'd best say so now before it's all too late, because I'll have no goings-on in my house under my own roof. Either you marry me and leave Jared alone or else you marry Jared and that's that. I could jolt him into proposing matrimony if you wanted him badly enough."

"I've no desire to marry Jared," I said, and it was true. I knew Jared would soon bore me; he was too uncouth, and because I knew I could outwit him I had no respect for him. But old Mr. Roslyn's wits were so sharp; I respected him enough to be sure that he would not bore me as Jared would. "I would rather marry you," I added in honesty. "Truly I would."

"Well, bless you for that, my dear, but may I ask why? Jared's a good-looking man, don't you think, and I'm sixty-two years old and ugly as sin! Explain to me why you say that."

"You're kind," I said, "and you understand. I want nothing else."

We were married a month later.

[5]

I had been married four years when I first saw Laurence Castallack. On the whole the marriage had turned out well enough; certainly my position was far better than it had ever been in St. Ives, even though I now had to work just as hard and sometimes harder than I had ever worked before. Life as Mrs. John Henry Roslyn, the wife of one of the more prosperous farmers in Zillan who owned his own land, was certainly respectable and secure, but it was also filled with a multitude of daily tasks such as managing the dairy, attending to the hens and pigs, cleaning and sweeping the house, laundering and ironing the clothes, and cooking, baking, brewing and distilling in order to ensure that there was always sufficient to eat and drink in the pantry. Fortunately I did have some help, but the deaf old woman who had worked for my predecessor died during my first winter at the farm, and her granddaughter Annie was too simple to work on her own initiative without constant supervision. I had brought Griselda with me from St. Ives to share my good fortune, but since she knew no more about managing a farmhouse than I did my responsibilities as mistress of the house weighed upon me all the more heavily. Matters did improve when my husband engaged two girls from Zillan village to help me with the cleaning and cooking, but I found I still went to bed exhausted every night. However, since my husband had discovered that he was not so young as he used to be where certain matters were concerned I was never kept from sleeping as soon as my head touched the pillow. My husband had had aspirations, it was true, and did occasionally manage to fulfill them during the first months of our marriage, but later his failures became merely embarrassing to us both and after our first anniversary he made no further attempts at intimacy.

I at least wasn't sorry. My husband was by no means repulsive and I was fond of him, but after a long hard day the last thing I wanted was to postpone the luxury of rest.

But it was not all drudgery. On Sundays I was able to escape from my work when we attended church, and on Sunday evenings I would practice my reading by studying the newspaper which I always bought when I went to market at Penzance on Thursdays. My husband was proud of the fact that I could read and write, and indeed I think he would have had no reservations about the wisdom of his second marriage at all if only he had been on better terms with his sons.

He and his first wife had had five children in all, but three had died in infancy and only the oldest and the youngest had survived. Joss was eleven years younger than Jared, so I did not expect them to be as close to each other as brothers can be, but Joss's older brother was so much a hero to him that he always took Jared's side in any family arguments. And Jared, of course, never forgave his father for marrying me.

Within six months he married the daughter of a Madron farmer, and my husband, relieved to end the uneasy atmosphere beneath his roof, ceded his son the tenant farm up the valley which Jared's mother had had as a dower when she married. The house was a mere stone cottage and the land was hilly and difficult to farm, but Jared was willing to accept any place which afforded him a measure of independence. He wasted no time in moving to the cottage and afterward took care to avoid his father as much as possible.

Joss soon followed his example and went to live with him. Unlike Jared, who had always been John Henry's favorite, Joss had never been on good terms with his father and I had found him a surly, difficult boy who had been hostile to me from the start. I was hardly sorry to see him go, but I felt guilty that my marriage had divided the family so deeply, and although my husband never reproached me I knew he reproached himself for not realizing that Jared's interest in me was more than a passing fancy, and for not foreseeing the rift that had developed in consequence between himself and his sons.

The fourth year of my marriage passed, and by this time I had grown accustomed to the life of a farmer's wife. I looked forward to the Corpus Christi Fair in Penzance and Feast Monday in St. Just and Harvest Festival in Zillan—I did not even mind preparing the feast at the farm to celebrate the end of the potato-lifting. I came to know all the villagers, from the farm laborers to the miners, the blacksmith to the carter, and although I never knew them well (for I was always regarded as a stranger) I also came to know their wives and families.

Even my surroundings now seemed less strange and more pleasing to my eyes. I loved the sweep of the hillside as it rose to the ruins of Chûn Castle, the square tower of Zillan church across the moors, the stone engine house of Ding Dong mine atop the hills to the east. And best of all I loved Roslyn Farm, the mellow bricks, the spacious rooms, the solidity of the dark, heavy furniture. I loved each uneven flagstone of the dairy, even the latticed windows of the parlor which were so tiresome to clean. In the summer I would open those windows and the scent of the wild roses would float into the house on the soft warm breeze from the moors and the bees would buzz around the honeysuckle. I loved it all; I was at peace. After years of struggle I at last had a home of my own, and the home was doubly precious to me since I had had to fight so long for what I wanted.

I felt no lack in my life. I was vaguely sorry that my marriage was not a romantic one, but would have considered myself a fool to have expected romance under the circumstances. I remember that occasionally I did wonder what it would have been like to have a child, but my childlessness did not upset me. I had never been as maternal as most women, and now the house was my child and it was the house on which I lavished my affection. So long as I had the house, I thought to myself, I would be safe, free from anxiety, blessedly secure.

So I thought my life pleasant enough as the time passed and the seasons came and went. Why not? I had never been more fortunate. It was not until I was thirty years old that I first realized life was merely passing me by, but then it was not until I was thirty years old that I first saw Laurence Castallack.

[6]

I met him in the evening when the light was golden and the air was still and there was a great peace on the ruined walls of

Chûn. It was March, a mild March when the spring flowers were already in bloom and the air was warm with the promise of summer ahead. We have mild winters in Cornwall; early springs are the rule, not the exception, and it was in the spring when I first saw Laurence, the spring of 1890.

It was a beautiful day.

After supper that evening Jared had called unexpectedly on his father, and because my head always began to ache when I saw Jared I slipped out of the house for a breath of fresh air. Why I decided to walk up the hillside behind the farmhouse I have no idea, but within minutes I was within sight of the top of the ridge and approaching the ruins of Chûn Castle.

The castle is not really a castle at all, merely a double circle of stone walls which have stood on top of the ridge since time out of mind, but the views from the walls are spectacular and I was not altogether surprised when I saw someone else was already there admiring the landscape. But then I saw not only that he was a stranger but that he was also a stranger of quality —and this did surprise me, for the ridge was remote and few of the visitors who came to Cornwall cared enough about a heap of stones to make the journey to the castle.

All we said to each other was "good evening," but I was to think of him for hours afterward. He had a sad face. His eyes were blue, unexpectedly gentle. What else is there to say? I have no power to describe him any more; descriptions are for people detached enough to observe, and apart from those first few seconds I was never a detached observer of Laurence Castallack.

I saw him several times after that at church on Sundays, and once I even came face to face with him in Penzance on market day. And each time I saw him something happened which I had previously thought happened only in the novels that Miss Charlotte St. Enedoc had lent me long ago at Menherion Castle. I felt weak. My heart hammered in my lungs and there was a quick sinking sensation in my stomach. Even my knees began to tremble.

Of course I soon found out who he was. Since strangers of quality were almost unknown in Zillan he quickly became a subject of interest among the villagers as soon as he began to attend matins at Zillan church every Sunday. He was, I was told, the owner of the large farm at Morvah where old Ned Sparnon had lived until his death recently; Mr. Castallack had inherited the farm from his mother, who had been a Waymark of Zennor. More than twenty years before he had married into the notorious Penmar family, but he and his wife, so gossip whispered, were divorced.

"But he can't be connected with the Penmars!" I protested to my most fertile source of gossip, Ethel and Millie Turner, who arrived daily at the farm to help me in the house. "The Waymarks, the Carnforths or the St. Enedocs—but not the Penmars!"

"Ah," chorused Ethel and Millie triumphantly, seizing the chance to voice one of their favorite observations. "There's bad blood in that family, that we all know."

And we all did. The Penmars were a wild family of jumped-up adventurers who lived in an enormous mansion called Penmarric on the far side of St. Just. The first Penmar had won the estate in the earlier part of the century by cheating the future King George the Fourth with a pair of loaded dice. Of his three sons, all of whom had been notoriously profligate, the youngest, Mr. Mark Penmar, had made a fortune by swindling in India before he had inherited the estate, and it was his daughter, Miss Maud, who had married Mr. Castallack. Miss Maud now lived in London, and Mr. Castallack lived with his two sons at the family home far away at Gweek. He was only spending the summer at Morvah, the Turner girls informed me—and as soon as I knew that I lived in dread that he would go away.

But he stayed.

Soon I knew not how to contain myself. I burned for him. I thought of him constantly. Yet there was nothing I dared do. Jared had of late been trying to drive a wedge between me and my husband by hinting that I flirted with Farmer Polmarth, a young unmarried neighbor of ours, and although I had convinced John Henry of my innocence I was too conscious that my past was yet again trying to repeat itself to feel confident that my husband trusted me absolutely. Soon all my old fears and dreads and my appalling sense of insecurity began to grip me again. If my husband were to suspect that I had succumbed to this wild infatuation with Mr. Castallack . . .

I felt quite faint at the thought.

I knew my husband had made a will in which he had left the house, together with a small income for its upkeep, to me for life, but I knew too that his own advancing years and the continuing rift with his sons had made him regret his marriage to a young wife; his suspicion and disillusionment had made him increasingly disagreeable as the months passed. I was well aware that if I gave him the slightest provocation he would remake his will to leave everything to Jared, who at present was to have only the reversion of the house together with a large part of the land and the tenant farm.

Blood always did run thicker than water under circumstances that were adverse. I began to feel as if I were walking on a razor's edge where one false step could send me toppling over the brink into the abyss of poverty below.

Yet by the time May came I was still trapped in the tangled meshes of my madness, still imprisoned by my determination not to lose everything I had by betraying any symptom of my lunacy. It was a Thursday when the disaster finally overtook me. For once I had stayed at home instead of going to market; having nursed my husband through a serious fever not long before, I was too tired to feel as well as I should have been. Annie had walked to Zennor to see her kin and Griselda had accompanied my husband to Penzance, so I was alone in the house.

I was just sitting in my room and reflecting in an agony of bitterness that I would soon be reaching my thirty-first birthday and still wasting whatever youth I yet possessed, when far away downstairs I heard the back door close.

"Who's that?" I called sharply at once.

But there was no reply.

In a sudden fever of excitement I raced downstairs, but when I flung open the kitchen door my hopes ended as abruptly as they had begun.

"So there you are, Janna," said Jared, amused. "I thought you might be at home."

The shock of seeing him combined with the violence of my disappointment made me tremble with rage.

"How dare you sneak in like that and frighten me so!" I stormed. "I've a good mind to tell your father—"

"—that you're sweet on Mr. Castallack of Morvah?"

The words struck me as hard as a blow. I had thought myself painstakingly careful in concealing my emotions. It had not occurred to me that a woman in love can betray herself in a thousand small but eloquent ways.

Jared laughed. "I'll bargain with you, Janna," he said confidently, amused how angry I was. "Fair's fair. Father's left you the house for life, hasn't he? Then promise me you'll give me the house when he dies if I give you a hundred pounds. I know I'll have that much coming to me. Promise me that and I'll see Father hears nothing of Mr. Castallack. If you won't promise . . . then I'll tell him what's going on and I'll see you get neither house nor coin."

"I'll see you penniless first!" I cried, my fury reviving. "You just try and make your word carry more weight with him than mine! He believed me when you made those accusations about Farmer Polmarth and he'll still believe me this time! You just try and make trouble and see where it gets you! You just try!"

There was a stillness, a second of hesitation. We stood close together, scarcely two feet apart, I looking him straight in the eyes, he looking at me with equal defiance. Suddenly an indefinable change came upon his expression; his dark eyes lost their hardness and the sullen line of his mouth softened.

"Well, you've plenty of spirit," he said. "I'll say that for you."

I stepped aside very quickly but not quickly enough. He moved faster than I did, and before I knew what was happening he had pulled me toward him with a jerk of the wrist and closed my lips with his own.

The room seemed to swim, tilt, blurr. I was rigid with revulsion, paralyzed with panic. I felt his huge hands, their backs matted with black hair, slide over my hips and move swiftly upward to my bosom, and all the while his tongue like some monstrous instrument of torture explored my mouth. I felt as if I were suffocating. The moistness of his lips mingled unpleasantly with my sense of taste, but as he pressed me against the wall I could not even twist my face from his.

Suddenly it was over. Jared's presence was withdrawn; I was left faint and gasping against the wall, but even as I opened my mouth to scream my vision cleared and I saw my husband watching us from the doorway.

The next day he rode to Penzance. He would not say why he went. He had not spoken one word to me since his early return from the market, and even though his silence had reduced me to tears he had stubbornly refused to talk to me.

Four hours later, just as he left the offices of his lawyers after signing a new will, he collapsed with a heart attack and died before he could be taken to hospital.

I would like to write that everyone was very kind to me, but they were not. I knew then who my friends were and who merely pretended to be my friends because I was the wife of one of the more well-to-do farmers in the parish. The rector Mr. Barnwell was as considerate and kind as I had expected him to be; he was the best kind of clergyman, wise, understanding and unprejudiced. My two daily housemaids Ethel and Millie Turner were also kind enough to stay with me for some hours after the funeral when I did not want to be alone, but I suspected they joined in the gossip about me once my back was turned.

Gossip was rife. The very air seemed thick with it.

"Have you heard?" someone said on Market Jew Street in Penzance as I went to see my husband's lawyers. "John Henry Roslyn . . . That's what happens when an old man marries a fast young woman . . . four years and he's dead! She's a sly one, I'll be bound. Fancy John Henry Roslyn, married all those years to that nice respectable woman, and then suddenly wedding a barmaid young enough to be his daughter . . . and we all know what being a barmaid means in a town like St. Ives, don't we?"

Even my husband's lawyers seemed to regard me with a prurient interest. My husband's new will was in the care of Mr. Trebarvah, the senior partner of Holmes, Holmes, Trebarvah and Holmes, the largest firm of solicitors in Penzance, and with Mr. Trebarvah when I saw him that morning was his assistant, a young man called Mr. Vincent. After Jared and Joss had arrived the will was read, and Mr. Trebarvah, translating the legal terms for us, explained what my husband had done before his death.

Jared had been cut out of the will; his little son Abel, who was two years old, inherited the money, the stock, the land and the tenant farm, although Jared, as co-trustee with Mr. Trebarvah, was allowed to administer this inheritance for the child till he came of age. Joss received his father's gold watch and twenty-five pounds. As for me, I was left with the house—and without a penny to support myself or maintain the house, yard and garden which had been devised to me not for life but in fee simple. The result, as I quickly saw, was that I would be forced to sell my inheritance while Jared, acting on behalf of his son, would be forced to buy if he wanted to recover his family home. My husband had kept his promise and left the house to me, but in such a way that it would be impossible for me to live there.

"So be it, Janna," said Jared, struggling to contain his rage. "We've both of us been punished. Name your price, and if it's a fair one I'll see you get your money. Mr. Trebarvah here can draw up the deed and see it's all done in a proper legal fashion, and afterward when the money's yours you can go and buy yourself a little cottage in St. Ives."

As soon as he uttered the words "St. Ives" I knew I could not and would not leave the farm. The farm was my home—the only true home I had ever had. It represented peace and security, a refuge from all those years of toil and hardship which had followed my dismissal from Menherion Castle. The house was mine and I loved it and no one, least of all Jared, was ever going to take it away from me.

"I won't sell," I said.

There followed a bitter and heated quarrel during which Mr. Trebarvah tried in vain to act as mediator and young Mr. Vincent looked both distressed and embarrassed.

"But you've got no money!" shouted Jared. "And if you want to make ends meet you'll have to replace the stock that's been left to me!"

"I've money saved," I said. But it was a lie.

"Even if you can replace the hens and cows you couldn't make ends meet!"

"That remains to be seen."

"Yes, you'll see well enough!" cried Joss. "We'll drive you out!"

"Really, young man," said Mr. Trebarvah, much scandalized by this threat. "That's no way to talk to a lady."

"She's no lady!" said Joss, trembling with hatred. "Ask anyone in St. Ives!"

And he stalked out of the room.

Jared and I left soon afterward. In the street outside he tried to bargain with me again, but I would not listen and ran all the way back to the inn yard where Cullis, one of the farm laborers, was waiting with the ponytrap. Within the hour I was back at the farm, shutting myself in the little sitting room behind the parlor where I kept my household accounts, and trying in despair to decide how I could ever get the money I needed.

I did not dare go to the Jews; I was too afraid that I would be unable to pay their rates of interest and would lose the roof over my head. I could approach a bank, but I thought the financiers there would look down on a mere farmer's widow when the rest of their clients were gentry or wealthy merchants.

It was then at last that I acknowledged the thought which had been at the back of my mind all the time and allowed myself to think of Laurence Castallack.

I knew he would help me just as surely as I knew no one else would. It did briefly occur to me that to sit down and write a begging letter to a gentleman with whom one was barely on speaking terms must break all recognized conventions of etiquette, but I dismissed the thought as irrelevant. Etiquette did not matter because he would understand.

So taking enormous care with my grammar and spelling, I wrote, asking him if he would call at the farm to advise me on a matter which I wished to discuss with a gentleman of quality and education, yet when the letter had been posted my courage ebbed and my confidence in him faded. Afterward all I could think with dread was: He will not come.

But he did come. He came when the rain had died away in the east and the May sunshine shimmered in a cloudless blue sky and the wildflowers blazed from the banks of the lane. He came in the afternoon in the long hours before supper, at the time when I was ironing, when my hair was untidy, when my black dress was drab beneath my shabby apron. And when I opened the door and saw him there he smiled and took off his hat, just as he always did, and there was nothing more to be said between us because we already knew all there was to say.

[8]

I had waited over thirty years without really knowing what I was waiting for, but at last the moment came and the thirty years were as nothing because time ceased to matter any more. It did not matter that I was no longer young. I was a woman; I was loved; I loved in return, and during our love the spring blazed into summer, a long, lingering, languid summer, and the whole world seemed reborn in my eyes so that each moment was doubly meaningful to me.

He would come in the afternoons, not every afternoon, only

twice or perhaps three times a week, and he would stay for two or three hours. It seems curious now and even painful to look back and see that out of the one hundred and sixty-eight hours of each week I did not spend more than nine hours in his company, but to me then the nine hours seemed a great wealth of happiness. I had never before been nine hours a week in the company of someone I loved; at first I was merely grateful that such hours could exist, but gradually I became restless and my yearning for him grew until the nine hours were a mere drop in the vast ocean of time and it seemed that all my days were spent longing for his arrival and dreading his departure. I wanted him every afternoon, not merely on two or three. I began to long for him in the mornings and evenings, not simply in the afternoons. And most of all I longed for him at night when I was alone in bed and the house was dark and still.

But I was afraid of seeming too eager, too immodest. He was shy, fastidious in his emotions, and I did not wish to alarm him by any frank declaration of feeling. So I schooled myself to be as restrained as he was, and forced myself never to complain when he took his leave, never to ask when he would be back, never to burst out saying how much I would miss him when I was alone. The years had taught me immense self-control, but even my self-control was no match for my emotions that summer. I endured it until July, and then one Wednesday when he was taking his leave of me I broke down and wept.

"I can't bear you going away," I sobbed. "I can't bear it . . . I love you so much . . . I want to be with you all the time . . ." All the things that a woman should not say to a man. All the emotions a clever woman should not express aloud to her lover. And I said them all. "Can you not come every day? I can't bear all these terrible partings and all the hours and hours till I see you again!"

"Janna dearest . . ." He was confused and upset. Despite the fact that he was a sensitive man he had had no idea of my feelings before that moment. "If I'd known you felt so strongly or minded so much—"

"I mind every hour I don't spend with you!" I was so distressed, so utterly devoid of self-control that I cried out, "Could we not be married? I would be a good wife to you—I would learn how to be a lady, to speak without any accent—I wouldn't be an embarrassment to you—"

I stopped. There was a terrible silence. But even before I could begin to feel appalled by what I had done he said in a low, unhappy voice, "But I cannot marry you. I would have told you from the beginning but I assumed you already knew. I'm not divorced. In the eyes of the law—not to mention the eyes of the church—I'm still a married man."

I looked past him. On the mantelshelf was a clock which he himself had given me, its hands pointing to half past four. It was a small attractive wooden clock with Roman numerals painted in black on the white dial. Ever afterward I remembered looking at that stolid comforting little clock keeping time with its stolid comforting little hands.

"Forgive me . . . If I had known your thoughts had turned to marriage . . ." And he began to explain that his wife had given him no cause for divorce, that divorce was impossible on the grounds of desertion alone, but I barely heard him. After a long while I managed to say, "Please, Laurence, think no more of it. I must apologize for behaving so very foolishly. You must be thinking I've quite taken leave of my senses."

If only he could have accepted my apology and responded with some light remark—then I could have maintained the shreds of self-possession I had summoned from the battered remnants of my pride and all would have been well. But instead he said, "Janna my dear . . . Janna darling . . ." And the compassion in his voice made me break down again and weep until my body shook with sobs.

I clung to him and he kissed me. From there it was but three paces to the bed, but after all was finished between us I was conscious as I always was of not having had enough of him, and the whole corrosive series of emotions began to wrack me all over again.

It was exactly as if nothing had happened, exactly as if nothing had changed.

[9]

It was two days later that I first saw Mark.

Laurence had naturally spoken to me of both his sons, and because I loved him so much I had been filled with a curiosity to see them so that I could glimpse their likeness to him in their features and mannerisms. When I had asked him if they resembled him closely he had talked at some length of Nigel, the younger boy, before adding that Mark shared his intellectual tastes. Despite the fact that he then went to great trouble to explain to me how anxious he was not to praise Mark too much for fear I would think him too boastful a father, it occurred to me as time passed that Nigel, not Mark, was the favorite son. This, I decided, was probably because Mark, although a dedicated scholar, was quiet and dull while Nigel, although less gifted intellectually, had more natural charm and grace of manner.

It amuses me now to look back and think how wrong I was.

I remember Mark as I first saw him, remember thinking him unprepossessing since he was small and pale and inclined to fat, but then I noticed that his hair was thick and dark, the kind of hair women long for but seldom possess, and that his shoulders had an unexpected breadth for one so young. Yet his eyes were his most unusual feature. They were black, blacker than the deepest mine shaft, and narrow, as if he surveyed the world warily and with constant speculation.

I did not trust those eyes. I trusted them still less when it became clear that he wished to pay me his precocious respects by calling at the farm. His boldness, coupled with his apparent indifference to my subtle hints that he was not welcome, annoyed me intensely but at the same time to my confusion I found myself admiring the boldness that annoyed me so much. Most boys of twenty are very lacking in polish, but he had an odd veneer of sophistication achieved, I suspected, by a combination of courteous manners, a quick tongue, a heavy dash of the aristocratic arrogance so common among the upper classes, and last but not least by his obvious experience in a matter of which a young gentleman of twenty is not supposed to be a connoisseur.

I did not like him.

Finally, after our initial meeting in Zillan churchyard, after a truly remarkable scene at the farm in which he routed Jared and Joss, who were making one of their disagreeable visits to pester me about the house, and after several social calls during which I was obliged to be polite for fear of arousing his suspicions, I managed to explain to him in no uncertain terms that I no longer wished to receive his attentions, and he took himself off for a week to St. Ives to sulk.

I was enormously relieved. The possibility that Mark might

have discovered his father's relationship with me had been a constant danger, even though Laurence never visited the farm unless Mark was spending the day, as he often did, in Penzance. I had hoped Mark would soon tire of being with his father and return to his friends in London, but he persisted in staying at that farmhouse which must have seemed both uncomfortable and isolated to him.

"You worry about him too much," said Laurence to me soothingly.

"But if he should suspect—"

"Such a thought would never cross his mind."

It irritated me that Laurence should have no idea of his son's true personality and should merely think him an overgrown schoolboy who had taken a naïve and touching interest in an older woman. Against my better judgment I said rashly, "I don't think he's half so innocent as you think he is! I think—"

"My dear, I know Mark better than you do. If you were a parent yourself you would understand that a father necessarily knows his own child better than any stranger can."

Long afterward when I look back it astonishes me that Laurence, who was an intelligent and sensitive man, should have been capable of hurting me so much without realizing it. Nothing could have hurt me more than this open reference to my childlessness. After years of indifference to maternity I now longed passionately for a child—his child—and at the beginning of our affair when I had thought he was divorced I had hoped that I would become pregnant and thus encourage him to marry me. My passion for him had made me oblivious to the reality of the situation; for a time I ignored the fact that my social station was so far inferior to his that I was unlikely to be his wife under any circumstances, but once I had learned that he was not after all divorced I came to my senses and, advised by Griselda, did everything I could to avoid the disaster of pregnancy.

But the longing for a child remained.

However, I think Laurence did sense he had hurt me during this trivial squabble about Mark's true nature, because as soon as we were ourselves again he began to speak of a plan he had in mind for the future to ensure that I would have all the security I would ever need.

"I made a new will the other day," he said. "It was a step I'd been contemplating for some time." He hesitated before adding,

"I'm not naming you in my will, Janna, to save you embarrassment, but I intend to provide for you before I die by creating a trust for your benefit. You need never have to worry about money again, I promise you."

"Please, Laurence!" I said lightly. "Let's not talk yet about you dying!"

It was the first of October. Within three days I heard in the village that he was confined to bed with a fever, and presently I heard that his condition had worsened and he was very ill. At last, unable to endure the horror of waiting for news, I set off to Zillan, ostensibly on the pretext of visiting my husband's grave but secretly in the hope of finding out more news than Griselda had managed to extract from the villagers. It was in Zillan churchyard that the rector found me and told me the news.

Laurence was dead. I had lost the only man I had ever loved and for the second time in six months I stood to lose the farm and all I possessed.

[10]

At first I was so overcome with the violence of my grief that nothing mattered any more, not even my future at Roslyn Farm, but at last Griselda succeeded in pestering me to my senses. Was the produce to go bad because I wouldn't rouse myself to go to Penzance? Did I want us to starve? It was all very well, she pointed out acidly, for delicate young ladies to go into a decline; they had the time and the leisure and the money to do so. I was less fortunate and it was about time I realized it. "Selfish 'ee art," grumbled Griselda. "Like yurr mother. Bone selfish."

She knew perfectly well that I could not endure to be compared to my mother. Sheer annoyance and a desire to prove her wrong made me rouse myself and attempt to pick up once more the threads of my day-to-day existence.

By the Sunday after Laurence's funeral I had managed to blunt the edge of my grief, but the thought of passing the fresh grave in the churchyard still filled me with dread and I would not go with Griselda when she trudged off across the moors to matins. Instead I sat in my sitting room and stared in despair once again at my accounts. I had barely enough money to last me to the new year. And after the new year . . . Tears pricked my eyes again as I looked at the list I had made of Laurence's loans to me. Some of the sums he had insisted I should regard as gifts, but the others I had been determined to repay one day somehow. Now they would never be repaid. I would have to sell the farmhouse to Jared and everything would be lost.

The flames of the fire blurred before my eyes. I was just about to give way and weep with my frustration and despair when there was a loud knock on the back door.

I jumped up.

If that was Jared come to pester me again about the house, I thought fiercely, I'd spit in his face.

Dashing my tears aside, I marched to the door and flung it open in a bold, angry gesture of defiance. But my visitor was not Jared.

It was Mark Castallack.

2

Henry was never considered a handsome man like his father but his youthful freshness captured Eleanor's fancy.

—Henry II,
JOHN T. APPLEBY

She, for her part, needed a protector . . . she found one in Henry of Anjou.

—King John,
W. L. WARREN

[1]

"Good morning," he said.

I stared at him blankly. "Good morning," I replied at last, and my voice sounded cold and unwelcoming in my ears.

There was a silence. I did not know what to say. We stood there facing each other until at length he said, "May I come in?" and as I held the door open for him he stepped past me into the kitchen.

"I apologize," he said, "if I'm calling at an inconvenient time, but I saw you weren't at matins and I wanted the chance to speak to you alone."

"It's not inconvenient." Silence fell again. I tried to say, "I was so sorry to learn of your father's death," but the words would not come.

The silence was on the point of becoming awkward when he said casually, as if it were the most obvious sentiment in the world to express, "I have come to offer my condolences."

For several seconds there was nothing, nothing at all, only those slanting dark eyes with their watchful expression, but then at last when I could breathe evenly again and the shock was a mere dull pain at the back of my throat I became aware of other things, the hens clucking in the yard beyond the open window, the birds singing in the eaves, the crackling of the flames in the kitchen range across the room. My mouth was dry. At last I managed to say politely, "How very kind." I did not say anything else. I was too busy thinking of Laurence, and all at once I did not mind how much the boy knew because I minded nothing save the fact that I would never see Laurence again.

"Perhaps we could talk in the parlor?"

"Yes. If you wish."

We were in the hall, then at the front of the house. I could no longer look at him. My eyes were blind with tears.

In the looking-glass I saw him sit down at the table, as if he were expecting a glass of wine to be brought to him, and tilt the chair backward, his hands in his pockets, until he could rock it gently to and fro on its hind legs. His air of casual indifference grated on me so much that I felt angry. Anger smothered my grief; within a moment my eyes were tearless and I was in control of myself again.

"Why have you come?" I said abruptly. "I presume you came for reasons other than to offer your condolences, but if you did not then I must beg you to excuse me. I am not feeling myself this morning and do not feel well enough to receive visitors."

He did not say how sorry he was that I was not feeling well. Perhaps he guessed that my indisposition merely stemmed from grief. Or perhaps he did not even believe I was indisposed. "Won't you sit down, Mrs. Roslyn?" was all he said, his voice idle and unconcerned as he continued to tilt his chair to and fro. "I feel I'm being discourteous by remaining seated while you yourself are still standing. It was ill-mannered of me in the first place to sit down without your permission, and I apologize. I had no wish to treat you as if you weren't the respectable widow you've always claimed to be."

"Mr. Castallack . . ."

"Please," he said, standing up abruptly and holding the chair out for me as a gentleman would for a lady, "do sit down and forgive my bad manners."

I sat down dumbly. He sat down opposite me. The table yawned between us, and outside the window the breeze from the hills made the thorns of the wild roses scratch against the pane.

"How is the farm?" he said politely. "I trust all is well with you."

"Thank you, yes."

"I'm glad to hear that. My father was actually worried about you, you know. His last words were concerned with your welfare."

I could not speak. I stared down at my hands and thought of Laurence saying in the voice I had loved so well, "You'll never have to worry about money again, I promise. You'll never have to worry about money again."

"If ever you need anything," said Mark Castallack, "I'm sure something can be arranged."

I looked up at him. His black eyes stared at me without expression. His hard masculine mouth curled slightly at the corners in a faint expression of amusement. As I averted my eyes from his face I saw his hand go into his pocket and bring out five sovereigns. The gold gleamed dully in the bright morning light.

"You must have many expenses to meet," he said, piling the coins neatly on the table before him with small precise movements of his hand, "and there's nothing more tedious than not having enough money to be able to live in comfort." He cleared his throat, picked up a sovereign and examined the face of it. I watched him, unable to look away. I was just thinking him totally absorbed in studying the coin when he looked across at me swiftly and our glances met.

I stood up and moved over to the fireplace.

The coins chinked. From the looking glass above the mantelshelf I saw he was putting the money back in his pocket. "Don't forget," he said, "that if ever you need any help you have only to ask and I shall do all I can to make some suitable arrangement."

I said quickly—much too quickly—my brain awhirl, "Well, as it happens . . ." I stopped.

He swiveled around in his chair to look at me. "You need help now?"

"I . . . I am in rather a trying position . . ." I bit my lip. "Perhaps," I said coolly, "if a loan can be arranged I could offer the house as a security . . ."

"Ah yes," he said. "The house. Yes, I'm sure something could be arranged, Mrs. Roslyn. I'm sure we could easily arrive at a convenient arrangement."

I wished he would not repeat the words "arranged" and "arrangement" so often. I did not like the way he used those words with such calculated repetition.

"Might I see the house?" he said casually. "If we're to arrange a loan I would be interested—purely as a formality, of course— to see the exact nature of the collateral you wish to offer."

"Very well," I said after a pause. "As you wish." I turned toward the door and he followed me, his movements indolent, his sharp narrow eyes absorbing everything there was to see. The palms of my hands were damp with sweat. I had to smooth them surreptitiously on my skirts as I crossed the hall.

"This is the dining room," I said, opening the door. "We used to use it at Christmas and Easter and on my husband's birthday. Otherwise we always ate in the kitchen." The solid oak table gleamed in the sunlight; blue china sat on the dark dresser. Laurence had loved the old oak furniture. It had been in the Roslyn family for many generations.

Mark said nothing. We went out into the hall again and I led the way to the back of the house.

"You know the kitchens, of course."

"Oh yes," he said. "I know the kitchens."

We went through the scullery and past the pantry and finally entered the dairy.

"This is very old," I said. "You can see how uneven the flagstones are. This is one of the oldest parts of the house."

"Yes. Is Annie not here today?"

"She's visiting her kin at Zennor. She walks over there once a month." I smoothed my hands against my skirts again. My heart was beginning to hammer in my lungs.

We went back through the kitchen and into the little sitting room behind the parlor.

"I used to sit here on Sundays and read the paper," I said. "We never used the parlor. That was always only for guests such as yourself." And Laurence, I might have added. I remembered how Laurence and I had drunk a glass of wine together when I had first invited him into the house. "What a charming room," he had said. He had loved the house as much as I had.

"There are one or two cupboards," I said, "and a little room off the scullery where we can fill the bath and wash, but otherwise there's nothing else to see."

"And upstairs?"

There was a pause. We were standing in the hall again. As I turned to face him I saw him glancing idly at the staircase.

"Oh," I said, "there's nothing to see upstairs, only a few rooms most of which are no longer used. And there's a loft, of course—a very good loft with a boarded floor. The servants used to sleep there in the old days, but now Annie and Griselda each have a room at the back of the house." I turned away again toward the parlor. My forehead was damp now and my hands so unsteady that I had to clench my fists to hide my shaking fingers. "Shall we go and sit down again? If you would like some wine—"

"I would like to see the rooms upstairs, if you please." He was impeccably polite, utterly bland.

"I—"

"Can that not be . . . arranged, Mrs. Roslyn?"

And then there was a long moment of nothingness, a void which nothing could fill. I could not breathe, speak or think. But the moment passed. They always pass, those long dreadful moments when you cannot bring yourself to believe the facts that are staring you in the face, and when they are passed and you believe, so much begins to happen at once that you feel confused. The next moment my heart was beating painfully, there was a sickness in my stomach and a hotness behind my eyes. I thought: I cannot. And then: It would not matter. And finally: He is offering me a loan with the house as security; there's nothing disreputable about that; the money isn't a gift; it's a loan, and what can be more respectable than a loan given for honest collateral? Everything else is irrelevant. Nothing else would count.

"Very well," I said politely. "If you wish." And we went up the old wooden staircase with the carved banisters to the landing above and I began to show him the back rooms.

"This is Griselda's little room . . . and Annie's . . ."

I was trying not to remember Laurence because I knew it would be best not to think of him. But I remembered just the same. Tears pricked like hot needles behind my eyes.

"This is the room Jared used to have . . . and over here is the one which belonged to Joss . . ."

I was moving as slowly as possible to give myself more time to think, but I could not think, reasoning was impossible, and all I could do was to tell myself that nothing could destroy my love for Laurence, least of all an episode so meaningless that it would soon pass from my memory into oblivion.

"And this is the box room," I said. "My husband kept his first wife's possessions here."

I was thinking so hard of Laurence that I could almost fancy that he was behind me. I thought: If I would turn now and glance over my shoulder I would see him; we would smile at each other and I would think: Never leave me, stay with me because I love you so much I cannot bear to see you go . . .

But he had left me. I was alone.

"And this is my room," I said. "It faces the moors, as you can see. My husband liked this view best of all, and I agreed with him." And I went to the window to gaze out over the view as if I had never seen it before in my life.

I heard the door close with a soft stealthy click. There was the faint squeak as the bolt was drawn, but I did not turn around. Presently I closed the window, which I had left open that morning to air the room, and drew the curtains.

There was a silence. I turned. He was standing, not looking at me, his glance on the little clock with the Roman numerals which Laurence had brought me from Penzance one day several months ago. I had loved it because it had come from him and yet at the same time had hated its little black hands for so cruelly marking each of the few brief hours he had spent in that room.

"What an incredibly ugly clock," said Mark, slipping off his jacket. "I suppose it was your husband's."

We said nothing else. We undressed, he very quickly, I with great precision as if every movement was of vital importance, and then at last when there was nothing else left to be done, we went to bed.

[2]

I expected nothing.

I did not love him. I had lost the man I loved and was full of grief. I was resentful but too wrapped up in my misery, too desolated by life's unfairness to feel either violently angry or violently humiliated. I felt nothing. I entered the episode so passively that I had already resolved to forget it the moment it was over, and one does not expect anything from an association begun in that frame of mind.

I did not want to expect anything. That would have betrayed Laurence, and it was Laurence that I loved.

So I went to Mark wanting nothing and expecting nothing, and suddenly it was all changed, just as it is in those nightmares when a familiar landscape becomes alien, and I found I did not know myself. I looked into those narrow black eyes, and it was as if I had never known myself, as if my own self were imprisoned in a stranger's body over which I had no control. And when he touched me, unhooking the fastenings of my bodice and burying his face in my hair as I let it fall past my shoulders, it was as if no man had ever touched me before and I forgot Laurence— yes, forgot him—forgot him as if he had never existed, because never in all my moments with Laurence had I imagined it was possible to experience what I experienced then with his son.

It was indescribable. No words ever invented could even begin to describe it.

When I awoke at last it was late afternoon and beyond the window the moors were already bathed in the golden October light. I lay where I was, not even wanting to move, my limbs warm and relaxed between the sheets, my eyelids heavy with drowsiness, my whole body satiated and at peace. The house was very quiet. All I could hear was the even breathing of the man beside me, but I did not look at him because I did not want to acknowledge to myself what had happened. I closed my eyes and let that slumbrous languor seep through me with its delicious drowsiness, and tried to pretend that it was Laurence beside me and that I had only to open my eyes to see the face I had loved so much, but suddenly his face was gone, I could not remember it, and all I could see were slanting eyes and that hard masculine mouth.

I sat up.

Mark did not stir. I looked at him. He seemed young and childish, his hair black against the white pillow, his lashes motionless against his flushed cheeks. I went on looking at him, but presently when I could look at him no longer I slipped out of bed and began to dress.

He still did not stir. I went on dressing, praying for tears or for some other release from the pain of shock, but I did not cry. I finished dressing, picked up the bolsters from the floor, twisted my hair into place. When I had finished I looked at myself in the mirror. My eyes were tearless. I thought I would look tired, but I did not. I looked young.

Twenty-five, perhaps. Or possibly twenty-six. I thought: I'm young—young! But I could not understand it; it was too hard to comprehend, but as I left the room and went downstairs I felt as light and free as air.

Griselda came out into the hall to meet me. I saw her look at Mark's hat on the table, but she said nothing and I said nothing to her. I went outside. The sun was warm; a breeze caressed the moors, and suddenly I was stumbling up the hillside until before me in the heather rose the ruined walls of Chûn.

I began to cry then, the tears welling soundlessly in my eyes and burning my cheeks. I went into the inner circle as if I could recall the ghost of the man I had first seen there seven months before, but there were no ghosts, only bitter memories of a romance between an ill-assorted couple, a farmer's widow aflame with the desire to make up for a wasted youth and a middle-aged scholar unable to tolerate a seventeenth consecutive year of celibacy. We had each been a convenience for the other; I saw that now. The only difference between us was that I had deluded myself by thinking I was passionately in love, while Laurence had recognized from the beginning that we were two strangers who, seeking an escape from loneliness, had stumbled upon an affection which manifested itself in diffident expressions of love three times a week during a long, empty rural summer.

That was all. It was a simple enough truth perhaps, but I might have gone to my grave without realizing it if I had not been confronted by a much more unwelcome truth during my enforced encounter with Mark Castallack.

As I began to cry again I tried to hate Mark for destroying the illusions I had lived with and loved for so long, but I could not. The instant I thought of Mark I began to wish myself back behind that locked door with him, and one cannot hate a man to whom one would give oneself again and again without a second's hesitation.

After a long while I turned once more, left the castle and moved slowly downhill to the farm.

Griselda was nibbling bread and cheese in the kitchen. Again neither of us spoke. Moving into the hall, I saw Mark's hat still on the chest, and in a fit of restlessness I returned to the kitchens and cut myself a large slice of cold pie from the plate in the larder. I found I was ravenously hungry and after the pie I ate an apple and some lemon curd tart. At last I was just beginning to feel that I had assuaged my hunger when I heard Mark's footsteps far away on the stairs.

I went at once to the hall.

When I saw him then it was as if I saw him for the first time. He looked older, poised, completely self-possessed, and his slanting eyes were shadowed with knowledge in a way I found curiously exciting. When he saw me he smiled. I could not understand then how I had ever thought him plain. I was in the middle of thinking what a striking face he had when he smoothed back a lock of hair with his hand and the sight of those short strong fingers reminded me at once of our hours together behind that locked door.

The color rose to my face; I felt my heart beating very fast.

"Will you stay and dine here?" I said evenly. "There's plenty of food if you're hungry."

"Thank you, but dinner will be waiting for me at Morvah, and I should be on my way." He paused and for some reason glanced at the closed parlor door. "However, I confess I'm thirsty. Perhaps some cider . . ."

"I'll fetch it for you."

When I returned with a full pitcher and a glass I found he was still in the hall, but the parlor door was now ajar. I wondered what he had wanted in there.

He drank the cider very quickly and set down the glass on the chest nearby. "May I call on you after dinner tomorrow evening?"

"Very well . . . but will you not come earlier and dine with me?"

"No," he said, "but I'll stay to breakfast." He smiled again. There was an expression in his eyes which I had seen and despised in other men but which in him seemed unbearably exciting. We stood facing each other two feet apart, and the spark between us was so strong that I felt if we touched each other it would flare as vividly as sheet lightning on a dark night. "Until tomorrow, then," he said after a pause. "Good day to you, Mrs. Roslyn."

"Good day, Mr. Castallack," I said wryly and held the door open for him as he stepped out into the porch.

When he was out of sight I closed the door and leaned against the panels. My knees were trembling again; physical exhaustion struck me with the force of a hammer. Picking up the jug of cider, I poured myself a measure into the glass he had used and carried it unsteadily into the parlor.

I was on the threshold when I saw the table. I nearly dropped the glass. Cider slopped over the rim, splashed my dress and stained the carpet. Then as my cheeks began to burn I set my glass down on the table slowly so that it would not spill again and picked up one by one the five gold sovereigns he had taken such care to leave behind.

[3]

Mark spent every night of that week at the farm. While he was gone I found myself incapable of doing anything except the most mundane chores such as dusting the furniture or feeding the hens, and in the end it was left to Griselda and Annie to do most of the work; on the grounds of economy I had not employed Ethel and Millie Turner since my husband's death. I did go once to market with Griselda but could not concentrate on my business and made a sadly inefficient muddle of my transactions. I lived for the evenings, but although I asked Mark more than once to dine with me at the farm he always refused.

His refusals made me angry and curiously humiliated.

"Am I not worthy to dine with you?" I demanded at last. "It's insulting to come here night after night and do nothing except—"

"Except?" He laughed, much amused by my confusion, and drawled, "Well, you must admit it's a very sizable exception!"

His levity annoyed me intensely. "But why should you refuse to dine with me?" I demanded. "I think I'm at least entitled to a reason!"

"You're not entitled to anything, my dear," he said politely. "I'm not answerable to you. I can do exactly as I please."

"Very well," I said, furiously angry, "be as independent as you please! I suppose you're still young enough to mistake a show of arrogance for an expression of mature behavior. As far as I'm concerned it couldn't matter less."

He laughed again. "I love to see you angry!" was his only comment, and then his hand was sliding across the parlor table and enclosing my own so that I felt the now familiar thrill of weakness shiver through my body, and his voice, the deep beautiful voice that attracted me so much, was telling me to be patient because in the end I would have everything I wanted. "When we dine together for the first time it's going to be a great occasion," he said, "not a mundane meal in this little Cornish farmhouse where you dined with your husband and received . . . other people. If you would only trust me . . ."

But I did not trust him. I had no faith in his grand promises, and his obvious dislike of the farm I loved so much rankled with me and made me feel resentful toward him. Young men, I knew, often made grandiose promises about the future with no intention of keeping them and I thought he was only pacifying me, smoothing over my resentment until I was once more a pliable convenience to be visited whenever he chose.

My distrust deepened when he departed the next day for the Castallack family home at Gweek. He had certain business affairs to attend to, he told me casually, and would be away from Morvah for a few days.

Two weeks passed and there was no sign of him. By this time each day seemed as long as a week. Finally to my horror I heard in the village that young Mr. Castallack had moved from Gweek to London and his housekeeper at Morvah did not know when he would be returning.

"But surely he must return eventually to Morvah!" I protested desperately to Griselda. "Laurence left him the house there—he wouldn't live at Gweek because Nigel gets Gweekellis Manor under the will and, besides, he and Mark are estranged. They quarreled violently when Nigel returned from abroad to find the funeral had been held without him and that Laurence had been buried at Zillan instead of at the church they attended near Gweek. And Mark wouldn't stay with his mother in London, because he doesn't get along with her, so in that case he must return to Deveral Farm at Morvah because he has nowhere else to go."

Griselda said she wasn't going to waste her precious time mooning over Mark Castallack and asking herself what he'd be doing next. Furthermore it was about time I pulled myself together, forgot about young Mr. Mark and gave serious thought to the question of remarriage. Those gold coins wouldn't last long, and then where would we be? If I was sensible I'd sell the farm to Mr. Jared, marry young Mr. Polmarth of Polmarth Farm, who had always regarded me with such favor, and escape all this constant worrying about where the next penny was coming from.

"Thomas Polmarth?" I said with distaste. "That uncouth, plain-looking yokel? No, thank you!"

"Don't 'ee be so high and mighty!" shrilled Griselda, losing her temper. "Just because thee's been a-courted by two gentlemen yurr head be turned and thee's all airs and graces! Thee'd best pull yurrself up, my girl, and put some sense in yurr poor addled mind. Gentlemen ain't be going a-marrying the likes of thee, so don't 'ee think they will. Gentlemen marry ladies, not fishermen's daughters. And don't 'ee forgets where 'ee comes from and what 'ee truly art! If 'ee thinks Mr. Mark's coming back here and marrying 'ee one day—"

"I think no such thing!" I said angrily, and it was true. Mark had indeed mentioned marriage to me once before Laurence had died, but he had been distraught at the time and I had not taken him seriously. Besides, at that time he was the last person I wanted to marry. Now I knew I felt differently, but despite my change of feelings I had not lost my common sense. "Mark was interested in me for one reason and one reason only," I said sharply to Griselda, "and that reason had nothing whatsoever to do with matrimony."

Griselda began to growl something about sin and damnation.

"Very well!" I cried, much exasperated. "So my behavior with him was sinful and wrong! But why should I not indulge in a pleasurable love affair for once? I've always been unlucky in love —I spent all my twenties in unfortunate circumstances—aren't I entitled now to a little pleasure with a man who attracts me? Surely God is not so cruel as to deny me the right to a little happiness after so much pain and misery! All I've ever wanted in life was security and love and if I can't have the one I think I might at least try and have the other!"

Griselda said what did it matter now anyway since it was clear as daylight Mark had taken when he wanted from me and moved on to someone else.

But she was wrong.

He came back two weeks later, just as I had given up all hope of ever seeing him again and was in my despair composing a cold note to remind him of his offer to grant me a loan. He walked into my house as if he owned it, strolled with the most insolent nonchalance into the parlor where I was writing my letter and greeted me as if it had been only yesterday since I had last seen him.

"I've been in London for the past three weeks," he said without offering even the briefest of apologies. "I had one or two tiresome family affairs to settle. Also my cousin Robert Yorke died and I was delayed in London on account of the funeral." Ignoring my coldness, which must by then have been very obvious, he glanced out of the window at the gray bleakness of the November afternoon and added carelessly, "I assumed you would realize that I was unavoidably detained."

"Unfortunately," I said icily, "clairvoyance is not among the gifts God saw fit to bestow upon me."

"Dear me," he said in such a gravely mocking voice that my cheeks flamed with anger. "I'm sorry about that. However, since God has seen fit to bestow upon you so many other admirable attributes it would no doubt be unfair to complain about such an inexplicable omission." And even before I could open my mouth to tell him what I thought of him he slipped a small square leather box into my hand and bade me open it.

The angry words died before they could be spoken. With fingers that were suddenly hot and unsteady, I fumbled with the catch, raised the lid and stared inside.

I saw a ring bearing an enormous sapphire. The sapphire had that warm slumbrous glow in shadow and that brilliant glitter whenever it caught the light. Around the sapphire were diamonds, bright, hard, multi-sided diamonds such as I had not seen since I had been a lady's maid long ago at Menherion Castle.

I could not speak. I was dumb. I stared at that exquisite ring and all I could think was: He did not go away and forget. I misjudged him. He thought of me when he was in London and finally he came back, just as he promised he would. He meant every word he said. He was sincere.

"It's . . . very beautiful," I heard myself say diffidently at last. "I—I have never had such a fine present before."

"I hope it will be the first of many."

After a moment I said, "Oh?" I was overcome; tears, absurd and unwanted, pricked my eyelids. "I thought you'd left me," I said suddenly, the words tumbling from my lips. "I thought you'd gone."

"After waiting for you for so many months?"

I looked up. Tears blinded my eyes, burned my cheeks, but they no longer mattered. Nothing mattered now because he had kept his word and he had come back to me and his attentions were not empty after all but filled with meaning and purpose.

"I didn't believe you," I said. "I didn't trust you. I didn't think you were so . . ." So ready to keep your promises, I almost added, but the words would no longer come. And as I halted uncertainly, my eyes so dim with tears that I could not see his expression, he leaned forward and took my hand in his and said gently in his beautiful voice, "Did you ever doubt that I would ask you again to marry me?" And I could not speak; it was as if I were in some dazzling dream which bore no relation to all those long years of toil and misery and insecurity behind me, and all I was conscious of was his hand hot and dry against my own and his dark eyes filled neither with cynicism nor speculation but with a message no man's eyes had ever held for me before. And the message was tenderness, not Laurence's pity and compassion, not Jared's lust, but tenderness, and beyond the tenderness stretching as far as the heart could read lay love, the love I needed, the love and peace and security I had longed for all my life.

"Will you marry me, Janna?" he said. "Will you?"

And I said, not even pausing to think, only obsessed by the fear that my lifelong desire might once again slip through my fingers, "Oh yes, Mark—yes, I will, yes, yes, yes . . ."

[4]

As soon as I had promised to marry him I was overcome with panic. Mark began to talk blithely of a wedding in London, a honeymoon on the Continent and renovations to Deveral Farm so that we could live there in comfort until he inherited Penmarric—and the more he talked the more frightened I became. At length when he paused for breath I managed to say in a small voice, "But, Mark, could we not be married in Penzance? Or Truro or Launceston or some other large Cornish town?"

"Penzance!" he exclaimed, much amused. "What an extraordinary idea! No, it would be much more practical to be married in London. My cousin Robert left me his townhouse in Park Lane, so we can stay there until we're ready to go abroad. You can have the opportunity to order some good clothes, look around the shops, buy whatever you wish—"

"But, Mark," I said, and I could hear my voice tremble, "I've never been away from Cornwall before. Penzance is the largest town I've ever seen. I—I would not know how to behave in London. I would make mistakes—it's so many years since I lived at Menherion Castle that I can't remember all the details of etiquette. All your friends would look down at me—your mother . . ." I nearly fainted with fright at the thought of Mark's mother. Words failed me.

"My darling," said Mark in his gentlest, kindest voice, "simply be yourself and I shall be more than proud to present you in any drawing room in London. If you're good enough for me you're good enough for everyone else as far as I'm concerned."

"But my voice—I don't speak as a lady should—"

"Your accent's so pretty! I love to hear you speak!"

"But I'm not educated! I know nothing—"

"You can read and write and that's all that matters. Too much education makes a woman unfeminine."

"Yes, but—"

"Listen," he said, kissing me, "you'll enjoy London—we can have a box at the theater, dine at some good restaurants, see all the famous sights—"

"But I shall have to meet your mother."

"Yes, it'll be tedious for you, I agree, but—"

"Tedious!" I felt faint again.

"She won't dare to make any unpleasant observations to you while I'm there. Besides, she's no longer living at the house in Park Lane. She's bought herself a house near Berkeley Square, so we need only see her once while we're in London. . . . There's no one else you need meet—one or two Oxonian friends of mine, perhaps, but that's all. You won't be meeting Nigel. He and I are still not on speaking terms."

The word "London" was still reverberating so loudly in my ears that I did not at first listen to his next words. It came as a shock when I heard him say rapidly: ". . . and while we're on the subject of my family I wish to make one point perfectly clear. I never want to discuss my father with you. Is that understood? I never want to hear you speak of him or refer to him in your conversation. He's dead. He's gone from your life and he's gone from mine, and that's all there is to say. I shall never speak of him myself and if I hear you speaking of him I shall be very angry. Is that clear?"

I was so startled by his vehemence and the rough edge to his voice that I merely said meekly, "Yes, Mark."

"Good." He rose to his feet and I rose too so that in a second we were face to face and he was taking me in his arms. We kissed. I had forgotten how weak and dizzy his embrace made me feel. I could hardly stand.

"Oh Mark, Mark . . ." We could not even separate from each other for long enough to go upstairs to my room. I remember lying on the sofa and then, when the sofa became too cramped for us, on the rug by the hearth.

Later, much later, when we were ourselves again and I was twisting my hair back into place before the looking-glass, he asked me if I had a gown I could wear that evening in Penzance.

"This evening?" I said stupidly. "Penzance?"

"At the Metropole Hotel," he said. "I was hoping that tonight at last we could dine together for the first time."

[5]

I said to Griselda, "He wants to marry me."

Griselda snorted.

"He does, Griselda. At Christmas. In London."

She gaped at me. "Lunnon?"

"He's going to marry me, Griselda. And I want to marry him. He's not as shallow as I thought he was. He keeps his promises —he means what he says, so I can trust him, Griselda, can't you see? I can trust him and feel secure."

"And the house? The house thee's so crazed for? What's to happen to the house?"

"I'll lease it to Jared. Mark and I will live at Morvah, and he says he'll make a little cottage for you, Griselda, a little home all your own! Oh, Griselda, I do love him! I'm not marrying him just because he's rich and well-to-do! If you knew how I felt— if you could understand—"

"Bewitched thee art. Bewitched and crazed. There's that boy, no more 'n one-and-twenty—"

"Oh do be quiet, you silly old woman! Really, you make me so angry sometimes I feel quite put out. Quick, get out the ironing board and let me press that pale-green gown Miss Charlotte gave me all those years ago. I think if I lace up my corset a little tighter I can still make the gown meet around the waist."

The news of my good fortune exploded in Zillan as furiously as fire in a tinderbox. At first my natural reaction was to feel exultant, but gradually my exultation faded and a bitter anger took its place.

"Maybe you'd have married me, Janna," said Jared, "if I'd been six inches shorter and a whole heap uglier and a rich gentleman instead of a yeoman farmer."

"Mrs. Roslyn," said my friend the rector with a tactfulness that could not wholly conceal his concern, "would it perhaps not be more prudent to wait until the spring? I realize that you and Mark both feel there's no point in waiting since you both know your minds so clearly, but I fear your haste will give rise to the most unfortunate gossip . . ."

"Gossip," said Griselda, "gossip, gossip, gossip. They thinks I'm deaf and don't understand, but I understands right enough. Fast, they says thee art, fast and scheming. And someone's been talking of thee and Mr. Laurence—Jared, maybe? Or that evil-tongued Joss. . . . Well, says they, well, if she can't get the father, they says, she gets the son. She gets what she can, they says, and her husband not yet one year in his grave. And there's Mr. Mark, they says, an innocent boy, they says, no more 'n one-and-twenty, and *clay*, says they, *clay* in the hands of a power-ful ambitious older woman. Terrible gossip there be all through Zillan parish and all through Morvah, Zennor and St. Just, and even as far as Penzance, Madron and Marazion—"

"Stop it, Griselda!" I cried. I felt close to tears with horror and resentment. "Stop it!" In a passionate wave of anger I exclaimed, "I'll be glad to leave here and go to London! I'm sick of all their vicious tongues! I'll be glad to leave Zillan parish and never speak to anyone in Zillan again!"

I left Roslyn Farm with Mark less than a week later.

3

She immediately married Henry.
— The Saxon and Norman Kings,
CHRISTOPHER BROOKE

*Henry and Eleanor were quietly married at Poitiers
without any pomp and almost surreptitiously.* . . .
— Henry II,
JOHN T. APPLEBY

[1]

I shall never forget the horrified amazement that assailed me
when I first saw the house in Park Lane which Mark's cousin
Robert Yorke had recently devised to him by will. I was already
stupefied by the long train journey from Penzance—I had never
been in a train before—and stunned by the enormity of the vast,
dirty, crowded, jumbled, confused city in which I found myself
late at night on that December evening, but when I saw the
townhouse I was so numb with shock that I forgot even the fear-
ful excitement of the journey and of my first sight of the London lights stretching away on all sides to infinity. I had fancied
"Park Lane" to be a pleasant little street in some modest neighborhood not unlike the superior residential areas of Penzance and

the house to be a simple dwelling a little smaller than Roslyn Farm but with one or two more servants. Yet to my horror I found myself in one of the grandest streets in London with the magnificence of Hyde Park on the one hand and the splendor of mighty mansions on the other. Speech instantly deserted me. I was so unnerved I could hardly bring myself to descend from the hansom cab.

A footman came out to meet us. And another. A butler hovered in the hall. There was even a third footman behind him. And the hall! A massive chandelier hung from an ornate ceiling. A beautiful staircase curved elegantly to the floor above. I stared blankly around me. The servants were bowing, the butler was murmuring courtesies. I think I smiled in acknowledgment. I cannot remember. All I do recall is that I thought at once with fright of the patched underwear in my valise, and I began to beseech Mark in a whisper to let me unpack the luggage myself. I had bought one or two items in Penzance before the journey but at his suggestion had left the essential purchases until reaching London. "But I must do the unpacking!" I urged wretchedly. "My clothes—"

"No." That was all he said. Merely: "No."

"But, Mark—"

"My dear, it simply isn't done. Do as I say." It was as if he were the one who had the ten years more experience of the world and I were the one scarce out of my teens. So overwhelmed was I by his manner and authority that I did not dare question him further.

Upstairs I found I had been allotted a vast bedchamber with a grandiose modern bed, resplendent furniture and somber paintings on the walls. The carpet was so thick that I could hardly walk upon it. Presently I was informed by the expressionless maid who was unpacking my belongings that there was even a bathroom nearby, and, seizing the chance to escape before she could discover my patched underwear, I hurried down the corridor in search of it. The bath was of white porcelain on little gilt legs and there was a basin with taps. I turned the tap. Water came out. I turned it off again. The water stopped. Becoming bolder, I investigated the room next door and discovered it was, as I had suspected, a water closet, the bowl very fancifully decorated with a royal-blue design on a white background. There had been a water closet at Menherion Castle, but none of the servants had ever been allowed to use it, and besides, the castle plumbing had never been very reliable—at least not back in the Seventies when I had lived there. Perhaps matters were so improved now that all the gentry had beautiful bathrooms and perfectly functioning water closets. Or perhaps they were simply more advanced in London than they were in far-off provincial Cornwall.

For a moment I was so absorbed with the novelty of my surroundings that I quite forgot to feel nervous.

That night after an informal supper we went to bed early. We slept in separate rooms, of course, to preserve the proprieties, but he slipped into my bed before dawn and stayed until it was light, so I was not alone the entire night. In fact the proprieties were hardly observed anyway since we were both unmarried and both sleeping under the same roof with the whole house to ourselves, but as we were to be married so soon and as we did not intend to mingle with society before our wedding, I supposed it did not matter that we paid such scant respect to the conventions.

The next morning for the first time in my life I had breakfast in bed, and afterward my maid offered to draw my bath for me. Oh, the wonder of that long hot bath! By the time I had finished it was almost eleven o'clock. Eleven, I thought, eleven! I remembered my days as a farmer's wife, the milking and the churning, the cooking and baking and cleaning, the ceaseless routine of morning activity. Yet here it was, eleven o'clock, and all I had done was have breakfast, lie in bed and take a bath!

I began at last to enjoy myself.

That day the dressmaker came, and, being a competent woman, she advised me at once on the wardrobe I required and made various suggestions about patterns and materials. It was an enthralling morning. After a late luncheon we took a drive in the park before visiting Bond Street and Oxford Street and viewing the amazing variety of shops. The next few days passed very quickly; Mark was making the arrangements for the wedding and I was busy trying on the new gowns which were beginning to arrive from the dressmaker's. I was just starting to adjust to my surroundings and to attain a small measure of self-confidence when Mark announced that the time had come to call on his mother.

Panic overwhelmed me again. I was literally shaking with fright. In vain Mark assured me that I looked so beautiful in my new clothes that he would have taken me to Buckingham Palace without a qualm. In vain he told me that his mother was only a middle-aged woman, very vain, incredibly arrogant and more than a little pathetic in her loneliness. In vain he reassured me that she was not the devil incarnate. All I could remember was that she was the haughty, domineering "Miss Maud Penmar" of Ethel and Millie Turner's gossipy reminiscences of the local gentry and the quarrelsome, discontented wife who had made Laurence so unhappy during the years they had spent together at Gweek.

"Oh, by the way," said Mark casually, "don't forget to address my mother as Mrs. Penmar. She never uses the name Castallack."

"Mrs. Penmar. Yes. I'll remember." I wracked my brains to think of an excuse I could use for avoiding that dreadful meeting, but there was no escape and at length we departed for the house in Charles Street.

"Oh, Mark!" I whispered in an agony of nervousness after an imperious butler had regarded us with a baleful eye and shown us into the morning room. "Could we not go away—leave before she comes? You could say I was suddenly taken ill, that I felt faint—"

"And have her instantly imagine you're pregnant and that I'm marrying you because I must? Certainly not!"

I was just about to give way to my panic and declare I did not care what motives for marriage she attributed to us when the door opened and a tall, handsome woman swept haughtily into the room and paused without the least embarrassment to survey me through a lorgnette. She had iron-gray hair, the black Penmar eyes which I now felt I knew so well, a tight, ill-tempered mouth and a strong masculine jaw. Rings flashed on her fingers. Her dress, of a grand shade of purple, was strangely becoming to her. As she let the lorgnette fall and came forward again toward me I saw she moved with the air of the privileged classes, the air of coming and going exactly where she pleased whenever she wished, the air of arrogance which had attracted yet irritated me when I had first met Mark.

"Well," she said disagreeably to her son. "This is a fine how-d'ye-do, I must say. At least she has good looks. I suppose one must try and look on the more fortunate aspects of the situation."

"Mama," said Mark in a voice of steel, "if you cannot receive us with the necessary minimum of courtesy, then pray do not bother to receive us at all. I don't have to have your consent to my marriage—"

"Very lucky for you, isn't it?"

"—and I certainly don't intend to go down on my knees and beg for your blessing!"

"I should think not indeed! I detest groveling. Very well, if you ring the bell and stop striding up and down like a bad actor playing Hamlet I'll ask Tipstock to bring in some sherry. Sit down, Mrs. Roslyn," she added, not bothering to look at me, and proceeded to lower herself into a formidable high-backed chair from which she could act the part of an inquisitor.

There followed a grueling quarter of an hour during which my prospective mother-in-law inquired ruthlessly into my antecedents. Mark had urged me beforehand to hide nothing and speak as boldly as if I were as proud of being a fisherman's daughter as she was of being a Penmar, but that was easier said than done. However, I spoke up as best as I could, telling her that my parents had died young, obliging me to go into service at an early age, and I somehow contrived to make it appear that I had worked at Menherion Castle until I had married my first husband; I also stressed that the Roslyns were not tenants but yeomen farmers who owned their own land.

"Hm," said Maud Penmar and took a large mouthful of sherry. She drank without any pretense of daintiness. "Well, that's all very respectable, I suppose. Is Janna your real name?"

"No, I was christened Jeanne after my father, whose name was Jean-Yves. But the Cornish cannot pronounce French names."

"He was French?"

"From Brittany, yes. There was a colony of Breton sailors in St. Ives."

"Do you speak French?"

"I've forgotten it all. It's so long since my father died."

"A pity. It would have helped if you spoke French." She set down her glass and turned to Mark. "When do you intend to be married?"

"Next week. I expect to have the special license any day now and I've made arrangements to be married in the Savoy Chapel—"

"Am I invited to the wedding?"

"I wouldn't dream of putting you in such an embarrassing position!"

"How tactful!" Their expressions became bitter as they stared at each other. Her mouth set itself in a hard narrow line. "Well," she said, not looking at either of us and pouring herself a third glass of sherry from the decanter, "I don't approve of your future wife—how could I?—but at least matters could be infinitely worse. There's no reason why Mrs. Roslyn should not acquire a certain air of gentility, and God knows there aren't many working-class women one could say that much for. She's clever and good-looking and if she makes an effort she could even be presentable. I wish you both well and hope you will always call upon me whenever you're in London."

The interview was over. Within minutes I was sinking down exhausted against the upholstery of the carriage and savoring the enormity of my relief that my ordeal should at last be behind me.

"Of course," said Mark abruptly, "she was most embarrassingly rude. I apologize for her. However, that's an ordeal we don't have to repeat. You need not visit her again—I've no intention of taking you back there to be insulted."

Relief made me charitable. "I don't think she meant to be insulting, Mark. She was merely a little outspoken, and I expect her outspokenness sprang from disappointment. She must have hoped you would make a good match."

"She of all people should approve of the fact that I'm marrying for love! She was angry enough with her father when he stopped her marrying Giles Penmar!"

"She wished us well, Mark—"

"Because she knew that if she did not I would not visit her again, and now that Cousin Robert's dead she's at last beginning to wish she was closer to her children. Her motives are entirely selfish and always have been. I despise her."

I did not answer. Despite all he had said I could not admit I was glad he was not more attached to her and glad I would not have to visit her frequently in the future. He remained silent also throughout the journey back to Park Lane, but at the house once more the uneasy atmosphere was quickly dispelled; on our arrival we found that a messenger had delivered our special license, and that very afternoon we set out for the Strand to make the final arrangements with the clergyman for our wedding.

[2]

We were married five days later on the morning of December the nineteenth. I wore a small but fashionable bonnet suitable for my widowed state, a blue silk gown cut in superbly stark lines which enhanced my figure while remaining the epitome of good taste, and the most elegantly uncomfortable pair of shoes my feet had ever encountered. Two Oxonian friends of Mark's were the only witnesses; it was a brief, informal affair, and afterward they joined us for a champagne breakfast at Claridges before leaving us free to return to Park Lane on our own. As soon as we reached the house Mark gave orders that we were on no account to be disturbed, and then we went to my room, locked the door and drew the curtains. I was so dizzy with the unaccustomed champagne and so elated that I was now Mrs. Mark Castallack that I went to bed without thought for any possible consequences, but later I was able to think carelessly: What if it was a risk? What does it matter now? And the sense of security was suddenly so immense that I was overcome with the miracle of my good fortune.

We went to the theater that evening. We had a box as if we were royalty, and I wore my finest new evening gown, white silk and tulle offset with black lace, and all the gentlemen looked at me through their opera glasses when they should have been watching the stage.

"Everyone's wondering who you are," said Mark, highly delighted. "You're the mystery of the evening."

The next morning the notice of our quiet marriage appeared in *The Times*. It was then at last, as I stared at the facts set down in black and white, that I was fully able to comprehend the magnitude of what had happened. I believe if I had been allowed then to think upon it for any length of time I would quickly have been beset by all manner of fears, but I was given no time to sit and think. Just as I was beginning to grow accustomed to the strangeness of London life and the dizzy pinnacle of society on which I now found myself, Mark told me that the arrangements had been made for our honeymoon and the next day I was swept off across the Channel to France.

[3]

I must have been the only woman on earth who did not fall in love with Paris the moment she set foot in it. I thought it a cold, dreary city full of grand buildings that were supposed to be famous landmarks and rude self-centered women whose language I could not understand. The men were full of false smiles and embarrassing attentions and I refused absolutely to go anywhere unless Mark was by my side. I felt strange, confused and lost.

"But since you're half French you should feel quite at home here!" Mark protested.

"My father was a Breton," I said, "and Brittany is different from the rest of France, just as Cornwall is different from England."

Finally to my relief we left Paris and took a train south to Monte Carlo, and although I remained convinced that France was an abominable country I did like Monte Carlo better than I had anticipated. It was a town set by the sea, and the semitropical vegetation there reminded me of the new Morrab Gardens in Penzance which were filled with palm trees and exotic shrubs. The weather was pleasant, and I might almost have enjoyed our stay if I had been able to conquer my aversion to the richness of French food and the constant flow of French wine. However, as time passed and my queasiness settled into a pattern of appearing remorselessly each morning I realized that French food alone might not be to blame for my malaise. I refused to consult a French doctor, but as soon as we returned to London in February I visited a physician in Wimpole Street who confirmed that I was going to have a baby.

I had not intended to spend the first year of my marriage battling the discomforts of pregnancy, but I had been careless since the wedding and was not altogether surprised by my condition. Finally I decided that since I did want children eventually it hardly mattered whether I began to have them that year or the next, so I resigned myself to the inevitable and even began to feel excited at the prospect of maternity.

Mark was anxious to stay in London so that I might have the best care and attention, but I could not wait to get back to Cornwall. I longed for a glimpse of the Cornish sea, the sweep of the moors, the stone engine houses of the mines. I wanted to breathe Cornish air again and tread on Cornish soil and sleep beneath a Cornish roof. I could hardly endure to remain a day longer in London, but at last, after an interval that seemed interminable, we boarded the train one mild morning in early March and began our long journey home to Cornwall, Morvah and Deveral Farm.

The farmhouse which I had glimpsed from a distance but had never entered was a plain unattractive building, very different from my own beloved Roslyn Farm, but it was spacious and the rooms were pleasantly furnished, so I felt I would be able to settle there well enough for the time being. The new plumbing which had been installed in our absence was a great luxury, and I was able to have a bath every morning whenever I decided to get up after breakfast. Mark had wanted me to consult a Penzance doctor who numbered the Carnforths of Carnforth Hall among his patients, but Dr. Logan was old and snobbish, so I decided instead to see the new young doctor in St. Just, Dr. Salter, who had attended my first husband once or twice during my years at Roslyn Farm. Dr. Salter, when consulted, advised me to take a little exercise after lunch if I felt well but otherwise to rest as much as possible, and although I was secretly amused at the notion of myself spending my months of waiting languishing on a chaise longue I decided to follow his advice and do as I was told.

Our stay in Monte Carlo had enabled us to escape much of the worst of winter, but we did not escape the Great March Blizzard, which raged for twenty-four hours, wrecking ships in Penzance harbor and blocking the railway lines at Redruth. This was a most unusual weather phenomenon and people spoke of it for years afterward. However, soon it was spring and before long spring was melting into summer. I continued to do very little. Sarah Mannack appeared to be an adequate housekeeper and was kind to poor Annie, who at first had trouble settling in her new home. Griselda, cantankerous as ever, had had "words" with Mrs. Mannack on more than one occasion, but since she was now comfortably established in her own little cottage nearby the situation in the kitchens was not as awkward as it might have been.

We received a few calls but did not entertain much on account of my condition. On the whole the people we saw most often were the Barnwells, for we still crossed the parish boundaries to worship at Zillan and occasionally we would lunch at the rectory after matins. Their daughter Miriam, who had disgraced herself the previous year by running off with young Harry Penmar, was like myself in "a delicate condition"—or so that tiresome woman Mrs. Barnwell confided to me cozily over tea one afternoon. Harry Penmar had married Miriam, so she was at least an honest woman, but he was up to his ears in debt as usual and I had a suspicion that Miriam might have begun to regret her impulsive elopement.

Time passed; Mark was busy working on some historical thesis which was much too learned for me to understand and seemed not to mind the quiet life we were leading. I was content enough at Morvah, but sometimes I longed to visit Roslyn Farm, and only the knowledge that I would have an unpleasant reception if I tried to go there enabled me to suppress the longing and stay away from that quarter of Zillan parish. I had leased the house to Jared but to appease my conscience had charged him only a nominal rent; there was no reason why I should have felt guilty where he was concerned, but he had had bad luck and I had always treated him coldly. His bad luck continued, however, for that summer two of his children, including his only son Abel, died of a sickness and his wife, who was one of those meek, faded women constantly on the brink of maternity, began a long period of miscarriages. I felt sorry for him, but he did not want my sympathy. He became more religious, I heard, and never missed chapel on Sunday. He had begun to attend the Wesleyan chapel at Morvah instead of the parish church at Zillan soon after I had married his father—in a gesture of defiance, no doubt, for he knew my husband did not hold with Methodists—but even after his father's death he continued to go there to worship with his family and Joss. In addition to this unexpected surge of religious zeal he became an active man in the community that summer and began to hobnob with the miners. Presently he organized a working-men's club in Zillan and used to make speeches there saying the miners should strike for better conditions and that they had as much right as the aristocracy to lead decent, comfortable lives.

"Very radical," I said distastefully to Mark, but Mark himself had a strange outlook for a young man of his class and responded to my comment with all kinds of intellectual reasons in favor of Jared's point of view.

August came. I had a month of waiting still before me, but by this time I was so bored with my uncomfortable shape and Dr. Salter's fussy insistence that I should rest as much as possible that I could hardly wait for the baby to arrive. By the end of the month I was just sighing for the hundredth time and wishing it were all over so that I could wear my beautiful London gowns again when the baby, as if responding to my impatience, decided to enter the world early and I was suddenly brought face to face with the ordeal of childbirth.

I had not imagined I would have any difficulty. I had always been a healthy person, and I think perhaps too at the back of my mind was the thought that as I had successfully survived my terminated pregnancy years earlier I would successfully survive this normal one. The one fact that I had failed to consider was that any woman who has her first baby when she is over thirty years old is begging for trouble.

My boredom changed to discomfort; my discomfort gave way to active pain; my pain gave way to fright, fear and nightmare. I cried out incessantly for Griselda. I shouted and screamed for Griselda, but there was only the midwife murmuring platitudes and later young Dr. Salter saying with useless kindness, "You must be brave, Mrs. Castallack. It will soon be over."

I cursed at him, saw his mouth gape at my language, and then at last Griselda was there, pushing her way to my side, her old face wrinkled with rage that she should have been kept from me.

I fainted. Afterward I thought: Never again. Never, never, never again as long as I live.

But then my son was placed in my arms, my poor ill-fated little son whom I was to love so much, and I forgot everything save the joy that I had given him life.

[5]

The happiness and pride that engulfed me after the birth were far greater than I had ever anticipated during the months of waiting, and with the happiness and pride came another emotion harder to define, a sense of exquisite security, as if God himself had solemnly promised that I would never be alone or unloved again. For the baby was so small, so helpless, so dependent on me, and I thrived on his dependence because it made me feel needed and loved and satisfied. It was then that I realized how empty my life had been without children. How could I ever have tolerated a childless future during my years at Roslyn Farm? I found it hard to remember how indifferent I had been to maternity then, for now I was so dazed with my new happiness, so dizzy with my unexpected bliss, that ecstasy was hardly the word to describe such overpowering euphoria.

We called the baby Stephen, which was Mark's second name and one which we both liked, and spent long hours hovering over his cradle as if neither of us could believe he was real. Naturally he was the most beautiful baby I had ever seen. I could hardly wait to leave my bed and display him to the world in his perambulator.

"I suppose he must take after you," said Mark. "He's certainly not like me."

For Stephen was fair. His blue eyes showed no signs of darkening and on top of his head was a hint of golden hair to come.

"Oh, it's much too early to say," I said at once, fearing a discussion of family likenesses in case the conversation should wander toward the forbidden subject of Laurence. "Stephen's eyes may yet turn darker and his hair grow black. At the moment he doesn't look like anyone. He's just himself."

This was perfectly true. I was about to begin a discussion of christening arrangements when Mark said suddenly, "Do you think he might be a little like my father?" and I was so surprised both by his uncertain tone of voice and by his reference to the forbidden subject that I could think of no easy reply.

At last I said, again repeating the truth, "It's much too early to perceive any family likenesses, Mark. Everyone knows newborn babies seldom resemble anyone, and Stephen's no exception."

He nodded, shrugged as if the subject were of no importance and turned aside.

"Mark . . ." I suddenly had an urge to confront this shadowy barrier between us and tear it aside. "Mark, about Laurence . . ."

"I don't want to talk about him," he said fiercely at once.

"Oh, if only you could see the truth and not be so consumed with jealousy whenever his name is mentioned! We had an affair. I was romantically attached to him and he, I think, was fond of me. We were two lonely people longing for a release from loneliness. He died. It finished. Now the entire episode is past history. You're my husband and I love you and you're the only man in my life and that's all there is to say."

"You don't understand," he said harshly. I was just thinking that he did not intend to say anything further on the subject when he burst out in despair, "You don't understand how I felt when I heard you were his mistress! You don't understand how much

I hated you—and him—and his insufferable hypocrisy . . ." He stopped. And then suddenly he said in a small voice, "I felt so very much alone. If Mr. Barnwell hadn't been so kind to me I don't know what I might have done."

I was distressed. The flash of tears in his eyes reminded me how young he was and my newly kindled maternal instinct was roused. "Oh Mark . . ." I began, but he would not let me finish.

"But that's all over now," he said abruptly. "Mr. Barnwell showed me how pointless hatred was, and besides I couldn't go on hating you when I realized . . ." He stopped again.

"Realized?"

". . . that I had to have you no matter how much I hated you because I loved you more than anything else in the world." He turned aside but I stopped him and raised my lips to his. I could feel the passion begin to shudder through his body, but as we lingered in each other's arms the baby awoke across the room and cried plaintively for attention in his high, lost little voice.

[6]

We had just completed the arrangements for the christening when Mr. and Mrs. Barnwell received news of a bereavement and we offered to postpone the ceremony for a few days in sympathy for them. Their daughter Miriam had died after giving birth to a girl, and since her husband died soon afterward of a liver infection caused, so the gossips said, by a prolonged surfeit of alcoholic spirits, the baby was brought to Zillan rectory to live with her grandparents. They called her Alice, a name which I did not like, and occasionally I went to the rectory to see her, but I thought her a puny, ugly baby not nearly as fine as Stephen, who was large and strong and (to my mind) quite perfect. He had a serene, contented face, beautiful little features and on top of his head there was now a smooth fair down which I liked to stroke with one finger. We engaged a nanny to look after him and so my maternal instinct was never strained too far by being obliged to tend him in the night when he cried or to change his linen when the occasion demanded it. Whenever I saw him he was at his best, and so I have no sullied memories of him, no recollection of any difficulties.

Spring came. Stephen grew. Mark was working on further historical researches again, but roused himself to take me in the ponytrap to Penzance once a week with Stephen and Nanny. We kept a perambulator at the Metropole, and on our arrival we would collect it and wheel Stephen up and down the esplanade or beneath the palm trees of Morrab Gardens before we all retired to the hotel for tea. I bought him toys, a white woolly dog, blocks of bricks, moving beads on a stick; he loved them all. Whenever he did something exceptionally clever with them I would take him in my arms and hug him and say to Mark how advanced and intelligent Stephen was, and Mark would laugh and share my delight and I was happy.

Those were the best times, when we could laugh and be at ease with each other, but in recent months such times had become infrequent and I was often aware of a constraint between us. It was not that we were unhappy; far from it. After Stephen's birth we had resumed our relationship in the bedroom without any trouble whatsoever, but marriage, as everyone knows, consists of more than a successful sharing of a double bed. I had not realized before my marriage that Mark was such a dedicated scholar, and my belated discovery of his passionate addiction to history was not altogether welcome to me. For hours and hours he would be closeted in his study, both in the morning and in the evening, and in the afternoons he would usually choose to go out for a walk by himself to "think." Once a fortnight he would go into Penzance on his own to lunch with his friend Michael Vincent, the young solicitor of Holmes, Holmes, Trebarvah and Holmes, and afterward he would call at Carnforth Hall, where the other young gentry of his own age congregated, but naturally I was never allowed to go with him on these occasions. I did not mind him seeing his friends, for all men like their own company from time to time, but I did mind being left alone for long hours with neither occupation nor conversation to divert me. Sarah Mannack ran the house so smoothly that there was little for me to do, and although I passed the hours planning redecorations to the house and engaging in the certain church charity work that was expected from the wife of a gentleman of means, I was often lonely and restless.

At length it occurred to me that my own inadequacies were in part to blame for my predicament and I at once set about trying to improve myself. I started reading novels again to widen my vocabulary and began to practice my writing by keeping a diary—not this present journal; that came much later after many years of practice, but a small memorandum of my daily activities. I bought an atlas for my geography, a child's schoolbook which explained English history in simple terms, an introduction to the study of French and a large dictionary to assist my spelling.

"But why this sudden urge to be scholarly?" said Mark, surprised, catching me amidst my books one day. "You know I dislike bluestockings!"

"Yes, but . . ." I hesitated. Then: "I thought you wouldn't be so reluctant to invite your friends here," I said in a rush, "if you knew that I—"

"My dear, any unsociable tendencies I may possess nowadays have nothing to do with you, I can assure you. I shall be more than happy to invite Justin Carnforth or Roger Waymark or Russell St. Enedoc to see us when I feel the time is right."

"I realize it might embarrass you if Mr. St. Enedoc were to remember me, but Mark, when I was at Menherion Castle he was only a little boy in the nursery—"

"Darling, I've just told you my unsociable mood at present has nothing to do with you at all!"

"Then why—"

"I merely feel that Deveral Farm is hardly the place to entertain on a respectable scale."

I was flabbergasted. I had thought my innovations had made Deveral Farm quite charming and comfortable enough for any friends Mark might have invited to see us, but evidently I had been naïve in supposing that the local aristocracy could be received in a former farmhouse.

"Perhaps we could have the Barnwells to dinner?" I faltered. "Or even Dr. and Mrs. Salter—"

"I think not," said Mark. "When we live at Penmarric we won't be asking them to dine with us, although no doubt we can invite them to lunch now and then as a gesture. So since this is the case I feel we should start as we mean to go on. We can't ask them to dinner now and then drop them as soon as we move to Penmarric. It wouldn't be the done thing at all."

"Oh," I said. I could think of nothing else to say. The very idea that the middle-class Barnwells and Salters would be socially inferior to us once we moved to Penmarric was enough to chill me to the bone. I could with a great effort be tolerably at ease when we lunched at the rectory and had supposed that with an even greater effort I could become accustomed to receiving Mark's friends among the local gentry, but the idea of a life surrounded entirely by the Carnforths and St. Enedocs of the county straight away filled me with panic. However, I suppressed my nervousness as thoroughly as I could and did my best to concentrate instead on Stephen's progress and the management of household affairs.

But I still had moments of acute uneasiness whenever I thought of the future.

To my relief Mark presently began to feel guilty about the quiet life we were leading, and one warm evening in early June, much to my excitement, he took me to dine at the Metropole. The evening was a great success. I had worked so hard at improving myself that I was now able to discuss a variety of topics with him. Taking my courage in both hands, I introduced the burning topic of the hour, Wilde's play *Salome*, which was destined to be banned from the London stage that year, and echoed the view that immorality should have no place in the arts, but Mark told me that in his view the trend toward such decadence was only just beginning. We talked of Kipling and Chesterton, I merely repeating the praise I had read in newspapers and magazines but Mark telling me that their popularity was due to the fact that they presented millions of people who led humdrum lives with the chance to sample glamor vicariously. It never ceased to surprise me that Mark's opinions should so often be at odds with the majority of other people's, and I could not decide whether this was the result of his advanced education or because he was still young enough to enjoy disagreeing with his elders. However, he paid me many compliments about my newly acquired knowledge and was presently so encouraged by my interest in his opinions that he spoke of politics—a subject about which he always claimed a woman should know nothing—and said he hoped that Mr. Gladstone would soon displace Lord Salisbury as Prime Minister and that Ireland would then at last be granted home rule.

"But they say the Queen does not like Mr. Gladstone," I said doubtfully.

He thought that was very funny. "My dear, we live in a democracy, not under a despotism! A man can vote as his conscience, not his sovereign, dictates!"

I was not entirely certain what either democracy or despotism meant, but I smiled too and we were so much at ease with each other that my sense of inadequacy and isolation seemed a nightmare of the past, a triviality which no longer existed.

It was late when we left the hotel. We were just walking over to the place where Mannack was waiting in the ponytrap when a little girl with a flushed face and bright eyes ran up to try to sell me a posie of flowers.

"No, thank you," said Mark curtly to the child and took my arm to draw me past, but I saw myself in each little beggar child in a tattered dress with no shoes and I stopped to fumble in my purse. "Here," I said, giving her threepence, and stooped to take the posie.

"Thank 'ee, lady." Her hand was burning. I stepped back, but Mark was already pulling me away.

"The child's ill," he said. "Don't go too near her."

But I had been near enough. Within days my cheeks too were flushed, my forehead burning, my eyes bright and aching. The doctor came and went and came again. Even the Carnforths' doctor, old Dr. Logan, visited me from Penzance. I lay in bed, my eyes closed, my thoughts jumbled and confused, and somewhere far away I heard Dr. Logan say, "There's a lot of scarlet fever in Penzance."

And after that there was a great dizzy darkness so that for a long time I knew not whether it was night or day until one morning I awoke and my eyes no longer hurt and I was better.

"You have a strong constitution, Mrs. Castallack," said Dr. Salter, satisfied. "You should recover very quickly now—if you do as I say." He had not forgotten how hard I had found it to follow his advice toward the end of my pregnancy.

I lay back on my pillows feeling weak but relieved that the worst was over, but even as I began to close my eyes I heard him say in a low voice to someone outside the door, "Make sure she's not told yet about the baby."

[7]

He died two days later from the sickness I had given him. Everyone was very kind. I was still weak when I was told the news, but I left my bed and went to the nursery. His poor dead little body was laid out in his cradle, his small serene face waxen in death, and suddenly the pain was more than I could bear and the grief more than could ever be released in tears. I wished he had been stillborn or had died soon after birth—anything but this dreadful death when he had a personality of his own which I had loved, his own character and individuality.

People kept writing kind letters; everyone was so kind, and no one was kinder than Mark. At last when everyone's hushed sympathy had left me dry-eyed and stony-faced he came to my room and sat down by my side.

"Janna dearest, forgive me but I must talk about the funeral. It's been suggested to me that the burial should be in Morvah churchyard, but I said that my father was buried at Zillan and that I wanted Stephen to be buried there too. I thought you would agree with me about that. . . . I saw Barnwell then and he consented and now the service is to be held the day after tomorrow. I've spoken to Salter, but he says absolutely positively that you're not well enough to go—"

"But I must!" I said wildly. "I couldn't stay away from my own baby's funeral!" With that sentence all my grief seemed to break within me; I began to shake with harsh sobs which tore at my breast and hurt my throat. I wept and wept, but he said nothing, only holding me very close as he waited for the first rush of grief to pass. At last when I was calmer I tried to speak again, but as I looked into his face I saw the drawn lines about his mouth and the sadness in his eyes and with great guilt I suddenly remembered that I was not the only one bereaved.

"Oh, Mark, I've been so selfish—forgive me—"

"Shhh . . ." He stroked my hair. "It's worse for you than for me, I realize that."

"Why? He was your only child too."

But he could not reply. We sat there for a while, united by our common grief, and it occurred to me in a bizarre moment of clarity that for the first time since our marriage we were a husband and wife and not merely a lover and his mistress.

[8]

I became pregnant soon afterward. My grief still ached within me, but now the grief was dulled by this new expectancy, and the sense of anticipation helped to fill the void of loss. I was just recovering slowly from my shock and returning once more to the familiar routine of my day-to-day existence when the event occurred that was to alter the course of our lives. Giles Penmar died at last at the end of December, and two-thirds of the enormous Penmar fortune, including the vast estate of Penmarric, fell abruptly into Mark's hands. My days among genteel middle-class society as mistress of Deveral Farm were over; my years among the aristocracy as Mrs. Mark Castallack of Penmarric were about to begin.

4

During the first years of the reign she was usually pregnant and so could not often travel with her hard-riding husband.

—The Devil's Brood,
ALFRED DUGGAN

For all the splendour of his household, Henry led a busy, rather drab and workaday life, hearing the constant suits that arose from the confusion of the civil war, settling disputes among his tenants, and ceaselessly investigating and prying into every aspect of the administration of his new realm. He was a severely practical man of business and his major concerns were to establish peace and order . . . to increase the revenues of the crown. . . .

—Henry II,
JOHN T. APPLEBY

[1]

Mark was by this time a very wealthy young man. In addition to the Penmar money he had inherited a modest part of his father's fortune and most of the money left by his mother's cousin Robert Yorke, who had died soon after Laurence at the end of 1890. Moreover he would inherit his mother's wealth when she died, so his expectations were still not exhausted. I did not pry into his financial affairs, for he gave me to understand in no uncertain terms that it was not a wife's place to meddle in such matters, but he did tell me once how much capital he possessed and the very sum made me feel dizzy with amazement. I could not imagine such vast resources; the very figure was meaningless to me simply because it was so large.

The only other major beneficiary of Giles Penmar's will was Mark's adopted cousin Clarissa. She returned to Penmarric from London for the funeral and two days after the service, much to our astonishment, she came to Morvah to call upon us.

According to all the Zillan gossips, Miss Clarissa Penmar had more than upheld the family tradition for wildness. It was notorious that she was very fast. Rumor had even whispered that there had been incidents with the Penmarric stableboys, although I found it hard to believe that anyone brought up a lady could ever have stooped so low. I had never met her, for Mark had been estranged from his relations at Penmarric, and even now when Clarissa called at Deveral Farm Mark refused to let me receive her.

"I'll see her alone," he said, a little white around the lips. "She and I are old enemies and I don't want you to be drawn into our quarrels."

I was surprised by this apparent aversion of his to Clarissa, for she was one of the most attractive girls I had ever seen and I would have thought her feminine blandishments would have appealed to Mark's susceptibility. However, I did not argue with him but merely waited with curiosity in his study as he spoke to her in the drawing room. I was just thinking I could not contain my curiosity a moment longer when I heard the door of the drawing room open. I waited, listening. To my amazement he took her down the hall to the kitchen and then upstairs to the floor above. So consumed was I by curiosity at this point that I could hardly force myself to stay in the study, but I knew Mark would be angry if I disobeyed him, so I contented myself with leaving the study door ajar and straining my ears to discover what was happening.

Presently they came downstairs again and paused in the hall.

"I still find it hard to imagine why you should want to live here, Clarissa," I heard him say frankly to her. "I'd have thought you would have had more of an interest in buying my house in London than my house here at Morvah."

"On the contrary," said Clarissa Penmar in her silky, well-bred voice, which I instantly distrusted. "I'm so bored with London! Bored, bored, bored! My dear Mark, surely you at least can understand? You forsook London society for this place—London society must have bored you just as much as it now bores me. I'm bored with the convention which expects girls to marry as soon and as well as possible, bored with dances and dinners and tedious social events, bored with having to stay either with friends in London or else entomb myself in that dreadful mausoleum on top of the cliffs—and why you want to live *there*, my dear Mark, I simply can't imagine—oh, I'm so bored with being bored! At least now that Papa is dead I have the means to do exactly as I wish and can come and go as I please. As soon as I heard Mrs. Barnwell talking about this house and saying how comfortable and pleasant your wife had made it, I knew I would like to try to live here for a while. I may not stay long but at least I would like to try it, if only for the sheer novelty of living in what was once a working-class farmhouse! I'm obsessed by novelty at the moment. Novelty is the only antidote to boredom, in my opinion, and for people like us the working classes must necessarily seem more novel than—my dear Mark, don't glare at me like that! *I* don't disapprove of you marrying a farmer's widow! Personally I think a love affair with someone of a lower class is rather stimulating."

And as I caught my breath in fury I heard Mark drawl, "Yes, I had heard of your partiality for the grooms of Penmarric. Good day, Clarissa. If you wish to buy this house you can notify my lawyers in Penzance and they will conduct the sale on my behalf." And he barely gave her time to say goodbye before he shut the front door with a bang.

Later when I heard that Clarissa had made up her mind to buy Deveral Farm I was glad that Mark disliked her so much. The parish of Morvah and the parish of St. Just shared a common boundary, and Deveral Farm and Penmarric were less than six miles apart. Clarissa was very much the kind of woman who fancied other women's husbands, particularly if she were living in a remote hamlet with nothing else to divert her, and six miles is hardly more than a hop, skip and a jump to a woman in that frame of mind.

The time had come to leave Deveral Farm, but Mark did not want me to cope with the strain of moving house when I was by this time far advanced in pregnancy and favored staying at Morvah until after the baby was born. However, I had an irrational fear of giving birth to another child in the house where Stephen had died, and although Penmarric was then the most depressing mansion imaginable I was passionately anxious to move without delay. Mark consulted Dr. Salter, they agreed to humor me, and on a brilliant summer day in May my second son was born at Penmarric in the great Tower Room which faced the sea.

[2]

This time the birth was easy, my recovery rapid. I decided I was right after all and that having a baby was a very simple affair. The baby thrived quickly; soon he showed signs of being as delightful as Stephen. I wanted to call him Mark after his father but Mark said it would be too confusing in later years, so we called him Marcus instead. His hair, scanty as it was, was so dark that I guessed it would turn into the thick black hair of the Penmars, but he had my blue eyes and my fair complexion, so it seemed he might grow up to resemble both of us. Soon I saw that his personality was more volatile than Stephen's; he cried more, laughed more and demanded more attention, but I could not help noticing he was not as forward as Stephen had been, nor as quick to learn new things.

But I could not pine at length for Stephen. There was no time. As soon as I had recovered from my confinement I found myself confronted with the challenge of that terrible old mansion which was now our home, and presently I discovered that there was such an incredible amount to do that all my energies were turned toward the task of making the place habitable.

Words almost fail me when I attempt to describe Penmarric. It was the sort of mansion that makes me pity the aristocracy who are obliged to spend their lives in such gloomy, drafty, dismal surroundings. It was built of the usual gray Cornish stone and the main part of the house was old, dating back to Elizabethan times, so Mark told me. There was even some evidence in the title deeds to show that there had been a fortified tower on the site before the house had been built, for the North Cornish coast had long been a prey to Irish pirates and Penmarric's position on top of the high cliffs would have been an advantage to the defenders. However, some of the present house was modern, new servants' quarters having been added earlier in the century by Mark's great-grandfather, the adventurer, and the entire house had been renovated a generation later to give it a fashionably Gothic appearance. Its appearance was actually the most engaging part about it; the exterior was fancifully decorated with a quantity of romantic pseudo-battlements and flying buttresses and roof gutters ending in gargoyles, and on either wing of the building was a squat round tower commanding superb views of the sea, the moors and the carns. It was certainly an impressive mansion from the outside. But inside! It was unbelievable. Peeling walls, threadbare carpets, skirting boards ravaged by mice and worse, mildew, damp, decay . . . I was horrified. The plumbing was primitive or nonexistent, the kitchens unsanitary and hopelessly old-fashioned, the housekeeping methods preposterously uneconomical. I asked the housekeeper to see the accounts; she referred me to the steward; the steward referred me back to the housekeeper. After much slyness and evasion I discovered some incomplete records which Giles Penmar had obviously never asked to see, and the very next day I told both the steward and the housekeeper that they might pack their bags and leave.

The butler was a nice old man, very devoted to the Penmars, and although I suspected he had become too fond of appropriating the best port in the cellar, I decided to give him a chance to turn over a new leaf. After that, turning from Medlyn to the rest of the staff, I discarded an overvirile footman and his pregnant scullery girl, sacked an insolent groom on the spot and put the fear of God into all the maids.

"Cleanliness," I said severely as they boggled at me round-eyed, "is next to godliness, as we all know. Now, when I enter a room in future I shall expect to see . . ." And I delivered a stern lecture about polished furniture, clean carpets, washed curtains, scoured pots and pans, scrubbed kitchen floors and food swathed in muslin to foil hungry mice. Inspired by the subject, I dropped dark hints about the fate which would overtake any servant who allowed cobwebs to flourish undisturbed in corners, and when I had finished at last I had made it abundantly clear that a new era was dawning at Penmarric and that there was no longer any room in the servants' quarters for the idle, the insolent and the irresponsible.

But new eras do not dawn unaided. For many months after our arrival Mark and I were immersed in our campaigns to improve the house until I began to think we would never be free to enjoy living at Penmarric; we would always have to struggle simply to exist there.

Secretly I cherished the notion of acting as my own housekeeper and fulfilling my ambition to be in charge of the domestic affairs of a large mansion, but of course, ironic though it seemed to me at the time, I was denied the opportunity to prove my skill. I was expected to employ a housekeeper; it would have looked exceedingly odd for a person in my new station to haggle with the tradesmen and deal constantly with the servants, and Mark wasted no time in pointing this out to me. But while I advertised for a housekeeper I engaged more staff, supervised the massive cleaning operations I had initiated, ordered new carpets and materials for new curtains. Mark had engaged an architect, and presently we all spent fascinating hours planning how that dreadful old house could be made not only habitable but pleasant. At last the interior was redecorated in light colors, new windows were installed so that the sunlight could blaze into the gloomy rooms, and the east wing (reputed to be haunted) was transformed into a suite of airy rooms for guests who, not knowing of the ghost's supposed existence, would not be disturbed by it. An army of plumbers installed two bathrooms, three water closets and running water in the kitchens. A family of cats colonized the mice's playground in the attics, a battalion of gardeners set out to reclaim the wilderness of the grounds, and by the end of that long arduous summer I began to feel I had the house in a condition resembling working order.

Meanwhile Mark was deeply involved with the estate. He had engaged a new bailiff and spent many hours investigating the affairs of the Sennen Garth mine, which had brought great wealth to the Penmars earlier in the century. I knew little about the tin and copper mines and had always accepted their stone engine houses as part of the landscape and their ugly slag heaps as a source of livelihood to poor men who did not have their own land to farm. "Fish, tin and copper!" ran the famous Cornish toast, but these three keys to Cornish prosperity were not listed in order of priority. Cornwall had been famous for its tin since time out of mind, but in fact in the nineteenth century the mines had produced more copper than tin. There were two world-famous mines not far from Penmarric—Botallack, which was perched on the edge of the cliffs and was truly a marvel of man-made ingenuity, and the Levant, which extended so deep into the earth and so far under the sea that it made the Penmars' mine Sennen Garth look small in comparison. The Penmars also owned a second mine, King Walloe, but King Walloe had been closed for many years and was no longer of profit to the family. Sennen Garth was hardly profitable either when we arrived at Penmarric; it was still operating but its output had dropped and fewer men were now employed there.

Mining experts were summoned from Dolcoath, the famous mine near Camborne, for consultations; their report was unfavorable and Mark, horrified by the working conditions in the mine and mindful of the enormous expense required to make the mine safe, let alone profitable, decided that Sennen Garth should be closed.

There was immediate uproar throughout St. Just and Zillan, where most of the miners lived. Deputations of protest arrived at Penmarric, and Jared led the miners in a noisy crusade to reopen the mine, but of course it was all a waste of time. Mark was adamant. The protests persisted, however, for the men thought that as he was so young he would retract his decision if they bullied him enough, but the tougher they became the tougher was Mark's attitude. He was as stubborn as half a dozen mules and more than a match for the discontented miners of the Cornish Tin Coast.

In the midst of all this turmoil Mark's mother arrived unannounced at the Metropole Hotel and wrote Mark a note to say she would not be kept away from her beloved Penmarric a day longer, no matter what excuses he might make to forestall her arrival.

"My God!" yelled Mark in a fit of temper. "As if I hadn't enough troubles without having her poking her nose around Penmarric and criticizing all we've done! How dare she come down here unannounced! How dare she! God, how I detest and abominate overbearing, domineering, arrogant women! I'm going to tell her exactly what I think of her high-handed attempts to gain admission to my house!"

But I could not help feeling a small twinge of sympathy for Maud Penmar. She had visited us only once since our marriage—after Stephen's birth she had stayed for a week at the Metropole in order to see her first grandchild—and I was sure that now she was anxious to see Marcus and revisit the house she had loved so much in her youth. I could not stop Mark quarreling with her, for they always quarreled violently whenever they met, but after she had shed one large and glassy tear and he had held her hand and told her she might stay a day or two after all, I did my best to be hospitable to her. But she was the most exhausting woman, and I was exhausted enough already, both on account of the reorganization of the house and the fact that I was expecting another baby in May. When Mark finally managed to send her off to Gweek to visit Nigel I was conscious of the most enormous relief and would have stayed in bed for a week if it had not been Christmas, one of the busiest times of the year for us all.

By this time the entire county had noticed our existence, and soon we were so overwhelmed with invitations of all kinds that I was thankful to be pregnant, thankful that I had the opportunity to escape if only temporarily from the more terrifying aspects of my new social station. When Dr. Salter gave me his usual advice to rest as much as possible I seized the chance to lead a quiet life and make renewed efforts to improve myself. Reading had widened my vocabulary and my accent had lessened, but I knew there was still Cornish in my voice and it embarrassed me very much. Finally in despair I advertised discreetly in the Penzance newspaper for a teacher qualified in phonetics and presently engaged a little old lady to come to Penmarric twice a week to help me overcome my defect.

Mark was surprised and protested that I spoke well enough to please him, but he did not protest for long and I suspected he was secretly more pleased than he cared to admit.

The new year came. Sometimes I would lie on the chaise longue and stare at those invitations from the aristocracy of Cornwall, and as I stared I would feel a shiver of panic edge its way down my spine. It was at moments like these that I would feel overcome by that now familiar burden of inadequacy and could think of nothing but Marcus and my future children living their lives in a world which I knew would never fully accept me. And I would say anxiously to myself: I hope I shall be at ease with them. And then with that terrible pang of dread: I hope they won't be ashamed of me.

Pregnancy was making me morbid, of course. I always made a resolution to beat back such gloomy thoughts and on the whole I succeeded, but sometimes, unable to help myself, I would remain low in spirits for hours at a time and would long uselessly—and ironically—for that quiet uneventful life we had once led at Deveral Farm.

My eldest daughter was born at the end of May when Marcus was a year old. I had taken a fancy to Tennyson's poetry during the last weeks of waiting, and his poem about the lonely moated grange where the heroine was entombed awaiting her lover had kindled my imagination. I saw the poor girl marooned in a place such as Penmarric had been when we had arrived, and my heart bled for her. When Mark asked me what we should call the baby I said unhesitatingly, "Mariana."

"After the girl in *Measure for Measure?*"

"After the girl in Tennyson's poem," I said, not knowing Tennyson had received his inspiration from Shakespeare, although Mark was quick enough to point this out to me.

"Well," he added, "it's a pretty name. But we must call her after you as well."

"Oh no, Mark! Mariana Janna—imagine it! Let her just be Mariana. Besides, I'm not fond of my own name."

"I am," he said. "Well, perhaps if we have another girl . . ."

We were not certain how many children we wanted but thought in terms of four or five. After Stephen's death I had had a frantic desire to have several children as quickly as possible to exclude the likelihood of ever again having to enter a silent nursery and wished only that children could come more rapidly than once a year.

But not long after Mariana's birth Mark said, "There's plenty of time and now we have two children—let's take care for a while and enjoy ourselves. I've been working very hard for a year and so have you in spite of your pregnancy. Why don't we go away for a couple of months' rest? I'd like to go to Italy or Switzerland, or perhaps France again. I feel I need a holiday."

Why I should have shrunk so absolutely from his suggestion I do not know. No doubt one of the reasons was because of my experiences on my honeymoon when my homesickness, insecurity and constant sense of inadequacy had set me against traveling in foreign places. Perhaps another reason was that I was struggling so hard to adjust to my new life at Penmarric that I simply felt I could not cope with the ordeal of a journey abroad. But whatever the reasons I knew at once that I did not want to go.

"Mariana is still too young for me to leave her," I began uncertainly, but to my dismay Mark saw through my excuse at once and made some sharp remark about it being a wife's duty to attend to her husband as well as to her children. This upset me, for I had made enormous efforts to please him and improve myself so that he would not be ashamed of me when we mingled with his social equals, but he made no effort to apologize and merely stalked away before I could protest the injustice of his remark. Afterward I tried to forget the conversation, but soon I found myself turning the disagreement over and over in my mind until at last, unable to endure worrying about it a moment longer, I decided to broach the subject of the holiday with him again.

"Mark," I said as the September sun blazed upon the terrace the next afternoon and the soft sea breeze fanned our cheeks, "Mark, about the holiday . . ."

He glanced at me, his black eyes veiled with the speculative expression I knew so well. "How curious that you should mention it," he said. "I was just about to introduce the subject again."

"Oh." I was so taken aback that speech deserted me.

"What were you going to say?"

"I . . . merely wished to apologize for—for not wishing to go just yet. But, Mark, I didn't mean I shall never want to go abroad for a holiday again! Perhaps next year—"

"Next year," he said cuttingly, "you'll be pregnant again and we'll still be unable to go."

Now it was my turn to be angry. "Would it be so odious to you if I were pregnant? I thought you wanted children!"

"Not all at once!" he retorted. "Why do we have to hurry so? Can we not spare a little time to enjoy each other's company? Why, think of it from my point of view—if you're capable of considering any point of view other than your own! You've had three children in four years, and while that may be very pleasing and satisfying to your maternal instincts it hardly enables you to act in a way which is pleasing and satisfying to *my* instincts! I think it's about time you considered me instead of yourself. I'm tired of being an occasional husband even if you thrive on being an occasional wife."

With an immense effort I kept a tight rein on my self-control. "Other husbands manage. Other wives have a baby a year."

"It's only the working classes these days who breed like a bunch of rabbits!"

"And I—as you never cease to remind me—am from the working classes! Is that what you mean? Are you trying to tell me it's 'not the done thing' to have a baby a year nowadays? Are you?"

"Oh, don't be so damned sensitive!" He was taut with annoyance. "Damn it, Janna, I'm not saying we shouldn't have a large family, but I simply don't see why we could not wait two years—a year even—before having another child."

"I haven't the time to wait," I said in a low voice, and now I too was trembling with annoyance, for the ten years' difference in our ages was a subject I never even liked to think about, let alone discuss with him. "I don't have all the time in the world."

"You have at least ten child-bearing years in front of you."

"Childbirth becomes more hazardous after the age of forty. That leaves five years, not ten."

"So you intend to occupy the next five years by having as many children as possible—and providing yourself with the excuse to avoid me for several months out of each year!"

"That's not true!"

"Isn't it true that a doctor doesn't recommend a woman to have sexual intercourse at certain times before and after her pregnancy?"

I hated it when he spoke so bluntly of such private matters. I felt demeaned by such frankness. I was no longer a barmaid or even a farmer's wife accustomed to hearing the crudest and coarsest conversations among those around me, and I resented Mark treating me as if I were.

But when I was silent he made no effort to change the subject. "Do I displease you in some way?"

"Oh Mark, don't be so absurd!"

"But to go to bed with me means less than it used to."

I told myself he was upset and struggled to suppress my resentment. "No—no, it doesn't but—" I strained for the right words, strove to make him understand—"but such times aren't forever, Mark—they come and go and then there's nothing left. But children—children are for always. Children are *there!* Children make a woman feel secure. Oh, Mark, do try and understand—"

"We seem to be having rather an abortive argument," he interrupted coldly. "I've told you I'm anxious for children. All I'm saying is that for one year I'd like to have you entirely to myself."

I said, unforgivably I know, but my patience was wearing thin: "And to think you accuse *me* of selfishness! You're much more selfish than I am!"

"I'm merely demanding what any husband has a right to expect!" We stared at each other. Then: "Will you come abroad with me next month for a holiday," he said evenly, "or won't you?"

"Mark, I've already tried to explain—"

"Yes or no?"

I thought of foreign cities, foreign people, the agony of being adrift in a strange and unfriendly land. "Perhaps next year—"

"Yes or no, Janna!"

I was only just beginning to get used to Penmarric. I could not face any more changes at the moment. It was his fault for not being more sympathetic, for not even trying to understand. "No," I said. "No, I don't want to go this year."

There was another heavy pause.

"I see," he said at last. "I assume that means you don't want to postpone your next pregnancy."

I seized at the opportunity to make an apparent concession. "I could try and postpone it," I said, affecting anxiety so that he would not guess how much I longed for another baby—and for another few months' respite from my social duties as mistress of Penmarric. "I don't wish to anger you, Mark. But . . . well, of course, one can never be entirely certain—I could not guarantee—"

"In other words," he said acidly, "you'll make no effort whatsoever to avoid a pregnancy while pretending all the while that you're taking immense trouble, and then once you're pregnant you'll say it was an unfortunate accident and beg my forgiveness."

It gave me such a jolt that he had seen straight through my attempt at deception that I was temporarily speechless.

"Well, let me tell you this," he said between his teeth while I was still at a loss for words. "If you won't sleep with me there are others who will. And if you find yourself pregnant before Mariana is a year old you'll spend your pregnancy wondering where I'm spending my evenings. Do you understand? And don't think I wouldn't be unfaithful to you if you shut your bedroom door often enough because I wouldn't hesitate. I've been patient long enough and I'm not going to be patient any more."

182

Such dark threats made in a fit of temper did not seriously disturb me since I knew well enough that I was the only woman in his life, but I was hurt that he should say such things and angry too that he should threaten me in that way.

"Mark," I said, still speaking levelly, "I have never, voluntarily, closed my bedroom door to you. I—"

"So far," he said, "you've closed it—voluntarily, since you chose to have children—for at least five months out of every year. But that was pardonable since we both wanted children and I was prepared to tolerate the situation. But at the moment I don't want children and if you become pregnant now after all I've said I'll take the news exactly as I would have done if you'd slammed the bedroom door in my face."

"My God!" I cried, my restraint snapping in two, my rage making me throw all pretense at calmness to the winds, "don't you ever, ever think of anything else except what can happen between us in the bedroom? Is it so utterly impossible for you to spend a night without . . ." And before I could check myself the profanity, the unmentionable word from the gutters, had slipped from my lips. I stopped at once, my cheeks burning, but I was too late.

He looked at me. Then he raised his eyebrows in an expression of amused distaste. "Really, my dear," he said in his most sarcastic London drawl, "you needn't have gone to such lengths to remind me where you come from, but since you remind me, I almost wish we were back at Roslyn Farm! There at least I could get what I wanted when I wanted it without all this fuss. What a pity I ever bothered to marry you! You were such a perfect mistress."

He stopped speaking. For one long moment there was an absolute silence save for the roar of the surf on the rocks far below. Beyond the parapet of the terrace the sea stretched to a misty horizon and the sun shone from a cloudless sky.

I turned and groped my way to the French windows.

I heard him say, "Janna . . ." but I did not stop. I opened the door, blundered against a small table, knocked over a vase of flowers. Presently I was in the passage leading to the hall. It was cool there, but dark after the brilliance of the afternoon light. I had difficulty in seeing. In the hall I thought: I want to go home. I hate this house. I hate it.

I went outside again and the drive stretched before me to the trees by the gates, and the contorted spinney thrust its twisted boughs toward that azure Cornish sky. As I crossed the lawn the sun felt warm upon my back and the distant moors, shimmering in the heat haze, seemed mysteriously to beckon me across the land which separated us.

I walked and walked. I walked to St. Just and I walked beyond St. Just and away from the road onto the moors which stretched into Zillan parish. The moors were gray-green, shimmering beneath that summer sun, and the rocks of Carn Kenidjack pointed jagged fingers to that brilliant southern sky.

I stopped, looked back.

He was following me, but some way behind, and when I stopped he stopped too. I thought I heard him call out to me, but I could not hear, I was too far away, and I turned and stumbled on once more through the heather to Zillan.

I went on walking. My feet began to hurt, so I took off my elegant shoes and walked barefoot over the moors, barefoot back into the past until in my mind's eye I was no longer on the moors at all but in the dirty reeking alleys of St. Ives. And suddenly I saw my father coming home from the sea, my poor, gay, generous father who was always so kind to me, and he was asking where my mother was and where he could find her. I saw the painted shutters of Shrimp Street, the coarse sailors, the smashed bottles, the drunken brawls. I saw hunger and want and hard times, the woman from the evangelist mission saying, "The wages of sin is death, my girl, and don't you forget it," the minister murmuring, "Poor child, such a sad case," and Griselda, dearest Griselda, holding me close to her and screaming at them all, "She's my kin! I'll keep her! Thee'll not take her away while I've breath in my body!" And I thought: I want Griselda. No one else. Just Griselda. I shall go and see Griselda because Griselda was always there, even in the beginning, and she's still there, even today.

I was confused then, thinking she was living at her little cottage at Morvah and not remembering until a minute later that she now had a cottage at Penmarric. I was walking in the wrong direction, every step I took carrying me farther from her, but still I did not turn back.

I went on into Zillan parish.

I walked and walked, and sometimes I turned to see if he had drawn nearer, but he kept his distance. And suddenly it was as if I were alone on the moors, as if I were a farmer's wife again snatching ten minutes of precious leisure, and before me at last lay the ruined walls of Chûn.

I went into the inner circle of stones and stood there. It was peaceful, sheltered from the wind. I stood motionless amidst the bracken and the soft grass, and glancing back over my shoulder, I watched him as he came toward me across the heather.

When he reached me I saw his eyes were veiled again, his mouth hard, his face closed and empty of expression. We stood perhaps six feet apart for ten full seconds and then he crossed the ancient turf which separated us and touched my arms slowly, lightly with his fingers.

I closed my eyes, felt the tears stab like hot needles behind my lids, tilted my head aside, but he kissed me just the same. And suddenly my knees were weak and my whole body trembled and I burned for him.

"Forgive me," he said. That was all. He made no excuses. Just the cool "Forgive me" in the voice I loved, and I forgave him because I loved him and because I had not realized before how desperately important it was that he should love me too. Yet he did love me. It was because he loved me that he had married me and not left me to struggle on alone at Roslyn Farm. So long as he loved me nothing mattered, nothing at all, and when I looked into his face then and saw that he loved me still I clung to him for one long shuddering moment as we embraced beneath that hot September sky. Our embraces became dizzier, unbearably urgent; at last we lay in the shadow of the castle walls, and it was there on the hard Cornish earth of the moors he was to love so well that my best-loved child was conceived.

5

By this time little Henry was the eldest of an increasing family. His sister Matilda had been born in 1156. In 1157 another son was born in Beaumont Palace, Oxford, and christened Richard. . . . The queen was kept busy, and must live in retirement for long periods every year. That gave Henry more scope for his adulteries. . . .

—The Devil's Brood,
ALFRED DUGGAN

[1]

When I first realized my condition I was extremely dismayed. First of all I was conscious of annoyance that I should have become pregnant unintentionally just like any refined woman who had no idea such a condition could be avoided, but presently my annoyance was replaced by my dread of having to tell Mark. Yet even my dread was lessened by my secret pleasure and relief; the ordeal of giving a ball at Penmarric in the new year could be postponed a little longer. We would have to extend the nursery, engage a nursemaid to help Nanny, tell Marcus the good news that soon he might have a brother to play with . . .

But first I had to tell Mark that soon he might have another son.

We were in London at the time; after the scene at Chûn I had told Mark I would go abroad with him as soon as he wished, but he, generously, had compromised by suggesting we spend a few weeks in the capital instead of making the more arduous journey to the Continent. In London we found everyone was talking of "The Books," Aubrey Beardsley's notorious *Yellow Book* and the more salubrious *Jungle Book* by Kipling. So agog was I to see the wicked Beardsley drawings that I wondered if I might acquire a copy secretly, but Mark bought a copy openly enough and even left it in an unlocked drawer so that I could peep at it whenever he turned the other way. He said he found the sketches "clever but facile" and "not altogether to his taste." They were not to my taste either, I soon discovered, for the drawings were much too bizarre to strike me as being "naughty." However, I did not admit to being disappointed, since it was the fashion for everyone to find them shocking, but merely turned my attention to other cultural events instead. We went to concerts, hearing the new Tchaikovsky symphony which had been first performed the previous year, and to the theater, sampling everything from the operettas of Gilbert and Sullivan to one of those dreadfully gloomy dramas by the foreign playwright Ibsen. We visited picture galleries, dined at a dizzy number of fashionable restaurants and paid the occasional nerve-wracking social call—and then at last after several weeks had slipped by I steeled myself once again to see my Wimpole Street physician.

". . . so you don't have to be musical to appreciate opera," Mark was saying that evening at dinner. "Opera is such a splendid spectacle independent of the music. Of course this new stuff by Richard Strauss is abominable, but some of the Italian composers. . . , Is anything the matter?"

When one has been dreading something continuously for several hours the anticipation is often worse than the event. For one long moment after I had told him he was so still that I felt my scalp prickle with fright, but then he shrugged and smiled and said lightly, "And after all that fuss! What a waste of breath that scene was! I should have known it was pointless to quarrel."

I said tensely, "This was not what I had in mind, Mark. I realize you must feel angry, but—"

"My dear, what right have I to be angry? You could hardly have become pregnant without my help. Let's try and forget that wretched quarrel and put it behind us once and for all."

So I made no more efforts to apologize, but I felt wretched, for I was sure he suspected I had deliberately sought such a condition. He was very thoughtful and considerate to me throughout the journey home and we even reached the point of discussing names for the baby together, but in the new year he became immersed in his writing again after a long spell away from his historical papers, and in February he traveled to London for three weeks to do some research. I missed him dreadfully. I hated eating alone in that enormous dining room, hated being waited upon so meticulously throughout each course, hated sitting on my own in that silent drawing room in the evenings. In the mornings I visited the nursery, but Marcus, though adorable, was hardly old enough to offer much companionship and Mariana was cutting teeth and very fractious. In the afternoons I tried to devote myself to my parish responsibilities and to my correspondence, but I was afraid of sending letters unless Mark had read them to ensure that they were correct, and whenever I picked up a pen I became so nervous that I found I knew not what to write. It was hard to know how to pass the time. When Mark returned home at last I was painfully glad to see him.

Yet even after his return I saw little of him. In the mornings he would work in his study. In the afternoons he would be out riding or walking or attending to estate matters and in the evenings he would once more be secluded with his books. Once a week, sometimes twice, he would go into Penzance and spend the afternoons at Carnforth Hall before dining with his old friend Michael Vincent, but I was careful not to object to this increasing taste for male companionship. I personally thought Mr. Vincent was a very boring man, but Mark was surely entitled to see as much of his friends as he wished and I did not want to weary him by complaining of his lack of attention.

The long dreary winter months crawled past. My housekeeper managed domestic affairs so admirably that there was little for me to do and presently my condition precluded me from fulfilling the majority of my parish duties. I visited the nursery and tried to make plans for the new baby, but for some reason I felt apathetic and could not summon the degree of interest needed to initiate the preparations.

Spring arrived, summer followed and at last it was time for the baby to arrive. He was born on the eighteenth of June and screamed with a vigor and determination that deafened us all. He stopped screaming only when he was placed in my arms, and then a great stillness descended on his minute crumpled face, and when he opened his eyes to look at me for the first time he seemed to survey me for a long while as if my presence had some mysterious significance for him.

I touched his hand gently with my thumb and forefinger, and from that moment on there was a bond between us, intangible, invisible but vitally alive.

I smiled.

Since Mark had chosen Marcus' name he told me I might choose the name for this third son of ours, so I called the new baby Philip for no reason save that it had always been my favorite name.

[2]

I loved all my children but some I did love better than others. Mariana once said to me years later in a fit of temper, "You only cared about the boys! It was only the boys who ever meant anything to you!" and although I denied it hotly it was true that my sons did interest me more than my daughters. For a long while Stephen, or rather Stephen's memory, remained closest to my heart, but that was probably because he was the first-born and his death had made his small personality especially poignant. Marcus was engagingly attractive with his blue eyes and shaggy dark hair; he had a winning air and I thought would grow very charming in later life, but he resembled me little; I could see myself neither in him nor in Mariana, and I had glimpsed only the faintest of likenesses between myself and Stephen, who had died before any strong resemblance could become pronounced. But from the start Philip was *my* son. He was fair, as I was, with wide, cool blue eyes and light thick hair. From an early age he was obviously ten times as clever as Marcus and much quicker in learning new things.

I doted on him. Marcus became jealous. "Take the baby away," he ordered Nanny. "Take it away. Don't want it."

"Run off and play with Mariana, Marcus," I said, irritated, but he clung to my skirts and would not let go.

"You spoil that baby, Janna," said Mark disapprovingly, coming home one day from Penzance to find me in the nursery as usual with Philip. "He'll take advantage of you later on."

"No, he won't," I said, "and I don't spoil him."

But I did.

Nanny became cross. "Excuse me, Mrs. Castallack," she said firmly one day. "Pardon me, madam, but how can I train Master Philip to be obedient and good when you never refuse him anything? He's growing very willful and thinks he needs only scream for something to get it. It's not right, madam, if you don't mind me saying so. When I was with the de Clancy family in Budleigh Salterton . . ."

And I was regaled with tales from Nanny's past of horrible children who had been idolized by doting parents.

I resolved I would have to be more sensible.

I think part of my absorption in the children was because of the lack in my relationship with Mark. I had imagined things would right themselves after Philip's birth and had resolved to try not to have any more children for at least two years so that I could give Mark my full attention, but the constraint between us persisted. I had made up my mind to go abroad if he wished, but now he did not offer to take me. He was deeply involved with his historical writings and had completed a second thesis on King John which he thought would further his career as a historian, and now when he spoke of going away it was not to the Continent but to Oxford to work at the Bodleian Library. Soon we had slipped into our old habit of rarely meeting except at mealtimes, and my dismay deepened when he again increased his visits to Penzance. He saw Michael Vincent two or three times a week now, and although I always waited up for him on those evenings he spent away from home he did not once come to my room on his return but slept in his dressing room across the passage.

In an effort both to please him and to draw us closer together I said at last, "Mark, why don't you invite your friends here instead of always visiting them in Penzance? They must think us very inhospitable."

"Oh," he said, "but I know you don't enjoy entertaining."

"I think I would enjoy it more now that I'm accustomed to life at Penmarric," I said, trying to convince myself as well as him that this was true, and soon I was no longer able to escape from the ordeal of giving dinner parties and Mark was once more talking of giving a ball after Christmas. The pace of life began to quicken; our social activities increased, and with my confinement now behind me I was drawn more into parish life and found myself very busy and occupied.

But despite this I scarcely saw Mark at all.

I tried not to worry, tried not to think of those ten years that separated us, tried not to think of my Tomorrow, that time waiting for me in the future when I would be middle-aged and Mark still in his prime. But I went on thinking of those ten years until finally came the moment when I could bear thinking of them no longer. One night when Mark came home late from Penzance I went to his dressing room to meet him and asked unsteadily if I had offended or displeased him in some way.

"Of course not!" He looked uncomfortable.

"Then why—lately—"

"The fault is mine," he said at once, "not yours. I've been tired and preoccupied lately." And the next day he did make a great effort to please me by lunching with me and the children in the nursery and by dining with me in the evening; he was courteous and charming, and for the first time for several weeks I forgot my depression entirely and was conscious only of happiness.

My happiness lasted five days. Then Mark rode into Penzance again for the day and that same afternoon I was summoned to the nursery, where Marcus lay ill with a high fever.

[3]

I was frantic with anxiety. Nanny said to me, "I'm sure it's nothing serious, madam. Young children do run high temperatures, but I think the doctor should be called just to be on the safe side." I sent at once for Dr. Salter and moved restlessly up and down the room as I waited for his arrival. I was thinking of Stephen, of course, remembering that dreadful silent nursery and his small waxen face in the cradle. I tried not to remember but I could not help myself. I began to picture Marcus dead, Philip falling ill, all my children dying . . .

I began to panic. Even after the doctor had arrived and diagnosed a moderate case of measles I could still hardly contain my fear and dread, and finally by the middle of the afternoon I felt so full of longing for Mark to be with me and soothe me with comforting words that I became desperate. Leaving the nursery, I fetched my hat and coat and ordered the carriage to the door.

"Drive me to Mr. Michael Vincent's residence in Penzance," I said to the coachman. By the time I arrived at the house Michael would be home from the office and Mark would be arriving from Carnforth Hall for dinner—or if they were both to dine at the Hall it would be an easy matter for me to drive there to find them.

The carriage rolled down the drive toward the moors.

It was half past six when I reached the pleasant residential district of Penzance where Michael had recently acquired a house. His housekeeper showed me into the drawing room and presently Michael himself emerged from the adjacent library.

He looked at me in amazement. "Janna!" he exclaimed, as if I were an apparition. "What are you doing in Penzance?" Recovering himself quickly, he remembered his manners and added, "I'm sorry—do sit down."

He was a typical bachelor, serious, plain and shy with the opposite sex; certainly whatever virtues he possessed as Mark's lawyer and friend he was no match for a woman who was as desperate and panic-stricken as I was that evening. It took me no more than five minutes to wring from him the fact that not only was he expecting to dine alone that evening but that, contrary to what I had been led to suppose, he had seen very little of Mark for some weeks. To make matters still worse I learned Mark could not be dining at Carnforth Hall that evening either since his contemporaries there, Mr. Justin and Miss Judith, were spending the week with the Trehearnes at Helston.

At last I managed to say after a long terrible silence, "Then where is he?"

And Michael did not answer.

"Please," I said, the panic rising within me in a huge silent tide, "if you know, please, please tell me! It's so urgent—surely you can understand—"

"Yes," said Michael suddenly, "of course I understand. Listen, I think I know where I can find Mark. If you'd care to wait here—"

"No," said my voice. "Tell me where he is."

"He may not be there."

"Tell me anyway. I don't want to waste time while I wait for you to go there and back to find out whether he's there or not. Tell me where he is."

"Janna, forgive me, but what you ask is out of the question.

I . . . Mark and I quarreled violently once because he considered—rightly—that I had abused his confidence. . . . I could not possibly—a second time—"

"Very well—tell me nothing! But once you leave this house to fetch him you can't stop me following you to see where you go! And you won't stop me from telling Mark later that you betrayed his confidence anyway!"

"But . . ." He was so horrified he could hardly speak. "But . . ."

"Give me the address," I said, "and I'll tell Mark I followed you there without you knowing it and that you were not to blame."

"Janna, please—I beg of you, be reasonable—forgive me, but I simply cannot—"

I lost my temper. All the strain and worry over Marcus merged with this new terrible shock that Mark had deceived me so that I lost my grip on my self-control. "No, I won't forgive you!" I blazed. "If Marcus dies without either of his parents beside him just because you won't tell me where Mark is—"

"But—"

"Oh damn you!" I stormed at him. "Curse you for a stubborn oaf and a fool! What do I care if Mark's amusing himself with some poor cheap woman down by the harbor? Give me her address, for the love of God, and let me go there and talk to him! This is an emergency, Michael—an emergency, can't you understand? You have a moral duty to tell me where Mark is so that I can find him as quickly as possible!"

"But it's a confidential matter—you cannot expect me to—"

"Oh, for God's sake! I'll take full responsibility, I swear it—full, total, absolute responsibility—is that what you want to hear? I'll see Mark doesn't blame you for anything. But if you don't tell me where he is I'll—I'll—"

"Wait." He went to his desk as if seizing any excuse he could find to postpone the moment of enlightening me and began to turn the pages of an address book with trembling fingers. As I watched he reached the letter P. "I think it's possible he may be visiting an acquaintance of mine," he said in a flat voice, "the —the widow of one of my clients. . . . Her name is Mrs. Rose Parrish. She lives at number twelve, Landeryon Avenue, which is about half a mile from here, the second turning on the left off the main road to Land's End."

"Thank you," I said and left him.

I went out to the carriage. "Twelve, Landeryon Avenue, Crowlas," I said to the coachman. "The second turning on the left off the main road to Land's End."

"Yes, m'm." He helped me into the carriage and closed the door.

I was alone.

I could not think clearly. I was dimly aware of pain but most of all of a searing conviction that life had again treated me unfairly. I had not intended to become pregnant with Philip; I had not intended to give Mark a rebuff. My pregnancy had been an accident, as much Mark's fault as mine, yet afterward he had used it as an excuse for infidelity with some wretched, common, miserable woman. I could visualize her all too plainly. Mrs. Rose Parrish, an ex-actress perhaps, with a little money, enough to afford a house in some drab lower-class neighborhood. She would be about forty, blowsily attractive with a witty tongue; Mark always preferred women older than himself.

The pain of discovery had vanished, drowned in the rising tide of my anger. I was still furiously planning what I would say when I saw him when the carriage stopped and the coachman called out, "Number twelve, m'm," as he scrambled down to help me dismount.

I glanced around feverishly. I was in a quiet middle-class neighborhood, not unlike the road where Michael lived. The house marked twelve was medium-sized and stood in a pretty garden of about one acre with bushes, shrubs, lawns and wide flowerbeds.

Mrs. Parrish obviously had enough money for a gardener.

I wasted no more time staring, but walked up the path to the front door and rang the bell.

A light in the hall was turned higher. I felt a void below my heart, a tightness in my throat, but it was a maid who opened the door, a young girl neatly dressed in uniform, her cap and apron immaculately starched.

I did not give my name but merely told her in my most imperious manner that I must see Mrs. Parrish at once. The parlormaid did not argue with me; I was shown through a small hall into a simply but tastefully furnished reception room, and as she lit the gas I saw there were flowers everywhere, bowls of delicately scented blooms on the window sill and the mantelshelf and the two side tables, while throughout the room was an air of elegance and refinement.

As soon as the maid had gone I walked to the bookcase and looked at the books. There were three volumes on the history of art, a picture book of the works of the Italian masters, an informative manual on water-color painting and a companion on sketching. There was another book called *Art Treasures of the National Gallery* and beside it a volume called *A Guide to Opera*. On the shelf below stood a biography of Mozart and a twin volume on Beethoven. I took one of the books out of the case and opened it. The pages were cut. I put it back again and as I turned away all I could think was: I should have let Michael come. I should have stayed at his house and waited.

And the panic, the dread and worst of all the fear overwhelmed me so that I could hardly stand for the dizziness before my eyes.

The door opened.

I turned slowly and looked at her.

She was young. At first I could not see her clearly, but I knew at once that she was young. She had good skin, a little pallid, and soft, fine, fair hair, awkwardly styled and somewhat wispy at the sides. She had pale blue eyes and light brown lashes which she should have darkened to make her more striking. I thought her looks anemic and her manner gauche before she smiled, and then—oh!—how pretty she was with her sweet young face and her naïve, enchanting expression, how radiant she looked! Her air of fulfillment was ravishing, and as I stared, unable to look away, she stepped forward, the folds of her evening gown moved slightly, and I saw that she was going to have a child.

I tried to speak, but no words came. I tried to summon the anger I had experienced in the carriage, but there was no anger any more, only the most dreadful pain. I prayed for the pain to cease, but there was no relief and the ache of shock throbbed through my brain till I thought I would faint.

But I did not faint. I stood motionless, my breathing uneven, and presently the girl said shyly, "I'm so sorry—I'm not quite sure—have we met before? Please forgive me if I—"

She was a lady.

I felt so crushed, so utterly overwhelmed that I had to sit down. I said, mumbling a little, not looking at her, "My husband . . . is Mark here? My little boy is ill . . . I wanted Mark . . . the doctor said . . ." I could not go on.

I stared at the pretty carpet beneath my feet and then the pattern blurred until it was all a mere red mist before my eyes.

After a long while I heard the girl say in an anxious, concerned voice, "How worrying for you! I hope it's nothing serious. I'll fetch Mark at once."

Light footsteps pattered behind her; a child's voice said, "Mama, let me stay up a little longer! I don't want to go to bed yet!"

"Hush, William." I looked up, saw her stoop over a little boy who was perhaps four years old. He had pale golden hair so that at first I thought he resembled his mother, but when he turned his head to look at me I saw Mark's slanting eyes in his small bright face.

"Who's that, Mama?"

"Shhh, William . . ." She led him out into the hall and closed the door behind her so that I was alone.

I sat there emptily. I thought: He has known her a long time. Certainly for as long as we've been married.

I thought of my other pregnancies then, not merely of my time carrying Philip. I thought of my unquestioned assumption that I was the only woman in Mark's life. The knowledge had given me self-assurance, confidence, the ability to cope with my new social position. I had felt secure and loved, yet all the time here in Penzance he had been visiting this young girl, keeping her in that respectable neighborhood, giving her books on painting and the opera, discussing his work with her, thinking, of course, what a mistake he had made by not asking her to be his wife.

I sat there, dry-eyed now, too appalled even to weep. Time passed. I went on sitting there, and when at last I heard his footsteps crossing the hall I only thought in detachment: I must pull myself together, behave as he would expect a lady to behave. No scenes. No shouting. No vulgarity.

As he opened the door I stood up and we looked at each other. His face showed nothing. His dark eyes were expressionless, his mouth hard. Presently he closed the door behind him and waited but when I said nothing it was he who spoke first.

"You say Marcus is ill?"

This made speech easier for me. I thought of Marcus lying in his cot in the nursery, his cheeks flushed, his eyes too bright, his forehead burning.

"Yes," I said unsteadily. "The doctor says it's measles but not a serious case. I shouldn't have been so frightened, I know, but poor Marcus was so fevered and distressed. I—it was foolish of me not to wait until you returned home—I shouldn't have come to Penzance, but—I—I started to remember Stephen—"

"Quite," he said. "I understand. Did Michael tell you I was here?"

"Yes, I . . . I forced him to give me the address. He said she was an acquaintance of his. He did not admit . . . acknowledge . . ."

"Yes. Did he not offer to fetch me?"

"I . . ." Words stuck in my throat. With a great effort I managed to say, "I'm afraid I behaved very foolishly and I shall have to apologize to Michael. He can't possibly be held responsible for this. The fault was all mine and he was in no way to blame."

"I see." He turned to the door again. "I suggest we leave at once. You have the carriage, of course?"

"Yes."

"My horse is at the inn. I'll send someone over later to collect him." He held the door open for me and we went into the hall. I supposed he had already taken his leave of Mrs. Parrish, for there was no sign of her and he did not pause to say goodbye. He led the way out to the carriage, helped me inside and then climbed in beside me as the coachman held open the door.

"Home, Crowlas, please."

"Yes, sir."

We set off on our journey to St. Just.

As we left Penzance he said, "I'm sorry this had to happen."

I could not answer. Tears were stabbing behind my eyes again and I was too afraid of breaking down and weeping and then not being able to compose myself sufficiently when we reached home. It would never do to show the servants that I was distressed. I could not endure the thought of them all gossiping about me behind my back.

As if he guessed my thoughts he said, "We'll discuss this further when we have more privacy." And after that the silence remained unbroken between us throughout the long journey over the moors to the north coast.

We arrived home. One of the footmen took Mark's hat and coat and told me the vicar of St. Just had called. We went upstairs, I not even able to look at him, and finally entered the nursery.

Nanny came to meet us. "Good evening, sir—good evening,

madam . . . yes, he's asleep now, poor little lamb, but he's still very feverish. Once the rash breaks out all over him he'll be better. He asked for you when you were gone, Mrs. Castallack, and I told him you'd gone to fetch his papa."

We went into Marcus' room to look at him. He seemed very little and defenseless, lying there so quietly with his small head resting on the pillow, and suddenly I was remembering Stephen again, remembering his tiny body laid out in his cradle and the silent emptiness of that deserted nursery. Stephen would have been four years old if he had lived, the same age as Mrs. Parrish's son. My mind began to blur with pain. As the picture of Mrs. Parrish's son flashed unwanted before my eyes all I could think was: Her child lived. Mine died.

"Where is Mariana?" Mark was saying to Nanny. "I trust she and Philip are being kept in a separate room."

Tears welled inside me. I knew I was going to cry and could not possibly hold back my tears a moment longer. I managed to say, "Excuse me . . . I'm a little faint . . ." and then I was out of the nursery and stumbling blindly down those dark clammy corridors to my room in the west tower. The sobs were almost suffocating me. When I reached my room I slammed the door, lay on my bed and cried until I was too exhausted to cry any longer.

After a long while I struck a match and lit the lamp. The great room, the famous Tower Room, yawned at me emptily. I walked up and down, my fingers trailing over the polished furniture, my mind a mass of confused painful thoughts, but at last I caught sight of myself in the looking-glass and halted abruptly to stare at my reflection. By some trick of the light my hair seemed so fair that it was almost silver. I lit a candle and walked slowly toward my reflection. Shadows cast odd lines about my mouth and eyes; grief made me bowed and somehow, mysteriously, smaller.

I stood looking at myself for a long time, too mesmerized to look away, for this was my Tomorrow, this was the future which I had known to be lying in wait for me, but now my Tomorrow wasn't tomorrow any more.

It was today.

My shoulders began to tremble again with sobs. I was just pressing my hands against my cheeks in a desperate attempt to control myself when behind me the door opened quietly and I knew at once that Mark had entered the room.

[4]

"Janna . . . dearest—"

"No, please . . . please don't. Please leave. I can't talk now. Please go."

"But I wanted to explain."

"I don't want to hear." I sat down, my hands over my ears, my eyes tightly closed to try to stop my tears from escaping. "I want to be alone. I can't talk. Please."

"Darling—"

"Don't touch me!"

"I simply wanted to tell you—"

"No—no, I don't want to listen!"

"—that you're my wife and I love you."

"Oh . . ." I cried. I cried for a long time. He sat beside me and held my hand, and after a while when there was not a dry inch left on my handkerchief he gave me his own handkerchief and bore with me without complaint as I blew my nose and tried to pull myself together. Finally when I was calmer he began to talk in a low voice about the past. He had had an affair with the girl before we had become husband and wife—even before we had become lovers—but after that initial incident he had been faithful to me until the months immediately before Philip's birth. He offered no excuses for himself, merely saying that it had been wrong of him and he was sorry. It had, he realized now, been wrong of him even to keep in touch with her, but he had treated her so badly in the beginning during the time he had spent with her in St. Ives that his conscience had obliged him to do all he could to make amends; he had borrowed money from Giles Penmar to support her during her pregnancy and later when his mother's cousin Robert Yorke had died he had had the means to buy her a house in Penzance so that she could live respectably in the manner to which she was accustomed. He had visited her occasionally as a friend and she had instructions only to communicate with him through Michael; their new relationship had proceeded along these correct and formal lines without difficulty until one day he had visited her in Penzance and—

"I don't want to hear any more," I said, pressing my hands over my ears, but once I was faced with his silence I immediately had an overpowering desire to make him speak. Before I could stop myself I was saying in a rush, "How could you have let her become pregnant again?" and my voice sounded high and unnatural in that quiet room. "How could you? I know most women of her—her class are ignorant of such matters and I would not expect her to know all the old wives' tales Griselda passed on to me, but could you not at least have—"

"Yes, of course I advised her."

"That was all you did? Advise her?"

He reddened but to my surprise held onto his temper. Perhaps he was too guilty to feel angry. "No, I did more than that."

"But then—"

"Most of the time." He turned aside abruptly. "But she was taking my advice from the beginning. It was unfortunate that she was unlucky, but you know as well as I do that there's no foolproof way of controlling such things. All a woman can do is to be careful and hope for the best."

"Nonsense," I said harshly. "One always knows when one's taking even the slightest risk. Even at Chûn I knew it was possible—unlikely, but possible—that I might conceive. If you want a foolproof way you simply don't take risks, that's all. That woman wanted another child. She fooled you. She wanted to be pregnant again."

He bent his head. I was just thinking he had no answer to offer me when he said at last, "She should be married. She should have a nice ordinary husband, half a dozen nice ordinary children, a respectable home—"

"Penmarric perhaps." I had to say it. I could not stop myself. "How well she would fit in here!"

"I could have married her if I'd wished," he said evenly. "But I didn't. I married you, not Rose."

"Rather an unfortunate choice, perhaps." I did not want to say such terrible things but some bizarre compulsion forced me to say them. "She would have been such a perfect wife and I—as you reminded me so frankly a year ago—would have been such an ideal mistress."

"I had you as my mistress," he said, "and I still wanted you to be my wife. Perhaps you forget."

I turned my head sharply and stood up. I was being stifled by pain again. I could not speak, but presently I heard him say, "Forgive me, Janna. Please. We'll start again."

I fingered the novel on my bedside table and thought of the books on music and art in that house in Penzance. He had gone back to see Rose Parrish even when her condition no longer allowed her to accommodate him. When my condition had placed me in a similar position he had gone away to London to study or to Penzance to amuse himself and I had been left alone at Penmarric.

"I was foolish," he was saying. "I admit that, but a lot of husbands stray occasionally; it seldom means much. They always come back eventually to their wives."

"Oh?" I said, trying to keep my voice as steady as his. "And do their wives always forgive them?"

"If they're sensible."

I spun around trembling, but when I looked into his face I was aware only of a great desolation as I tried to imagine what life would be like if we remained estranged. There would be no divorce, of course. I knew little of the matrimonial laws, only that there had to be adultery but that the wife could not divorce her husband for adultery alone. There probably would not even be a formal separation. He would want to keep up appearances and avoid a scandal, and so we would go on living at Penmarric, he continuing to live the life he enjoyed so much while I—I would be cut off, isolated, more lonely than I had ever been before, imprisoned forever in solitary confinement behind those iron walls of class. Such a situation could only have been tolerable if I had hated him, but I did not hate him. In spite of all that had happened I still loved him and wanted him and knew I could not endure to exist beneath the same roof with him in a state of estrangement.

"Well, perhaps . . ." I faltered. Tears pricked again behind my eyes. "For the sake of the children—"

"Never mind the children," he said roughly, his calm patient manner forgotten. "They'd be better off with separated parents than with parents who were merely together for their sake—and I know what I'm talking about! No, I want a reconciliation because I want *you*, and unless you want a reconciliation because you want me I think we'd best make arrangements to live apart."

"I do want you." My voice was unsteadier than ever. My heart felt as if it were bursting. "I do, I do, I do . . ." And as the room blurred and I closed my eyes with the pain, he took me in his arms and kissed me on the mouth.

We were reconciled. The incident was closed. I had postponed my Tomorrow, but from that day onward I always felt that I was living on borrowed time and I never fully trusted him again.

6 *. . . he had already married Eleanor. However, he and Rosamonde resumed their relationship and another son was born, who was named Geoffrey. . . .*

—The Conquering Family,
THOMAS COSTAIN

The King's eldest son was now at a suitable age to begin his formal education.

—Henry II,
JOHN T. APPLEBY

There may have been disagreement over the education of the children . . .

—The Devil's Brood,
ALFRED DUGGAN

[1]

We did not speak again of Mrs. Parrish for some months. Mark had decided that she should move to Truro many miles away, and although he visited the town in order to find a house for her there he did not refer to his visit when he returned. In the new year I managed to say off-handedly one evening, "I suppose Mrs. Parrish has had the baby by now," but all he said was "Yes, another boy, unfortunately," and his manner was so abrupt that I did not dare to ask any more questions on the subject.

We spent a busy Christmas. All Mark's contemporaries seemed to be either marrying or proposing to marry, and there was a stream of parties and balls. Roger Waymark was married now, Russell St. Enedoc engaged, and Justin Carnforth had fallen in love with a pretty empty-headed little debutante and was talking of a wedding in the spring. Judith Carnforth had made herself unpopular by marrying a banker, but, poor girl, she hardly had the looks to secure a more suitable match, and since she was now well into her twenties I suppose she thought that any marriage was better than being left on the shelf. Another young spinster well into her twenties was Clarissa Penmar, although Clarissa was so attractive she hardly merited the classification "on the shelf" since she could surely have married any time she chose to do so. She had not lived much at our old home Deveral Farm after she had purchased the property but had instead divided her time between London and the Continent with a freedom unprecedented for an unmarried female. But she was of age, she had no guardians, and she had the means to do exactly as she pleased. Her fortune, inherited from her adopted father Giles Penmar, no doubt encouraged her to maintain her independence; it might have been Giles's intention to persuade suitors to overlook her uncertain reputation by giving her an enticing dowry, but Clarissa had ignored the purpose of his generosity by dallying with her suitors at a safe distance from the altar. Sir James and Lady Carnforth, always very strait-laced, would no longer receive her at Carnforth Hall, but Clarissa was hardly the person to worry about the hostile attitudes of the local aristocracy.

In the autumn of 1895, shortly after my discovery of Mark's infidelity, she returned to Morvah and settled there, much as a brilliant butterfly would rest for a while in the shade before returning to flutter among the exotic blooms in the sun. The Barnwells invited her to Zillan rectory to see her niece, her brother Harry's daughter Alice, and she in turn invited them to lunch at Deveral Farm, but apart from the Barnwells she saw no one and it was hard to understand what she could be doing to occupy her time.

"Having a love affair, I should think," commented Mark with a flash of his characteristic coarseness, but although I had my doubts about this theory I soon discovered that it was absolutely true.

I made the discovery at—of all places!—my own beloved Roslyn Farm. The lease I had granted Jared five years before had expired, and, seizing the opportunity to revisit the house I had loved so much, I managed to persuade Mark to allow me to return there for a visit on the pretext of inspecting the property before granting a new lease. Naturally I was not allowed to go alone; Mark said flatly that he had no intention of returning to the place, but he asked Michael in his position as family lawyer to accompany me and arrange the details of the new lease with Jared, and so early in the new year Michael and I traveled together in the Penmarric carriage to Roslyn Farm. Since I had assumed complete responsibility for prising Mrs. Parrish's name and address from him that day in Penzance there was no ill-feeling between us, but whenever we met there was an awkwardness in the atmosphere that was well-nigh impossible to ignore. However, we spent the journey to Roslyn Farm uttering empty little politenesses to each other to pretend we had forgotten the disastrous scene at his house, until at last to our joint relief we reached our destination, left the carriage and walked up the path to the front door.

Oh, how I loved that house! I stepped across the threshold of the front door and its mellow atmosphere enveloped me so that I was immediately at peace. Children were wailing and there was a commotion in the kitchen but I was oblivious to all distraction. I was home. I went into the parlor and there was the same solid furniture, the same table where I had sat facing first Laurence and then Mark so many times, the same sofa and rug where Mark and I had made love after I had agreed to marry him. When I went to the window and stared at the overgrown front garden that I had tended so carefully the years seemed to fall away as if by magic and I felt so pleasantly comfortable, so unutterably secure.

"Roslyn never had another son, did he?" Michael was saying, listening to the sound of childish chatter in the distance. "I remember your first husband leaving money and property to the little boy Abel, and I remember the money and property reverting to Roslyn when the child died. The death must have been a sad blow for him."

Masterful footsteps in the hall prevented me from replying. The next moment the parlor door was flung open and Jared himself entered the room.

He looked well. He was thirty-six, just as I was, and his face had the glow of good health and prosperity. He was heavier than before, but it suited him; he looked exactly like the successful farmer and pillar of the working community he had become.

"Good morning, Janna," he said. He did not stand on ceremony. There was no bowing or calling me Mrs. Castallack. "Good morning, Mr. Vincent."

"Good morning, Mr. Roslyn."

We settled down to discuss business. Presently when he showed us over the farm I was interested to see that although the house was dirty and untidy the farm itself was in excellent condition. There were new outbuildings, more cattle, more poultry.

"You seem to be prospering," I said politely to Jared.

His eyes met mine. "I think so," he said.

We signed a new lease for a further five years, and presently his wife brought in wine although she did not stay to drink with us.

"You have a fine family, Mr. Roslyn," said Michael sociably as she closed the parlor door. "How many children are there now?"

"Five girls surviving," said Jared abruptly and added, looking me straight in the eyes: "Not all wives are so successful at providing their husbands with sons."

I was so taken aback that I said nothing at all. I had expected hostility from him in the form of a curt, abrupt manner, but I had not expected hostility in the form of a bitter compliment. And suddenly for one second as our glances met I saw how it was with him and wondered—as indeed I had wondered before—how changed things might have been if he had been as ready as his father to propose to me when we had first met long ago in St. Ives.

I was still trying to think of something to say to break that awkward silence when from the front garden came a girl's laugh, loud and clear, and the echo of feet on flagstones. All three of us glanced out of the window simultaneously; and all three of us saw Clarissa Penmar.

She wore her hair loose and did not look like a lady at all but more like a gypsy with her dark eyes and olive skin. Her attire was most improper, so improper that I could hardly believe my eyes. It was true that the sport of bicycle riding had been popular for some years now and it was true that females often did ride bicycles for pleasure and needed a certain freedom of movement unhampered by a respectable habit, but I had never in my life seen a girl wear a cyclist suit when she had no intention of riding a bicycle. Clarissa wore trousers. "Knickerbockers" would in fact be a more accurate description, but whatever they were they were outrageous. She also wore a short mannish coat of matching material and beneath the stark lines of this masculine attire the voluptuousness of her figure was most indecently evident. She wasn't even wearing a hat; a piece of vulgar red ribbon tied her hair back from her face while the wind whipped at her black curls. She looked wild, exotic and utterly unprincipled.

Beside me I heard Michael take a short painful breath but I did not look at him. I was too busy looking out of the window, for beside Clarissa was my younger stepson, Jared's brother Joss.

I had not thought of Joss and Clarissa together before, but now when I did I saw at once that they were alike. They were much the same age, both at odds with the world, both ready to defy and scorn anyone who crossed them, both fiercely independent. Joss too was dressed carelessly. As if demonstrating his rejection of the conventions he had discarded his farmer's smock and wore a pair of dirty breeches torn at the thigh, a coarse shirt beneath an unbuttoned sheepskin coat, no neckcloth, no hat and muddy boots. He was smiling at her. I had never seen Joss smile like that before, never seen his sullen face light up and his blue eyes sparkle with good humor. For a moment he looked so uncannily like his father that I could not take my eyes off him, but then as Clarissa laughed a second time I was again aware of the two of them together and noticed with shocked incredulity that they were hand in hand.

Beside me I heard Jared check an exclamation and mutter a hasty "excuse me" as he left the room.

"Good gracious me!" I exclaimed to Michael incredulously. "Did you ever see such a sight?"

But Michael was white to the lips, his eyes blind with the pain of memory, and I remembered at last that he had loved Clarissa once years ago and had never looked at another woman after she had lost interest in him.

"I'm sorry," I said quickly. "I had quite forgotten. Let's go at once. We've finished our business and there's no need for us to stay."

He followed me wordlessly into the hall just as Jared entered it with Joss and Clarissa behind him. There was a silence before I said coldly, "Good morning, Miss Penmar. Good morning,

Joss. Jared, you will forgive us if we leave now—I wish you luck and hope your success and prosperity continue. Please thank your wife for the wine."

Jared took my hand in his. His skin was rough, his fingers thick, his palm unexpectedly wide. I had forgotten what enormous hands he had. "Thank you, Janna. Good day, Mr. Vincent."

"Good day, Mr. Roslyn." He was looking at Clarissa.

She stared back at him insolently without a trace of embarrassment. "Hullo, Michael! What a long time it's been since I last saw you!"

"Yes," he said. The poor man was blushing painfully. "Yes, indeed."

I moved past Joss and waited for him to open the front door, but he merely stood regarding me with his usual rudeness.

"Joss!" said Jared harshly. "Remember your manners."

Joss looked me up and down, opened the door and lounged against the doorpost so that I was obliged to push my way past him. He was quite the most disagreeable young man I have ever encountered.

"What's troubling you?" he inquired with a sneer. "Did you look so disapprovingly at Mr. Castallack and his father when they showed a taste for a working-class companion? At least Clarissa's more fortunate than they were! I'm not from the gutters of St. Ives."

"Really?" I said. "You both look as if you belong there. Good day." And I swept down the path to the waiting carriage without looking back.

Michael stumbled after me.

"Back to Penmarric, Crowlas," I said sharply to the coachman and paused for Michael to offer me some assistance as I climbed into the carriage, but I waited in vain for good manners that morning. Poor Michael was too upset to be aware of what was happening, and although later I made an attempt at conversation he was too sunk in depression to respond. Deciding it would be kinder to ignore him, I stared out of the window, my mind still on the extraordinary scene at the farm, and so absorbed was I with my thoughts that I barely noticed the creaks of the carriage as it surmounted the ridge and rolled downhill once more toward the sea.

"I must confess," I said to Mark later, "I was very shocked. A young lady like Clarissa! You should have seen her! So abandoned, so—so blatantly immoral! Frankly I was horrified."

"I can see why Joss is interested in her," said Mark cynically. "She's well off—very rich by his standards—and she has the farm at Morvah, which is the finest farmhouse in the parish with a considerable amount of land. It's true the land attached to the house is leased to Farmer Rosemorran and has been since my father lived there, but the lease is an annual one and can be reclaimed without a long wait. He's after her money and her property. He's tired of living at that hovel of a tenant farm on his brother's charity. He's anxious to come up in the world."

"Well, she'll never marry him," I said distastefully. "She's not that much of a fool. She's dallying with him just as she used to dally with the Penmarric stable boys, and soon she'll tire of him and go back to London again to find someone of her own class."

But I was wrong. A week later the banns were called for the first time, and within a month, much to the amazement of the county and the delight of the village gossips, Clarissa had changed her name to Roslyn and Joss had at a stroke become one of the wealthiest young men in western Cornwall.

They were not received, of course. Clarissa had cut herself off from her class by her behavior, and Joss was certainly not presentable in any drawing room. They were married by Mr. Barnwell at Zillan church, and no one was at the wedding save Jared and his family together with Mrs. Barnwell and the Barnwells' granddaughter, little Alice Penmar. After the wedding they lived at Deveral Farm and presently Joss reclaimed the land from Farmer Rosemorran and began to renovate the outbuildings and buy stock. How Clarissa adjusted to her new life as a farmer's wife after her years of carefree irresponsibility I have no idea, for I seldom saw her. Occasionally I glimpsed her in Penzance, but we did not speak to each other and in any case Joss would not have permitted her to make any sociable overtures either to Mark or to myself.

Needless to say, local gossip was of the opinion that she married because she had to, but as winter passed into spring and she retained her figure the gossiping tongues were silenced. It seemed that after all she had married for love, that in Joss, with his rebelliousness and coarse vulgarity, she had found what she wanted at last after her years of searching among the brilliant ballrooms of London.

"Well, good luck to her," said Mark, shrugging the incident away as I continued to marvel at the match. "I hope she's happy."

He was too busy to spend much time dwelling on Clarissa's *mésalliance*.

The thesis of his on King John had been published by an Oxford journal and later reprinted by a London publication of note. He was beginning to make a name for himself in academic circles, and in the spring of 1896 he went away again to study a series of documents called the Pipe Rolls, which I understood to encompass the household accounts of medieval royalty. I did not go with him on that occasion, but when toward the end of the year he invited me to accompany him to Oxford for a month or two while he did some more research, I accepted willingly enough. I knew better than to refuse, but I found Oxford a cold, formal place with forbidding old buildings and an air of such advanced scholasticism that I felt at once pitifully aware of my lack of education.

"Never mind, Mrs. Castallack," said one of the professors to me with a smile after I had made some appalling historical *faux pas*. "Lovely ladies were never intended by God to pursue the quest for knowledge!"

But I felt sure Mark was embarrassed by my all too obvious ignorance.

However, the weeks away from Penmarric brought us closer together than we had been for some months, and when we returned home I felt my effort in making the journey had not been wasted. Early in 1897 when I told him I was again expecting a baby we were both pleased, and in August, two years and two months after Philip's arrival, I gave birth to another son in the Tower Room of Penmarric.

This time it was Mark's turn to choose the name. The baby was christened Hugh, not a name that appealed to me, but the infant made no protest and slept tranquilly through the service. He was small, much finer-boned than Philip, but Philip had always been unusually large. At the reception following the christening, Marcus made himself ill by drinking a glass of champagne when no one was looking, Mariana refused to sit down for fear of creasing her dress and Philip pulled off his sister's straw hat and jumped on it.

"You horrid, horrid boy!" cried Mariana, who was a very feminine child and loved all her clothes but especially her hats. "I hate you!" And she boxed Philip's ears so resoundingly that he sat down and cried until the room was deafened.

"Mariana, how naughty!" I said, much irritated by this fuss and fearing the guests would think my children very ill-behaved. I stooped and gathered Philip to me. "There, there, precious . . . hush, Mama's here."

He looked at me mistily with great tear-filled blue eyes. My heart ached with love for him.

"Now, now!" said Nanny's voice sternly from close at hand. "What's all this to-do? Who stamped on this hat?"

"*He* did!" wailed Mariana. "I hate him!'

"Oh, do be quiet, Mariana," I said crossly. "You quite make my head ache. The hat's by no means ruined." I turned to Nanny. "I think the children are getting tired and overexcited."

"Yes, ma'am," Nanny agreed. "I'll take him away and put him to bed." And to my exasperation she scooped up Philip and carried him away to the nursery.

Time passed. Hugh, although small, was evidently strong and healthy. He too was fair like Philip and had inherited my blue eyes and my features, but I often wondered whom he truly resembled. As he developed more personality he seemed to have a little of everything, a little of Marcus' winning charm, a little of Philip's striking looks, a little of Mariana's irritating fastidiousness. He seemed intelligent without being unusually precocious. Presently as he began to walk he showed himself tough enough to survive copious nursery fights with Philip, and ultimately I suspected he had a belligerent streak in his nature.

But Nanny thought otherwise. "It's Master Philip, ma'am," she told me bluntly when I raised the matter with her. "It's he who's the trouble-maker in the nursery."

I privately thought she was prejudiced against Philip. To make up to him for any slights he might or might not have received at her hands, I was especially loving toward him whenever I visited the nursery.

When Hugh was a year old some news reached our ears about the Roslyns of Morvah. Clarissa had given birth to a girl after more than two years of marriage and, so the local gossips reported with malicious satisfaction, had had a difficult time, so difficult that the doctor had told her it was unlikely she would have any more children. I could not fathom how the gossips knew such delicate details and suspected much of the news was pure invention, but it was true that the child was born and that it was a girl. They called her Rebecca after Joss's mother, my predecessor at Roslyn Farm. Joss and Clarissa were still beyond the pale as far as society was concerned and seldom even made the effort to go to church or chapel, but once a month Clarissa would go on her own to Zillan rectory to see her niece Alice and have tea with the Barnwells. Alice was less than two years older than Marcus. I had half a mind to invite her to Penmarric when we engaged a governess for the children, for Mariana was always complaining she hated little boys and had no little girls to play with.

It was the fashion for children just then. All Mark's contemporaries seemed to be busy perpetuating their illustrious family names. I remember thinking that it would be pleasant for my own children later on when they needed friends of their own age, but that made the shadow cross my mind again, the dread of the passing years, and I would become morbid and depressed.

When Hugh was sixteen months old I said to Mark, "I would so love another baby."

He had no objection but he laughed and said, "You're not tired of children yet? With three noisy sons and one very vociferous daughter?"

When I answered, I was expressing the thought most dominant in my mind. "Next year I shall be forty," I said, "and once one is forty childbirth becomes more difficult and hazardous. I only have a few months left now."

"You speak of forty as if it's the end of the world!" he said, amused. "I'm sure it can't be as bad as all that!"

He was twenty-nine.

My second daughter was born in December at the very end of the nineteenth century. I would not allow her to be called Janna, so we called her instead by my true name, Jeanne, and she was christened directly after Christmas. Three days later the old year was gone, and although the Astronomer Royal said that the end of the nineteenth century should officially be recognized as the thirty-first of December 1900, we took little notice of this in distant Cornwall and welcomed the new century at the end of 1899. The twentieth century! I remember we were all very gay, a little overawed by the prospect of entering a new era, but excited too as if the best was yet to come and the promised land lay ahead for every one of us. We celebrated New Year's Eve that year in the most splendid manner imaginable and never once guessed as we heard the church bells chime across the moors at midnight that they were ringing the death knell for big houses like Penmarric and for a way of life that supported us all.

[3]

It was the time of the Boer War and the newspapers were full of England's struggles in South Africa against the farmers of Dutch descent. Since it was a highly controversial issue not only between Tories and Liberals but also between Liberals and other Liberals, the war soon became a leading topic of conversation whenever the subject of politics could be suitably introduced into a social gathering. A wave of patriotism which swept the country led to a wave of enlistment; young men joined regiments and left their homes to risk their lives in that faraway foreign land.

"You wouldn't enlist, would you?" I said to Mark in a moment of fright after Russell St. Enedoc had left St. Ives for London before being sent overseas to the war. "You're not anxious to fight, are you, darling?"

But I need not have worried. Mark, as was usual where politics were concerned, held unorthodox views which the majority of his class did not share. "Certainly not!" he said sharply. "I wouldn't dream of enlisting. To begin with I think all war is utterly monstrous and quite inexcusable unless one's own family and land are being threatened. Secondly, I disapprove of the British Empire when its foreign policy dissolves into jingoism, and finally I'm not at all sure the Boers haven't a right to determine their affairs as they wish without outside interference. I'm not in favor of their unfortunate attitude to the black people, but a show of force by the mightiest nation on earth isn't going to do anything except convince them that their attitudes are worth holding on to. Soon they'll be martyrs and world opinion will think the British Empire nothing but a big bully too fond of waving the big stick. No, my dear, I've better things to do than join in a war of which I most strongly disapprove!

Nobody is more of a patriot than I am, but I've very little confidence in politicians and even less confidence in wars. When I look back over past history and think how much misery and suffering they caused to so many people and usually for a net result of absolutely nothing, I can only think how remarkable it is that the human race never learns from past experience."

So he did not enlist. However, his brother Nigel did not share his views and presently set off for South Africa. I had not met Nigel, since he and Mark had remained estranged since their father's death, and soon I heard that we were destined never to meet. He was killed in action in 1900 and, being unmarried, left his money and his property to his mother.

"Good heavens!" said Maud Penmar with her typical lack of any emotion resembling sentiment. "What shall I do with the wretched house? I don't want it! Do you? Have it if you want it, by all means, and the money too. I want no part of any Castallack inheritance."

She came down to visit us after receiving the news of Nigel's death, but although I was prepared to sympathize with her in her bereavement she hardly seemed to need my sympathy. "He was a nice boy," she said plainly, "but foolish. Mark was right not to enlist. What's the point of going six thousand miles to fight a bunch of rustic foreigners? Let the colonials settle their own disputes! After all, what did they go to the colonies for in the first place? To weep on the bosom of the mother country as soon as they have a tiff with some other white men who cannot even speak English? I don't know what the Empire's coming to these days and I told Nigel so, but all Nigel said was that moral issues were at stake and that it was his moral as well as his patriotic duty to go to war. Well, of course I am entirely in favor of patriotism and moral duties, but it does all seem very sad to think I shall not see Nigel again just because the present-day colonial is markedly lacking in the spirit which built the Empire."

"I'm sure," I said cautiously, "that you'll miss him very much."

"Yes, doubtless I shall," she agreed moodily. "I did not know him as well as I know Mark, but he was a nice boy. Kind, very kind. . . . I was fond of him. But when I left Gweek he was hardly two years old and I didn't see him again until he was grown up. Now Mark was different. I saw Mark continually throughout his childhood."

"Three times in twelve years," said Mark.

"Yes, but . . ." They began to wrangle again, spoiling for a fight as always, and the subject of Nigel's premature death was temporarily forgotten.

"I suppose I ought to retain Gweekellis Manor," said Mark later without enthusiasm. "There have been Castallacks at Gweek for hundreds of years. No doubt I ought to keep the estate in the family." He worried over the problem for some time, but finally in 1901, just before the Queen's death, he managed to lease the house and estate for a term of fifty years to a retired Indian Army colonel and thus ridded himself of the place while still keeping the title deeds.

He had formed the habit of going away three times a year to London or Oxford to do research and I had at last grown to accept the fact that I saw less and less of him. His latest project was a study of changing social conditions in the twelfth century, and he already had publishers anxious to produce the book as soon as the manuscript was ready. He was well known at Oxford now; he had even been offered an academic post, but he had no wish to become involved with lecturing and other faculty activities and was content to continue his work as a writer. But the academic world attracted him; I could see how much he looked forward to his visits to Oxford and could judge from his letters how stimulating he found the atmosphere there. Slowly, almost imperceptibly, the tenor of his habits changed; he visited Oxford more often, stayed longer, wrote fewer letters. Presently he rented rooms there. "Well, why not?" he said blandly. "I'm tired of staying in the same old hotel and I like a place of my own where I can entertain my friends."

"Yes, of course," I said stiffly. "I understand."

But I did not. Depression enveloped me. I was forty-one, then forty-two. My hair was no longer the same rich color but paler, dimmed with an increasing number of white hairs which I could no longer hide. But my figure remained good and my skin belied my years unless the light was unexpectedly harsh. I told myself I was still attractive, still beautiful, still desirable, but as the months passed and Mark spent more time away from home it became useless to try to deceive myself any more.

He no longer wanted me. It was almost as if he had outgrown me, just as he had outgrown Cornwall. The phase of his life when he had enjoyed playing the gentleman of leisure running a country estate was finished, and now he was back once more where he belonged, in the libraries of Oxford, in the drawing rooms of the upper classes, in the society of the most brilliant intellectuals of his day. He belonged in a world where there was no place for me among people to whom I would seem provincial, narrow and—worst of all—uneducated.

He denied it, naturally. "I would ask you to come with me more often," he said, "but I know how you hate to leave Cornwall."

This was true enough, but when I offered to come with him he always had an excuse for going alone, and I knew that his talk of my accompanying him had been a mere gesture of courtesy, an empty politeness that had no meaning. Yet we did not quarrel. He was careful always to be pleasant and courteous to me whenever he was at Penmarric, and so there were no scenes, only perpetual constraint, which was worse than any scene would have been, and after a while my distress became dulled and I could hardly believe we had not always lived together in that fashion.

I knew I was unhappy, but I tried my hardest not to give myself time to think about it. I involved myself with my home, the parish and my neighborhood acquaintances to a greater degree than ever before and kept myself constantly occupied. And the farther Mark and I drifted apart from each other, the closer I became to the children.

They were growing up. Their personalities, blurred in early childhood, were becoming clearly defined. I knew Marcus would always be affectionate toward me, full of candid charm and engaging conversation; he was gregarious and enjoyed having plenty of people around him. I began to recognize an antagonism in Mariana, a resentment of discipline, an inclination to be bossy. She and Marcus were inseparable companions, being only a year apart in age, but it was she, not Marcus, who dictated what games should be played, she who always had the last word. Philip refused to stand such bossiness. He went his own way, conducted his own amusements, and in his wake like a little pale shadow trailed Hugh, a willing but often unwanted companion. Jeanne was still a baby and so somewhat apart from the others, but I thought her a pretty, docile child, quite different from her willful older sister. I became very fond of her. Like Philip and Hugh she was fair, but nonetheless I did not believe she greatly resembled me. Occasionally her serenity reminded me of Stephen, and because of this I felt a warmth toward her that I never felt toward Mariana. I always claimed later that I loved all my daughters equally, but for many years, particularly while they were children, it was Jeanne who remained my favorite.

It was 1902, the year of the new King's visit to Penzance and St. Michael's Mount, the year when I might have been presented to royalty as befitted my place in county society. But I was not presented. Mark was away at Oxford at the time and although he wrote and urged me to accept the invitation to the Mount and go there in the company of the Carnforths, my courage failed me and I was unable to face the ordeal of a social occasion of such magnitude without my husband at my side. Besides, the Carnforths did not ask me to accompany them, and I was not so ill-mannered to press for such an invitation when they had obviously decided I would be better off at home. Nanny and I took the children to the station to wave at the royal party as they arrived in Penzance, but after that we returned to Penmarric and I did not see the King again.

In fact I had too many other matters claiming my attention at that time to dwell for long upon the royal visit to Cornwall. Mark had been considering the children's education and presently announced to me that he had made arrangements for Marcus to go away to preparatory school in Surrey before he was sent to Eton at the age of twelve.

This was no sudden shock to me, for I had long known that my sons must be sent away from home to receive a gentleman's education, but nevertheless now that the time had come I could not help being filled with misgivings. Marcus was only nine years old and loved his home so much! My heart ached when I thought how homesick he would be far away in Surrey.

However, Marcus himself seemed delighted with the prospect and for a time at least I managed to ignore my misgivings.

"I'm going to school!" he chanted with glee and crowed smugly to Mariana, "No more lessons with you and Alice and Philip and Miss Peach!" Miss Peach was the governess; little Alice Penmar, a very plain child, came over to Penmarric from Zillan rectory during the week to learn her lessons with my children and had shown a surprising aptitude for her studies. I supposed she had inherited her aptitude from her grandfather the rector since neither Harry Penmar nor Miriam had had the reputation of possessing a nimble intelligence.

"You and Mariana and Philip will have to do your lessons

alone now, Alice," declared Marcus proudly. "*I'm* going to school."

"Well," said Alice, who had a very acid tongue for one so young, "I wish you joy of it. I'm glad it's not me."

"You're jealous!" said Mariana. "Marcus can't wait to go!"

This was certainly true. But on the day of his departure he cried all the way to Penzance station, and on the platform he clung to me and wept that he did not want to go at all.

I was horribly distressed. If it had been any of my other children perhaps I would not have been so upset, but Marcus was such an affectionate child that it wrenched my heart to think that we were sending him away all on his own as if we no longer loved him. It was no consolation for me to tell myself that his grandmother was meeting him at Paddington Station and would look after him until the time came for him to board the school train from Waterloo the next day; Maud Penmar was such a hard, unsympathetic woman, and Marcus would be so lost and bewildered . . .

"Don't send me away," he was sobbing pathetically, burying his face against my skirts. "Please. I'll be so good you'll never scold me again."

"Oh Marcus!" I could not bear to see him looking so pathetic. I felt the tears streaming down my cheeks as I hugged him. "Marcus darling, we'll take you home—you shan't go."

"What's all this?" Mark, who had been organizing the luggage, reappeared beside us on the platform. "What's all this fuss and nonsense? Come, Marcus, this won't do at all. Pull yourself together and be your age—it's high time you stopped clinging to your mama's skirts. Now, have you got everything? Then take my handkerchief, blow your nose and get on the train at once. We don't want it to leave without you."

Marcus sobbed into his father's handkerchief.

"Mark . . ." I began but broke off as I saw his expression.

"I think," he said, "you'd better wait outside in the carriage." And later when the train had gone and he was in the carriage beside me his first furious words were "That's the last time I ever allow you to see your children off to school!" He was keeping his voice low so that there was no chance of Crowlas overhearing our conversation beyond the cramped interior of the carriage. "Marcus would never have become so distressed if you had remained calm—he looked to you for support and you gave him none. The whole unfortunate scene was entirely your fault."

"But I couldn't help—"

"No, you couldn't help it because you don't know any better, but in future you'll say goodbye to Marcus at Penmarric. Sensibly. Without any ill-bred embarrassing scenes."

And it was then at last that we had our long-postponed quarrel.

I said I was sick of him always sneering at me, always hinting that I wasn't good enough for him, always behaving as if I were too common, too uneducated and too old to matter to him any more. Mark said that was a pack of lies and I was obviously too distraught to know what I was saying, so I reminded him how he spent most of the year away from Penmarric and how even when he was at Penmarric he took care to avoid me most of the time. He said that he thought he was doing me a kindness by leaving me alone; he was well aware that I had never forgiven him for his affair with Rose Parrish because ever since I had found out about her I'd never been the same in bed. Besides, it was patently obvious that now I no longer wanted more children I found my marital obligations not only unattractive but also so unbearably tedious that I was anxious to escape from them whenever I could.

"That's not true!" I cried. "It's just not true! I do love you still—I do want you—but can I help it if your behavior toward me makes me feel so nervous that I sometimes seem cold and ill-at-ease? The truth is that you're just using my apparent coldness, my failure, as a convenient excuse! If you can convince yourself that I no longer want you you'll consider you have a right to go elsewhere—which is all you truly want to do anyway!"

"If you cannot face the truth squarely, there's no point in discussing the matter further," he said. "I think we've spoken quite enough on the subject. There's nothing more to be said."

We drove on to Penmarric. We did not speak. On our arrival home we went our separate ways, I to my room, he to the library, and the gulf of our estrangement yawned between us until it seemed to me as if it were an abyss no bridge would ever span again.

[4]

He came to my room that same night. I suppose he regretted the quarrel as much as I did; certainly we both tried to make amends, but afterward I felt convinced not only that I had failed him but that he had found it no more rewarding than I had. He had simply made the gesture to be kind to me; I was certain in the cold hard light of early morning when I looked at myself in the mirror that he could have had no other reason for coming to my room, and all I knew was that I did not want him to come any more if he simply came on account of kindness.

As I dressed that morning I stared out of the window at the rain slewing into the stormy sea, the ugly black cliffs surrounding that bleak ugly mansion, and after a while it seemed to me that I would be much happier if I were not continually worrying about maintaining the shreds of our old relationship. It was obvious that Mark no longer wanted me, and if I could only reconcile myself to this truth and accept the fact that our physical relationship was dead, then his indifference could no longer hurt me. Perhaps I would no longer even mind so much that he went to other women—for I knew Mark too well by this time to assume naïvely that he was not unfaithful to me whenever he had the chance. I knew he had other women. What I should also have known was that I did not have to demean myself by competing for him as if I were his mistress, utterly dependent on retaining his favors. I was his wife, the mother of his children and the mistress of his house, and nothing could ever change that.

At breakfast when we had a moment of privacy I said to him carefully, "If you don't wish to come to my room in future I quite understand. I apologize for the scene in the carriage yesterday. I didn't mean to place you under any kind of obligation in regard to our affairs as husband and wife."

He looked at me for a long moment. At last all he said was a curt "It's your decision."

"I merely thought it would be easier for both of us if—"

"Quite." But he wasn't listening to me. When I was silenced he said with that coarse bluntness I had always detested, "Sleep alone if you wish but don't expect me to follow your example."

I tried not to let him see how much his words hurt. I simply said, "I'm sure you'll be very discreet" and turned my head away sharply so that he should not see my tears.

He did not bother to reply and a second later he had left the room. I was on my own, listening to the sound of his footsteps dying away in the distance until at last all sound faded into nothingness and there was nothing else to listen to except the silence.

My chair toppled over as I sprang to my feet. I went after him, but he was gone by the time I reached the hall and when I stopped the silence wrapped itself around me in thick suffocating folds. It was hard to breathe. I glanced around wildly, ready to clutch at any small trifle that would help me maintain my self-control, but there was nothing, only the dark shadows of that deserted hall, and at the top of the stairs the cynical smile of the first Penmar as he looked down at me from his enormous frame and brandished his pair of loaded dice.

7

The disparity of age between Henry and Eleanor was perhaps primarily responsible for their growing animosity; at forty-five she had passed the prime of her beauty, while he, eleven years her junior, was still in the full vigour of his lustful passions.

—King John,
W. L. WARREN

Eleanor began to dislike her husband. Presumably he was now more blatantly unfaithful even than before. . . .

—The Devil's Brood,
ALFRED DUGGAN

[1]

Late summer melted into autumn; a mellow light came to the moors, a cooler wind blew in from the sea, and at last to my embarrassment and regret it became increasingly evident to me that I was going to have a child.

The news was as unexpected as it was unwelcome. It was the first time Griselda's old-wives' tales had proved of no use to me in preventing such a situation, for all my other pregnancies had either been wanted or at least due to a carelessness that I had not regretted later on. But this time I had not been careless. I had not wanted another child, and when my unfortunate condition was confirmed I was at first so disgusted that I could not even bring myself to tell Mark what had happened. However, there

221

was no need to tell him immediately. Concealment was easy enough for the first few months, for he went away soon after the child was conceived and spent some time at London and at Oxford before returning to Penmarric for Christmas. Even then we saw so little of each other that he did not guess anything was amiss, and in the new year he returned to Oxford so that I was once more on my own.

He had bought a house now, a manor house in a village called Allengate not far from Oxford, where he could entertain his friends in greater style. He said it was more comfortable than living in rooms and that anyway he preferred a house in the country to cramped quarters in a town. He even invited me to join him at Allengate Manor, but of course he knew I would refuse; he knew how I had hated Oxford during my one and only visit there, how uncomfortable I had been among his intellectual friends. My one consolation was that he planned to live at Allengate only during the academic year, and when he left Penmarric in early January he promised to return at Easter to see the children during Marcus' school holidays.

When he did return I was seven months pregnant and no further concealment was possible.

I sensed he was as embarrassed as I was by the situation, although as always he remained courteous and considerate.

"Are you feeling well?" he said. "I hope you're not doing too much and the vicar of St. Just isn't pestering you too hard on parish matters."

"No," I said. "I feel very well." It was true. Despite the fact that I was now almost forty-four and much too old, in my opinion, for having a baby I was in excellent health and Dr. Salter was pleased with me. Even when the time for the birth came there was no trouble. Elizabeth was born in June, a dark, plain, heavy baby with little to commend her save her prompt arrival in the world. My confinement was brief, my recovery rapid. After the christening I left her in Nanny's care with relief, and although I paid my usual visits to the nursery they were paid more out of a sense of duty than any deep emotional feeling toward the new baby. She had inherited Mark's dark slanting eyes, the first of my children to do so, and against my will I was reminded of Mrs. Parrish's elder son, whom I had glimpsed briefly years ago. Poor ugly little Elizabeth! I regret to say I held her looks most unfairly against her, but try as I would I could not overcome my irrational prejudice.

Meanwhile the time had come for Philip to be sent away to school with Marcus, who was by this time thoroughly enjoying his career as a schoolboy. I was pleased that he had settled down so well, yet sad that he should now be so independent and no longer as reliant upon me as he had been before. He was now very much the eldest child and looked down with scorn upon Philip and Hugh, who had not been out and about in the world as he had.

"Are there moors there?" said Philip. "Are there mines? Is it near the sea?"

"Of course not!" Marcus said loftily. "The school is near London and the countryside is full of woods. It's quite different."

"How stupid it sounds," said Philip. "Why should I want to go there?" And to his father he declared boldly, "I shan't go."

"You'll do exactly as you're told," said Mark curtly, "and no nonsense."

"I shall run away," said Philip. "You can't make me stay there."

"If you run away," said Mark, "I'll give you the best hiding you've ever had in your life."

They stared at each other in open hostility, and suddenly I could not help but notice Philip's resemblance to his father, the strong will, the stubbornness, the unyielding determination to get his way. He took no notice of Mark's threat. The first time he ran away he was apprehended within a few miles of the school, but the second time he was missing for three days. I was dreadfully distressed and Mark even came home from Oxford to be with me while we waited for news. Finally Philip, dirty, exhausted and tear-stained, arrived at Penmarric and rushed headlong into my arms.

"We can't send him back!" I said, appalled, to Mark. "We can't! Please, Mark, please let him stay!"

"Certainly not," said Mark. "He has to learn his lesson—he has to learn that he can't always have his own way. I'm not giving in to him, and the sooner he realizes it the better. He's going straight back to school and I'm going with him to deliver him in person."

"But—"

"Blame yourself if the situation is distasteful to you! If you hadn't always spoiled him so atrociously from the cradle onward he wouldn't be so unmanageable now!"

We quarreled bitterly and parted in anger. The next day Mark set off with Philip to the east, and after he had delivered Philip to the school in Surrey he went to Oxfordshire and remained at Allengate until December.

I saw little of him after that. He returned to Penmarric for a week at Christmas and a week at Easter, but in the summer he was asked to give a series of lectures to graduates interested in twelfth-century monasticism and he stayed at Oxford throughout all the summer months. Soon the new academic year had begun and I knew I would not be seeing him again before December. We did correspond irregularly about the children, and he remembered all their birthdays with meticulous care, but gradually as summer passed into autumn I began to feel more isolated than I had ever felt before. My parish activities seemed dreary, the mechanical round of social calls futile. Finally in November I felt so desperately low in spirits that I resolved to make the journey across the Tamar and visit the boys at their school in Surrey. Their half-term weekend was in early November and they were permitted to go out for the weekend of three days with their parents, so I wrote to them both to tell them of my intended visit.

It happened that Marcus had already accepted an invitation to stay with a school friend in London; the school friend's parents had bought theater tickets, and since it would clearly have been awkward for him to cancel the arrangement I did not press him to do so. Instead I met Philip at the school early on the Saturday morning and after we had visited the village tea shop so that he could drink lemonade and eat two currant buns I asked him how he would like to spend his holiday.

I had fully expected him to list a number of things he wanted to do in London, for I had already asked the townhouse staff to prepare themselves for our visit, but to my surprise he had other very different plans.

"I want to go to Brighton," he said firmly. "There are downs there like moors, and there's the sea. One of the masters at school lives there—we can go to London and get a train from Victoria Station, he said. There are lots of schools there and I want to see if I like it. If I do I shall ask Papa to let me change schools. I want to be by the sea."

So the matter was settled. We journeyed down to Brighton easily, much more easily than I would have believed possible, and found ourselves in a pretty seaside town with attractive townhouses and esplanades and a strange foreign-looking palace that had been built years before by the Prince Regent. The driver of our hired cab took us to the largest hotel that was open all the year round, even in November, and the manager offered me a most pleasant suite of rooms overlooking the sea. I accepted the offer at once, and the porters began to bring up the luggage.

"This is delightful!" I exclaimed to Philip, pleased because the town was more congenial than I had anticipated and because the hotel was luxurious and comfortable. "How clever of you to suggest we come here!"

That evening we decided to dine in the hotel dining room rather than in our suite, so I put on my best gown and saw that Philip was clean and tidy before we went downstairs together soon after eight o'clock. The hotel at first seemed as quiet and sedate as when we had arrived, but presently we heard the murmur of voices from the dining room and I supposed that there were more guests staying at the hotel than might have been anticipated at that time of the year.

As we went into the dining room the headwaiter came up to us and bowed. "A table for two, madam?"

"Yes," said Philip before I could speak. "A corner one, please."

"Hush, Philip!" I was amused but a trifle embarrassed by his precocious treatment of the eminent headwaiter, but the latter merely smiled and said kindly, "Of course, sir! This way, please."

I was just stepping forward to follow him when Philip said, surprised, "There's Papa."

There was a void below my heart. I felt my breath catch in my throat. And then I looked across to one of the tables on the other side of the room and saw Mark with Rose Parrish and their two sons.

[2]

She still looked young and pretty. Why not? She was no more than thirty-five. She was dressed in a beautiful, expensively cut gown and there were diamonds at her throat. Age had improved, not detracted, from her looks, and although I had always remembered her as pretty, now her prettiness seemed more mature, more striking. She was happy too. She was laughing, her expression gay and carefree. Beside her were the two boys, the elder good-looking with more than a hint of the familiar Penmar features, the younger as blond and cherubic as a choirboy.

"Mama," Philip was saying urgently. "Mama."

Mark chose that minute to catch sight of us. I saw his expression change.

"Madam?" said the headwaiter, returning to my side when he saw we were no longer following him to the table in the corner.

Mrs. Parrish had seen us. I saw the laughter die from her eyes and the color ebb from her face.

"Mama," said Philip, tugging at my hand. "Why is Papa with those people?"

I said to the headwaiter, "Pray do not trouble to seat us at a table. We shall be dining elsewhere."

The headwaiter looked astonished but I did not care. I turned, walked blindly out of the dining room into the brightly lit hall and began to stumble up the staircase. My breath was coming in short, uneven gasps and I felt ill with shock.

"Mama!" Philip was behind me, treading on my heels. "Mama, what is it? What's the matter?"

I was crying. I tried not to but I was unable to control myself. I fumbled for a handkerchief and tried to hide my tears from him.

"Didn't you want to see Papa? Who's that woman? And who are those boys? Are they at school here?"

Of course, I thought, it would be their half-term too. Mark had come down from Oxford to see them and take them out. He had made no effort to see his legitimate sons, but for Mrs. Parrish's children he was prepared to travel from Oxford to Brighton.

"Mama, please!" He was frantic. "Please talk to me! Who are those people? Why is Papa here?"

"I . . . will explain . . ." We reached the suite. I fumbled in my handbag for the key to the door and felt the tears wet on my cheek.

"You're crying," said Philip.

"No." I found the key, fitted it in the lock.

"He's made you unhappy." He turned and began to walk off down the corridor back to the stairs. "I'll go and talk to him."

"No, Philip!" I cried. "No, no! Come here at once. Don't you dare go downstairs!"

He hesitated. I had never spoken to him so harshly before.

"Please," I said. "Come here, Philip, and don't be disobedient. Please."

He came without a word. We went into the suite and I closed the door. The maid had already been in to light the gas and the room was well lit and warm. After a moment I sat down by the fire and stared into the flames in an attempt to compose myself.

"Tell me," said Philip, kneeling on the floor and pressing close to me to secure my attention. "Tell me. I want to know. Please, Mama. Don't cry."

"I'm not crying, Philip." I was more controlled now. My voice was stiff and level. I tried to swallow but my throat still ached too much. After a while I said, "The woman is called Mrs. Parrish. She's a widow, an acquaintance of Papa's. The boys are her sons."

"Is it their half-term? Are they at school here? Why did Papa come to see them and not Marcus and me?"

"I . . . don't know . . . I suppose there was some reason—"

"That's not fair," said Philip. He scrambled to his feet. "May I go down and speak to him?"

"No—please, darling, please. Stay with me."

There was a knock at the door.

I started violently. I rose at once to my feet but before I could speak Philip said, "That'll be Papa. Perhaps he's come to apologize." He crossed the room, wrenched the handle and pulled open the door.

Mark stood on the threshold. He was alone, and suddenly I felt so faint that I had to sit down again.

"Hullo, Philip," he said. "What a surprise to see you here! Where is Mama?"

Philip said nothing but merely stared at him stonily. Mark took no notice. He came into the room and when he saw me he held out his hands.

I looked away.

At last he said, "Why did you bring Philip to Brighton?"

"I . . . it was merely . . ." My voice was unsteady. I had to stop.

"It was my idea," said Philip from beside me. "I had heard there were schools in Brighton and I wanted to see what sort of

227

place it was. I was going to ask you if I could go to school by the sea. It's got nothing to do with Mama. It's not her fault."

"No one," said Mark, "is implying that anything is Mama's fault."

There was a silence. Then: "Why are you here?" said Philip with the bold insolence that Mark could not tolerate. "Are those boys having half-term? Why did you see them and not Marcus and me?"

"Perhaps because they have better manners." He turned to me. "What have you told him?"

"Nothing. Only her name."

"I must talk to you alone," he said abruptly. "My suite is down the corridor. I suggest you come there with me for a few minutes."

"No," I said strongly, "I'm not going into any suite of rooms you share with that woman."

"Please, Janna!" He was dark with anger. "Not before the child."

"I don't care," I said. "I don't care. I've never been so humiliated in all my life as when I walked into the dining room and saw you sitting there with her—with your sons."

"They're not his," said Philip. "They're hers. You told me—"

"Listen, Janna—"

"No, I won't! Where does she live now? Is it in London? Ah no, of course she must be at Oxford—at your new house at Allengate! How stupid of me not to have guessed before! I suppose she's masquerading as your housekeeper."

"I refuse to discuss this in front of the child. He shouldn't be present."

"How dare you dictate to me what should be done with my children! What right have you to interfere with them when you do nothing but ignore them for the best part of the year? How am I to explain to Marcus and Philip why you preferred to see William and his brother at half-term? How dare you pay such attention to your bastards!"

His hands were on my shoulders. He was shaking me. "For Christ's sake!" He was so furiously angry that he did not even check the profanity. "Have you no sense, no discretion, no—"

"Stop it!" shouted Philip. He drove his small fist into his father's thigh and tried to tear Mark away from me. "Stop it, stop it, stop it!"

"You see how you're upsetting the child?" He took Philip by the scruff of the neck and disengaged himself from the child's grasp but Philip flew straight back into the attack.

"No, Philip." I caught his hand and pulled him to my side. "It's all right, darling, it's all right." I stooped and hugged him tightly. He looked at me, his blue eyes clear, his face white and strained, and then suddenly his mouth trembled and he began to cry. I pressed him to me and looked up at Mark with blazing eyes.

"This is your fault."

"I beg your pardon, but it was not I who chose to make such a disgraceful scene before the child! I suggest you come to my suite at once and we can discuss the matter alone and in privacy."

"I have nothing to say to you."

"Don't be so absurd! There's much to discuss, even if it's merely the question of whether we should seek a divorce."

The shock was so harsh that for a moment I could not breathe. I managed to stand up. "Divorce?" I repeated blankly. "Divorce? But that's impossible. It's out of the question. It's unthinkable."

"You've never considered it? I thought perhaps since you refused to live with me—"

"I've been waiting month after month for you at Penmarric!"

"You could have been with me at Oxford—I gave you the chance, but you refused. I asked you to live at Allengate."

"Yes—with Mrs. Parrish as housekeeper!"

He went white. "I refuse to discuss this with you in front of Philip."

"Very well," I said, anger making my voice sound cold and hard. "We'll go to your suite." I turned to Philip. "Darling, I won't be long, only a little while, but there's something I must talk about with Papa. There's no need for you to worry or be upset. When I come back we'll have dinner here together in our rooms. Will you be all right here by yourself?"

"Of course." But his voice was faint, his mouth stiff and white-lipped.

"If you want us, Philip," said Mark, not unkindly, "my rooms are at the very end of this corridor. The number on the door is seven."

Philip said nothing but turned away and went over to the window to watch the sea.

We left him, walked in silence down the corridor and finally entered a larger, even more luxurious suite. At first I thought the sitting room seemed bare of all trace of personal occupancy, but then I noticed a schoolboy's cap tossed casually on the chaise longue. When I was closer I saw the name tape sewn in the lining, the name of the younger boy who had been born so soon after Philip, and because the name seemed in some mysterious way to be an omen to me, a glimpse of dark days to come, I picked up the cap and traced the letters on the tape with my fingers.

His name was Adrian, a name I had not heard before. Adrian Parrish.

Mark closed the door. Suddenly there seemed nothing to say, nothing that could ever be said between us. The pause in the quarrel had destroyed it; there seemed to be nothing remaining of my initial anger; I could not even recall the shock I had experienced on hearing the word "divorce." I was only conscious now of bewilderment that I should still, even after all these months of estrangement, be so overwhelmingly jealous and resentful. I had accepted the fact that he must have other women; why could I not accept Rose Parrish? There seemed no logical reason, only a painful awareness that Rose Parrish symbolized so much more than the fact that my marriage had failed. To me she was the symbol of a youth I would not know again, of a class I had never entered, of a world in which I had never been at ease. She was the personification of all my unhappiness, and it was as if in looking at her sweet gay face I had gazed on everything I had ever wanted but never quite managed to attain.

"Well, I must say," said Mark's cold voice from a long way away, "that was a particularly distasteful scene to enact before our son."

I sat down in an uncomfortable high-backed chair and tried to think what I should do, but my mind was too confused and I could not even manage to reply.

"It's because I think it of vital importance that such scenes should be avoided in the future that I suggest we separate permanently with a view to seeking a divorce when it becomes possible for us to do so. I have no grounds for divorcing you, as I'm sure you realize, but if I leave you now and insist on remaining at Allengate without your consent you will eventually be able to seek a divorce on the grounds of adultery coupled with desertion. I believe the period of desertion has to be at least two years, so we would have to wait before commencing proceedings, but unfortunately since you cannot divorce me for adultery alone there's no other alternative open to us. Now, I know divorce will mean a considerable amount of scandal and I'm sure a great many people will disapprove and be shocked, but I dare say most of the criticism will fall upon me and frankly I'm willing to endure a great deal to terminate this situation in the most expedient way available. You know and I know that our marriage is irrevocably finished. My one concern now is that we act in a way most beneficial to the children, and in my opinion it would be much better for them in the long run if our marriage was officially ended in the divorce court."

I heard myself say woodenly, "I fail to see how the shame and disgrace of a divorce would benefit them in any way at all."

"And I fail to see how two hostile parents, hopelessly at odds with each other, would be of any benefit to them whatsoever! Come, Janna, be reasonable. You're still thinking of yourself, you see—you're still not considering the children! Now if we were to handle this in a discreet, sensible way—"

"You're not thinking of the children either," I said. "It's not because of them that you want a divorce. You want a divorce for one reason and one reason only. You want to marry Mrs. Parrish."

For a moment he hesitated. Then: "I don't deny," he said slowly, "that I hope to remarry eventually, but—"

"Well, you'll never remarry," I said, "because I'll never divorce you. Never as long as I live." Tears blurred my eyes and my thoughts blurred too until my mind was a confused jumble of stark, painful images. In a flash I pictured the servants' gossiping, the neighbors' insincere condolences, the tittle-tattle, the smirks and the backchat. I saw myself in the past, my struggles to improve myself, my enormous efforts to live the life that was required of me, the strain, the fears, the agonies, the self-consciousness, the loneliness and the misery. A divorce would mean that it had all been for nothing. My one consolation had always been that I was his wife and that no one, not even Mrs. Parrish, could take that title from me. How could I possibly consent to a divorce? It would make a mockery of all my past effort and endurance, and besides . . . I could not bear to lose him to Mrs. Parrish. "I won't divorce you," I said fiercely, and the very word "divorce" rang through the air in a terrible challenge to my security. "I won't."

I could see he was very angry but somehow he managed to hold on to his temper. "Please," he said in a level voice. "Please try and be reasonable, Janna. I know it's humiliating for us both to have to admit to the world that our marriage is a failure, but surely isn't it futile and pointless to go on as we are at present? And what's more, it's very bad for the children. Come, even you must see that! Now, if we can be unselfish and put the children first I'm sure we can work out a separation which would be infinitely better for the children and yet not too distasteful to us both—"

"I won't agree to a separation," I said, "and I won't agree to a divorce. If you decide to leave me, that's your decision, but please don't expect me to condone it."

"If you're worrying about the money, I would naturally make you a generous financial settlement and you could continue to live at Penmarric—"

"No," I said.

He stared at me. "What do you mean?"

"If you leave me, I'm not living at that place any more."

"But—"

"I hate it," I said, the words tumbling from my lips, "I hate Penmarric, I hate it. I hate holding those horrible dinner parties, paying and receiving those dreadful calls. I hate all those enormous cold rooms and never being able to do anything without some servant watching. I've hated all those months I've spent there alone without you. If you leave me, I won't stay at Penmarric. I'll go home. I'll go and live at Roslyn Farm. I never did like Penmarric anyway, not even in the beginning. I was always homesick for the farm and for Zillan."

He looked at me as if I were mad. "But, my dear Janna . . ." He was at a loss for words. "My God, you can't go back and live on a farm like some common working-class woman! You can't possibly do such a thing!"

"I want to go home," I said. "That's all I want. I just want to go home. I don't want to live at Penmarric any more if you leave me."

"Look, Janna, you must try and pull yourself together and be sensible about this. You've been mistress of Penmarric for eleven years. All your surviving children were born there. You cannot

—and I mean *cannot*—go back to Roslyn Farm now. I don't think you realize what you're saying."

"I can go back. And I will."

"Then how can I possibly let you have custody of the children?"

I did not hear what he said at first. I could not comprehend what he was saying. And then suddenly I saw it all, saw my cherished security crumble into dust, my children growing up strangers, not loving me, not caring, leaving me to face old age alone.

"You wouldn't take them away from me," I said. "You wouldn't be so cruel."

"No indeed—I was going to suggest that they should live with you for most of the year and come to the townhouse in London for a few weeks to see me either during the Christmas or the Easter holidays. But God Almighty, Janna, how can I consent to my children being taken away from Penmarric and brought up on a farm? How can I possibly agree to such a thing?"

"If you try and take them away from me I'll contest you in court. I'll engage lawyers—London lawyers—"

"Do you seriously suppose that any High Court judge is going to make a custody order which allows upper-class children to be brought up on a working-class farm?"

"And do you seriously think," I said, fear making me icily controlled, "that any High Court judge will make a custody order which permits a man's children to be brought up by his mistress instead of by their own natural mother?"

"Yes, I do," said Mark without hesitation. "The test is not whether I'm living discreetly with a woman who's not my wife but which environment is going to be most beneficial to the children. And if you think any judge is going to consider it more beneficial for the children to be brought up as members of the working classes on some remote Cornish farm—"

"Then I'll stay at Penmarric! I'll make the sacrifice!"

"Would you, Janna? Would you? Are you sure you would not promise the court to remain at Penmarric and then spend more and more of your time at Roslyn Farm? On second thoughts, I believe that even if you stayed on at Penmarric I should nonetheless ask the court to take the children away from you. I don't think I could trust you to bring them up decently without poisoning their minds against me, or giving them a false picture of why our marriage came to an end."

"In other words, you've decided to spite me by not letting me have the children!"

"Haven't you just done your best to spite me by refusing me a divorce?"

"You have no right to demand a divorce! And I have every right to demand my children!"

"Try convincing a High Court judge of that! I think you would have a most unpleasant surprise, particularly when I tell him—"

"I'll convince him! But if you think I'm going to divorce you—"

"If you consent to a divorce I'll be lenient about the custody of the children."

"Even if I live at Roslyn Farm?"

"I can't answer for what the judge will decide if you leave Penmarric."

"I see! So in other words you hoped to lure me into seeking a divorce by promising to let me have the children and then once you obtained the divorce you'd turn around and insist that I was deprived of the children anyway! Well, I'll never divorce you and I'll never give up the children—and don't think either that you can trick me into giving them up!"

"You're not keeping those boys."

"Nobody," I said, trembling, "nobody on this earth is going to take my sons away from me. If you try to separate me from Philip—"

"And Philip is the one child who must at all costs be separated from you! That at least is plain to see! Look here, Janna, I'll not stand by and see that boy ruined by you—"

"How can I ruin him! I love him! I love all my children, all of them—I love you, but you're so infatuated with that shamelessly immoral woman—"

He hit me. He gave me a sharp stinging slap across the cheek with the palm of his hand. As I gasped and stepped back, speechless with fury, I saw his narrow black eyes blaze with rage.

"You bitch," he said. He did not shout. His voice was low and filled with the most bitter contempt. "Oh my God, you bitch. And you hypocrite. You damned hypocrite."

It was as if he had struck me again. I stepped back another pace, flinching from his words, and found myself at last with my back to the wall. "Mark," I said suddenly. "Mark, don't."

"Oh yes!" he said. "Oh yes, yes, yes! I'm going to tell you just what I think of you! I'm going to make you see yourself for the first time in your life! You're going to take a long, long look at yourself, my dear, and this time you're not going to pull down the veil of hypocrisy to hide what you don't wish to see."

"Mark, please—"

"All this talk of love! All these melodramatic protestations that you love me, love your children! My God, you don't even know the meaning of the word! You don't love me—you never loved me! All you loved was the money I could offer you, the security, the comfort and the luxury and—as a specially pleasant bonus—the sexual gratification in the bedroom. And don't think you can make me believe you truly love the children either! You simply love the security they represent and the idea that there are six more people in the world to adore you and tell you you're wonderful! Why, you don't even really love Philip—you're only so obsessed by him because he looks like a little masculine reflection of you, and let's be honest, Janna, let's not pretend any more, let's admit the truth to ourselves without hypocrisy, there's only one person on this earth whom you do love and that one person is yourself! Why else do you put yourself first the whole damned time? Why else is everything always subjugated to what *you* want and what *you* desire? You're a selfish, vain, egocentric woman—cold, empty and emotionally sterile."

I began to blunder my way toward the door. My voice said as if from a long way away, "I'll not hear any more of this."

"Oh yes, you will, my dear," he said. "Oh yes, you will." And before I could stop him he had darted in front of me, locked the door and pocketed the key.

"Let me out," I said unsteadily. "Let me out at once."

"No," he said, "no, I won't. We haven't resolved the future yet, if you remember. We haven't resolved the future of our children. All we've resolved is a few home truths about your character, which you're trying to pretend you haven't heard, but now you *are* going to hear me, my dear, because I'm not going to talk over your head any longer in such an incomprehensible manner. I'm going to talk to you in your own language

235

for the simple reason that that's the only language you'll ever understand."

He stopped. I looked at him. I was trembling from head to toe, my head ached and my mouth was dry. I could not speak.

He took out a gold sovereign. And another. And he laid them on the small table which stood beside us by the door.

"There'll be four hundred and ninety-eight more of those a year for the rest of your life," he said, "if you let me have the children without any unnecessary dramatic scenes. If you can manage to conduct yourself with the minimum of good taste, I'll even let you come to visit the children at Oxford whenever you wish and allow them to visit you at the farm if I bring them to Penmarric. The money will, of course, be in addition to the maintenance allowance which I shall be legally bound to pay you."

I said at once in a shaking voice, "I don't want the money. I want my children. Please. I'll stay at Penmarric—I'll do anything you like, but—"

"Then give me a divorce."

But I knew that once he had the divorce he would make renewed efforts to deprive me of the children. I knew now that once he had the upper hand he would never consent to letting them stay with me. "No," I said, shaking my head blindly. "Not that. Not divorce."

"I'll pay you for it. How much do you want? Tell me how much you want and I'll pay whatever you ask."

"I don't want money!" My eyes smarted with tears. My voice was harsh with pain. "I don't want it!"

"Dear me!" he said with that cutting London drawl I had always hated. "Dear me! Are you trying to tell me in all seriousness that you're not for sale? How times have changed!"

"I've never been for sale! Never!"

He laughed. I flew at him. I was blind with rage and hatred. I tried to hit him but he merely caught my wrist and flung me away from him so that I slipped and fell upon the chaise longue.

"You've never been for sale?" he said, looking down at me. "Well, well, well. How we do deceive ourselves, to be sure." His voice changed. "Old John Henry Roslyn didn't buy you, I suppose, when he offered you money and a roof over your head in return for your favors? Oh no, I quite forgot! He married you! That makes it all respectable, doesn't it, and you don't even have to explain to yourself why you left that bar in St. Ives and went to live with a man you didn't love. Perhaps—knowing your talent for self-deception—you even managed to persuade yourself you did love him! But what about the times before old Roslyn? Was that really the first time you'd ever consented to go to bed with a man for the sake of money and a roof over your head? You always told me you were a virgin before Roslyn married you, but you weren't a virgin, were you, my dear? There'd been other men before him! A woman with a face and figure like yours doesn't stay chaste till she's twenty-seven. No, there were other men who paid for your services and the only reason why Roslyn was any different from the others was because he happened by chance to be a decent man and he offered to marry you. And later—why, your actions speak for themselves. When Roslyn died and left you short of money, what did you do to get the money you needed? No, don't try to tell me you would have gone to bed with my father for sheer romantic love alone! He kept you at that farm and you went to bed with him so that you could stay on at that house! And when he died so inconveniently, what did you do next? Why, I only had to put five sovereigns on the table and you took me straight upstairs to your room. You sold yourself to me for five pounds, my dear, and don't ever fool yourself into believing you did it for love! But then the gods favored you, didn't they, because I was so childishly infatuated with your very beautiful and very desirable body that my common sense deserted me and I decided I could not rest until I paraded you to the world as my wife. What good fortune! What incredible luck! Here was a rich young man begging to marry you! Of course, he was rather young and undeniably plain, but with a little mental effort you were ready enough to believe yourself in love with him. It was all so easy, wasn't it? A few nights here, a few nights there, and lo and behold! You're a lady living in a mansion and mingling with the aristocracy! Never mind how you got there—no need to think about that now—push it to the back of your mind. You're a lady now—or so you think, but you see, that was the whole tragedy, wasn't it, my dear, you never were a lady and you never could be. You're a whore. You always were and you always will be. Some women never change."

He stopped speaking. Nothing happened. After a long moment I thought: I must go. I must leave. I can't stay here. But it was strangely difficult to move. Presently I managed to stand up. I could not look at him but I knew he was still standing watching me. I could feel his anger and hatred, and suddenly I was conscious of nothing save the most dreadful foreboding and the desire to escape from that room.

I stumbled to the door, rattled the handle, but it was locked. I spun around. "Let me out!" I cried. "Let me out of here! Let me out!" Claustrophobia was overwhelming. As I turned to rattle the door again, I knew with that intuitive instinct that women possess that something even more appalling than the preceding scene was about to take place between us. "Let me go!"

I heard him drawl casually, "Let you go? Certainly—if you'll first let *me* go and agree to a divorce."

I whirled around to face him and found with a shock that he was standing right behind me. My nerve snapped. I lost control of myself. "You'll never make me agree to a divorce!" I shouted at him, and my voice grated Cornish in my ears. "We're husband and wife and we'll always be husband and wife and you'll never make me take one single step that'll make things otherwise —you'll never make me do one single thing I don't truly want to do!"

There was a split second of utter silence. I sensed a void in the room, then an overpowering blast of a primitive savage emotion.

"No?" he said very politely. "We'll see about that." And then the politeness was discarded like a mask and I saw what he wanted in revenge.

I stepped backward. "Don't touch me."

"Why not?" He moved forward. "You're my wife, aren't you? Isn't that what you've been trying to tell me? That you're my wife and I'm your husband?"

"Keep away from me!"

"Hardly the right response for a devoted wife to make!"

"If you dare lay one finger on me—"

"I'm laying every finger I've got on you, you bitch, to prove to you what a bloody hypocrite you are!"

"Get away from me—I hate you!"

"And by God I hate you too," he said between his teeth and slammed me back against the wall.

I screamed and screamed but the door was shut, the windows were closed and the walls were thick. No one heard. No one came. And when at last he let me go and we could look at each other in hatred the silence closed in upon us and shrouded the memory of our dead love like a pall. As soon as I was fit to leave I asked him again for the key of the door and he gave it to me without speaking.

I left him. I left the room. I left Penmarric and aristocratic society and all the luxury and grandeur which money could buy. And as I stumbled sobbing down the corridor and out of his life all I could think of was not of the future, not of Philip, not even of the terrible humiliation I had just endured, but of Mark, of my husband, of the man I had once loved more than I would have believed it possible to love anyone. I thought numbly: I did love him, I did—oh God, tell me that I loved him once! But God was silent, God did not speak, and all that was left was the truth, which was much too terrible to face and Mark's own bitter voice saying politely, "You're a whore. You always were and you always will be. Some women never change."

III

ADRIAN: 1904-1914

Good and Evil

> *He was distinguished from his legitimate half-brothers by his consistent attachment and fidelity to his father. . . . His history is chiefly one of quarrels with his half-brothers.*
> —"Geoffrey of York,"
> ENCYCLOPAEDIA BRITANNICA

> *Geoffrey, Henry's natural son, though quarrelsome and high-spirited had always been faithful and earned the praise of his father who [said]: "You alone have proved yourself my lawful and true son, my other sons are really the bastards."*
> —Oxford History of England:
> From Domesday Book to Magna Carta,
> A. L. POOLE

> *That Henry had been sincerely in love with [Rosamund Clifford] was made clear by what he did for her and her two sons . . . the second, Geoffrey, seems to have been a great favourite with the king.*
> —The Conquering Family,
> THOMAS COSTAIN

1

*Giraldus mentions that the King, who had been a
secret adulterer, began openly to live with Rosamund
Clifford.*

> —The Oxford History of England:
> From Domesday Book to Magna Carta,
> A. L. POOLE

*As royal mistresses go, she was not expensive, and did
not aspire to influence policy. In fact she was popular
with certain ladies of good birth and impeccable
morals.*

> —The Devil's Brood,
> ALFRED DUGGAN

[1]

I disliked my half-brother Philip Castallack from the first moment that I saw him. I was eight years old at the time, almost nine;
my birthday was on December the eighteenth and this made me
exactly six months younger than Philip, whose birthday was on
the eighteenth of June. I first saw him at Brighton.

I never cared for Brighton after that.

Even in later life I never returned to that elegant and popular
seaside resort. Even now whenever I hear someone mention the
word "Brighton" I think not of the Regency terraces, the shingly
beach or the docile sea but of Philip with his tough, hostile mouth
and frosty eyes and later, much later, of my father lighting a
cigar and saying so carefully in such a meticulously casual tone

of voice, "I'm afraid I have something to say which should have been said a very long time ago."

That was the first time I realized that good people may do bad deeds. At least, that was how I phrased it in my child's vocabulary. "But, Papa," I said, "if you and Mama are good, how could you ever do something that was bad?"

"Nothing is black and white in this world, Adrian" was all he could say in reply. "One cannot divide people into two categories and neatly label one 'good' and the other 'evil.' When you're older you'll understand. Life isn't like that."

But I was young and I did not understand. His words confused me and made me feel uncertain. I liked to label everything. I liked to know where I was. I had a passion to identify objects, people, scenes—anything—and then classify them neatly in my small mind so that life might conform to a sensible, comforting, logical pattern.

"Everything in the world is part of a design," my mother had said to us when we were very young. "Everything has meaning and purpose and a place in the pattern of existence, only it's not always possible to understand what that design is. Only God can understand the design, because He invented it. It's like a magic puzzle. We can't expect to understand everything. Some things are beyond the bounds of human understanding, but if we trust in God and believe in Him, no harm can come to us. We must have faith in our part of the design—in the part He has given us to play, and if it appears dissatisfying to us we must always realize that He knows best and that everything is part of a pattern more perfect than anything any mortal can ever visualize."

The idea of life being a design like a jigsaw puzzle enchanted me. I loved to sift through the jagged pieces and fit them together. For the first eight years of my life the idea that I would ever come across a piece that could not be made to fit into the puzzle would have seemed to me both nonsensical and alarming —if such an idea had ever crossed my mind, but of course it did not. I viewed the world with perfect serenity. Everything was part of a pattern. Everything fitted in. The world became familiar, almost cozy in its warmth and friendliness and security.

And then, out of nowhere, came Brighton.

My short past had not prepared me for it. I was born in Truro, a pleasant Cornish cathedral town, but I did not regard myself as Cornish, for we moved to England when I was two years old and my first memories are not of Cornwall at all but of our house in London at St. John's Wood. It was not a large house and my mother had no servants apart from a gardener and two daily women, one of whom came in to clean and the other to cook. Years later the Castallacks were to say to me incredulously, "But who brought you up?" and I, not knowing what they meant, retorted, "Mama, of course! Isn't that what mothers are for?"

"But you had a nanny," they said, "when you were a baby. You must have had a nanny."

"Mama took care of us from the beginning," I said, fearing that a nanny was something every decent person ought to have had, but William said easily, as if it were the most natural thing in the world, "She wanted to, you see. She wanted to. She chose to do without a nanny."

She did choose to be without resident servants; that was undeniable. At first I wondered vaguely if we were poor and even asked her once if she would like me to go out and sweep chimneys to make some extra money for her, but she only laughed and exclaimed, "Oh, Adrian darling, just like poor little Tom in *The Water Babies!*" and gradually I realized that we would never be poor because Papa was very rich. Mama preferred to live simply. She could have had a bigger house and more servants but she chose to live in that quiet tree-lined road in north London in that peaceful, sunny little house. It was more restful, she said, and much less extravagant.

It was more private too. When Papa came to visit us she simply told the daily servants not to come in for a few days. "It's more fun if we can all be alone together," she said, "and I do so hate to think of servants watching us the whole time. I love to be a little more secluded now and then." It meant that she was much more busy, but she did not mind. She had to do all the cooking and cleaning herself although William and I helped her with the shopping. William used to run many errands for her. He was four and a half years older than I was and was allowed to go out on his own since Mama knew he would not be run down by a cab or lose his way in the bewildering network of London streets.

Papa did not visit us often, at least not when I was very young, and so on each occasion that he did come it was a great event.

Mama would instantly cancel all her social duties, even church charity work; the vicar used to be annoyed when she let him down at short notice, but he merely had to endure his annoyance. When Papa was coming everything else was set on one side. The house was cleaned from top to bottom and the larder was stocked with the most delicious food the shops could offer. Mama moved out of the spare room where she always slept when she was on her own and returned to the main bedroom with the double bed and the thick carpet and the water-color paintings on the walls. Vases were filled with flowers, silver was polished, William and I were dressed in our best clothes and Mama took her finest gowns out of their dust covers in the wardrobe.

I used to become sick with excitement. Every time I heard the clatter of horses' hoofs on the road outside I would dash to the front window and stand on tiptoe to see if the carriage had stopped. William, infuriatingly casual, would be pretending to read the morning paper and pausing occasionally to nibble his fingernails. Mama would wander from room to room, her eyes bright, a spot of color on each cheek, her fingers clasped together as if she could not bear the agony of waiting one moment longer.

Finally, after a seemingly infinite space of time, a hansom cab would draw up at the gate and Papa, carrying his luggage himself, would walk up the garden path to the front door.

Papa was, as Mama used to say, a very foreign-looking gentleman. He did not look like an Englishman. "Which is hardly surprising," he used to say, "since I was born and bred in Cornwall." He was dark, with thick hair as black as jet, an oddly pallid skin and arresting dark eyes which had a peculiarly magnetic quality. We could not take our eyes off him whenever he opened his mouth to speak, but whether that was because we all unashamedly idolized him or because of any hypnotic powers he might have possessed, it would be difficult to say. He was only an inch or two taller than Mama and a trifle stout. "Well-built," said Mama. "What a fine figure he has!" She never, of course, forgot either of us once during his visits, but it was always unquestioned that Papa came first. Our duty was not to claim her attention at such times but simply to help her make his visit as splendid as possible.

I used to talk about history with him. Papa was a historian—"A very brilliant scholar," said Mama—and led such a busy life between his researches at Oxford and his estate in Cornwall that he did not have time to visit us for long.

"Indeed," said Mama, "he's so busy that we must consider ourselves very, very fortunate that we see him at all." She would often say that when his visit had ended and he had gone away. The flowers would droop in their vases, and she would droop a little too, becoming quieter, sighing now and then, putting away her fine gowns and taking out her well-worn day dresses once more. The servants would come back; life would go on; everything would be as it was before.

She would write to him, of course. I was five years old when I was able to read the name on the envelope and learned that Papa's surname was different from ours. I said to William, "Why isn't Papa called Parrish too?"

"Because he's not," said William tranquilly.

"Then why aren't we called Castallack?"

"Because we're not."

"Why?"

"Oh, honestly, Adrian, all you ever do is ask why this, why that, why the other! You're the nosiest little nuisance I ever met. We're not called Castallack because Mama *chose* not to be called by that name. She told me all about it ages ago. She promised her father she would always call herself by his name, which was Parrish, and that her children would be called Parrish too. He had no son and it was his dying wish that the name Parrish shouldn't be wiped from the face of the earth."

"I see," I said, satisfied, recalling countless dying wishes in fairy tales and picturing Grandfather Parrish on his regal deathbed with his beautiful daughter kneeling heart-broken beside him. In fairy tales she would be the good princess and after the death of the king her wicked stepmother would shut her up in a tower until her prince came to set her free.

It was hard to know which I enjoyed most—fairy tales, legends or historical myths. "When I'm grown up," I said to Papa one day, "I shall go on a crusade like Richard Coeur de Lion and wear a white cross on my chest and rescue damsels in distress—"

"That was St. George," said William loftily, "and anyway, silly, there aren't any more crusades."

"Then I shall make one," I said firmly. "I shall go out into the world and fight Evil."

"To fight *is* evil," said Papa, but he was smiling at me and holding my hand in his, and suddenly I was so pleased merely to be walking down a street with him that it did not matter that his words made no sense to me. I could feel my heart almost burst with love for him because he was so good and wise and kind.

"Why doesn't Papa live with us always?" I said to Mama longingly. "Why doesn't he stop being busy and come to live with us in St. John's Wood?"

"He does live with us when he can," said Mama reasonably, "but he has great committments at his estate in Cornwall and of course he has work to do at Oxford. We mustn't expect him to come more often."

"Dear Jesus Christ," I prayed idly, watching the sunlight stream through the church's stained-glass windows as the vicar reached the most boring part of his sermon. "Please make Papa come to see us more often. Please make him come to live with us. I'll be good forever and ever. Thank you. Amen."

Since I saw no reason why such a natural and reasonable request could be refused I was not in the least surprised when my prayer was promptly answered. Papa had decided to spend most of the year in Oxfordshire so that he could conduct his historical research and writing within easy reach of the library there, and when he bought an old manor house in the village of Allengate ten miles from Oxford we all left St. John's Wood to be with him. He still had to spend Christmas and Easter at his distant Cornish estate which had consumed so much of his time in the past, but apart from these two holidays and a week or two during the summer months he promised he would be living with us all the year round.

At first the prospect seemed too splendid to be true. I spent some hours thinking nervously that the unknown Allengate Manor might be a horrible place, but I need not have worried. The manor was the most beautiful house I had ever seen, and so enormous after our little house in St. John's Wood that we could hardly believe our eyes when we first saw it. There were acres of grounds, including lawns, flowerbeds, a vegetable patch, an orchard and even a sunken rose garden. Beyond the lawns a stream ran a tumbling course through tall beech woods and was dammed at one point to form a small pool. Near the house were the stables, and next to the stables was yet another outbuilding, this one housing the carriage and the ponytrap. We had to accustom ourselves to the presence of grooms and gardeners and, inside the house, a butler, a parlor maid, a scullery maid, a 'tween maid and a cook.

"Papa must be very rich," said William, amazed, to Mama. "How can he afford all this?"

"Darling, Papa is a gentleman of considerable means and he is very used to living in this way. Such gentlemen do not have to worry about money. Now, we must try and adjust ourselves as smoothly as possible to his way of life because he was always able to adjust himself so easily to ours when he visited St. John's Wood."

William said slowly, "Papa is really much grander than us, then."

"Yes, darling, much. As you know, my poor papa was only a country doctor and he and I had a very modest house in Devon with only a cook and a gardener to help us. Your papa has always been accustomed to large houses and grand surroundings and innumerable servants. He is of the aristocracy even though he has no title, but I am simply from the middle classes. But it doesn't matter. You needn't be one jot ashamed that so far you've only had a modest middle-class upbringing. There's nothing shameful about that at all. The middle classes are the backbone of England and Papa is as proud of that fact as I am. Heavens, we can't all be born with silver spoons in our mouths! The most important thing is not that you should be aristocrats but that you should be gentlemen. A true gentleman may go anywhere in the world and be both accepted and respected by all levels of society."

It did not take us long to settle down at Allengate, and soon I had decided that I liked it much better than St. John's Wood. The only aspect of life at Allengate that I did not like was the pretend game. We had never had to play it at St. John's Wood, for Mama had never invited guests to the house while Papa was there, but at Allengate she would assist Papa in giving dinner parties for his friends and when the friends came and we were presented to them we had to pretend that we were not Papa's sons but his wards and that our real father had died some years before.

I can still remember Papa telling us that we had to play the pretend game. It was the night before we moved to Allengate and he was alone with us while Mama was in the kitchen.

"You see," he said in an odd voice, "if people realized that you were my sons yet did not have my name they would think all kinds of bad things about Mama. So in order to protect Mama—"

"But why would people think bad things about her?" I said, mystified.

"You're much too young to understand," said William grandly, and added to Papa, "Yes, I can see why we must pretend for Mama's sake, but why can't we simply change our name from Parrish to Castallack? Wouldn't that be much simpler?"

"I'm afraid," said Papa, "that's not possible, William. You see—"

"Of course it's not!" I was scandalized. "Remember the promise Mama made to Grandfather Parrish, William!' I turned to Papa again. "Papa, I still don't see why anyone should say nasty things about Mama."

Papa tried to speak but took a mouthful of brandy instead. His cigar had gone out. As he laid its mangled body down upon the plate I saw to my amazement that his fingers were trembling.

"Adrian, you're such a baby," said William, exasperated. "I know you can't help it, but you are. People might think he and Mama weren't married if they misunderstood the situation and that would be very horrible for Mama, so—"

"I don't understand." My filing and classification system had been put out of joint. "How can there ever be any question of Mama and Papa not being married? How can people have babies if they're not married to each other?"

"Oh, honestly!" said William, scarlet with embarrassment. He looked at Papa under his lashes and twisted uncomfortably in his seat. "They just can, that's all. Marriage is just the blessing of the church and children don't have anything to do with it, except that marriage is a holy thing and children are supposed to be the result of a holy thing. That's why no one wants to have children without a marriage because if they did it wouldn't be holy."

"Children after marriage are good, you mean," I said, classifying again after my uncomfortable moment of confusion. "And children before or without marriage are bad and unholy. I see." I turned to Papa again. "You mean people might make a mistake and think we were all wicked and sinful if we didn't play the pretend game."

"Children are innocent victims," said Papa, not looking at us.

His hands were dissecting the cigar and tearing it to pieces. "No one would think badly of either of you. But they would indeed think Mama was sinful and wicked."

"How cruel!" I said angrily. "Mama's the best person in all the world! In that case, let's play the pretend game and then no one will ever have the chance to think such horrible things."

So we played the pretend game, but I hated to listen to Papa saying, "These are my two wards, William and Adrian Parrish," and although she never said one word to us about the situation I knew that Mama hated it too. The guests were always kind and interested and usually asked us one or two questions but sometimes they looked at one another and I wondered if they had seen through our pretense. Everyone always looked very hard at William. I knew why. William had inherited Papa's unusual eyes although otherwise he looked much like Mama.

I looked like nobody. My eyes were bluer than Mama's and a different shape. My hair was fair but darker than Mama's and not so fine and silky. I did not resemble Mama at all in features, but neither did I resemble Papa except in one small respect. My hands were like his. They were squarish hands with strong fingers and crooked thumbs, odd hands, rather ugly.

Time passed and at last came the summer of 1904 when Mama and I had to travel to London together to buy my uniform and all the quantity of shoes and other garments I needed to begin life at boarding school. William had already been going to preparatory school at Rottingdean near Brighton for two years and was by this time well accustomed to leaving home for long periods at a time, but as summer drew toward autumn I became more and more nervous at the prospect of going away and secretly longed to remain at Allengate and continue to do my lessons with the vicar every morning.

Mama seemed nervous too when she and Papa came to the station to see us depart, and for a panic-stricken moment I thought she did not want me to go any more than I wanted to leave. But then she smiled and I decided she was not nervous at all, only excited and happy that I should be on the brink of a new adventure.

"Just think how nice it will be for you to have William there," she said, "and what fun it'll be for you to mix with boys of your own age again after all those solitary lessons with the vicar! Of course I shall miss you very, very much—" she stooped to kiss me—" but I shall come down to the school at half-term as usual, and I shall mark each day on the calendar to make the time pass more quickly."

The thought of seeing her at half-term cheered me up enormously. I even managed to say in an interested voice, "When is half-term? Will we have long to wait?"

"I believe it's in early November," said Mama, and Papa added at once, "Mama and I will both come down and we can all spend the weekend together at Brighton."

[2]

Brighton.

I liked it at first. I was enjoying my life at school after a shaky start and the usual wretched first nights which every small new boy must expect, but even though I was enjoying myself it was still pleasant to escape from Rottingdean for three days and drive into Brighton with Papa and Mama.

"Brighton is a fascinating town," said Papa. "There's much to see."

Grand, elegant Brighton with its splendid esplanade, its Regency houses, its fantasy of a palace, the antique shops of "The Lanes," the opulent hotels which faced the sea! We admired it all, from the white cliffs out toward Rottingdean to the smooth green Downs that rose behind the town toward the Devil's Dyke. Beautiful, spacious Brighton! How fortunate we were, we thought, to be at school near such a colorful and individual seaside town.

Papa took a suite in the largest, grandest hotel, and on Saturday night we all went down to the hotel dining room for dinner.

We ate one course. It was onion soup, very delicious. We had ordered the next courses and were waiting for our fish.

"Papa," I said, "was George the Fourth a good king or a bad king?"

He smiled. "Adrian, one of these days you'll learn that nothing in this world is black and white. You cannot divide people neatly into—"

He stopped.

"Yes, but, Papa . . ." I began and then I stopped too.

Mama was deathly white. They were both staring past me over my shoulder. I swiveled around, very frightened, to see what had given them such an appalling shock, but there was no one there except a woman with a boy of about my age.

Then I noticed that the woman was staring at Mama and Papa with an equally appalled expression. As I watched I saw the boy tug at her sleeve and speak to her before turning to look at us again. For a split second his eyes met mine. His were frosty, hostile and bright with an emotion that might have been either anger or fear or simply indignation. He had fair hair, fairer even than Mama's, and a powerful build, which made me identify him automatically with the current school bully. As I stared at him, fascinated, the woman backed away from us. She was a tall woman, perhaps a little older than Mama, and she wore a flashy gown—or at least it probably seemed flashy to me because Mama tended to dress simply in quiet pastel colors. She had pale gold hair, very elaborately dressed, and the frosty eyes I had first noticed when I had seen the boy.

The headwaiter was beginning to flutter around her like a moth infatuated with a dazzlingly brilliant flame.

"Who is it?" said my voice much too loudly. "Who is she?"

Nobody answered. The woman turned and went rapidly out of the room while the boy ran after her, trying to catch her sleeve as if he too were seeking an explanation.

Papa stood up.

We all looked at him immediately but he did not speak. He did not even see us. He was walking away from our table as if he were indeed under one of the spells I had encountered so often in my favorite fairy tales. A voice from my memory began to recite silently: And the evil enchantress cast a spell over the good prince and imprisoned him in her bower for a thousand years . . .

"Mark," said Mama. "Mark."

To my horror I saw that she was dreadfully distressed. I turned away, very frightened now, and looked at William, but he looked as frightened as I was.

"Papa!" I cried, standing up and running after him. "Papa, don't go! Don't leave us!"

He stopped, looked down at me. After a moment he looked back over his shoulder at Mama.

He came back to our table.

"Rose," he said. "You understand. I shall have to speak to her. We can leave here tonight."

Mama nodded. It was as if she could not speak.

"I shan't be long. Stay here with the boys and try and finish your dinner."

She nodded again and picked up her fish knife as if the fish were already in front of her. "Yes, Mark. Of course."

He was gone. We were alone. Mama was trying not to cry. I remember thinking, my fear mingling with my anger: He's made her unhappy. He shouldn't have done that.

The waiter arrived with our fish. We sat looking at it for a moment.

"Please eat," said Mama in the rapid voice she kept for partings on station platforms. "Please, darlings. Don't let it get cold."

I looked at William. He pushed away his plate, so I pushed away mine.

"Mama," said Willam. "Please tell us. Who—"

"William, I'm sorry but I simply can't. I know it's silly of me but I can't talk about it. You'll have to ask Papa."

I said in a small voice that trembled, "Is it bad?"

"Yes," said Mama, "but don't be frightened. There's no need to be frightened at all. Papa will explain everything when he comes back."

We did not say anything after that. We merely sat and waited for Papa. When the waiter came to remove our plates Mama with our consent canceled the rest of the order.

"We can have a tray sent up to our room," she said, "if we feel hungry later on."

We went on waiting for Papa. We waited a long time.

"Could we go and sit in the drawing room?" I said, shifting uncomfortably on my high-backed chair.

"No," said Mama. "Papa told us to stay here, and we shall stay here till he comes back."

We went on waiting.

At last William said suddenly, "Here he is."

I swiveled around. He came toward us slowly, not hurrying, and I noticed that when he looked across the room he looked not at Mama but at us. His face was very white and he had two red marks across his cheek as if he had scratched himself too violently with his fingernails.

"Well," he said, "that's settled." He added to Mama, not looking at her, "I'm so sorry, Rose. I'm so very sorry."

Mama did not speak.

"It's all right," he said, taking her hand but still not looking at her. "It's all over, Rose. I finished it. It's over once and for all. No more unexorcised ghosts. No more Christmases and Easters in Cornwall. No more living two lives."

"Mark—"

"I finished it, Rose. It's over."

"Mark, please—"

"I finished it, you see. I ended it once and for all."

"Please," whispered Mama, "please look at me."

But he could not. He pulled back his chair and sat down and all he could say was "It's over. I finished it."

Very slowly Mama stood up.

"Don't go, Rose!"

"I want to wait in the drawing room." Her voice was faint. "Please explain to the boys."

"Rose—"

"I'm quite well," she said. "It's nothing. I just don't want to be here when you tell the boys."

"Rose, my darling Rose . . ." He stood up clumsily and looked at her for the first time. I could not see his expression. "It was so squalid," he said, mumbling so that it was difficult to hear him. "So sordid. I cannot begin to explain—"

"I understand."

"You cannot. It's too bestial for you to understand."

"It doesn't matter. Nothing matters as long as you—"

"I do. More than anything else in the world."

They looked at each other. We looked at them but they did not see us. My mother was crying.

"Then everything is all right," she said, turning away so that we should not see her tears, "isn't it?"

"Let me come with you to the drawing room."

"No . . . please, Mark. The boys—"

"Yes," he said. "Yes, of course. The boys."

"I'll wait for you in the drawing room."

"Very well."

We all watched her as she walked away out of the dining room and disappeared from sight. Finally Papa sat down again opposite us, motioned the headwaiter and ordered a glass of brandy. As we watched him in silence he selected a cigar, lit it and then said slowly, "I'm afraid I have something to say which should have been said a very long time ago."

We waited, staring at him. Presently the headwaiter brought

him a glass of brandy and Papa drank half of it as soon as it was put in front of him.

After a long silence he said, "I expect you both wondered who the woman and the little boy were."

We remained silent. "I suppose they were acquaintances of yours," said William uneasily at last.

"Yes," said Papa. "They are." He fidgeted with his cigar and added without expression, "The boy is my son."

We gaped at him.

"Our brother, you mean?" I said, my heart pounding fast.

"Your half-brother. The woman with him was his mother."

"You mean . . ." I was confused. I could feel my filing and classification system begin to disintegrate. "Isn't it illegal," I said at last, "to have two wives at once?"

"I have only one wife."

"Did the lady have a baby even though she's not married to you?"

"She is married to me," said Papa. "Your mother is the one who isn't married."

We looked at him dumbly. He took a mouthful of brandy and began to crush his cigar to pulp again.

"I'm sorry," he said, more to William than to me. "I should have told you long ago, but we were all so happy and somehow the opportunity never seemed to present itself."

William said nothing.

"But how could you and Mama have decided to have William and me?" I said. "You knew it was bad."

"Yes," he said. "It was bad."

"But, Papa, if you and Mama are good how could you possibly do something that was bad?"

"Nothing is black and white in this world, Adrian. One cannot divide people into two categories and neatly label one 'good' and the other 'evil.' When you're older you'll understand. Life isn't like that."

William said so icily that I hardly recognized his voice, "Why didn't you marry Mama? Why did you marry that other woman?"

"Because I thought I was in love with that other woman. I did not realize how much I loved your mama."

"Do you love her?"

"Very much."

"Then why don't you divorce your wife at once and marry her?"

"I have no grounds for obtaining a divorce," said Papa evenly. "I would marry your mama if I could, but I can't."

I said cautiously, tracing a little pattern on the tablecloth to help me concentrate, "It's just as if you really were married to Mama, though. We're just like any other family really."

"Yes, indeed. In fact we're more of a family than many families I know."

"Well," said William in a loud, rude, disagreeable tone that was quite unlike him, "in that case I can't think why anyone bothers to get married. If one can live just as happily without God's blessing and be a family just like anyone else, why is there an institution of marriage at all? If you marry the wrong person and everything turns out to be a mess all that happens is that lots of people are made unhappy and you can't marry the person you should have married in the first place. If you never marry anyone, then no one would ever be unhappy. I shall never, never get married, never as long as I live." And he pushed back his chair abruptly and ran out of the room.

I stared after him and then turned to Papa. He looked shaken and old. There were dark shadows under his eyes and deep lines about his mouth.

"Never mind, Papa," I said, taking pity on him because he looked so tired. "We can play the pretend game a little differently, that's all. We can pretend to ourselves that you and Mama really are married."

He shook his head without speaking.

"Papa, was it not true about Grandfather Parrish wanting Mama to keep his name?"

"No, that was a story Mama told—foolishly or otherwise—in an attempt not to hurt you when you were younger. It was a great pity she—I—did not tell you the truth from the beginning."

I traced another pattern on the tablecloth. "Does God think I'm sinful and wicked?"

"No, of course not."

"But you and Mama are."

"We love each other. God will understand and forgive us."

"Are you sure?"

"Of course! How could God ever think Mama was wicked?"

"But she did a wicked thing."

"Everyone does wicked things," said Papa. "Only saints are good all the time and I don't love Mama because she's a saint. I love her because she's human."

"Then it's all right for people to live as if they're married when they're not because God will forgive them."

"No, I didn't say that." As always, he was endlessly patient with me. "What I'm saying is this: That if two people love each other as deeply as Mama and I do, yet for some reason cannot marry although they want to very much, then I do believe that God, being merciful, will forgive them for their sins. But for two people to have a casual affair—that is to say, to meet, to act for a few hours, days, months, as if they were married yet possessing no intention whatever of marrying each other—that's the sort of relationship which is wrong and which God doesn't forgive easily. God can forgive love but not lust."

"How can you tell when it's love and when it's lust?"

"Adrian," said Papa, "if there was a simple answer to that question there would not be nearly so many unhappy husbands and wives. . . . But that's something you can't possibly understand at the age of eight. Come, I think it's time we joined Mama in the drawing room and found out what's happened to William."

Mama was alone. Papa left me with her while he went off to discover where William had gone.

"Poor Mama," I said, hugging her. "Don't look so sad! I don't mind in the least! It doesn't make any difference to me so long as God isn't cross with us for being bad. But Papa says we're good anyway." I had a bright idea. "Let's go upstairs to our sitting room," I suggested, wanting to cheer her up, "and I'll read aloud to you from the book I've brought with me from the school library."

"No, darling, the hotel manager is changing our suite. Papa decided he didn't like the rooms and so the manager said we could have another suite instead."

"Oh, I see . . ." I fidgeted. "Is the lady staying here with the boy?"

"No, they've gone to another hotel. Papa was going to leave too and take us somewhere else but when he heard she was going he decided simply to change suites. So we must wait here until the porters have finished moving our luggage and everything is ready."

We waited for some time, Mama looking at a magazine and I sitting beside her so that I could see the pictures.

"You're not still sad, are you, Mama?"

"No, Adrian. Not now."

Papa came into the drawing room alone at last and walked over to us. "William's gone to bed," he said. "We had a long talk together." He glanced at me. "You should be in bed too. It's very late."

I suddenly became aware of a great emptiness. "I feel hungry," I said surprised. "Very hungry."

Mama smiled a little. I was relieved to see her smile again. "I think I'm hungry too! Perhaps we could have a tray sent upstairs for us, Mark."

"What a good idea," he said. "I'll order it straight away." He took her arm, stretched out to grasp my hand; together we left the drawing room and began the journey upstairs to the privacy of our new suite of rooms.

The evening was over. But nothing was ever the same again.

[3]

The next morning I said to William, "Do you mind?"

"Yes," he said, "but I'm never going to let it show. I'm going to go through life pretending I don't give a damn."

I was rather shocked by this swear word although after six weeks at boarding school my ears had become accustomed to this sort of vocabulary. "Why?" I said, not understanding his defiance.

"Because *they* don't give a damn. They don't mind not being married—they don't care what people think. They say they'd like to be married—well, of course they have to *say* that, but they can't be married so they don't care. And why don't they care? Because they know they're as good as any husband and wife. Well, I'm going to be as good as any legitimate son, and I shall think of myself as legitimate, but if anyone ever calls me a bastard I shan't knock his teeth in because that would show I cared, so I'm going to laugh and say 'what the hell' and then no one can ever, ever insult me because I shan't care enough to feel insulted."

I listened to him, dazed. I had never heard William talk with such passionate intensity on any subject before. After a long moment I said, "What's a bastard?"

"Us," said William. "It's a swear word like devil and bitch and bloody."

I was shocked. "Well, if anyone ever calls me that," I said at once, "I shall fight him. I'll knock him down and beat him till he apologizes."

"Save your energy! It's not worth it!"

"But I must!" I said, even more shocked. "It's a matter of principle! Nobody's going to go around calling me bad names when I'm good."

"But you are a bastard, you little silly! It's true!"

"I'm not bad," I said stubbornly, clinging to my pattern, my neat classification and my immaculate filing system, "and no one is going to go around calling me bad names."

"Then you're just asking for trouble," said William. "Practically begging for it."

But I did not believe him.

[4]

We began to hear more and more about the Castallacks after that. Appalled, we learned that the boy we had seen at Brighton was not an only child; he had two brothers and three sisters, and —most appalling of all—Papa wanted to bring all of them to Allengate to live with us.

"It's very kind of Papa to think we might like other children to play with," I said to Mama after she had informed us of this proposal, "but please tell him not to worry. Allengate is just right for you, Papa, William and me. I don't think we want any other people here, thank you."

"Absolutely not!" said William loudly. "And I think it's quite wrong of him to suggest it."

"Well, really!" said Mama strongly. "Shame on you both! Think how fortunate you are! You have a beautiful home with everything you could possibly want and two parents who love each other. I think you should spare a thought for others less fortunate than yourselves. Those children have been brought up in a dreary isolated mansion with parents who have been too preoccupied by unhappiness to spend much time with them, and now that their mother is seeking a judicial separation from Papa it must seem to them that fate has treated them even more harshly than before. You should be anxious for them to come to Allengate, if only so that you can show them what a truly happy home is like."

I hung my head in shame but William said abruptly, "I know Papa said he couldn't divorce their mother, but why can't she divorce him? If she's seeking a judicial separation why can't she seek a divorce? And what's the difference between divorce and a judicial separation anyway?"

"Divorce is a very drastic step," said Mama, "and Mrs. Castallack may have found herself unable to take it for moral or religious or social reasons. A judicial separation means that she will remain Papa's wife—but in name only. He is not allowed to treat her as if she were his wife and she cannot expect him to visit her as he did in the past."

"That sounds just like a divorce," I said, puzzled.

"It's similar in some ways. But in a judicial separation the marriage still exists, while in a divorce the marriage is dissolved so that the parties are free to marry again."

"She should divorce him!" said William angrily. "What's the point of insisting on only a judicial separation? It's not fair!"

"I know her decision—right or wrong—is very distressing for us," said Mama without hesitation, "but we must all three of us remember that it's even more distressing for Papa because he hates to see any of us unhappy. So we must be very careful not to complain to him. Also Papa has so many other worries at this time that it's all the more important that we shouldn't add to them in any way. For example, I know he's most concerned about those six children. He and Mrs. Castallack cannot agree where the children shall live now, and that's why he's had to make these frequent journeys to London ever since you both came home for the holidays—he was obliged to consult the judge since only the judge can make a firm ruling on the matter."

"Will the judge decide in Papa's favor?"

"We don't know what he will decide yet. But I thought you should know that the children may all be coming here to live. Mrs. Castallack has been behaving a little unwisely and so the judge may even decide that she should not be allowed to keep her daughters with her. But whatever happens to the girls it does seem almost certain that Papa will receive custody of the boys, so—"

"All the boys?" I said. "Even the one at Brighton?"

"Philip? Yes, of course. He's only a little older than you and so I'm sure you'll soon become good friends with him."

I was silent. I knew even then that Philip and I were not destined to be friends.

At the end of the Christmas holidays William became ill and I was not allowed to go back to school until I was safely out of quarantine. He had diphtheria. Mama devoted every hour of the day to nursing him while Papa, looking ill with exhaustion himself, spent his time traveling between the sickroom at Allengate and the courts of law in London. However, at last I was allowed to return to school, and William, who was by this time a little better, was left to recuperate slowly at home. Mama took him abroad to Switzerland for two weeks in March to complete his convalescence. I felt envious of him enjoying himself among the Alps while I was having to work so hard at school.

When I came home for the spring holidays, Papa met me at the station and there on the platform beside him was a thin, pale William recently returned from Switzerland.

"William!" I bounced over to him joyously. "Did you have a nice time? Thank you for your postcard! Is your heart still strained?"

"My blood pressure is high," said William grandly, "but otherwise I'm well, thank you."

Papa embraced me and patted the top of my head. "Did you have a good journey?"

I nodded, looking around the platform. "Where's Mama?"

"She's waiting for you at home," said Papa, "with the children."

I stood stock-still. William's eyes, dark and watchful, met mine for a moment. He made a fleeting grimace.

"All the children," said Papa casually as an afterthought. "I brought the girls and Hugh up a week ago and Philip and Marcus arrived here from their school in Surrey the day before yesterday. Now let's find your luggage and start the journey home."

As soon as we were alone I hissed to William, "Why didn't you write and tell me? You didn't say a word about it in your letters!"

"Mama asked me not to, because she didn't want you to worry when you were so far away at school. Anyway I couldn't write when I was ill—"

"What are they like?"

"Well, Marcus is a fairly decent sort of fellow, and Hugh's harmless enough and the girls are just girls, but Philip is the absolute end. He's the most detestable little brute I've ever met."

The hackles rose on the back of my neck. "I knew he would be," I said. "I knew it. I shan't go near him."

"You'll have to. He's sharing your bedroom with you."

"What!"

"There aren't enough bedrooms to go around. I'm sharing with Marcus, and Papa said that as you and Philip were the same age—"

I left him. I marched down the platform, accosted Papa and announced in my firmest voice, "Papa, I don't want to share my room with anyone except William. Could you arrange it so that—"

"Into the carriage, Adrian," he said abruptly. "We don't discuss family affairs on station platforms."

In the carriage I tried again. "Papa, I don't mind sharing with William, but I don't want to share with—"

"You'll do as you're told," he said in a sharp, hard voice he had never used to me before, "and no nonsense."

I was silenced. I stared at him, my cheeks burning, and thought in misery: We don't matter any more. The other children come first. And the tears pricked unexpectedly behind my eyes as the carriage rolled on toward Allengate.

[5]

Mama came out to meet us and embraced me as warmly as ever. She looked so completely unchanged and so utterly serene that I hugged her for a moment longer than usual. When I released her at last and turned to the open front door I saw that two pairs of blue eyes were inspecting me curiously from the doorway.

"Adrian darling," said Mama, "here are Hugh and Jeanne. Hugh is seven and a half and Jeanne is five."

I looked at them coldly. The little girl turned and ran shyly away into the hall, but the boy smiled at me. He had a peculiarly sweet smile, open and frank. His golden hair and light blue eyes gave him a look of effortless innocence.

"Come along, Adrian," said Papa. "Where are your manners?" My cheeks burned again. "Hullo," I said to the boy.

"How do you do," said Hugh with winning politeness, and held out his hand.

After a moment I shook it and turned away. "How are you, Mama dear," I said clearly. "Thank you for your lovely cards from Switzerland."

"Did you like them? It was so beautiful there—next time you must come too and see it for yourself." She took my hand tightly in hers and squeezed it. "Come in and meet Marcus and Mariana."

Marcus was already in the hall. He was tall and sturdy with an encouragingly friendly smile.

"Hullo, Adrian," he said, also offering me his hand to shake. "William has talked so much about you. It's nice to see you at last."

His eyes, light blue like Hugh's, were so clear and frank and unconcerned. For some odd reason I did not trust them. For a second I imagined myself taken from my mother and from Allengate and sent to live among strangers; it occurred to me that the very last thing I would do in such circumstances would be to feel friendly toward my new companions. I thought: They're pretending. They hate us as much as we hate them. They don't really want to be friends.

We went into the drawing room. Seated on the window seat in a classic pose was the prettiest little girl I had ever seen. She had black hair, beautifully arranged, a pink and white skin and those same clear light eyes.

How odd that they should all have those horrid eyes was my reaction, and suddenly I was remembering Brighton, the woman with the flashy gown, her frosty ice-cold stare.

"Hullo," said Mariana, smoothing the folds of her exquisite white dress, and looked me up and down with a quick flicker of her long black lashes.

I shuffled my feet, overcome by her femininity, and was glad when Hugh said brightly, "Did you see any motorcars on the road, William?"

"Only one."

"What fun! Mariana, we should have gone to the station with them as Papa suggested and then we would have seen a motorcar!"

"I don't like motorcars," said Mariana.

Mama said, "Jeanne! Don't be shy, dear—come over and say hullo to Adrian!"

But the little girl who was standing behind the sofa only hid her face in Mama's skirts and would not look at me.

"Ring for tea, Rose, would you?" said Papa, coming into the room. "Marcus, where's Philip?"

There was an awkward silence.

"I don't know, Papa," said Marcus.

It seemed so strange to hear a complete stranger address my father as Papa. I didn't like it. It made me feel angry.

"Well," Papa was saying abruptly, "if Philip doesn't want any tea that's his business and he can go hungry. Are you hungry, Adrian?"

"Yes," I said. "Starving."

I must have sounded unusually belligerent, but he merely smiled at me and suggested that I go to the cloakroom to wash my hands while Finch the parlor maid was bringing in the tea.

I escaped, but instead of heading for the downstairs cloakroom I ran across the hall and raced upstairs to my room.

A baby was crying somewhere. I grimaced and, beside myself with fury at the thought of my own home being invaded by a tribe of unwanted strangers, I kicked open the door of my room with such a savage bang that it nearly fell off its hinges and walked, still trembling with indignation, into my own private sanctuary.

But it was no longer private. There was a second bed against a far wall; my book shelves had been moved; there was another chest of drawers over in the corner. I paused, simmering with resentment to see my room rearranged without my consent, and then, aware that I was being watched, I spun around and saw the boy I had seen at Brighton.

He was sitting down. On my bed. My noisy entrance had disturbed him, for he was rubbing his eyes as if he had been asleep.

We stared at each other.

"That's my bed," I said.

He did not answer. He went on staring at me.

"Get off."

He said nothing. I was just about to grit my teeth and fly into the attack when he stood up and went over to the table. He had been writing a letter. I saw a white scrap of paper torn out of an exercise book and a series of marks made by a blunt pencil.

"Adrian!" called Mama from the hall. "Tea's ready!"

"Coming!" I yelled. I gave the boy one last stare, but he had his back to me and did not turn around. I left him, returned slowly to the hall and caught Mama as she was emerging from her little sitting room.

"Mama," I said rapidly, "why can't I share with William? I don't want to share with Philip. Why do I have to share with him?"

"Darling, you must try not to be so selfish. Poor Philip is very unhappy at the moment because he did not want to leave his mama, and his mama tried to disobey the court order and keep him, which made the whole matter even more upsetting than it was already. It's very important that we show Philip that he's welcome here and that we want him to be happy, and how is he to think he's wanted if you refuse to share a room with him? William is sharing with Marcus and they're getting on very well together. Marcus is such a nice boy and I'm sure Philip is too when he's not so unhappy. Do try and like them, darling, please. For my sake. I don't want this to become a quarrelsome, unhappy home."

"I don't think Papa should have brought them here," I said stubbornly. "Why should we have to put up with them? That's not fair. It's bad."

"Adrian, please. I know it's hard not to be jealous—"

"I'm not jealous! I just can't see why Papa couldn't let Philip's mother keep him if she wanted him so much! And why are the girls here anyway? I thought she was going to be allowed to keep them! What happened?"

"It's all much too complicated to explain in detail. First of all the judge gave custody of the boys to Papa and custody of the girls to Mrs. Castallack while she remained at Papa's house, Penmarric, but then Mariana didn't want to stay at Penmarric without Marcus and Papa, so Mrs. Castallack tried to exchange Mariana for Philip in direct contradiction to the judge's orders. This made the judge angry, and when Papa asked him to amend the order Mrs. Castallack opposed it in such an overwrought, ill-advised way that the judge was angrier than ever and amended the order entirely in Papa's favor so that Papa acquired not only custody of all the children but also the right to choose whether

Mrs. Castallack may see the boys or not. She is still allowed to visit the girls, and while she remains at Penmarric they will be allowed to visit her there, but she may not see the boys without Papa's permission. It's a most difficult and sad situation."

"But why couldn't Papa let her keep Philip and end the matter peacefully? I don't understand."

"Sometimes it's not good for little boys to be brought up without a father."

"You brought William and me up and Papa was hardly ever here in the beginning!"

"That was different."

"Why?"

"Darling, I really can't go into involved explanations. You must just take my word for it that it's better for Philip not to be with his mama. Now come along into the drawing room and let's have tea."

I thought: Even Mama is changed. She has become secretive and impatient and even a little cross. She never used to be cross with us. Not before *they* came.

I felt so depressed then, so miserable, that my appetite deserted me and I could hardly eat any tea.

Afterward I shut myself up in the attic with my trains but even then I was not allowed to enjoy myself in peace. Papa came to interrupt me with Hugh.

"Hugh loves trains," he said. "I thought you would like to show him your collection."

"Please," said Hugh winningly. He looked around wide-eyed at my train collection. "Papa, this is much nicer than my collection at Penmarric."

"They're much the same, I think," said Papa distantly and left Hugh alone with me as he returned downstairs to join Mama.

"What a beautiful collection," said Hugh to me sincerely as I struggled with my anger and resentment. "How lucky you are. May I play with them?"

I swallowed, making an immense effort.

"I'll be very careful," said Hugh. "I promise."

"All right," I said.

We played for a short time together but presently I felt I wanted to be alone, so I left him playing happily by himself and went outside.

William and Marcus were playing French cricket on the lawn

while Mariana sat daintily on the swing and watched them. William was even laughing. I turned away abruptly toward the woods.

"Come and join us, Adrian," called Marcus.

"No, thanks."

"Come on!" shouted William.

I shook my head.

"Oh dear," I heard Marcus say with a sigh, "I hope he's not going to be like Philip. I do so hate everyone being nasty to one another."

"Adrian," said William with cold severity, "is never nasty to anyone."

"Well, of course I didn't mean . . ."

I moved rapidly out of earshot. In the woods I padded along to my favorite tree and climbed up to my favorite branch. It was peaceful there. I began to feel better but on my way down some minutes later I discovered that some vandal had carved the initials P.C. on the trunk.

Philip Castallack.

He had even defaced my favorite tree. I was so livid that I ran at once to the house to get a knife and immediately set to work to alter the initials. I turned the "P" into an "A" by adding a straight stroke to the right and the "C" into a "P" by rounding it into an "O" and adding a stem.

It was at supper when I saw him again. As I entered the room he was already stuffing himself with sausages and mashed potatoes.

"Are you usually in the habit of scratching your stupid initials on every nice tree you find?" I said to him at once.

He did not answer.

"Careful, Adrian," said William. He, Marcus and Mariana were also eating supper with us in the dining room; Papa and Mama were to dine alone together later, while Hugh and Jeanne had already had their supper in the nursery with the nursemaid and the baby Elizabeth.

I said to Philip—clearly so that he should not misunderstand, "If you carve your initials on a single tree again I'll fight you."

He took no notice. Marcus cleared his throat unhappily.

"Shut up, Adrian," said William.

I was furious. "How dare you take his side!"

"I'm not taking anyone's side," said William, helping himself to another sausage. "I just don't want everyone fighting everyone else, that's all. It's not worth it."

"Horrid," agreed Marcus with relief. "I do so hate scenes."

"After all," said Mariana, bored, sipping elegantly at her glass of milk, "what does one tree matter?"

"Well of course," I said, "you're just a girl. You wouldn't understand."

"Oh!" said Mariana. "I'm so bored with boys! Why didn't Aunt Rose have a girl if she had to have a baby in the first place? I wish Alice was here."

"Who's Alice?" said William.

"A friend of ours," said Marcus. "She used to do lessons with Mariana at Penmarric."

"I even wish Nanny was here," said Mariana, squashing her mashed potato very flat. "I know I used to grumble at her but I did quite like her really. Even stupid old Miss Peach—"

"Did Papa sack Miss Peach?" said Marcus, worried. "I couldn't gather what went on while Philip and I were at school."

"Oh, it was ghastly," said Mariana, stifling a yawn. "All those tedious scenes when Papa came down to Penmarric after you boys had gone back to Surrey! You can't imagine how dreary it was. Nanny went around weeping and said she wouldn't be parted from us but she wouldn't go and live in any household where the mistress was a fallen woman—whatever *that* means—and Miss Peach sobbed and wailed and said the same thing and then Papa sacked them both on the spot before they could change their minds. Actually I think Nanny would have changed her mind because she doted on us all so much, but Papa wouldn't have her any more because she'd been nasty about Aunt Rose. I can't think why they should have been nasty about Aunt Rose when they hadn't even met her. Personally I think Aunt Rose is a lot sweeter and nicer than—"

"Poor Nanny and Miss Peach," said Marcus very quickly, "and poor Mama. How very upsetting it must have been for her. I wish Philip and I could have been there to help."

"You wouldn't have seen much of her even if you'd been there, because I was there and I hardly ever saw her. She spent most of the time weeping all over the place or having migraine or going to London to see lawyers. Dr. Salter kept rushing in saying, 'Oh, Mrs. Castallack, you must rest, you mustn't do this, mustn't do that, mustn't go to London' and she didn't take any notice. She didn't look well, though. She looked all pale and she didn't bother to do her hair prettily and she'd put on weight and seemed to sag so that her clothes didn't look right on her. I heard Nanny say to Miss Peach that it was shocking for her to be in such a condition at such a time, and Miss Peach agreed."

"Poor Mama," said Marcus again. He looked white. "I hope she's all right. I'm glad Nanny and Miss Peach were sorry for her."

"You should have heard the other servants," said Mariana. "I thought they'd be against Papa and sorry for Mama but they weren't. They said she should have known what to expect when she married a Penmar—isn't it funny how they always think of Papa as being a Penmar like Grandmama?—and that if she knew any better she wouldn't be making so much fuss. They said that that's what happened when you gave yourself airs and graces and tried to pretend to be what you weren't. They said—"

"Shut up," said Philip.

I was so surprised to hear him speak that I dropped my fork with a clatter. We all stared at him.

"It's true!" said Mariana defiantly. "And if you really want to know, Nanny and Miss Peach weren't truly sorry for her either. Miss Peach said—"

"Shut your stupid little mouth."

"Philip, don't," begged Marcus. "Don't. Please."

"Honestly!" said William. "What a way to speak to a girl!"

"I don't care," said Mariana, tightening her beautiful rose-colored mouth into a hard, angry line. "He's the last person I expect to be polite to me. I wish Mama had been allowed to keep him at Penmarric. I can't think why Papa wanted him here anyway."

"Look, don't let's talk about it any more," said Marcus. "It's too upsetting and when I think about it my stomach goes into a peculiar knot and I don't even want to eat any of this nice supper. Let's talk of something else."

"Why don't you run away?" said Mariana to Philip. "I wish you would. Good riddance to bad rubbish."

"Honestly!" said William again, appalled. "Do you usually talk to one another like this in your family?"

"How can I run away?" shouted Philip to Mariana. "If I run away Papa will bring me back and beat me and Mama will be put in prison for disobeying the judge! How can I run away?"

"They wouldn't put Mama in prison," said Marcus, white to the lips. "They wouldn't do that."

"They would! She told me! 'You have to go with Papa,' she said to me, 'because if I keep you they'll put me in prison for disobeying the judge. I'm not allowed to keep you any more,' she said, and she cried and cried so that I could hardly hear what she said—"

"She didn't cry when she said goodbye to me," said Mariana. " 'Goodbye, darling,' she said, 'I'll miss you so much.' Phooey! She couldn't have cared less. She was quite content to say good-bye to me when she thought she was getting you in exchange. She didn't deceive *me*! I knew!"

"She was probably thinking good riddance to bad rubbish."

"Oh! You horrid beastly boy!"

"Mariana, don't, don't . . ." said Marcus in agony, but he was too late. Mariana had smacked Philip resoundingly across the cheek, and he, springing to his feet, shoved her away so violently that she fell against the wall and burst into tears.

"Honestly!" said William for the third time. "Where on earth were you brought up, Philip? Did no one ever tell you not to strike a girl?"

"Don't cry, Mariana," said Marcus, dreadfully upset. "Please. I can't bear it. Don't cry."

Mariana sobbed, heart-broken, into a dainty lace handkerchief.

"Look here," said William to Philip, "I think you'd better apologize. I think—"

"Who cares what you think!" yelled Philip, scarlet with rage. "Who are you anyway? Who do you think you are, giving me orders, telling me what to do—"

My mother walked into the room.

We all turned to face her. Mariana stopped sobbing and allowed Marcus to help her to her feet. There was a silence.

"Dear me," said my mother tranquilly. "Your dinners will all be quite cold! I did at least think you'd all be too hungry to quarrel with one another while you were eating. William and Adrian, sit down and finish up your food, if you please, and I don't want anything left over on the side of the plate. Now, Mariana dear, what's the matter? What happened?"

"Nothing," said Marcus before Mariana could speak. "Nothing at all. We're quite all right, thank you, Mrs. Parrish."

"Are you all right, Mariana?"

271

Mariana blew her nose and cast a sidelong glance at Marcus. "Yes, Aunt Rose."

"Good. Now sit down and finish your meal. I've brought another jug of milk in case anyone would like some more. Would you like some more, Philip?"

Philip walked out of the room without a word.

"Mama," I said in a wave of fury, "Mama, Philip was to blame. Philip hit Mariana and she—"

"Adrian," said Mama very strongly, "I do not want to hear anyone telling tales about anyone else. Marcus and Mariana have not complained about Philip. If you were not involved in the disagreement which they had then you have no business to complain either."

Some dark emotion too violent to be analyzed made me lay down my knife and fork and push back my chair. "I'm going to bed."

"Very well, dear," said Mama. "I expect you're tired after your journey. I'll come up and say good night to you in a quarter of an hour."

I stumbled upstairs, trembling with rage, and found with surprise that Philip also was getting undressed for bed. We did not speak. I went to the bathroom, washed, came back and read a few pages of my book as I lay on my bed and waited for Mama.

She came five minutes later. Philip was already in bed with his eyes closed.

"Have you been to the bathroom, darling? Did you wash behind your ears?"

"Naturally," I said in a cold voice.

She smiled, and suddenly I clung to her and pressed my face against her breast.

She kissed me. "Don't forget your prayers."

I began my usual recitation of the Lord's Prayer with the appropriate appendices. ". . . and-God-bless-Mama-and-Papa-and-William-and-all-the-poor-and-suffering-Amen," I ended, and stole a glance at Philip's inert form as I rose from my knees and slipped into bed.

"Good night, darling." She kissed me again and tucked me in. "Sleep well."

"Good night, Mama."

She went over to the other bed. "Good night, Philip," she said and kissed him too on the cheek.

He said nothing. He was pretending to be asleep but I knew he wasn't. She tucked him in and straightened the covers. Presently she blew out the light and left, closing the door behind her.

There was a long silence.

"Are you a heathen?" I said boldly into the dark. "Don't you say prayers?"

No answer.

"I think you're a heathen," I said. "I think you were brought up a heathen and your mother's a witch."

"And I think," he said in a loud, clear voice, "that you're a bastard and your mother's a slut."

I did not even hesitate. I tore back the blankets and shot across the room like a bullet from a gun.

He was waiting for me.

We met head on in a savage fight.

Unfortunately he had the advantage. He was bigger than I was, tougher and stronger. As my strength began to ebb I began to be frightened.

"Pax!" I gasped, fighting for breath. "Pax!"

But Philip did not abide by the traditional schoolboy conventions of warfare. He went on fighting. I was about to humiliate myself by opening the door and running away when there were footsteps in the passage and the next moment Papa walked into the room to discover us both on the floor punching each other.

Light from the corridor streamed into the room. Papa gave an exclamation, picked us up by the scruff of our necks and shook us sharply.

"What's all this?" He let us go and lit the gas. "I was just coming to say good night to you both," he said curtly. "I thought you were both supposed to be in bed, not scrabbling around on the ground like a couple of guttersnipes. Who was responsible for this?"

"He was," said Philip and I together and stared at each other in rage.

"Liar!" yelled Philip. "You started it! You insulted me!"

"You insulted me worse!"

"Not till you insulted me!"

"Be quiet!" said Papa in such a strong voice that we both jumped. He turned to me. "Was it you who called the first insult?"

"Yes, but—"

"Now, listen to me, Adrian, and listen very carefully. I'm not

273

going to tolerate this sort of behavior. The next time I find you picking a quarrel like that you'll get a thrashing. I'm going to have peace and order under this roof, and I'm not going to stand any sort of nonsense from any of you if you try and fight whenever you think my back is turned. You'll behave properly, and if you don't behave you'll get beaten." He swung around on Philip. "Are you listening to me?"

"Yes, sir."

"Then I suggest you take this as a last warning and pull yourself together before I get out my cane. You'll be civil to your brothers and civil to your sisters and civil to Aunt Rose. And you'll speak when you're spoken to and remember your manners. I've had enough of your rudeness and I don't intend to let it go unpunished any longer."

"Yes, sir," said Philip flatly.

"Now get into bed, both of you, and go to sleep. I'll be looking in here again later tonight with my cane, and if I find either of you awake you'll be in trouble."

He waited. We got into bed without a word. I closed my eyes very tightly so that the tears should not escape.

When we were both settled he extinguished the light, went out into the corridor and closed the door. He did not even say good night. He walked off down the corridor to the stairs, and I was left alone in the dark room with a boy I despised.

We did not speak to each other, but we did not sleep either. I lay crying soundlessly for a while, but when my tears had stopped I stole a glance at him. My eyes were accustomed to the dark and the curtains were not quite closed, so I could see him. He had his eyes open and was watching the pattern the moonlight made on the ceiling.

I wondered bleakly what he was thinking about.

The next morning I made an effort to atone for the wrong I had done in causing the fight.

"Would you like to play with my trains?" I said sullenly as we dressed.

He looked at me. His light eyes were cold with scorn. "Thank you," he said, the two words a mockery of politeness, "but I'm much too old to play with trains."

After that there was no going back. We were bitter enemies and were to remain enemies for more than twenty years to come.

2

Richard had a robust dislike for Geoffrey.
—The Conquering Family,
THOMAS COSTAIN

*[Geoffrey] proceeded to show he had the makings of
a good fighter.*
—Henry II,
JOHN T. APPLEBY

[1]

As the holidays passed we began to settle down slowly. I was
hurt when William spent so much time with Marcus, but since
Marcus enjoyed riding and fishing better than I did I could not
blame William for becoming friends with him. Besides, Marcus
was only two years younger than William and therefore more of
a contemporary for William than I was. Mariana showed no interest in their outdoor pursuits but liked to sew or look at
Mama's London magazines for ladies. She and Mama would go
into Oxford together occasionally to the shops; Mama would
help her with her sewing and supervise her piano practice. The
younger girls I seldom saw. Edith the nursemaid looked after
the fat baby Elizabeth, and although Jeanne occasionally fol-

lowed Hugh when he went upstairs to play with my trains she would spend most of her time in the nursery. Hugh and I became cordial toward each other, but I did not like the way he still remained friends with Philip while assiduously cultivating my good will.

"You'll have to choose between us," I said, not trusting this ambivalent relationship which defied classification. "You can't be friends with both him and me."

"Why not?" said Hugh innocently, and I found to my irritation that it was very hard to give him an adequate reply.

So Hugh went on playing with my trains and borrowing my books but whenever I was occupied elsewhere he would be running after Philip and ignoring my existence. Right from the beginning I was aware of his cunning ability to face both ways.

Philip and I went on fighting, of course. Sometimes Papa interrupted our fights and sometimes he did not, but when he did discover us fighting we were both beaten and he would be very angry indeed. William kept telling me to leave Philip well alone but I seemed completely unable to follow his advice no matter how hard I tried to do so. Part of the trouble, I think, was that Philip and I were so close to each other in age. If he had been either much younger or much older than I we would not have seen each other so often, but as it was we were constantly getting in each other's way and our personalities grated on each other remorselessly.

In the end I was almost relieved to return to school for the summer term. I had had more than enough of Philip trying to requisition my favorite tree, Philip digging a hole (he called it a mine) beyond the stream and muddying the pool where I sailed my boats, Philip saying Allengate was a pretty poor sort of place compared to Cornwall and the Cornish Tin Coast. I had grown very tired of hearing about Cornwall and had soon made up my mind that I would never go there under any circumstances. However, as Mama pointed out to me, since Cornwall had been their home it was only natural that all the Castallacks and not merely Philip should talk about it nostalgically from time to time.

Once a week they would hear news of Cornwall when their mother's letter arrived; Papa would read the letter aloud to them after breakfast on the morning of its arrival although William and I, of course, did not stay to hear what was said. Then every

Sunday after church they would all settle down to write their individual letters back to her, and Mariana would yawn and say, "What a bore! What on earth shall I say?" and Jeanne would bring her crayons and draw a picture of a house and a sun and a tree; Philip would fill one page with blunt pencil marks and Hugh would write, "Dear Mama: I hope you are well. I am well. There is no news here, I regret to say. Love from Hugh." Only Marcus would write the sort of letter I would have written to my mother. He would fill two pages of paper with his large, generous handwriting and would always conclude by saying, "We all miss you very much and are longing to see you again soon. With much love from your devoted son, Marcus."

I used to join these writing sessions to write to my best friend at school, and occasionally I would wander around the table and surreptitiously peep over their shoulders to see what they had written.

Toward the end of August their weekly letter from Cornwall did not arrive. Instead there was a letter addressed to Papa, and all the Castallacks at once thought their mother had written to him to suggest an occasion when she could see her children again.

"Perhaps Papa's given her permission to come here," said Marcus, looking hungrily at the letter as it lay waiting for Papa at the breakfast table. "I know she's not officially allowed to see us boys, but if Papa consented it wouldn't matter about the judge and the order. And Papa hasn't actually said that he'll never let us see her. He's only said that we can't see her 'for a while.' Do you suppose 'a while' could mean seven months? It's seven months since I last saw her in Cornwall. Perhaps he's even going to allow us to go down to Cornwall to visit her!"

"How boring," said Mariana. "That awful tedious journey to Penzance! I don't think I shall go."

"I shall," said Hugh.

"I shall," echoed little Jeanne.

We all looked at Philip. He did not speak. His eyes burned like blue flames in his tense white face.

Papa opened the letter as soon as he came into the room. He was expressionless. We all watched him avidly, and when Mama came into the room I saw she was watching him too. On finishing the letter he glanced across at her.

She said, "Is it—"

"Yes," he said. He folded the letter neatly and put it away in his wallet. He said nothing else.

"Dear me," said Mama absent-mindedly, "I've just remembered I must speak to Edith about something. Excuse me."

"Papa," faltered Marcus as she left the room, "is—is Mama coming for a visit? Are we going to see her?"

He looked up, surprised. I could almost feel the Castallacks holding their breath.

"Good gracious, no," he said casually. "Your mother is much too preoccupied at the moment for visits. She's just had another baby."

There was an absolute silence. Nobody spoke.

"Another boy," said Papa. "A brother for you all."

We all stared at him. I was curiously aware of William laying down his knife and fork.

Papa poured himself a cup of coffee.

"Another baby?" said little Jeanne, pleased. "That's nice! Does Elizabeth know yet?"

"No, not yet." He smiled at her. "Do you want to go and tell her the news?"

"Oh yes! May I, Papa? May I tell her?"

"Of course you can. I'll come with you. Hugh, do you want to come and tell Elizabeth with us?"

"Not especially, thank you, Papa," said Hugh politely.

"Finch," said Papa to the parlormaid who entered the room as he was leaving it, "I'll be back in five minutes. Don't serve my eggs and bacon till I return."

"No, sir." She followed him out of the room after collecting a pile of dirty plates from the sideboard. The door closed. We were alone.

We looked at one another.

"How odd," said Marcus. He looked at William and began to blush. "I don't understand that at all."

"Why not?" said Hugh, greatly interested. He already had a precociously prurient interest in the facts of life.

"I don't understand it either," said William flatly. "I didn't realize he was still on good terms with your mother last year."

"If you ask me," said Mariana, "I think it's in bad taste to have a baby at that age. She's too old for that sort of thing. And *another* boy! As if I hadn't enough brothers!"

"I can't think how it could have happened," said Marcus,

still blushing. "He's hardly seen her lately. I didn't think he visited Penmarric at all last year once the Easter holidays were over."

"Well," I began, anxious to demonstrate my worldly knowledge, "it's quite plain what must have happened. He must have seen her nine months ago. Now let me see. Nine months ago would take us to—"

Philip pushed back his chair. His face was so ashen that it seemed greenish in color. Without a word he ran out of the room and we heard his footsteps rushing across the hall.

"Where's he gone?" said Hugh, startled.

Far away the door of the downstairs cloakroom banged shut noisily.

"November," said Marcus. "How odd. I thought that was when they quarreled."

"Oh really, Marcus, what does it matter?" said Mariana impatiently. "The wretched baby's been born and that's all there is to it. I wonder if it'll be sent to Allengate."

"Yes," said Marcus, "but I still don't understand—"

"Mariana's right," said William. "It doesn't matter now. What the hell. I don't care." He got up clumsily from the table. "I don't feel like breakfast. I'm going riding."

He went out of the room. Marcus and Mariana began to argue about whether the baby would be sent to Allengate or not. I toyed with a lump of scrambled egg, then pushed back my chair and ran after William.

He was saddling his horse.

"William—"

"Shut up," said William. "Don't talk to me."

"William, please!" I began to feel a wave of panic edge unpleasantly down my spine. "I don't think I quite understand and I want to know. Does it mean that at Brighton—"

"Well, of course that's what it means! Don't be such a stupid little ass! Don't you know anything about the facts of life?"

After three terms spent among ninety boys ranging in age from eight to thirteen I had acquired a shadowy idea of such basic biology but still found the whole business bewilderingly grotesque. I began to grasp at facts which I could understand more easily and tried to arrange them in some sort of orderly classification.

"But, William," I said, "if Papa loved Mama—"

"Shut up," said William.

"—why did he kiss *her* and everything? Does he love *her* as well as Mama? I don't understand."

"Oh God," said William, "it's so obvious it's painful. You're such a baby, Adrian. I know you can't help it, but—"

"Then tell me! Explain! I want to know!"

"There's nothing to tell. Papa was living with two women at once for years and years, that's all, and he didn't stop till Mrs. Castallack decided to have a judicial separation. It just goes to show what a sham marriage is. Even if he'd been married to Mama he would still have lived with Mrs. Castallack whenever he had the chance—what happened at Brighton would still have happened no matter which one he'd been married to. Marriage doesn't mean anything at all. He had two women to choose from, so he had them both."

"That was wrong of him," I said at once. "That's bad."

"Not bad. How could it be? Papa's not a wicked person."

"But if Papa loves Mama—"

"Oh, for goodness' sake stop talking as if it were all one of your fairy tales! I don't believe true love exists. Papa just likes Mama better than Mrs. Castallack now, that's all. He lives with her because he likes her best. But when it comes to just sleeping and the other thing, it doesn't matter who he likes best and he'll just do it if he has the right opportunity. He probably gets tired of doing it with the same person all the time and likes to have a change now and then."

I was hopelessly at sea. "But of course there's such a thing as true love!" I protested. "They've both told us they love each other! So why was Papa deliberately unfaithful?"

"He wasn't unfaithful! He's not even married to Mama!"

"He was unfaithful to her," I said stubbornly. "She loved him and he loved her and it was just as if they were married. But he betrayed her. I simply don't understand it at all."

"Well, obviously he still loves Mama best because here he is still living with her." He turned his back on me. "It was just a casual thing with Mrs. Castallack at Brighton don't you see? It didn't mean Papa liked Mama any the less, it didn't mean anything special. . . . When I'm grown up I shall have casual things and never get married, and if I find someone I like better than anyone else I'll live with her and still have casual things when I feel like it."

"But that's wicked!"

"Why? I think it's more wicked to get married and make all those promises to love someone forever when you know you'll probably break those promises later and hurt people who didn't deserve to be hurt in the first place."

"But . . ." I felt dizzy suddenly. My head was beginning to ache. "Marriage and true love are good," I said stubbornly, "but casual things are wrong. Papa told me. God forgives true love but not casual things. Papa told me at Brighton. I shall never, never have any casual things and if I love a person I shall try and marry her if I can. It's sinful to love a person and not marry her if nothing stands in your way. It's fornication."

"Oh, don't be such a beastly little prig," said William, leading his horse into the yard. "You know as well as I do that if it hadn't been for fornication neither of us would be in this world at all."

"But, William—"

"Be quiet, damn you! Can't you see I don't want to talk about it?" His eyes shone with tears. "Leave me alone!"

And he turned, mounted his horse and set off at a gallop to the comforting solitude of the woods.

[2]

I was dreadfully upset and felt sick with bewilderment. After a long while I managed to find Mama alone in her sitting room. She was busy doing her household accounts.

"Mama," I said wretchedly, hovering around her like some restless fly. "Do you mind about the baby?"

She did not answer immediately. She was busy examining the butcher's bill.

"I feel sorry for the poor little baby," she said at last, "coming unwanted and unloved into the world."

"Are you angry with Papa?"

"No."

"Why?"

"Because I love him too much ever to be angry with him for long."

"Did you know the baby was coming?"

"Yes, Papa told me some time ago."

"Were you unhappy when he told you?"

"Not for myself. I knew by then that Mrs. Castallack was seeking a judicial separation and that Papa would not be returning to her any more."

"But weren't you angry when Papa caused the baby? He shouldn't have caused the baby, surely. That was bad."

"Not in the eyes of the church," said Mama. "Papa had a moral duty to try to live with his wife even though they made each other unhappy. When husbands and wives live together it's natural that they should have children. However, now everything is changed because he and Mrs. Castallack are legally separated and he is no longer obliged to live with her, so there won't be any more children."

I slowly began to feel better. "So Papa really did love you best all the time. He just saw Mrs. Castallack now and then because he was trying to be good." I fidgeted absently with the calendar on her desk as I digested the information. "But, Mama—"

"Yes?"

"I know it was good of Papa to do his duty, but wasn't it upsetting for you whenever he went to see Mrs. Castallack?"

"I expect it was upsetting for Mrs. Castallack," said Mama, "whenever he came to see me."

"But—"

"Everyone gets upset sometimes, Adrian. But you see, I love Papa so very much that I can never be upset with him for long."

"Then you're not feeling hurt now because of the baby? It's just that I don't want him to make you unhappy again like you were at Brighton. You're not unhappy, are you, Mama?"

"No, darling, of course not! You mustn't waste your sympathy on me. Think of the poor little baby instead—now he really does deserve your sympathy. I can't think what will become of him."

"Won't he come here?"

"Not for at least a year. He must be with his mother while he's still so young. After that, I don't know. No doubt the judge will have to be consulted again, although Papa isn't anxious for the child to come to Allengate."

"Why?"

"Oh . . ." She was totally absorbed in adding up a column of figures. "Reasons. . . . Now, darling, I think you'd better run along and let me finish these horrible bills. And don't, please, be worried and anxious any more. There's absolutely nothing for you to worry about."

I did in fact feel better after that. Later William reverted to his old careless self again and apologized to me for being so bad-tempered in the stables. No one else seemed to be disturbed. Marcus and Mariana played croquet together; Hugh and Jeanne loyally weeded the patch of earth that Philip had requisitioned near his "mine" and dignified by the name of garden. Philip himself had gone off somewhere in the woods as usual. Fat little Elizabeth tottered onto the lawn with Edith the nursemaid and tried to pull up the croquet hoops, and Mama played with the baby for a while in the shade. It was exactly like any other day.

But in spite of my comforting conversation with Mama and the seeming normality of everyone around me I still felt oddly lost and dissatisfied.

[3]

Papa did not go down to Cornwall for the baby's christening. He did not even speak of the baby except to tell us what it had been called.

"Jan-Yves!" said Mariana distastefully. "How peculiar!" And afterward she added privately to Marcus, "How common!"

"Not a very suitable name for a young English gentleman," said Papa dryly to Mama. "But I've no intention of being provoked into contesting the choice." He made it sound as if Mrs. Castallack had chosen the name to annoy him.

"Jan-Yves is Cornish for Jean-Yves," Marcus explained to us cautiously, "and Jean-Yves was the name of Mama's father. He was French and lived in St. Ives when he was alive. He was in shipping."

"Oh, I would so love to see the new baby!" sighed little Jeanne. "Papa, can't we go down to Cornwall and see Mama and the baby soon?"

"Not at present, my dear," said Papa kindly, stroking her long golden hair. He was very fond of Jeanne. "Perhaps later."

"When?" said Philip.

"We'll see," said Papa.

He always said that. He said that until Christmas, and after Christmas he simply said, "I'm afraid you can't visit Mama at present. She's left Penmarric and gone back to Roslyn Farm, and the judge won't permit you to visit her while she lives there."

Apparently, I learned to my astonishment, Mrs. Castallack had been a farmer's widow before she had married Papa, and she still owned the farm, which was near Papa's estate, Penmarric. However, the judge was naturally reluctant for the children to be brought up on a mere farm when they could live at a place such as Allengate Manor, and it did not seem to me in the least surprising that he would not allow them to visit her in these circumstances. But the Castallacks found his decision harder to accept than I did.

In the end Philip said to Papa, "It doesn't really matter where she lives, does it? You wouldn't have let us visit her anyway, even if she'd stayed at Penmarric, because she wouldn't have left Penmarric if she'd thought she would be allowed to see us there. But while she was at Penmarric you had to pretend you might let us visit her. Now she's gone to the farm you don't even have to pretend any more. You're never going to let us see her."

But all Papa said was "The judge ruled that she is allowed to see the girls and I have no intention of disobeying his ruling on the matter. Since the girls can't visit her at the farm I intend to arrange a meeting at the townhouse in London when the time is right. It's true you boys aren't allowed to see her at the moment unless I consent, but I think it would be ill-advised of me at this stage if I ignored the judge's decision to grant me absolute custody and allowed your mother rights she doesn't legally possess. However, if all goes well and everyone behaves satisfactorily, the judge may well see fit to modify his ruling on the matter in due course. Until that time there's nothing further I can say on the subject. The decision was made by the judge, not by me."

"You made him make it!" cried Philip. "And you could make him unmake it if you wanted to!"

"Indeed I could not! The judge reached an independent decision after meeting your mother and myself and talking to all of you. I intend to abide by the order of the court, that's all. It's as simple as that."

That all seemed very reasonable to me but the Castallacks remained upset and Philip was convinced that Papa was only obeying the judge to the letter in order to make Mrs. Castallack as unhappy as possible.

"As if Papa would do that!" I scoffed privately to William.

It did not occur to me until much later that Papa must have been very angry when Mrs. Castallack sought a judicial separation instead of a divorce and that angry men seldom act in a calm, dignified, reasonable manner.

In the new year while we were at school for the spring term, Mrs. Castallack, accompanied by a friend of Papa's called Mr. Vincent, journeyed to Oxfordshire from Cornwall to see the girls. None of the boys was there to greet her; Hugh was by this time at a preparatory school near Banbury, Philip was still at school in Surrey and Marcus was in his second term at Eton.

"Mrs. Castallack did not choose to come to Allengate," wrote Mama, who had been visiting a friend of hers in London at the time, "but Papa decided that it would be best for the girls not to leave their new home where they've all settled down so well, and so he withdrew his original proposal that the meeting should take place at his townhouse in London. He did wonder if Mrs. Castallack would come in view of the fact that his decision would make her journey more difficult and her visit more arduous, but I myself felt she would not be deterred from seeing her daughters no matter how adverse the circumstances, so I wasn't at all surprised when she agreed to come to Allengate. I'm glad Mariana, Jeanne and Elizabeth had the chance to see their mama again, but I fear poor Philip will be very distressed to hear that he did not share their opportunity, and Marcus quite broken-hearted . . ."

Philip came home from school at the end of term in a towering rage. As soon as he saw Papa he walked straight up to him, his fists clenched, his chin tilted, his head held high.

"Mama was here three weeks ago to see the girls," he said, his voice much too loud. "You only let her come when I was away at school, and you told the headmaster not to let her see me when she called at school on the way home to Cornwall."

Papa said levelly, "The judge has ordered that it would be best for you not to see her for a while. It's a temporary measure made in your own best interests. I explained it to you before."

"But she wanted to see me!" Philip cried. His voice was trembling. "How can it be in my best interests not to let her see me? How can it be?"

Mama took pity on him. She stooped and kissed him and took him in her arms. I was conscious of my usual pang of resentment to see her pay him attention. "You mustn't be upset, Philip dear. I'm sure you'll be able to see your mama before too long."

He tried to push her away. "I don't want you saying nice

things." His voice was high with grief. "Leave me alone."

Ungrateful little beast, I thought.

Mama was upset. "Mark—"

"That will do, Rose," said Papa abruptly and she was silent.

Later Marcus said to Philip, "I've been talking this over with William. I don't think Papa's going to let Mama see us for a long time, and I don't think the judge will change the order for a long time either. I know Papa talks about it being a temporary measure, but how temporary is temporary? I don't think he wants us to see her till we're grown up."

"The order can't last forever," said Philip. "I'll make him tell me when it stops."

But Papa's answer was unsatisfactory. He told Philip that although the judge might reconsider the order if he felt the circumstances warranted it, he would always, in amending or confirming his earlier decision, be guided by what he felt were the best interests of each child. In Papa's opinion the judge was unlikely to change the order as it affected Philip until Philip himself was at least sixteen years old, and there was no question of the order expiring conveniently at an earlier date.

"I'll show him!" muttered Philip afterward. "I'll show him! When I'm sixteen I'm off. I'll be big enough then to fight anyone, even a judge. As soon as I'm sixteen I'll leave school and go and live with Mama at the farm and Papa can go to the devil for all I care."

And he drew up a five-year calendar, hung it on the wall at the foot of his bed and meticulously began to cross off the days.

There was something about this merciless attention to passing time that chilled me. I would look at the last month, June 1911, and as I wondered what would have happened by then I could feel uneasiness grip me like a vise. I tried to imagine what I would be like at fifteen and a half and decided that I did not like the idea of growing up at all.

"If only the years would pass more quickly!" Philip would say, beside himself with impatience. "If only I were a man!"

As if in answer to his wishes he began to grow. By the time he was thirteen he was unusually big for his age. At fourteen his voice had broken and he was six feet tall. At fifteen he could have passed for a young man of twenty. Awkwardness, lankiness, spots, pimples, shyness—all the banes of adolescence—passed him by and left him unmarked. Even I, who hated him, had to admit he was the most striking youth I had ever seen. Marcus, who would normally have appeared an exceptionally prepossessing young man as well, was overshadowed by Philip's enormous golden splendor, and even William, who was reasonably good-looking, seemed nondescript in contrast.

To my disgust I became plainer and plainer. For a long time I would not grow and remained humiliatingly short. Then when I did grow I grew so fast that I became painfully thin.

"Like a skeleton," said Hugh with interest. He also was very small, so my sudden growth was encouraging to him.

None of my clothes fitted me. My feet became too big and whenever I tried to fold myself neatly into an armchair my limbs seemed to sprawl uncontrollably in all directions. My voice broke in the worst possible way and squeaked ignominiously whenever it was vitally important for me to maintain a deep pitch. My skin troubled me. Every aspect of puberty was an unspeakable embarrassment. I was miserable.

"Don't worry," said William encouragingly. "It doesn't last forever. You'll probably turn out presentable enough in the end."

But I could not believe him and instead wasted many futile minutes envying the Castallacks their good looks. Only Elizabeth was fat and plain, although no one knew whether the baby Jan-Yves was ugly or not. Jan-Yves had not been summoned to Allengate. Mrs. Castallack had left him behind at Penmarric when she had returned to her farmhouse and he was being brought up there by a nanny. I thought this was unexpectedly correct of Mrs. Castallack, since according to the judge's order she was not allowed to see or bring up any of her sons, but Mariana and Marcus thought it was odd and would discuss the subject from time to time.

"Since Papa doesn't want it at Allengate you'd think that Mama might like to keep it at the farm," Marcus said.

"Since Papa doesn't want it and Mama won't live with it," said Mariana, "it must be odd."

"An imbecile, you mean?"

"Or else it's a creature so ugly no one can bear to look at it." Mariana shivered daintily at the thought and Marcus looked solemn.

In fact every year Papa said he must go down to Cornwall to pay a visit to his estate—and to his youngest child—but somehow he never managed to make the final arrangements for the long journey to the west country. It was really amazing how something always turned up at the last minute to detain him in Oxfordshire, and then talk of a visit to Penmarric would be postponed until the end of the next academic year.

Mrs. Castallack did not visit Allengate again but instead requested that she visit the girls at the townhouse. Papa refused. Mrs. Castallack then went to the judge, who told Papa that the girls should be allowed to go away with their mother for two weeks to a suitable place. Mrs. Castallack took them to Exmouth, but the visit was not a success because Elizabeth cried all the time for Mama, and Mariana sulked because she had wanted to stay at the townhouse and see the London shops. Even Jeanne, who had been looking forward to visiting the seaside with her mother, seemed glad to be back at Allengate again, and after this unfortunate episode Mrs. Castallack appeared to withdraw more completely into Cornwall and seemed unable to face the annual tussle with Papa about where and when she could see her daughters.

Later that year Papa's mother died, but since William and I had not met her the news of her death hardly affected us. Papa even told us it was not necessary for us to attend the funeral in spite of the fact that she had been our grandmother. However, all the Castallacks except for Elizabeth were dressed in black and made to travel to London with Papa for the service. None of them wanted to go.

"I was terrified of her," confessed Marcus. "When she came to Penmarric after Uncle Nigel died I thought she was a witch. I was frightened to death."

"So was I," agreed Mariana. "She was horrible—so loud and noisy. She shouted all the time."

"Thank goodness *we* don't have to go to the funeral!" I said to William, but somehow as I watched them go away with Papa in the carriage to catch the train to London I was aware of a mysterious feeling of exclusion.

The years that followed were comparatively uneventful. I hated my first year at Winchester, but then became accustomed to life at a public school and drowned my miseries by throwing myself wholeheartedly into my work. I was given excellent reports. Papa was pleased with me and I felt satisfied that in this field at least I outshone the Castallacks. Marcus' scholastic ability was unexceptional and in some subjects he was even below average. Philip did well when he felt like it but repeatedly failed to shine at any of the arts; his strong points were mathematics and science, neither of which interested me in the least. Hugh, judging from his accounts of school life, seldom bothered to work but—amazingly—never failed a single examination.

There was something a little mysterious about Hugh. I often had the feeling he was much cleverer than most of us supposed.

Apart from William and I, who were both at Winchester, all the others were at different public schools. Papa said this eliminated the risk of one brother outshining another in the close-knit community life and the development of unnecessary jealousies, so after Marcus went to Eton, Philip was sent to Rugby and Hugh to Harrow. As for the girls, they had a governess, a Miss Cartwright, but at sixteen Mariana was sent abroad to a finishing school in Geneva and returned after six months with a wardrobe of French clothes, a grownup hair style and a conversation consisting entirely of her forthcoming debut in London and all the eligible men she would enslave during the course of the Season.

"Mariana dearest," said Mama, "you must try to converse on other subjects or people will think you very vain, always talking about yourself. Gentlemen are not attracted to girls who are too self-centered."

But Mariana was too excited about the coming Season to take much notice. A dowager friend of Papa's mother was going to present her and act as her chaperone. Papa spent much time at his townhouse in London, and it was arranged that a ball would be given there for Mariana at the end of May. Philip, Hugh and I would be away at school and were anyway considered too young to dance with the girls who were to be present—"Thank God!" said Philip, who hated dancing—but Jeanne and Elizabeth were to dress up in their party frocks and watch with Miss Cartwright for an hour at the beginning. Marcus, who was eighteen and in his last year at Eton, was going to get special leave to come down to London for the occasion, and William, now almost twenty, would also be there. After leaving Winchester and spending several months on the continent to "broaden his outlook" he was toying with the idea of going up to Oxford in the autumn of 1911. I did not think he would go. He disliked studying and was secretly pining to lead an outdoor life pursuing the traditional occupations of hunting, shooting and fishing. However, that summer he had nothing to do but enjoy the

London Season and was already looking forward with pleasurable anticipation to all the pretty girls he would meet.

Girls embarrassed me. I did not know what to say to them and decided that most of them were too empty-headed to merit my attention. Certainly Mariana, who was still talking nonstop about her wretched presentation to the King and Queen and her equally wretched ball, seemed one of the most empty-headed girls I had ever met.

"Oh, Aunt Rose!" she cried. "You will come to the ball, won't you? Please say you'll come! I couldn't bear it if you didn't!"

But Mama was unwell with an infection and her health did not permit her to go to London.

For a time I wondered if Mrs. Castallack would come to her daughter's coming-out ball, but this possibility was never mentioned and I suspected Mariana was secretly glad to be spared the presence of a former farmer's wife at such a select occasion. Certainly she never once suggested to Papa that her mother should be present.

In fact by this time the Castallacks' attitude toward their mother was uneasily ambivalent. Marcus had first sought permission to visit her on his own when he was sixteen, but after Papa had promised him that once he was no longer a schoolboy he could visit his mother whenever he pleased, Marcus had agreed to wait another two years until the end of his final term at Eton. It occurred to me then that although Marcus was genuinely anxious to visit his mother he was also nervous about the prospect of seeing her again after such a long absence and was much more easily persuaded to delay his reunion than he should have been. I noticed too that apart from Philip, who still threatened to leave school on his sixteenth birthday and fight anyone who tried to stop him, the others were by no means overcome with the urge to see their mother again without delay. "I wish I could run away with you to Cornwall, Philip," said Hugh, but when Philip started to encourage him Hugh said perhaps he ought to wait until he too was sixteen. "How lovely it will be to see Mama again one day!" Jeanne would sigh occasionally, but meanwhile she was more than content to live at Allengate with Mama. So was Mariana. And as for Elizabeth, it was hard for her to remember that she had not always lived in Oxfordshire and that Mama was not her own mother after all.

"Pretty odd sort of mother you've got," I could not help commenting after Mariana had remarked that since her mother had not bothered to see her for years one could hardly expect her to bother to come to the ball—even if she were invited. "Well, I suppose it takes all sorts to make a world."

Of course Philip had to be near enough to overhear me and make a fuss. "You're bloody well right it does!" he yelled at me. "But at least my mother doesn't sleep with a man who isn't her husband!"

"Why, you—"

William and Marcus came into the room just in time to drag us apart.

"My God," said Philip, white with rage. "I can't wait to get out of this bloody house! Thank God I'll be sixteen in June. I've had enough of living with a couple of bastards who ought to have been shoved into an orphanage as soon as they were born instead of being brought up to think they're as good as I am! Just you wait. If you ever try to set foot in any house of mine I'll kick you right out into the gutter where you belong!"

"Oh God," I said with a calculated yawn, "why on earth would we try to set foot in any beastly house of yours? That would be the one dwelling on earth which I at any rate would avoid like the plague."

He spat on the floor at my feet and walked out of the room. The door slammed with a thunderous bang behind him.

"Adrian Parrish," said William as he and Marcus regarded me wearily, "will you ever, ever learn any sense?"

"Why blame me?" I shouted, beside myself with fury. "It was his fault! He slighted my mother and I'll not stand by and see her insulted! You may think yourself sensible to keep quiet, William, but you're not—you're weak! What's the good of having principles if you're not prepared to fight for them?"

And as they looked at me in blank astonishment, I yelled, "Oh, go to hell, both of you!" and rushed headlong out of the room in a rage.

[4]

Mama could not seem to rid herself of her infection. After Mariana's ball, which all the society papers called "a brilliant occasion," Jeanne and Elizabeth stayed on with Miss Cartwright in London, and Papa, leaving Mariana in the care of her chaperone, returned alone to Allengate.

Toward the end of term he wrote me a short note to tell me to go to the townhouse when I left Winchester for the holidays; Mama was still unwell and the doctors had advised that no children or young persons should go to Allengate while there was a risk of infection.

William met me at Waterloo. He had been in London at the townhouse throughout the Season and so had no firsthand news from Allengate.

"How's Mama?" I said anxiously.

"I don't think she's very well. Papa's hoping she'll get a little better so that he can take her abroad to Switzerland."

"Oh?" A faint dread shadowed my mind and made my heart beat faster. "It's nothing serious, is it, William? I mean . . . she's on the road to recovery, isn't she?"

William did not answer. He wasn't even looking at me.

"William?"

"Papa's coming back from Allengate this evening to see us. We'll know more then."

Panic swept over me. I took his arm and shook it. "What's wrong with her? Tell me! What is it? What's the matter with her?"

He looked at me levelly. His eyes were calm but opaque. At last he said in an odd voice, "Papa told me she has tuberculosis." And then in a tumbling rush, his eyes blind with pain: "I think she's dying."

3

When she died Henry had a splendid tomb made for her before the high altar in the nunnery of Godstow near Oxford.

—King John,
W. L. WARREN

[1]

She died.

We were with her at the end. Even Mariana, who had looked forward for months to the grand finale of her first season, abandoned the yachting at Cowes and traveled back to Allengate. It was August. Everyone was at Allengate at the end except Philip, who had left Rugby at half-term, quarreled violently with Papa and caught the train to Cornwall on the morning of his sixteenth birthday.

Papa wrote to him, telling him of Mama's death and informing him of the funeral arrangements. I saw the letter on the hall chest. It was addressed to Philip Castallack Esq., Roslyn Farm, Zillan, near St.-Just-in-Penwith, Cornwall.

"He'll never come," I said to William, "he never cared. He was the coldest, most unfeeling brute I ever met. Mama just wasted her time being good and kind to him because he didn't care a jot for her. I'm only glad we don't have to suffer his presence at the funeral."

The funeral.

I had not been to a funeral before. I had not seen anyone dying before either. I found I was consumed with the most overpowering fear of death and an unbearably painful obsession that God was cruel and unjust.

"There can't be a God," I said to William. "Why does Mama have to die when she's still young? And from tuberculosis, that horrible, distressing disease! Nothing makes sense any more. Nothing."

But Mama had said to me, "There's a pattern. Never, never doubt that there's a pattern. There's a pattern always. Everywhere. In everyone."

And at the very end she had said, "Be loyal to Papa."

She died, and the house was still. The flowers drooped in their vases and the petals fell softly to the ground like tears. It rained. That summer had been the finest in living memory but now it rained and went on raining, and the letters began to come and the flowers, so many beautiful brilliant flowers, invaded the house as if to replace the flowers that had faded away. And when the funeral was held at the little church at Allengate, the people came, dozens of people, Papa's friends from Oxford, servants from the village, her own friends from St. John's Wood, mourner after mourner, and none of them either knew or cared what wrong she had done because it no longer mattered and now all that was left was the goodness and it was the goodness that people remembered and for which they came so far to grieve.

The Castallacks grieved. Philip—naturally—was absent, but all the others were there. Mariana and Jeanne wept through the entire service and little Elizabeth, who was now eight years old, wept with them. Hugh was white and still; Marcus was ashen, his fingers twisting endlessly at his crumpled handkerchief; William cried. But I could not cry. I was beyond tears. And beside me Papa's face was lined with grief and his hair was gray and he was old.

It was quiet in the churchyard and very peaceful. The clergyman read aloud from his book and the sun shone again as the coffin was lowered into the grave. He went on reading and I thought: Where is the pattern? Show me the pattern. If a pattern exists let me see it and give me some glimpse of what it all means.

A breeze ran invisible fingers through my hair. I glanced away, unable to watch any longer, and as I looked up I saw Philip crossing the churchyard toward us, a single red rose glowing in his hand.

[2]

Afterward Papa left my side and went over to him. I heard him say, "Why didn't you send me a telegram to let me know you were coming? I would have arranged for you to be met at the station so that you could have been here in time for the service."

"Would you?" said Philip, insolent as ever in his rudest voice. "I thought you told me when we parted company in June that you would never lift a finger to help me again. You told me never to ask you for anything for the rest of my life."

Anger swept away my grief in a black ungovernable tide. I wanted to shout at Papa, Tell him to go away! We don't want him here! Tell him to go back to Cornwall and never bother us again!

But Papa touched Philip on the shoulder and said gently, "My dear Philip, I often say words in anger and regret them later and I've no doubt you do too. I'm more pleased than I can say that you made the effort to come back for the funeral. I hope you will at least stay with us for a few days before going back."

"I'm never staying under your roof again," said Philip, and with a shock I heard a tremor in his voice. "Never."

"Please. I won't try and persuade you to go back to school or leave Cornwall. I simply don't want us to remain estranged."

He shook his head. "I want to get back to Zillan to my mother."

It was then that Papa said, his quiet voice lacerating my aching sense of loss, "How is your mother?"

I turned and ran. I ran back into the church and hid myself in a back pew behind a pillar. Great sobs tore at my throat and shuddered through my body. I cried and cried as if I were a child of five instead of a youth of fifteen; I cried for my mother and I cried for myself, and as I cried the past closed its doors soundlessly behind me and I was left alone in a cold present without even the courage to look ahead into the future.

William found me an hour later.

"We were looking everywhere for you," he said. "I was getting worried." He sat down in the pew beside me and put an arm around my shoulders. "Come on, old fellow," he said. "Please. You must stop now. You must try and make an effort to be your usual self again. Mama's gone and nothing's going to bring her back. Least of all tears."

"Oh, but . . ." I could not speak. "What's to become of us?" I said painfully at last. It was still very hard to speak. I seemed to be capable of using only simple, awkward words. "While Mama was alive everything was always well . . . but now she's gone nothing's . . . certain . . . safe."

"Why, you little ass, don't be so silly! What do you think's going to happen? Do you think Papa will summon us to his study, grow a couple of horns, start breathing fire and tell us not to darken his doorstep a day longer? I *am* surprised at you! Why this sudden lack of faith in Papa? Obviously he'll look after us and take care of us, just as before. Don't be so ridiculous!"

Papa did summon us to his study to discuss the future, but he waited until September when our grief had become dulled and I was reluctantly beginning to think about returning to school. Allengate had long seemed deserted and forlorn; Mariana, promising tearfully to order a becoming selection of black gowns, had returned to her chaperone in London after the funeral, and Marcus had departed for Cornwall to make the long-postponed visit to his mother; Miss Cartwright the governess had taken Jeanne and Elizabeth to Bournemouth for a month, since Papa felt that a holiday by the seaside would be beneficial to them after so many sad days at home, and Hugh had gone to stay for a week with a school friend of his in Norfolk. It was on the evening of Hugh's departure, when Papa was finally alone in the house with William and myself, that he asked us to join him in his study after dinner and I knew instinctively that he wanted to discuss the future.

"Well, William," he began in a friendly voice, "since you've said no more to me on the subject I've made no arrangements for you to go up to Oxford next month. But I trust you've by now decided which profession you wish to adopt. What decision have you reached?"

William went red. I felt sorry for him, for I knew he disliked the studying which adoption of a profession would entail and had no vocation for such a convenient solution as the Army or the Church. It was his misfortune that he had not been born a country squire with a comfortably unearned income awaiting him at the age of twenty-one, but Papa had made it clear to us some time ago that although he intended to leave us legacies in his will we should always expect to have to earn our own living. Mama had also explained that it was natural for Papa to take this attitude since he disapproved of any young man leading an idle life, and since Mama had accepted this attitude as correct I too had accepted it without complaint. But now I found myself becoming angry. Marcus had just left school but no one had mentioned that he must think of earning his living. In fact Marcus seemed to take it for granted that he would spend his twenties enjoying himself without doing a stroke of work. It suddenly seemed grossly unfair to me that William, who was actually Papa's eldest son, was supposed to fend for himself financially while Marcus was free to do exactly as he pleased without worrying where the next penny was coming from.

"Well, Papa," said William uncomfortably after an awkward pause, "I'm afraid I'm finding it very difficult to come to a decision about this. The truth is that the only thing I really want to do seems to be out of the question, so I'm rather at a loss to know what I should do instead."

"I'm very much in favor of people doing what they really want to do," said Papa. "What is it you have in mind?"

"Well . . . to be honest, I would like to manage an estate and spend most of my time out of doors in the country, but I know a bailiff is a very lower-class occupation and I couldn't expect you to approve of it."

Papa looked surprisingly interested. "Estate management is a skilled job," he said agreeably enough. "It's not a career I would have preferred you to choose, certainly, but if you really want to pursue this, William, then I shan't stop you—in fact it's possible I may even be able to give you a start and see that you have a training on a large estate."

William brightened and leaned forward in his chair. "That's

very good of you, Papa! Did you . . . was there any particular estate you had in mind?"

Papa took a cigar from the box on his desk. I stiffened instinctively, then forced myself to relax. Even after seven years Papa's cigars would remind me of that dining room at Brighton.

"Yes," said Papa, making a great business of lighting his cigar. "Yes, as a matter of fact I did have a certain estate in mind."

I knew then. I stared at him but he did not look at me; he was too busy shaking out the match, and suddenly I was back at Brighton and Papa was saying through a cloud of cigar smoke, "I'm afraid I have something to say which should have been said a very long time ago."

"Which estate is that, sir?" said William innocently.

"Penmarric," said Papa.

There was a silence. I clenched my fists and looked at the carpet and gritted my teeth so that I should not speak.

Papa began to explain. He said he had decided to sever his ties with Oxford for the time being and return to Penmarric to work on a book. He was always able to write well in Cornwall, and besides Penmarric was his home and he was beginning to miss it. As for Allengate, he had decided to sell it. He was sure we understood why. The house was so full of memories for him—for all of us—of Rose ill . . . suffering . . . dying . . . He did not want to live here any more. Besides, he was sure we would like Cornwall. We had both been born there, and although we might find the Cornish Tin Coast strange at first he felt certain we would soon settle down—

"I'm not going there," I said violently. "I'm not going to Penmarric. I absolutely refuse. I've no intention of being publicly humiliated."

"We can maintain the fiction that I'm your guardian."

"Yes—the fiction no one believes!"

"Adrian, what on earth does it matter what a few village gossips think? You must learn not to be so sensitive! Try to take a mature, sensible attitude—as I'm sure William will—"

"William!" I exploded. "William will just take the line of least resistance as usual, but I'm not like that! I stand up for what I believe in and—shut up!" I hissed at William, who had managed to kick me on the foot—"and I don't think it's right or just for you to to drag us back to Cornwall and parade us as your . . . your . . ."

"I'm merely trying to do my best for you."

298

"You're not! You're discriminating against us—just as you discriminate against William when you say he has to earn his living while we all know Marcus can be a gentleman of leisure for as long as he likes! It's unfair! You treated Mama as if she were your wife—you should treat us as if we were your legitimate sons!"

"I would hardly have suggested you came to Penmarric unless I had wanted to treat you as my legitimate sons. But I can only treat you as legitimate up to a certain point, and beyond that point I cannot go if I'm to remain fair to my legitimate children. Now don't interrupt me or I swear I'll lose my temper too and then we'll both be sorry! You're nearly sixteen years old and it's high time you began to view this situation realistically. Your mother was not my wife. It was a great pity she wasn't, but there it is. One can't undo the past. One must merely learn to live with it. She was my mistress. You know that and I know that and nothing we say is going to make that fact otherwise. I loved her, I treated her as my wife, I would have married her if I'd been free to do so, but she was my mistress. You are my illegitimate sons. You must face that. Illegitimacy is unfortunate, I admit, but it needn't in the long run prove to be a handicap. You've both been given a decent education and upbringing. If you do well in your chosen professions and live your lives as satisfactorily as possible I doubt if anyone will ever even question your parentage."

"But—"

"What I'm saying is this: Don't waste time pretending you're not illegitimate and reading insults into every nuance of my behavior toward you. Face your illegitimacy, see it for what it is—a handicap which need not ultimately affect you at all—and make up your mind to live with it as best as you can."

"Yes—at Penmarric of all places!"

"If you can learn to live with it at Penmarric you can live with it anywhere in the world."

"I won't go there!" I was on the verge of tears suddenly. "I'll go to America. I'll—"

"My dear Adrian, you won't solve your problems by running away from them. And how are you to fulfill your ambition to lecture in history at a university if you leave on the next boat to America without completing your education?"

I was aware of him getting up and coming around the corner

of his desk toward me. I wished William wasn't there. I felt sure I was going to make a fool of myself and I did not want him to witness my foolishness.

"William," said Papa, "we'll speak again later about your profession." And when William had gone he stooped over me and put an arm around my shoulders and said in his kindest voice, "Poor Adrian, how very confused you are. I'm sorry."

But I did not want his sympathy. "I'm not in the least confused," I said rapidly. "It's crystal clear that we're an embarrassment to you and that you're only inviting us to Penmarric out of respect for Mama's memory. It's equally clear that you feel you must put your legitimate children first—"

"In my affections? I never said such a thing."

"But . . ." It was no use. I could not go on, and as the words stuck in my throat there was nothing for me to do but fight a losing battle with my tears.

"Listen," he said. "I do want you at Penmarric—and not merely out of respect for Rose's memory. Do you think I couldn't make other arrangements if I secretly wanted to rid myself of you both? If I didn't want you in my house any more now would be the ideal time for me to get you off my hands. But I do want you in my house. Now try and trust me, please, about this move to Cornwall. If I thought you were going to be unhappy there I wouldn't force you to come, but I think you'll like it. Promise me at least that you'll try to like it."

I managed to nod.

"And promise me you'll never again think I don't want you in my house. Will you promise me that?"

I nodded a second time.

"Well, in that case," he said, relieved, a note of encouragement in his voice, "our troubles are over, aren't they?"

But they were only just beginning.

[3]

I could not bear to say goodbye to Allengate. I packed my possessions into a trunk, as Papa requested, but when it was time for me to leave for Winchester I left the house pretending I would be returning to it as usual for the Christmas holidays. I think if I had allowed myself to admit I would not be living there again I would have found it intolerably painful to turn my back on it. The only step I did take in recognition of the fact that I would not be at Allengate again for some time was to give my savings to the vicar's wife and ask her to see that flowers were placed from time to time below the fine headstone which Papa had had erected above Mama's grave.

In some ways it was a relief to get back to school. I flung myself into my work again and tried to forget the world beyond the school walls, but letters from Papa kept arriving regularly and I found it impossible to shut out the world as completely as I would have wished. William wrote too, of course. He did not write very erudite letters but they always seemed to be full of news.

". . . so Mariana is engaged," he wrote at the end of September. "She had a lord, a baronet and an honorable wanting to marry her, so of course she chose the lord. His name is de Leonard, a baron, I think. Pots of money, of course . . ."

"Dearest Adrian," wrote Mariana's flowing hand, "thank you *so* much for your divine letter! Of course, it's wonderful news and I'm quite fantastically happy. Darling Nick is just what I've always wanted and I know titles and money don't matter a scrap but they *are* rather fun! Imagine me—Lady de Leonard!!! Nick has a beautiful country house in Kent, but I think we'll spend most of the time in London (Upper Grosvenor Street). My ring is GORGEOUS! Of course I know material things are quite unimportant but somehow they do make one feel more *comfortable*, if you know what I mean . . ."

Papa wrote to say he had insisted on a year's engagement since Mariana was only seventeen, and so the wedding date had been provisionally set for September of the following year. Mariana was now with him at Penmarric, but her fiancé planned to visit Cornwall directly after Christmas and I would have the chance to meet him then.

But I did not want to think of the Christmas holidays I would have to spend at Penmarric. I turned in relief to William's next letter—only to discover that William had written of nothing but Penmarric, how much he loved the spectacular scenery, how amazed I would be when I saw the house, how surprising it had been for him to see the portraits in the gallery and realize what a telltale feature his Penmar eyes were.

". . . you're lucky you don't resemble the Penmars in any

way," he added cheerfully. "At least you'll be spared the old butler giving you funny looks whenever he thinks your back's turned! Incidentally, talking of the Penmar looks, wait till you meet the youngest member of the family. Jan-Yves is without doubt the most obnoxious infant you could possibly imagine. Poor little devil! He's ugly, rude, loud, disobedient, dirty and looks like something the gypsies left behind. However, for some reason he's formed an overpowering attachment to me and follows me wherever I go. The little beggar doesn't like anyone else, so I suppose I should feel flattered. Do you know his mother hasn't been to see him once? Not once! And she only lives a few miles away at Zillan. What a strange woman she must be! The more I hear about her the more thoroughly dislikable she seems, but the others seem enraptured with her and even Mariana's attitude seems to have melted a little. And if you think *that's* a surprise, let me tell you that Papa no longer makes any attempt to stop them from seeing their mother and says they can go to Roslyn Farm as often as they like. It's almost as if he no longer cares now that Mama is dead. . . .

"Anyway, Marcus and the girls have fallen into the habit of visiting the farm every Saturday for lunch, but Jan-Yves won't go and personally I don't blame him. Even when Papa encouraged him to go he wouldn't listen. Between you and me I think he dislikes Papa almost as much as he dislikes his mother, in spite of the fact that Papa is now bending over backward to be nice to the child. You'd be amazed how remorselessly patient and even-tempered Papa is being in the face of so much deliberate provocation, but he seems determined to be as long-suffering as possible toward the little devil. . . . I wonder what you'll make of all this when you arrive. Looking forward to seeing you. . . ."

It was December. The term was drawing to its end, and at last on December the eighteenth, 1911, I left Winchester and began the long tiring journey to the west, to Cornwall and to my new home.

It was my sixteenth birthday.

4

King Henry had now another son, John. . . . He was a dear little boy.

—The Devil's Brood,
ALFRED DUGGAN

Their mother, who had long ceased to enjoy any con-jugal felicity, had in fact for some years lived apart from her husband, ruling with her son Richard over her own inheritance in the south.

—Oxford History of England:
From Domesday Book to Magna Carta,
A. L. POOLE

[1]

I had not been west of Truro. I arrived at Penzance, the train sweeping along by the sand of Mount's Bay, and there before me rose St. Michael's Mount, shimmering in the December sun, a shining pinnacle of medieval splendor afloat on the sparkling Cornish sea. I felt the strangeness of Cornwall then, the antiquity, the echo of a lost nation whose language had faded away so that one forgot they were a different people with a different past. My memory sharpened; suddenly I seemed to hear my mother saying to us long ago in St. John's Wood: "Papa is a very foreign-looking gentleman."

But my first favorable impression of Cornwall quickly faded when I met William on the station platform, for behind Wil-

303

liam, treading on his heels, was a very small, very ugly urchin. He had thick black hair, a rebellious sulky mouth and the black slanting eyes of the Penmars. As I stared at him he put out a small pink tongue and jeered at me.

"This is Jan-Yves," said William. "I'm sure you recognize him from my descriptions. Jan-Yves, this is my brother Adrian."

"Hullo, spotty," said the urchin.

"Stop that, fatty," said William.

"I'm *not* fat!"

"And Adrian's not spotty. Now run along and make yourself useful. Take Adrian's overnight bag—that's right, is it too heavy for you?—very well, and take it out to Crowlas and the carriage. Thank you."

The urchin grabbed the suitcase out of my hand and trundled away, staggering a little, toward the entrance.

"What a perfectly frightful child," I said in distaste. "How do you put up with him?"

"Oh, he's a nice little beggar really. . . . Let's get out to the carriage."

The journey to Penmarric was entirely spoiled by the tiresome child. He bounced around the carriage, interrupted all attempts I made at conversation with William and boasted about what he was going to do when he was grown up.

"I'll be a genius," he said, looking at me impudently with his narrow black eyes, "and I'll be rich. I'll be so rich everyone will beg me to like them, but I shan't. I'll throw them over the cliffs and watch them get mangled on the rocks below."

I said cautiously to William, "Y a-t-il une malade de la tête, peut-être?"

"He's trying to shock you," said William placidly. "So far he thinks he can only get people's attention by shocking them. Isn't that so, Jan-Yves?"

The child laughed uproariously and aimed a cuff at William's chest. William absent-mindedly parried the blow and patted the child's head as the carriage crawled on toward Penmarric.

Of course I disliked the Cornish Tin Coast as soon as I set eyes on it. It was so different from the trees, lanes and picturesque villages of the Oxfordshire countryside; here everywhere was stark and ugly, for there was not a tree in sight and the houses of the mining villages were gray and somber. The scars of the mines, most of them derelict, were a hideous blight on that godforsaken landscape, and even before we reached the point in the road which gave me my first view of my new home I felt I already knew what I could expect.

"There it is!" cried the child. "There's Penmarric!" He turned to me and his little black eyes shone. "I lived there all alone," he said proudly, "just the servants and me. It was my very own castle. Until *they* came. But I'll get it back one day."

It was a gray sprawling monster of a building, and when we drew closer I found myself sneered at by bleak walls, leering gargoyles, tall chimneys, sightless windows and grotesque pseudo-battlements.

"Nice, isn't it?" said William. "I like it."

I was speechless. As we got down from the carriage the front door opened and Papa came hurrying out to meet me.

"Adrian! Welcome to Penmarric!"

Jeanne was behind him and Elizabeth.

"Hullo, Adrian!" said Jeanne breathlessly. "How lovely to see you here! Isn't it the most beautiful house you ever saw? It's so exciting to be home!"

"Hullo," said Elizabeth. "Cook has made a very special cream tea for you with the very best Cornish cream. The food here is very nice indeed."

Marcus was in the doorway. "Hullo!" he called. "Do you fancy a sea view? We've given you Philip's old room so you can look out toward Land's End. It's an awfully nice room."

Mariana came flying across the hall. "Adrian, what fun! Do come in! Do you like my ring? The central diamond is terribly fine, isn't it? I think it's the most divine ring I ever saw in my life—"

"Medlyn," said my father to the butler, "tea in ten minutes in the drawing room, if you please. James, take the luggage upstairs, would you?"

The footman leaped forward with alacrity.

"I'll show you your room," Marcus offered. "I do hope you'll like it. I expect it'll be nice to have a room to yourself after all those years of sharing at Allengate."

We went up the great staircase and into a long gallery. In spite of myself I had to stop to look at the portraits on the walls.

"Past Penmars," said Marcus humorously. He gave a quick Gallic shrug of the shoulders. "Odd-looking crowd, weren't they?"

There was an immense gloomy corridor. Marcus opened a door and we went into an enormous room with a high ceiling and solid Victorian furniture. Beyond the window was the sea.

"Very nice," I said politely.

"Do you like it?" said Marcus with eagerness. He was always so anxious for people to like everything and be happy. "It's a nice view, isn't it?"

"Lovely," I said.

"There's a bathroom quite near—go to the end of the corridor, then to the right and you'll find it's the first door on the left. Come downstairs as soon as you're ready. One of the footmen will tell you where the drawing room is."

"Good. Thank you, Marcus."

"See you later!" He smiled at me.

"Yes."

He went out, closing the door behind him, and I was alone at last.

I looked around me slowly. I hated it. It was the most chilling mansion I had ever seen, and I knew at once that I would not be happy there.

[2]

Hugh arrived the next day from Harrow. He paused at Penmarric just long enough to eat dinner and enjoy a comfortable night's rest and then the next morning he had saddled a horse and was riding off to Zillan to see his mother. He was gone all day but arrived home just in time not to incur Papa's displeasure by missing dinner.

"She looks well, doesn't she?" said Marcus to him. "Did you think she'd changed much?"

"Not particularly," said Hugh, considering the question with care. "Her hair was whiter but otherwise she seemed much the same. I thought she looked marvelous for her age."

"She was longing to see you," said Jeanne. "She could hardly wait. 'Oh how lovely it'll be to see Hugh again!' she said last Saturday. 'I can't wait till he comes home!'"

Hugh smiled his peculiarly sweet smile and looked complacent. "She said how good-looking I'd become," he said serenely, "and said she was sure I'd soon be as tall as Philip. God, I hope she's right! It's simply not fair that I should be so short. Everyone's tall except me."

"Did you take Mama a present?" said Marcus anxiously.

"Of course! I bought her some French perfume in London on the way down from Harrow. It was very tasteful," said Hugh fastidiously, "and highly suitable for her personality. I spent a long time choosing it."

"How lovely!" breathed Jeanne. "Was she thrilled?"

"Very," said Hugh. "I knew she would be. I thought it was rather a good present."

"Did you have a nice lunch?" said Elizabeth with interest. "Did Mama make any Cornish pasties? She makes them very nicely indeed."

"No," said Hugh. "Griselda made some old stew full of herbs. Frankly it wasn't very palatable but I ate it to be polite."

I said, fighting once more to overcome that insidious sense of exclusion, "Who's Griselda?"

"Oh, an awful old hag," said Hugh casually. "She must be at least ninety. I think she was Mama's old nurse once."

"We had a lovely time at the farm last Saturday," said Elizabeth. "We had a little elderberry wine for elevenses, and quite the nicest honeycakes I've ever tasted."

"Honestly, Lizzie," said Mariana, looking up from writing her daily letter to her fiancé in London, "don't you ever think of anything except your wretched little stomach?"

"Was Mama pleased about your engagement, Mariana?" said Hugh with interest.

"My dear, simply thrilled. She was so sweet. She said I had the most beautiful hands, just right for diamonds, and—"

I was becoming rather tired of Mariana's diamond ring.

"—and she said it was a wonderful match for me, and how pleased she was. I must say, I do think Papa has treated her a little meanly, don't you? I suppose he had his reasons for making it so difficult and upsetting for poor Mama to come to see us when we were at Allengate, but . . . anyway, I said that *of course* she must come to the New Year's Eve ball Papa's giving for Nick and me and *of course* she must meet Nick as soon as he comes down to Penmarric after Christmas. . . . Although to be perfectly frank that's going to be just the tiniest bit awkward. I mean, how on earth am I going to take Nick to that awful farmhouse? I do wish Mama didn't live there."

"I can't think why she does," agreed Hugh. "It's hard to imagine a woman of Mama's delicate tastes and refined habits actually *choosing* to live at a farmhouse in preference to Penmarric. Good God, they haven't even got a proper lavatory! It's distressingly primitive, to say the least."

"Mama could come to tea at Penmarric to meet Nick," suggested Marcus. "That would solve the difficulty without embarrassment to anyone, and I don't suppose Papa would object."

"What a good idea! I'll ask him about it at dinner."

When we were alone I said to William, "We won't have to meet her, will we?"

"Mrs. Castallack? No, of course not! Look, I'll tell you what we'll do—when Philip brings Mrs. C over here to have tea, let's ride over to Zillan and pay a visit to the rectory. The rector's a nice old man and his granddaughter Alice Penmar is a sort of adopted cousin of ours. Her father was a foster-son of Giles Penmar, who lived here before Papa did, and her mother was the rector's only child. Her parents are both dead and she was brought up by her grandparents at the rectory, but Mrs. Barnwell, her grandmother, died recently, so now Alice keeps house for her grandfather. She's rather fun. She's not pretty but she's amusing. I think you'll like her."

"How old is she?" I said suspiciously, for girls still made me feel awkward and I did not enjoy their company.

"My age!" William laughed. "Much too old for you! Don't worry, I'm not trying to pair you off. She'll probably be calling at Penmarric some time this week to see Mariana, so you'll soon have the chance to meet her."

"I don't feel like meeting anyone at the moment," I said obstinately. "I'd much rather be on my own and not have to make the effort to be sociable."

And despite all William's efforts to dissuade me I spent the first few days after my arrival at Penmarric in solitude. I walked around the grounds, scrambled down to the cove below the terrace, explored one or two caves, but then the weather broke and the cliffs were wreathed in mist and I had no inclination to go out of doors. I kept a fire going in my room and spent long hours reading my way through Papa's collection of novels by Anthony Trollope.

I even kept to myself at Christmas. They made a fine Cornish celebration of it at Penmarric, but I felt a stranger still, an outsider still dogged by that persistent feeling of exclusion, and I remained in the background as much as possible. Everyone else was very merry. William and Marcus got tipsy on one or two occasions and chased the maids around the mistletoe; presently they began to ride into St. Just in the evenings, or even out to Zennor or Zillan to drink at the local pubs, and often they would not return to Penmarric until late at night.

I went on sitting in my room or perhaps venturing out for brief walks by myself, and all the while I would think with pricking eyes of past Christmases, of Allengate and of my mother.

People called at Penmarric to see us. Young Peter Waymark called from Gurnards Grange at Zennor; George and Aubrey Carnforth and their sister Felicity rode over from Carnforth Hall, which stood between Penzance and Marazion. There were parties, invitations, calls to be repaid, but I avoided them all.

"Do come," said William. "Please! Why won't you come? Look, nobody knows about—"

"It's got nothing to do with that," I said.

"They think we're just a couple of obscure poor relations with Penmar blood in our veins! Nobody thinks that Papa—"

"I don't care. I hate parties and I don't want to meet anyone."

"But parties are fun, Adrian! Girls are fun! You're missing such a lot!"

But I shook my head obstinately and retreated still further from all opportunities to be sociable.

Fortunately after Christmas Mariana's fiancé Nicholas de Leonard came down from London and everyone was too busy entertaining him to concern themselves with me. However, Jan-Yves did not share my pleasure at being ignored, and confided crossly to me one morning that he was sick and tired of "that stupid lord" taking up all William's time.

"I wish he would go away and take Mariana with him and never come back here again," he added darkly. "I hate both of them."

"Don't you like any of your family apart from William?" I said, exasperated. "It's unreasonable to dislike everyone except him!"

"Why?" said Jan-Yves. "Marcus always tells me to go away and play whenever I come near him, Mariana looks at me as if I was a dead starfish washed up on the beach, Hugh has never spoken one single word to me except 'hullo,' Jeanne's silly, Elizabeth eats all my food, and you're always trying to get William's attention and take him away from me. You're as bad as the lord and I don't like you either. And I don't like Papa because he brought *them* back here without my permission and I don't like that new nanny because she slippers me and I don't like old Cartwright-governess because she's a stick-in-the-mud. I liked my old nanny," he added unexpectedly, "the nanny I had before *they* came. But she drank gin and had to go. Papa didn't even ask my permission either. I went to her room and found her packing her bags. I said I'd run away with her but she said I mustn't although I think she wanted me to because she cried. Poor Nanny! Is it so bad to drink gin?"

"Very," I said and tried to get rid of him but he stuck to me like a leech.

"Have you met my brother Philip? I haven't and I'm not going to either. He lives with *her*. I hate her more than anyone else in the world. I'm never going to meet her as long as I live. Nobody's going to make me meet her."

"Why don't you like her?" I could think of nothing else to say.

"Because I don't." He looked around mysteriously, then grabbed my hand to draw us closer together. "You know how if you see a bit of rubbish on the floor you pick it up and throw it away in the wastepaper basket?"

"I suppose so, yes."

"That's what she did to me. I was four months old and she picked me up and took me to Nanny and said 'throw it away!' But Nanny didn't. Nanny kept me secretly and looked after me. I know that's true because Nanny said it was."

"I can't believe your mother ever said—"

"Well, she went away, didn't she?" said the child. "And she never came back. She must have thought Nanny had thrown me in the wastepaper basket. Otherwise why didn't she come to see me? Anyway, I'm not going to meet her. She's coming to tea tomorrow to meet the stupid lord and Papa says I must be there but I shan't be. I'm going to go with you and William to tea at Zillan rectory."

But Papa had foreseen Jan-Yves's reaction to Mrs. Castallack's visit and took care to lock the child in his room the following afternoon to prevent him playing truant.

"Poor little devil," said William as we jogged over the moors toward Zillan.

I had not been to Zillan before. It was a moorland parish east of St. Just and south of Morvah, and to my surprise I found the little village was pretty in its austere Cornish manner, and the church had a fine Norman tower.

"Our grandfather is buried there," said William, "and our eldest half-brother who would have been only a few months younger than me if he'd lived." When I did not answer he added to me abruptly, "For God's sake, Adrian, I do wish you'd brighten up a bit! I hope you're not going to sit through this tea party in glum silence or I shall be most horribly embarrassed. Do cheer up a little, there's a good chap. I hate to see you so down."

"I'm sorry." I sighed. "It's just that life seems so beastly sometimes."

"I think it's fun," said William. "Don't worry, it won't seem beastly forever! You'll enjoy it again presently, I dare say."

When we reached the rectory we tethered our horses and walked around to the porch. As we approached, the front door was opened and a tall thin girl of about twenty with dark eyes, a sharp nose and a clever mouth smiled at us across the threshold. "Good afternoon!" said Alice Penmar in an attractive contralto voice. "How nice to see you both!" And she regarded me with that keen interested stare which I had come to know and dread.

"Alice," said William, "may I present my brother, Adrian Parrish. Adrian—Miss Alice Penmar."

"How do you do?" I said politely.

"At last!" said Alice. "I was wondering when you were going to deign to make your debut in west Cornish society. Frankly I was even beginning to doubt that you existed! Every time I called at Penmarric to see William or Marcus or Mariana I never even caught so much as a rear view of you. I can't think why you hid yourself away. You look eminently presentable to me and even quite friendly—what a relief! I feared you might have some frightful defect which everyone was too polite to mention."

I blushed. Shyness overcame me. I managed to smile.

"Come in," said Alice kindly, "and meet Grandpapa."

We went into a large old-fashioned drawing room and the rector stood up to greet us. He was, I supposed, about seventy years old, but his spare frame was agile and his eyes were brilliantly alive. He had extraordinary eyes, deep-set and lustrous. His hair was silver, giving him a distinguished appearance.

"Grandpapa," said Alice, "this is Adrian Parrish."

He looked at me and he knew. I saw the recognition flicker in his eyes although he suppressed it quickly enough. How he knew I had no idea, for I had no marked physical resemblance to my father, but he knew.

"How very nice of you to come," he said, and he took my hand and smiled at me as if he were greeting a long-lost friend. "What a very pleasant surprise!"

I smiled at him in return. I longed to ask him how he knew, why he was so unusually glad to see me, but I knew it was the wrong moment for such questions and that they could not be asked until we were alone together.

As if he could read my thoughts, he said, "We must have a long talk later. I want to hear all about you." And when he stretched out his hand and touched me on the shoulder it was as if I had reached the end of a long journey, and before me at last I saw the pattern again and knew that I was no longer alone.

[3]

He said to me later, "The Castallacks have called here several times since their return. They were all so full of praise for your mother. She must have been a very remarkable woman."

"Yes," I said. "She was." Alice was over by the window showing William some photographs she had taken during a visit to St. Ives. They were laughing together. I said clumsily to the rector, "She was a very . . . good person."

"Mark was fortunate to have such a person to look after his children so well. I have known Mark—your guardian—a long time, you know. Since he was William's age."

"Oh?"

"Yes, he was not a happy young man. He had difficult times. But he was tough. He survived. The Penmars have a strong streak of durability in their blood, and your guardian was no exception."

"I suppose," I said, "life is so awful sometimes one simply has to be tough to be able to face it at all."

"Dear me! You sound as if you've suffered the tortures of the damned! Has life really treated you so badly?"

That made me stop and think. "No," I had to admit at last.

"No, it hasn't. Apart from my mother's death I've been most extraordinarily fortunate. I do know that. It's just that I feel so unutterably depressed by the—the injustice in the world. It seems so unfair that people should often have to suffer for no reason or for something that they can't help. There's so much evil and suffering in the world, and since my mother's death it's seemed to me especially unbearable that there's so little I can do about it. In fact I feel that all I can do is turn my back on the world and retreat from it—pretend for as long and as often as I can that all the evil and suffering don't exist."

"But that will hardly help you or anyone else!" The rector leaned forward urgently. His eyes were so dark and brilliant that I found it impossible to look away. "You must face these things. Confront them! Don't hide your head in the sand and hope they will go away with wishful thinking. The world can indeed seem a better place to you—but only if you contribute to it, for no cause was ever helped by the passive, the apathetic and the uncommitted. Don't retreat into yourself by pretending the world is so distasteful that you have no place in it! Step out into the world and take your place in it and don't be afraid any more."

[4]

After that I decided that I would attend church at Zillan in future. Everyone at Penmarric attended church in St. Just, the nearest of the mining villages, and Papa in particular felt himself obliged as the largest landowner in the parish to worship at the parish church, but when I asked him for permission to go to Zillan instead he made no objection. Indeed I think he was pleased that I liked the rector so much and said that the rector had been very kind to him years ago after his father's death.

The only obstacle confronting me in my intention to attend church in Zillan was Mrs. Castallack. Her farm stood in Zillan parish, and I soon heard that she never missed matins on Sunday. It was unpleasant for me to realize that she was one of Mr. Barnwell's flock, but fired by my conversation at the rectory, I told myself resolutely that her presence at matins would be of no consequence to me—or if it was it oughtn't to be. But I was more worried about Philip's presence than his mother's, for I felt sure he would at once think I was trying to cause trouble if he saw me in Zillan church, and I did not want any violent scene with Philip. Finally I decided to attend evensong instead of matins, and this worked out very well. Before the end of the Christmas holidays I went twice to the evening service at Zillan, and each time the rector invited me to have supper afterward at the rectory. The first time I was very shy, especially of Alice, but she soon put me at ease with her quick, effortless conversation, and on my second visit I actually enjoyed talking to her. We spoke of Anthony Trollope's novels and discussed the character of Ferdinand Lopez in *The Prime Minister*.

"Attractive rascal," said Alice. "It's odd how many girls fall for a man who's absolutely no good. What a funny thing love is."

"Yes, it must be," I said seriously and blushed when she laughed.

"You're rather sweet!" she said in her frank, abrupt manner, and patted me fondly on the head as if I were six instead of sixteen.

I think it was then that I began to suffer the first stirrings of calf-love.

Since she was such a frank person I soon learned what she thought about a great many things. She was deeply interested in current events, and although she had always lived in such a remote village far from the hub of London life she knew far more than I did about contemporary politics, social questions and the great public issues of the day. In my desire to emulate Papa's taste for history I had always been too concerned with the past to be interested in the present, but now all that was changed. It was Alice who opened my eyes to the fact that today's events would be tomorrow's history, and I began to read the newspapers avidly in my efforts to match her knowledge and give a new depth to our conversations.

Alice was a Liberal, I discovered, and an admirer of Sir Edward Grey, the foreign secretary, despite the fact that he had been recently criticized for pursuing a policy which had led England dangerously close to war the previous summer.

"But you have to take a firm line sometimes," said Alice. "Especially with the Germans. How can anyone talk of placating the Germans when they do nothing but build their wretched submarines and challenge our naval supremacy? I'm glad Churchill's at the Admiralty now—he at least has the right ideas about expanding the navy so that the Germans won't outdo us.

He'll do a lot better there than he did as Home Secretary—oh, he and that horrid little Lloyd George! When I think of how they handled the entire question of women's suffrage . . ."

It was then that I learned that where women's suffrage was concerned Alice was more radical than many of the Liberal members of Parliament.

"But do you really think all women should have the vote?" I said doubtfully, having grown up with Papa's theory that women should have no part in politics.

"Why not?" said Alice. "Do you think it's either right or just that a person should be discriminated against for something they cannot help?"

"Certainly not!" I said fiercely, thinking of my illegitimacy, and suddenly found myself a supporter of women's suffrage. However, I retained enough of my old convictions to add, "But I think the suffragettes go much too far. I'm not surprised Churchill and Lloyd George lost patience with them."

"Unfortunately," agreed Alice, "there are always fanatics in every good cause and they're always the ones that get the publicity. No, much as I dislike Churchill's attitude I wouldn't attack him with a horsewhip as that woman did the other day. That only convinces people that women should never have the vote under any circumstances."

"What would women do with the vote anyway?" I said, veering back again toward my conservative views. "Take Mariana, for instance. She couldn't care less whether she has the vote or not. All she can think about is marrying a lord, living in London and wearing her wretched diamond ring."

But Alice, who was supposed to be Mariana's friend, was careful not to say too much against her. Mariana was always glossed over, I noticed, and since Alice seldom spoke of Philip either I assumed that he too found little favor with her. In fact the only person whom Alice openly confessed to disliking was Mrs. Castallack, and soon I found myself acquiring some information which I had never heard mentioned by my half-brothers and sisters.

"I have an aunt," Alice told me. "She was Miss Clarissa Penmar and was brought up at Penmarric, but she married a farmer, one of Mrs. Castallack's stepsons by her first marriage, a man named Joss Roslyn. They have one of the biggest farms at Morvah now. Joss's brother Jared and his family used to live at Ros-

lyn Farm after Mrs. Castallack's marriage to your guardian—
they were tenants, and Jared always understood that his family
home was to be his for a nominal rent for the rest of his life—"

"It was a five-year lease, Alice dear!" said the rector, coming
into the room in time to hear this last sentence. "And Mrs. Castallack waited till the third term expired before she evicted him!"

"Yes, but it was a mean trick really, Grandpapa! Fortunately
for Jared, Adrian, his brother Joss bought him a farm and land
at Morvah, so everything ended happily, but if Joss hadn't had
Aunt Clarissa's money—"

"Alice dear! There's no need to go into that—"

"Yes, but, Grandpapa, she did give him all her money when
he married her, didn't she?"

"Yes, but that's none of our business, my dear, and you know
that as well as I do."

I was sorry when I had no more opportunities to spend my
Sunday evenings at Zillan rectory, but in mid-January I returned
to school and was away from Penmarric until the end of March.
When I next saw Cornwall spring had come, the roadside verges
were ablaze with wildflowers, and the sunshine was sweeping
across the bleak landscape to that dark and brilliant sea.

[5]

Following the established tradition, Marcus had spent a few
months abroad before returning to England for Mariana's September wedding; he was in Paris by the time I returned to Penmarric at the end of March. Mariana had gone to London to
spend the Season at the townhouse with her chaperone, and
Papa was also in town combining some research with one or two
long-term arrangements relating to the coming wedding. At Penmarric Jeanne and Elizabeth were already discussing bridesmaids'
dresses, and Jan-Yves, determined not to be left out, was making
himself obnoxious by demanding to be a page. William was so
busy with estate matters during Papa's absence that I soon realized I would see little of him. Presently when Hugh came home
from Harrow and began his daily treks to the farm again I became tired of solitude, and one day, more out of boredom than
any better reason, I followed him cautiously on horseback as he
rode over the moors to Zillan.

I decided I was curious to see the farm for which Mrs. Castallack had abandoned Penmarric. Obviously it was a house of character. I had no intention of walking to the very walls, but I thought it might be fun to encircle the place from a distance, and besides I was tired of reading and the weather was fine enough to tempt me out of doors.

I set off in Hugh's wake. I did not see him turn around once as we left St. Just and took the road to Morvah, and he still did not turn when he left the road and followed the bridlepath up onto the moors.

A decayed signpost by the bridlepath read: "TO CHÛN, ZILLAN AND DING DONG MINE," and suddenly Cornwall was all around me, the great tracts of the moors heavy with memories of a bygone civilization, the towering summit of Carn Kenidjack bursting black granite toward a cloudless sky. We rode on, and the land was wild, prehistoric, forgotten. Heather and bracken whispered together beneath the salt breeze from the sea, and far below us on the coast was the headland of Pendeen and the engine houses of the Tin Coast.

We reached the summit of the ridge. The view was extraordinary. I could see south to St. Michael's Mount shimmering in the blue of Mount's Bay, north to Morvah and the sea, east to the engine house of Ding Dong Mine and west to the mighty crest of Carn Kenidjack. Directly in front of me, further along the ridge, Hugh and his horse seemed to be disappearing slowly behind a heap of weathered rocks.

I was puzzled but when I rode nearer I saw what it was. It was an ancient hill fort, its stone walls still standing, and suddenly I remembered my father speaking once at dinner of the "castle" which still stood on the ridge at Chûn.

I rode warily through the heather to the castle walls.

There was an outer ring and an inner ring. I rode into the inner ring on the assumption that the place had two exits and that Hugh had entered by the first and left by the second. I was wrong. Just as I was reining my horse to a halt in the middle of the inner circle Hugh's voice said coolly behind me, "What the devil are you doing, following me like that!"

I swiveled around in the saddle. He had dismounted and was standing with his horse in the shadow of the walls. I dismounted too and turned to face him.

"I'm sorry," I said readily. "I didn't intend to spy on you—I realized you were going to the farm. But I was bored and wanted a ride, so I thought I would see which route you took. By the way, what's this? Is it Chûn Castle?"

"Yes," said Hugh, who cared nothing for history. "It is." He smiled his wide charming smile. "Why didn't you tell me you wanted a ride? We could have ridden over together."

"I . . . thought perhaps you might have wanted to be alone."

"No indeed! You're the solitary one these days, not me! I'm glad to see you. Look, come with me down to the farm! Philip's taken Mama into Penzance today and I'm only riding over there because Griselda promised to make me a special pasty to celebrate the start of the holidays. Come with me and help me eat it!"

I said uneasily, "I don't think I'd better."

"Oh, come on! Mama and Philip will have been gone at least half an hour by now. Look, don't be silly—do you think I'd ask you to come if I thought for one moment they'd be there? I don't want Philip yelling at me any more than you do!"

I gave in. "Very well," I said. "If you're sure—"

"Positive. Come on—it's only just down the hill in the valley and I can almost smell the pasty already! What a long time it seems since breakfast!"

We led our horses out of the castle and mounted again before setting off down the hillside into the valley below.

"There's the tenant farm," said Hugh. "That belonged to Jared Roslyn, who lived at the farmhouse while Mama was at Penmarric. When Mama evicted him later she bought him out of the tenant farm as well because she didn't want him living on her doorstep after she'd returned to Roslyn Farm. Anyway the cottage would have been too small for him. He and his wife have eight daughters and one son. Eight girls! Imagine! And they're all called funny names like Chastity, Fidelity and Continence."

"Not really, Hugh!"

"Well, Faith, Hope and Charity, then!"

We laughed together.

"Jared Roslyn is at Morvah now, isn't he?"

"Yes, he and his brother Joss have adjoining farms. Joss has got pots of money but he won't spend it—except to help his brother. His wife used to be a lady but you'd never guess it now, Mama says. Mama doesn't like any of them. There's a feud."

"A feud?"

"Yes, nobody likes Joss Roslyn. He's a real bastard." He cleared his throat. "Sorry, old chap—unfortunate word. No offense meant."

But I was already thinking of something else. "Wasn't Joss's wife brought up at Penmarric? Why did she marry a farmer?"

"*Amor vincit omnia,*" said Hugh suavely, "or so they say."

"Are there any children?"

"There's a girl. I saw her once ages ago before I went to Allengate. She was a year younger than me."

We were within sight of the farmhouse, and with surprise I saw that it was beautiful. Above the slate roof rose mellow chimneys, while beneath the roof quiet gray walls slumbered peacefully in the morning sunlight; there were climbing plants around the porch, honeysuckle and a rambling rose.

After tethering our horses by the stable we walked around through the farmyard to the back door.

"Griselda!" yelled Hugh, stepping into the old-fashioned kitchen. "Griselda! Where's my pasty?"

There was a patter of feet. A servant woman, obviously simple-minded, appeared and said something unintelligible.

"Hullo, Annie," said Hugh. "Has Griselda made my pasty?"

A door opened at the far end of the kitchen. An old crone in a black dress and black shawl shuffled into the room.

"Griselda," said Hugh, "have you made that—"

She said something in a violent tone of voice, and I saw with a shock that her finger was pointing at me. Her voice was so heavily Cornish that I found it impossible to understand her.

"Oh, this is a school friend of mine," said Hugh, exercising his talent for telling plausible lies. "He's staying at Penmarric."

The old crone went crimson and began to shout at him. I watched in great alarm and at the same time marveled at her lack of restraint; she did not behave like a servant at all. It was as if she were the mistress of the house.

"Rubbish, Griselda," said Hugh politely. "I don't know what you're talking about. Is my pasty ready, please? If it is, I'll take it and go outside."

The old crone muttered something and shook her head.

Hugh said to me, "It'll be ready in ten minutes. Come and have a look at the rest of the house."

I followed him silently into the passage. As he closed the door he said, "She knew who you were."

"How?" I felt chilled by this apparent clairvoyance. "How could she know?"

"God knows! Don't worry, if she says anything to Mama later I'll insist that she made a mistake and that you were Aubrey Carnforth. You're about the same height and build as Aubrey. . . . Now, this is the hall and through here is the parlor . . ."

I followed him through the rooms. They were beautiful, the furniture old and solid, the spaciousness infinitely pleasing to the eye. Everywhere was spotlessly clean and well-kept.

"What a lovely house," I said with genuine admiration. "I like it much better than Penmarric. It's so warm and comfortable and serene."

"How odd! It doesn't appeal to me in the least—I much prefer Penmarric! Penmarric is so much more civilized, don't you think?"

"Because it has a couple of proper lavatories?"

"Well, plumbing is an advantage, you must admit." He was quite serious. He seemed to have no aesthetic appreciation whatsoever of the farmhouse. "Do you want to see upstairs?"

"May I? I'd like that."

Philip had a room facing the moors. On the table by the window were several books on the Cornish Tin Coast, including a volume entitled *A History of the Levant Mine*. I picked it up and flicked through the pages, but Hugh was already going out into the corridor again, so I put down the book to follow him. Mrs. Castallack had a pleasant room next door with an old-fashioned four-poster near the window and an enormous wardrobe along one wall.

I glanced around. "What a funny little clock!" I exclaimed, wandering over to the mantelshelf. "I like it! Do you know where it came from?"

"Haven't a clue," Hugh said. "Do you really like it? I think it's hideous. . . . Come over and look at the view. Isn't it fine?"

We admired the view together and then returned to the kitchen. The pasty was ready. We took it outside, found a sheltered spot behind a stone wall and settled down to an early lunch.

It was delicious. Presently Hugh fetched some cider, and when we had finished both cider and pasty we lay on our backs and watched the wispy clouds drift across the blue sky.

Hugh fell asleep.

I got up and wandered off in search of a lavatory, however

primitive, but when my search proved abortive I stepped behind the barn instead. Afterward I moved back toward the house and stole a glance into the kitchen. No one was about. I went in, feeling nervous, and wandered through those beautiful rooms again, my fingers trailing lightly over the furniture. No one disturbed me. I went upstairs and the floorboards creaked beneath my feet. The door of Mrs. Castallack's room was ajar. I went to the window, then to the bed, then to the fireplace. The little clock sat ticking on the mantelshelf, and as I touched it I looked over my shoulder as if I half-expected to see someone watching me but there was no one there, only a bird singing on the sill and the curtains blowing lightly in the wind.

I left, walked into Philip's room, picked up the book on the Levant Mine. To my surprise I found it interesting. I sat down and began to read, and the minutes slipped idly away as morning merged into afternoon.

I was just thinking that I should return to Hugh when I heard a door slam.

I got up, put back the book and went out into the corridor.

From the hall a Castallack voice said, "Perhaps you left it upstairs."

But it was not Hugh who spoke. It was Philip.

I stopped, rigid with horror, and as I felt the sweat break out on my forehead I heard him add, "I'll go up and look."

I wanted to run. I looked around wildly at the closed doors of the landing and my panic was so great that I could not even decide which room I might choose as a hiding place.

And then she spoke. Her voice was low and soft, like surf breaking on a beach far away, and she said, "No, don't bother, darling. I'll go upstairs and find it. I think I know where it is."

I could not breathe. My heart was hammering so hard that there was a pain in my chest. I still could not move, but as the stairs creaked beneath her feet I suddenly knew what I must do. I walked forward to the head of the stairs. I went out to meet her, and below in the hall Philip was saying, "I wonder where Hugh is. He said he'd be coming over this morning. I must ask Griselda if—"

I saw her. She looked up at me, and I saw those cool light eyes which I had first seen so long ago in that dining room at Brighton. When she saw me her eyes widened. Her hand flew to her throat and I heard her sobbing gasp of fear.

She looked as though she had seen a ghost.

She said a name, a man's name, a name I knew, but before I could speak Philip was pushing past her, Philip was rushing up the stairs toward me, Philip was shouting, "You bastard, get out of here! Get out, get out, get out—"

I went downstairs. As she turned and stumbled away from me I called out, "I'm sorry. I didn't mean to come. I'm sorry."

She slammed the parlor door.

"You damned bastard!" Philip was still shouting. "If ever you show your face here again—"

Hugh was in the hall. His eyes were that same cool blue.

"It was he who suggested I come," I said in a shaking voice to Philip. "He said it would be all right. He said—"

"Absolute lies," said Hugh. "You insisted on coming. You followed me all the way to Chûn." He turned to Philip. "I did my best to turn him out, but—"

"You liar!" I shouted. "You miserable rotten—"

Philip hit me on the jaw. I fell backward against the hall chest, picked myself up and moved to the front door. Philip was edging in to hit me again. I wrenched open the door, stumbled out into the porch and ran down the path to the lane. The air was sweet with the smell of herbs and the sun still shone serenely from that limpid southern sky.

I looked back.

She was watching me from the parlor window, but before she stepped behind the curtain I had a glimpse of her face. It was white and crumpled as if she had been crying, and as I made my way blindly to the stables to get my horse I wondered if she was upset simply because I was her husband's bastard or upset because she had thought for one long terrible moment that I was the ghost of my grandfather Laurence Castallack, come back from the dead to remind her of the past.

5

The lady Alice was sent to the court of King Henry
. . . it seemed all to the good that he was said to have
taken a fancy to the child.

—The Devil's Brood,
ALFRED DUGGAN

The heir of [Brittany's] duke was a daughter named
Constance . . . the Breton barons hated Norman dom-
ination.

—Oxford History of England:
From Domesday Book to Magna Carta,
A. L. POOLE

[1]

I rode into Zillan village. I had stopped crying by the time I reached the rectory. I was completely composed. Alice was out buying milk and eggs from a neighboring farm, the cook told me, but the rector was in his study preparing his Sunday sermon.

I talked to him there for a long time.

"Am I like Laurence Castallack?" I said. "Am I?"

He smiled. "Yes," he said, "there's a likeness. I must confess that that was one of the reasons why you interested me so much from the first time I saw you. Laurence and I were old friends."

I made an enormous effort. It cost me a great deal but I managed to say, "He was my grandfather. My guardian is my father, not a distant cousin."

After that everything was easy and I did not want to cry any more. "Poor Mrs. Castallack," said the rector later. "Yes, no doubt it did give her a severe shock to see you—and to see you in such an unexpected manner. What an unfortunate thing to happen! Hugh was very wrong to have tried to wash his hands of you but I expect he was more afraid of falling into his mother's bad books than of incurring your anger. . . . You must make allowances, you know. Mrs. Castallack was not an attentive mother—she had too many troubles of her own—and as a result her children are perhaps overanxious to win her attention and favor."

"I don't know why they bother with her!" I said fiercely. "She was content to live without them for nearly seven years!"

"Ah, now you're speaking too hastily." And he began to talk about Mrs. Castallack in such a calm, dispassionate voice that soon I had forgotten that he was speaking of a woman I had resented so intensely for so long and was listening instead to the story of a woman who had suffered an orphaned poverty-stricken childhood, raised herself with great difficulty to the respectable level of a farmer's wife and then jeopardized her happiness by an unwise marriage which had finally brought her nothing but the most bitter distress.

"Poor woman," said the rector, "she was caught between forces which she could not master at all. I was seriously worried about her when the courts deprived her of the children. She had a difficult pregnancy which she had to endure without one single gesture of assistance from her husband. She was, believe me, greatly to be pitied."

I was silent. I had not thought of Mrs. Castallack from a sympathetic viewpoint before and the experience was so novel that I found it hard to know what I wanted to say. In the end all I could say lamely was "If she'd given my father a divorce I don't suppose he would have been so harsh to her about the children's custody." But even as I spoke my words seemed to condemn my father and exonerate Mrs. Castallack from blame.

The rector said simply, "The marriage meant a great deal to Mrs. Castallack. Also she was convinced that even if she had divorced your father he would still have tried to deprive her of the children. You mustn't judge her too harshly."

"No," I said with an effort. "I can see why you say she was to be pitied, but . . ." I stopped but the next moment I was saying, unable to help myself, "My mother was to be pitied too."

"Yes indeed," said the rector at once. "She must have had many appallingly difficult times."

"Then my father was wrong to hurt them both so much," I said, trying to sort it out. "It was my father who was at fault."

"Not entirely," said the rector. "In a way they were all at fault—your mother, your father and Mrs. Castallack; it would be unjust to blame your father alone. He did wrong, certainly, but he was far from being a wicked young man. He was lonely. He longed for affection from his father, but Laurence was—without meaning to be unkind—more inclined to show his deepest affections toward others. He expected no affection from his mother, who was a very difficult woman. He was a plain young man, not particularly attractive to the ladies, who was anxious to find companionship of a certain kind whenever he could. In many ways it was inevitable that he should have entangled himself in such an unhappy domestic situation."

We talked for some time longer, and soon I began to feel infinitely better. When Alice returned presently from her shopping expedition I stayed to lunch and by the time I was on my way back to Penmarric that afternoon I had fully recovered from my visit to the farm.

On my arrival at Penmarric I discovered to my disgust that Hugh had planted himself in my room to wait for me.

"Adrian!" He sprang to his feet in concern as I came in. "God, I was getting worried about you! Look, old chap, I'm terribly sorry about that scene at the farm—"

I had had more than enough by that time of his talent for facing both ways and I told him so, but he was so full of apologies and winning smiles that I found it impossible to be furious with him for long.

"After all," he pleaded, "how was I to know Philip and Mama would return early from Penzance? How was I to know that Mama would take the wrong handbag with her by mistake and that she and Philip would reach Market Jew Street to find they had only half a crown between them? It was just a piece of the most awful bad luck."

"Well, all right," I said reluctantly, not wanting to be uncharitable. "But if you turn against me again as you turned against me today at the farm, that's the end of all friendship between us. I don't believe in having a friend unless he can stand up for me when I'm in trouble."

"I absolutely agree," said Hugh. "So we're friends again? Good! I'm so glad. Look, why don't we ride into Penzance together one day next week? I went over there the other day with Philip and I discovered the most fascinating shop down by the harbor. Come to my room and I'll show you one or two of the things I bought there."

To my disgust I discovered that his purchases consisted only of three postcards, each a garish photograph of a scantily clad woman in an artificial pose.

"They're called 'semi-classical' poses," Hugh explained. "Classical means nude. I tried to get some completely classical cards but it was no good—the man refused to sell them to me. However, you're tall and could easily pass for at least eighteen—if you came with me I'm sure the man wouldn't refuse to sell them to you."

"But why on earth do you want to buy them?"

"Why, to look at, of course!" He gave me a scandalized glance. "Don't you do that sort of thing at school?"

"No, I'm too busy working or reading or trying to play cricket."

"Girls are much more fun!" He sighed. "If only I wasn't so short! If I were two, three, four inches taller I'm sure I could have any girl I wanted just by snapping my fingers."

"I wouldn't want to be in that position anyway," I said flatly. "I expect I shall get married one day, but until then I don't want to have anything to do with girls. I find the whole business of casual affairs repulsive."

"Really?" said Hugh. "I find it utterly fascinating. I say, you're not in love with a boy at school or anything, are you?"

"Do you have to be so absolutely revolting?"

"I take it that means no. In that case, why aren't you interested in girls? I spend almost every day wondering what it's like to . . . incidentally, I found out from that shop where I bought the postcards that there's a woman who does it with boys our age. But she charges a guinea. Rather pricey, isn't it! I don't suppose by any chance—"

"You're not seriously considering seeking out some common prostitute!"

"No," said Hugh, "just toying with the idea."

"Honestly, Hugh!"

"Well, why not? Everyone else goes to bed with women, so

why shouldn't I? I'd go and see that barmaid Tilly at Zillan, but Marcus goes to her and I don't want her telling Marcus when he comes home from the Continent that I've been taking his place during his absence. He's quite silly enough to let the news slip out to Papa, although why Papa should object I don't know since he spent seven years at Allengate going to bed with . . . sorry, old chap! I didn't mean to say that, I just wasn't thinking. No offense meant. . . . Actually the girl I'd really like to go to bed with is right here at Penmarric. You know Hannah the tweeny? I must say, I rather fancy her. Have you noticed her mouth? She has very full lips. I think it might be fun to kiss her. And she's got the most marvelous bosom. . . . Hey, where are you going? What's the matter?"

But I shook my head blindly without replying. I felt sickened by his conversation and wanted to be alone.

"Wait!" He followed me and caught my arm. "I'm sorry— look, let's forget about girls for a while—I was only joking half the time anyway! Let's go for a walk along the cliffs—it's a fine afternoon and it seems a pity to waste it indoors."

I tried to get rid of him, but when he refused to take no for an answer we went outside together and strolled along the cliff path past the deserted engine houses of the Sennen Garth and King Walloe mines. Soon St. Just was on our right while the sea lay to our left. Passing Cape Cornwall, we skirted the mighty workings of the Levant mine and walked on along the scarred cliffs to Botallack before turning inland to Carn Kenidjack and wandering up onto the moors. Finally after several minutes of stiff climbing we sank down in the heather to rest. I lay on my back, my hands behind my head, and tried not to think of Hugh's postcards and his obsession with the 'tween maid's anatomy, but presently Hugh propped himself up on his elbow and disturbed me.

"There's a girl coming," he said, his eyes narrowed against the bright light. "A girl on horseback."

"Semi-classical?" I inquired with suitable sarcasm.

He did not answer. I went on looking up at the sky and displaying a pointed lack of interest.

"How odd," said Hugh. "I don't recognize her. Yet she must be someone of consequence if she's riding her own horse. Perhaps she's a friend of Peter Waymark's sisters and spending a holiday at Gurnards Grange. But why is she out riding alone?"

Curiosity conquered me. I levered myself into a sitting position.

The girl was close to us now but it was difficult to tell if she had noticed our existence. Certainly if she had she gave no indication of it. She was young, younger than us, and she had long straight black hair which she wore brushed back from her face. A small hat, perched on top of her head, kept her hair in place and prevented it from blowing across her eyes. Her riding habit was elegant but old-fashioned, as if it had been handed down to her from someone else.

"She's very pretty," said Hugh.

I thought she was too. We watched her approach and at last she looked at us and tilted her chin up haughtily in rejection.

We both rose to our feet as if we were puppets governed by the same strings.

"Good afternoon!" called Hugh.

She stared at him. Her eyes were dark and proud. "Good afternoon," she said with a faint air of disdain and prepared to ride past us.

"It's a beautiful afternoon too!" persisted Hugh with a reckless determination I could not help but admire. "Beautiful weather for a holiday!"

The girl raised her slim, dark eyebrows; a faint smile curled the corners of her wide mouth.

"I live here," she said coolly and spurred her horse to the gallop.

We watched her race away from us across the moors toward Morvah.

"Who is she?" Hugh was saying. "Who is she? Who *is* she?"

"How should I know? You're the native of this part of the world, not I!"

"But damn it, who *can* she be! Unless . . ." He stopped.

"Yes?"

"She might be a Roslyn."

"Of course," I said at once. "That must be it. She must be the daughter of Alice's Aunt Clarissa. That would explain why she had such a ladylike appearance."

"Good God!" said Hugh. He was still staring after her. "Little Rebecca Roslyn! Last time I saw her she was six years old, wearing a pinafore and talking with a Cornish accent!" He could not get over it. He kept referring to the incident all the way back to Penmarric. Finally he said in disgust, "But I can't even call at her house to invite her to come riding with me! That bastard Joss Roslyn would chase me off his land with a pitchfork."

"If she has such an unpleasant father," I said, trying to console him, "maybe she's not particularly nice either."

"What does being nice have to do with it?" said Hugh, very fractiously, I thought, and retired without even so much as an apology to the solitude of his room.

[2]

I was to see Rebecca Roslyn again before the year was out but meanwhile I was soon preoccupied with her cousin Alice Penmar once again. At Penmarric Jan-Yves had hounded the housekeeper into giving notice, and when discussing this item of news with Alice during a visit to the rectory I was suddenly smitten with the brilliant idea that Alice might like to be the new housekeeper. She had often mentioned the fact that if she did not keep house for her grandfather she would be obliged to earn her living by keeping house for someone else, and Mr. Barnwell had once privately regretted to me that Alice met so few people at Zillan rectory and wished matters could be otherwise. Much excited, I decided that my idea would suit everyone to perfection and I became determined to pursue it.

"William," I said with unintended overtones of *David Copperfield*, "tell Papa that Alice is willing."

"Very well," said William agreeably, "but why don't you tell him yourself? You were at the rectory when the subject was discussed and I wasn't." In my enthusiasm I had already mentioned my idea to Alice, who, after protesting that she could not leave her grandfather even if she were offered such a post, had allowed the rector to convince her that he had no wish to confine her to Zillan rectory for the rest of his life.

"No, you tell Papa, William," I said. "You're the bailiff and he'll listen to you on business matters."

For I was shy about Alice. I did not want anyone to know how much I liked the idea of her coming to Penmarric to keep house for us all, and I did not want anyone to know how pleasant I thought it would be to discuss current events with her after dinner in the evenings and perhaps walk in the grounds with her after lunch whenever she had a few minutes to spare.

Papa first of all said Alice was too young to be considered

for such an important post, but when he invited Alice to lunch to discuss the matter he soon changed his mind. Afterward he said, sounding surprised, "She seemed a capable, self-assured girl. I liked her. We agreed that she should accept the position on a six months' trial basis—that at least will take us until after Mariana's wedding. Then if either of us find the arrangement unsatisfactory we can terminate it without any hard feelings on either side." And to Jan-Yves he added, "If you once play on Alice the kind of practical jokes you played on Mrs. Hollingdale you'll get a good caning—is that understood? I've had enough of your pranks at the servants' expense and my patience is exhausted."

"Pooh!" said the child rudely, but Papa let the rudeness pass. In spite of his threats he always seemed curiously reluctant to discipline Jan-Yves.

I went back to school for the summer term soon after that, and for twelve weeks I heard about family affairs only through the letters I received from Papa and William. Mariana had paid a fleeting visit to Penmarric to discuss the wedding arrangements, and much to her fury Papa had said that since Jeanne and Elizabeth were to be bridesmaids it was only fair that Jan-Yves should be granted his burning wish to be a page.

"Papa bends over backward to be nice to the little beggar," wrote William, "but I don't believe it makes any difference whatsoever to Jan-Yves's ingrained dislike of him. Incidentally—and this'll surprise you!—Jan-Yves is now meeting his mother once a week and saying good morning to her. This came about because Alice likes to attend matins at her grandfather's church and now that I've got the hang of the new car I drive her over to Zillan each week. Naturally Jan-Yves couldn't bear to be left out of an expedition that included a motorcar—" And you, I thought dryly "—so he comes with us, but only on condition that he greets his mother afterward. Papa was very firm about that. I find I don't mind seeing Mrs. Castallack at all—of course we always keep our distance from each other—and if she minds seeing me that's her concern, not mine. But she can't mind so very much or she'd go to evensong."

But later he wrote: "Mrs. C's causing trouble again. On Nick's behalf Mariana asked me to be an usher at the Great Wedding, which I must say I found very flattering, and everyone thought this was a fine idea—except Philip and Mrs. C. Philip wrote to Papa and said they wouldn't be at the wedding if I was to be an usher, and furthermore that if we were to be staying at the town-house he'd take his mother to stay at a hotel. So I expect I shall have to step down. Rather a shame, isn't it? When you think how Mama provided a home for the Castallacks for seven years you'd think Mrs. C could put up with us for a day or two, but evidently she doesn't see the situation in that light."

I was incensed by this news and wrote back demanding to know what Papa had said in reply to Philip's letter, but William was vague. Papa had postponed making a decision on the subject and was at present involved in quarreling with Marcus.

"Marcus went broke in Monte Carlo," William wrote shortly after his twenty-first birthday in May, (God knows what he was doing there out of season! He was supposed to be somewhere else) and wired Papa for money. Papa was furious, since this was the third time Marcus has got into this sort of scrape, and wired him to come home. Marcus wired back to say he'd borrowed the money and had no intention of coming home early as he was having such a marvelous time. Papa was livid. I've seldom seen him so angry. He immediately sent another wire saying Marcus was to come home pretty damned quickly if he still wanted to go up to Oxford in the autumn and Marcus sent a wire saying he couldn't see why Papa was making so much fuss. Papa then wired: 'Kindly cease wasting borrowed money on expensive telegrams stop Your behavior is insolent, impertinent and totally irresponsible stop Be at Penmarric by Friday or else I shall be in Monte Carlo promptly to bring your Grand Tour to a conclusion decidedly lacking in grandeur stop MSC.' I know the telegram word for word because I had to go to Penzance to send it! Poor old Marcus. Anyway, he came home fuming on Friday and he and Papa had the most almighty row. Marcus actually vomited afterward. Poor chap, he does so hate scenes and unpleasantness. It turned out that he'd fallen violently in love with a French cabaret dancer in Monte Carlo and had been sending her two dozen red roses every day, wining and dining her in the most expensive restaurants and assuming optimistically that his money would last forever. . . ."

When I returned to Penmarric for the summer holidays I fully expected to find a strained atmosphere existing in the house, but Marcus had evidently made his peace with Papa and Papa himself seemed to have forgotten the quarrel. However, I noticed that Marcus spent more time visiting his mother. He went over there with the girls for Saturday lunch as usual, but he had fallen into the habit of dining at the farm during the middle of the week and calling whenever he happened to be in the neighborhood.

I saw Mrs. Castallack at matins on the first Sunday after my return. I did not see her enter the church since William and Alice had formed the habit of arriving early and taking a front pew, but I turned around during the first hymn and glimpsed Philip's golden head at the back of the building. When I glanced around again I saw his mother beside him. She wore black and looked almost young from a distance. I did not dare stare at her too long for fear our glances would meet, so I spent the rest of the service looking steadfastly ahead of me toward the altar.

But throughout the service I remained uncomfortably aware of her presence.

"Do you like your mother any better yet?" I asked Jan-Yves after he had said his weekly "Good morning" to Mrs. Castallack and had rejoined us as we all wandered over to the rectory for lunch.

"No," said Jan-Yves. He scowled. "Why does she bother with me? She never did until Papa started to. I wish they'd both go away and leave me alone. I wish my old nanny could come back instead of them. She really did like me and it wasn't just a pretend-like either because if it was just a pretend-like she wouldn't have saved me from the wastepaper basket when I was a baby."

"You and your wastepaper basket!" I said, laughing at him, and he stuck out his tongue at me as he skipped ahead to join William.

After lunch the rector and I played chess outside in the garden, Alice wandered down to the far border to cut some flowers for the drawing room, and William took Jan-Yves for an afternoon walk on the moors. Some time passed. I was just wondering if Alice would finish arranging the flowers soon and come to join us when there was an interruption. The side gate opened by the back door, light footsteps crossed the yard outside the scullery, and the next moment I looked up and saw a girl moving over the lawn toward us, an empty basket swinging from her hand.

It was the girl Hugh and I had seen riding on the moors in the spring, the girl we had assumed to be Alice's cousin, Rebecca Roslyn.

She looked different, younger. Her hair was tightly plaited instead of being allowed to trail wild and free down her back, and her gingham dress was severely cut to give her a childish look. It was also too small for her. I noticed uncomfortably that she was beginning to look like a woman, and to my furious embarrassment I remembered Hugh's postcards and felt my cheeks begin to burn with a long slow blush.

"Ah, good afternoon, Rebecca!" called the rector. "More cheese from Deveral Farm? How kind of your mother to remember us!"

"There was a chicken too," said the girl, "and some bantams' eggs. I've just given them all to Cook." She spoke carefully, as if she were for some reason listening to herself, and as she spoke she glanced fleetingly in my direction. When the rector introduced us I could see at once that she remembered me.

"How do you do, Miss Roslyn," I said, stammering a little.

"How do you do, Mr. Parrish." She looked around as if she did not expect me to have come to the rectory alone, and presently she asked, "Where's your friend?"

"You mean the boy I was with when we saw each other by Carn Kenidjack last Easter? That's my cousin Hugh Castallack. He's not with me today."

"I see," she said and seemed to lose interest.

I was just feeling inexplicably disappointed when Jan-Yves and William reappeared after their walk, Alice brought out some lemonade and we all sat down on the lawn to enjoy the sunshine and the languid summer air.

William, I noted enviously, began a conversation with Rebecca without any difficulty at all. They talked of Morvah, where she lived, and then of Penzance.

"I'm at a small boarding school there," said the girl, and I noticed again her trick of speaking too precisely as if she were in elocution class. "It's horrid. Dad didn't want me to go but Mama thought I should learn how to embroider tablecloths and say 'please' and 'thank you' in French."

The word "Dad" struck a jarring note in her carefully phrased speech and made me remember that her father was a farmer.

"Don't you enjoy being with other girls of your own age?" said the rector kindly.

"Not particularly. Most of them are snobs and I don't like them."

"I don't like girls either," said Jan-Yves at once. "Whenever we go to the beach I kick down all the sand castles that belong to girls."

"I must commission Elizabeth to knock down a few of yours one day," said William and glanced at his watch. "Well, sir, I think we'd best be returning to Penmarric—"

"Oh, William, we must stay to tea!" exclaimed Alice. "Cookie's made a special cake! Do let's stay."

In the end we all stayed and had a pleasant tea party on the lawn. It was the girl who moved first. She picked up her basket and scrambled to her feet.

"I must go," she said. "Dad'll be furious if I'm late for tea."

"But you've just had tea!" protested Jan-Yves, and then added enviously, "But he doesn't know that. I see. You're going to get two teas instead of one just by keeping quiet."

She laughed. "I meant high tea! Supper! Dinner—whatever you want to call it." She turned to the rector. "Thanks very much for the tea, Mr. Barnwell. Thanks for the lemonade, Alice."

"Look, I'll tell you what, Miss Roslyn," said William. "We'll give you a lift home. There's plenty of room in the car and we'll be driving home via Morvah anyway."

"No, please, don't bother—"

"Good gracious, it's no trouble at all! It'll save you a long walk and make sure you're not late for your evening meal."

"It's all right, Rebecca," said Alice. "We can drop you at the end of the lane."

"Could you? I wouldn't want Dad to think—"

"I know," said Alice and turned to say goodbye to her grandfather.

Presently we all climbed into the car. The hood was down; I sat on the back seat with Jan-Yves on my right and Rebecca on my left while Alice sat in the front with William. After Jan-Yves had elbowed himself enough room in which to bounce up and down behind William's shoulders and yell encouragement into his ear I found myself sitting rather too close to Rebecca. She did not seem to mind. I was uneasily aware of her thigh, warm and firm, being pressed against my leg, and when I stole a glance at the rest of her body I could not help noticing certain aspects of her figure beneath the childish gingham dress. I began to feel too hot. In an effort to turn my thoughts elsewhere I tried to concentrate on the scenery and take an intelligent interest in the conversation.

"How are your Roslyn cousins, Rebecca?" Alice was inquiring. "How are all the girls?"

"They're well, thank you. Patience is still walking out with Will Pryde. They've been walking out over two years now."

"Walking out where?" said Jan-Yves.

"It's a phrase meaning 'partaking of each other's company with a possible view to getting married,'" said William. "Don't interrupt."

"Charity wants to go into service at Gurnards Grange but Uncle Jared won't let her because young Mr. Peter Waymark's reputation is supposed to be . . ." She stopped and I saw she and William were looking at each other in the driving mirror.

"Go on!" William laughed. "I won't tell Peter!"

"Well . . ." Rebecca was confused. "Since Charity is a little flighty . . . Do you know my cousin Charity Roslyn, Mr. Parrish?"

"No, but she sounds most interesting. Is she as pretty as you are?"

They looked at each other in the mirror again and the girl gave an exquisite blush.

"Do keep your eyes on the road, William," said Alice irritably. "I don't want to end up in a field."

"Simon Peter still suffers from asthma," said Rebecca in a rush as if to draw a veil over William's compliment, and I heard the Cornish lilt creep into her voice as she forgot her elocution lessons. She added, more to Jan-Yves than to me: "That's my youngest Roslyn cousin. He's nine, but you wouldn't think it because he's so small and sickly."

"I shall be seven next month," said Jan-Yves. "And I'm never ill."

"Poor little Simon Peter," said Alice absently. "Such a shame. All those eight sisters of his are such healthy strapping girls too. Perhaps he'll be stronger when he grows up."

The car surmounted the ridge and ran slowly downhill into the parish of Morvah. The village lay half a mile below us, its tiny church basking in the late afternoon light, and beyond the village the fields stretched to the cliffs and the sea. It was a perfect summer day.

"This is fun!" said Rebecca suddenly. "I've never been in a motorcar before. It's much more exciting than a ponytrap. I wish . . ." She stopped.

I looked at her. She was staring at the road ahead and her face was white.

Alice said abruptly, "Pull up here, William, and let Rebecca out."

"No!" cried Rebecca and ducked down behind the seat so that the soft curving front of her body was pressed against my thighs. "Drive on to the village! Don't stop! If he sees me get out of a motorcar—"

"He's seen you," said Alice. "You were too late. He's waving his stick."

I was so absorbed in the embarrassing physical sensations which Rebecca's posture aroused in me that for a moment I was too dazed to realize what was happening. In confusion I glanced around to discover the cause of all the fuss. William had halted the car by this time, and I now saw that he had had no choice in the matter; ahead of us, parked firmly in the middle of the road, was a thin, wiry farmer in his forties with scanty graying hair and bright angry blue eyes. As the car engine idled uneasily he moved, striding forward toward us and waving his big stick.

"Who is it?" Jan-Yves was hissing. "What does he want? Who is he?"

"My uncle Joss," said Alice grimly. "What bad luck, Rebecca! Is there anything we can say to explain—"

"No." Rebecca was fumbling with the door handle, but William had already sprung out and was moving swiftly around the bonnet to open the door for her.

Alice leaned forward. "Good afternoon, Uncle Joss! We were just giving Rebecca a lift back from the rectory. Do you know Mr. William Parrish, the bailiff at Penmarric?"

The man turned on Rebecca. "What did I tell you?" he shouted at her. "Didn't I tell you that if you ever so much as looked at any of them bloody Castallacks, I'd—"

"Please, Uncle Joss," said Alice. "Let me take the blame. It was I who encouraged Rebecca to accept the lift. I—"

"You be quiet!" He swung around again on his daughter. "Didn't I tell you? Didn't I?"

Rebecca said stiffly, "Mr. Parrish isn't one of them, Dad. He's just the bailiff."

"Bailiff! You know well enough who he is, my girl, and don't you go a-standing there and telling me you don't know it as well as all Morvah, Zillan and St. Just knows it! He's as much a Castallack as that ugly little brat in the back seat!"

"I don't know what you mean, Dad."

"Christ Almighty, girl, you've been born and bred on a farm—

don't give yourself such airs and graces! Don't try and tell me you don't know what I mean!"

"I'm sorry, Dad. Honest. I didn't mean no harm." She was trembling. I was just thinking I would jump out of the car myself to defend her from any more of this monstrous onslaught when William said politely, "I'm sorry you should take such exception to your daughter's conduct, Mr. Roslyn. May I confirm what Alice has said and repeat that the fault is ours and not Miss Roslyn's? She did in fact decline the lift at first, but we persuaded her to accompany us against her wishes. Miss Roslyn, I apologize for causing you so much distress and embarrassment. Please forgive us. Good day, Mr. Roslyn." And he turned his back on the man without another word and walked briskly around to the driving seat.

"Don't you come near my girl again!" yelled the man after us as William released the brake. "You leave her alone!"

We drove on downhill into Morvah.

Jan-Yves kept saying, "Who was he? Why was he so horrible? What did he mean? Why doesn't he like us?"

"I'm terribly sorry, William," Alice said as we turned west toward St. Just. "I do apologize."

"My dear Alice, what on earth for? It wasn't your fault."

"But he was so abominably rude—"

"Good gracious me!" said William blandly. "I'm not going to get upset about some nonsense which an ill-tempered Cornish farmer yelled at me on a nice peaceful July afternoon! I couldn't care less. What does it matter anyway? We all know he's an unpleasant man with a fanatical grudge against the Castallacks. I'm sorry for Rebecca, that's all. I'm sure he'll give the poor girl a terrible time."

"William," said Jan-Yves. "William, I don't understand. What did he mean when he said—"

"He was just being rude, Jan-Yves. He has a grudge against us. The best thing to do is to forget the whole scene ever happened."

"But what did he mean when he said—William, are you a Castallack? Isn't your name Parrish after all?"

"For goodness' sake!" I burst out, maddened by his persistence. "Can't you stop asking questions?"

"But he said—"

"Yes, he did," said William. "No, my name's not Castallack, Jan-Yves, but since you ask you might as well know the truth.

337

I don't believe in hiding things from children. I'm not your cousin. I'm your brother, your half-brother. We had the same father but different mothers."

"William!" I shouted at him. I could not bear Alice to hear. The whole scene was suddenly a nightmare. "Shut up, William, shut up—"

"It's all right," said William. "Alice hears gossip just as everyone else does. I'm sure she knows anyway."

"But . . ." I could not go on. I sat back in the seat in misery and screwed my eyes tight shut so that I could not see Alice's face.

But I still heard her voice. She said, "Please, Adrian, don't be upset. It doesn't matter to me in the least."

"Wait a minute," said Jan-Yves with intelligent precision. "This is very peculiar. Wasn't Papa married to your mother?"

"No. That's why our name isn't Castallack."

"I see," said Jan-Yves, satisfied. "Like Bella the kitchen maid and Davey the stable boy. How nice! I *am* glad! I knew you were too good to be just a cousin."

And he sat back comfortably in the seat and began to pester William with questions about Joss Roslyn.

As soon as we arrived back at Penmarric I went to my room and locked myself in. I felt exhausted and miserable. First there had been the ordeal of seeing Mrs. Castallack in church, and then, as if that were not enough for one day, I had had to endure that humiliating scene with Joss Roslyn. As I slumped on my bed in weariness my only thought was: How could Papa ever think that illegitimacy isn't a handicap? And I began to long hopelessly for Allengate and for my mother.

I tried to visualize the future. Perhaps when I went up to Oxford Papa would allow me to spend my vacations either at my rooms there or at the townhouse in London, but the beginning of my first term at Oxford was still more than two years away. Until October 1914 there was nothing I could do but tolerate as best as I could the interested stares, the gossiping whispers and all the miseries inflicted on me by my being obliged to live at Penmarric. But in 1914 I would be free; in 1914 I could begin again with a clean slate in new surroundings. Impatience overwhelmed me. Seizing pencil and paper, I drew up an enormous calendar, just as Philip had done long ago at Allengate, and hung it on the wall so that I could cross off the days.

6

They agreed upon a marriage between Henry's eldest daughter, Matilda, and Henry the Lion, Duke of Saxony and Bavaria. . . . As the King's eldest daughter she was provided with a magnificent outfit.

—Henry II,
JOHN T. APPLEBY

Geoffrey was the favourite bastard of the Old King. . . . Though his life was passed in quarrels he was personally devout and even chaste, a virtue very rare in a Plantagenet.

—The Devil's Brood,
ALFRED DUGGAN

[1]

It was the August of 1912. Far away at the other end of Europe trouble was brewing in the Balkans, but not even Alice could summon much interest in the squabbles of such remote and barbaric peoples. At home the endless succession of labor strikes seemed to have subsided at last; Ireland had become troubled again, but since Ireland was perpetually troubled this was hardly a novel item of news, and although there was a bill afoot to broaden the franchise (much to Alice's satisfaction) I privately thought it had no hope of being passed by the ultraconservative House of Lords even if it did manage to survive a vote in the Commons. In short it seemed an unexciting time of the year, and unable to divert myself from my private problems by studying a series of absorbing issues at home and abroad, I was reluctantly obliged to confront the approaching spectacle of Mariana's elaborate society wedding.

The ceremony, which had been arranged to take place in Westminster at St. Margaret's on the second Saturday in September, was to be followed by a lavish reception at Claridges. William had agreed not to be an usher, but Papa still had not approached us on the subject of where we would be staying during our visit to London, and we were just wondering if Mrs. Castallack had decided after all to stay at a hotel when Papa summoned us to his study to discuss the matter with us.

"After some indecision my wife has agreed to stay at the townhouse," he said, fidgeting with a cigar as if he could not make up his mind whether to light it or not. He did not look at us. "She and I are traveling to London together tomorrow. She decided to stay in London for a fortnight before the wedding so that she could order some new clothes and accustom herself to London society after such a long absence." He looked at us directly with his opaque eyes and added without expression, "There's no question of a reconciliation, but we wish for Mariana's sake to assume some semblance of a marital façade to display to the world for the occasion."

We said nothing. We simply looked at him, and against my will I thought of my mother rushing with shining eyes to the door of our house in St. John's Wood and running down the path into his arms.

"Philip will join us early next week—he'll probably travel up to town with Marcus and Hugh. Miss Cartwright and Nanny will bring the girls and Jan-Yves three days before the wedding. I don't know what you two would like to do—I leave it to you to decide when you want to leave Penmarric. By the way, I've made arrangements for you to stay with Michael Vincent's brother Peter and his wife. They have a house near Russell Square, and I thought it would be more pleasant for you to stay there than in a hotel. Michael will also be staying with them, so you won't be entirely among strangers. After you've decided when you want to arrive in London perhaps you could write a line to Peter Vincent informing him of your arrangements. I'll give you his address."

After a pause William said, "Thank you, sir. It's kind of Mr. Vincent to have us to stay."

"Well, Michael and I are such old friends and I've met Peter on a number of occasions . . ." He talked on fluently for a minute or two about the Vincents and we listened to him in polite silence. Then: "About money," he said, opening a side drawer of his desk. "Of course you'll find it expensive in London and I do want you to have a pleasant stay and go out and about as much as possible. I thought I'd give you a little extra so you can do as you please without having to worry about exceeding your respective financial limits."

"No, thank you, Papa," I said. "Please don't bother. It's really not necessary."

"Not in the least, sir," said William, "and besides, you have enough expense with Mariana's wedding without being over-generous to us as well."

"Nonsense! I insist—"

"No, thank you, sir," I said strongly.

"No, thank you, sir," said William. "It's most kind of you but we'd rather not accept."

He shrugged, closed the drawer of his desk again without looking at us. "As you wish."

There was a tense, awkward silence. I stood up clumsily. "Then we'll see you in London, Papa," I said. "In case I don't see you before you leave tomorrow, I hope you have a good journey."

"Yes indeed, sir," said William, standing up also. "And thank you for making the arrangements. Good night."

"Good night, Papa," I said, opening the door.

After a pause he said, "Good night" and began to shuffle the papers on his desk into a heap.

We went. We crossed the hall, and I began to run up the stairs to the gallery. William followed me to my room. When the door was closed at last and we were alone we looked at each other.

"Rather bad taste," said William, "wasn't it? Trying to buy us off like that."

A draft from the window made the gas flicker. I went over to the frame and tried to stuff part of the curtain down the crack. It was damp and cold in the room, and since it was August no housemaid had been up to light the fire.

"I'm not going," I said.

"We must. It wouldn't be fair to Mariana not to go."

"Mariana wouldn't notice!"

"She might. Mariana's not as hard and conceited as she seems sometimes. I think she's surprisingly sensitive underneath all that grand talk. Besides, she's always treated us as if we were her brothers—look how she asked me to be an usher! She needn't have asked me on Nick's behalf like that, but she did. She really wanted me to be one."

The gas flickered again.

"Frankly," said William, "I don't trust Papa an inch over this business. I think he's angling for a reconciliation. Why else should he tolerate the idea of spending two weeks—two weeks!— under the same roof as that woman? God Almighty, they weren't under the same roof longer than two hours at Brighton and look what happened there!"

"Stop it!" I shouted. I could not bear to think of Brighton. Whenever I thought of Brighton now all I could remember was my mother crying yet struggling to hide her distress from us, my father returning to the dining room yet unable to look her in the eyes. "I don't want to talk of Brighton," I said fiercely. "I don't want to talk about it."

It was as if he had not heard me. "After all," he was saying, "let's face facts. Mama was the only person who could keep him away from that woman and even she couldn't keep him away all the time—" He must have noticed the acuteness of my distress then, for he stopped abruptly. The next moment the familiar casual expression had swept back across his face and he was giving a careless shrug of his shoulders to dismiss the subject. "Oh, what the hell," he said idly, wandering over to the door. "Everything'll turn out all right, I dare say, and it's silly to waste time worrying about something that may never happen. . . . Well, I think I'll go to bed. Good night, old chap. Sorry I was so down."

But I did not answer him. He went, easing the door gently shut behind him, and I was alone in the flickering yellow light. The wind moaned across the cliffs; the rain hurled in from the sea to explode against the glass pane. Presently I went to the window and stared out for a long time upon the darkness of the Atlantic, and as I stared I thought of Brighton, of a gray November sea pounding restlessly on an ugly shingle beach. My mind twisted through the past as if searching feverishly for an elusive memory, and then from the recollections of those last days at Allengate I heard Mama say, "Be loyal to Papa," and I hid my face in my hands as I began to cry.

[2]

After Papa had gone to London Hugh began to hover at my elbow again and suggested that we could have a moonlight picnic in the cove in belated celebration of his fifteenth birthday. He had the entire exploit already planned, I soon discovered; a bottle of home-made wine had been secretly imported from Roslyn Farm, twenty cigarettes had been smuggled into the house from Penzance, and he was thinking of asking Hannah the tween maid and her sister to drink and smoke with us.

"No thanks," I said shortly. "I'm not interested." I was still feeling upset after the scene with Papa, but that evening I became full of remorse at my ungraciousness toward Hugh and decided to seek him out to tell him I had changed my mind. By that time it would be too late to invite the girls and I would be spared the embarrassment of watching Hugh display the precocious interest he had already expressed in Hannah's anatomy.

But I was fated to be embarrassed that evening. After searching the house for Hugh without success and even journeying down to the cove in case he had decided to hold his party without me, I concluded he must have gone to bed early and made my way patiently to his room.

"Hugh?" I called, knocking on his door. "It's Adrian—can I come in?"

There was a noise as if a glass had been overturned and the faint creak of a mattress. Seeing no reason on earth why he might not wish me to enter, I turned the handle, opened the door and walked into the room.

He was in bed with Hannah. I almost but not quite caught them in the act of fornication.

[3]

As I was getting dressed the next morning he sneaked into my room and closed the door softly behind him.

"I'm terribly sorry about last night," he said charmingly, an anxious look in his eyes as if he feared he had given me offense. "You see . . ." And he launched into a long story about how potent home-made wine was and how he had met Hannah entirely by accident and . . . "Well, I had absolutely no intention of beginning anything, but almost before I knew what was happening . . . well, I'm sure you can understand how it was."

As he paused for reassurance I stared at him. His eyes were wide and frank. An engaging half-smile hovered at his mouth. He looked as if he had never had a dishonest thought in his life.

"I don't believe you," I heard myself say in an unexpectedly hard voice. "Last night wasn't the first time. You've been playing around with that silly little maid for weeks."

It was odd how certain I was that this was true. Memories of his fascination with the semi-classical postcards, his prurient conversations the previous holidays and his talent for telling lies all converged in my mind to eliminate any doubts I might otherwise have harbored about whether he was telling the truth or not.

"So you knew all the time!" said Hugh. He laughed before relaxing in relief. "Why on earth didn't you say so? I've been putting on an act for you for ages because I was afraid of shocking you and losing your friendship! And I did want us to stay friends because I knew that as soon as you began to take an interest in girls we could have such fun together." And suddenly he was confessing everything, how he had blackmailed Hannah into sleeping with him the previous holidays by threatening to tell Papa that he had seen her coming out of "a certain someone's" bedroom in the early hours of the morning—I assumed he was referring to Marcus—and how after the first time he hadn't had to blackmail her any more. "She thought I was inexperienced," he said, satisfied. "It really surprised her to find out how much I knew."

"You mean—before Hannah—"

"Yes, I went to that prostitute in Penzance but I wouldn't honestly recommend that. She was old," said Hugh fastidiously, "and used a very vulgar scent. I had no desire to go back to her afterward."

"But . . ." For a moment I was speechless. "How could you?" I said at last. "Of all the sordid things to do I think that's about the most degraded I can imagine. And you were fourteen—fourteen years old! It's almost too disgusting to talk about!"

His eyes changed subtly. They were lighter, clearer, more expressionless. "My dear Adrian, you talk as if there were an eleventh commandment saying, 'Thou shalt not fornicate at the age of fourteen'!"

344

"I can't help it," I said, upset. "I'm sorry, but I think it's so—so low, so utterly despicable—"

He lost his temper. With a jolt I realized I had not even known Hugh had a temper to lose. The smile was wiped off his face, the urbane affability fell away like a mask, and into his eyes blazed the violent, ungovernable rage of the Penmars. It was then that I saw the real Hugh, saw beyond the surface resemblance to his mother to the personality which lay beneath, and the personality was the personality which spoke silently from the Penmar portraits in the gallery, the personality of an adventurer, a clever, dangerous adventurer without scruples of any kind.

"Damn you!" he yelled. His eyes glittered. His face was scarlet with fury. "Damn you! You bloody prig, don't you dare preach to me!"

"I wasn't preaching. I was just telling you—"

"You were just telling me what a bloody stupid prig you are! You don't know anything, do you? No, don't bother to tell me how well you do at school—I don't care if you get a hundred percent in all your exams, the fact remains that you still don't know one damned thing about anything that matters. You can't imagine, can you, what it could be like to be the cleverest, best-looking member of a large family and yet be so overlooked that most of the time no one knows whether you're there or not! If no one appreciates me inside my family, why shouldn't I spend time with people who admire me as a person in my own right? Hannah may seem just a 'silly little maid' to you but to anyone who knows anything about life at all she's a prize any man would be glad to win—and if you really want to know, she says she finds me the hell of a lot more exciting in bed than your bloody bastard of a brother!"

"Why, what do you—are you trying to say—"

"Yes, I thought you hadn't guessed! I suppose it must be very shocking to you to realize your beloved William isn't as perfect as you think he is!"

"You say one more slander about William and I'll—"

"I've often wondered why Papa was so besotted with his bastards. Of course he's more besotted with you than he is with William, but—"

So confused was I, so stunned, that all I could say was an automatic "Papa doesn't have any favorites."

"What!" He stared at me incredulously and then burst out laughing. "Could I possibly have heard you correctly? Did you really say 'Papa has no favorites'? Why, you silly fool, how dare you stand there and say such a thing when we only had to spend one night at Allengate to discover who *his* little blue-eyed boy was!"

But all I could say was "It's not true. It's just not true."

"It *is* true, damn you! It *is* true!" He was so angry now that he could hardly speak. "Christ Almighty, do you think we haven't noticed how Papa is always talking to you at meals, sitting with you on the terrace, discussing history with you in his study? Do you think Marcus has never worried in case Papa should leave all his money to you in his will? Do you think you're not the main reason why Philip won't visit Penmarric? Has it never occurred to you that Philip won't be friends with Papa not just because Papa put his mistress before his wife but because he puts *you* before *us*! How do you think we felt when we were bundled off to Allengate and thrown into a house where you and William were the little lords of the manor? Why, it was as if we, not you, were the bastards! We hated you! We always hated you! We still hate you! Mariana didn't even want you at her wedding to embarrass us all publicly—but she had no choice in the matter! It was no good telling Papa that he couldn't bring his favorite son to his daughter's wedding. But let me tell you this: When Papa dies, you'll be out and William with you. We've had enough of you bastards to last us a lifetime and as soon as we get the chance we're going to kick you as far away from us as we possibly can."

I managed to say, "If you call me bastard just once more—"

"Bastard," said Hugh and spat on the floor at my feet like a guttersnipe.

I hit him. We fought each other to a bloody, bitter standstill. I was bigger than he was and had a much longer reach, but he was muscular and tough. We fought until we were gasping with exhaustion and stopped only when someone flung open the door of my room to interrupt us.

It was William. "What on earth's going on in here?" he demanded in amazement. "I could hear you from the end of the corridor! What the devil—"

Hugh spun around, his fury undiminished. "—you," he spat at William in the language of the gutter. "—you both, you bastards."

And as William's eyes widened he pushed past him and slammed the door in his face as he left the room.

I sank slowly down on the bed.

"For God's sake!" exclaimed William, stupefied. "What was all that about? I've never seen Hugh so angry! What did you say to him? What happened? Tell me!"

But when at last I was able to speak again all I said was "I'm not going to that wedding."

[4]

William and I talked for two hours, but I would not change my mind.

"I'm not going," I said. "We're not wanted. They all hate us, even Mariana."

"Rubbish!" said William. He was becoming angry himself. "Hugh's lying as usual, and you know it. He lost his temper and invented slander after slander. It's simply not true."

"I don't care what you say—I'm not going!"

"Papa'll be furious!"

"Let him be," I said flatly. "But I'm not going to London."

"Well, there's no need to sound so angry with *me*!" said William, half amused, half exasperated. "I'm not the one who's been causing all the trouble!"

But of course I was angry with him too. I had long since suspected that his evening outings with Marcus to the neighboring pubs were hardly made for the sole purpose of drinking beer in a convivial atmosphere, but I had yearned to give him the benefit of the doubt and now that I could no longer do so I felt that he had somehow failed me. It was as if I shared his weakness; I felt guilty and humiliated, and I resented him for demeaning himself in my eyes.

"Look, old chap," he was saying reasonably, "you needn't stay long in London. If you came up for the wedding and then went home immediately afterward—"

"I don't care what you say," I said violently. "You might just as well save your breath, because I'm not going to that wedding and neither you nor anyone else is going to persuade me to change my mind."

I kept my word. Everyone else went to London but I stayed

behind at Penmarric. I did not even go over to Zillan to church because I was afraid Mr. Barnwell would be disappointed by my behavior, so I went to church at St. Just instead and spent most of my time in my room or out walking on the moors. It was then, when I was entirely alone, that I began to write. I tried prose first. I attempted a project Papa had mentioned once and began to write my autobiography, but I was too young still to see my youth in perspective, so I put the manuscript away in the drawer where it was to lie untouched for another twenty years. After that I tried poetry. I liked this better. For long hours I would sit by the window and stare out to sea as I tried to arrange my thoughts into a stimulating but flawless verbal pattern.

I had written six poems and had tentatively entitled them *Pastoral Reflections of an Unhappy Youth* when my solitary existence came abruptly to an end. Two days after the wedding Papa came home alone without warning from London and summoned me at once to his study.

[5]

"I hope you can explain your absence to me," he said curtly, "because I certainly couldn't explain it to Mariana. She was most upset."

"I'm sorry," I said, swallowing uncomfortably. "I didn't think she would notice that I wasn't there."

"Of course she noticed! I must say, I thought it was extraordinarily selfish of you not to come. I had told you on several occasions that I wanted it to be an especially happy day for Mariana and I certainly implied that it might be necessary for all of us to make one or two sacrifices to ensure that her day was as perfect as possible." He took a cigar and began to fidget with it. "Well, of course it wasn't an easy situation!" he said abruptly. "Of course it was difficult! Do you think I wouldn't have preferred you and William to stay at the townhouse? I knew you wouldn't like being boarded out with the Vincents, but it was the best I could do and I hoped you would be sensible enough to understand and forgive me—for Mariana's sake, if for no one else's. I knew it would be awkward and even distasteful for you at the reception to see my wife and myself together, but I hoped you would be generous enough to tolerate it—at least for an afternoon! But no—you made no effort. You did not even attempt to help me in any way. I confess I'm very disappointed in you."

I stared down at the floor. "I'm sorry."

"Do you think it didn't cost me an effort to have an amnesty with my wife for two weeks? Do you think it was easy for me?"

"I—"

"Well, it wasn't." He stared angrily at the cigar. "It was damned hard. If it hadn't been for Mariana . . ." He stopped to light his cigar.

"Papa, I'm very sorry. I realize now how selfish I was. I was upset at the time—I didn't think . . . I had heard gossip that Mariana didn't want me at the wedding and that she was secretly embarrassed by the fact that William and I would be present—"

"Whoever said such a thing?"

I colored and shook my head. "I'd rather not say."

"Well, more fool you for believing it! I might add that Mariana is a great deal fonder of you and William than she is of Philip and Hugh. She was certainly a lot fonder of Rose than she ever was of my wife. Didn't you realize that?"

I hung my head and said nothing.

"You heard one ridiculous piece of gossip and immediately felt you weren't wanted! Adrian, you must learn not to be so sensitive! How many more times do I have to say that to you? You really must toughen your outlook or your vulnerability will completely overwhelm you. I'm especially disappointed because you seemed to have overcome your difficulties to a large extent during the past year. You've been happy here, haven't you?"

I swallowed again but still could not speak.

"Haven't you?"

"Yes, I suppose so. But—"

"Yes?"

"Papa, when I go up to Oxford—couldn't I spend the vacations at the townhouse? Or at Oxford itself? I—I really have no affinity with Cornwall. I would prefer—"

"We'll talk about that when the time comes." His voice was so abrupt that at first I thought he was angry, but then suddenly I realized he was hurt.

"Oh, Papa, I didn't mean—"

"Look, Adrian." His cigar had gone out. He mashed the burned stub into the tray and leaned forward toward me. "I merely want you to be happy. That's all. Try to remember that everything I do, no matter how outrageous and unjust it seems, is done with that aim in mind. If you really don't want to live at Penmarric after you go up to Oxford I won't try to detain you, but you're too young at present to live away from home during the holidays and anyway I don't want you to feel lonely and unwanted any more than you yourself do. Try to understand."

"I do understand, Papa—I'm sorry, I didn't mean to hurt you. Please forgive me."

"I'm only hurt when you get this absurd idea into your head that you're not wanted here. By the way, who did tell you that piece of nonsense about Mariana not wanting you at the wedding? Did Philip say something after church one Sunday?"

"No."

"But it was one of your brothers, wasn't it?"

I did not answer.

"Well, Marcus is incapable of saying anything unpleasant, and if Philip said nothing on the subject the culprit must have been Hugh. What a tiresome child he is! He doesn't say more than half a dozen words to me when we meet, he writes me one letter a term in which he says absolutely nothing, and now apparently he's been stirring up trouble while my back was turned! If he's indirectly responsible for your absence from the wedding I shall damned well summon him here to my study and tell him what I think of his talents as a trouble-maker!"

"No, Papa, please . . . please don't."

"Why not?"

"Because it would prove—at least, he'd think it would prove—that he wasn't your favorite and I was."

"I have no favorites," said Papa.

"I told him that, but he didn't believe it. He thinks you treat your legitimate sons unfairly."

"Absolute nonsense. I treat all my sons exactly the same. If Hugh wants me to take more interest in him he should stay at Penmarric more often instead of running over to Roslyn Farm every day after breakfast. No doubt his mother's been fostering the idea that I don't treat her sons as well as I treat you and William—I wouldn't be at all surprised if she were to blame for the whole unhappy situation! She's always tried to turn the children against me, and now I see she's having more success than I anticipated. First Philip, now Hugh. . . . Philip hardly spoke to me while we were at the townhouse. If I thought it would make any difference to his attitude toward me I would go to court and try and prise him out of that farmhouse with the help of the judge and some form of the 'ward of court' legal machinery, but it's too late for all that now, too much has happened, and it would only serve to make Philip's estrangement from me deeper and more bitter than ever. Yet I keep worrying about him. It's all wrong for him to be buried alive with his mother on a remote Cornish farm." He began to crush his cigar to pulp. "She's trying to win over Jan-Yves now," he said wryly, "but she's not succeeding. Poor little devil! He can sense that she's not interested in him for himself, only for his usefulness to her in her private war with me. Poor little Jan-Yves. I should have had him at Allengate, I knew it was my duty to send for him, but there was Rose, looking after six of my wife's children without complaint, and I couldn't bring myself to ask her to look after a seventh, least of all such an unwelcome reminder of—"

Brighton, I thought.

"—well, never mind. It's done now. For better or for worse it's done. I shouldn't be speaking to you of such things. The very last thing you want to hear about is my very bitter and very sordid estrangement from my wife."

"There's no chance of—of a reconciliation? William and I were wondering—"

"Good God, no," he said. "Never." He added again in a bleak, cold voice, "Never." He pushed away the ashtray and the mangled cigar and stood up. "Let's change the subject. You have two letters to write—you do realize that, don't you? One to Mariana, to apologize for your absence, and one to Mr. and Mrs. Peter Vincent to apologize for any inconvenience caused them by your failure to arrive to stay at their house as arranged."

"Yes, Papa."

"Then we'll say no more about the matter. Your behavior was very unfortunate and greatly to be regretted, but there it is. It's past now. Write the letters and we'll consider the incident at an end."

"Yes, Papa. Thank you. I'm very sorry."

"I know you are. Never mind. I'm sorry too if you've been unhappy." He smiled at me, and suddenly all my cares dissolved until I felt as happy as I had felt long ago in the days before I had ever heard of Brighton. When I smiled in return he said, "How like my father you look when you smile!" and we laughed and were at ease with each other and it did not occur to me until much later that amidst all Hugh's lies there might have lurked a small unpalatable core of truth.

[6]

"It was a lovely wedding," said Jeanne with a sigh. "Mariana looked like a princess. There were hundreds of people there and the traffic in Parliament Square was held up. All the ladies wore such beautiful dresses, but Mama wore the most beautiful dress of all—except for Mariana's, of course. So many photographers wanted to take pictures of her afterward."

"Everyone said how beautiful my page's costume was," said Jan-Yves. "I was photographed afterward too. I had to spell my name to a newspaper reporter and he said he had never heard of such a name before. He thought Yves was spelt E-v-e."

"I liked the reception at Claridges best," reflected Elizabeth. "The wedding was boring really—all that standing around and listening to the clergyman—but Claridges was lovely. I had half a glass of champagne and three of the most delicious meringues. I tried caviar too, but I liked the meringues better."

Nobody could stop talking about it. They talked of the wretched wedding until I felt I wanted to shout "Stop!" and clap my hands over my ears.

"It was good to see Mama and Papa together again," said Marcus. "They got on splendidly together, I thought. I was nervous in case there was an awkward atmosphere, but I needn't have worried at all. They behaved just like any other married couple at the reception, and afterward they went out to dinner together. Not alone, of course, but at least they couldn't have objected to each other's company too much or they would have made some excuse not to be together."

"There's no question of a reconciliation," I said to William privately. I had by this time sufficiently recovered from the shock of Hugh's revelations to feel ashamed of my anger toward William earlier; I saw now that Hugh had wanted me to be shocked and I was angry with myself when I realized how ably

I had obliged him. It still upset me to think that William's standards fell short of my own, but I had firmly resolved to face up to this unwelcome fact and not turn my back on him and try to pretend that neither he nor his weakness existed. Such an attitude, as Mr. Barnwell had already convinced me, solved nothing, and besides . . . it was impossible for me to remain estranged from William for long. Now as I reassured him about the impossibility of a reconciliation between Papa and Mrs. Castallack I was glad I was able to set his mind as fully at rest as my own mind was. "Papa said a reconciliation would never happen," I explained to him. "He said it was out of the question."

"Did he say that? What a relief! The more I saw them together the more convinced I became that she would be coming back to Penmarric. You know, in all fairness to her I have to admit that no one at the reception would ever have guessed she had once been a farmer's wife. I almost found myself admiring her a little despite the fact that I was worried stiff about a possible reconciliation."

Alice was the only one who did not seem to have enjoyed the wedding much.

"I'm not at my best at large grand gatherings," she told me frankly. "I always feel shy and want to hide behind the nearest curtain."

"You don't, Alice!" I could not believe it.

"Indeed I do! Ask Mr. Castallack! He found me quivering behind a potted palm and came over especially to talk to me. How kind he is! I'm very fond of him."

Papa evidently approved of Alice's presence at Penmarric, for after the wedding he asked her to stay on permanently as his housekeeper and even, so William told me, raised her salary. This was hardly surprising, for she was excellent at her job. It was true that she was young for the position, but the Penmar name had a certain sentimental value for the servants, especially those such as Medlyn the butler, who could think of her fondly as "Young Mr. Harry's daughter." But whether her success was due to her name or to her natural efficiency in household affairs, the fact remained that Papa did not have to worry about domestic matters at Penmarric any more and could concentrate fully on his work.

It was in November, just after Mariana had returned from her honeymoon and written sketchily to us that "everything was divine," that Papa had a book published on the career of Stephen Langton and his relationship with King John both during and after the Interdict. It was fascinating to read, and during the Christmas holidays Papa and Alice and myself had some most interesting conversations on the subject after dinner in his study. Alice enjoyed history almost as much as she enjoyed studying current affairs. Her grandfather had an extensive library at the rectory and she was surprisingly well read.

The new term began and soon it was spring and we were all home for the holidays. Marcus, down from Oxford for a few weeks, was at the townhouse for the beginning of the Season and presently wired Papa for "a little extra money."

Alice commented shrewdly to William, "Marcus has probably met a rich fast crowd at Oxford."

But William would not join in criticism of Marcus and merely said Marcus had a great many expenses to meet.

"Fiddlesticks," said Alice. "He's hopelessly extravagant."

Afterward William remarked privately to me, "Alice is a very bossy sort of woman. She always thinks she's right."

"That's because she usually is," I said, springing at once to her defense.

"Even so she shouldn't insist that she's right in such a dogmatic manner," said William. "It's unfeminine and I don't like it."

But Alice seemed impervious to his disapproval and they continued to bicker at intervals, particularly over the political situation at home and abroad.

It was 1913. At home the House of Lords had thrown out the bill to extend the suffrage, just as I had foreseen, and the suffragettes had become even more militant in consequence.

"And I can't say I really blame them," said Alice, "although I do think the use of violence in those circumstances can't really be justified."

"They'll never get the vote at this rate," said William. "Just as well, if you ask me."

"I don't think I ever did ask you," said Alice, "but surely isn't it narrow-minded to judge all women by the activities of a group of extremists?"

The House of Lords had also thrown out a bill designed to ameliorate the perpetual troubles in Ireland.

"It's a pity the Lords ever survived the constitutional crisis of 1911," commented Alice tartly. "Now of course there'll be civil war in Ireland."

"It's no more than the Irish deserve," said William. "They're always squabbling among themselves anyway. Of course they're quite unfit for self-government."

"Not quite as unfit as that collection of fossilized relics at Westminster," said Alice.

Abroad the second Balkan war was stirring, but everyone was confident that Sir Edward Grey would keep Britain uninvolved and control the dispute through his usual skillful diplomacy.

"There'll never be a war," said William. "None of the European heads of state wants such a thing—that was made abundantly clear when that last Balkan crisis cropped up."

"Yes, but how long can Sir Edward Grey keep up this neutrality policy?" said Alice. "There must surely be times when one simply can't stay neutral."

"Exactly!" I agreed. "Anyway, I think war can be noble if it's waged in the name of justice and liberty."

"I don't know about it being noble," said Alice, "but I can see times when it could be necessary—inevitable, in fact."

"I can't," said William obstinately. "Why should we get involved in Russia's endless squabbles with Turkey and all that Slavic bickering at the other end of Europe?"

"Austria is interested in 'all that Slavic bickering,'" said Alice promptly, "and who's hand in glove with Austria, I'd like to know?"

"The Kaiser'll never bother us," declared William. "So long as he can dress up in splendid uniforms and parade his soldiers as if he were a child playing with toys, he'll be absolutely harmless. He won't make any trouble."

"Nonsense," said Alice. "Grown men who play with real soldiers under the mistaken idea that they're mere toys are a menace to the civilized world."

"What a gloomy Cassandra you are, Alice!" said William, but his good-humored comment could not quite hide the note of irritation in his voice. "But I'm afraid I still think there won't be a war."

"Churchill thinks there will be!"

"Churchill's an irresponsible warmonger!"

"I don't think there'll be a war—for a while anyway," I interposed as the conversation threatened to become too acrimonious. "But if war did break out I'm sure it would only be because someone flouted all the principles of civilized behavior so outrageously that we would have no choice except to intervene.

After all, when there's an open conflict between good and evil—when one's very principles are at stake—one simply must defend what one believes to be right. There's no better reason for fighting, in my opinion."

At least they both agreed with me about that. I sighed in relief. I did not like to listen to them arguing since I always felt trapped in the middle; I usually agreed with Alice, but I did not want to support her too enthusiastically for fear of being disloyal to William.

Summer came. The second Balkan war was maneuvered delicately into peaceful waters by the statesmen of Europe and Sir Edward Grey rose to new heights of popularity.

"I told you so," said William to Alice.

"Well, I never said there'd be a war this year, did I?" said Alice, but I could see she was annoyed that William had been right and she had been wrong.

Mariana and her husband arrived for a visit at the end of July, but Cornwall was clearly too provincial for them and they did not stay long. Papa spent some time in Oxford after they had gone, and while he was away Penmarric reverberated with Jan-Yves's tantrums as he declared he would not go to boarding school in September. When Papa returned from Oxford I thought he would find this rebelliousness very tiresome, but he took a lenient attitude toward the child's stormy scenes and soothed Jan-Yves by promising to visit the school at half-term with William.

Christmas arrived at last. I was eighteen years old now, very tall and still much too thin, but my skin was clearing and I no longer felt so ungainly whenever I entered a room. I decided life was improving, and as winter melted into spring I began to think with pleasurable anticipation of the prospect of going up to Oxford in the autumn. When my final term at Winchester ended in July I felt sad to think my school days were closed at last, but I did not feel depressed for long and soon I was back at Penmarric and resuming my discussions of current events with Alice.

However, the news at that time was enough to revive my depression. There had been more trouble in the Balkans, but no one was taking that very seriously since we all knew from past experience that trouble there could be controlled by diplomacy. The real troubles were at home. The suffragettes were setting buildings on fire, firing shots at trains and even bombing churches. Civil war was breaking out in Ireland. And then, slowly it began to dawn on everyone that even the grave disunity at home could be eclipsed by the waning power of diplomacy abroad. From the beginning of that summer and even after the assassinations at Sarajevo I think we had assumed that the neutralist policy would keep us out of trouble and that if we kept calm the crises abroad would blow over in their usual fashion. Now, suddenly it began to dawn on the general public that Europe was divided into armed camps, diplomacy was grinding to an impasse and the third Balkan war, far from blowing over, was in fact billowing into a massive conflict.

Yet still there was talk of peace. I was just reading a report in *The Times* of a speech made by Lloyd George in which he had said that the international situation had been much worse in 1913, when Papa said to me unexpectedly, "Would you come into my study for a moment? There's something I want to show you."

Thinking that perhaps he had made an additional amendment to his current manuscript (an article on that intriguing character William Marshal), I followed him willingly to his study. I always felt flattered when he chose to discuss his work with me and was continually eager to show my interest in his writings.

However, this time I was mistaken about the purpose of his invitation. When we were in the study he turned not to the papers on his desk but to a gold watch lying on a side table.

"I found this the other day," he said, picking up both the watch and its chain. "I have a perfectly good watch myself which my father gave me when I was twenty-one, so I hardly need another. I want you to have it. I almost decided to wait until you were twenty-one, but then I thought I would give it to you now in token of your successful career at Winchester and to wish you well for your coming years at Oxford."

He held it out to me. I was so overcome with surprise and pleasure that I found myself unable to speak. However, after accepting the watch and holding it in my palm for a moment I was about to exclaim, "How beautiful it is!" when I saw the inscription on the back and fell silent.

There was a pause.

"It was my father's watch, as you can see," said Papa. "It was a twenty-first birthday present from his own father but in spite of its age it still keeps excellent time—probably because it's had no wear and tear for a quarter of a century. I had it overhauled in Penzance last week. It's in perfect working order."

I stared at the engraving. LAURENCE CASTALLACK, said the inscription. 22ND MARCH, 1864. I stared at it for five silent seconds before saying slowly, "This shouldn't come to me."

"Why not?" said Papa. "You're the one who's most like him. He would have wanted you to have it. It would have pleased him more than you could ever imagine to know that I had a son who resembled him."

"But . . . what will the others say?"

"I should hope they won't be so childish as to make any adverse comments! I shall give my personal belongings to exactly whom I please. If I gave the watch to Marcus he would probably pawn it and spend the money sending roses to the latest woman to catch his fancy. If I gave it to Philip he would refuse to accept it and if I gave it to Hugh—but damn it, why should I give it to him? I want to give it to you! Take it and wear it and enjoy it, and if anyone feels mortally insulted tell him to complain to me and I'll answer his complaints in person."

I made no further protest. I was too thrilled with the watch. I thanked him as adequately as possible, but as I went outside to find William I still could not help wondering with a pang of uneasiness what my half-brothers would think when they heard of Papa's unexpected generosity.

7

The King [gave a] ring, set with a sapphire of great price, to Geoffrey . . .

—Henry II,
JOHN T. APPLEBY

It was not absurd to suppose that . . . he, the favourite bastard, might have a chance to seize the English crown.

—The Devil's Brood,
ALFRED DUGGAN

The boys—for they were still only boys—had their grievances and were filled with eagerness to rebel against their fond but masterful parent.

—Oxford History of England:
From Domesday Book to Magna Carta,
A. L. POOLE

[1]

To my surprise the reaction to Papa's present was indulgent to the point of indifference.

"What an awful old relic of Victoriana!" drawled Marcus when I boldly wore the watch that evening. "My dear chap, you're more than welcome to it!"

"Does it work?" inquired Hugh politely and, on hearing that it did, commented, "It'll probably break down before long. Those old watches usually do."

Jeanne, who at fourteen was all breathless enthusiasm, exclaimed, "Oh, but it's beautiful! Even if it does break down you could always wear it simply for show, Adrian!"

"Certainly he could!" said Marcus genially. "It's really an intriguing period piece, if you like that sort of thing."

On the whole I thought they took the news fairly well.

It was a full two days afterward that Marcus said to me at breakfast, "Are you doing anything this morning? You wouldn't like to come riding with me, would you? It's a beautiful morning and I'm bored with riding alone."

I was surprised, for Marcus had never made such an invitation before, but I saw no reason to be suspicious. He probably was bored with riding on his own. William was too busy with the estate these days to ride for pleasure during the working week, and Hugh was always either at the farm or away on private expeditions of his own.

"Very well," I said after my moment of hesitation. "Yes, it's a perfect morning for a ride. Where do you want to go?"

"Oh . . . why don't we ride up on to the moors around Carn Kenidjack?"

"Fine. I'll go and change. See you in the stables in about ten minutes."

We rode down the drive and along the road into St. Just. It was a clear morning with a cool breeze gusting in from the sea. Beyond St. Just we followed the road toward Botallack, Pendeen and Morvah, and eventually branched away onto the bridlepath that led across the moors.

The weatherbeaten old signboard was still standing. I looked at its faded arm as we rode past and read the familiar inscription: "To Zillan, Chûn and Ding Dong Mine."

"Why don't we ride out to Chûn?" called Marcus. "We'd have a first-class view from the ridge today."

"All right."

I had a pang of uneasiness when I remembered how Hugh and I had been to Chûn before visiting Roslyn Farm two summers ago, but the uneasiness passed. It was an exhilarating morning for riding, and as we rode past Carn Kenidjack the wind whipped scudding white clouds across the sky and sent fleeting shadows across the heather. Presently when the path allowed us to ride two abreast Marcus began to talk of Oxford, relating amusing anecdotes of his life there, but soon the path narrowed again and conversation became difficult. We tried to talk once or twice, but the wind whipped away our words as soon as they left our lips and after a while we gave up the attempt and traveled in silence across the heather. We passed Carnyorth Circles, crossed the lane which later joined the road from St. Just to Penzance, and rode onto the moors again by skirting the edge of Woon Gumpus Common. We were climbing steadily now and at last we reached the ridge to find before us, rising from the heather, the ancient walls of Chûn.

"The view's clear, isn't it?" called Marcus over his shoulder. "How blue the sea of Mount's Bay is!"

The view was indeed superb. I stared at the south for some minutes before turning north to Morvah and the cliffs.

"Let's rest for a moment in the castle," suggested Marcus. "We can shelter behind the walls out of the wind."

"All right."

We reached the outer walls of the castle and, dismounting, led our horses into the inner enclosure. I was just about to hitch the reins to a convenient rock when a well-remembered voice drawled behind me, "Well, well, well! Fancy seeing you here!"

I spun around. Philip was lounging casually against the walls, and Hugh was beside him.

"Well, well, well!" echoed Marcus with elaborate surprise. "What a coincidence!"

They smiled at one another and then all turned to look at me. As the smiles gradually died from their eyes I felt my heart begin to bump uncomfortably against my ribs.

"Please don't bother to pretend," I said quickly to Marcus. "I can't think why you considered it necessary in the first place. If you'd told me that you, Philip and Hugh had something you wished to discuss with me at Chûn I would willingly have come of my own accord."

"You know damned well you wouldn't have done anything of the kind," said Philip. "You'd have told Marcus to go to hell."

I checked the angry reply which rose to my lips and instead said politely, "That's a matter of opinion. However, since I'm here I'm perfectly willing to discuss whatever you wish. What is it you want to talk about?"

There was a silence. I was aware of their cool light eyes appraising me with hostility. I clenched my hands and waited.

"Do let's sit down," said Marcus suddenly. "After all, there's no reason why we should all stand around dramatically like characters on a stage. Do you smoke, Adrian? Have a cigarette."

"I don't smoke, thank you," I said stiffly and watched him take out a packet of cigarettes to offer Philip and Hugh.

They all lit their cigarettes. We sat down casually, Philip with his back to the ancient walls, Hugh on a slab of rock nearby, and Marcus and I on a patch of grassy turf. Although the sky was still streaked with high white clouds the sun was warm and the horses tossed their heads impatiently as they waited for us.

"Who's going to conduct this meeting, Marcus?" demanded Philip. "You or I? You seem very reluctant to start."

"I was just trying to think of a civilized approach to the problem," said Marcus with engaging frankness. He smiled at me. "I'm awfully sorry about all this, Adrian old chap, but the fact is we're all rather—well, rather embarrassed about certain things, and we thought that if we could all have a little talk together—"

"Oh my God, Marcus!" said Philip. "Call a spade a spade, can't you?" He leaned forward, and as he moved I realized I preferred his blunt honesty to Marcus' determined efforts to appear friendly. "Look here," said Philip directly to me. "There are some things we want to know. First of all, why did Father give you Grandfather's gold watch?"

After a moment I said, "He wanted me to have it."

"Why?"

"Because he felt Grandfather would have wanted me to have it."

"Why?"

"He said I was the one who was most like Grandfather."

They digested this unwelcome statement in stony silence.

"You have no right to that watch," said Philip narrowly at last.

"I have every right to it," I said. "It belonged to Papa and he gave it to me, as he was legally entitled to. There's no law against accepting a gift from someone entitled to give."

"You seem to be getting on very well with Father at the moment."

"We're on good terms with each other, certainly."

"What kind of game are you playing?"

"I don't understand you."

"Has he given you money?"

"Of course! I make no secret of the fact that I have an allowance."

"I mean has he given you large sums as a gift over and above your allowance?"

"No, but if he had it would be none of your business."

"It certainly would. You're not entitled to his money."

"If he chooses to give me what is his to give I most certainly am entitled to it."

362

"Has he discussed his will with you?"

"Yes, as a matter of fact he did once. He told us that although William and I could expect a legacy the bulk of his fortune would go elsewhere and we would always have to earn our living."

Hugh said casually, "Was this recently?"

"The last time the subject came up was three years ago."

"Three years ago?"

"Yes. It was after my mother died."

"Past history really."

I said nothing.

"He hasn't discussed his will with you recently?"

"If he had," I said, "it would be none of your business, and I should hold it as confidential information. If he wished to discuss his private affairs with any of you he would presumably do so in person."

"You're hoping, of course, that the legacy's a large one."

"I'm certainly not expecting it to be large. Otherwise Papa would hardly have told me I'd have to earn my living."

They stared at me.

"You see, Adrian—" Marcus began, but he was interrupted.

"I'll handle this, if you don't mind, Marcus," said Philip. He looked at me directly again. "If you think for one moment," he said to me at last, "that you can cheat us all out of our inheritance—"

"I've just said—"

"Never mind what you just said! You were referring to something that was said three bloody years ago, and we're not interested in past history even if you are! We're interested in the present— and the future. We think—"

"If you think for one moment," I said, trying to keep my temper, "that I'm conducting some monstrous plot to swindle you all, you must be completely mad. I don't want your wretched inheritance! I detest Penmarric! I don't deny that Papa and I get on well together, but if Papa happens to prefer me to you, Philip Castallack, I for one wouldn't blame him. What have you ever done to give him cause to feel affectionate toward you? You never even come near him! If he prefers me to you, you have only yourself to blame!"

"So you *are* trying to wangle your way into his affections and get him to make a will in your favor," said Philip at once. "We thought you were. Hugh and Marcus have both noticed how you've been attracting attention to yourself recently by pretending to be interested in his work. They've noticed how you've been spending hour after hour with him in his damned study. They've noticed—"

"Steady on, Philip," Marcus said nervously. "Steady on."

"If you're not trying to steal the inheritance," said Hugh smoothly, "give Marcus Grandfather's gold watch in token of your good faith."

"My word is my good faith!" I yelled at him. "If you weren't such a bloody liar yourself you'd understand that! Grandfather's watch is mine and it stays mine and that's all I have to say on the subject." I began to stand up.

"Sit down," said Philip. "We haven't finished."

"You have as far as I'm concerned."

"Sit down!"

"Like hell I will!"

We stood facing each other, fists clenched, muscles taut. For the first time in our lives he was no longer taller than I was.

"Please!" exclaimed Marcus, scrambling nervously to his feet. "Do let's be civilized. No violence—nothing sordid. Please."

I stepped back a pace, shrugged my shoulders, shoved my fists into my trouser pockets. "What else do you wish to say?" I said crisply to Philip.

"Just this," said Philip. "Just this. Marcus and I both need money and we're not going to tolerate any attempts you may make to stand in our way. If you want to show us your good intentions you'll help us by doing two things. First, you can find a copy of Father's latest will and see what it says. You have access to his papers, and if he catches you in his study you can always claim you're looking for some manuscript or other—good God, you can think up an excuse! Judging from what I've heard, you spend half your time in the study anyway. When you've found the will, show it to Marcus and Hugh and replace it again as soon as they've read it. We want to see how the money is divided so that we can ask for a portion in advance."

"If you're suggesting I should sneak into his study and pry among his papers like some common thief—"

"You want to show us your good intentions, don't you?"

"I don't display my good intentions by stooping to such degrading behavior!"

"Damn you, Adrian, you're not going to stand in our way!

We want that money and we want to know what's in that will and if you don't bloody well do as you're told—"

"Yes?" I said. "What's the next threat?"

"—Marcus will see there isn't a soul in all Oxford who doesn't know your true relationship to the eminent historian Mark Castallack. You'll find everyone sniggering at you behind your back when you go up for your first term in October."

The wind hummed over the stone walls and cooled my cheeks. I kept my head, managed to remain calm.

"Marcus wouldn't have the guts to be such an out-and-out bastard," I said, stammering a little over the hated word but otherwise speaking strongly enough. "That's an empty threat if ever I heard one. Very well! So you want me to do your own dirty work for you and find out about the will and now you know my answer. I shan't. What was the second favor you wanted to ask me?"

They were all furious. Marcus was red at the implication that he was too weak to carry out a threat, Hugh was white with indignation that I should be so annoyingly insubordinate, and Philip was speechless with rage at my refusal to be brow-beaten.

"Well?" I said. "What was it? You may as well tell me. What was the second thing you wanted me to do?"

Philip managed to control himself. As he began to speak, the sun went behind a bank of clouds and the wind whistled eerily over the darkened landscape so that his voice sounded distorted and far away. "Go to your friend Alice Penmar," I heard him say deliberately, "and find out if she's taken your mother's place in Father's bedroom."

[2]

After a long silence I managed to laugh. "You're mad," I said and turned away to my horse.

"Adrian, if you don't cooperate with us and do your best to help, it'll be patently obvious that you're simply out for what you can get where Father's concerned. If you had a single spark of fraternal feeling—"

"Don't you dare speak to me of fraternal feeling!" I whirled around, blind with rage. "Fine brothers you've all been to me! Why, I believe if I fell off my horse and broke my leg you'd ride straight on and leave me without a second thought! You're the most shallow, worthless bunch of scoundrels I've ever met and I feel sorry for Papa having to tolerate you all and try to fulfill his obligations where you're concerned. And if you're despicable enough to suppose that Alice Penmar, a clergyman's grand-daughter, a decent, honest, moral girl, would ever—"

"Father doesn't let outward respectability bother him," said Philip. "Look at your mother."

"My God, you—"

"Please, Philip," said Marcus tightly, "don't speak of Aunt Rose like that. In fact don't even mention Aunt Rose. It's not right."

"Besides," said Hugh blandly, "we're discussing Alice. Aunt Rose is irrelevant to the conversation except possibly as an illus-tration of Papa's tastes in that direction. Now let's try and con-sider this dispassionately without getting all hot under the collar and losing track of the argument. I'm sure you're intelligent enough to understand, Adrian, that we're interested in Alice be-cause we're anxious to get some sort of lever over Papa. For example, if he shows reluctance to give Marcus and Philip a portion, it may be necessary to exert a little pressure of a certain kind—you understand? Now, considering the available facts, I think it's highly probable that he has his eye on Alice. Whether anything's happened yet is a moot point but as far as I can see it's very likely that something will. Consider the situation. Papa, as we all know, has to have some sort of woman in the back-ground, and no matter how devoted he was to Aunt Rose I don't suppose he's been utterly celibate since she died. However, re-cently he's hardly moved out of Penmarric. He's been here all summer working, and meanwhile living in the same house—keep-ing house for him—is this young woman of twenty-two, unrelated to him by blood in spite of her surname, unmarried and—if I may use a farmyard phrase since there are no ladies present—ripe for the plucking. No, wait! Don't interrupt! Hear me out! This much is in Alice's favor: She's young, she's quick-witted and she knows how to listen when he rambles on about history. How-ever, she's also plain and dark—have you noticed how Papa seems to prefer fair women?—and she's too thin with practically no bosom at all. The question is therefore as follows: Does her youth—men of Papa's age like young girls—and her intelligence outweigh her obvious lack of physical excitement? Considering that Papa's probably had enough physical excitement to last him a lifetime and that he's getting to an age when looks cease to be as important as personality, I think the answer is probably yes. In which case—"

"If you were to talk to her," said Philip to me, "test her on the subject, observe her and Papa when they're together—after all, you're the one who's always with them! If you could manage to establish that there was some sort of illicit relationship between Alice and Father—"

I hit him very hard on the jaw.

He reeled, toppling over, spinning against the ancient walls, and as he fell he gave a shout of rage and pain.

"Oh God," said Marcus, looking sick, "oh God, I knew this wouldn't work. I knew it."

"Be quiet!" Hugh spat at him and swung around on me. "You'll be sorry for this. You'll regret it when you go up to Oxford. All we wanted you to do was just to give us the minimum of cooperation to show your good faith, but you couldn't even give us that! We gave you the chance to be friends and join us, but you deliberately turned your back. And as if that wasn't enough we have to endure your insufferable priggishness and listen to your self-righteous, hypocritical justification for your self-righteous, hypocritical conduct!"

I tried to hit him too but he dodged the blow. Philip was picking himself up, spitting blood and using foul language. I was outnumbered.

"All right, you bastard," said Philip, "now you're really going to wish you'd never come here. Get out of my way, Marcus."

I had no choice. I turned, ran and vaulted into the saddle of my horse. Hugh tried to stop me as I whipped the horse out of the inner circle, but Marcus caught his arm and I was able to wrench myself free. I rode out of the castle gateway and galloped off along the ridge as fast as my horse would carry me, and when I glanced back over my shoulder I saw the three of them standing by the outer walls, Philip still rubbing his jaw as he stared after me.

[3]

By the time I arrived back at Penmarric I was shaking from head to toe with a nervous reaction to the scene at Chûn, and the knuckles of my right hand were raw and swollen. I went upstairs to the bathroom, found some antiseptic lotion and bathed my hand, but I was still so shaky that finally I slipped down to the dining room and helped myself to a mouthful of brandy from the sideboard. After that I felt better. In the privacy of my room I tried to think clearly. There was nothing I could do. I could not run to Papa like a lost child and announce dramatically that his legitimate sons were plotting against him. That sort of behavior would smack too much of the telltale sneak. And I certainly could not run to Alice and say how upset I was that Philip, Marcus and Hugh suspected her of being Papa's mistress. I was helpless. All I knew was that a bottomless rift had opened between myself and my half-brothers and that if Marcus were sufficiently malicious my anonymity of status would be jeopardized at Oxford.

I thought: I must leave Penmarric. I have to get away.

Yet I hated to think I was fleeing from my half-brothers and the unpleasantness they had created. Some element of stubbornness in me rebelled against taking a course of action which I might later judge cowardly and weak. I went on considering the problem, my thoughts twisting restlessly as I sifted each minute of the scene at Chûn, and at last I began to think with an uneasy clarity of my friend Alice Penmar.

I knew that there was no immoral relationship between her and Papa. I knew nothing of love affairs but I could remember how different Mama had always been in Papa's presence, how bright and joyous and gay. Alice was always exactly the same. I could remember too how Papa had looked at Mama sometimes; he had not once looked at Alice as he had looked at my mother, and in fact his attitude toward her was so obviously paternal that I wondered why I could not dismiss the notion of a relationship between them without any difficulty at all. But I could not dismiss it. I kept thinking of Hugh's repellently logical analysis of Alice's flaws and attractions to a man such as my father, and not for the first time I had the uneasy suspicion that beneath Hugh's questionable statements there might lurk a small unpalatable core of truth.

It was not impossible for Papa to fall in love with her.

He would not love her as he had loved Mama, of course, but he would like her and respect her and perhaps if she were willing—

I tried to tell myself that she would not be willing, but I could not.

My mother had been willing.

I got up, went downstairs again in a fit of restlessness and began to pace up and down the billiard room. I found I was unsure of my own feelings, aware of a confusion in my thoughts. In my own way I loved Alice myself, and at one time when I first knew her I had admired her to the point of adolescent infatuation, but I knew well enough now that my feelings for her were those a brother might feel toward an older sister to whom he was deeply attached. I had not once felt toward Alice that embarrassing chain of physical reactions that had accompanied my meetings with her cousin Rebecca Roslyn; in fact my love for Alice, even at its most fervent, had always been entirely on an unreal, idealistic plane. But I did love her. She was very dear to me, and the thought of her being sought by my father for an immoral purpose was distasteful in the extreme.

I stopped by the window and stared out onto the terrace. The urge to escape from Penmarric now was so strong that it made me feel dizzy. It was not simply because my half-brothers were openly my enemies. It was because I could not bear to watch a second version of my father's association with my mother, another unfolding of a love that could not end in marriage, another episode in which two good and decent people became entangled in a sordid and degrading relationship. I was filled with revulsion. All my worst memories of Brighton welled up inside me in a wave of nausea and all I was conscious of thinking was: I must leave. I have to get away from Penmarric. I can't stay here any longer.

Voices echoed in the hall.

Philip said, "Tell my father we want to see him, Medlyn. At once," and Hugh added something else that I could not hear.

Far away across the hall I heard old Medlyn quaver, "No, Mr. Hugh, I haven't seen Mr. Adrian. I thought he was out riding with you, Mr. Marcus, sir."

I went out into the passage in time to see them disappear into Papa's study and close the door.

Medlyn ambled away across the hall. It was quiet. I went into the drawing room next to the study but the wall was thin, being a mere partition erected when the old gunroom had been divided into two; when voices were raised in anger I could hear too much that I did not want to hear, so I walked through the open French windows into the summer morning outside. At the far end of the terrace I leaned on the parapet and stared out to sea. Surf boiled on the black rocks of the cove far below and the sea was flecked with white before ending in a hard angry horizon.

I watched the sea for a long time. Finally I straightened my back and returned to the French windows, but before I could reach them I heard Alice call from the drawing room beyond.

"Philip!" Her voice was sharp and clear. "Philip, may I speak to you for a moment?"

I drew back, not knowing why, and waited, leaning against the wall by the open window.

"Please," she said. "Just for a moment."

He came. The door banged behind him and he said roughly, "I'm sorry, Alice, but I'm not anxious to delay here. I've just quarreled with my father."

"I know," she said. "I listened. I heard every word."

I tried to move away but could not. I was riveted to the ground. I heard Philip say, "Then perhaps it's true that eavesdroppers never hear any good of themselves! Now if you'll excuse me, Alice—"

"Listen, Philip." For the first time I was aware of the tension in her voice, although she still spoke with a swift precision. "You were wrong in assuming I was—or might become—any more than simply your father's housekeeper. Your father has always treated me with the greatest propriety, and even if he had made any advances I would have rejected them. He's not the man I love."

"Oh? Well, to be frank I don't give a damn who you love or who you don't love, and I'll talk to you some other time, if you don't mind. I'm not in the mood to talk to you now."

"Please, Philip. You can't be unaware of the way I feel. I loved you from the very first moment that I saw you after your return to Cornwall, and I've loved you ever since."

"My God, Alice, do you really have to make such a fool of yourself? Of all the embarrassing, ridiculous confessions—"

"But it's the truth, Philip, the truth! I don't love your father, I love you! I shall never love anyone else except you! I—"

"God Almighty," said Philip, wrenching open the door, "as if I didn't have enough to cope with without having a hysterical woman screaming foolishness at me. Leave me alone! I'm not in love with you! Go away and stop being so silly!"

"Philip, please—please listen—"

But he went out into the hall and slammed the door in her face. I waited, speechless and stricken, listening to the dreadful

370

aching silence that remained, and finally as I leaned against the wall and pressed my burning forehead upon the cold stone I heard her harsh, painful sobs as she began to weep.

[4]

The war came.

I enlisted, of course. I did not even hesitate. I did not have to run away from Penmarric because I was called away by my country, summoned by my patriotism, inspired by the notion that if I could not wage a violent battle against my family I could at least go and fight the Germans in a good, glorious, noble war waged for the benefit of the world.

I braced myself, prepared to ride into battle bearing aloft the standards in which I believed so passionately, prepared to die if necessary for the cause I thought so worthwhile.

But I did not die. Nor did I ride into battle on a milk-white charger like some mythical crusader lost in the corridors of time. I went to the trenches. I went to places from which no man save I returned alive.

I saw war, and of course it was evil, the most appalling evil I could ever have imagined to exist on the face of the earth. I went out and I met evil face to face, and it was then at last that my soul was stripped naked before my eyes and I saw a truth so terrible that I felt as if I were a part of that evil and that my standards were as dust. For I had been at war all my life. I had always been fighting. I had fought my father and fought my brothers and fought most bitterly of all against the pattern which God had marked out for me from the moment I entered the world.

And when the trenches ran with blood and the air reeked of putrefaction and my comrades died like flies at my side, all I thought was: God Almighty, let me get home to Penmarric and I swear I'll never go fighting again.

IV
PHILIP: 1914-1930
Truth and Falsehood

Contemporaries held varying opinions about the character of Richard I. He was hot-tempered and irresponsible, generous and accomplished . . . above all he was a superb soldier.

> —The Oxford History of England:
> From Domesday Book to Magna Carta,
> A. L. POOLE

The young Duke was later called "Richard Oc e Non"— "Richard Yea and Nay"—because he always said exactly what he meant; his yea meant yea and his nay meant nay. He never troubled to dissimulate and he scorned lies. . . . He minced no words in telling his father what he thought of Henry's treatment of his Queen.

> —Henry II,
> JOHN T. APPLEBY

Richard was his mother's favourite.

> —The Conquering Family,
> THOMAS COSTAIN

The company of his mother may have affected Richard's character. . . .

> —The Devil's Brood,
> ALFRED DUGGAN

1

*The crusade was Richard's dominating passion. . . .
He worked with a singleness of purpose to remove
every obstacle that might stand in the way of its early
and successful achievement.*
　　　　　　　　　—Oxford History of England:
　　　　　　　　　　From Domesday Book, to Magna Carta,
　　　　　　　　　A. L. POOLE

*It is not too much to say that he had dedicated his life
to the service of the Holy Places.*
　　　　　　　　　　　　—The Devil's Brood,
　　　　　　　　　　　　ALFRED DUGGAN

[1]

It was the war that brought my mine back to life. I cared nothing for politics or for world events, but I cared about my mine. Making money or winning fame for myself or moving in county society never interested me, but I cared for my mine and all I ever wanted was to search for tin beneath the Cornish sea and one day have a son who would care for my mine when I was no longer there to care for it myself.

There were other things I cared about, of course. I cared for farming, which had always interested me, and I cared for the farmhouse where I went to live when I was sixteen, and I cared for my mother. It would be untrue to say that my mother was the only person who ever understood me, because I don't think she

375

did understand me half the time, but she understood what I wanted, and what I wanted was that mine.

My mine. Sennen Garth. I used to dream of it during the years of my childhood when I was far from Cornwall and the Cornish Tin Coast. I dreamed of reopening it and making it the grandest mine in all Cornwall. I dreamed of making it a greater mine than either Botallack or the mighty Levant, which were world-famous for their copper and their tin. I dreamed of a day when all the way around the world tinners would say, "Sennen Garth! Now that's a mine for you! That's a hell of a mine!" and I would dream of visiting the tin mines of the Rockies—or of anywhere in the world—and the miners there would look at me and say, "Sennen Garth!" and the name would be so famous that I would be offered a job in a tin mine anywhere and at any time because Sennen Garth was my mine, my cause, my life's work, and the greatest name in Cornish mining history.

The psychiatrist said to me years later, "Why are you so interested in mining?" and it was very hard to give him an answer. I was Cornish and most Cornishmen are supposed to be born with either a miner's candle or a fisherman's net in their hands, but I had five brothers and none of them had any inclination to be a miner. Nevertheless I think the truth was simply that I was a born miner. Some men are born painters or musicians. Some men are born lawyers or doctors. I was a born miner, and in case you think all mining consists of is chipping away at a bit of rock with a hammer, let me say that to be a first-class miner requires years of apprenticeship, plenty of hard-won skill and that mysterious flair which means more than all the skill and experience put together.

However, there was no reason why I should have been a miner. First, I was born in the wrong class and second, the mine—my mine—had been closed before I was born. There were mines nearby certainly—the famous Levant was on the cliffs by St. Just, our nearest village—but my father did not own the Levant and there was no reason why I should ever have had any connection with the mining industry. My father owned two mines on the western reaches of the Tin Coast. King Walloe, which had become defunct in the mid-nineteenth century, was flooded to the adits, but next door, its passages making a honeycomb of the cliff, was Sennen Garth. There was tin there still but it was too expensive to get it out of the ground and the mine wasn't an economic proposition any more.

Or so my father said when he closed the mine two years before I was born.

My father never cared about the mine.

But I cared. The mine called to me. It was dead, but its specter beckoned me across the forsaken landscape and the wind whistled to me as it swept through the ruined engine house. For almost as long as I could remember Sennen Garth was my cause, my life's work, and in fighting for my cause I fought my father and stayed fighting him till the very day he died.

[2]

All psychiatrists want to do, I discovered, is to ask questions about your childhood. But it wasn't much good asking me those kind of questions, because frankly I hardly remember my childhood at all. It's not that my memory is always bad. It's just that it's erratic. What I do remember of my childhood I remember with vivid clarity, but I remember so little that I can almost count my memories on the fingers of one hand. I have no intention of recalling those memories in detail, because, contrary to popular psychiatric belief, I don't believe childhood plays an important part in shaping people's lives and I want to talk about the more vital times after the outbreak of the war, I want to talk about when I was a man, when my life really began, when my cause came alive at last. So don't expect me to indulge in lengthy reminiscences about the days when I was a small boy running around in short trousers. There are other more important things to talk about than that.

However, I suppose I should briefly sum up the facts which are in some degree relevant to my later life. After all a miner doesn't just show a stick of dynamite to a wall of rock and expect an explosion straight away; you have to drill the holes, pack the charges and light the fuses before you can expect to blast your way forward into the lode.

I was born in Cornwall and until I was nine years old I lived on the Cornish Tin Coast close to the mines which had made Cornish tin and copper a legend since time out of mind. That's the most basic fact about me. Nothing else is as important as that, not even the fact that when I was nine my parents separated and I was taken away to Oxfordshire to spend my next seven years far from the Cornish Tin Coast. My father had decided to abandon my mother in order to live with his mistress and their two bastard sons, and since he was a man of considerable wealth and standing he had no trouble persuading the judge who legalized the separation to deprive my mother of the custody of all her children. This step was taken under the pretense that my mother wasn't "good enough" for her children. She was a former farmer's wife who had been born in a fisherman's cottage in St. Ives, and although ever since I could remember her no one could have guessed she was other than a lady born and bred, there were always people who enjoyed reminding themselves and others of her origins. My father was one of those people. He stressed to the judge that he wanted his children to be brought up by a "lady" in a "gentleman's household," and the judge, who came from the same class as my father, naturally agreed that this was of vital importance. My father's mistress was judged a lady and the estate in Oxfordshire where he kept her in luxury was recognized to be a gentleman's household. Class meant everything; immorality, so long as it was conducted in a discreet and civilized manner, could be overlooked; my mother didn't have a chance.

It would be easy to say I loathed my father's mistress Rose Parrish and her sons, my half-brothers William and Adrian, but it wouldn't be entirely true. I did loathe Adrian certainly; he was the most pugnacious little bastard anyone could ever wish to meet and he was all the more dangerous because he looked like a cherub and was capable of the most sickening displays of piety whenever he wanted to impress his parents. I can still remember him kneeling by his bed and reciting devoutly, "God bless all the poor and suffering" while his mother watched with pride. But as soon as she was gone the prayers would be forgotten and he would be fighting me as soon as he had the chance. Why he had such an overwhelming urge to fight me I have no idea. He had so much and I had so little, only my memories of my mother and Cornwall, only my determination that as soon as I was sixteen I would leave the house at Allengate and never spend another night beneath my father's roof again. But Adrian was determined to be enemies with me and so enemies we remained throughout all the seven years I spent in that abominable house. William I could tolerate; he never bothered me and spent most of the time with my brother Marcus. And Rose Parrish?

She was like a good nanny. At first I was rude to her and sullen and disagreeable as well, but how can you keep on being rude to someone who simply turns the other cheek? She was a good, decent, honest person whom my father had dragged through the mud. There! I needn't have said that, need I? But it's the truth, and if there's one thing I despise it's a man who twists the truth to suit his own ends.

However, I don't want to dwell on the unhappy memories of my childhood. They're over now and best forgotten. There's only one other person I want to mention in connection with my early years, and that's my grandmother.

I disliked her at first because she reminded me of my father, but she took a fancy to me for some reason and at last I thawed toward her when I discovered she shared my love of Cornwall and the Cornish Tin Coast. I made this discovery during a weekend my mother and I spent in London when I was nine; since my mother was unwell at the time my grandmother took me to tea at Claridges and the next day invited me to lunch at her house in Charles Street. There I found that she had several books on Cornwall, and so pleased was she with my interest in them that she lent me her favorite, *A History of the Levant Mine*. I regret to say I never returned it to her, but she couldn't have minded much because when she died a year or two later she left me all her books on Cornwall and the Cornish Tin Coast.

Afterward when I was savoring my legacy I thought how fortunate it had been that we had met in London that weekend, for there was no doubt I wouldn't have been there at all if my mother and I hadn't first met my father elsewhere under unpleasant circumstances. It had been my half-term weekend; my mother and I had decided to go on an outing to Brighton—a fine idea in itself, but the entire expedition was ruined when we happened by the most extraordinary piece of bad luck to choose a hotel where, unknown to us, my father and Rose Parrish were staying with William and Adrian. There was a confrontation in the dining room. I'm sure it was all very dramatic but I don't remember it well. The part I remember most clearly now is leaving the hotel afterward, catching the train back to London and the next day having tea with my grandmother.

My parents separated directly after that. For me Brighton was the beginning of the road which led to those seven years' exile at Allengate, so it's small wonder that I've never once been back there.

However, so much for family history. And now that I've got

that out of the way I can turn to the beginning of my career as a miner—and to my earliest memories of my mine, Sennen Garth, my cause, my life's work.

[3]

I remember the Levant mine, magnificent Levant, one of the greatest tin mines in Cornwall, and the last mine in the Duchy where copper was mined on a commercial scale. The Levant mine was high on the cliffs overlooking Cape Cornwall, and when I was a child the Levant beckoned me like some gigantic magnet pulling at a small pin. I used to slip away from home whenever I had the opportunity and fraternize with the miners' children so that I could hear about mining at first hand, and soon I was learning from my friends about their fathers who worked at Levant, fabulous Levant, its main-shaft pole supporting its unique man-engine sixteen hundred feet from top to bottom, its galleries running fathom after fathom out under the sea, its immense wealth packed into enormous lodes of tin. Often I would walk down to Cape Cornwall and watch the water draining through the launders and out of the adits, and often the water would run red as blood from the ore in the rock. I used to hang around the engine houses which hoisted the ore and pumped the water. There would be men shoveling coal into the furnace, spinning machinery, the hiss of steam. The bucket, or skip, was raised from the galleries below and its load of crude ore dumped in a wagon which would take it to a floor where it could be pounded by sledgehammers. For the mine lived and breathed like some enormous animal; it was an entity with a life of its own, and when I realized this I looked at the deserted mines, the abandoned ones like Sennen Garth which had been left to die, and I wanted them to live again, to live as Levant lived, because there seemed to me suddenly nothing so forlorn and sad as a dead mine that had been allowed to die.

I remember the mine captain at Levant, the mine captain saying to me, "You can't ride the man-engine to the bottom of the mine, boy, you're too small. You'd miss your footing and fall down the shaft. You can't go down the mine."

"But isn't there a lift?" I said, not understanding. "I'll go down in that."

"A gig?" He broke out laughing. "This is the Levant, boy," he said. I can still remember the way he said "Levant." "This is the *Levant*," he said, and it was as a believer might speak of Jerusalem. "The miners go down to the levels on a man-engine."

The man-engine was like some gigantic prehistoric monster. I'll never forget the first time I saw the man-engine at the Levant. The captain took me to the edge of the shaft and explained to me how the mechanism worked.

"The wooden rod plunges, see—up, down, up, down. Up twelve feet, down twelve feet. There are steps all the way down at twelve-foot intervals on the rod, and corresponding platforms—sollars, we call them—on the sides of the shaft. The rod comes up, you step on, grab the handle—see?—and then the rod plunges down twelve feet and off you get onto the sollar. The rod swings up again, you get on the next step, drop twelve feet, step off onto the sollar, wait, step on, step off—and so on. It takes half an hour from top to bottom."

I was speechless with wonder, and when I found my voice I again pestered him to let me ride the machine. But he still refused.

"Not while you're so small, Master Philip," he said, "and even when you're bigger I wouldn't take you down without Mr. Castallack's permission."

I tried the mine at Botallack, but they wouldn't let me down there either. It was then, to compensate myself for my disappointment and to satisfy my craving to go below ground, that I turned to the dead workings of Sennen Garth.

I found a shaft on the cliffs with a ladder stretching down into the darkness. After stealing a candle and matches from the Penmarric pantry I went down the ladder and took possession. I was seven years old then, too young to know how lucky I was that the ladder ran unbroken from top to bottom, or how fortunate it was that the shaft was a small one which could be descended by a child without risk of exhaustion. I reached the bottom. Far above me was an oval patch of blue sky and around me were damp rocky walls and the black opening of a passage. Beside myself with delight, I lit the candle and set off undaunted into the death trap of the disused workings.

Although I had no idea where I was, I discovered later that I had been in the oldest part of the mine, the maze of the western reaches which bordered on the flooded King Walloe mine next door. The walls were damp, the smell odd, the ground hard but wet beneath my feet. I was hypnotized with excitement. Presently I came to a fork, chose the left branch and reached a place where the tunnel divided into three. As I took the left passage again I began to go downhill and suddenly I heard water, a great roar of water that seemed to grow louder and louder until, rounding a corner at last, I found myself in a huge cave where a large machine clanked without ceasing to channel the water into a launder.

With a leap of joy I thought I had discovered a man-engine, but it was only a water wheel, a primitive pump which went on draining the mine night and day even though there was no longer any need to keep it drained. For Sennen Garth, unlike King Walloe, was only partially flooded; the bottom of the mine alone was under water, and at that point the bottom of the mine was still many fathoms away.

For a long while I sat and watched the pump, but at last I glanced around more carefully and noticed an interesting rock at my feet. I stooped to pick it up. A second later I had dropped my candle, the flame was extinguished and I was plunged into darkness.

A great peace came upon me. I felt a quietness despite the roar of the water, a feeling that I had been in the place before—which was nonsense, because of course I hadn't. My immediate reaction was: This is what it's like to be dead and in heaven—or a spirit waiting to be born.

I sat there for several seconds in the dark. I still wasn't afraid. It wasn't that kind of darkness. When I became aware of myself again I felt around for my candle, relit it and returned slowly to my shaft to crawl back to the surface once more.

Later when I happened to mention to my friend the mine captain that I had begun to explore Sennen Garth, he nearly fainted on the spot.

"If you were my son," he said grimly when he had recovered, "I'd beat the hide off you for that. Now listen to me, boy. You want to live to be a man, don't you? Then don't go down those old workings on your own! No miner goes into danger without a mate to help him, if needs be. Above all he doesn't go into an area without anyone knowing where he's gone. Supposing you'd slipped and broken your ankle down there? Who do you think would have found you? Supposing you'd fallen down a winze—a shaft linking one level with another? If you're wandering along not looking where you're going—well, you'd never see the light of day again. Besides, those old workings are honeycombed like a maze—you could get lost in them and never find your way out. Those old galleries are unsafe too. Have you ever heard of a cave-in? Do you know what happens when timber supports are so rotten that one finger-touch will send them crumbling into dust? If there was a cave-in in the western reaches of that mine, do you know what would happen?"

I shook my head, admiring his knowledge, wishing I could speak of mines with such authority. "No, sir," I said respectfully.

I shall always remember what he said then. It's the clearest memory of my childhood. "The water would come in from King Walloe," he said, just as a baptist preacher might have thundered, 'Fire and brimstone will rain down from heaven.' As I looked duly impressed he added, "The mine next door to Sennen Garth is flooded to the adits. That means that when you're at, say, the hundred-fathom level in Sennen Garth you have an enormous amount of water—thousands of gallons—standing over you in King Walloe next door. Think of it as if you were standing beside a mighty water tank with sides as thin as paper. One prick in those thin walls and the water would rush through and the whole face of the tank would collapse. The western reaches of Sennen Garth are dangerous as all hell let loose. You keep away from that mine."

But nothing could keep me away from Sennen Garth. I was more careful, certainly. I left notes hidden in my room in case I had an accident, took a ball of string with me so that I would not lose my way in the labyrinth, but I went on exploring the mine. I was just beginning to think I knew the old workings like the back of my hand when my parents separated, I was sent to Allengate, and for seven years I did not see any mines, least of all the mines of the Cornish Tin Coast.

That was how I came to know Sennen Garth. That was how it came to be my mine, my cause, my life's work, because once I'd taken possession all I wanted was to make it live again as Levant lived and to restore it to its position among the greatest mines in Cornwall. Almost all the best memories of my childhood were linked with that mine.

But the very best memory had nothing to do with the mine at all.

I remember going home.

On my sixteenth birthday I quarreled with my father and took the night train to Cornwall. The next morning in Penzance I left my luggage at the station until I could collect it later, hired a horse from the nearby inn and rode out of town.

The moors rose before me in the sunlight like a mirage of the promised land.

It was all so beautiful, you see, each particle of heather, each swaying frond of bracken, each wildflower by the wayside. I saw the ruined engine houses of the deserted mines of Zillan parish, the square tower of Zillan church, the gray huddles of scattered farms, and once I stooped from my horse to touch the stone walls which bordered the road as if I couldn't believe my return wasn't a dream. But it was real enough. I rode on, too drunk with joy to hurry, and the black tors were jagged against that flawless sky and the air was cool and fresh upon my face.

Zillan village lay to the east of me; the farm, Roslyn Farm, where my mother had lived since the separation, lay to the west. I left the road, turned up the lane, and still I couldn't bring myself to hurry. The land was so beautiful, so foreign yet so familiar. My heart ached with love for it. I thought of all those long dreary years at Allengate which now lay behind me forever, and tears pricked my eyes because I was free at last and I was home.

I saw the house.

And someone saw me coming. The front door opened and I saw her standing in the shadows of the porch.

I hurried then as I had never hurried in my life before. I slid off the horse and started to run. I ran and ran, my feet stumbling on the wet earth, and as I ran she ran too, and the scent of wild roses floated toward me on the soft wind from the moors.

[4]

It was three years later when Jared Roslyn rode up to the back door of the farmhouse with the scheme that was to bring my mine back to life, but during those three years I had tried every means I knew to persuade my father to open Sennen Garth again. First of all I tried writing to some groups of well-known mining speculators or "adventurers" as they were called in the old days, to urge them to approach my father and ask him to grant them a sett, but although I had some friendly replies none of them showed enough interest to begin negotiations. My father's gesture of closing the mine in the Nineties after seeking advice from the famous mining experts of Dolcoath was still remembered, and although my father's opinion of Sennen Garth might have been questioned in mining circles, no one questioned the opinion of the experts. No one seemed willing to believe me when I stressed that the mine had been closed for practical reasons unrelated to the remaining wealth beneath the ground, and that to judge from the old maps and books I had inherited from my grandmother there was plenty of tin still left if anyone cared to invest some money in bringing it to the surface. Everyone merely assumed that too much money would be needed for such an investment and that the returns might not be half so rewarding as I myself felt they would be.

After that I approached my father in person. By then Rose Parrish had died, Allengate Manor had been sold and the entire family—including my bastard half-brothers—had returned to my old home Penmarric in St. Just a stone's throw from my mother's farm in Zillan. Presently my oldest sister Mariana decided to marry some overbred boor with a title, and when we all gathered at the townhouse in London for her wedding I seized the opportunity to speak to my father about the mine. I thought I presented my case very convincingly, but I got nowhere at all with him. The truth was that he was in an exceedingly bad mood, and when I saw his mind was closed against anything I proposed my mood became as bad as his, so we ended up shouting at each other in our usual fashion. I had no idea then why he should have been so bad-tempered, but I discovered later from my mother that he had asked her to return to Penmarric—for *my* sake! Of course that was his way of saying he did not like me living at the farm. I practiced farming in my spare time when I wasn't riding over to Levant or Botallack to learn as much as I could about mining, and the thought of any son of his cleaning out a pigsty was no doubt horrifying to him. Fortunately my mother refused to be bullied back to the place where she had been so unhappy, and retorted that she and I were both more than content to remain at Zillan. However, I doubt my father was serious about this proposed reconciliation, for he had admitted willingly enough to my mother that he had no intention of removing William and Adrian from the house even if she did come back, and I fail to see how he could have expected her to live in the same house as his bastards.

After the failure of my attempt to reason with my father I tried to force his hand by resorting to blackmail, but even that was a fiasco. It was my brother Hugh who invented the scheme, but my brother Marcus was as quick as I was to back him up. Marcus had the quaint idea that as he was the eldest legitimate son and the heir to Penmarric my father should finance his revels at Oxford with an inexhaustible supply of blank checks. Hugh wasn't nearly such a fool as Marcus. Though in many ways my direct opposite—he had no regard at all for the truth and nothing would have induced him to soil his hands with manual labor—he was such good company that I found myself forgiving him his more irritating qualities. And he was clever. It was he who suspected that the current housekeeper at Penmarric, Alice Penmar, was my father's new mistress and that my father might do much to avoid a scandal, and it was he too who thought of forcing Adrian to provide us with the proof we needed for a showdown. It seemed a first-class scheme at the time, but in the end it came to nothing. Adrian, playing the role of noble martyr with his usual sickening piety, refused to yield under pressure and when we were obliged to confront my father prematurely without evidence, my father made short work of demolishing our hopes. Marcus was reproved for "continual immaturity," Hugh was labeled "a capricious child with a talent for mischief" (Hugh, who had dreamed up the entire scheme!) and I was informed that I was obviously still suffering from my "small boy's infatuation with the mine."

That finished it.

I started to yell at him and soon he was yelling at me. I accused him of unjustly favoring Adrian, and he said yes, he damned well did favor Adrian because Adrian was the one son who behaved as a son should behave toward his father. I told him that was a load of horses' excrement and that he favored Adrian because he had preferred Adrian's mother to mine. I was so angry that I made the mistake of referring to Rose Parrish as "that whore." My father at once went white with rage and shouted that my mother was the whore and that he had once paid her five pounds to go to bed with him. I called him a bloody liar. Marcus then said he was sorry but he felt sick and would we please excuse him, and Hugh somehow managed to melt away into the hall before I was even aware that he had left the room. Without any form of moral support I knew there was nothing else for me to do but retreat ignominiously in their wake, so I spat on the floor and walked out with as much dignity as I could muster after such a disastrous defeat.

But even then I wasn't allowed to leave Penmarric at once. Alice Penmar cornered me, confessed she had been eavesdropping and swore she wasn't my father's mistress because she would much rather be mine. Considering she had spent her childhood calling me a "rude foul-mouthed little pest," I suppose the situation was not without its humorous side, but unfortunately I wasn't in the mood to be amused and merely suggested to her in the crudest of Anglo-Saxon terms that she should go and have intercourse with herself instead.

I admit I behaved badly to her, but since she'd been brought up in a rectory I don't suppose she understood half of what I was saying anyway. When I made the effort to apologize to her the following Sunday after church she told me with perfect composure that she realized we had both been unusually upset at the time and that as far as she was concerned the incident was closed and I was to think no more of it.

I followed her advice with relief.

As if to divert my attention from the memory of those scenes at Penmarric, the war broke out a week later. I thought at first that this was the last straw, the final slice of ill-luck I needed to end all my hopes for reopening the mine, but I was wrong. I had just made up my mind fiercely that no one would make me enlist no matter how many white feathers might be handed to me and that no one, not even the King himself, could ever drag me away from Cornwall again, when I had a visitor. One cloudy morning at the end of 1914 I heard horse's hoofs ring out in the yard of my mother's farm, and on going to the window I saw to my amazement that my visitor was none other than that pillar of the working-class community, Mr. Jared Roslyn of Morvah.

[5]

I knew Jared Roslyn just as he knew me, but we had never spoken to each other. He was the elder of my mother's two stepsons by her first marriage, and both he and his brother Joss had been her enemies for nearly thirty years. My father was as unpopular with them as my mother was, so I had not expected either brother to show any sign of friendliness toward me, and when Jared Roslyn came riding up to the farm on that mild December morning I instantly assumed he came on some hostile mission. My first reaction—caused by my guilt—was that he had come to tell me to enlist at once as every other young man had done and to fight for my country against the Germans; I had long been afraid that someone would drop hints to me on the subject, and although I was popular in the parish I had begun to think that people were looking at me askance. I fully expected to receive a letter any day from my father asking me why I had not followed the example of Marcus and Adrian, both of whom had enlisted at once, but in fact I received no such inquiry from Penmarric. My mother took my part, of course, and declared my work on the farm was of vital importance, but there were older men, too old to fight, who could have managed the farm in my absence. Even William, whose position as bailiff was as important as my role at the farm, had volunteered for the army, and the only reason why he was still at Penmarric was because he had been declared medically unfit for military service; a bout of diphtheria suffered in childhood had left him with high blood pressure and the suspicion of a weak heart. As soon as I saw Jared Roslyn I concluded he had come to remind me of my patriotic duty.

Having given free rein to my guilty conscience, I then became more rational. Jared was a lay preacher in the Wesleyan chapel and a leading man in his community, but it was hardly likely that he would dare hand me a white feather and roundly harangue me for cowardice.

Finally I had to admit to myself I was baffled and went out into the yard to meet him.

He was a big man, as tall as I was, and Cornish-dark with a black beard. He must have been over fifty but he had few gray hairs and still carried himself like a young man. Considering we had never spoken to each other, I knew a fair amount about him; he had an anemic-looking wife who was obviously terrified of him, eight buxom daughters, and one pale undersized boy in whom he was clearly disappointed. The boy was a couple of years older than my youngest brother Jan-Yves and had just surprised everyone by winning a scholarship to the nearest grammar school. Of the eight daughters, all of whom had the most preposterously Puritan names, three were now safely married to local men, four were at home under the stern supervision of the paterfamilias, and one, Charity, had become a fallen woman and was publicly disowned by her family; she had been in service at Gurnards Grange, the Waymarks' home at Zennor, and, according to Hugh, who always managed to hear the gossip, had been dismissed for fornication in the pantry. Not in the least daunted by this just reward for her sins, she had found employment as a barmaid in St. Just and for over a year had maintained the honor of being the best whore from Land's End to St. Ives. However, the urge to settle down had overtaken her and presently she had left her lodgings at the pub, where she still continued to work at the bar, and moved to a little villa facing the sea on the outskirts of the town. It was common knowledge that everything in the cottage, from the lace curtains in the bedroom to the geraniums in the window boxes, had been provided for her by my half-brother William Parrish, who also exercised his discretion as my father's bailiff and allowed her to live there rent free.

It was small wonder that Jared Roslyn had disowned an offspring who flourished so embarrassingly only a few miles from the working-men's club he had founded for the miners who lived in Zillan parish.

I crossed the yard toward him. "Good morning," I said curtly. "What do you want?"

I saw no reason to be polite to him. It would have been foolish to speak as if we were old friends.

His glance flickered over me from head to toe. His dark eyes were hard but no longer hostile. "A word with you," he answered, equally direct in his manner. His voice, deep and Cornish, surprised me for some reason; perhaps I was merely surprised to hear him speak. "We needn't trouble your mother. It's you I want to see."

I felt more baffled than ever. "Just a moment," I said abruptly and turned to tell the Turner girls in the kitchen that my mother could stay out of the way. After they had scurried off round-eyed to find her, I asked Jared Roslyn into the house and led the way through the kitchens and hall to the parlor. He followed me without a word, and as I closed the parlor door behind us I remembered that the house had been his home once and that he had probably loved it then as much as I loved it now.

"How can I help you, Mr. Roslyn?" I said, spurred to a reluctant courtesy. "Please sit down."

"I'll stand." He had gone to look out of the window but now he turned to face me. There was a short silence as our glances met. "I've heard a lot about you," he said at last. "Good things mostly."

I was so surprised I was speechless. This was the very last observation I would ever have expected to hear from him. I was still staring at him blankly when he added, "It takes guts not to follow the crowd. I don't know why you haven't enlisted and I don't care. I don't hold with wars. Men should live in brotherhood and not murder each other in violation of the Commandments. Besides, you're needed here—now. In a way it's a miracle you're still here, but then God moves in mysterious and wonderful ways. I'm beginning to see His Hand in this and His Providence." He spoke simply with complete sincerity. In spite of the fact that I had outgrown religion a long time ago and went to church only to please my mother, I was impressed. After a moment he said, "You look like your mother. I might have married your mother once long ago. A pity I didn't. I could have done with a son like you."

It seems ridiculous to admit it now but I was touched, even moved, by what he said. My father had never said anything to suggest he did not regard me as a nuisance, a cross he had been assigned to bear as part of his parental duties. Everything I had done had been wrong, foolish and misguided in his eyes, even if it had not been positively bad. Yet here was this stranger whom I had been brought up to dislike, and he was saying he had heard good reports of me and that he wished I could have been his son instead of my father's.

"I'm glad you've heard good reports of me," I said uncertainly, still taken aback by his words, "but how could they be of interest to you?"

He said, "We have a mutual interest, I think."

"Mutual interest?"

"Sennen Garth."

There was a silence. We stood there, just he and I in that house where he had lived long ago, and I realized that here at last was my ally, someone who understood, and he was talking of the mine, my mine, Sennen Garth, which I longed to transform into the greatest mine of the Cornish Tin Coast.

"I've had many a tussle with your father over that mine," he was saying. "The first time was when he closed it down after he had moved to Penmarric. Many good miners out of work, there were, with starving families. Those were bad days. I led deputations to persuade him to reopen it, but he was stubborn as a dozen mules. He was young then—two or three years older than you are now maybe. Very polite he was, but stubborn. Unreasonable. Once he'd made his decision there was no deflecting him."

"He's always refused to reopen the mine," I said, the words tumbling out of my mouth. "He's mean with his money and won't take a risk, but I know there's tin there, Mr. Roslyn, I know it because I've seen the old maps and I've been down the Levant and I *know*. There's a lode under the sea, running westward—"

"I've talked to miners who said the same thing. Now listen to me, boy, and listen carefully. Have you ever thought that this war may be the saving of Sennen Garth? You read your newspapers, no doubt—you'll know we're short of tin. If we could interest the government in the mine—if we could persuade them there's plenty of tin still there in the ground—"

The sudden comprehension so overwhelmed me that I felt dizzy. "Christ Almighty."

"Hold your tongue, boy, blasphemy won't open the mine any more than your father will. Now listen to me—are you listening? I've got a number of depositions from men who used to work at Sennen Garth twenty years ago before your father closed it. They all testify that there's tin still left in the mine and probably more below the lowest level—after all, your father didn't close the mine because it was worked out; he closed it because it wasn't a money-making venture any more, because he wasn't prepared to invest more money to make it a money-making venture, and because he'd as lief live with the mine closed for good as having it provide a livelihood for honest working men. I've also got a deposition from the men of Levant about the probability of there being a rich lode under the sea, and I've got a deposition from a young mining expert from Redruth called Alun Trevose who gives it as his opinion—being impartial—that the Government would find it well worth their while to investigate the possibilities of reopening Sennen Garth. I've got any number of depositions. Now all I want is someone to present that case to the Government. I could present it myself and go to London and do my best, but I'm not a miner and I've no technical knowledge should they want to question me. I've talked it over with the miners, men who live in St. Just and Zillan, and they all mentioned your name. You're known to love the mines like a miner; you've been down the Levant often enough. Everyone speaks more than highly of you."

I was dumbfounded. My face began to burn with pleasure.

"Of course you're young," said Jared Roslyn, "and just a boy in some ways, I dare say, but the miners I spoke to thought of you as a man who could act like a man and think like a man as far as the mine's concerned. You've also got one great advantage, be it unjust or not; you've been reared as a gentleman. You'll know how to talk to the Government and they'll listen to you more readily than they'd listen to a Cornish working man. Well, there it is. Will you go to London for us and present our case?" And as I began to stammer he added, "You'd best think it over. I don't want to be accused of rushing you into any rash judgment. I'll be at the Working Men's Club in Zillan tonight—come over after eight and give me your answer, if you will."

"You needn't wait till eight for my answer." I was so excited I could hardly speak. "I don't need time to think it over. I've been thinking about that mine for over twelve years. I'll go to London for you and get that mine opened and, by God, I'll find that tin and strike that lode if it's the very last thing I ever do."

2

Warcraft was his specialty and everything else was sacrificed to indulging it.

It was no use his enemies taking refuge in castles, for Richard would detect a weakness in even the most allegedly impregnable of them and exploit it with precocious skill.

—King John,
W. L. WARREN

[1]

I needed money then, not much, just enough for my fare to London and to pay for my meals and my hotel. Also I had discovered that my best suits, which I had put away in the wardrobe on my return to the farm over three years ago, no longer fitted me. I had filled out; hard work had made me muscular and the material of my jackets now strained across my shoulder blades and refused to meet across my chest. My mother had money saved, but I hated to ask her for anything, and nothing on earth would have induced me to go crawling to my father. In the end I approached Jared. He was astonished to hear I had no money, I suppose because he believed that anyone who spoke as I did should have too much money for their own good.

"Look," I said bluntly, "I'm a working man, just as you are. The farm makes enough profit to enable me to live very simply, and now I no longer have to ask my mother for a share of my father's maintenance payments, but I only have seven pounds of my own in the bank and nothing more, so if you can't help me I'll have to borrow from somewhere else, and frankly I'd rather borrow from you than from a professional moneylender. And don't suggest I borrow from my mother. She's supported me financially for long enough and I don't want her to support me any more."

He didn't ask me why I couldn't approach my father. He knew, just as everyone knew, that my father and I were estranged. Instead he said with reluctance, "I haven't much money to spare myself, but I wouldn't want to see you in debt to the moneylenders. I'll talk to my brother Joss. He married a rich woman and has only one child to provide for. He'll lend me the money."

So I got the money and had a new suit made and after Christmas I went to London to see our member of Parliament. He said he would look into the matter. I said that wasn't good enough. He became annoyed, but when I reminded him of my father's power in the Duchy and how many votes he could influence he said he would speak to the Minister. I hung around a few days longer, wishing I was back in Cornwall and wondering how they were managing without me at the farm; I had never liked London, and London in wartime was even more depressing than when the world had been at peace. Peace now seemed a thousand light-years away. "I give the Germans exactly six months!" Marcus had declared before leaving Cornwall to enlist, but he, like so many others, had been hopelessly optimistic.

The war was dragging on. All the action had taken place within the first four months and now matters had reached a stalemate— or so it seemed, although since information was scarce rumor was rife and it was hard to know what was really going on. However, it was generally agreed that the British Expeditionary Force under Sir John French had done well after crossing to France in August; it had reached Mons in time to thwart the Schlieffen Plan and prevent the Germans reaching Paris; it had forced the enemy back across the Aisne, and presently at Ypres it had halted the German advance to the Channel. But now in December both sides had paused to replenish their supplies and it was hard to forecast what might happen next. Both sides were evenly matched and there was no hint that a clear-cut victory was just around the corner.

I was made more aware of the war while I was staying in London. In Cornwall it was easy enough to think of the conflict being confined to France, but in London I was conscious that the war had reached across the Channel to lay drab, dank fingers upon a city which had been until so recently the most brilliant, most opulent and most colorful capital in Europe. Men in uniform, unending speculation on the war, rabid Germanophobia, new rules and regulations, a drop in the quality of food and service—the war permeated everything. It was a gray, grim winter in a gray, grim city and I grudged every moment I was kept waiting by those incompetent politicians.

While I was waiting I heard a rumor of compulsory enlistment if the recruiting campaigns did not measure up to expectations, but the news was a false alarm. Patriotism ran so high that everyone was in a fever to enlist, and no one suspected then that the war would be so lengthy and the casualties so high that compulsory enlistment would become necessary. I relaxed. It was not that I was unpatriotic. I would have defended Cornwall to the last ditch if the invaders had tried to advance across the Tamar, but I saw no point in rushing off to France to fight a bunch of foreigners who were causing trouble because some fool had got himself shot in Sarajevo. I had my own wars to fight anyway. I hadn't the time to run around France killing Germans when I was needed in Cornwall to fight the battle for my mine. Besides, why shouldn't the French fight their own battles? If they'd had more backbone Britain wouldn't have been dragged into the war and I wouldn't have been placed in such an embarrassing position.

I was just thinking I would have to send home for more money when I heard that the high-ranking civil servant who advised the Minister on matters such as my mine would be willing to give me an appointment, and presently I went to Whitehall with my member of Parliament to see him.

He was an ill-tempered aristocrat with a dissolute mouth and eyes weary from worry and overwork.

I tried not to show how nervous I was. Making a great effort, I kept my voice forceful and began the concise speech I had prepared for the occasion.

"Yes, yes," he interrupted me irritably, his hands twitching the copies of the miners' depositions before him, "but who owns this mine?"

"A man called Mark Castallack, sir."

"Castallack? The historian?"

"Yes, sir."

He looked at me oddly. "Didn't you say your name was Castallack too?"

"Yes, it is. He's my father."

"Your father! Good God, why on earth didn't you say so!" He gave me a conspiratorial smile as if to say, "So you're one of us after all." When I refused to return his smile and waited politely for him to continue, he was somewhat taken aback. It took him several seconds to think of what to say next. "What is your father's present position in regard to the mine?" he inquired distantly at last. "Was he a shareholder before the old company became defunct? I assume it was once a company with capital, shares and so forth."

"Yes, sir, it was." I was glad the interview had become more formal again. The atmosphere of a cozy chat would hardly have helped me to state my case succinctly. "However, the Penmars —my grandmother's family who owned the mine—were never content to be just landowners taking a percentage of the dues. They were adventurers—speculators and shareholders, that is—as well as landowners, and they were the moving force in floating the old company and seeing it established. They owned two-thirds of the shares, and even when the company was wound up they of course remained the landowners. For the last couple of years I've been trying to persuade both my father and various well-known adventurers to reform the company, but my father's not interested in spending his money in that way and the adventurers these days seem to be wary of the old mines, especially after what happened at the mine East Wheal Rose in the Eighties —although there are plenty who say Wheal Rose was closed just when the greatest wealth of all was within reach. . . . But to return to Sennen Garth, there's no doubt that it's still a rich mine. First of all there's tin left in the old workings. No one denies that. Second, there's tin beneath the lowest level of the old workings. No one seriously denies that either. Third, the greatest wealth of all can most probably be reached by extending the mine out under the sea, just as they've done at Levant and Botallack.

In those depositions you'll find expert mining opinion which re-inforces this probability. Why, you may ask, in these circum-stances does the mine remain closed when it obviously has such a great potential? Sir, that's a fair question and I'll tell you the an-swer. It's because considerable capital investment is required and investors are fighting shy of the Cornish tin mines because econ-omists in London—who know nothing of Cornwall—have been spreading a rumor for a long time that the Cornish tin industry has moved into an irreversible decline. It's the attitude that's to blame, sir, not the facts. If the Government now backs Sennen Garth, you'll revive not just my mine but the whole Cornish tin industry. You'll give the investors faith and you'll get your tin. You can't miss! And as far as Sennen Garth is concerned, it would really be a very simple operation. All you would have to do would be to get a new engine, drain the bottom of the mine—"

"What does your father think about all this?"

I tried to keep my temper. "Sir, my father's not a miner. He knows nothing about mining and very little about Sennen Garth. That's why I'm here."

He smiled cynically. "Have you ever been down a mine?"

That was the moment when I nearly punched him on the nose. He spoke of the mine as one might speak of a lavatory.

"I've studied mining for a long time," I said abruptly, "and I've been down the Levant mine at St. Just more times than I can remember." How I managed to hold onto my temper I don't know. "I was sent here by the miners of St. Just," my voice was saying reasonably, "because they believe I know what it means to be a Cornish tinner. I wasn't sent here because I'm my father's son. That's why I made no effort to trade on his name when we first began our conversation. It was the men of St. Just who sent me, not my father."

"Are you a Socialist?"

I saw red. By this time I was clinging onto my temper with both hands and sweating with the strain.

"Frankly, sir," I said, "I've no more use for politics than you have for mining. In my opinion in such a time of national crisis any talk of internal politics is pretty damned irrelevant. The only reason I'm here talking to you now is because I've got something you want and you've got something I want, and what we both want is for England to win this bloody war. If we two can reach an agreement as quickly and painlessly as possible we'll both of us benefit but England would benefit most of all. Why don't we concentrate on the facts instead of wandering off into side issues and wasting time? What the hell does it matter who my father is? What the hell does it matter if I'm a Socialist or not? Is that fact going to help England win the war? The important fact is that there's tin in this mine, probably ten times as much tin as anyone even dreams there is, and if you agree to finance—"

"You can regard that as agreed," he said coolly. "I'll advise the Minister to sanction the reopening of the mine and grant the appropriate funds since the prospects are evidently so promising. You're right. We need every ounce of tin we can get." And as I stared at him dumbly, unable to believe the magnitude of his words, he added, "How old are you?"

"I . . . Twenty in June, sir."

I fully expected him to say, "Then why the devil aren't you in France?" but he did not. All he said was "You're a very unusual young man. You should go far." Then he rose and shook hands and the interview was over and I never saw him again.

Within two weeks Government officials were at Penmarric to talk to my father; within a month the preliminary operations were being organized, and at last on one morning at the end of March the main engine was christened "Castallack" with a bottle of port, the engine house was decorated with spring flowers, and every man with mining in his blood came from miles around to cheer the resurrection of the Sennen Garth mine.

[2]

That was when I first met Alun Trevose.

He was a mining expert from Camborne's East Pool and Agar, one of the men whom Jared had approached when he had been gathering his depositions, and he too believed in the wealth of Sennen Garth and the existence of the lodes under the sea.

He was just like me really. Not obviously like me—not like me in appearance or background or education, but like me in the ways that mattered. We thought alike, felt alike, acted alike. For he was a born miner, just as I was, a man with a passion for mining that equaled my own, and I knew soon after I had met him that this was the best friend I would ever have, anywhere at any time.

I had had plenty of friends at school but none of them had shared my interests. By this time I did not expect to make such a friend, and when I first met Trevose I wasn't even sure I liked him. He was half Welsh, half Cornish, totally Celt. He had been born in Redruth, where his father had been a miner, but at the age of eight he had gone to South Africa, where his father had chased easy money in the gold mines. That hadn't lasted long; the dust of the gold mines can play havoc with a miner's lungs and then not even the best pay in the world can stand between you and an early grave. At sixteen Trevose was back in Redruth and vowing to spend the rest of his life in Cornwall instead of following his father's example and dying on foreign soil. He had been married, but that hadn't worked out; his views on God, the upper classes and women soon became famous throughout the more conventional circles of the mining parishes, and at first people were suspicious of him, distrusting his nasal South African accent, which had supplanted the native speech of Redruth, and rating him little better than "one of they furriners" with "powerful uppity ideas." But there was Cornish blood in Trevose and he didn't remain an outsider for long. He knew mines and he knew tin and he knew how to lead men below ground, and after a time people forgot his strangeness and learned to live with his eccentricities because he was a good man to have around and kind too for all his roughness and coarse speech.

I liked him long before he could permit himself to like me. It went against the grain with him to be other than surly to someone with my kind of background.

As a miner he was an expert. No other word could do him justice. Sometimes I felt he could almost smell tin a hundred yards away behind a wall of granite. He was young, only ten years older than I was, but I trusted him more than I would have trusted a man twenty years his senior because he had the mysterious flair of the born miner and it was this flair that seemed to speak aloud to me and identify him as a man after my own heart.

He was with me on all those preliminary surveys of Sennen Garth, and it was he who organized the draining of the lower levels. A Government official had been appointed "managing director" of the mine and another official was acting as purser, but neither of those civil servants knew much about the Cornish tin mines and their principal purpose was to keep a watch on the expenditure of Government money. From the beginning it was understood that I was in charge of operations, but since I was young and inexperienced I knew I needed someone whom I could rely upon to give me good advice. There was no shortage of advice itself; endless streams of interested miners, anxious to work for "tutwork or tribute" in exploiting the possible new lodes, were continually at my elbow, but Trevose was the one I trusted. When we finally sank a shaft farther below sea level and began to strike out under the sea, it was he who decided on the level to sustain and it was he who went on believing that we would blast our way into wealth.

"There's tin there," he said. "I know it."

The Government began to worry about expenditure and the civil servants suggested we should concentrate on mining the tin which remained in the old workings, but in fact it had turned out that there wasn't nearly so much tin left in the old workings as everyone had thought there was. Soon I began to realize that the entire success of the venture depended on whether a series of rich lodes really did exist beneath the sea. I still thought they did, but now the amount of speculative risk involved seemed greater to me than ever before and I could understand why adventurers had fought shy of Sennen Garth for more than twenty years.

"Relax," said Trevose. "There's tin there, waiting for us. I can feel it."

So we went on under the sea and the walls ran with water and the noise of the pick and the hammer and the drill nibbled at our ears, but there was no lode of tin. The miners began to look worried. The old men at the surface shook their heads wisely and said there were no seams below the sea at that point and that they themselves had said so all along.

"They don't know bloody nothing from bloody nothing," said Trevose. "We'll go lower." And we sank a shaft to the two-hundred-and-forty-fathom level far out under the Atlantic Ocean.

My father, visiting the mine out of interest, inquired politely if we had met with any success.

"Not yet," I said defiantly, "but it'll be very soon now." But in the darkness of a hope strained to unbearable limits my own faith began to waver. Those months exploring the mine and searching fruitlessly for a new lode had made me realize how ignorant I was, how little I knew in comparison to Trevose. I was merely an inexperienced boy thrust by circumstances into a position of authority. The more I worked with Trevose the more convinced I became that I knew nothing. I had been wrong about the extent of my knowledge, I thought in despair; perhaps I had been wrong too about the mine.

"There's tin here," said Trevose one morning in 1915. "I can smell it."

Above the ground it was raining and a clammy mist was blowing in from the sea, but down at the two-forty level it was as hot as hell and we were all naked to the waist. The dust from the previous explosions had settled and we were back drilling holes for the next fuses again. Our mechanical drill had developed a fault, and so we were relying once more on the traditional method of beating an upper with a seven-pound hammer. Trevose, like any miner worth his salt, was ambidextrous in this skill, but I found it hard enough with my right hand to wield a heavy hammer for minute after minute in a hot underground hole far below the sea. In most of the mines around St. Just a miner wields a hammer and turns the drill rods single-handed, but this takes practice and I was inexperienced, so I turned Trevose's borer while Trevose himself focused his concentration on wielding the hammer. Even though I was comparatively inactive sweat was pouring off my body and dust was pricking my nose and making me uncomfortable. But at last when the holes were deep enough Trevose called for dynamite. The charges were packed, the fuses left dangling; having made sure that all was in order, we packed our belongings together and retreated from the stopes while Trevose was left behind to fire the charges. That day there were six of us in our "pare," or working party, Trevose and I and four "hard-rock" men, two of whom had come from Botallack, which had closed at last a few months ago; the other two were Zillan men who had been subsisting on part-time employment at South Crofty after the unsuccessful attempt to reopen Ding Dong mine in 1912.

Trevose was flicking the sweat from his face; we stood there, the others swarthy, I fair-skinned, all of us covered with dust, and seconds later after the distant roar of the explosion hot air blasted down the gallery like a breath from the devil's furnace.

"Now you bloody hell of a mine," said Trevose, "give us that tin or by God I'll blast you into the House of Water and flood you to the bloody adits."

We had to wait a long time for the dust to settle and then we went back.

It was a mess. Rocks and rubble were piled high. We groped our way forward just as a tram arrived to cart away some of the debris. The dust prickled again in my nose and made my eyes water.

Trevose said, "I smell tin."

I stared around. There was so much sweat and dust in my eyes that I could hardly see. I sniffed but I could smell only the acrid fumes of dynamite.

"Can you see anything?" said Trevose.

I looked at him, but he was gazing around vaguely at nothing in particular.

I stared and stared until I thought I would go blind.

And then I saw it.

I stumbled forward over the rubble, and the breath was rasping in my throat and my heart was hammering in my lungs. I tripped, fell and arrived on all fours by the chunk of rock which had attracted my attention.

And there it was. It wasn't much, just a dark rock with flecks of white in it, but to me it was more valuable than a bucket of gold. For the flecks of white were white quartz stringers, the plainest indication that at last we had stumbled on wealth, and as I stared at that magic rock in my hands I knew already that the lode would be an enormous lode, vast, mighty and fabulously rich.

"Hey!" yelled Trevose, having made sure that I was the first to discover it. "It's here! We done it, boys, the bloody lode's here! Come see what the boss has turned up for us! If we ain't at the beginning of a bloody champion lode as big as a bloody church I'll be hauled up in the skip and stamped with my own bloody hammer!"

They came running. I said in a voice that didn't sound like my own, "It was you who found it first, not me." But he wouldn't hear of it.

"No," he said at once. "It was you who found this lode, sonny, make no mistake about that. You knew it was here long before I'd ever been near Sennen Garth. If it wasn't for you we'd none of us be here today, and if that's not a bloody fact I don't know what is."

But I was dumb by then, wanting to laugh and shout aloud

with joy, yet struggling to control my tears, so I could not argue with him. I just stood there, overcome with emotions too deep to understand, and the candlelight from my helmet shone steadily into the darkness and onto the tin I had come so far to find.

[3]

St. Just was in an uproar. It so happened that my discovery coincided with payday at the Levant and everyone set out to drink to the new lode at Sennen Garth. The mine captain at the Levant stood me a drink and shook me by the hand; everyone wanted to buy me ale or cider and shake me by the hand, but I had no wish to get drunk, so after I had accepted drinks from the mine captain and Trevose I paid for a couple more out of my own money so that I wouldn't feel obliged to keep pace with those around me. Egged on by his friends and by several glasses of draft cider, Trevose launched into the first verse of the "Furry Dance" while old Granddad Penhellick rushed away to get his fiddle. The barmaid, Jared's renegade daughter Charity, was so excited that she kissed me on both cheeks and pulled me outside into the square so that we could dance together. I was too happy even to be embarrassed by such attentiveness. As I was protesting my inability to put one foot in front of the other in time to music, wives and sweethearts came running up the streets to the square to find out what was going on. Soon everyone was dancing. Even the children were joining in. At the climax of the celebrations I was carried aloft around the square amidst a host of cheering people, and when I had rescued myself from this undeserved tribute, I found Charity Roslyn again at my elbow.

With a hospitality that William Parrish would have deplored, she invited me to her cottage for a bite of pasty and a mug of beer. Not being hungry and preferring to drink with my friends at the pub, I declined. She then declared herself mortally insulted and asked me why I didn't like beautiful raven-haired barmaids who lived up to the name they'd been christened.

"And I'm charitable to you tonight, Mr. Philip," she promised. "Everything free, all secrets kept and no questions asked—"

"William Parrish would have a question or two to ask if he could hear you!"

"William Parrish!" sniffed Charity, tossing her black curls.

"He don't have as much say with me as he likes to think! If he'd marry me it'd be different, wouldn't it, but powerful set against marriage he is, even with those girls who be good enough for him, let alone those that ain't. And if he won't marry me I'll not answer to him as if I was his wife. I'll do as I fancy."

But I did not feel in the mood for anyone's charity that night when I had so many other more exciting things on my mind, so I eluded her as tactfully as possible and returned to the bar. The celebrations continued so long that it was very late when I rode into the yard of my mother's farm and unsaddled my horse in the stable.

My mother was waiting up for me, not knowing what had happened to delay my return.

"We did it!" I shouted as I ran across the yard toward her. "We found it! We struck the lode!"

My shouts rang out over those silent moors. It was as if I were calling to the ghosts of long ago, the generations who had worked in Cornwall since time out of mind, but I wanted to call all tinners everywhere, I wanted to shout the news to the whole world, because my mine was alive again, my mine had come back from the dead, and my mine was going to be the mightiest mine in the history of the Cornish Tin Coast.

[4]

Jared Roslyn, meeting me the next day in St. Just, invited me to his farm for a glass of wine, and, not wishing to offend him, I accepted. I found his house gloomy and his unmarried daughters oppressively eager to draw attention to themselves, but I liked his son, Simon Peter, and thought that even though he was puny for a boy of twelve he had a sharp intelligence and seemed genuinely interested in mining. I was about to leave when Joss Roslyn arrived with his wife, a fat, gray-haired, sullen-looking woman, and the atmosphere of hospitality at once degenerated into awkwardness.

"So you made your peace with the Castallacks, Jared," said this obstreperous and thoroughly dislikable man. "Well, it's your business who you allow to cross your threshold, and your business who you allow your daughters to be acquainted with."

"There's nothing wrong with young Mr. Philip," said Jared

at once. "If it hadn't been for him there'd still be out-of-work men leaving the area to save their wives and children from starvation. Say what you will about his parents, but he's an honest upright young man and there are others who'll say the same thing. He doesn't get drunk and he keeps the Commandments and he goes to church on Sundays, and if that kind of young man isn't fit company for my girls I'd like to know the kind that is."

"I don't care what kind he is," said Joss Roslyn with his talent for demonstrating that his mind could only travel along a single track, "but there's bad blood in his family, that we all know, and bad blood always tells."

I wasn't going to let that pass without comment. One good blow below the belt deserved another, so I did something I wouldn't normally have done and used the unfair weapon of my background against him. "My dear Mr. Roslyn," I said in my best public-school drawl, "you surprise me. I would have thought you found bad blood attractive since you took such painstaking care to marry a Penmar."

The man went scarlet with rage, but I noticed his wife gave me a bitter smile before I turned my back on them both and took my leave. She had been an adopted daughter of my father's predecessor at Penmarric, but Joss Roslyn had taken advantage of her penchant for working-class lovers and had managed to marry her, money and all. The marriage had produced one child, a girl who was now about seventeen, and for some time Hugh had been exercising his compulsive need to flirt with danger where women were concerned by carrying on a secret intrigue with her. The one girl in all Cornwall any Castallack should have avoided was Joss Roslyn's daughter, so to Hugh of course she was totally irresistible.

"I hope Hugh does manage to marry Rebecca," I said angrily to my mother over the kitchen table that evening. Although I enjoyed Hugh's company from time to time I was becoming increasingly disenchanted with his taste for fornication, fabrication and general deviousness. "He's exactly the kind of son-in-law that bastard Roslyn deserves."

But my mother did not like this slight on her darling Hugh, who was always so charming and devoted to her, and said tartly that any child of Joss Roslyn's was the last person she would ever choose to have as a daughter-in-law.

My mother clung especially to Hugh at that time because

she was frightened he would choose to enlist. He was eighteen now and had finished his schooling at Harrow that summer.

"Will you enlist?" I asked him bluntly when he arrived home from school at the end of July. "Or will you go up to Oxford?"

"I don't know," mused Hugh, suave as ever. "It's a tricky situation, isn't it? If I go up to Oxford everyone will immediately point a finger at me and call me a coward idling my time away in peace and leisure while my contemporaries are dying for their country, so the temptation is to enlist. However, it's better to be alive and a coward than dead and a hero, so I might go up to Oxford after all. If only there was some convenient middle course!"

"Well, if there is," I said, "I'm sure you'll find it."

He did. He had a friend at Harrow whose father was a colonel who knew someone who knew someone else who . . . It was interminable. The upshot of it all was that he was promised a safe little ADC job well away from the front lines if he enlisted then and there, so he decided to take the plunge and volunteer for the army.

"Compulsory enlistment is only a matter of time anyway," he told me. "Even if I did go up to Oxford I might be hauled down by force or else recruited as soon as I was due to leave. Then I'd probably end up in the trenches and once you're in the trenches you're as good as dead, as far as I can gather."

It was 1915. By this time everyone was realizing that this was an entirely new kind of war in which there was no limit to the catastrophes that could happen, no precedent for the total involvement of civilians as well as soldiers, and no end seemingly in sight. The casualties already staggered the imagination. In May of that year Asquith had reconstructed his Government in an attempt to reorganize matters at home to cope with the hideous crises abroad, and now there was a new ministry, a ministry of munitions headed by Lloyd George, and the talk was all of manufacturing munitions quickly enough to keep pace with the need of the army in France. But soon concern for supplies at home began to rival concern for supplies abroad. The Zeppelin raids had been too sporadic to have widespread effect, but the German blockade of the British Isles meant that food became scarcer and poorer in quality. Even in Cornwall we noticed the difference and I felt glad we lived on a farm and were not entirely dependent on the shops for our supplies.

But we were well off in Cornwall; across the sea the disasters continued, the Dardanelles and Gallipoli at the other end of Europe, the unending bloodshed of the trenches nearer home. Adrian was in the trenches. So was Marcus, although the two of them weren't together. Every day I would get hold of a newspaper to see if any major disaster had overtaken their regiments, and every day I fully expected never to see either of them again. It was then that I was filled with guilt that I should still be at home even though by that time I had no reason to feel guilty. I was needed at the mine. I was doing a vital job producing tin to use against the enemy. If compulsory enlistment came I could obtain an immediate exemption.

Yet still I was aware of guilt.

William Parrish was obsessed with it. Whenever I met him in St. Just he would say how inadequate he felt not being able to do anything useful in the war.

"You're seeing that twice as many crops are grown on the Penmarric estate, aren't you?" I pointed out to him as if in stemming his guilt I could also stem my own. "Someone's got to devote time to the country's agriculture to see we don't all starve! Besides, could you help having diphtheria when you were thirteen? It's not your fault you're unfit for service."

But it was no use. He was embarrassed by his safety and was pining for the reek of stinking trenches and the ragged roar of guns.

When Hugh went away in the autumn of 1915 William was the only one of my father's sons still at Penmarric. Jan-Yves was away at school, and when he returned he did not come to church at Zillan with William and Alice any more but accompanied my father to church at St. Just as consolation for the others' absence. That meant my mother and I never saw him—not that I cared, for he was a sullen, disagreeable little brute, but my mother was saddened by his stubborn hostility and spent long hours regretting it. Why she should have felt this way never ceased to surprise me. Jan-Yves had been an unwanted child, and she had suffered so much during the pregnancy and birth that when he was born she had taken an understandable aversion to him. Since he was technically in my father's custody she had seen little of him until he was six years old, but from the very first moment that she saw him again after the long interval her aversion disappeared and was replaced by a most irrational obsession. It made no difference to her that he was ugly and rude. He was her child and she loved him and she was filled with regret that she had played little part in the first six years of his life. My mother was a very maternal woman, devoted to all her children, and so she was all the more upset that an aversion resulting from a difficult pregnancy could have caused her to act out of character where Jan-Yves was concerned.

Fortunately although Jan-Yves never visited us, my younger sisters traveled to Zillan every Saturday to have lunch at the farm. Jeanne was nearly sixteen now and liked to practice cooking in the farm kitchen. Elizabeth tried too but was seldom successful. Her bread was soggy, her scones as hard as bullets and her cakes sank in the middle.

"Never mind, Lizzie," said Jeanne, who had an inexhaustible repertoire of feminine platitudes. "Think how clever you are at your lessons. You can't be good at everything."

"Phooey!" said Elizabeth, aggrieved. "What does it matter if the cake sank in the middle? It still tastes the same." She tossed back her pigtails, a round little girl with a face like a currant bun. "I don't care."

"Poor Lizzie," my mother would say to me afterward with remorseless regularity. "So plain."

Jeanne was plain too, although I did not say so. Her hair, fair in childhood, was now brown and she was too tall for a girl. She had a pleasant face and a bright smile, but she was no longer as pretty as she had been as a child.

"Sixteen is an awkward age for a girl," said my mother, still hoping Jeanne would recapture some of her former glory one day. "She'll look better later. At least she has excellent features and isn't grossly overweight."

Mariana, on the other hand, was still as good-looking as ever. She was widowed in 1916, her husband being one of the twenty thousand men killed in a single day's fighting during the bloodbath of the Somme, and arrived at Penmarric in swaths of black crepe to recuperate from the shock. I was prepared to make a nominal effort to be sympathetic when she arrived at the farm to see my mother, but she refused all gestures of sympathy.

"I don't want people being sad and sorry for me," she said. "That makes me feel all the worse. I don't want to cry and I don't want to think about death and the war. Let's talk about something else."

And she proceeded to talk in her affected London way of how

dreary it was at her husband's mansion due to wartime economies and how she detested her mother-in-law.

"Will you stay long at Penmarric?" I inquired, thinking she might want to return to her family, but she made a gesture of distaste.

"Oh God, if it's not one dreary mansion it's another! I'm sick of cold, soulless mansions! I think I might go and live in the townhouse, but it's so dull in London with the war on and so depressing. Oh, how boring this war is! How boring and hateful and beastly!"

And she burst into tears.

Emotional feminine scenes have always embarrassed me, so I chose that moment to withdraw, but after Mariana had gone my mother said to me, "I wonder if Mariana was happy with Nicholas? I know it's a terrible thing to say, but I half wondered during the course of the conversation if she wasn't actually glad to be a widow—while hating herself for being glad, of course. She struck me as being distressed for all the wrong reasons."

I yawned. "Even if she wasn't happy with Nick she was happy with her house in Upper Grosvenor Street and her mansion in Kent and her cartload of jewelry. I shouldn't worry about it, Mama."

"But material possessions really mean so little," said my mother, who believed, as all good women believe, that a woman should marry for the purest possible motives. "I'm not saying Mariana married Nicholas for his title, but she was so young—eighteen is too young for many girls to know their own minds—that she mightn't have realized the shallowness of her feelings until it was too late. Also she's so beautiful that Nicholas might have wanted to marry her for all the wrong reasons."

Since my brother-in-law was dead this discussion struck me as being too academic to take seriously. However, not wanting to be tactless, I smothered a second yawn and nodded my head in agreement.

"I wonder why she didn't have a baby?" said my mother, still worrying over the situation. "They were married two years before Nicholas had to go to France and most young girls of her age and upbringing are mothers by the time they celebrate their first wedding anniversary."

"Quite," I said, bored by this unending feminine speculation, and took the bowl of scraps out into the yard to give to the pig.

My mother continued to worry about Mariana and even went so far as to write to my father to say he should insist that Mariana stay at Penmarric until the war was over.

"It will make her feel more secure," said my mother, "to be in a familiar environment, and besides, a young widow should live a quiet life after such a bereavement. Grief can lead to impaired judgment and she might remarry too soon before she had recovered sufficiently to know what she was doing."

Personally I disagreed with this, but I realized I couldn't be expected to understand a bereaved female, so I said nothing. In my opinion Mariana was much too calculating to let bereavement impair her judgment and was already cheering herself up with the prospect of hunting for husband number two.

My father wrote back to my mother to say he agreed with her letter, so presumably he tried to persuade Mariana to stay in Cornwall. But as I had suspected, Mariana was anxious to jump back on what remained of the aristocracy's social merry-go-round. Friends in Scotland invited her to stay and after declaring that Penmarric was "positively too dreary to tolerate a second longer" she went north to Edinburgh and spent the next two years flitting from one country mansion to the next like a lost butterfly.

"Not at all proper for a young widow," said my mother, but by this time she sounded more disapproving than anxious. "She'll get herself talked about if she's not careful."

"Come, Mama!" I said in an effort to dispel her gloom. "What's wrong with visiting friends?" But my mother pursed her lips and shook her head and—to my relief—kept her darkest thoughts to herself.

I had too much on my mind at that time to bother myself about Mariana. We had found considerable wealth under the sea and both the miners and the Government were well satisfied. However, our success meant that there was so much to organize that often I did not get below ground at all but was kept busy attending to endless details at the surface. We hired more miners, organized the shifts, appointed the shift bosses, employed men to work at the surface in attending to all the subsidiary jobs required to keep the mine in order. Sawyers and carpenters were kept busy working at the timber which the mine was now devouring as fast as we shipped it to St. Just. Pitmen began their task of regular inspection of the pumps, and in the count house there was paperwork to do, forms to fill in, accounts to keep. I engaged an experienced purser to assist the inadequate civil servant whom the Government had appointed and spent long hours with my father's solicitor, Michael Vincent, who kept hovering around to see that everything was done according to the law. My own position still remained theoretically vague, but in practice I continued to be in charge. How I managed this I don't know, but despite my inexperience Trevose never took a big step without consulting me and neither did the Government's puppet of a managing director and neither did the purser. I was the boss. It was all most mysterious, but since the net result was that I spent as much time as I could below ground with the miners I was happier than I had ever been in my life before.

The Government paid me a generous salary, part of which I gave to my mother and most of which I put in the bank. I had more respect for money than I had had when I had walked out of my father's house in London five years earlier, but now that my mine was well provided for money was of little interest to me.

The months passed. I had just managed to absorb myself in my work so entirely that I had forgotten all my worries, even my guilt about the war, when my father sought me out a week before my twenty-first birthday and steam-rollered me into accepting his invitation to dine at Penmarric.

[5]

I had seen my father now and then since the mine had been re-opened, for he would usually attend the regular monthly meetings held to discuss the mine's progress, but it had evidently been his decision to interfere as little as possible with the proceedings, and since he seemed determined to remain in the background as far as the mine was concerned, we managed to avoid quarreling with each other. We might have seen each other more often than once a month, I suppose, but we did not. To be honest I must admit that this was my fault, not his. He had congratulated me after the lode had been discovered and had several times invited me to Penmarric to see him, but I had always found an excuse for not accepting his invitations. I would have refused this invitation to dinner too if it had come in the form of a written note, but it did not. This time he was too clever for me. He turned up at the mine, met me when I came out of the "dry" one evening and publicly issued the invitation. Since we were surrounded by a dozen miners, all with their ears flapping, I found myself unable to think of a reasonable excuse, so I accepted. It was for that same evening, so I could not even invent an excuse later on. I did try to say I had no evening clothes to wear, but he said we would dine informally; Jeanne and Elizabeth had gone for a week to Exmouth with their governess, Jan-Yves was at school and William was to be out for the evening; we would dine alone together.

"My mother—" I began.

"I have the note written to send to your mother," he said. "One of the stable boys can ride over to Roslyn Farm with it at once."

He had thought of everything.

"Very well," I said ungraciously. "If you like."

We rode back to Penmarric together, neither of us speaking, and on entering the house we went to the library while we waited for dinner to be served.

My father offered me a drink.

"I never touch spirits," I said.

"How wise. Perhaps you'd like some cider?"

"Beer."

"Certainly," he said and told the butler to bring me a bottle from the pantry. There was a new butler at Penmarric. Old Medlyn had retired to nurse his gout at last, and James, the first footman, who turned out to be Young Medlyn, had taken his father's place. Young Medlyn was a soft-footed fifty-year-old, very deft and sure of himself. I wondered how he got on with the housekeeper, but of course I did not like to introduce the subject of Alice Penmar.

My father tried to make conversation with me about the mine, but I wasn't interested in discussing it with him, so I said little. In fact I wasn't interested in discussing anything with him, and he soon realized his mistake in inviting me to dine at Penmarric as if we were old friends.

Dinner was a disaster. He tried to talk about the mine again, but that was still no good. Presently he asked me about my friends and on hearing that they were all working-class men he asked if I was still in touch with any of my school friends.

I said I wasn't.

He asked if I heard from Peter Waymark, George and Aubrey

Carnforth and Francis St. Enedoc, all of whom were my contemporaries fighting overseas.

I said I hadn't.

He asked me if I ever saw the Waymark girls, Peter's two sisters, who lived at Gurnards Grange.

"No."

"I suppose you don't meet many girls."

"No, I have enough on my mind at present without coping with women as well."

"Perhaps you're wise. It would be a pity if you fell in love now and wanted to get married. It's a mistake to marry too young."

I helped myself to more vegetables. "You should know," I said.

We were silent for some time after that. Finally it was he who spoke first.

"It's your twenty-first birthday next week, isn't it?" he said. "How unfortunate that the war's on and everyone's away! However, we should have some sort of celebration. What would you like to do?"

"Stand my friends a round of drinks in the pub," I said. "Play darts with Alun Trevose. Have dinner with my mother."

"Why don't you bring your mother to dinner at Penmarric? The girls will be here and we can invite—"

"No thanks."

"Perhaps you would prefer to come on your own for a short time. We can all drink your health in champagne."

"No thanks."

He shrugged. "As you wish."

We finished our meal. After the cloth was drawn he offered me a glass of port, which I declined, and I was just wondering if I could make my escape when Young Medlyn tiptoed into the room with an envelope on the silver salver.

My father took one look at it and went white to the lips.

"This just arrived, sir," whispered Medlyn. "Special messenger. Penzance post office."

It was a telegram.

My heart began to thump against my chest. I thought: Adrian's dead. Then as I stared at my father I thought, unforgivably: Serve him right. But I clamped down on the thought at once and tried to hope for his sake that Adrian was alive.

My father took the envelope. Medlyn backed away and hovered by the sideboard. Finally, not being able to invent an excuse to linger in the room, he padded away into the hall and closed the doors softly behind him.

We were alone.

"Dear me," said my father, tearing open the seal. "I'm afraid this must be bad news."

He took out the slip of paper, unfolded it methodically and stared at it for a long time.

I heard myself say rapidly in an uneven voice, "Is it Adrian? Is he dead? Is Adrian dead?"

He looked up at me. His face was ashen and his eyes were bloodshot with pain. "No," he said. "Marcus." He got up then, levering himself to his feet like an old man, said "excuse me" in a very polite voice and walked blindly out of the room into the hall.

3

The sudden death of the Young [Henry] from dysentery was a sad blow to his father. . . . The Young Henry was the only member of the family who gave no evidence of political sagacity, military skill or even ordinary intelligence but such, after all, are not looked for in a fairytale prince. . . . He was tall, handsome, gay and splendidly improvident.

—King John,
W. L. WARREN

Richard was practically an independent ruler in Aquitaine. He . . . behaved as though England were a foreign power.....

—The Devil's Brood,
ALFRED DUGGAN

[1]

After a while I read the telegram. Marcus hadn't even been killed in action. He had died of dysentery three weeks after his twenty-third birthday.

I got up, walked to the window, drew the curtain. Outside lay the grounds of Penmarric, the lawn where Marcus and I had raced when we were children, the Cornish night air cool beneath the pale evening sky. I remembered the last time I had seen him, heard his voice and his careless laugh and his confident "I give the Germans exactly six months!" I thought how he had irritated me, how impatient I had been with him, how often I had dismissed him as a fool.

My blunt nails bit into the palms of my hands.

I began to walk up and down the room and every few minutes I would pick up the telegram and read it again. In spite of myself I began to remember all the things it would have been best not to think about, how much he had enjoyed life, how much he had hated fighting, how little he had deserved this early grave. Even his manner of dying seemed undeserved; Marcus should have stopped an enemy bullet and died a hero's death, but no—even that was denied him. Instead he had rotted away with some disgusting disease and now he was dead, I would never see him again, and death was the end because there was no God, no after-life, nothing at all except nothingness and non-existence and non-being.

There was sweat on my forehead. My hand shook. I went through the hall and let myself out of the front door into the drive. I stood there, taking great gulps of fresh air, and then I ran to the stables, got my horse and set off down the drive at the gallop. I rode as hard as I could, as if I could outpace my primitive and shameful fear of death; I rode until my horse was sweating with exhaustion. I rode until I reached St. Just and then I dismounted, entered the pub and ordered the largest shot of brandy I could buy.

[2]

Mr. Barnwell came from Zillan rectory to be with my mother, and my father even rode over from Penmarric, but there was little either of them could do. As for myself I felt useless, too aware that I could not help her, too upset by what had happened, too resentful that my father should have intruded on her grief and attempted to supplant what small comfort I might have been able to offer her. When he and the rector left at last I could only feel relieved, despite my secret reluctance to shoulder the burden of my mother's distress. I hated to see her unhappy. I couldn't stand to see her grieve. But I stood it and tolerated it as best as I could until gradually she became resigned to her loss and began to pick up the threads of her normal life again.

However, she was fated to have more than her fair share of bereavement in 1916. In the autumn her great-aunt Griselda died at last, and although Griselda had been a difficult old woman my mother was saddened to lose her. Griselda had cared for her during her childhood, and in turn my mother had later cared for her; a lesser woman would have abandoned such an unpresentable reminder of a poverty-stricken past, but even when my mother had been mistress of Penmarric she had seen that Griselda lived comfortably in her own little cottage on the estate.

1917 came. In retrospect I think 1917 was the worst year of the war—at least for those of us who remained in England. It's easy now to look back and say things can't have been too bad because peace was only a year away, but at the time peace seemed more remote and the war more oppressive than ever. By this time shortages of all necessities were chronic; we learned later that at the end of April the stores of food for the entire country could be stretched to last only six weeks. The German U-boats were trying to starve us into submission, and during the first few months of the year nearly two million tons of shipping ended up at the bottom of the sea. Easy now to look back and say that the U-boat sinkings propelled the United States into the war and made the vital difference in the balance of power, but at home the long-range view was obscured by the immediate consequences of rationing, deprivation and hardship.

In London Asquith had been ousted and the Government was in the hands of Lloyd George—a good thing, I thought, since Asquith's gentlemanly passivity hardly lended itself to effective wartime leadership, but by then the discomforts of civilian life had reached the point where a new hand at the helm made little difference to the man in the street. Abroad the muddled bloodshed streamed on unabated; an advance of five miles wiped out thousands more of our men at Passchendaele, while Russia, in a state of military collapse, was dissolving into revolution. Not that we cared much in Cornwall about Russia, but we did care about the carnage at Passchendaele.

The toll of death and the misery of the bereaved were appalling.

Among my Cornish contemporaries, George Carnforth had been killed in 1915 and now two years later his brother Aubrey followed him to the grave; their father Sir Justin was already a widower, so through the war he had lost his entire family apart from his daughter Felicity. Peter Waymark was still alive, I heard, and so was Francis St. Enedoc, but many of the humbler men of Cornwall had found foreign graves, and I was hardly surprised when my mother developed a morbid preoccupation with Hugh's safety. In vain I told her time and time again that Hugh was much too far from the front lines to get himself killed; she remained convinced she would never see him again, and to make matters worse Hugh was a hopeless correspondent. On the rare occasions when he did make the effort to put pen to paper we learned little from his letters except that French lavatories were primitive and that French food was a sadly overrated commodity, but in a private letter which he addressed to me at the mine he admitted being both bored and homesick; French women were all the same and none of them could hold a candle to Rebecca Roslyn. Had I seen Rebecca at all? He wrote to her every week in care of Charity Roslyn at Charity's cottage in St. Just, but he hadn't heard from her lately and he was afraid Joss Roslyn might have discovered that they were exchanging letters. Could I try and see Rebecca and find out what was happening? Was there some other man paying attention to her? I was to tell her when I saw her that he spent all day thinking about her and couldn't wait for the war to be over so that he would be able to see her again.

For the first time it occurred to me to take his fancy for Rebecca seriously. When Charity confirmed that Rebecca was head over heels in love with him and had been since the age of thirteen I began to think he really might marry her eventually, but I said nothing to my mother for fear of upsetting her and merely wrote back to Hugh that Rebecca was as anxious for his return as he was.

"If only the war could be over," my mother would sigh again and again. "If only Hugh could come home . . ."

Adrian came home. He was wounded in the October of 1917, and although the wound left no radical disability, he was confined to a military hospital for some weeks. When he was discharged he was judged unfit for further service and by Christmas he was back at Penmarric after an absence of more than three years.

Both Jeanne and Elizabeth were enraptured with him. He had won a few colored ribbons for bravery, which was creditable enough, of course, but to the girls this was an excuse to speak of him with bated breath and shining eyes. I had to remind them both sharply not to mention his name in my mother's presence.

"I wish you would try to like Adrian, Philip," said Jeanne timidly when my mother was out of the room. "He's such a good, kind, worthwhile person. I was always surprised you didn't get on well with him."

"We had nothing in common," I said shortly, "and we were always getting in each other's way."

"Well, it's your loss," said Elizabeth, outspoken as ever. She sat on the kitchen table, her shoulders slouched forward as usual, her black hair straggling around her pudding face, her black eyes watching me with a challenging stare. Her stomach curved generously below the waistband of her skirt, and beneath her jacket her breasts had a middle-aged sag to them. The onset of adolescence had done nothing to improve her looks. "He and I have had some simply inspiring discussions about God and Life and Civilization and all that kind of thing. Oh, if only I could go to school! I'm sick of being taught by that ninny Miss Cartwright! I'm hoping Adrian can help me persuade Papa to drop this mid-nineteenth-century notion of his that education for women is 'not quite nice.' Adrian at least can understand how horribly frustrating it is for me—I mean, how on earth am I ever going to appreciate the glories of Greek civilization if I can't tell an alpha from an omega? It's so unfair not to let me go to school!"

By chance I saw Adrian soon after that in St. Just. He and William came into the pub one evening just as I was leaving it. I supposed I ought to say something, so while William wandered on ahead I made an effort to be pleasant.

"Hullo," I said. "Welcome home. Congratulations on all your medals."

He smiled at me readily enough, and as he smiled the light fell across his face and I saw the lines about his mouth and the white scar at the corner of one eye. He was painfully thin and walked with a limp.

"Thanks," he said. "It's wonderful to be home. Congratulations on your success at the mine." And as I nodded and stepped past him he added, "Won't you join us for a drink?"

"I have to be getting home," I said and went out abruptly into the square without waiting for his reply. I considered I had fulfilled my obligations toward him and had no intention of pursuing the conversation further.

But he had other ideas. I saw him twice after that and each time he tried to badger me into having a drink with him. In the end I was obliged to be frank.

"Look," I said, "don't let's pretend because I can't stand hypocrisy. I dislike you and you know damned well you dislike me. It's always been that way and as far as I'm concerned nothing's changed. Now leave me alone and don't come bothering me again with your hypocritical overtures of friendship."

At that he reverted to his old pugnacious self again and abandoned his saintly "let's-be-nice-to-each-other" attitude, which he had had the gall to tell me he had developed while fighting in the trenches. I knew he only wanted to emphasize the fact that I had stayed at home and he hadn't. However, after an exchange of insults we parted enemies again, turning our backs on each other and walking angrily away in opposite directions, and the wall of our hostility stood repaired and resurrected between us, a towering monument to those bitter memories of the past.

[3]

Early in 1918 Jeanne was sent away to a finishing school at Eastbourne to learn a few airs and graces, but she was so miserable away from home that my father allowed her to abandon the school after only one term. However, Jeanne's fleeting absence from Penmarric had one satisfactory result. Lizzie managed to persuade my father that with Jeanne gone it was pointless for him to retain the governess who had nothing left to teach her remaining pupil, and my father grudgingly gave his consent for Lizzie to attend Cheltenham Ladies' College, the famous girls' public school. Almost bursting out of her school uniform with excitement, she departed for her first term at the end of April and we saw no more of her at the farm for several weeks.

Meanwhile Lizzie's hero Adrian had decided to go up to Oxford to read history. I was conscious of relief that I would no longer run the risk of meeting him in St. Just, but I was too preoccupied with other more vital matters to think much about Adrian just then. At last the war really did begin to look as if it were drawing to a close; earlier in the year the Germans had advanced on the Somme, at Ypres and on the Aisne until they were once more on the Marne, but after that Foch, Haig and Pershing turned the tide until by the end of September the German High Command was thinking in terms of peace. Finally on the eleventh of November the Armistice was signed; the war had ended at last amidst universal relief, but even before the cheering had died away I was worrying about my mine.

The Government's nominal lease was due to expire at the end of the year; the country's economy had been stretched to the limit during four years of massive warfare, and now that the need for tin was no longer so vital the Government was anxious to rid itself of the mine and turn it back to private enterprise.

Fortunately there was every reason not to close the mine, for we weren't losing money and there was still plenty of tin waiting under the sea, but the mine did require more capital investment. Shaftmen complained the skip road needed repairs, timbermen presented me with a long list of galleries where rotten timber posed a threat to safety and the pitmen were forever complaining about the pumps. In addition to all this, there were missing rungs on shaft ladders, worn rails on the main tramming level and the gig needed overhauling.

It was the question of safety that concerned me most. Any mine is potentially a dangerous place, but some mines are safer than others and I wanted my mine to be as safe as I could possibly make it. I felt I owed that at least to my friends who had no choice but to go beneath the ground every day to earn their daily bread, and besides I was no more anxious than they were to work in a possible death trap. The owners of the other mines along the Tin Coast could do as they pleased; their mines weren't my concern and there were always men like Jared Roslyn to conduct crusades for better working conditions on behalf of the miners who were employed there, but Sennen Garth was my concern and I was prepared to go to any lengths to see that it was the safest mine in Cornwall.

Good maintenance was the key to safety—but good maintenance costs money, and money was something I didn't have.

Since I was convinced my father wouldn't lift a finger to finance the mine out of his own pocket, I went first to London to see if the Government would grant the mine a subsidy, but the Government, entangled with financial problems of a far greater magnitude than the Sennen Garth mine, was not in the mood for subsidies. It was only then that I gritted my teeth and rode to Penmarric to beg my father to keep the mine safe—and thus keep it alive, for without capital investment I knew it would soon be doomed. The issues of safety and survival were no more than two sides of the same coin, although I hardly expected my father to see beyond the figures of his current bank balance to the question of the miners' well-being.

However, to my surprise he was much more agreeable about it than I'd anticipated; perhaps I had underestimated the fact that Sennen Garth, despite its maintenance problems, was still very much a going concern. In the end he agreed as landowner to float a new company—"as my contribution to the postwar unemployment problem," he was careful to explain to me, "and because if there are gamblers willing to invest money in a speculative venture they might just as well invest their money in Sennen Garth" —and granted me a concession to mine the land in whatever way I thought fit. However, despite all his remarks about gamblers and speculative ventures I noticed he was quick enough to buy up sixty percent of the shares as soon as he had the chance. At first I thought his Penmar blood ran more strongly in him than he cared to admit, but soon I realized he was following a policy of controlling the company with an iron hand.

"The mine lasts only so long as it can pay its own way, Philip," he said to me. "If it goes into the red don't expect me to put additional capital into it over and above my shareholdings. Not one penny more of my money goes into that mine, so you'd better be sure you organize the concern in the best possible way."

"You won't need to put a penny more of your money into the mine," I told him shortly. "With your dues as landowner and your dividends from the shares you'll be making more profit than you would ever have believed possible."

"I wonder," said my father.

And presently I wondered too. On inquiring further into the mine's position, I learned from my purser that the net profits had dropped alarmingly. Wages had risen; it cost more to get the tin out of the ground; the tin market was in a shaky state and the price of tin wasn't what it should have been.

"It's monstrous!" I protested. "We're getting as much ore out of the ground as we used to in the old days—the records show that. Yet we're only making a quarter as much money."

"The economic climate is different today," said the purser, a sharp, sensible, middle-aged man called Walter Hubert. "You'll have to increase the mine's output if you want your profits to be as substantial as they used to be."

With new equipment, I thought, new methods, more men . . . With the new capital I had been able to modernize much of the mine and thus raise the general standard of safety to an acceptable level, but much still needed to be done and I had only been able to afford to concentrate on the essentials. To employ more men was out of the question; I was already starting to worry about what would happen if the cost of living rose much further; the miners would want more pay and there would be even less profit than there was already.

It was 1919. I was only just beginning to realize the extent of my problems concerning Sennen Garth, but even then I was dimly aware of the struggles with my father which lay ahead of me. The mine absorbed me as always; now I was bent upon the task of infusing it with new life, and so immersed was I in the mine's problems that I found it difficult to pay any attention to my family. But 1919 turned out to be quite a year. Hugh came home belatedly from the war and eloped with Rebecca Roslyn, Mariana found her second husband, and Adrian abandoned his historical studies at Oxford after deciding that what he wanted more than anything else was to be a clergyman of the Church of England.

[4]

I was not in the least surprised that Mariana had chosen to marry again, since she had been husband-hunting seriously for over two years, but I admit I was surprised and disgusted by her choice. Her husband was a childless widower, fifty-nine years old; he was also Marquess of Lochlyall and master of a townhouse in Edinburgh, a summer residence at North Berwick and the usual hundred-room Highland castle somewhere at the back of beyond. Mariana married him quietly one April morning in Edinburgh and afterward wrote a long letter to both my parents explaining why she had not announced her intentions earlier. She had no valid excuse, of course, for keeping her parents in the dark, but she rambled on for several pages about how she had been having such a difficult emotional time in Scotland and had been so prostrate with nervous tension after being pestered by two suitors for over a year that finally she had washed her hands of both suitors and married the Marquess at the first available opportunity. Since the Marquess was "an older man" he made her feel "secure" and "perfectly at peace." She "adored" him and "trusted him absolutely." Everything was "divine." Eventually, she promised, she would bring him down to Cornwall to meet everyone and we would see how sensible she had been to marry someone so "mature" and "kind" who was "the perfect gentleman in every respect." She absolutely knew we would all "adore" him and "heartily approve" of her choice.

What my father thought of this rigmarole I have no idea, but my mother was very dubious and said she did hope Mariana hadn't rushed into the marriage too impulsively.

I made no comment. Mariana was old enough to know her own mind by that time, and if she wanted to live in Scotland with a man old enough to be her grandfather that was her business, not mine.

As for Adrian, I wasn't much surprised that he had reverted to the pious inclinations he had shown as a child. I could easily picture him wearing a surplice and invoking his congregation to ask God to bless all the poor and suffering. It occurred to me with relief that once he was a curate he would be assigned to some faraway parish and I wouldn't have to see him any more, and to be honest I admit I found the thought a pleasant one.

But with Hugh's marriage I was much more heavily involved.

We were at the station to meet him when he came home from the war. His discharge from the army had been delayed by the fact that his cushy little ADC job was just as hard to ditch as it had been to acquire and the VIP whom he was supposed to assist had been busy after the Armistice with security measures regarding the peace treaty negotiations at Versailles. However, now the treaty was signed and Hugh was almost home again; my mother, beside herself with excitement, kept clutching my arm as if she were afraid she might topple over with her joy. I felt excited myself. It had been a long time—over three years—since I had seen him, and distance, as everyone knows, lends enchantment. I forgot his more unfortunate tendencies and remembered only what a good companion he was and how amusing it would be to see him again.

As the train drew into the station we saw him lean out of the window to look for us, and my mother broke away from me and ran down the platform toward him. Within seconds the train had halted, the door had opened and he was falling into her arms.

He looked well, his hair bleached to a pale gold by foreign sunshine, his eyes vivid blue against his tanned skin. He was only twenty-one but seemed older, and his body looked fit and tough and muscular beneath his uniform.

"Trust you to come through the entire war without a scratch," I said. "I might have known."

We were still laughing together a second later when my father and Jeanne arrived to provide the welcoming contingent from Penmarric. Elizabeth and Jan-Yves were away at school, and I was relieved to notice that there was no sign of either William or Adrian.

After the first confused moments of the reunions, my father said to my mother, "Would you and Philip like to come to Penmarric for lunch? Only Jeanne and I are at home today, so it would be pleasant if you could both join us to welcome Hugh back to the house."

"Well," said my mother, considering the invitation and looking up at me for advice. "Yes, perhaps—"

And then, suddenly, with no warning at all, Hugh left us. He flew down the platform like a bullet from a gun and as he ran I saw Rebecca Roslyn running toward him from the station entrance. She wore a drab coat, but beneath it blazed an emerald green dress, and as I watched I saw her black hair escape from its fastenings beneath her ineffectual little hat and stream behind her like a banner in the wind.

She hurtled into Hugh's arms and stuck there. The embrace that followed was so intimate that it bordered on indecency, and everyone turned to gape at the exhibition.

"It's Rebecca Roslyn!" said Jeanne, surprised. "I didn't know Hugh knew her!"

I glanced at my parents. Their expressions were not encouraging. My father's narrow eyes became narrower and his hard mouth became harder, while my mother's wide-eyed astonishment gradually gave way to a wide-eyed disapproval.

"Well, well," I said, amused. "What a dramatic reunion! Are you going to invite her to Penmarric as well, Father?"

"No doubt Hugh's already done so," my father said.

He had. They came toward us hand in hand, smiling sunnily at each other, oblivious of everyone except themselves, and when they reached us they turned and smiled sunnily at my parents.

"Rebecca and I are engaged," said Hugh with pride, the suave cynicism I knew so well displaced by a sincerity I hadn't known he possessed. "We've waited over three years for this moment, haven't we, darling? We were secretly engaged before I went away, but we agreed not to tell anyone until I got home again."

My parents were struck dumb. Jeanne opened her mouth as if to say, "How wonderful!" but closed it again in uncertainty.

"That's nice," I said, amused. "Congratulations."

"Congratulations," said Jeanne quickly, following my lead. "How exciting." But she sounded nervous about it.

My mother looked at my father. My father looked at Rebecca.

"Do your parents know about this yet?" he said not unpleasantly. "Does your father approve?"

The girl blushed, still starry-eyed. "I haven't told my parents yet, Mr. Castallack."

"Then isn't this rather . . . premature? I presume you intend to ask Mr. Roslyn's permission, Hugh, for his daughter's hand."

"Come, Papa," said Hugh, happy as a lark and just about as unconcerned, "you know what Joss Roslyn would say if I did! Rebecca's twenty-one in August, so we'll get married as soon as possible after that. We all know Roslyn won't approve of the marriage, but there's no reason why we shouldn't get married as soon as Rebecca no longer needs his legal consent."

"I see," said my father in his politest voice. "Very interesting. Well, the station platform at Penzance is hardly the place to discuss such important family matters. I suggest you lunch with us at Penmarric, Miss Roslyn, and we can discuss the situation in more detail later."

"I've already asked her to lunch," said Hugh gaily, "and she says she'll come. Will there be room in the car, Papa, or shall Rebecca and I hire transport of our own?"

"There'll be room for you both in the car," said my father shortly. He turned to my mother. "Janna, if you would care to travel with us in the car, Jeanne can go in the ponytrap with Philip. It would be more comfortable for you and I'm sure you want to talk to Hugh."

We sorted ourselves out and presently Jeanne and I set off in the ponytrap as the car roared away from the station ahead of us.

"Well!" I said. "That's set the cat among the pigeons! I wonder what line Father will take. It's obvious he and Mama will be opposed to the marriage."

" 'The course of true love never did run smooth,' " murmured Jeanne, who was incurably romantic at heart. "She's pretty, isn't she? I can see why Hugh likes her. Oh, I don't care if it *is* unsuitable! It's lovely to think of them writing to each other for nearly four years, each faithful to the other . . ."

Knowing Hugh's sexual inclinations, I doubted if he were capable of maintaining a strict celibacy for four years, but naturally I couldn't say this to Jeanne. She was already taking the dewey-eyed feminine view of the situation and planning what she should wear at the wedding. I wondered what would happen at Penmarric.

In fact what happened was predictable enough. For once my parents were in complete agreement with each other; neither of them wanted a grandchild who had Joss Roslyn's blood in his veins. After lunch my father said to them in his politest voice that while he and my mother bore Rebecca no ill-feeling whatsoever they really felt they couldn't accept the engagement until Hugh had obtained Roslyn's consent.

"Well, of course we'll get married anyway," said Hugh nonchalantly in private to me later. "After Rebecca's twenty-one who the hell cares what our parents think? Besides, I don't see how Papa can disapprove of the marriage for long—he married when he was younger than I am to a woman of a lower class than himself."

"And look how that ended!"

"Yes, but that's no good reason for assuming my marriage will automatically end in the same way!"

"True . . . It's a pity she is who she is. I don't think they would be half as opposed to the idea if she was anyone but Joss Roslyn's daughter."

"But God damn it, that's not her fault! Poor girl, she's terrified of him. I can't wait to get her out of that house. She's had a miserable existence there, and now her mother's ill things are ten times worse than they were already."

"What's the matter with her mother?"

"I'm not sure. I'm afraid it might be serious because she refuses to discuss it with Rebecca."

There was a pause. After a moment I said curiously, "You weren't faithful to Rebecca in France, of course."

"I didn't fall in love with anyone else. She's the one I love."

"But you—"

"Oh God, of course I made use of the camp women! What the devil have they got to do with it? Could you conceivably exist for over three years without having a woman of any description?"

I was silent. I had never understood Hugh's compulsion to go to bed with a woman whenever he had the opportunity. It was true I had sometimes considered having a brief affair in an attempt to discover why such a pastime should be so irresistible to him, but I had never met a woman who had attracted me enough to override my wariness of all the risks that were involved. I had no wish for rumors of any bad behavior of mine to reach my mother's ears. I don't say she wouldn't have understood if I had had my fling with the village girls, but she had suffered enough from my father's fornications, and I didn't intend her to suffer from mine.

In an effort to change the subject I said abruptly to Hugh, "What are you going to live on when you get married? You'll need a job—Papa won't give you anything while he's in a hostile mood, and it's no good expecting a penny from Joss Roslyn."

"Oh . . ." Hugh yawned as if this were a very minor detail. "I'll get some job which pays the maximum of money for the minimum of effort. I'll think of something." He smiled at me lazily with his innocent blue eyes. "I've always been rather good at making money."

I smiled too, but if I had known where his future source of income was to come from I wouldn't have smiled at all. Unknown to us both, our friendship was already sailing blithely toward the waiting rocks to wreck itself beyond repair.

[5]

They married six weeks later after running away to London immediately after Rebecca's twenty-first birthday. Somehow they had managed to keep their engagement a secret from Joss Roslyn, but Rebecca had told her mother, who had encouraged the affair as vigorously as she could whenever her husband's back was turned. But the vigor she possessed was too weak to give them more than token support; she died a month before Rebecca's birthday and was buried according to her wishes—and contrary to her husband's—at St. Just by the Penmar family tomb.

What Joss Roslyn thought of his daughter's elopement so soon after his wife's funeral can well be imagined. He shut himself up in his farmhouse for a week, spoke to nobody and allowed his anger to simmer in silence. When he left the house again he rode to St. Ives—"To see his lawyer there," said my mother's servant, Ethel Turner, who always knew everything, "to cut Miss Rebecca out of his will, as like as not. Joss Roslyn got a powerful lot of money when he upped and married Miss Clarissa Penmar, that we all know, and he won't be a-wanting Miss Rebecca to get the money now."

My parents were at first as furious as Roslyn, but Hugh had enough charm and cunning to wind anyone around his little finger if he tried hard enough, and he soon softened my mother's heart with two treacly letters in which he laid on the sentiment with a shovel while begging his darling mama's forgiveness. I wasn't in the least surprised when she finally relented far enough to have them to stay at the farm when they returned to Cornwall from London and even gave them the tenant farm up the valley as a wedding present; this was a cottage which had belonged to Jared Roslyn, but my mother had bought him out when she had returned to the farm to live and it had been empty for some years. I supposed I ought to offer some sort of a wedding present, so I offered to pay to have plumbing installed, the walls painted and the chimney swept.

"Oh, that would be kind!" exclaimed Rebecca with shining eyes. "Thank you so much." She turned to her husband. "We'll have a home of our very own after all, Hugh!"

"Yes," said Hugh, who had always turned up his nose at agricultural dwellings. "That'll be nice."

The next day he rode over to Penmarric to try to make his peace with my father.

On the whole he had more success than I had anticipated. My father refused to pay him an allowance in future or offer him any financial help, but he said he would like to see Rebecca again and asked Hugh to bring her to Penmarric to dinner at the end of the week. When they arrived he gave them a dinner service and a canteen of silver and said he hoped they would have a happy married life together; he was too clever to give them a check in lieu of a gift, and even as it was Rebecca had a struggle to prevent Hugh pawning the silver. However, they were now on speaking terms with my father and were accepted at Penmarric, so Hugh felt he had made a step in the right direction. He was confident he would soon be able to persuade my father to renew the monthly allowance, and I had a suspicion my father would in the end capitulate, finance the marriage and forgive them.

Unfortunately Joss Roslyn was not prepared to follow my father's example. He stormed over to the farm on the Sunday after their return from London and told Rebecca in front of us all that he never wanted to see her again and that as far as he was concerned she could go to the devil along with her mother.

We all rose to speak. Hugh was scarlet with fury, my mother pink with indignation, and I've no idea what color I was. But Rebecca silenced us all. Up till that moment she had always been so quiet and polite that my mother had privately called her colorless, but now at last we saw the real Rebecca and it soon became clear that the word "colorless" no longer did her justice.

We gaped at her.

"Don't you dare speak of my mother like that!" Her words rang out across the farm kitchen, and her quiet overrefined little voice was suddenly harsh and wild and full of Cornish. "My mother was a true lady and why she married you I'll never know since you never had a good word to say for her morning, noon or night. Once you'd got your filthy hands on her money you never had a moment's time for her! I know! She told me! You only married her so that you could set yourself up in a big house with a lot of land and try and make yourself out to be a land-owning gentleman. You—a gentleman! My God! You weren't even fit to shine my mother's shoes, let alone share the house she lived in!"

"You be quiet!" shouted Roslyn. "I loved your mother! She married me because she thought she didn't want to be a lady any more, but when she found herself a farmer's wife she didn't like it any better than she liked being a lady at Penmarric! She was a bad wife to me, always grumbling and complaining and never having the house straight or the cooking right and the milk always going sour in the dairy—"

"—because you wouldn't pay for more servants! You—with all the money she gave you when you married her! You wanted her to be a household drudge like Uncle Jared's wife with a baby every year and—"

"You shut your cursed mouth about a baby every year and go down on your knees to thank God you were born at all! She didn't want any babies! She wouldn't even give me a son! All I got was one miserable daughter and after that she says she's never going to have no more children again—"

"—because she didn't want to bring any more daughters into the world and have to listen to you moaning because they weren't boys! She knew the kind of man you were! How do you think I felt, not knowing why you never seemed to show any spark of affection for me? I thought I was ugly, afflicted with some terrible defect. Do you imagine I didn't want to get out of your horrible house? I only stayed there for Mother's sake and once she was in her grave I was thankful to leave it. You can keep your ill-gotten money and your grand farmhouse and your prosperous lands! I don't want any of them. I've had enough of you—more than enough—and if you don't want to see me or speak to me again, that's the best news I could ever wish to hear."

We all began to speak at once, Hugh threatening him with violence, I shouting at him to get off my land, my mother telling him he should be ashamed of treating his own flesh and blood so unkindly. He listened to no one. Instead he spat on the floor, told us he hoped we'd be damned for all eternity and stalked out into the yard to his horse.

Rebecca burst into tears.

While Hugh and my mother fussed around her I went out to the yard after Roslyn, but he was already riding off over the moors to Morvah; all I could do was stand and watch him till he disappeared from sight.

After this incident Hugh and Rebecca stayed two weeks longer under my mother's roof and then coaxed my father to let them stay at Penmarric while their cottage was being made habitable. I was relieved to see them go. I was tired of returning from the mine each night and being obliged to waste the evening talking to Hugh. I had nothing to say to Rebecca, and the atmosphere emanating from the pair began to be wearisome. I was bored with all their intimate smiles and meaningful looks and exasperated when I was kept awake at night. My mother had lent them her bedroom, which was the only room in the house with a double bed, and as I had the room next door all the louder accompaniments of sexual intercourse were audible to me. I couldn't have cared less how often Hugh wanted to make love to his wife, but I didn't see why I should have to lose sleep on account of his extended honeymoon.

To my surprise my mother was also relieved when they moved from the farm to Penmarric.

"I was becoming irritated with Rebecca," she confessed. "We nearly quarreled at least twice. You know, I don't believe she's half as meek and mild as she would like us to think she is. The more I see of her the more willful and opinionated she becomes.

If Hugh's not firm with her from the beginning he's going to find her quite a handful later on."

"Personally," I said, "I think she's the one who's going to find her partner a handful. How on earth is he going to find the money to support them? He shows no inclination at all to earn a living and do an honest day's work."

But I misjudged him. The next morning I was sitting at my office desk in my hut near the count house and trying to sift through a mountain of paperwork which the purser, Walter Hubert, had said wasn't truly "within his province." It wasn't within mine either, but Walter was overworked and I'd refused his request for a clerk in order to economize, so I had no alternative but to attempt the work myself. I was just wondering gloomily if I would be able to get below ground before the bell rang for the change of shifts when there was a knock on the door of my hut.

"Come in!" I yelled, hoping it was Walter coming to tell me the work was within his province after all.

The door opened. A shadow fell across my untidy desk. I looked up.

"Good God!" I said, amazed. "What are you doing here?"

"Offering my services," said Hugh, casually debonair in his best country tweeds. "You wouldn't like a hand with the accounts, I suppose? I can promise you I'm exceedingly clever with money. I was wondering if you'd like to take me on as your assistant purser, chief clerk and general factotum."

4

Geoffrey* was married to Constance, the heiress of Brittany, and assumed the title of duke of that rugged corner of France. . . . Eleanor had disliked her Breton daughter-in-law from the beginning.

—The Conquering Family,
THOMAS COSTAIN

The trouble with Geoffrey was that his honey-tongued eloquence was merely a top dressing on a scoundrelly hypocrisy. Roger of Howden can hardly mention his name without an epithet of abuse, and thought him the real trouble-maker among the brothers.

—King John,
W. L. WARREN

[1]

"Try me," said Hugh. "I could learn what has to be learned. I'm not a fool."

It was an attractive proposition. As soon as I had recovered from my astonishment I began to consider his offer seriously. To my reluctance I had been more and more involved with the business side of the mine since Walter Hubert had become too busy to cope with all the paperwork single-handed, but the more involved I became the more I realized that I hated to work in my office and grudged every second I was kept from the mine. But if

---

* The third of Henry's legitimate sons to survive infancy. To be distinguished from Geoffrey of York, Henry's favorite bastard.

I had Hugh to help Walter run the office, deal with the freight company, haggle with the middle men, supervise the payroll, cope with the insurance schemes and hack a path for the mine through the jungle of administration it was possible I could spend most of the working week down the mine with the tin. It would be more than pleasant to have Hugh take my place in dealing with the more boring aspects of management, and since Walter was no longer young Hugh could be trained to take over from him completely when he retired.

"I wouldn't want much to start with," said Hugh modestly. "Just enough to keep body and soul together."

"How much do you have in mind?"

"How much are you prepared to spare?"

We looked at each other. I looked right into his innocent blue eyes and I knew. He was just out for what he could get. He would never understand that every penny of profit had to be plowed back into the mine to stoke it up into the best and safest mine in all Cornwall. As soon as Walter's back was turned he would prey upon the profits, altering a figure here, a figure there, a figure somewhere else, and while he lived off the fat of the land my mine would be slowly choked to death in an economic noose.

I wondered what to say. I couldn't tell him I didn't trust him and suspected he was a dishonest adventurer out to line his own pocket as lavishly as he could. Nor could I admit that I thought he might outwit me even though I watched him like a hawk. I couldn't say, "You're much too crooked and much too clever and I don't want to have anything to do with you." On the other hand I didn't want to lie about it either. As the silence lengthened I wondered why this situation had not arisen before; I had realized long ago that Hugh was untrustworthy. However, since I had never had to put him in a position of trust, the more unpleasant aspects of his personality had never bothered me. Our interests had not conflicted before, but now that they did I found myself placed in a situation which was not only damned difficult but damned embarrassing as well.

"Look, Hugh," I said carefully at last, "I can't really afford to put another man on the payroll at the moment." That was true anyway. "The mine badly needs new equipment," I said, warming to my theme, "and although Father has put capital into the mine in the past he's always vowed not to put in a penny more, so we're entirely dependent on the mine's profits. We haven't even been able to pay a dividend yet because we still need every penny we can make. I'm sorry."

"I see," he said, still pleasant and friendly. "Let me put it another way, and you may see the situation differently. You're making money out of this mine. The mine pays you a salary. Papa and the other shareholders may not have made much so far but during the next few years it seems clear they're assured of getting their money back plus more besides. In other words, regardless of how close to the red you are at this moment, there's money in this mine and I don't see why I shouldn't join you and Papa in making a little profit out of the family business. After all, I'm Papa's son, just as you are, and if you're allowed to work here I don't see why I should be turned away."

"I don't think you understand the position," I said. "I need money for that mine."

"I need money too," he said. "I need money for my wife, and next June I'll need money for a child as well."

"Oh? That was quick work, wasn't it?"

He looked at me. Some indefinable change in his expression put me on my guard.

"Is there anything wrong in conceiving a baby on one's honeymoon?"

"You've only been married a couple of months," I said. "You can't blame me if I comment that it must have been a quick conception."

"I suppose you think I've been sleeping with her ever since I came back from the war."

"To be frank I couldn't give a damn whether she was a virgin or not when you married her, but knowing you I shouldn't think she was allowed to hold on to her virginity that long. Now about the mine—"

"She was a virgin."

"If you say so."

"And if you ever dare to make any slighting remark again about my wife—"

"All right, she was a virgin! For Christ's sake, what does it matter anyway! She was a virgin and now she's an expectant mother and you need money to finance your venture into fatherhood, and I'm sorry, I'd like to help you, but I can't afford to put you on the payroll and that's all there is to say."

"I'm afraid not," said Hugh politely. "I'm sorry you're being so obtuse over this, I really am. I hoped we would be able to come to some amicable arrangement which would benefit us both, but I see I shall have to go to Papa after all and ask him to coax you into a more reasonable frame of mind."

"Father! What the hell's Father got to do with this?"

"I was under the impression he owned the mine—and sixty per-cent of the shares."

I stood up. He stood up too. I clenched my fists and grabbed hold of my temper and kept calm. "Look, Hugh," I said. "Let's get one thing straight. I run this mine. I decide who goes on the payroll. I'm the boss."

"Interesting. I'll tell Papa that. He might disagree with you."

"My decisions are final! I'll stand for no interference, and he knows that. If you think you can force yourself into this business and worm your way into the money—"

"It's a family business and I'm entitled to a share. I hate to phrase it so crudely, but since you're being so obtuse I see I shall have to spell it out for you: I want my cut and if you don't give it to me I'll make trouble for you. It's as simple as that."

"Why should Father listen to your complaints? You're so much out of favor with him that he won't even give you an allowance!"

"Papa will be impressed by my sincere wish to earn an honest living in the family business," said Hugh, his voice syrup-smooth. "And how delighted he'll be when he hears he's going to be a grandfather! I wouldn't even be surprised if he invited us to live at Penmarric and made his will in my favor. Since he has to leave his fortune to someone, why shouldn't he favor the one son who's married, settled, stable, hard-working, respectful, pleasant, anxious to please and thoroughly commendable in every possible way? There's a lot of money to be made in this part of Cornwall, Philip, and if you weren't so in love with a dirty old mine and content to live as an artisan you'd go chasing the money yourself instead of leaving me to pocket it from under your very nose. But your loss is my gain! If I play my cards carefully and all goes well, I'll invite you to dinner when I'm master of Penmarric and maybe if you ask me nicely enough I'll write you out a check to help support your godforsaken bloody mine!"

"Get out," I said between my teeth. "Get out or I'll throw you out. And never come back here again."

"Do you think I don't understand why you don't want me at the mine? Do you think I don't realize what's going on in your mind? The mine comes first, doesn't it, Philip! Every penny you possess, every drop of strength in your body and every ounce of ambition in your soul is sacrificed to that mine. You won't even give your own brother a job and a salary because you can't bear the thought of any sum, however small, being diverted from Sennen Garth. You're not interested in anything except feeding and nurturing that bloody mine! You don't have any vices not because you want to be pure but because that mine is every vice rolled into one. And what the hell is the mine anyway? A hole in the ground! A dark passage in the bowels of the earth! A sweating cavern a mile from the light of day! And for *that* I'm denied a job and the chance to work in the family business!"

"Well, of course I would hardly expect you to understand! You're not a Cornish tinner. You don't understand what the mine means and you never will."

"Oh, come, Philip, you're no more a Cornish tinner than I am! You're just trying to satisfy some extraordinary obsession you have!"

"If you don't believe I'm a true Cornish tinner born and bred you ask Alun Trevose or Willie Halloran—or any miner who's ever worked alongside me! They'll tell you! They know me and they know what I am!"

"And what are you?" said Hugh. "A cold-blooded bastard who surrounds himself with working-class men, lives with his mother and can't even get bedded by the hottest whore between Land's End and St. Ives."

I hit him, but he was ready for me. He dodged, swung an uppercut at my jaw, spun me back against the wall. He tried to leave then but I wouldn't let him. My temper was gone; a mist swam before my eyes; I was blind with rage. As he opened the door I grabbed him by the collar, shoved him back and lashed out with my fists. But he was quick on his feet, nimble and agile. I couldn't close in and whenever I tried to get to grips with him he would pack a solid punch to the body and knock me aside. But I kept going. I was just thinking I'd finally cornered him and was just gasping out, "Now, you crooked little liar," when he hit me below the belt. I jackknifed with the pain. As I lay winded on the floor I was dimly aware of him opening the door, slipping outside and slamming it shut behind him before he walked away.

It took me several minutes to recover. When I could walk again I went to the first-aid post, told Jack Priske, who was in charge there, that I'd had a fall, and took a shot of brandy from the medicinal bottle. After that I felt better. I looked at my face in the mirror. I was bruised across one cheekbone and my lip was cut, so I took out my handkerchief, found a clean patch and pressed it against my mouth. After a moment I took the handkerchief away and looked at it. Scarlet flared against the white linen and suddenly—for no reason—I was remembering Mariana's wedding, Mariana passing beneath a stained-glass window which had made a scarlet gash of her mouth. The next moment I vomited. Fortunately I managed to get outside before making a mess of the first-aid room, but Jack Priske began fussing around me and telling me I should go home and rest.

"I'm all right," I said shortly. In truth I did feel better for having vomited. I supposed the tension of the scene with Hugh had combined with his blow below the belt to give my stomach a tough time, but now I was better all I wanted was to go down the mine and find my friends. "I'm fine," I said to Jack. "It was nothing. I'm fine now." And still sucking the blood from my cut lip, I began my journey to the two-forty-fathom level far out below the Cornish sea.

[2]

Trevose called Hugh a lunatic and said his insults were a load of rubbish. "Lunatic" and "rubbish" are the best printable translations of the words he used.

"The trouble with Mr. Hugh," said Trevose sourly, "is that being a bloody gentleman he don't know nothing about being a bloody miner down a bloody mine. 'Course you're as good as any Cornish tinner! 'Course you love your mine! Any man who's ever worked with you'd say the same bloody thing. Mr. Hugh's jealous of you, sonny, that's what he is, just bloody jealous because you're twice the man he'll ever be and with more friends than he'll ever have and if that's not the bloody truth my name's not Alun Trevose." Trevose's worst insult was to call someone a gentleman. I began to feel better. "Bloody cheek," said Trevose. "Bloody gentleman." In fact he used the word "bloody" only once during his tirade, but it serves as a useful substitute for his other obscenities. I told him then how I'd refused Hugh a job and why.

" 'Struth!" said Trevoce. "You do have your troubles with that family of yours, don't you?"

But the worst of the troubles were still to come.

My father took Hugh's side, said that it was highly commendable that Hugh wanted to work in the family business and told me to employ him without further delay.

"I won't," I said, "and I'll tell you why. I don't trust him. He'd be filching money from the accounts whenever my back was turned."

"Rubbish!" said my father. "The plain fact of the matter is you don't want Hugh at the mine because you won't admit that you're lax with the paperwork and that your office is a shambles. You won't admit Hugh could be more than useful to you in straightening out the administrative mess you now have on your hands—"

That put me in an awkward position because I knew I did need help in the office. But I wouldn't admit I needed Hugh. "I'll employ someone else to help me," I said, "but I'm not employing Hugh. You can't make me employ him."

"Why not? It's not your mine, you know, although I admit I've let you treat it as if it were. But it's not yours. It belongs to me, and not only does it belong to me but I also control the company—"

"Yes, but—"

"—and I sign the checks."

That threat was all I needed to make me lose my temper. I shouted at him for several minutes, but all the time I knew I'd lost because the mine desperately needed money to keep it both open and safe and my father's fortune was much too vital to ignore. He could threaten to fire me and stop my salary—I could have stood that, for if necessary I would have worked for nothing —but I couldn't let him withdraw his financial support from the mine. In the end all I could do was repeat stubbornly, "I'll work with a clerk at the count house, but I won't work with Hugh. I don't trust him and I think it would be a mistake to employ him. And beyond that I have nothing else to say."

"Very well," said my father, "but Hugh goes on the payroll whether you like it or not. I fail to see why he should be penalized for your pigheaded and unreasonable attitude."

At first I thought I couldn't possibly have heard him correctly. "You mean I must pay Hugh a salary even though he won't be doing a stroke of work?"

"Precisely."

"And pay the new clerk as well?"

"Naturally."

"But that means we'll be paying two salaries instead of one!"

"Your decision, not mine."

"But the mine can't afford it!"

"Then if you really care about the mine you'll agree to work with Hugh."

"God . . . damn . . . you . . ." I felt sick with rage. "I won't work with Hugh!" I shouted. "I won't. I'll put most of my salary back into the mine to compensate for the loss, but I won't work with him! Damn you both to hell!"

And with that I turned my back on him, strode out of the room and slammed the door as violently as I could behind me.

But later when my rage had cooled it occurred to me in bitter disgust that Hugh, not my father, had had the last laugh. He had said on his return to Cornwall that he wanted a job earning money in the easiest possible way, and now all he had to do was to sit around on his backside being a gentleman of leisure while my hard-earned profits from Sennen Garth flowed gently into his bank account.

[3]

We were the last mine west of Cape Cornwall now. We were one of the last mines alive in the entire county. For the year was 1919, and on the twentieth of October 1919 the Levant came to an end.

It wasn't quite the end perhaps, for the mine did linger on for a few years afterward while the miners worked the levels above adit, but it was the end of Levant as we all knew it, the end of a mine which ranked with Dolcoath, Cook's Kitchen and Botallack as one of the greatest mines in Cornish history.

Fabulous Levant! To me—and to many others—it was unparalleled in its magnificence, the mightiest mine in Cornwall, the richest in copper and tin of all those rich mines on the north Cornish coast. But now Levant was dead. It was hard to believe at first. St. Just mourned the loss in stricken silence as the news swept through England and flickered around the world. Levant was dead. Levant, the mine which was so vast that no man knew the fullest extent of its workings, the mine that went far out under the sea and sank to levels hundreds of fathoms below the Cornish cliffs. Fabulous Levant! The mine where the miners traveled to work on that monstrous invention of a man-engine which carried each man on a thirty-minute ride into the heart of the Cornish earth, wondrous awe-inspiring Levant where the lodes were as big as a cathedral and the miners' singing would echo as if they were in a mighty church. Unique Levant! There wasn't a tinner alive who didn't know its name and admire it as one of the most incredible mines of them all.

But Levant is dead now. It began to die on one calm October day in 1919, and when it finally closed for the last time after its lingering death, its splendor was ended forever and its levels were abandoned to the rats and rising waters. You can go back to the outbuildings still, you can walk among the ruins decaying above Cape Cornwall and pick your way across the slag heaps grown over with weeds; you can see the ruined engine house still standing on the cliff and sometimes on a quiet night you can almost hear the roar of the furnace and see the miners laughing as they leave the "dry." You can go to the surface of the Levant because the surface is still there. But you can't go down to the bottom of the mine.

For on the twentieth of October 1919 there was a disaster. Nearly forty miners, all of them known to me, never saw the light of day again. In the evening they were riding to the surface as usual when suddenly with no warning the man-engine collapsed into the shaft with a grinding roar, and after that there was nothing except dust and dead bodies and the weeping of the women at the surface.

The equipment was faulty, people said. Not enough money had been spent on maintenance. The Levant was old and dangerous and no longer even very profitable. It must stay crippled. There was nothing else to do but let it die.

And after that there was a terrible quiet on the Cornish Tin Coast, as if it had been brought home to us at last that we had been born at the end of an era which had endured for thousands of years and that we were the last of the Cornish tinners who would ever mine the Cornish tin. All the mines were dead or dying and Sennen Garth was one of the handful left alive.

[4]

It was in 1920 that I first met Helena Meredith. Old Algernon Meredith, who owned the only mansion in Zillan parish, died at the ripe old age of ninety-six, and since he had been a bachelor his estate reverted to his cousins, the Warwickshire Merediths. There had been Merediths at Polzillan House for many generations, just as there had been Carnforths at Carnforth Hall and Waymarks at Gurnards Grange, but since old Meredith had been bedridden for thirty years with arthritis few people apart from the rector had seen him and only the oldest inhabitants of Zillan could remember days when Polzillan House had not resembled a nursing home. But in 1920 there was a promise of change. A certain Gerald Meredith arrived with his sister to take up his inheritance, and all the tongues of Zillan parish were soon wagging themselves into exhaustion as the gossip flew back and forth like a ping-pong ball.

However, it soon became clear that Polzillan House was to remain a nursing home; young Meredith had been wounded in the war and was confined to a wheelchair.

"However," said my mother, "his sister seems perfectly able-bodied. He's lucky to have her to look after him."

But I was too deeply involved with the mine to care much about the new inhabitants of Polzillan House.

"We should call on them, Philip," said my mother. "Perhaps we can call on Saturday and take Jeanne with us. It would be nice for her to meet a young man, even if he is in a wheelchair. I wonder if he's convalescing or whether the wound is permanent? I wish Mark would take Jeanne to London now that the war's over and give her a season. I know she refused to go last year, but he should have insisted—or at least he might have taken her to London and arranged for her to meet a few people informally. She'll be twenty-one next Christmas and she's never had any young man taking her out and about and entertaining her. And now that Peter Waymark is married and the Carnforth boys were killed in the war . . ."

I ceased to listen. I was obliged to listen to my mother worrying about Jeanne's marital future at least six times a week.

". . . and his sister is very pretty," said my mother. "I saw her in church last Sunday when you had to miss matins to get the vet for that cow."

"Hm."

"She's really a very good-looking girl. Fair hair and green eyes, an excellent complexion and an elegant figure. I believe her name is Helena."

"Hm."

"Philip, are you listening to me?"

"Yes, Mama. You said you believed her name was Helena." I hoped she had no intention of acting as a matchmaker for me as well as for Jeanne. I hated to be told how to organize my life.

In fact Helena Meredith was every bit as good-looking as my mother had promised she was. I found her pleasant. In contrast her brother was fractious and evidently resented his helplessness bitterly. I disliked him at once, but Jeanne, whose ability to sympathize was more extensive than mine, was filled with compassion and thought him very courageous in his adversity.

"I wish I could be a nurse," she said to my mother as we walked back to the farm after calling on the Merediths. "If the war hadn't ended I would have asked Papa if I could have been a V.A.D. Do you suppose he would let me study nursing?"

"I don't know about your papa," said my mother, "but I wouldn't approve at all. You're much too young to waste yourself being worked to the bone in some large hospital, and young girls of your class don't become nurses anyway."

"Yes, Mama," said Jeanne. She never argued with my mother. The subject of nursing didn't arise again between them but I noticed how quickly Jeanne became friends with Helena Meredith and how often she used to visit Polzillan House to see the invalid. I heard Helena in turn was often at Penmarric, but since I never went there myself I seldom saw her except at church on Sundays.

At first my mother was pleased that Jeanne saw so much of the Merediths, but as the months passed she began to worry about the scope of Gerald Meredith's disability and had second thoughts about encouraging Jeanne to visit Polzillan House. To my discomfort she tried to persuade me to find out more about his paralysis.

I was reluctant to interfere, but I did see that my mother felt it was her duty to find out more about Meredith and I also saw that it was my duty to help my mother. The trouble was I couldn't think how to set about it. I didn't get on well with Meredith anyway, and even if I did I couldn't very well call on him and demand to know if he were capable of sexual intercourse. At last it occurred to me that the key to the problem lay in Meredith's feelings toward Jeanne; if he were either indifferent to her or uninterested in matrimony it would hardly matter how impotent he was.

Having brooded over the situation for some time, I came to a decision. The next day at the mine I went to the telephone in my office and asked the operator if Mr. Gerald Meredith had had a telephone installed at Polzillan House. He had. I asked to be connected, and when the butler answered the bell seconds later I wasted no time in asking to speak to Helena.

[5]

I invited Helena to dine with me at the Metropole that evening, and when she accepted I gritted my teeth and steeled myself to ask my father for a favor. I needed his car and chauffeur for the evening since it was out of the question for me to drive Helena into Penzance in my mother's ponytrap, and I foresaw he would be reluctant to grant me any favors as we had been on worse terms than usual for some months. But I was wrong. To my surprise he almost fell over himself trying to be helpful when he heard why I wanted to borrow the car and told me I was welcome to both car and chauffeur whenever I liked. Having solved the problem of transport with such unexpected ease, I returned home early to Roslyn Farm to have a bath and try on the dinner jacket I had not worn for years. I had had a bathroom installed at the farm at the end of the war more for my mother's convenience than for my own, but as I grew older I admit I did enjoy the comforts of modern sanitation.

"Yes, I'm home early today," I said to my mother when she arrived home later from a visit to Zillan. "I shan't be in tonight. I'm taking Helena Meredith out to dinner at the Metropole."

"Oh!" cried my mother, for all the world as if I had produced six white rabbits out of my trouser pockets, and immediately began to flutter around me like some overanxious butterfly. "Your shirts—I haven't ironed them yet—your dinner jacket—I'm sure it'll have to be altered—"

I did wish she wouldn't make so much fuss. By the time my father's chauffeur arrived that evening it was a relief to escape from the farm and concentrate on my evening with Helena.

I was out of touch with fashionable society and had no idea what was happening in London, but of course I had not forgotten how to behave at a place like the Metropole; ten years of rural living hadn't affected my memory of manners instilled in childhood. The Metropole was still the same stuffy hotel with the pseudo-French menu and the palm-court atmosphere, but I was astonished by some of the diners. There were several women with short hair and skimpy dresses and ugly necklaces, and one was actually smoking in public. If this was Penzance, was my reaction, what on earth could London be like? I thought, amused, how shocked my mother would have been by such changes in feminine conventions.

"Thank God you're not looking like those people over there!" I said frankly to Helena. "I've never seen such a hideous collection of women."

She laughed. "I'm glad you say that! I was beginning to feel not only old-fashioned but decidedly dowdy as well."

"Nonsense!"

After we had ordered I turned the conversation to the subject of her brother and asked if his health showed any signs of improvement, but she told me frankly enough that he was a permanent and not a temporary invalid and that nothing further could be done to improve his health.

"That's tragic," I said, picking up my soup spoon as the waiter approached with the first course, "but at least he's not totally paralyzed. I suppose that's one good thing."

She gave me a fleeting glance. Her eyes were cool and green, like the color of the sea around the offshore rocks of Cape Cornwall. "Yes," she said. "He can move from the waist upward."

I made a great business of tasting my soup and saying how good it was. She said her soup was good too. We smiled at each other.

"I hope Jeanne isn't pestering your brother too much," I said carelessly. "It seems she's always at Polzillan these days! I hope she's not boring him."

"Good gracious, no! Far from it! You've no idea how he's changed since Jeanne began to call regularly. She's given him an interest in life and he doesn't get so depressed or maudlin as he used to. He looks forward to every one of her visits."

"That's a relief," I said casually. "I was afraid he was too polite to ask her not to call so often."

She shook her head. "No, he enjoys seeing her immensely. I think he's very fond of her."

"I think she's fond of him," I said.

"Yes, I think so too." She was calm and self-possessed. I liked the way she didn't simper or blush at the least hint of an awkward subject.

"Do you think he loves her?" I said after a moment.

"Possibly," said Helena. She raised her cool green eyes to meet mine again before glancing away. "But of course," she said, "there can be no question of marriage. If Gerry does love her he'll keep it to himself. He knows he can't expect a girl like Jeanne to tie herself to a man in a wheelchair."

That was what I had brought her to Penzance to find out. I relaxed in my chair with relief and started to enjoy my food, but of course the evening wasn't over and I had to sustain the effort of making conversation. I had been well brought up. I could almost hear Rose Parrish say seriously in her light, gentle voice, "One cannot take a lady out to dinner and then proceed to ignore her."

But the rest of the meal passed easily enough. I asked her about her family and the place in Warwickshire where she had been born. Her mother had died when Helena was three and her father had been killed in the Boer War; Gerald was her only surviving relative.

"I thought of living on my own when the war was over," she said. "I was sure Gerry would get married and if he did I didn't want to stay on in his house and get in his wife's way. But then Gerry was wounded and I felt I should really stay with him as long as I was free to do so."

"He's fortunate to have you with him," I said with mechanical courtesy and added as an afterthought, "You have the means to live on your own if you wish?"

"Oh yes," she said, unperturbed. "My father had unusual ideas for a man of his generation and decided to leave his money equally between us."

"I see," I said impassively, just managing to conceal my amazement. For Gerald Meredith kept a well-heeled establishment at Polzillan House. There were plenty of servants to maintain the rambling old mansion in perfect order, several gardeners to attend the immaculate grounds, numerous grooms to look after the well-bred horses. I couldn't help wondering if the establishment was financed by Meredith alone or with his sister's help.

". . . so Gerry and I were independent of each other even before Cousin Algernon died," she was saying. "I'm much more fortunate than many girls."

"So old Meredith—your cousin—left his estate to your brother—"

"No, he died intestate. Isn't that amazing? You would think at the age of ninety-six he would have a will all ready for his death, but he didn't. Gerry and I inherited the estate equally as next of kin."

"Ah," I said. I was too astounded to say anything else. It had never occurred to me that she might be an extremely wealthy woman. Not that it mattered to me. I didn't care about money although I would have welcomed a few pounds to spend on new equipment for the mine. However, one hardly sells oneself into marriage merely to buy several hundred feet of ladders and a few thousand yards of piping.

Presently we went outside for a stroll along the esplanade. The night air was cool but not unpleasant; a full moon shone, transforming the sea into a hypnotic pattern of black and silver, and I stopped to stare out over the water. I never tired of watching the sea; I could watch the surf of the north coast and the meek little waves of the south with equal fascination.

Beside me Helena was refreshingly silent and I gave her credit for good taste. Most women would have made some comment about how lovely the moonlight was.

I decided then that I liked Helena Meredith. There was nothing displeasing about her. Her slim figure was always well dressed; her appearance never jarred the eye and her fair hair and light eyes appealed to me. I also admired the way she never said anything silly or mawkish, and most of all I admired her for her self-possession. Here was a woman, I thought, who would be incapable of initiating an embarrassing scene. I felt drawn toward her, and when we parted at the end of the evening I thought vaguely that I might ask her to dine with me again some time in the future.

The next morning I found my mother waiting agog at the breakfast table.

"You can relax," I told her as she hovered around me with the eggs and bacon. "He's incurably paralyzed from the waist downward but he has no intention of proposing. I'll have three slices of toast, please, and some of the new chunky marmalade."

"And how was Helena?" said my mother. "Did you have a nice time?"

"Yes, it was pleasant. Aren't you interested in what Helena said about her brother?"

"Yes, of course. I'm sorry, what did you say she said? I wasn't listening."

I repeated the news patiently.

My mother was seriously alarmed. "But Helena can't *know* her brother wouldn't propose!" she exclaimed at once. "Supposing he asks Jeanne to come to Polzillan as his nurse and companion? Naturally she would have to marry him, and Jeanne's quite foolish and softhearted enough to say yes even if he proposed under such adverse circumstances! Dear me, it's all most worrying. I think I shall write to Mark. I'm sure he has no idea how dangerous the situation has become, and I think the time has come for him to be warned."

"But is it really necessary to interfere?" I asked frankly. "Jeanne's always wanted to be a nurse and she obviously enjoys Meredith's company or she wouldn't visit him so much. Assuming she knew beforehand that he was impotent, why shouldn't she marry him if she wants to? She's over twenty-one, and if she doesn't have a mind of her own by this time I think it's high time she started to develop one."

My mother was shocked. "Darling, I don't think you quite understand the situation. Of course Jeanne mustn't marry him! It doesn't matter how old she is. She must be prevented from making such a terrible mistake."

"But would it be such a mistake? Supposing she doesn't care how impotent he is. Supposing—"

"Really, darling, must you be quite so crude? If she doesn't care about such matters, then she should. She should marry to fulfill her role as a woman, not to be an unpaid nurse to a cripple."

I sighed in the face of this unanswerable feminine platitude and decided to concentrate on my breakfast without attempting any further comment.

Throughout the events that followed I kept firmly in the background. My mother went to Penmarric for a conference with my father; my father wrote to Mariana and my mother spoke to Jeanne. Between the two of them they reduced her to a state of abject misery and packed her off to Scotland to spend the summer with Mariana.

"With a stroke of luck," said my mother, "she may meet some eligible man and make a suitable marriage. I hear Edinburgh is a very sociable place and of course Mariana will know all the right people."

But Jeanne didn't marry. She stayed in Scotland from the summer of 1921 to the autumn of 1922, and then without my parents' approval she entered a small religious order which sent its nuns to nurse the sick in a charity hospital in London.

[6]

My mother was naturally upset by Jeanne's decision and for a while avoided thinking about it as much as possible by concentrating on her grandchildren. Hugh's daughter, Deborah, had been born in the June of 1920, but since I refused to have anything to do with Hugh and had no interest in babies I avoided the christening and made no effort to see the child afterward. This was hard on my mother, who of course doted on the baby and would have liked to have discussed it constantly with me, but it was no good my pretending an enthusiasm I didn't possess and after a time she became reconciled to my attitude.

Mariana's son, Esmond Mark Duncan Donald Alexander, Earl of Roane, was born six weeks after Deborah in early August. Since Mariana's husband was over sixty by then I supposed that represented some sort of achievement, but personally I thought it was embarrassing. However, I was careful not to comment because I knew my mother's first marriage had been to a man over sixty when she had been about Mariana's age and I didn't want to hurt her by a couple of thoughtless remarks. In truth my mother's situation had differed from Mariana's in one important respect; my mother had been John Henry Roslyn's wife in name only and had come to the farm more as his housekeeper than as his wife; marriage for her then had been the most expedient way of keeping up her respectability in a household consisting of three unmarried men, and although my mother's delicacy on such matters had stopped me from asking her outright, I knew her well enough to assume she and old Roslyn had always had separate bedrooms.

The news of her grandson's arrival in Scotland sent my mother into the expected frenzy of delight. It had been a sore point with her that Mariana had so far made excuses not to bring her second husband down to Cornwall for inspection, but now all was forgiven and my mother's one concern was that Mariana might be dilatory in presenting the baby to her. Mariana wasn't. After a visit to Penmarric on which she was accompanied by a nanny, a nursemaid and her own personal maid but not by her husband, she launched into an ecstatic correspondence with my mother and sent her a steady stream of photographs of the baby and clippings of his blond hair and long letters about how wonderful he was. This was much more surprising than the facts would suggest at first glance. First of all Mariana wasn't the sort of woman one would expect to enter into the role of motherhood with such zest, and secondly she and my mother had never been close. But now all that was changed. Mariana became the Favorite Daughter, and soon I was so bored with hearing about the prodigious infant Esmond that my mother no longer bothered to read Mariana's letters aloud to me.

"Oh, all these dreary children!" said my sister Elizabeth, echoing my own point of view on a visit to the farm at the end of the summer holidays. "I'm bored to tears with this incessant baby talk! I can't wait to get back to Cheltenham and escape from Deborah and Esmond, the joint eighth wonder of the world!"

I was amused by this, but my mother naturally was annoyed.

"I do hope you're not becoming too much of a bluestocking, Lizzie," she said politely. "It's well known that men despise aggressively intellectual women and prefer girls with softer, more feminine tastes. If you go around openly declaring your lack of interest in motherhood, you can hardly expect men to do anything except shun you whenever you enter a room."

"I couldn't care less," said Lizzie. "Most men are stupid anyway. I'm not even sure I want to get married."

"Well, dear, unless you do something about your appearance soon it's possible no one will ask you. Is it really necessary for you to eat so much? It makes you too stout and all those sweet things give you spots. And do you really wash your hair once a week? Greasy hair is so unattractive."

"Very well," said Lizzie angrily. "My hair's greasy and I'm fat and a bit spotty. But I for one don't care! *You* may think that the most important thing for a woman is to be beautiful and marry successfully and have lots of marvelous children—why shouldn't you? That's all you've ever done in life! What's so special about that anyway? Any fool can get married and have a baby. I'm going to do something exceptional!"

I felt I should intervene. "Shut up, Lizzie," I said abruptly. "You're being very rude to Mama."

"Well, she was beastly rude to me!" shouted Lizzie in a rage. "Why should she expect me to be polite back? Parents take the most outrageous liberties with their children and then expect to get away with them—no, I won't apologize, Philip! If you weren't so besotted with Mama you'd see it was her fault to start with. Oh, men are so exasperating! Jan-Yves's the only one who's got any sense." And she flounced out of the farmhouse. Since she returned to school a week later it was some time before we saw her again, and she never once wrote to my mother from Cheltenham.

By the time Jeanne entered her convent in the autumn of 1922 Lizzie had left school and was up at Cambridge reading classics. I was surprised that my father consented to this since I knew he was basically opposed to higher education for women, but evidently he had abandoned the struggle to oppose Lizzie's masculine thirst for knowledge and Lizzie proceeded to fall head over heels in love with academic life. We still saw little of her, but shortly before the Christmas of 1922 she returned to Cornwall for a couple of weeks and on the day after her arrival she called at the farm to see us. Not expecting a visitor, my mother had gone to Zillan, but as it was a Sunday I was at home and found myself obliged to entertain Lizzie in the parlor till my mother returned. At first I wondered what on earth we could find to talk about, but I needn't have worried; I had forgotten that Lizzie always had plenty to say for herself and soon I had long ceased to worry about where the next word was coming from.

"—so I think even you'd feel sorry for him these days," she was saying as I recalled my wandering concentration. I had become bored during her lengthy eulogy on the subject of Cambridge. "After all, Marcus is dead, Mariana's in Scotland, Jeanne's in the convent, I'm away at Cambridge, Jan-Yves's at Eton, and as far as Papa's concerned you're a total write-off. Who has he got left to keep him company? Of course Hugh calls two or three times a week and practically falls on his nose being the dutiful son, but he and Papa haven't got much in common and soon get politely bored with each other. It's true Adrian's coming home this week for Christmas, but he's too busy learning to be a clergyman and doing social work in his spare time to be much at Penmarric these days. That leaves William, but he's hardly much of a companion for Papa since he spends at least three evenings a week with Charity Roslyn—I do wish he'd marry her! Who cares if she *was* the local tart anyway?—so really, when you come to consider the situation it's awfully lucky that Papa has Alice. If it wasn't for Alice I think he'd be horribly lonely."

Alice Penmar.

I thought of the disastrous scene before the war in my father's study. Alice had been in love with me in those days—or so she had said, but that was long ago now, long, long ago, and times had changed and people had changed with them.

"Interesting, isn't it?" Lizzie was saying blandly. "I don't get on with Alice myself—she's much too bossy and self-opinionated for me!—but I have to admit she's a good conversationalist and nobody's fool. She always dines with Papa, you know, if William's spending the evening with Charity and there's no one else at home. She and Papa are very . . . friendly."

After a moment I said with care, "Does she go out of her way to be friendly toward him, do you think?"

"You mean is she his mistress?" said Lizzie with interest. "I don't *think* so. Jan-Yves and I have private bets about it. He thinks she is but I'm not so sure. I simply don't think Papa could possibly be *that* desperate. Alice just isn't the type. I'm not saying all unchaste women have to look like Charity Roslyn, but I do think they have to have a certain something, and whatever it is I don't think Alice has got it. She's so prim and proper and spinsterish! I simply can't imagine her and Papa—well, you know . . . But Jan-Yves disagrees. He says Alice is just the type who would fall from virtue out of sheer frustration. What do you think?"

It was on the tip of my tongue to ask her about Jan-Yves, whom she mentioned so often, but I did not. I had no real interest in him; we never saw each other since he never visited the farm, and it had long seemed obvious to me that we would remain strangers all our lives.

"What do you think, Philip?" repeated Lizzie, recalling my thoughts to the subject of Alice Penmar. "Can you visualize Alice as a fallen woman?"

I gave a short laugh and moved to the window to see if my mother showed signs of returning from Zillan. "You have an emancipated line of conversation, Lizzie. Is that the result of an advanced education?" But even as I spoke several different ideas were flickering through my mind. I was thinking that there was talk of changing the divorce laws so that a woman could sue for divorce on the grounds of adultery alone instead of adultery coupled with desertion. I was thinking that the last thing my father would ever want would be to see the granddaughter of his old and valued friend the rector of Zillan involved in an unsavory scandal. I was thinking that if I was careful, if I had sufficient proof, if the laws were changed in my mother's favor, I might just possibly have found my father's Achilles' heel and an Achilles' heel might be more than useful to me if severe difficulties over the mine's future arose in the years ahead.

"It's certainly an interesting idea," I heard myself say at last to Lizzie. "I'll have to think about it."

[7]

I ran into trouble with my father again soon after that. There had been a lull since our last quarrel, but presently I knew we were sure to clash again. In 1923 after paying fair dividends for three years, Sennen Garth had a bad year and went into the red. There was an accident resulting from faulty equipment and naturally I had no choice but to replace the equipment immediately in order to maintain the standards of safety for which the mine was now well known. Since there was no ready money available, however, I had to take out a loan. The loan wasn't much, but I had to pay interest on it and so more good money went down the drain.

The situation at the mine made me try again to persuade my father to reverse his decision on Hugh's sinecure, but my father clung on as firmly to his decision as I clung to mine and Hugh remained a gentleman of leisure. Hugh's fortunes reached a new unjust zenith that year; he was playing the stock market so cunningly that he could afford to take Rebecca to London and live like a lord during their stay there; moreover, his financial affairs improved at home as well; his father-in-law died of pneumonia, and although Joss Roslyn had disinherited Rebecca and left his money and property to Jared's only son Simon Peter, Jared offered on his son's behalf to let her have her old home at the rent of a peppercorn a year. Rebecca didn't want it, but Hugh had other ideas. I could well imagine him rubbing his hands in delight at the opportunity to make some extra money. When they moved to Morvah to take advantage of Jared's offer Hugh leased the cottage which my mother had given him as a wedding present, and on arrival in Morvah he leased the Deveral Farm lands to the highest bidder. Then, having assured himself of a more comfortable home and a larger income, he settled himself on his backside again and prepared to idle away some more time with his wife and child. As far as I could gather they spent their time picknicking or swimming in one of the nearby coves. Hugh was a good swimmer, and I could imagine him passing his afternoons demonstrating his aquatic skills to his admiring wife and then sunbathing languidly with her on the beach. It was a fine life, I supposed—if one liked to be idle. Certainly there was no one who enjoyed being idle more than Hugh.

My father and I had another bitter correspondence on the subject of Hugh's sinecure, but it was a waste of time. As the mine teetered on the brink of financial disaster I couldn't decide whether I hated my father more than Hugh or hated Hugh more than my father.

It was 1924, the year Ramsay MacDonald led the Labour party to power for the first time. I voted for his party, just as most of my friends did, although my mother was horrified by my gesture and saw my political views as "improper." Despite her background—or perhaps because of it—she firmly believed that it was a matter of good taste to vote Conservative, just as it was a matter of good taste to go to church every Sunday, hold one's knife and fork correctly and avoid short skirts.

"But, Mama, things have changed since the war," I pointed out reasonably. "We have to have a new Government with new views to fit the new times. The country's in an appalling mess—the poverty among the working classes, the misery—"

"They should work all the harder instead of grumbling so much and going on strike," said my mother firmly. "If you want to get on in life you have to work hard and not sit back in idleness."

"But how can they work when there are no jobs? There are millions of unemployed and the numbers grow every day. These people have spent four years fighting for their country—and for what? To line up every day at the labor exchange? To face the humiliation of being unable to earn money to support their families? To live in condemned hovels because of the housing shortage? There have got to be some radical changes to improve things, Mama, and the Conservatives are hardly known for their radicalism. Neither are the Asquith Liberals, and the Lloyd George Liberals aren't much better. Look what a mess the coalition government's made of things! We need something quite new now, not more of the same ineffective recipe."

"Merely because an idea is new," said my mother tartly, "doesn't necessarily mean it's any better than old and proven ideas."

I gave up. It was no use trying to persuade her to abandon her ingrained convictions, but when Ramsay MacDonald came to power I remained convinced that matters would soon improve throughout the country. They did improve slightly at Sennen Garth, but even though it was a better year for the mine I still had to take out another loan. Walter Hubert was beginning to look grim whenever the subject of money was mentioned but I didn't care. I was determined that 1925 was going to be the year when matters would be righted and loans paid off.

But although I didn't know it then the mine's faint improvement was destined to last only a short time longer than the Labour Government—nine months. By the beginning of 1925 I was beginning to worry again, but I was still optimistic enough to be able to suppress my doubts most of the time. I was in a cheerful frame of mind when I rode back to Zillan one May evening from the mine—and found my mother entertaining the last person on earth I would have expected to see in the parlor of Roslyn Farm. At first I thought it was my father. I heard his laugh ring out as I crossed the hall, and his voice drawling lazily, "So there we were! Wasn't that amusing?"

My mother laughed too. I had not heard her laugh so spontaneously or so happily for a long time.

I was amazed. Wondering why my father had chosen to call and display such extraordinary good humor, I flung open the door and walked into the room.

They were sitting at the table, just as my mother had sat facing my father when he had called to see her after Marcus had died. I still thought it was my father. It was not until the man turned and I saw his unlined face, his black hair untouched with silver and his cynical, humorous mouth so different from my father's that I knew who he was.

It was Jan-Yves.

[8]

"Philip!" he said gracefully. "How nice!" And despite his voice, his drawl and his marked physical resemblance to my father, I seemed to hear an echo of my mother in his manner and choice of words.

He stood up. He was six inches shorter than I was but tough and well-built. I remembered him as being a fat child, but now he was merely stocky and muscular. He moved with a curious grace, again unexpectedly reminiscent of my mother, and despite his calculating Penmar eyes he had a wide, innocent smile which reminded me at once of Hugh.

I distrusted him.

My mother was saying with shining eyes, "Isn't this exciting, Philip? After all these years! I could hardly believe it when I saw him riding down the hill from Chûn."

I managed to say to Jan-Yves, "I thought you were up at Oxford?" I knew he had gone up to Christ Church in the autumn of the previous year and since it was still only May I was surprised to see him back in Cornwall again. "What are you doing in Zillan?"

"Mending my ways," said Jan-Yves with his innocent smile. "Is it ever too late to reform? Egged on by Papa and Mr. Barnwell and my conscience, I decided to ride over to Roslyn Farm bearing the olive branch of peace. Mama quite naturally nearly fainted with shock, so to revive her we selected the best bottle of elderberry wine and—well, here we are! It's as simple as that!"

Of course it wasn't as simple as that at all. It turned out that he had been sent down from Oxford for some reason which he glossed over with great adroitness, and it seemed obvious enough to me that having blotted his copybook so badly with my father he had decided to compensate himself by seeking a little attention elsewhere. When I went outside later to see him off I was about to say as much to him when he launched into a speech full of such lavish praise for my mother and such lavish regret that he had not visited the farm before that I was caught off my guard, and before I knew where I was I was promising to have a drink with him after work the next day in the bar of Charity's pub in St. Just.

"Marvelous!" said Jan-Yves with enthusiasm. "I'll be looking forward to it!" And swinging himself up onto his horse, he flashed his wide smile at me once again before riding jauntily off up the hillside to Chûn.

I watched him till he was out of sight. Despite my natural inclination to return friendship with friendship, I couldn't help thinking that Jan-Yves was after something much less innocuous than mere maternal love and filial affection.

I didn't trust him an inch.

[9]

But I saw Jan-Yves before I was due to meet him in the pub the following evening. I saw him the next morning at the one place on earth I wouldn't have expected to find any of my family —at the two-hundred-and-forty-fathom level of the Sennen Garth mine. It was a Friday morning and I had been with Trevose far out under the sea to inspect the blasting area and check the stopes. We were on our way back to the main shaft when we saw one of the shift bosses, Willie Halloran, coming toward us and with him, looking odd in some borrowed overalls, was Jan-Yves.

"Good God!" I said, amazed. "What the hell are you doing down here?" Part of my amazement was due to his guts in coming down the mine. Most laymen were wary of going so far below the earth's surface and did not care for the experience at all. "What is it?" I demanded. "Has something happened?"

"I'm afraid it has. I was sent to fetch you. Can I have a word with you alone for a moment?"

I stared at him. Beside me Trevose said, "I'll wait at the shaft for you, sonny" and walked away down the gallery with Willie Halloran. The light from their helmets flickered on the moist walls and cast ghostly shadows up and down the level.

"What is it?" I repeated sharply.

"It's Hugh."

"Hugh?"

We looked at each other. There was an odd expression in his eyes.

"Has something happened to him?"

"Yes, he had an accident. Swimming. He and Rebecca and the child were picnicking at Portheras Cove. He misjudged the current."

"You mean he—"

"He was drowned," said Jan-Yves and added with a grimace of pain, "Rebecca saw it all."

5

Geoffrey was fatally wounded in a tournament. . . .
> —King John,
> W. L. WARREN

When Richard announced publicly that this money, rightly his and unjustly detained by his father, would be used to strengthen the northern defences of Aquitaine, it seemed that open war between father and son must soon be waged with full vigour.
> —The Devil's Brood,
> ALFRED DUGGAN

This dramatic scene was the occasion for the last rebellion. . . . Undutiful as Richard's conduct certainly was, he had great provocation.
> —Oxford History of England:
> From Domesday Book to Magna Carta,
> A. L. POOLE

[1]

All I could say was "But Hugh was a good swimmer. He was always first-class at swimming."

Jan-Yves said "yes"—nothing more, just the one syllable, and after that we were silent.

Around us the mine was dark and comforting in its familiarity. I turned aside, stared down the gallery into the blackness.

"Rebecca wasn't swimming. She was paddling with the child. She heard Hugh cry out, but—"

"Be quiet." I turned and began to walk on down the gallery to the main shaft. "I don't want to hear about it."

He was silent again. His footsteps echoed behind me, and around us was my mine, Sennen Garth, the last working mine west of St. Just, the mine that had turned Hugh into my enemy and kept us estranged month after month, year after year.

We walked on, still not speaking, just Jan-Yves and I walking toward the land from beneath the Cornish sea.

At last I said, "Who sent you?"

"Papa."

"When did the news reach Penmarric?"

"About an hour ago. Jared Roslyn rode over himself and told William. I was with William at the time. We didn't know what to do. In the end William told Alice and Alice broke the news to Papa. Then Papa and William went over to Morvah in the car to see Rebecca and be with her when the police arrived. There'll have to be an inquest although God knows when they'll ever find the body."

I tried not to listen. I let my fingers trail against the rocky walls and timber props of my mine and tried not to think of the sea above me, the beckoning breakers, the lethal currents and the jagged teeth of the offshore rocks. People drowned every year in Cornwall. Strangers, holiday-makers, people who either knew nothing of the Cornish sea or who fancied they knew everything there was to know—they were the ones who got sucked to their deaths by whirling water and pounded to pulp on the waiting rocks. All you needed to get drowned in Cornwall was either total ignorance or total vanity. Either you didn't know the currents existed or else you thought you could outswim any current on God's earth.

Vanity. It didn't matter how much you enjoyed living, how successful you were at making money, how cleverly you had managed to survive a world war without a scratch; it didn't matter how much talent and charm and cunning you possessed; you could have a first-class brain and first-class good looks and enough potential to launch any career you chose, but one single moment of vanity could bring it all to nothing. A flash of vanity and you were gone, wiped out, blasted beyond recall.

"What a waste," I said to my mine, "what a bloody waste."

"What did you say?" said the boy behind me.

"Nothing."

I thought of Hugh all the way home, but I didn't think of those last years of estrangement. I thought of other better days, because they seemed more real to me than those times after we had quarreled. I wouldn't have quarreled with him if it hadn't been for my mine; or if I had I would have forgiven him long ago and patched up the friendship, because despite everything I had liked Hugh and he was the one brother whose company I had actively sought. I hadn't meant the mine to come between us. I hadn't meant it to happen that way.

I rode on over the moors, and around me the sun shone, the bracken swayed and the gorse was in bloom. When I reached the farm I broke the news to my mother as gently as I knew how, and afterward I sat with her and suffered her tears and tried as I had tried so often before to take my father's place at her side.

[2]

It was a month before they found the body. I had a moment of panic in case I was asked to identify it, but my father went to the morgue to make the identification and no one suggested that I should be present.

After that came the funeral.

There was no escape from that.

The funeral of an elderly person—Griselda, for example—is a mere ceremony, a gloomy ceremony certainly, but an experience which usually only grazes the emotions. When you're old you expect to die; you've had your life, lived it and no one can live forever. Death is inevitable, and its inevitability serves to numb the emotions. But the funeral of a young person is a totally different experience. The funeral of my own brother, dead in the prime of life just before his twenty-eighth birthday, was the worst ordeal I had ever endured on consecrated ground.

It was unspeakable.

Everyone was there. Mariana even came down from Scotland with her small son, and Jeanne left her convent in London. The service was at Zillan and the body was buried beside the graves of my grandfather Laurence Castallack and my eldest brother Stephen, who had died in infancy. The rector, now over eighty but ageless as ever, was very kind to my mother afterward and suggested that I take her home to rest as quickly as possible.

All my mother could say was "All my boys. All my beautiful boys." And she cried until her face was lined and old and exhausted and she looked every one of her sixty-six years.

"Well, you still have me," I said, thinking I was offering her consolation, but to my distress she began to weep more violently than ever.

"Oh, Philip, Philip . . ." I could hardly hear what she said, and suddenly I no longer wanted to hear what she said because the knives of memory were grinding in my brain, just as they always did when I saw her unhappy, and long-forgotten scenes were crawling out into the light from the darkest corners of my mind. I stood up, but as I moved she cried out, "Don't throw your life away too, don't lose your life in the mine—I couldn't bear it, Philip, if you were killed. I don't know what I'd do."

I saw her crying when I was taken away from her and sent to Allengate. I saw her crying at the townhouse in London during the ill-fated half-term weekend that had marked the beginning of the final rift between my parents. I saw her crying at—

My mind snapped shut.

"Mama . . ." My voice was speaking even before I had decided what to say. I was having to make such an effort to stay in the room that the sweat was breaking out on my forehead and every muscle in my body ached with tension. "Mama, listen— please . . . Nothing will ever happen to me in Sennen Garth. Nothing. It's my mine and I know. It won't kill me. I know and love it too well. You need never be afraid that I won't come home from the mine."

But she was not in the mood to believe me.

Later the rector called and after that she was better. I managed to persuade her to have an early night and also suggested she cancel an invitation she had made to Mariana to visit the farm next day, but she was longing so much to see her grandson Esmond that she refused to agree to such a cancellation. Privately I thought she was making a mistake. I went to bed depressed but found to my surprise the next day that Mariana's visit was a welcome opportunity to take my mind off the harrowing memories of the funeral. She arrived for morning coffee at eleven, and with her in my father's chauffeur-driven Rolls-Royce was my nephew Esmond. Her husband, as before, was in Scotland; this time he was recovering from a mild stroke and his health had not permitted him to attempt the long journey to Cornwall.

"Darling Archie," said Mariana, remembering him at last. "He was so sorry not to be able to come with me to Penmarric." Her glance flickered quickly over the farm parlor with her usual casual disdain. "He's longing to meet you, Mama—I wish you'd come up to Scotland to visit us sometime." She began to talk of her three homes, the townhouse in Edinburgh, her place by the sea at North Berwick, her mansion in the Highlands. "I just adore Scotland—honestly! I have so many absolutely divine friends in Edinburgh . . ." The divine friends all seemed to have masculine names. I looked closely at her. She was in her early thirties now but looked no older than twenty-five. I studied her hard Penmar mouth, cold eyes and bleakly perfect features and wondered how anyone so artificial could ever attract so many admirers.

"Philip," said my mother suddenly as I stifled a yawn, "why don't you show Esmond around the farm? I expect he'd like to see the animals."

"Oh!" cried Mariana before I had had time to look unenthusiastic. "What a lovely idea! Esmond darling, you'd love that, wouldn't you? Run along with Uncle Philip, there's a good boy, and make sure you behave yourself."

I wasn't interested in children. They bored me and I hadn't the patience for them. But I liked Esmond. There was no reason why I should, since he was the son of a sister I had never liked and of an elderly Scottish peer I had never met, but for the first time in my life I found a child who caught my attention and held it. At the start I did not intend to take him for more than a cursory tour of the farm, but he was so well-behaved and intelligent that I found myself smiling at his questions and taking trouble over my replies. He was still a few weeks short of his fifth birthday, but he was tall for his age, fair-haired and blue-eyed, and suddenly I saw myself in him so strongly that I understood why it was that men wanted sons and cared that there was someone to come after them when they themselves were gone.

I was thirty years old. It occurred to me for the first time that if I were to die tomorrow as Hugh had died I would leave behind nothing except a tombstone in Zillan churchyard, a few memories among the miners of Sennen Garth and a number of possessions in my bedroom at Roslyn Farm.

I knew I ought to marry, but the knowledge blunted my enthusiasm for a son and made me feel listless. There was no woman I wanted to marry. I had never been in love. I found the idea of marriage depressing and decided that it wouldn't hurt if I put it off for another five years or so. Why should I hurry to get married? I was happy enough as I was.

But Esmond had disturbed me. Long after I had waved goodbye to him I kept remembering his small bright face upturned to mine, and although it was some time before I saw him again the memory of his visit to the farm never entirely faded from my mind.

[3]

With the funeral over at last the memory of Hugh's death began to recede slowly and life reverted to a more normal pattern. Adrian returned to the Oxford parish where he had just become a curate; Lizzie returned to Cambridge, where she won a first in her final examinations and decided to stay on at Girton for further studies; and Jeanne stayed at Penmarric instead of going back to her convent. When questioned about her decision to leave the Order she would only say that while she had enjoyed the nursing she found she hadn't the vocation to be a nun.

"Thank goodness for that!" said my mother to me afterward. "Now perhaps if Jeanne bought herself some smart clothes and had her hair styled fashionably and made an effort to meet more people—"

But Jeanne had other ideas. She wanted to live quietly at Penmarric, take an interest in parish affairs and do some charity work.

"But Jeanne," said my mother, horrified, "that's all very well for a married woman, but it would be so dreary for a young unmarried girl."

"Then I'd like to be dreary, if you don't mind, Mama."

"But you'll never meet any men if you just—"

"It's no good simply meeting men, Mama, one has to attract them as well. I found that out when I was in Scotland with Mariana. And I'm not attractive to men."

"Fiddlesticks!" said my mother angrily. "Absolute nonsense! Any girl can attract a man if she wants to. It's simply an attitude of mind."

"It's an attitude I don't possess, then," said Jeanne, nearly in tears, and ran out of the room before anything more could be said.

"Poor Jeanne!" said Jan-Yves to me later when the women were washing the dishes and we were alone. "But she's quite right, of course. She's not attractive to men. Lizzie's ten times more attractive than Jeanne, if you ask me, but Mama's never going to believe that because Jeanne is technically pretty and Lizzie isn't technically anything except plain and plump."

Jan-Yves was often at the farm those days. I did not resent his presence—on the contrary, I was glad he had stepped forward to fill the void Hugh's death had created for my mother—but I still distrusted him. He showered my mother with presents, which was all very commendable, but I often wondered what it was he was trying to buy. I wondered too where he got the money to pursue this present-giving policy and suspected he had Hugh's talent for doubling a small income by various questionable ways and means.

Hugh's posthumous son was born during the first week of 1926. There was some ridiculous controversy over his name in which I had no intention of involving myself, and my mother and Rebecca refused to speak to each other after Rebecca had omitted to invite us to the christening. After that there was open warfare between them, but as in all feminine quarrels it was no more than a storm in a teacup with emotions running absurdly high on both sides.

I had other more important matters on my mind to spend much time thinking of my nephew Jonas.

The mine was in deep trouble again. Walter Hubert was fending off creditors, the men were seeking higher wages to meet the rising cost of living, and I needed more money to open up a new level and buy new equipment.

"We've got to get another loan," I said. "We must."

But Walter shook his head. "This is a bad time for raising capital, Philip. The postwar prosperity boom is being affected by the rise in unemployment; the economic climate is getting more and more uncertain and money's tight. Ask Mr. Vincent or your father, by all means, but I doubt if we're in a position to issue more shares, and if we take out a third loan on top of the two we already have I think you'll find yourself in very real trouble before long."

"But I've got to have the money!" I thought about it day and night. I was just discussing the subject with Walter for the umpteenth time when my father astonished me by turning up at the mine and asking for an audience.

I was desperate by this time, and this visit from my father made me more desperate than ever. I was afraid he was going to suggest cutting our losses and closing the mine, and I was right. He did. He put it well and his mild manner was calculated not to give offense, but that was what he wanted. He was suggesting a halt—"Temporarily," he said, "until the economic situation improves"—but I knew him too well to believe that. Once he had that mine closed no one would ever get him to open it again.

Presently all the machinery and equipment would be sold to pay the debts and the levels would be finished, flooded, forgotten.

I began to plead with him. It went against the grain and I was humiliated, but I would have gone on my knees and crawled a hundred miles for that mine, so I gritted my teeth and pleaded as well as I could. To do him credit, he did listen. He kept telling me I was fighting a losing battle, but he did listen, and in the end he did write the check the mine needed so desperately and I knew I'd won.

But it was only a reprieve.

"Now listen to me," he said in his coolest voice as he handed me the check. "That's the last penny you'll ever get out of me for the mine. Do you understand? The very last. And if that mine doesn't show a profit by the end of 1926 I'm closing it. Is that understood?"

"Yes, sir," I said, hardly listening, my fingers caressing the slip of paper in my hands. "Thank you, sir. You won't regret this."

"Won't I?" he said. "I fully expect to. Good day, Philip. I'll not trespass any longer on your valuable time. I'm sure the mine needs you more than I do."

And he walked out of the hut, slammed the door behind him and stumped angrily off across the yard, but I was too excited by my hard-won victory to pay attention to his sourness.

I spent every penny of the money. I organized the development of the new level and the working of the new lode. I gave the men new pep talks about how vital it was that we should bring to the surface every scrap of tin we could lay our hands on. I worked all day with them far out under the sea, worked until I barely had the energy to come home at night and roll into bed; I toiled at that mine with every ounce of strength I possessed as if I could inject my own vitality into its tired old veins, but my efforts were all for nothing.

For 1926 was the year of the General Strike; 1926 was the year all industry dependent on coal suffered a blow below the belt. Even before the year was over I knew that Sennen Garth was bankrupt and that its working life had once more come to an end.

[4]

The General Strike lasted for only nine days in May, but the coal miners' strike, the original cause of the great disruption, lasted another six months. I was torn two ways by what was happening. On the one hand I was behind the miners, who lived on a pittance that could not possibly have enabled them to live decently, but on the other hand I knew a rise in the coal miners' wages would eventually mean additional demands from my own men, which Sennen Garth could hardly afford to meet. But gradually as the months passed I no longer had any choice except to condemn the strike. The shortage of coal affected Sennen Garth's output until finally there was no fuel to feed to the furnaces and all activities above and below the surface ground to a halt.

Incoming monies were reduced to a trickle and finally ceased completely. Outgoing monies mostly in the form of wages roared on. And still there was no sign of the coal miners ending their strike and turning the lethal tide of economic disaster.

Finally in September my father called an extraordinary meeting at Penmarric for all those who were in any way connected with the administration of the mine. It wasn't technically a shareholders' meeting, although there were shareholders present, but since my father controlled the majority of the shares no one doubted that the outcome of the meeting would be the outcome of any formal meeting of shareholders that convened later to discuss the situation. The purpose of this prior meeting was to give those who were most intimately concerned with the mine the chance to formulate a clear policy for the mine's future—assuming, of course, that the mine had a future, and I was damned sure that was more than most people were willing to assume.

At the meeting presided over by my father were Michael Vincent, the company's solicitor, Stanford Blake, the senior partner in the firm of accountants who audited the company's books, Walter Hubert the purser, and Sir Justin Carnforth, who, like my father, had a substantial financial interest in the mine. With me when I arrived at Penmarric to confront this unpromising gathering were Jared Roslyn, who had long been famous for championing the causes of the working men of the district, and, since he had almost as much say in Sennen Garth's affairs as I did, Alun Trevose.

Both of them were pessimistic.

"Face up to it, sonny," said Trevose. "We'll never talk your dad out of this one."

"I know your father," said Jared grimly. "Stubborn as a dozen mules. If he's made up his mind to close that mine neither you nor I nor anyone else is going to persuade him to keep it open."

"We'll see," I said. That was all I would say. "We'll see."

I didn't intend to let my father get the better of me either now or at any other time.

But I had to admit he was clever. He conducted the meeting in a formal, businesslike manner which allowed no room for loud expressions of disagreement. First of all he summed up the financial plight of the mine and called on Blake and Walter Hubert to verify this. Then he spoke of creditors; Michael Vincent was asked to explain the legal position of bankruptcy. Finally he spoke of the possibility of raising more money; to issue more shares, even to float an issue of preference shares for the existing shareholders, would be a risky venture which would probably result in—at best—a mere postponement of the inevitable. My father then said he himself was not inclined to invest a penny more in the mine, and Sir Justin Carnforth agreed with him and said he wouldn't recommend the other shareholders to invest more money in the venture either. Walter Hubert said he had already explored the possibility of a loan from the banks, but loans were difficult to obtain at that time and the mine's present position was considered insufficient to constitute collateral.

Having pointed out that Sennen Garth was broke and that no one was going to lift a finger to save it, my father then said he thought it must be my turn to speak. Did either of my associates care to make any comment on the situation? Perhaps Mr. Trevose would like to speak first.

It was typical of my father's cunning that he should have chosen Trevose, the least experienced of negotiators, to speak first.

"Well, sir," said Trevose rapidly in the nasal accent he had acquired as a child on the Rand, "all I can say is that it's a fact that that mine's still honest-to-God rich—there's plenty of tin left down there under the sea, and under normal conditions—"

"But these are hardly normal conditions, would you say, Mr. Trevose? A lot of tin beneath the sea is no use to us if we can't afford to bring it to the surface."

"What he means, Mr. Castallack," said Jared swiftly, "is that under normal circumstances the mine would have made a fine profit for you, and there's no doubt that when things get back to normal and the Labour Party returns to power to put the country right . . ." He allowed himself a purple passage of Socialist propaganda before steering his way back to the mine and painting a dramatic picture of the poverty and suffering which would overtake the miners and their families if Sennen Garth closed down. Twenty years' experience as a lay preacher had sharpened Jared's inborn flair for rhetoric; he had no qualms about extracting every ounce of melodrama from the situation and flaunting it in a thunderous voice before his audience. By the time he had finished I almost had tears in my eyes myself for the starving little children who cried for a crust of bread while my father dined off the fat of the land at Penmarric.

But of course my father was interested neither in Socialist propaganda nor in the brand of demagoguism in which Jared excelled. All he was really interested in was his money, which was, as far as he was concerned, tied up in a bad business investment, and at last he interrupted Jared as politely as possible in order to make this clear.

All Jared could say in resignation was "So you're determined to close the mine."

"After a formal meeting of the shareholders, yes, I'm afraid I see no alternative."

There was a silence. We sat there around that long table with the light from the chandeliers playing harsh tricks on aging faces, and the silence went on and on and on until I thought it would never break. I waited. Everyone waited, but finally one by one they all turned to look at me, and I knew that the time was right and that I could put off the moment no longer. The silence was almost audible now. I seemed to hear it humming in my ears.

I said to my father, taking care not to speak too loudly, "If you close that mine I'll break you."

There was nothing then, just he and I facing each other as we had faced each other so often in the past, and between us like a death's-head lay the gigantic shadow of my mine, Sennen Garth, the last working mine west of St. Just.

He went white, but from anger, not from alarm. He was furious that I had embarrassed him before his friends and revealed our hostility so blatantly before Jared and Trevose. At last he managed to say, "You leave me to assume, therefore, that you have no useful comment to make in regard to my decision."

"Only that I mean what I say. Close that mine and I'll make you regret it. That's all." I stood up. "Jared," I said. "Trevose. There's nothing more to be said." And I turned without another word and walked out of the room.

6

*It is impossible to know what the Old King was up to
with Alice. She may have been his mistress, as most
contemporaries believed. . . .*

—The Devil's Brood,
ALFRED DUGGAN

*The King and Richard played out the last act of
Henry's tragedy. . . .*

—Henry II,
JOHN T. APPLEBY

[1]

I knew exactly what I was going to do.

I had had the plan in my mind for a long time, and when the
matrimonial laws had been changed the previous year I had
known it was a plan which I could put into operation whenever
I chose. Now at last a woman could divorce her husband on the
ground solely of adultery; and since I knew my mother would
always do all she could to help me I knew too that I could place
my father in an awkward and difficult position—if only I took
the time and trouble to lay my plans correctly.

For I was wary. I could remember that other time twelve
years ago before the war when we had threatened my father
with such ignominious results, and I had no wish to make the

same mistake twice. It was no good accusing him of adultery without some form of proof that he was misconducting himself, but Jan-Yves had often told me he would swear on the Bible that Alice was my father's mistress and I thought it would hardly be difficult to get the proof I needed from him.

However, to my disgust I found this was harder than I expected. When I managed to have a conference with him the next day in my office it soon became clear he had no evidence whatsoever for assuming Alice and my father were having an affair.

"It was only a guess," he was driven to confess at last. "I don't know anything positive. Nobody does. Nobody knows the truth—"

"But you told me you were convinced it was true!" I shouted at him, and then clamped down on my anger. "Well, I believe it's true anyway," I said flatly, "and so would any lawyer if the facts were presented to him in the right way. If you could testify to Mama's solicitor that you've seen Alice and Father—"

"I'm not testifying anything!" He was white with fright. "I'm not standing up in a court of law and giving evidence against my own father! Do it yourself!"

"Don't be a bloody fool," I said, exasperated. "It'll never get to court! All I want is enough evidence to enable Mama's lawyers to get as far as serving a petition—if such a move proves necessary. It may not even be necessary to go that far. I'm going to write him an ultimatum first of all and see how he responds to that. But if that doesn't work I'll go to the solicitors in St. Ives who handle the St. Enedocs' affairs and show Father that I mean what I say."

"But suppose there's nothing between him and Alice?"

"He'd have to drag her through the dirt trying to prove it. No, he'll never let the case get beyond the preliminary stages, but I still need your help to get the plan moving."

He looked at me. The small pink tip of his tongue slid around his lips. He had an expression of strained calculation on his face as if he were involved in some fantastically complicated gamble. At last he said slowly, "I don't think I could risk it. If Papa found out he'd disinherit me." He glanced up at me with his sharp little eyes. "You'd have to make it worth my while financially, otherwise I might lose out all along the line."

I suppose my contempt must have shown in my face, for the next moment he burst out passionately, "No, I won't take a penny of your damned money! Nobody's going to accuse me of selling my own father for gain! I'll do what you want but I won't take a penny for it. I'm not disloyal."

Personally I failed to see how he could have been more disloyal and thought the question of the money utterly irrelevant, but I wasn't going to bother to understand his tortuous line of reasoning. I had guessed that the rift existing between him and my father since his dismissal from Oxford had never fully healed, so I was prepared for his behavior, but I was still disgusted. It was then that I made up my mind about him after my years of indifferent distrust; to me he was a mere overgrown schoolboy who continued to cling to a juvenile talent for mischief, a worthless individual too shiftless to be trusted and too futile to be taken seriously. He was obviously another Hugh with no purpose in life except to acquire easy money. Yet he hadn't Hugh's charm or maturity or able brain. Hugh, I felt, had had redeeming qualities. This ugly, cowardly, disloyal, hypocritical, avaricious, sly, stupid lout had none at all.

I despised him. Suddenly incredulous that he could ever have been held in esteem by my father, I said as an afterthought, "Are you really Father's heir? Has he really made his will in your favor?"

He looked at me swiftly as if he were suspicious, then gave a quick shrug of his shoulders. "To be frank, I haven't actually seen the will. But who else can he choose now that Marcus and Hugh are dead and you're more estranged from him than you ever were before? He won't give it to the bastards. William told me Adrian wouldn't accept anything except a token legacy anyway and that both of them had been told more than once that they must always expect to earn their living."

I turned abruptly, went to the window, stared at the sea. I was imagining myself trying to work with Jan-Yves over the mine, having to ask him for money, struggling with him as I had had to struggle with my father. Revulsion swept over me again, a disgust mingled with anger that there should be so little justice in the world. I couldn't understand how anyone could believe there was a God. The world was so corrupt, so obviously condemned to perpetual injustice.

"Adrian arrives home today for a visit," said Jan-Yves nervously, fumbling with the door handle. "You're not going to deliver that ultimatum just yet, are you? I'm sure Adrian will think I had something to do with it."

He was even scared of Adrian. My patience snapped. "Oh, for

God's sake get out," I said wearily. "We've said all there is to say anyway."

"But the ultimatum—"

"That's my concern, not yours."

"All right," he muttered and slipped out of the door as fast as his legs could carry him.

I watched him until he had disappeared from sight and then turned back into my office with a grimace. I didn't trust him to be any more loyal to me than he had been to my father, and I couldn't help feeling he would be a highly unreliable witness if his talent for perjury were ever put to the test in court.

[2]

To my surprise my mother had grave misgivings about my plan, and although she agreed to do what I wanted she remained doubtful of the plan's success.

"I'm sure Mark would never misbehave with Alice," she said. "She's not at all the sort of woman who would attract him and besides she's the granddaughter of Mr. Barnwell, one of his oldest, most respected friends. . . . Yes, I know Rose Parrish was from a similar sort of background, but I can hardly believe Mark would make such a fool of himself twice! As for Alice, well, I wouldn't be surprised if she had her eye on being mistress of Penmarric one day—after all, she's given ten years of her youth to that house; surely she must regard it as some sort of investment! —but I think marriage would be what she had in mind, not an affair."

But I was not convinced. Privately I thought that my mother's deep sense of propriety made it impossible for her to see the situation in its true perspective, and that same night after she had gone to bed I sat down at the kitchen table and wrote the ultimatum. It took some time and several drafts but in the end I felt I had said all that I wanted to say. When it was completed I read it through again.

"Sir," I had written. "This is to inform you that my mother has a strong desire to avail herself of the new remedies arising from the recent innovations in the field of matrimonial law. Neither she nor I wish to institute what may prove to be some exceptionally sordid legal proceedings, but unless you mend your ways and revise certain regrettable opinions which you hold on a matter which I need not trouble to name to you, you may expect to be the defendant in a petition for divorce on the grounds that you have been committing adultery with Alice Penmar. In case you think this is a mere idle threat which cannot be substantiated, I must tell you that I have sufficient evidence of adultery to justify my mother initiating the petition through her solicitors. In case you think too that this would be a quiet divorce with the details kept to a minimum I assure you that it won't be anything of the kind. You got off lightly with Rose Parrish. This time you won't. Bearing in mind the shame and humiliation and pain you've caused my mother in the past I don't think you can possibly term as unjustified any attempt she may make to obtain a divorce from you now and enable you to taste a fraction of the suffering she has had to endure since you married her in 1890. Unless I hear favorably from you my mother will consult her lawyers a week from the day you receive this letter. I remain unfortunately, sir, your son, Philip Castallack."

After reading the letter for the final time I decided that it would serve its purpose, so I put it in an envelope and sealed the flap. Then I went to bed and snatched what sleep I could before dawn.

It was after nine when I arrived at Penmarric to deliver the letter, and the house lay quietly in the September sunlight as I rode up the drive. The lawns were white with a premature frost and the flowers were pinched after the chill of the night. Leaving my horse with a groom, I went up to the front door and rang the bell.

One of the footmen opened the door, but the butler was in the hall almost before I had crossed the threshold.

"Good morning, Medlyn," I said. "Is my father in the dining room?"

"He's not up yet, Mr. Philip. He wasn't feeling so well this morning. Is there a message?"

I hesitated, fingering the envelope in my pocket, and as I paused by the front door a well-remembered voice called out, surprised, "Good morning, Philip! Isn't it rather early for social calls?"

A shadow fell across the wall below the first Penmar portrait; the next moment my half-brother Adrian Parrish, looking unclerical in a pullover and slacks, was strolling down the stairs toward me.

We looked at each other, and as I looked into his eyes I saw back into the past. Hatred gripped me like a vise and made me wooden.

"How are you?" I said. "I suppose you're doing well."

"Well enough, thanks," he said. "Life's treating me kindly at the moment."

That was no surprise. Life had always treated him kindly. Probably half my resentment of him sprang from the fact that life had treated him a damned sight better than it had ever treated me.

The injustice of the world sneered at me again. I turned aside, taking the letter from my pocket.

"Give this to Father, would you?" I said, holding it out to him. "With my compliments."

Before he could reply I was on my way outside to fetch my horse.

[3]

Jan-Yves was in my office when I reached the mine. He had overheard the scene in the hall with Adrian and had immediately run out of the house, taken the short cut along the cliffs and reached my office seconds before my arrival. It turned out that he had had second thoughts about the entire scheme. He was sorry but he really didn't think he could go through with it.

"You bloody—!" I yelled at him, falling back on Trevose's vocabulary in my rage. "Can't you make up your mind about anything? You're not even worth the shirt on your own back! Are you such a bloody coward that you can't even stick to a decision once you've made it? You sicken me! I wish to God I'd never bothered with you!"

"And I wish to God I'd never got involved with you and your damned mine!" he yelled back at me. "Don't you dare call me names and tell me I'm not worth the shirt on my own back! What kind of a man do you think you are anyway? No, don't tell me how wonderful you are to your mother and what a hero you are at the mine! Don't tell me what an outstanding example you are to the community! My God, to think you have the nerve to say *I* sicken *you*—why, however much I sicken you it's nothing compared to how much you sicken me! You make me want to vomit!"

I hit him, not hard, just enough to knock him over and make the room spin a little before his eyes. He shook himself, recovered his balance, scrambled to his feet.

"Get out," I said.

His eyes were empty. He rubbed the place on his jaw where I had hit him and watched me with those empty black eyes. I had cut open his lower lip; I had to suppress a shudder as the blood trickled down his chin.

"You'll regret that one day," he said. "I have a long memory. You'd be surprised if you knew how long it is. I don't forget easily."

I stepped forward, crowding him, but he turned without hurrying and pushed open the door. Cool air from the yard outside fanned my cheeks. Beyond Jan-Yves I could see across the slag-heaps and along the coast to Penmarric.

He stepped outside. I was just about to slam the door after him when I saw him freeze and whirl to face me.

"Adrian's coming," he said.

[4]

Miners working underground can sometimes hear a disaster even before it reaches them. If water floods the galleries above them the air is trapped and the pressure rises in their own gallery until the men can hear a high-pitched ringing in their ears. If your ears begin to ring, that's the time to get out and to get out as fast as you can because that's disaster time and by the time the noise stops you may not be alive to hear the silence.

I wasn't underground, but I felt as if I were. I stood there high on the Cornish cliffs on that cold September morning and my miner's sixth sense told me it was disaster time and I seemed to hear that high-pitched ringing in my ears telling me to escape.

But there was no escape. Not this time. This time I was trapped.

I turned my back on the doorway. "He probably wants you," I said to Jan-Yves, "not me."

I rustled some papers on my desk, tried to find a cigarette. When I next looked up Jan-Yves was back in my office and closing the door behind him. "Something's happened," he said, frightened. "I don't want to see him. I don't want to see anybody from Penmarric."

"Pull yourself together, for Christ's sake." I found a cigarette, lit it. I wanted to turn him out but my strength had deserted me and we stood there, the two of us, six feet apart, and waited in silence for what was to come.

We went on waiting. I was just wondering how he could possibly be taking so long when I heard the clatter of his horse's hoofs in the yard and the next moment the ring of his riding boots on the old granite paving stones as he walked up to the hut.

"Oh God," said Jan-Yves violently, and as if he could not bear the strain of waiting a moment longer he reached out and pulled open the door.

Adrian was on the threshold, but Adrian didn't see him. Adrian saw no one except me. Adrian brushed aside Jan-Yves much as one would brush aside a troublesome fly and took two long paces toward me until we were inches apart from each other in that small, quiet room.

"You've killed him," he said to me. His voice shook. His blue eyes brilliant with hatred blazed into mine. "You bloody murderer, I hope you rot in hell."

[5]

There was a long, long silence. And then at last I realized Adrian was speaking again, this time in a lower, more even voice.

"Papa received your letter," I heard him say flatly. "He opened it and read it. I was there. I saw him. When he had the stroke a few seconds afterward I was able to raise the alarm and get help immediately, but even then it was too late." He swung around on Jan-Yves. "I suppose you were in this with Philip."

"I . . ." Jan-Yves was trembling. Tears ran down his cheeks and transformed him into a child again. "I didn't mean it, I didn't want anyone to know, please don't tell anyone—"

"My God, your father's just died and all you can do is worry about what everyone will think of you! To hell with you both." He walked out of the hut into the yard but then paused to look back at me. "And if you so much as set one foot inside Penmarric, Philip, I swear I'll—"

"You're swearing rather a lot for a clergyman," I said, "aren't you?"

That was all I said. I stood there and watched him turn his

back on me and vault into his horse's saddle and all I said was "You're swearing rather a lot for a clergyman."

Jan-Yves started to cry again. Leaving him alone with his histrionic self-pity, I walked out of my office and went down the mine. I went to the old shaft I had explored as a child and climbed down into the honeycombed workings of the western reaches. I worked my way down from level to level, picking my way in and out of that tangled labyrinth which bordered King Walloe, and as I walked I thought to myself: My mine, Sennen Garth, the last working mine west of St. Just. My cause. My life's work.

The words went round and round in my brain and meant nothing because after all they were only words, and words don't mean anything, not really, and all the angry words I had ever addressed to my father had no meaning except that they were spoken because of the mine. Everything I did was because of the mine, because I *was* the mine, because I loved it and it meant something to me, just as music speaks to a musician and paint to an artist. He had had no more right to close that mine than any man has a right to tear up a manuscript or deface a painting. But he hadn't understood, he had never understood, and suddenly I wanted him to understand, I longed for his understanding, I thought: If only he could have understood we could have begun again; I didn't mean to hurt him; I didn't want him to die.

I was at sea level. I found one of the adits, waded through a pool of water and walked out through the cave at the foot of the cliff. The tide was coming in. Surf burst against the rocks of the cove and thundered on the sand. I turned, blinded by spray, found the cliff path and began the long climb up to the engine house. A squall was sweeping in from the sea as I walked to the village to collect my horse from the inn and ride up into the hills to Chûn. The castle walls were wet with rain and the wind was cold as it whipped along the ridge. Shivering, I flicked the horse's reins and headed him downhill to the farm.

When I arrived I found my mother alone in the kitchen as she cleaned the brass.

"Philip!" She dropped an ornament in her surprise and didn't even stoop to pick it up. "What's happened? What is it? Why are you home at this hour?"

I said abruptly without stopping to think, "Father's dead. He had a stroke and died earlier this morning."

I was just in time to catch her as she fainted.

When she had recovered consciousness I carried her up to her room and gave her some brandy. At last I managed to say, distressed, cursing myself for my stupidity, "I'm sorry—please forgive me. I didn't realize the news would affect you so much after all this time."

"Why should you have realized?" She had mastered her tears and was brushing them away. "I never said anything." After a moment she added, glancing at the mantelshelf, "That funny little clock, ticking my life away . . . 'What an incredibly ugly clock,' he said. 'I suppose it was your husband's.' He didn't like the clock. We laughed about it afterward, but I never told him where it came from. I can see him still . . . He was only twenty-one. He wore black because Laurence had died. He looked well in black. People said he was plain but he never seemed plain to me, not when I knew him better. I had everything then, everything a woman could ever want, and I threw it all away."

"But, Mama—"

" 'Some women never change,' he said, but oh, I could have changed! If only I could have understood before, but I never understood until we quarreled and after we quarreled it was too late. If Brighton hadn't happened—"

I fumbled with the catch on the window, but it was stuck. I started to wrestle with it, shaking the frame.

"—I think I could still have got him back, but after Brighton I hated him even more than I loved him and there was no going back from that."

The window flew open. I leaned out over the sill but I could still hear her voice.

"I couldn't forget Brighton," she said. "That was the whole trouble. I couldn't forget Brighton."

I left the window and made for the door. "Mama, I'm going to Zillan to fetch the rector. I think he ought to be with you." I gave her no chance to argue with me. Running out to the stables, I saddled my horse again, and five minutes later I was riding as hard as I could across the moors toward the village where my parents had first seen each other in the churchyard on one summer afternoon long ago.

Later after the rector had gone my mother said she wanted to see the body. I would have given much to avoid going to Penmarric, but since it was my duty to take her I got out the ponytrap in the afternoon and drove her to St. Just.

The last thing I wanted to do was to see the body in the Tower Room, but my mother shrank from being alone, so I went with her up the wide staircase and along the gallery and corridor. And with each step I took I found I was consumed with the most primitive of fears, fear of death, fear of guilt, fear of terrible dark emotions which I could not name. I felt that if I saw the body I would vomit, but because I could not allow my fears to get the better of me I followed my mother into the Tower Room and forced myself to look down at my father's corpse.

I looked upon his face. But suddenly the only face I could see was Jan-Yves's face, so like my father's, Jan-Yves as he had been that morning with the blood running from his cut lip, Jan-Yves saying, "You'll pay for that one day," in my father's voice. Then all I could see was the blood, the blood running from his mouth until it seemed that the corpse itself was bleeding, and I felt the room begin to tilt beneath my feet. I groped my way out into the corridor and leaned against the wall. When my vision cleared I saw with a shock that I was no longer alone; Adrian was there, watching me, and as soon as I saw him I was able to straighten my back, close the door and flick the sweat from my forehead.

"I heard you were here," he said, "and I thought I should tell you that I've been making the necessary arrangements. Jan-Yves, of course, is quite incapable of organizing anything." Our glances met; I could see he despised Jan-Yves as much as I did. "I intend to ask Mr. Barnwell to hold the funeral at Zillan. Papa always said he wanted to be buried there with his father, and I don't think the vicar of St. Just will take it amiss."

I nodded without speaking and began to move away down the corridor.

"Oh, by the way," said Adrian in a voice of steel. "No one knows what was in that letter except you and me. Everyone knows there was a letter but I merely said you had threatened him about the mine. I didn't think it would serve any useful purpose to reveal the contents—not because the letter reflected badly on him but because it reflected so appallingly badly on you. I burned it. I trust I did the right thing."

I didn't answer. There was nothing I could have said except "thank you" and I couldn't even say that. I walked away, and as I stumbled down the stairs to the hall I thought that never during all my stormy visits to Penmarric to see my father had I felt so humiliated by him as I felt then when he reached out from beyond the grave and shamed me before the brother I despised.

[8]

I had no wish to go to the funeral, but of course I had to go. It was irrelevant that I detested funerals and in this case felt no grief for the corpse in the coffin. I was the elder of my father's two surviving legitimate sons, and I had to be there not only because convention demanded it but because my mother would need my support at such a distressing time. She even said to me beforehand, "I'm so glad you'll be with me at the funeral, Philip," and after that there was nothing I could do to avoid the ordeal which lay ahead.

So I put on my black suit and black tie and took her to Zillan. Everyone was there, county names from all over Cornwall and from beyond the Tamar, representatives from London, from Oxford, people I had never met, and the humble people were there too; all my father's tenants had walked over from St. Just, all the servants from Penmarric, even the Roslyns had come over the hills from Morvah. The church was overflowing with people and the graveyard was full of people and everywhere there were flowers, enormous wreaths, lush bouquets, even small bunches of wildflowers, all perfumed and beautiful and dying, and their fragrance filled the church and lingered on the still September air.

There were newspaper reporters, a correspondent from *The Times* who wanted to know about his work, and I had nothing to say to any of them. I could only say, "I'm not a historian. I know nothing about it," and what I was really saying was "We were estranged. His work meant no more to me than my work meant to him," but nobody realized that, no stranger realized what had passed between us. His publishers shook me by the hand and said how sorry they were, and I was dumb; I had nothing to say. "What a delightful man he was," said his friends at

Oxford. "He'll be very sadly missed." And: "He was good to his tenants," said a farmer. "And to his servants," said Young Medlyn, and the cook said, "He was kind."

I listened to them, but it was as if they were talking of a stranger. I tried to remember him being kind and delightful but I couldn't; all I could remember was my voice saying clearly in the dining room at Penmarric, "If you close that mine, I'll break you."

And he had died.

I had to face everyone, all the mourners, and worst of all I had to face the men who had heard me speak those words to him at Penmarric—Sir Justin Carnforth, cold and barely polite; Walter Hubert, silent with discomfort; Michael Vincent, trying so hard to be civil; Stanford Blake, rigid with dislike. Even when I had finished facing them I still had to face my family, and my family treated me as if I didn't exist.

Mariana said, "Mama darling—how terrible this must be for you" and took care to see her back was turned in my direction.

Jeanne said, "Mama . . ." and then was overcome with tears as she caught sight of me.

Elizabeth stayed with Jan-Yves and kept her distance. The Parrishes were with Alice Penmar and took care that I was never too close to them. Alice's face looked white and pinched and there were dark circles beneath her eyes; she looked ill and full of grief.

From behind me the rector's voice said, "I trust you're going to Penmarric now, Philip. Would you care to travel in the car Adrian has hired for me? I'm not used to motoring and would be grateful for your company."

I said, not looking at him, "I have to take my mother home."

"Oh no," he said. "That's all arranged—I've just been talking to your mother. The Turner girls will see her home and at a time like this she'll be much better with women around her. And naturally you'll want to go to Penmarric to be with the rest of your family for a short while. I believe there's a small cold luncheon."

I shook my head. "No," I said. "No." I couldn't say anything else. "No, I can't go."

"I think you should. There are some obligations no man can remove from you."

I looked at him. His face was old, his body frail but his eyes were young. His eyes never changed. I looked into those eyes and saw he knew everything, even that I wanted to escape, yet still he was asking me to go to Penmarric as if my father and I hadn't been estranged.

"They expect you to go," he said. "I think you should."

The chauffeurs were drawing up the cars at the lych-gate. I said unevenly, "Very well. If I must," and we walked together down the path away from the church.

We passed the journey in silence. The car made heavy weather of the hills and the engine roared laboriously as the chauffeur steered us over the moors to St. Just.

We were the last to arrive.

"Where is everyone?" I said nervously. "Where have they all gone?"

"I think they'll be in the drawing room. Michael Vincent was going to read the will." His hand was on my arm. He had surprisingly strong fingers. "You'll want to hear, of course, what provision has been made for your mother."

"Oh yes," I said blankly. "Yes, of course." It hadn't occurred to me. When I followed him into the drawing room I found to my discomfort that all my family were assembled and the meeting had been delayed until my arrival.

Nobody spoke to me. There was a vacant chair by the fireplace, but when I turned to offer it to the rector I found he was already seated next to Alice.

I sat down uneasily.

"Now," said my father's lawyer and oldest friend Michael Vincent, "I think we can begin." He had the will in his hands, and as he spoke he opened it up and prepared to read from the beginning.

I had a craving for a cigarette. I began to fumble in my pockets for the packet I had with me and hoped none of the women in the room would mind if I smoked.

". . . last will and testament . . ." Vincent's voice was clear and incisive. Everyone was still.

". . . hereby bequeath . . ."

I struck a match.

". . . following legacies to my children and grandchildren: To my daughter Mariana, Marchioness of Lochlyall . . . To her son Esmond, Earl of Roane . . ."

Mariana and Esmond already had more than enough money of

482

their own; my father's legacies to them were small, a token gesture of affection.

". . . to the children of my deceased son Hugh . . ."

Two more token legacies followed to Deborah and Jonas. The tokens were more generous this time.

"To my daughters Jeanne Castallack and Elizabeth Castallack, to ensure that they will be provided for should they not wish to marry . . ."

The legacies were no longer token. I glanced at Jan-Yves. He was chalk-white, his eyes black as pitch.

". . . to my daughter-in-law Rebecca Castallack for as long as she shall remain a widow . . ."

I wondered what Hugh would have thought of that. Personally I thought my father had been more than generous to Rebecca in granting her any income however small.

". . . to my wife Janna Castallack, to ensure that she receives the same income after my death . . ."

I sighed in relief.

". . . following legacies to the sons of Rose Parrish: to William Parrish in token of all he has done to help me in the administration of the estate of Penmarric . . . to Adrian Parrish to assist him in the pursuance of his vocation . . ."

So my father had kept his word after all about the Parrishes. No large legacies, just a fair-sized gift. My cigarette went out and I had to strike another match.

". . . following legacies to my servants: to my housekeeper Alice Penmar with many grateful thanks . . ."

It was a good legacy for a housekeeper, a poor one for a mistress. In any event it was calculated not to give rise to unfortunate comment.

". . . to my butler James Medlyn . . ."

Every servant was remembered, right down to the scullery maid. The list seemed interminable.

Vincent cleared his throat and turned yet another of the pages.

"After payment of all the above legacies and bequests . . . after payment of all taxes . . ."

This was it. I glanced at Jan-Yves again. He was the only one who hadn't been mentioned so far.

". . . all that part and parcel of land known as Penmarric in the parish of St. Just-in-Penwith in the Duchy of Cornwall . . ."

The legal phrases droned on remorselessly.

". . . the house . . . all my personal chattels in the house with the exception of my papers, writings, articles, manuscripts . . ."

It was endless.

". . . and the mine known as Sennen Garth . . ."

My mine. Sennen Garth. The last working mine west of St. Just. My mine left to a worthless lout I despised.

". . . including all rents, profits . . ."

My mine, I thought, my mine. My cause. My life's work.

"I hereby devise and bequeath . . ."

He stopped.

There was utter silence. Then:

". . . to my son Philip Castallack," said Michael Vincent and looked me straight in the eyes.

7

*Why did Richard and the Old King always get on so
badly? In many ways their characters were alike. . . .*
                                         —The Devil's Brood,
                                              ALFRED DUGGAN

*Richard was crowned king on 3 September 1189 in
Westminster Abbey. . . . He was anxious to be off on
the exciting adventure of a crusade. Already before he
was crowned he had ordered a muster of ships.*
                                         —King John,
                                              W. L. WARREN

[1]

". . . on trust for life," said Vincent, still looking at me, "and on
his death to . . ."

He was saying something about how the estate would pass to
my son when I died, or if I had no son either to Jonas or to Jan-
Yves as I should appoint by will. But I didn't really hear him. I
didn't hear anything. All I knew was his voice saying, " 'To my
son Philip Castallack,' " my head ringing with those legal phrases,
my mind not understanding, not even trying to understand, only
trying to accept that it was mine—on trust but mine—mine for life,
for as long as there was breath in my body, for as long as I
could wake each morning and look upon the Cornish moors. All
the residue of the Castallack fortune, every brick of Penmarric,

every square inch of ground within the boundary walls, every fathom of the Sennen Garth mine. The tenant farms, the rows of cottages in St. Just, the black cliffs, the golden sands. The rhododendrons and the hydrangeas and the azaleas, the heather, the brambles and the gorse. All that part and parcel of land known as Penmarric in the parish of St. Just in the Duchy of Cornwall.

And he had left it all to me.

I had cursed him, abused him and threatened him but it was as if I had never spoken a word. I had walked out of his house long ago after scoffing at his money and sneering at all he had done for me, but it was as if all our past quarrels were meaningless. I had thought he had hated me as much as I had hated him, but now it was as if the hatred had never existed and our estrangement had been nothing but an illusion created and fostered by the mine.

And now he had left me the mine. And the money to keep it alive. He had left it all to me, but suddenly I didn't want it because the gift was so terrible to me that I felt as if it were an invisible rod beating me to the ground. I wanted to retreat, to fling up my arms to protect myself, to run and hide and claw my way to safety, yet there was no going back. I had nowhere to run, no way of turning back the pages of the past. My mistakes were all made and now that my father was dead nothing could undo them. He had left me the mine and the money, and now I had to live with them. I had to eat in the dining room of Penmarric and hear my voice say, "If you close that mine I'll break you," to present checks to the bank and hear my voice from the past shout, "You never give me a penny of your damned money!" to go down the mine every day and listen to my memories crying, "You never understand! You've never tried to! You've done nothing for me all my life!" So many terrible memories; and I had to live with them all.

I stood up. They all looked at me. Vincent had been reading the passage in which my father had appointed Adrian as his literary executor, but as I rose he stopped. I looked at my sisters, Mariana smart and pretty, her blue eyes ice-cold; Jeanne pale and drawn; Elizabeth cool and hostile. I looked at the Parrishes, at William, large and untidy, his humorous mouth unsmiling, at Adrian, tall and spare, his expression shadowed with an emotion I could not read. I looked at Alice, saw her contempt for me in her tight-lipped face, and then I looked at the rector. He knew. His face was inscrutable yet filled with the knowledge of what that will meant to me. He knew. There was knowledge in Jan-Yves's face too, not the rector's knowledge but another knowledge far more bitter, and I saw then that he had known all along about the will. It was the will that had brought him to Roslyn Farm, the will that had spurred him to ingratiate himself with my mother and thus with me, the will that had obliged him to involve himself in my schemes. He had written off an inheritance from my father and was angling for a possible inheritance to come; he had been planning for the future, making sure he was on the right side when my father died.

I stood there looking at them all, and I saw that they were as estranged from me as I was from them. None of them cared. Why should they have done? I hadn't cared for them. All I had cared for was my mother and my mine.

I went out of the room. Nobody said anything. Nobody stopped me. I walked out of the house, down the drive, across the cliffs to the mine, but there was no comfort at the mine, no solace, only the dark mystery of the main shaft and the repellant blast of air from the furnace, and in the end I went on, into St. Just, out toward Morvah, up into the hills, to the moors, to Chûn. I walked and walked and walked. I noticed nothing, I felt nothing. I didn't even know where I was going. When I reached the castle I almost went down the hill to the farm but then I knew it was too soon, I couldn't bring myself to tell her. The knowledge was obscene. I wanted to talk about it, to try and unload that terrible burden from my mind, but there was no one to talk to, nothing except the sweep of the moors and the occasional gust of rain, and far away on the skyline the ruined engine house of Ding Dong mine.

I walked on to Zillan.

The village was quiet now after the departure of the crowds who had flocked to the church to mourn. There was no one about. I went into the deserted churchyard, and it was peaceful. My father's grave was heaped with flowers, and the scent floated toward me as I moved down the path. A breeze stirred the exotic blooms, and as I looked at them I remembered that none of the wreaths had come from me. My mother had sent flowers in my name but she had paid for them. I hadn't spent one penny of my own money in providing an adequate funeral. Not one single penny of my money.

I told myself it was futile to wish I had paid for the flowers. What difference could it possibly have made? My father couldn't see the flowers, couldn't know who had given wreaths and who hadn't. To be overcome now by an absurd compulsion to lay still more flowers on that already overcrowded grave was not only superstitious but inexcusably sentimental as well.

And yet . . .

I was at the wall of the churchyard. My mind had ceased to reason; I was conscious only of the large wild daisies still blooming beneath the shelter of the old stones, and I found myself stooping to tear the stalks off at the root. I didn't hurry. I just went on picking the daisies one after the other until suddenly my eyes were blind and I could no longer see.

The flowers fell lightly from my hands. The ground at my feet was strewn with their petals but all I could see was a white blur, and suddenly I put my hands over my eyes and leaned against the wall and cried as I had not cried since I was a child long ago in times I had long since tried to forget.

I cried for a long time. Afterward I felt no better, only empty and sick. I sat on the ground, my back to the wall, and stared at the flowers on the grave, and there was nothing to think about; it was all too late for wishing the past could have been otherwise, and although I tried to pray I couldn't, I had no belief. I went on sitting there in the churchyard. I had lost all count of time. And then just as I had noticed the lengthening shadows I heard the click of the lych-gate far away and knew that I was no longer alone in the churchyard.

I waited. I heard his footsteps on the path, saw his dark suit black against the gray tombstones. I saw him walk to my father's grave and close his eyes in prayer, and when he opened his eyes again he saw me watching him as I sat with my back to the ancient wall among those ancient forgotten graves.

We looked at each other for a long time, just he and I, just Adrian Parrish and Philip Castallack, and between us lay the mighty wall of our joint past, a monumental wasteland of hostility which had separated us for more than twenty years.

He took a step toward me, then a step back. It was more than he could do. After a moment he turned, walked quickly down the path and disappeared into the shadow of the porch.

And the wall between us crumbled into dust, the wasteland became a mere mirage of past jealousy and I was free.

I went after him. At first I thought he had gone into the church but I was wrong. He was still in the porch, still lingering as if he didn't know what to do, his hand on the old iron ring which lifted the bolt and opened the door. My shadow fell across the doorway; he looked up, and there we were, face to face at last, and—for the first time in our lives—equals.

[2]

"But we were always equals," said Adrian. "That was the whole problem. We each wanted the best for our mothers and both of us—in our different ways—gave our father a tough time in consequence. No wonder we never got on. How could we? We were traveling the same road all right—but in opposite directions so that when we met it was always in a head-on collision."

I couldn't grasp what he was saying. I couldn't believe what he was telling me.

"You thought you were the only one who ever gave Papa a hard time? My dear Philip! I might not have used the same tactics as you did but I'm sure there were times when he was at his wits' end to know what to do with me. Yes of course I was a little pest at Allengate. Wouldn't you have been if you'd been in my shoes? I was jealous and insecure and haunted all the time by the dread that my illegitimacy made my position inferior to yours."

He had feared his position had been inferior to mine. I couldn't take it in. My mind balked at it.

"Yes, of course I did my best to get on well with Papa—why not? It was my best insurance against that enormous insecurity. When I wasn't worrying him silly with my erratic behavior I did all I could to win his affection. Yes, I did like history and yes, I did share some of his interests, but would I have liked them so much if I hadn't so often been falling over myself to win his approbation? I wonder. You see, I wasn't really very like him at all. I realized that clearly when I went up to Oxford after the war and tried to follow in his footsteps."

I tried to say something, but there were no words. All I could do was listen.

"I saw the truth then," said Adrian. "I realized that I liked history well enough—but as a hobby, an intellectual exercise.

Nothing more. I could never have made a good historian. I hadn't the . . . how shall I put it? I hadn't the passion for it."

The passion.

"But Papa was different. History was his passion. It was his cause, his life's work. Have you ever read any of his books? Have you ever read any of his articles, his theses? Didn't you hear of the academic feuds he had with other historians whose views were opposed to his own? Didn't you hear of his great friend at Oxford—the one he quarreled with and brought to ruin? No, I don't suppose you did. You weren't interested in history, after all. You were too busy with your mine."

My mine. I was dumb. Speech was beyond me.

"I tried to pursue history as Papa pursued it, but I couldn't do it. The hours of patient research, the fanatical attention to detail, the total self-absorption in the events of long ago to the point where you can sink yourself into the personalities involved and think as they thought—no, it was beyond me. I hadn't the ambition. But Papa had the ambition. I think if I'd presented an original historical thesis which had been heavily criticized by academic experts I would have fled in shame and hidden myself in a corner to lick my wounds, but Papa wasn't like that. He was tough and he didn't care how much criticism he had to face because he was convinced he was right and they were wrong. He rode roughshod over all opposition because nothing else mattered to him except the views which he believed to be true. With him, historical truth as he saw it was so important that nothing was allowed to stand in its way, not even an old and valued friendship. But I couldn't have been that ruthless. It's not in me. I was really so dissimilar to him. We were cast in such different molds."

There was a silence. At last I managed to say something. I don't remember what it was.

"No, it was a logical will," said Adrian. "It was just and fair. He knew Jan-Yves was too immature to cope with a large inheritance. He knew it would have been foolish to leave the estate to either William or me—not simply because we were illegitimate but because neither of us needed it. William has no ambition; he's happy enough as he is, and I—well, what would a clergyman want with a large inheritance? It would have been more of a hindrance than a help to me, and I never liked Penmarric anyway. That left you. But you needn't think he was forced to leave it to you simply because there was no one else.

He wanted to leave it to you. That makes sense, doesn't it? When it came down to the basic facts, what did all the quarrels matter? You spoke a language he could understand. That was what mattered. He seldom saw you but he didn't have to see you often to know you well because you both spoke the same language and it was the language he had spoken all his life."

I said nothing. There was so much I could have said but none of it would have been enough.

"You didn't know him," said Adrian, "but he knew you. That was how it was. That was the truth. You never really knew him, did you?"

[3]

I said carefully to my mother, "He left it all to me, except for some legacies and your annuity. He left me everything. On trust. It's mine for life and then it goes to my son—or if I have no son, then to one of my father's male descendants who bears the name Castallack and was alive at the time of my father's death. That means either Jan-Yves or Jonas—but not Esmond—and I can choose in my will which one of them shall inherit the estate from me."

She could not believe it. I kept repeating it to her, and still she repeated even my repeated words as if she could not believe her ears. She thought, just as I had, that Jan-Yves would be the chief beneficiary under the will. "So you won't have to worry about the mine any more," she said at last, and then exclaimed, "Oh, Philip, I'm so happy for you! But—"

"Yes?"

"I suppose . . ." She hesitated before adding uncertainly: "You'll live at Penmarric now, of course."

"Well, I suppose I should, but—"

"Oh, but Philip, you must! Naturally I'd love you to stay on here, but I do realize it would be quite wrong to expect you to stay at the farm now that this has happened. Now that you have Penmarric—and the mine . . . well, you'll want a son to leave them to, won't you? You'll want to get married. I wouldn't want you to think that you can't get married and go to live with your wife at Penmarric; you mustn't be afraid to leave me at the farm. You're not holding back because of me, are you? Because I'd love you to get married and have children, darling—truthfully,

I don't think anything could give me greater pleasure than that. . . . You do want to get married, Philip, don't you? You do want to have children?"

"Well, of course, Mama!" I said, laughing. "Have I ever said that I didn't?"

In truth for the first time in my life I didn't find the idea of marriage displeasing. I remembered my nephew Esmond and thought how good it would be to have a son, someone whom I could bring up to take an interest in the estate, someone who would love the mine as I did and keep it alive after I myself was dead. I knew I should get married. However, I decided I would wait a little longer until everything was settled, the taxes and legacies had been paid and I knew where I stood financially. There was no hurry. I had waited thirty-one years to get married, so one more year would hardly make any difference.

I went on planning for the future. Soon I was no longer thinking of marriage. The idea of finding a wife had once more slipped to the back of my mind and instead my thoughts had reverted, just as they always did eventually, to the mine.

But it wasn't just my mine now. It wasn't simply Sennen Garth, the last working mine west of St. Just. It was the mine I owned and controlled. It was the mine no man would ever close again.

[4]

The accountant Stanford Blake told me it would take a great deal of money to keep the mine alive and said I would be surprised to discover that Penmarric was an expensive house to run. He also reminded me that my financial resources were still limited since I could not touch a penny of the capital my father had left me in trust, and advised me to talk to the bailiff and housekeeper so that I could get a clearer picture of the annual expenditures that had to be met.

The very next day I went to Penmarric to talk to Alice Penmar.

"I'm so glad you asked to see me, Philip," said Alice in her politest voice, "because I was going to ask to see you. I wish to hand in my notice and will leave whenever you find a suitable replacement. I hope that's not causing you too much inconvenience."

We were in the drawing room at Penmarric, both of us standing facing each other before the fireplace. She wore black. Her hair was scraped back from her plain face and there were hard lines about her thin mouth. Her eyes, like her grandfather's, were inscrutable.

"On the contrary," I said, "that's most convenient. I had planned to dispense with a housekeeper as an economy and to ask Jeanne to run the house for me instead."

"Really?" said Alice. "Well, I hope Jeanne can manage. She knows nothing whatsoever about housekeeping."

"I haven't discussed the idea with her yet. If she's unwilling, then I'll be obliged to find someone to replace you, but I'm more than anxious to economize as much as possible on household expenditure."

"Quite," said Alice.

There was an awkward pause. I wondered, as I had wondered so often before, if anyone would ever know the whole truth about her relationship with my father. Why had he had a stroke? Because the accusations in my ultimatum were every bit as true as I had suspected they were? Or because they were so far from the truth that the very thought of them was too appalling to contemplate? I supposed I'd never find the answers to those questions now. My father was in his grave and Alice wasn't talking.

"Are you seeking a position elsewhere?" I said tentatively to break the silence.

"Oh no," said Alice, cool as the iceberg that sank the *Titanic*. "I'm marrying Sir Justin Carnforth and moving to Carnforth Hall."

I've no idea what kind of expression that produced on my face. Stupefaction was probably hardly the word to do it justice.

"The notice is to appear in *The Times* on Monday," said Alice. "My grandfather will be so pleased to see me settled at last, I've no doubt, and I think everything will work out very nicely. Sir Justin, as you know, has been a widower for some years and has actually been anxious to marry me for some time. But the moment never seemed right until now."

"I see," I said. I groped for the suitable words. "I must congratulate Sir Justin when I next see him. I hope you'll be very happy."

"Thank you," said Alice neatly. "I'm sure I shall."

There was another pause.

I couldn't help myself. I was too used to saying exactly what I thought to hold the words back. "I suppose," I said, "my father knew all about this."

"Oh yes," said Alice. "We often discussed it. He was most anxious for me to take advantage of such a splendid opportunity, and he used to worry in case I spoiled my chances of becoming Lady Carnforth—spoiled them by delaying, I should say—but I weighed up the situation and decided Justin could wait for a while. And he did, bless him! Wasn't that fortunate? But then I'm rather good at weighing up situations."

"Yes," I said, "I'm sure you are, Alice."

"I was in love with you once, as you know, but in the end you forced me to see I was wasting my time. Well, that was all right. Every girl should fall violently in love once and chalk it up to experience. So I chalked it up. What else could I have done with a situation like that? Anyway, after a while I got over you and began to count my blessings. I was so privileged being able to keep house for your father. He had such a fine academic mind and I enjoyed his company so much. He worried because he thought people would talk if we dined alone together and so on—he worried especially during the war when everyone was away and we were often on our own at Penmarric—but I told him not to worry. I had the situation weighed up. People might talk, but so long as they couldn't prove anything nothing they said would matter." She stopped, then smiled at me. "And nobody ever proved anything," she said, "and what's more nobody ever will. I knew I had the situation weighed up correctly. . . . Please excuse me if I leave you now, Philip, but I'm so busy at present and have so much to do. Oh, by the way, you will come to the wedding, won't you? It'll be some time in the spring, I expect." And leaving me still speechless before the hearth, she sailed casually out of the room.

I had seldom in all my life felt so foolish.

[5]

Jeanne was reluctant to try her hand at housekeeping, but after I had promised her that I intended to marry before long and that her position would be only temporary she agreed to give the idea a try. After that I spoke to William about reducing expenditure on estate matters, but on the whole I didn't consider he was much help. His attitude seemed to be that he was already keeping expenditure to a minimum and to economize further would be a mistake. After making a mental note to investigate William's efficiency further as soon as I could spare the time from the mine's affairs, I abandonned William and turned my attention once more to Jan-Yves.

"So what do you intend to do with yourself?" I asked him sardonically. "Sit around on your backside and hope I appoint you my heir?"

I'll say this for Jan-Yves: If he was pressed hard enough he could speak up well in his own defense. When I contrasted this unexpected courage with his panic on the day of my father's death, I found him an even odder mixture than I had found him before. He was a mass of contradictions. Nothing he did seemed to make sense.

"If you think I like being idle you're wrong," he said abruptly. "I don't want to be a gentleman of leisure living on your charity and I'm not afraid to work. If you'll employ me I'll work at the mine."

"In what capacity?" I inquired, never thinking for one moment that he was in earnest. "As an apprentice below ground?"

"If you like," he said without batting an eyelid. "When can I start?"

We stared at each other. My God, I thought, he's serious. He really would go down the mine. He's got more guts than I gave him credit for.

"I'll start at the bottom," said Jan-Yves doggedly, "and work my way up—to the count house. I think I could be useful to Walter Hubert, but I'll see what goes on below ground first, and if you don't think I'm in earnest about it why don't you at least try me to find out how much in earnest I am?"

After a pause I said, "It's all right—you don't have to crucify yourself to get back in my good books."

"I'm not thinking of your good books, I'm thinking of my future! I want to live and work in this part of Cornwall. It's my home. So why shouldn't I want to find out all I can about mining and then work in the family business? I don't think my decision's as extraordinary as you seem to think it is."

"Perhaps not." I thought about it. I was still inclined to distrust

Jan-Yves as much as I had distrusted Hugh, but I was impressed by his offer to begin work below ground and was willing to believe he meant to do an honest day's work when he was given the opportunity. Besides, the situation at the count house had changed since Hugh had offered his services; Walter Hubert was getting old, and Slater the clerk hadn't the ability to be more than a mere assistant. If Jan-Yves proved himself at the mine perhaps he could be trained to take over from Walter and become purser one day. "All right," I said suddenly. "We'll try it and see what happens. I'll speak to Trevose about it tomorrow and ask him if he'll show you the ropes. If he doesn't object you can start next Monday."

I still could hardly believe he meant what he said. And when I spoke to Trevose about Jan-Yves's progress a week later I could hardly believe Trevose meant what he said either.

"Funny about that kid brother of yours," he said to me as we drank a pint of beer together at the pub. "He's a plucky little bastard. He doesn't like that mine and he hates being under the sea and he's scared stiff of dynamite but he's game for anything. No airs and graces either. No talking high and mighty as if he was the cat's bloody whiskers. I like him."

I was amazed. Trevose seldom admitted liking anybody and was always sparing with his praise. In fact I was so amazed I would have pondered on the miracle for much longer if by that time I hadn't been so involved with the future finances of the mine. I went to see my bank manager in Penzance presently about the possibility of a loan, but his response was not as positive as it should have been—or so I thought.

"My dear Mr. Castallack," he said to me apologetically, "I don't want to be unhelpful, but you do realize, of course, that these are extraordinarily difficult times. I'll be absolutely delighted to give you half the sum under discussion. With great difficulty I might manage to give you two-thirds. But more than that—well, I'm afraid it's not possible." And he began rambling about the estate being on trust and the depressed state of the mining industry until I was so exasperated that I left more abruptly than I should have done.

Outside his office on Market Jew Street I decided to cool my anger by going for a walk through the town, through the winding back streets above the harbor and over the hill to the esplanade and Morrab Gardens. I could not believe that even with my inheritance behind me it would be so hard to lay my hands on some ready money. I walked on fuming. My thoughts began to run in a series of "if onlys." If only I had capital I could draw on. If only I could sell Penmarric and put the proceeds into the mine. If only—but there were a hundred "if onlys" and none of them solved my problems.

I needed money.

I needed a son.

I stopped and stared out to sea. If I could marry a rich woman both my problems would be solved.

I swung around. Before me stood the Metropole Hotel, where I had dined five years earlier with a very rich woman indeed.

Of course! I smiled in delight. The perfect solution. I would marry Helena Meredith.

And feeling pleased with my inspired idea, I turned, left the sea and walked briskly back to the center of the town, where my chauffeur was waiting for me with the Penmarric car.

8

[Richard] used England as a bank on which to draw and overdraw in order to finance his ambitious exploits abroad. . . . "I would sell London," Richard is reported to have said, "if I could find a suitable purchaser."

—Oxford History of England:
From Domesday Book to Magna Carta,
A. L. POOLE

Everything was sacrificed to raising money. . . . Everything was for sale.

—King John,
W. L. WARREN

[1]

Of course I wasn't such a fool as to imagine I was in love with her, but I was honest enough to admit to myself that I did not now expect to fall violently in love with anyone, and since this was the case I decided I might as well make the best of the situation. I didn't love Helena, but I liked her and respected her and saw no reason why we shouldn't have a successful marriage. I might be marrying her primarily for her money, but I was prepared to try hard to make her happy and I did find her attractive. I couldn't have tied myself to anyone I disliked, not even to save Sennen Garth.

I had no idea whether she found me attractive or not, but I supposed I could be considered eligible enough now that I was master of Penmarric, and on the one occasion when I had taken her out to dinner we had found plenty to say to each other. But as soon as I thought of that evening nearly six years ago at the Metropole I began to feel worried. Perhaps she had resented the fact that I hadn't asked her out a second time. Perhaps she had suspected my motive for dining with her and resented the fact that she had been used. Whatever her feelings on the subject it was essential that I transform our present prosaic friendship by injecting a shot of romance and behaving as if for some reason I had noticed her for the first time. It would certainly be no use trampling over the conventions like a bull in a china shop and saying in my usual blunt way, "Look, I've known you for six years and now I've suddenly realized I like you and your money would be more than useful to me. Why don't we get married?"

That wouldn't do at all. I must be delicate, subtle, even crafty. For this particular role I had to act out of character.

I worried about the problem for some time, but eventually hit on the idea of having a small dinner party at Penmarric for about eight or ten of my contemporaries in order to attract Helena's attention and put our relationship on a new footing. Jeanne and I would be the host and hostess, and in addition to Helena and her brother I decided to invite William, Jan-Yves and possibly my sister-in-law Rebecca, whom I had seen little of for some months on account of her estrangement from my mother. I had no grudge against Rebecca; my quarrel had been with Hugh, not with her, and even the bitterness I had felt toward Hugh had ebbed since his death. In addition to Rebecca I still needed another female guest to make up the numbers, and since I thought I should flaunt my county background in front of Helena I decided the last guest would have to be Felicity Carnforth, Sir Justin's only surviving child. Felicity, a horsey, hearty girl in her mid-twenties, was something of a joke, but I couldn't think of anyone else to invite. Peter Waymark's sisters were married now and the St. Enedoc girls were away in London; even Lizzie, who would have been a convenient solution, was spending Christmas with friends in Cambridge.

The dinner party was held on Christmas Eve and much to my amazement went far better than I had expected it would. I began by being absurdly nervous, but I soon recovered myself and after dinner I managed to sit next to Helena in the drawing room and pay her a compliment or two. That wasn't difficult. She wore pale green and had her hair piled on top of her head and was without doubt the prettiest woman in the room.

Presently I said casually to her, "I hope we'll be able to see more of each other now that I lead a more conventional existence."

"Conventional?"

"I was hardly conventional when I lived at the farm and worked at the mine. When I move to Penmarric in the new year things will be different."

"Not too different, I hope," she said with a smile. "You mustn't change radically now that you're master of Penmarric."

"If I do," I said, "it'll be for the better, I promise you."

And we smiled at each other.

I invited her to lunch at Penmarric the following week and took to calling regularly at Polzillan House. Every move I made met with nothing but success; no scheme could ever have gone so meticulously according to plan. By February I considered it was time for a visit to the Metropole again since I had now maneuvered myself into a position where I could explain away our previous visit there, and after traveling to Penzance in the Penmarric car we ate a first-class dinner in the Metropole's grandiose dining room. I was hesitant about mentioning the previous visit, but presently when Helena herself referred to it without embarrassment I saw at once that she bore me no grudge and that there was no need for any awkward explanations. So relieved was I to discover this that I even suggested we leave the table for a dance, but I think she knew I disliked dancing, for she suggested a stroll outside on the esplanade instead.

Unlike that other night when we had walked together along the esplanade, the sky was overcast and there was no moonlight. In Morrab Gardens the palm trees were shivering, their fronds sighing longingly for their native tropics. The sea thudded amiably on the beach and a cold breeze blew into our faces from the southwest.

I thought quickly. I had seen her now with great regularity for six weeks. We knew each other well by this time. The one awkward obstacle between us, the abortive dinner of six years ago, had been painlessly overcome. So far I had treated her with a more than friendly interest and had conducted a keen but decorous pursuit; unless she was stupid (which she wasn't) she must have realized by this time that I wasn't pursuing her without purpose, and matters had now reached the stage when a more concentrated interest was required unless I were to risk her becoming bored. I remembered that there was a new doctor, a young man called Donald McCrae, who visited her brother several times a week; I knew nothing about him, but his presence, however innocent, in her life was sufficient to remind me that she could attract other suitors besides myself. If I, hesitated too long or failed to live up to her expectations of how a man should conduct a romance I might wake up one morning to find she was engaged to someone else.

"I must have been blind six years ago," I said lightly. "Imagine dining with you once and then never dining with you again!" And as she turned to smile up at me I took her in my arms and stooped to kiss her.

I was surprised how warm her lips were. I had somehow always imagined women's lips to be flabby and cold. But hers weren't. They were warm and firm, pleasantly moist.

"Mmmmm!" I said, startled.

She sighed, closed her eyes for a moment, and when at last she opened them again I saw without doubt that she loved me.

[2]

It was all easier than I had imagined it would be. After the evening in Penzance I saw her several more times during February and by early March decided that I ran no risk in proposing earlier than I had anticipated. Accordingly on one of those mild springlike March mornings when the air was enticingly warm, I took her for a walk over the moors and after a suitably romantic scene among the walls of Chûn I asked her if she would marry me.

I had my arm around her. I felt her shudder and thought for an aghast moment that she was going to burst into tears, but she didn't. Jeanne would have done perhaps, or a thousand other women, but not Helena. Of all her many admirable qualities there wasn't one I respected more than her indestructible self-possession.

She turned to look at me. Her eyes seemed to burn with joy. Her lips, slightly parted, were upturned to mine. After we had kissed I said, teasing her, "Does that mean yes?"

"Of course," she said.

Her intensity made me uneasy, but I was flattered all the same. I was conscious of a warm glow of satisfaction at the thought of a difficult task successfully accomplished. It was a pleasant feeling.

The news of our engagement was received with varying degrees of excitement and surprise, ranging from my mother's predictable ecstasy to Jan-Yves's stupefaction. Why he was so surprised I had no idea, although I suspected he had made up his mind I would remain a bachelor and had become so accustomed to regarding himself as my heir that the prospect of my providing him with a usurping nephew was too distasteful to accept readily. William was pleasant, Gerald Meredith affable enough to call for champagne and Jeanne was almost as thrilled as my mother. Even Young Medlyn swelled with feudal approval on behalf of the Penmarric servants.

"That's very good news, sir," he purred. "Very good news indeed. I'm sure we all wish to congratulate you, sir, and offer you and Miss Meredith our very best wishes."

My friends at the mine received the news with a roar of approval and everyone except Trevose pressed around to shake my hand and clap me on the back. Trevose sulked. I had expected this, but privately I thought he was being unreasonable. There was no harm in being a misogynist but it was a mistake to expect everyone else to give women as wide a berth as he did.

Fortunately by evening he had pulled himself together and was in the pub with the others to drink my health. He made no effort to apologize for his surliness—I knew him better than to expect an apology—but he was friendly enough, so I pushed the incident with relief to the back of my mind and forgot about it. I had too many other matters on my mind at that time to bother myself with trivialities.

We had decided to get married on the first Saturday in July, and while Helena began to make the preliminary arrangements I tackled the problem of what should be done about the members of my family who were then living at Penmarric. I knew William would be willing to move out once I moved in, for he had already told me as much after my father's death and had suggested that it might be easier for us both if we kept our relationship on a friendly but businesslike footing. After consulting him about his preferences I granted him a nominal lease of an old stone house on the outskirts of St. Just; the previous tenant, a retired seaman, had died a month ago and the house had been vacant since his death. The house was larger than any of the village cottages, had an acre of garden and was structurally sound. William was pleased with this arrangement, and I was pleased too to think he was comfortably settled away from Penmarric; when he moved into his new home I wrote him a check to help him with his expenses, but he considered I had done enough for him and I saw later from a glance at my bank statement that he had never presented my check for payment.

However, he did accept a check from me shortly afterward in lieu of a wedding present; at long last Charity had bullied him into marrying her and had dragged him along to the nearest registry office. Nobody went to the wedding except Jan-Yves, and William never once referred to it afterward although Charity took care to wear the largest wedding ring she could lay her hands on and had a great time displaying herself to St. Just as Mrs. Parrish. Why William bothered to marry her I have no idea. It was true Charity had blackmailed him by refusing to keep house for him in his new home unless he married her, but William could have had another working-class woman on the terms he wanted—or, for that matter, he could have had a woman of his own class if he had reconciled himself to the idea of marriage. But William had a horror of marriage. He was eccentric on the subject, and I had always been surprised that someone so conventional should not only preach free love but practice it as well. However, if he had decided to abandon his unorthodox views, that was his business, not mine, and all I could do was wish him well while I wondered skeptically how long the marriage would last. I had a feeling both of them would soon find fidelity more trouble than it was worth.

From William I turned to Jan-Yves. In a way I felt sorry for him. He was in the unenviable position of having a small weekly wage, no capital and nowhere to live except Penmarric, and I couldn't help thinking his circumstances were not entirely deserved. Since my father's death I hadn't been able to find any fault with him; he was behaving well about a marriage which would probably result in excluding him from any part of the Penmarric inheritance; he had worked hard at the mine, won Trevose's respect (I still found that hard to believe), assimilated a detailed amount of knowledge rapidly and had now replaced Slater the clerk in giving Walter Hubert an able helping hand with the accounts.

I decided to be generous to him, so finally I gave him enough

503

money to build a house and leased him some land at a nominal rent. I couldn't dispose of the land outright, of course, because of the trust, but the trustees thought a house would constitute an improvement to the estate and raised no objection when I told them what I had in mind. Jan-Yves said he was grateful, but I could see he had difficulty in believing the scheme was free of some hidden flaw and I doubted even then whether despite our recent cordiality we would ever fully trust each other.

Having provided for my brothers, I had my sisters to consider. Lizzie was still engaged in advanced academic studies at Cambridge, and there seemed every likelihood that she would make her home there; she was already provided for financially under the terms of my father's will, so it seemed she presented no problems for the present. That left Jeanne. An unmarried woman was always entitled to a place in her brother's house, so after breakfast one morning I told her she could live at Penmarric for as long as she liked.

"Oh, Philip, how kind of you!" she exclaimed, but then to my surprise she hesitated. "However, I . . . well, I do have other plans. Gerry must have someone to be with him once Helena leaves—he'll be so lonely on his own, and no professional nurse can ever be as sympathetic as . . . well, as someone who cares for him, and so . . . well, I'm not quite sure how to explain, but I—I've promised to marry him. Now I don't expect Mama to understand, but—"

"Understand!" I exploded. "She'll have a fit!" And then as I saw the tears spring to her eyes at my tone of voice I added hastily, "As far as I'm concerned I wish you well—you're old enough to know what you're doing, you've been in love with the man for years, and if that's the kind of marriage you want, good luck to you. But as far as Mama's concerned—"

"I shall write her a note." She had it all planned. "I'd rather explain everything in writing. If I try to explain matters to her face to face I know I shall get flustered and say the wrong thing."

In the end, of course, I was the one who had to deliver the note, but when the news was duly presented to her my mother was more exasperated than upset.

"I didn't think anyone could be quite so stupid," she said with an impatient shrug of her shoulders. "It's simply beyond my powers of comprehension. How absurd Jeanne is! Well, if she wants to make a fool of herself, let her, that's all I can say, but

I hope she doesn't fall violently in love with an able-bodied man once she's a married woman."

So Jeanne too began to wear an engagement ring, and when she wasn't talking about Helena's wedding in July she was talking about her own wedding in October. I began to be very tired of hearing about nothing but weddings and tried to keep on the sidelines as much as possible, but my mother kept asking me such questions as who was to be best man, when was I going to make arrangements for the honeymoon, hadn't I better write to Mariana if I wanted Esmond to be a page, and I found it was impossible to leave all the wedding arrangements to Helena. Helena was busy enough as it was; wedding invitations were sent out, the reception as Polzillan House was organized, the trousseau was bought in London and designs for the bridesmaids' dresses were chosen. And all the time spring was galloping into summer until I felt I had never known that the seasons could pass so quickly.

Since I had no close friends of my own class I eventually had to ask Jan-Yves to be best man. I couldn't think of anyone else to approach. The choice of a place for the honeymoon worried me for a time as I had no wish to be away from Cornwall for long, but Helena suggested Torquay, which I had heard was not unlike Penzance, and I agreed to that with relief. A honeymoon in the next county was hardly very adventurous, but I could always take her abroad later on when I felt more in the mood.

Not unnaturally I thought about the honeymoon a great deal. I wasn't nervous, but I was undecided about how I should approach it. I was determined nothing should go wrong and confident that I could cope with the situation, but I could see that to make sure I knew what I was doing I should indulge in some discreet practice beforehand. The trouble was that there never seemed to be any time. I was occupied all through June not only by the approaching wedding but by the mine and hardly had a single free evening. Besides when I was free I was usually too tired to make the required visit to Penzance. I kept putting the moment off until finally it was too late and I knew I wouldn't be able to find the time to go. I was annoyed with myself for not making more effort earlier, but not particularly worried. Any healthy man in his prime of life was capable of sexual intercourse, and since Helena was a virgin she would have no idea whether I was experienced or not when the time came for us to spend our first night together. I shrugged away the situation and spent no more time worrying about it. I was sure it would all sort itself out satisfactorily.

The night before the wedding Jan-Yves, William and all my friends from the mine joined me at the pub to cheer me up on my last evening as a bachelor, and the beer and cider flowed until there wasn't a sober man in the house. Trevose even had to be carried home, a phenomenon never before witnessed in St. Just. Fortunately I managed to avoid such a humiliation, but I was more drunk than I had ever been before, so I must have come close to following in Trevose's footsteps. At last when the evening was over, William tottered back to his new home on the outskirts of the village, Jan-Yves went to bed with Charity's successor behind the bar, and I staggered back to Penmarric and fell asleep for the last time in my old room which faced the sea.

[3]

The wedding was set for two o'clock at Zillan. When Jan-Yves and I were ready the chauffeur Tredinney drove us there in the Penmarric car, and since we were early I prepared to idle away a few minutes in the front pew. But I wasn't allowed to idle for long. The rector appeared for a word with me; Peter Waymark, who was an usher, arrived with his wife. Other guests began to appear, and, glancing over my shoulder, I saw Mariana and Lizzie with the Carnforths; they were both staying at Carnforth Hall with Sir Justin and Alice, who were just home from their honeymoon. Mariana's husband, now a chronic invalid, had once again been left behind in Scotland. Rebecca came with my nephew Jonas, a tough two-year-old with Hugh's eyes and Rebecca's wide sullen mouth; Jonas's sister Deborah, who was the youngest bridesmaid, was by that time at Polzillan House with Esmond, the page, and the two adult bridesmaids, Jeanne and a friend of Helena's from Warwickshire called Charlotte. After Rebecca's arrival I saw Helena's other friends from Warwickshire enter the church; I had met them the week before while they had been staying at Polzillan House and now recognized each one in turn. The St. Enedocs came from St. Ives, the Trehearnes from Helston, the Kehellands from Lelant, the Tregothas from St. Erth; I lost count of the county faces I knew so well. The Penmarric and Polzillan servants, stiffly dressed in their Sunday best, tiptoed into the back pews, and at the far end of the church beneath the bell tower sat a few of the miners from Sennen Garth, the ones who had been successful in the lottery held to decide who should have the limited number of temporary seats available. Trevose by his own choice was not among them.

My mother arrived, looking beautiful as usual, and sat down between Mariana and Elizabeth in the row behind me. Something told me she was trembling with excitement, but when I turned around to whisper a greeting to her she seemed serene enough. Beyond by the doorway I could see the last of the guests arriving. William slipped in with Charity and a pace behind them, much to my surprise, came Adrian. I hadn't thought he would bother to come down from Oxford for the wedding and had sent him an invitation only as a courtesy.

I thought of my father's funeral and the truce we had reached afterward, but that seemed long ago now, long, long ago, and the memory of it was blurring in my mind. I wondered what my father would have thought of my marriage. I supposed he would have been pleased, although it was hard to imagine him being pleased with me.

It was good of Adrian to have come.

Two o'clock struck and the organ went on playing and more time slipped away but at last there was a murmur of excitement by the porch and I knew that Helena had arrived.

The organ changed key. We all stood up. I turned to look at her. The odd thing is that now I can't see her at all; there's a blankness in my memory so that when I try to recall how she looked or what she wore I can remember only a void in white, an emptiness behind a floating veil. I can remember Jeanne, Deborah and Helena's friend Charlotte in long pale blue dresses. I can see Esmond, proud and dignified in his page's costume. But I can't see Helena. All I can remember thinking is that she looked even more striking than usual but the details are lost to me, lost and gone beyond recall, and even when I look at the photographs now years later they seem not only remote but unreal as well.

But I married her. That much I do remember. I remember those words of the wedding service which everyone seems to think so gracious and which I've always thought merely embarrassing; I can remember Jan-Yves giving me the ring, remember the touch of metal cold against my dry fingers. I can remember the rector saying a few words to us in private before the altar, but what he said I've no idea, for that's gone too now, gone with all the other forgotten memories of the past, and finally I remember walking down the aisle and out of the church into the faded sunshine of a cold June afternoon. All the village had turned out for the wedding. There were cheers and shouts and a storm of confetti, and I remember smiling and waving as I climbed into the car with Helena to drive to Polzillan House.

I can remember the reception, tables of delicacies, champagne in buckets, a wedding cake like an ivory tower. Jan-Yves made a witty speech, but I merely said a few words of thanks, and afterward there was only talk and laughter and the incessant clinking of glasses. I can remember talking to innumerable people about nothing, trying to talk to Esmond but never being able to say more than a sentence to him without being interrupted.

Esmond. Seven years old, tall and straight-backed with candid eyes and a strong mouth. That was all I wanted now, a son like Esmond, a son of my own whom I could bring up to love Sennen Garth as I loved it. Seeing Esmond made me realize fully how little the wedding meant to me. I loved Helena in my own way and I was glad to be married and I didn't grudge her one minute of the celebrations, but the proceedings seemed so irrelevant to my way of life, such a waste of time and effort and money. But everything went well. Everything had gone well from the start, ever since I had decided to marry Helena. I had no cause to complain.

We left for Penzance at six o'clock. I had decided against traveling to Torquay on the first night of the honeymoon, so I had booked a suite at the Metropole which in Helena's eyes had a number of sentimental memories for us. We had a hard time escaping from Polzillan, however. Everyone had to crowd out into the drive to see us off; everyone had to wish us goodbye. I kissed my mother, shook Jan-Yves's hand to thank him for his role in the service, and made a point of saying goodbye to Esmond.

"Come and stay with us at Penmarric," I said to him. "You won't forget, will you? Don't go back to Scotland and forget all about us."

"No, Uncle Philip, I won't forget. Thank you and Aunt Helena very much for letting me be a page and giving me the gold pen." He was well-mannered without being unnaturally polite. I thought again how much I liked him and wondered as I had often wondered before how a woman like Mariana could have produced such a son.

We left at last, the chauffeur edging the car through the throngs of people, and within half an hour I was signing the register at the Metropole.

We were shown to our suite. The furnishings were the monstrosities one would expect in a place like the Metropole, but I supposed such grandiose luxury was not out of place on one's honeymoon. At least there was a good view of the sea. We changed, she in the adjoining bathroom and I in the privacy of the bedroom, and when I was ready I wandered into the reception room and stepped out onto the balcony to watch the evening light on the water as I waited for her.

At dinner the conversation took a reminiscent turn as we recalled previous evenings in that dining room, and when the meal was over I escorted her outside for our traditional walk along the esplanade. At last, after the final edge of the afterglow had faded from the sky and the moon had risen, I suggested it was time to go to bed.

"Very well," she said calmly, but I saw the faint color in her cheeks and knew that she was nervous.

I wasn't nervous. I just wanted to get it over with. The prospect of my first night with her had been on my mind for so long that now I was more than ready to face it squarely and put it behind me.

As we reached the hotel I murmured, "I think I'll have one more cigarette out here before I go in. Why don't you go on ahead upstairs?"

She smiled, agreed, and walked quickly through the doors to the hall of the hotel. For the first time for several hours I was alone.

I lit a cigarette, walked over to the railings of the esplanade and watched the moonlight glittering on the dark waters. The sea was calm; I felt at peace. Finishing my cigarette, I ground it to ashes under my heel and walked back across the road to the hotel. Faint strains of music reached my ears from the dining room; the murmur of conversation floated to meet me from the drawing room close at hand. I mounted the stairs, my feet sinking into the thick carpet, and moved without hesitation down the corridor to the door of our suite.

She was ready for bed. She wore some pale floating garment and as I entered the room I could see her reflection in the dressing-table mirror. Her hair, thick and luxuriant, cascaded over her shoulders and stretched halfway down her back. I was about to tell her how beautiful she looked when she turned to face me with a smile.

"I was just taking off my make-up."

I stooped to give her a kiss. "Do you wear any? I've never noticed."

She laughed. "How like a man!" she said lightly and raised a slip of linen to her mouth to wipe off a trace of pale lipstick.

It was then that it happened.

I looked at her and went on looking. I stared at her and went on staring. It was such a simple little gesture, the linen pressed to her mouth, the trace of red when she took the linen away, but suddenly it wasn't simple at all. It was complex—and horrible. The room blurred, the years fell away and my memory spun out of control in a crazy plunge into the past.

I was by my father's corpse, my imagination making the blood run from his mouth just as the blood had run from Jan-Yves's cut lip that same morning at the mine.

I was watching my own cut lip in the mirror after my worst quarrel with Hugh, pressing my handkerchief against my mouth and seeing the blood flare on the white linen.

I was at Mariana's wedding as the stained-glass window made a scarlet gash of her mouth.

I was everywhere at once—Penmarric, the mine, London—but all the while I was somewhere else because someone was crying. I could hear low, harsh, choking sobs. They went on and on and on. Terrible, racking, painful sobs. I couldn't get them out of my ears—I tried to stop my ears with my fingers but still I heard that dreadful weeping and suddenly my memory opened up like a chasm at my feet and I knew where I was.

I was back among the worst memories of my life, back amidst all the blood and violence and suffering I'd tried so hard to forget. I'd thought I'd never have to live through those memories again, but I was wrong. Time had been displaced, the clock put back.

And I was there.

[4]

I was at Brighton with my mother. My mother was all alone and she had no one to protect her except me. My father came and when she started weeping and shouting at him he took her by the shoulders and shook her. I tried to fight him but I was too small, so I couldn't fight him, I couldn't protect my mother, I had to stand by and watch while he took her away, and I knew he was going to hurt her, I knew he was, and I waited and waited for her to come back but all the time he was hurting her and there was nothing I could do to stop him. And then at last she came back. I heard her coming down the passage and she came very slowly and fumbled for the door handle as if she couldn't see what she was doing and I was suddenly so frightened I had to hide my face because I was afraid she might have been disfigured. That was when I heard the sobs. She came into the room and they were all I could hear, and when I managed to look at her I saw her bright hair was disheveled and her neck was scarred with strange marks and her lip was cut and bleeding. She was pressing a handkerchief against her mouth and when she took the handkerchief away it was soiled and bloody.

"Oh God," she kept saying. "Oh God. Oh Christ. Oh God, help me. Please help me." But God didn't lift a finger to help her; my father had hurt her till she was bruised and scarred and bloody and God had just stood by and watched. No doubt He was still standing by as she sobbed for help, and although I tried to help her I couldn't. I couldn't stop her sobs or ease her terrible pain. At last she went into the bathroom and when I heard the water running I knew she was trying to wash the pain away, but she couldn't; it was stamped in her indelibly, and nine months later . . .

Nine months later Jan-Yves was born. I was ten years old. I didn't know then what the word "rape" meant, but I damned well knew what had happened at Brighton. My mother had been raped almost under my nose and I hadn't been able to do anything about it. No wonder I felt so guilty I wanted to forget Brighton by wiping the entire incident from my mind. My mother had been all alone in the world with only me to protect her and I had let my father rape her—I had stood by while he had hit and bruised and hurt her—and afterward I had felt that by the very act of doing nothing I had connived at his guilt until I was every bit as responsible as he was for my mother's terrible suffering.

[5]

Someone was saying, "Philip, Philip, what is it? What's the matter? Philip! Please, Philip, speak to me! What's happened?"

It was Helena. I was in Penzance. I wasn't in Brighton with my mother any more, but somehow that made no difference. It was as if Brighton had become Penzance and my mother had become—

"It's all right," I said. "It's all right."

But it wasn't. It was all wrong. I was beginning to shake from head to foot.

"Philip darling—"

"I'm going to have a bath," I said and fumbled my way past the double bed into the adjoining bathroom.

I closed the door, locked it, leaned against the panels. Presently I managed to vomit. I bent over the basin and retched as if I could rid myself of my memories of Brighton, but they remained steadfastly in my mind. I could still see every detail; I didn't even have to close my eyes. Everything was brilliantly clear, each image rippling through my memory like a strip of moving film.

I struggled to suppress the memory. I had pushed it to the back of my mind for more than twenty years and what I could do once I could do again. I'd get over it. I had to. I had to pull myself together.

At that point I raised my head, looked in the mirror over the basin and stared into my own eyes.

I knew then.

I was at once gripped by panic. I—who had scorned panic in others, who had despised panic as a manifestation of cowardice— I was struck down and paralyzed by fear. I could not move. I began to cry as my mother had cried at Brighton, my body racked with great silent sobs, my cheeks burning with the tears I couldn't stop. I was shivering. In a clumsy movement I wrenched on the taps of the bath and let the noise of the water drum in my ears, and because I was helpless and didn't know what else to do I took off my clothes, got into the bath and began to wash myself, soaping each limb, rubbing my back with the flannel, dashing water across my face to eradicate all trace of that shocking loss of self-control.

But still I couldn't get a grip on myself. Stepping out of the bath, I started to dry my limbs with a towel.

I began to pray. I had been an atheist for twenty years and I began to pray. Please, God, please. Help me. Please.

Tears of helplessness blinded me once more. I tried to clean my teeth but couldn't see what I was doing. At last, dashing away the tears, I again looked at myself in the mirror. I had to pull myself together. After all, if the worst came to the worst there were excuses. It wasn't the end of the world. I had shamed myself in my own eyes by behaving in such a ridiculous manner, but I had had no witnesses. Only I knew that I had panicked, given way to fear, cried and even tried to pray. No one else knew that except me. No one would ever know, least of all Helena.

I tied a towel around my waist, gathered my clothes together and blew my nose on the tail of my soiled shirt. I walked to the door. To open it and cross the threshold into the next room required more courage and more will power than I had ever been called upon to display before. For three terrible seconds I could not nerve myself to move, but at last I reached out, turned the handle and stepped into the living nightmare of the room beyond.

[6]

Soon after dawn when the room was growing lighter I got up and began to dress. I found a pullover and a pair of slacks and extricated an old pair of shoes from my suitcase. I had just finished putting them on when Helena said quickly from the shadows of the bed, "Philip?"

"I can't sleep," I said. "I'm going for a walk."

She said nothing. I slipped out of the room, the key safely in my pocket, and padded downstairs to the hall. The night porter, dozing at his desk, let me out and I stepped into the clean air of early morning and ran across the road to the sea. Without thinking I headed east, past the harbor where the fishermen were already at work, past the lighted windows of their cottages, through the town to the beach beyond the railway. My footsteps left harsh prints in the sand as I walked toward Marazion, and before me in the hard light of dawn St. Michael's Mount rose out of the dark waters of the bay, a fairy-tale castle, an ivory tower as unreal as the wedding cake towering above the table of my own wedding breakfast.

I sat down on the sand to watch the light changing on the shifting sea. I watched for a long time and at last the water hypnotized me and I slept. When I awoke my body was shivering with cold; hauling myself to my feet, I stumbled quickly back to Penzance to find a café that opened early for the fishermen, a place where I could drink some tea and be on my own. There was a place near the harbor. I bought tea at the counter and hid myself in a corner while I drank it. Time passed. It was seven o'clock, then seven-thirty. I bought another cup of tea to buy myself time, but time wasn't for sale and soon it was quarter to eight.

I didn't know what to do. Our train left the station at nine-thirty and we had agreed to breakfast lightly in our rooms at eight. But I didn't want to go back to the hotel. I couldn't face Helena. I was panicking again, giving in to my fear, wanting only to retreat, hide myself, be alone to think.

I stared into my tea. If I didn't go back to the hotel what was the alternative? Where could I run away to? Where could I hide? I was being absurd. There was no alternative. I had to go back to the hotel, breakfast with Helena and be on the train to Devon at nine-thirty. What else could I do? Cut short my honeymoon after the wedding night? The idea was inconceivable. What would everyone say? What would they think? I clasped my hands together, closed my eyes and tried to arrange my thoughts in a logical formation. The most important thing, as I saw it, was that no one should know. Nothing was more important than that. The thought of anyone knowing the truth was enough to make me sweat. No one must know. Helena knew but she wouldn't say anything. She was too proud to tell anyone what had happened, or failed to happen, between us. Everyone else would assume that we'd spent a normal honeymoon. For a moment I wondered if matters would be different at Torquay, but I didn't allow myself to hope that they would be. I was incapable then of foreseeing far into the future, but I knew that as matters stood at that hour I was incapable of making love to any woman, let alone my wife. The memory of Brighton would take longer than the three weeks of the honeymoon to fall out of sight into the bottom of my mind.

I finished my tea and went outside. It was drizzling. When I reached the Metropole at last I made myself buy a paper, just as I would have done if nothing had been wrong, and walked upstairs to our suite.

She had ordered breakfast and it had already arrived. When I came in I saw that she was sitting at the table by the window with her cup of coffee steaming before her as she stared out to sea. She turned to face me but I looked away.

"Sorry I'm late," I said carefully, sitting down opposite her and reaching for toast and marmalade. "I didn't realize the time. I walked along the shore to Marazion."

After a pause she said, "You must be very tired."

"I can do without much sleep once in a while." I looked around for the teapot but there wasn't one. "Did you only order coffee?"

"Oh . . . yes, I'm sorry. I didn't realize you liked tea for breakfast."

"It doesn't matter." I poured out some coffee, slopping it over the brim of the cup into the saucer. After a short silence I said casually, still not looking at her, "I'm sorry about last night. I—"

"Oh please . . . please—it doesn't matter."

"—stupid of me. I suppose I drank too much the night before at the pub, and then with all the champagne at the reception—"

"I understand. Please don't worry. It's all right."

"Yes, but I can't understand it—I can't think why—"

But I knew. I understood.

"—never happened before—"

The stupid thing was that there was no need to lie. I needn't have said anything, but I couldn't stop myself. I had to cover up the truth, so I lied and went on lying.

"—in the past—"

"Please, Philip—don't let's talk of it any more. I understand, and anyway . . . well, what does one night matter? There'll be plenty of others. Please don't worry about it. I hate to see you upset."

"I'm not upset. Just annoyed."

"Well, don't be—please! For my sake!"

"I can't help it," I said. "I am." I opened up the newspaper, pretended to read it and then glanced at my watch. "There's not much time, is there? I suppose I must hurry or we'll miss the train."

But we didn't miss the train. We arrived at the station, found our reserved compartment and settled ourselves for the journey, and soon after half past nine we were on our way out of Cornwall as the train headed east to the Tamar.

9

[1]

On the third day I went to the public library, dug out a
medical dictionary and tried to make sense of the jungle of technical terms there, but I wasted my time. The days dragged past.
To make matters worse the weather was bad and there seemed
nothing to do. I was restless and ill-at-ease. I longed to return
to Cornwall, to the mine, to the life I knew and loved, but was
too afraid of what people might think if I returned early from
my honeymoon; besides, when I had mentioned to Helena the
possibility of cutting short our visit to Torquay she had been so
upset that I hadn't pursued the subject further.

"Please, Philip," she begged. "Please—not that. If you don't
want to stay here perhaps we could go somewhere else? I
wouldn't mind that. But to go back so abruptly to Penmarric—

oh no, Philip, please! If you love me don't take me back there before we're due to return."

I didn't know who was more unhappy, she or I. There was no pretense between us any more. I no longer bothered to make an effort to entertain her. She spent most of the day reading in the privacy of the hotel while I wandered alone through the wet streets and across the rain-soaked sands, and in the evening she would sit for a time in the hotel drawing room before going upstairs to bed and I would go out to a pub where I could drink in peace. I could no longer talk to her. Her presence unnerved me so much that I couldn't wait to escape for a few precious hours of solitude. I became obsessed by my inadequacy, so conscious of it that I could think of nothing else. It was both mysterious and baffling. Helena embarrassed me so acutely now that I no longer felt any degree of arousement in being with her, and after a while I couldn't help wondering if the fault was with her and that I'd be all right with someone else. It was useless to try to push the thought from my mind. Once it was there it stayed there and I had to find out what the answer was. One evening after dinner I picked up a prostitute, but that was no good—on the contrary it was worse than I could have imagined it would be—and afterward I paid her again as if by paying I could somehow erase my humiliation and my grief and my pain.

Pain made my throat ache and pricked my eyes like hot pins. I was awash with pain, soaked in it. I didn't know it was possible to be so unhappy. I longed for my home, not for Penmarric but for my room at the farm, longed for the comfort of dining with my mother in the farm kitchen, longed for my mine, for the galleries far out beneath the sea, for tin ore beneath my fingers and tin dust pricking in my nose. I longed for my friends too, for my fellow miners, for Trevose. I ached for their rough talk and good-natured companionship. They would be at the pub, I knew; they'd be drinking slowly, pausing for a game of darts or skittles. I could picture them all. Willie, Tom, Harry, Dave, Jack, Ray—and Trevose, always Trevose with his ugly face and his stocky build and his callused miner's hands with their black-grimed broken fingernails. It seemed an eternity since I had last spoken to Trevose.

I said to the clerk at the reception desk, "Is there a telephone I could use?"

"Yes, sir, just down the corridor by the billiard room."

"Thank you." I found the kiosk, squeezed my way inside. Within five minutes the landlord of the pub in St. Just was on the line, and, adopting a Cornish accent to disguise my voice, I asked if Trevose was in the bar.

"Yes, he's here. I'll fetch him for 'ee."

I waited, and suddenly there he was, terse and suspicious.

"Hullo?"

It was hard to speak because it was so good to hear him but I managed to say, "And how's the mine doing without me?"

"Jesus Christ!" he said, thunderstruck. "What the hell are you doing on the bloody phone?"

"Making sure my friends aren't on strike in my absence." There was a lump in my throat. Tears stung my eyes. "How are things going?"

"Fine!" he said brightly in the tone of one unaccustomed to addressing an inanimate instrument. "No news. Everything as usual."

"Good."

"What's it like where you're at?" he said perkily. "Been much rain?"

"Too much. We're at Torquay in Devon."

"Torquay? Is that like Penzance?"

"A little."

"How's Mrs. Castallack?"

"She's fine. Look, have a drink for me and tell the boys I'll be back at the mine on Monday. . . . Will you be at the pub on Saturday evening when I get home? Maybe we could meet for a drink."

"I'll be there. I'll eat my tea and be at the pub by seven."

"I may be later than that but you can order a pint of bitter for me if you're there first."

"I'll do that! So long, sonny, all the best. I'll be seeing you."

"Seven on Saturday. 'Bye, Trevose."

I put back the receiver, fumbled for a handkerchief and blew my nose. I felt better. There were only four more days to go now. Four more days would soon pass and then I could go back to Cornwall, to Sennen Garth, to my old way of life and old friends and old habits.

I could hardly wait to leave.

[2]

When we arrived at Penmarric on Saturday afternoon we found all the servants lined up to receive us in the traditional fashion. Helena was presented with a bouquet of flowers by the cook's niece and Young Medlyn made a speech. At last when our official welcome was behind us and we had dined alone, I slipped away to the village and stayed drinking with my friends till closing time. I felt better after that. On returning home I found Helena had already gone to bed, and rather than disturb her I slept on the couch in my dressing room. As a result I succeeded in having the best night's sleep I had had since my marriage. I felt my old self again when I awoke the next morning and didn't even balk at the tradition of taking Helena to church at St. Just so that the villagers could have their weekly glimpse of the Master and Mistress of Penmarric paying their respects to a nonexistent God.

Afterward at Penmarric we lunched with William and Jan-Yves. Jan-Yves, who was staying with William and Charity, had so far made no plans to build a house for himself and I began to suspect he had already spent the money I had given him for the purpose; the answers he gave when I questioned him about his future plans were ominously vague.

As always it didn't take me long to feel annoyed with him. He really was a tiresome youth.

Meanwhile Helena was inquiring after Charity and expressing surprise that she hadn't joined us all at Penmarric for lunch. There was nothing of the snob about Helena. She knew what Charity was and what she had been but she was still willing to be friendly toward her—within limits, of course. She wouldn't have invited Charity to dinner—or to a lunch that wasn't informal, but she meant well and I didn't blame her for paying lip service to the conventions.

However, William was more of a snob than Helena and evidently saw nothing strange about keeping his marriage morganatic. "Charity's shy of Penmarric," he said lightly, "and of you too, I think, Helena. You'll have a hard time getting her to call here."

The prospect didn't seem to bother him too much. He showed

no signs of trying to change his wife or raise her up to his own social level, so I supposed he was content for her to remain as she was. It was certainly a curious marriage. I couldn't see how it could ever be a success.

After our guests had left Helena and I motored over to Zillan to see my mother. I enjoyed the couple of hours we spent with her, and by the time we returned to Penmarric I was feeling less embarrassed by Helena and more at ease in her presence.

In the hope that now I was in a better frame of mind everything might yet be well between us, I went to bed with her. But it was useless. The next morning I avoided the mine and nerved myself instead to stop in St. Just to see Dr. Salter.

It was difficult to tell him, but I managed it somehow. I was so strung up over the business that I had a hard time keeping calm, but I controlled myself so that he didn't see how upset I was. I liked old Salter. He had brought me into the world, and there's something comforting about a family doctor who knows not only one's own medical history but the history of one's family as well. After listening sympathetically he proceeded to act as if the matter were no more than a transient inconvenience and told me not to worry.

"Often happens on honeymoons," he said cheerfully. "Honeymoons are often a sadly overrated part of getting married. All that strain and stress beforehand—by the time you board the train with your bride you're physically exhausted! I'm sure this is nothing for you to concern yourself about."

I began to feel better. When he had examined me he straightened his back and took off his spectacles.

"Absolutely nothing wrong with you," he said emphatically. "No reason on earth for you to worry—in fact I strongly advise you not to worry. Don't rush. Let things take their time. The more you worry the more difficult you make things for yourself."

The enormity of my relief was beyond description. After so much wretchedness it was wonderful to hear someone tell me everything was going to be all right.

"By the way," he added as an afterthought, "when did you last have intercourse?"

The question was like a blow between the eyes.

I saw he had not understood, but although I tried to tell him

521

the truth the truth refused to be spoken. In the end I said evasively, not looking at him, "I haven't been near another woman since I began to take an interest in my wife."

He laughed, made some jovial comment about being out of practice and that he had no doubt all would soon be well.

"And if it isn't?" I said.

"Well . . ." He paused to consider this unlikely possibility. "Come back and see me in a fortnight's time if you're still having difficulty, and we'll discuss the situation further."

I thanked him, shook hands and walked away from his house toward the mine. But my relief was gone, my depression was crawling back to repossess me and a chill wind blew toward me as I turned to face the sea.

[3]

I went back to him two weeks later. He was surprised to see me and treated the matter much more seriously.

"You'd better have a more detailed examination," he said. "I happen to know there's an excellent man at Falmouth who's an expert on this kind of trouble. Could you travel to Falmouth to see him?"

I could and did. The doctor at Falmouth was an ex-navy man, salty and blunt. I trusted him at once and became sure he could help me, but he couldn't. After I had seen him several times he merely sat back in his chair and told me there was nothing he could do.

"The tests were all negative," he said tersely. "There's nothing physically wrong with you."

I felt desperate. My nerves were stretched tight with the strain. "There must be something wrong," I said. "There must be. I don't understand."

"If you want a second opinion I could recommend you to a man in London—"

"No, I trust you. If you say there's nothing wrong with me I believe you." I twisted my hands together, trying to think what I could do next. "I don't understand" was all I could say. "I just don't understand."

There was a silence.

"Look," he said at last with a gentleness I wouldn't have expected from him, "I'll tell you what I'd advise you to do. I'd advise you to go to London and see a doctor I know in Harley Street—"

"But I've already told you," I said blankly. "I trust your judgment. If you say there's nothing physically wrong with me I believe you. I don't want a second opinion."

"This doctor isn't interested in that branch of medicine. He's a psychiatrist."

"A psychiatrist!" My nerves snapped at the insult. Tension made me lose my temper quicker than I would normally have done. "A psychiatrist! No thanks, I'm not having anything to do with that kind of nonsense—I'm not paying out money to some bloody quack when I'm as sane as you are! If you seriously think—"

"It's you who should be doing the serious thinking, Mr. Castallack."

There was a silence. After a moment he leaned forward in his chair and began to talk rapidly in a sharp, abrupt voice. "Listen," he said. "You're not a fool. You're an intelligent man of thirty-two and there's no reason why I should beat around the bush with you. I'm not going to tell you there's nothing wrong with you whatsoever. There is. There's something very wrong with you, but it's not something I'm able to cure—it's not even something I know much about. So I suggest you go and see a doctor who specializes in this field of medicine. It's the logical, sensible thing to do, can't you see? All I've proved is that there's nothing wrong with you physically. Well, that's fine but it's not going to help your relationship with your wife, is it? It doesn't cure your problem—whatever your problem may be, and you do have a problem, make no mistake about that. For some reason you have a block in your mind which is preventing you from achieving a normal sexual relationship. I don't know what that reason is. You may. Or you may not. You may have an inkling of an idea what it is but it's a safe bet to say you really have no knowledge how extensive the block is or how you can overcome it. You need help—but it's a help that I'm unable to give you. So take my advice and go to London to see this man because he's an expert and he'll find the problem, whatever it is, and help you to try and overcome it and lead a normal life."

There was another silence. I no longer found his suggestion insulting, but I was still unwilling to admit the solution he proposed was either right or necessary. I knew what was wrong with me. I knew what kept getting in my way. It was the memory of that scene at Brighton. I didn't need a psychiatrist to tell me I couldn't help connecting sex with violence and suffering, and I couldn't see how he could offer me a cure when the only possible cure could lie in my will power to overcome my aversion.

But then I remembered that night at the Metropole. Will power hadn't been much help to me then. If will power was all that was needed to cure me I wouldn't have been sitting there in that room in Falmouth.

"You think a psychiatrist would cure me?" I said slowly.

"I don't know, but at least there'd be a chance. Why don't you give it a try?"

I thought of Helena. I didn't want her to be unhappy. I thought of the son I wanted. The memory of Esmond flashed tantalizingly before my eyes.

"All right," I said abruptly. "What do I have to lose? Who is this psychiatrist and how do I make an appointment to see him?"

[4]

". . . so that was why I couldn't make love to my wife," I told the psychiatrist. It was odd how easy it was to talk to him. He didn't say much, so the onus was on me to fill up the silence. I'd thought he'd fire questions at me the whole time but it wasn't like that at all. "I couldn't make love to her because as soon as she wiped off her lipstick I was reminded of my mother at Brighton. Well, it's understandable, isn't it? I associate sex with memories of my mother suffering. I couldn't make love to my wife because the idea of sex left me cold instead of exciting me."

I looked around the room. It was quiet and peaceful. A plant drooped from a pot in a corner and the Venetian blinds were slanted so that the light fell obliquely across the floor.

"After that first failure," I said, working it out carefully, "I was held back not so much by the memory of Brighton—although that was still there—but by the fear of failing again. The more I failed the worse it got. That makes sense too, doesn't it?"

He nodded. He was a little man, a foreigner, with sad dark eyes and a small drooping moustache. I wondered what he was thinking about me and thought I could make a guess or two at the diagnosis lurking behind his silence. I decided to put him back on course.

"I suppose you think I'm in love with my mother," I said. "Isn't that what all you disciples of Freud would think? I was reading about Freud the other day in the encyclopedia."

He said nothing but permitted himself a polite smile.

"Well, that's a lot of nonsense as far as I'm concerned," I said. "My mother and I are close and I'm not ashamed to admit it, but she doesn't have much influence on how I run my life and I've always gone my own way without being tied to her apron strings. We do get on well together, it's true, but if her circumstances had been different it's possible I might not have chosen to spend all those years living with her at the farm. I'd have set up house on my own somewhere, I dare say, or shared rooms with someone my own age as one does at school—or as the undergraduates do up at Oxford. I enjoyed living at the farm and I liked my mother's company, but to tell the truth I did get a bit tired of all those women—my mother, my mother's great-aunt, my mother's servants. . . . Still, it would be wrong to complain. I always had plenty of friends of my own sex and whenever I wasn't at the farm I was always in the company of men. But you see I couldn't have left my mother at the farm. I was all she had. She had no one else to look after her. My brothers and sisters were too busy leading their own lives and my father had opted out of all his responsibilities where she was concerned, but at least I was there—at least although my father had left her she had me standing by to take his place. Well, I mean, I couldn't have left her, could I? It wouldn't have been right, and I didn't want to leave her anyway. As I said, I liked living at the farm, although farming never meant as much to me as my life at the mine. . . .

"What drew me to mining? Oh, I don't know. I was just a born miner, I suppose. I was always unconventional. My father tried to cast me in the traditional mold—you know, public school, upper class and so on—but I wasn't standing for any of that. He and his class! They'd made my mother unhappy and I didn't want anything to do with them. I left public school as soon as I had any choice in the matter and went back to live among the miners. My father was furious, but he couldn't stop me. He tried to keep the mine closed then, but I got it open. I fought him over that mine. The mine meant so much to me. I suppose it's hard for you, a foreigner, to understand the magic of the Cornish mines. It's as if the mines are alive—sometimes they seem to live and breathe like people. A lot of the Cornish mines are called women's names—Wheal Mary Anne, Wheal Margery, Wheal Harriet—because the miners like to think of the mines having personalities of their own. My mine is called Sennen Garth. No one knows why except that Sennen is the name of the nearest fishing village beyond St. Just. The mine next door is called King Walloe because at one time it was rich enough to keep a king in luxury all his life . . . or so they say. But King Walloe's dead now. My father wanted Sennen Garth to stay dead but I got it alive again, I got it back on its feet. . . .

"It's warm down the mine. Sometimes it's hot as hell. It's wet and dark and exciting. It's an adventure. Yes, I suppose it's dangerous, but I'm careful—only a bad miner takes foolhardy risks—and I know I won't get killed there. I'm never afraid in my mine. I never have to worry about anything when I'm there. Outside above ground I always have so many worries and distractions, yet when I'm in my mine I'm always at peace. But I don't suppose you could ever understand.

"My father didn't understand. No, we didn't get on. Perhaps we were temperamentally too alike—I don't know. All I know is that he was a damned bad husband to my mother and a damned bad father to me. Maybe he didn't mean to be. Maybe I never really knew him, but that's my opinion on the subject and I don't expect to revise it in the foreseeable future. I was sorry when he died and guilty too because he died in the middle of one of my quarrels with him, but to be honest he wasn't much help to me when he was alive, and he certainly wasn't much help to my mother either. Why, even before they separated I remember how often he used to leave her alone at Penmarric. No wonder she turned to me for companionship! She never got companionship from him. . . .

"Yes, I was her favorite. What of it? I was the best of the bunch anyway, so I'm not surprised she singled me out from the others. The others couldn't have helped her as I did, and she needed someone to help her back in those days when . . . well, as far back as I can remember. Yes, as far back as I can remember I was looking after my mother and keeping her company, and the older I grew the more necessary it became to take my father's place at her side and step right into his shoes. Hell, what else could I have done? It was my duty, wasn't it? My mother was all alone in the world and she had no one else to look after her except me. Of course I had to take his place! Damn it, I wanted to take his place! I was sick to death of seeing her so unhappy and all I wanted was to look after her so that no one could ever make her unhappy again. She was so beautiful, you see, she was such a unique and exceptional woman, and it seemed all wrong that she should have to suffer so much. I couldn't bear to see her unhappy." I looked at him. It was suddenly vital that he should understand. "You do see, don't you?" I said. "I just couldn't bear to see her suffer. That's all it was really. I just couldn't stand to see her unhappy."

[5]

To my surprise the psychiatrist didn't seem to place nearly so much importance on the scene at Brighton as I did. I managed to get him to agree that it was an unpleasant scene to have witnessed, but when I tried to persuade him to confirm that my mother's suffering at Brighton was the reason for my present impotence with Helena he remained infuriatingly noncommittal.

"But if Brighton is unimportant," I demanded, determined to prise a judgment out of him, "why is it that it always comes between us whenever I try to make love to my wife?"

"I thought you said it didn't always do that. I believe you told me this happened merely on the first occasion—" he consulted his notes—"although naturally you were aware of the memory afterward."

"Yes, but—"

"The scene at Brighton is of importance, of course," he interrupted, "I did not say that it was unimportant. But the scene at Brighton in my opinion, Mr. Castallack, is a mere symptom—a symptom of a much more fundamental maladjustment." I must have looked disbelieving, for he added, "Consider it from this point of view: There is a command built into your mind which says: Do not have sexual relations with a woman. You're not aware of this command, yet it exists and sends out signals you can't ignore. When you first had the opportunity to enter into a sexual relationship with your wife the command promptly sent out its signals to stop you—and the signal in this case was the long-repressed memory of Brighton. A drastic signal, perhaps, but it was a drastic event, was it not? For the first time in your life you were being virtually forced to form a sexual relationship. You could not escape from it. It was unavoidable. So the signal had to be so powerful that it would pull you up short on the brink—which it did."

"Well, no doubt that's all very clever," I said dryly, "and I know the human brain is capable of all sorts of things and I certainly wouldn't be so presumptuous as to argue with you, but what's the solution? What do I do to cure myself? How can you help me?"

He smiled mirthlessly and shook his head. "There's no quick cure, Mr. Castallack. It isn't as if the trouble was a headache for which you could swallow two tablets and presently feel your normal self again. I believe I can help you, but I shall have to see you again many times before any marked improvement is possible. It's necessary, you understand, for you to talk to me at much greater length, particularly about your childhood and your early years. You've given me an admirable thumbnail sketch of your parents and background, but I must have more than a series of thumbnail sketches if I'm to help you as much as I would like to."

I stared at him in dismay. "But that's not possible!" I exclaimed angrily. "I have my work in Cornwall, my business interests! I can't keep coming up to London every week to talk to you. Good God, Penzance is nearly three hundred miles from London! It takes hours to get here from there."

To his credit I must admit he seemed as dismayed as I was. "But I would have to see you at least once a week," he said at once. "Indeed, in the beginning I would prefer you to come twice a week. Is there no possibility that you could stay in London for a time?"

"None at all. I have to be in Cornwall."

He sighed heavily and was silent.

"Come, sir," I said sharply, "there must be something you can do! You must be able to give me more immediate help than that! Why do I have to visit you so many times? Can't you diagnose the trouble now and tell me what's the matter?"

"You have to discover the truth for yourself" was all he said. "That may take a long time. If I were to talk to you now in abstract terms you would not only disbelieve every word I said but you would also be unable to relate them to your own situation."

"Then I see no solution," I said flatly. "I can't stay in London and you can't help me if I go back to Cornwall. I see no solution."

"Is that because you don't want to see a solution, Mr. Castallack?"

I grabbed my temper and kept calm. "Naturally I want a solution," I said coolly, "but I admit I'm at a loss to know how to find one. Perhaps you have a suggestion to make on the subject?"

He hesitated. "You might try writing everything down," he said with reluctance. "Write an account of your life—as detailed an account as you can possibly make it—and when you've finished it, post it to me. I shall read it and study it carefully, and then when you are next in London perhaps you could make another appointment to see me. I'm afraid that's the best compromise I can suggest."

"But I'm not a writer!" I stared at him angrily. "I'm not used to writing!"

"You are an educated man. You can spell words and form sentences. Try it."

"But I—"

"It's the best compromise I can suggest, Mr. Castallack," he said politely, cutting short the argument, and after that there was nothing more I could say except "thank you" and "goodbye."

I was tempted to "chalk the episode up to experience," as Alice would have put it, and forget about that visit to London, but I didn't. I suppose my position was too desperate not to clutch at any straw I could lay my hands on in my sea of troubles, so as soon as I got back to Penmarric I shut myself in my father's study, found paper and ink and began to write.

The odd part was that I took a fancy to it. Perhaps writing wasn't such an alien hobby to me after all, for my father had been a writer and my mother had for years kept a diary voluminous enough to make Queen Victoria's journal look like a tear-off calendar. At first I could do no more than make random jottings, but gradually I became more coherent and now—years later— I find I can attempt to edit my writings and shape the most important parts into some sort of order. No, I didn't send the manuscript to the psychiatrist as he had requested. No, I never saw the psychiatrist again. Why? Because I hadn't finished the first draft of my life story when I found the solution to my troubles, and once I'd found the solution and accepted it there was no need for me to see a psychiatrist any more.

For after six months I came to terms with myself. After six months of misery and embarrassment with my wife I asked myself: What can I do to be happy? What can I do to put an end to this wretched situation? And the answer was surprisingly simple. All I had to do was to recognize the truth. I had to admit my failure, meet it face to face and resolve to live with it. It was hard, of course, but I forced myself to confront the facts.

I didn't love my wife. I didn't want to be a husband. I didn't even want to be a father except to provide an heir for Sennen Garth one day. Least of all did I want a conventional existence as master of Penmarric. I had to live there with Helena certainly —there was no way out of that—but I decided I wasn't going to let either Penmarric or Helena stop me from living the kind of life I had to live in order to be happy. After all, there was nothing wrong with enjoying myself at the mine, dining more often with my mother at the farm and spending more time exploring the cliffs with Trevose on fine Sunday afternoons. I became more determined than ever to live as I wanted to live and not live as society dictated I should. No more doctors. No more psychiatrists. I'd had enough of all that. I'd had enough of Helena too although I tried always to be as kind to her as possible since I knew I'd given her a rough deal and I wasn't so inhuman that I didn't feel guilty about the emptiness of our marriage.

I went my own way.

I knew it was wrong. I knew I was treating my wife badly by ignoring her and I knew I was destroying my marriage by pretending it didn't exist, but by that time the desire to revert to my old ways was so strong that I could no longer make any effort to resist it. Cautiously I began to enjoy life again—but unknown to me I was already enjoying myself on borrowed time.

For ahead of me, not far ahead of me now, lay the world's end and retribution. It was 1928. I had two years left, although I didn't know it then—not two years of being alive, naturally, or I wouldn't be here to tell the tale, but two years of living and being able to explain why there was some point in being alive. But I didn't know that. Fortunately I couldn't see into the future.

My family seemed not to realize anything was wrong with my marriage, even though I had told Helena she could seek a divorce whenever she wanted one and that I wouldn't blame her if she decided to leave me for someone else. However, she didn't leave me and the issue of divorce was thus put in abeyance. It was true that the marriage could have been annulled, but I would have opposed that and Helena herself never suggested it. She too had her pride, and soon I saw she was just as anxious as I was to keep up the façade of our marriage and pretend to everyone that nothing was wrong. The only time when she came close to betraying her true feelings was when Jeanne married Gerald three months after our own wedding. The ceremony was not as pathetic as it might have been since both the bride and groom looked so happy throughout, but Helena broke down and wept. Nobody thought this was odd since women are supposed to weep at weddings, but I doubt if Helena would have wept if she hadn't been thinking how ironic it was that her own husband was no better than her brother in his wheelchair.

There was no honeymoon, since Gerald wasn't strong enough to travel, and after the wedding Helena spent an increasing amount of time at Polzillan House. Sometimes I wondered if she spent too much time there, but I felt sure Jeanne was too ingenuous to suspect there was anything amiss between Helena and myself.

No one suspected anything.

I saw little of William apart from our routine meetings to discuss the affairs of the estate, and Jan-Yves was too involved in his own affairs to pay me much attention. His house had remained unbuilt and he had had no home of his own since my marriage, but at Christmas he created a sensation by announcing his intention to marry Felicity Carnforth. Felicity was the hearty spinster I had invited to the first dinner party I had given as master of Penmarric. She was six years older than Jan-Yves, an heiress and bore a striking resemblance to the back end of a tram.

"I suppose you're making no secret of the fact that you're marrying her for her money," I said, trying to hide my contempt.

"None at all," said Jan-Yves cheerfully. "Felicity thinks it's a marvelous idea and so do I. As a matter of fact, we get on very well together. I know she's plain, but she's funny and sensible and she's got a good sense of humor. I see no reason why we shouldn't be just as happy as you and Helena are."

There was no point in commenting on this and in fact I sensed any further discussion might prove dangerous, so I merely wished him well and let the subject lapse. My mother received the news of the engagement with mixed feelings. Her sentimental streak made her disapprove of the fact that Jan-Yves was obviously not head over heels in love with his fiancée, but her good sense pointed out to her that it was a good match for Jan-Yves not only financially but socially as well. Finally she decided to give the marriage her blessing and began to plan what she should wear at the wedding at Easter.

Fortunately my mother was the last person to suspect anything was wrong between Helena and myself. She visited us frequently, for she liked Helena and was fond of her. In fact her attitude to Helena contrasted sharply to her attitude to her other daughter-in-law. Relations between my mother and Rebecca had worsened, not improved, with the passing of the years.

"She's so common!" my mother would say distastefully. "Deborah should be brought up to be a lady and sent away to a nice girls' school to escape from that unsuitable rural environment, but Rebecca won't be bothered. I can see Jonas will grow up into a very working-class young man unless something's done about him. What a tragedy Hugh died when he did! He would have taken better care of the children and kept his wife in order. . . . I wouldn't be at all surprised if her morals were rather loose. Her mother Clarissa Penmar was a most immoral young woman and that sort of thing often runs in families."

So my mother turned from Rebecca to Helena with relief and never breathed a word against her until July came and with it the day of our first wedding anniversary.

"Helena does want children, doesn't she?" she said to me anxiously. "She's not making any effort to avoid having them?"

"No."

"Dear me, I hope . . . Of course, she *is* very slim. Sometimes slim women have difficulty in conceiving as well as in giving birth—or so Griselda used to say."

"My God, Mama, give the girl a chance! We've only been married a year!"

"Yes, but by the time I celebrated my first wedding anniversary I already had Stephen . . ."

I reassured her, changed the subject and when I felt myself becoming upset I merely told myself that it didn't matter, that nothing mattered so long as she didn't find out the truth.

Esmond came to stay for a month that summer. I had a wonderful time with him. We went riding over the moors together and exploring the coast and at his request I took him down the mine and showed him around. He came alone to Penmarric; Mariana was busy in London, where she had been involved in a society divorce suit, and had wanted Esmond to be out of the way while the case was being heard. She herself was neither doing the divorcing nor being divorced, but she had obviously been implicated in an unsavory scandal, and from the newspapers I took care to hide from my mother I realized Mariana had achieved a certain notoriety in London circles.

But Esmond and I didn't talk of Mariana. We talked of riding and mining and Cornwall, and I enjoyed myself so much during his visit that I was thoroughly upset when the time came for him to go. After that I felt more depressed and more lonely than I had ever felt before, and it was then, at the emptiest phase of my life, that I turned at last to Alun Trevose.

10

Richard was suspected of sodomy. . . . Certainly he liked men, especially the trouvères of north France; in spite of the differences in rank, these artists were his constant companions.

—The Devil's Brood,
ALFRED DUGGAN

The crusade of Richard I belongs to world history. . . . But he found it necessary to withdraw his troops and to abandon for ever the hope of recovering the Holy City [after] the last event of this costly enterprise.

—Oxford History of England:
From Domesday Book to Magna Carta,
A. L. POOLE

[1]

Of course Trevose had always been there. It wasn't as if I had just discovered him out of the blue. He had been my closest friend for a long time, the friendship beginning when I was twenty and a novice at the mine, and the ten years which separated us had never seemed to matter. But I had been different in those days when we had first known each other. I was young then, wrapped up in my dreams for the mine and believing that everything I touched would turn to tin if I tried hard enough. Now I was changed. I knew what it was to fail and keep on failing no matter how much I wanted to succeed. I no longer believed myself to be invincible. I was disillusioned, cynical and isolated, and the more I became aware of my isolation the more I longed to confide in someone. But there was no one to confide in except Trevose, my best friend, and my troubles were too private even for his ears. I went on suffering my isolation in silence but gradually as the months passed I contrived to confide in him by implication.

I never mentioned Helena to him, never spoke of my marriage. I sought his company on Sundays, stayed up late drinking with him, had him to an informal supper at Penmarric when Helena was dining at Polzillan House. Inch by inch I saw he guessed what had happened and that although he didn't know the exact truth he knew, as no one else knew, that Helena and I were privately estranged. Yet still we didn't speak of it; I never referred to my marriage and never mentioned to him openly that all was not as it should have been between Helena and myself. But I knew that he knew, and I waited for him to make some move to indicate that he was ready to listen if I wanted to confide.

It was in the summer of 1929 when it happened. We were out walking one Sunday morning along the cliffs when everyone else was at church, and suddenly he said without warning, "What happened between you and your wife?"

The sea breeze blew in lightly from the northwest. I heard the surf crash at the foot of the rocks far away and felt the gorse scratch at my trousers as we followed the cliff path to Zennor.

"I've always wanted to know," he said, "but didn't like to ask. I didn't want to seem too familiar. None of my business anyway."

After a moment I said, "I don't want anyone else to know about it."

"Sure. I understand. Stands to reason."

We walked on a little farther and the sun shone and the translucent water around the offshore rocks of Gurnard's Head was the color of Helena's eyes. "It was no good," I said at last. "I shouldn't have married."

"I told you," he said, and the ugly colonial accent which predominated in his voice blurred in sympathy and became softer, more Cornish. "Didn't I? I told you."

"You told me."

We walked on, turning out onto the spur of Gurnard's Head. The cliffs were black and sheer, the white foam frothing on the rocks far below.

"Everyone's different," said Trevose. "Some people have to get married and some people have to run around after women and some people don't. Not all people are alike. Stands to reason."

"Yes."

"You're like me. I knew what suited you better than you yourself did. You ought to have listened to me."

I laughed at him, mocking his seriousness for some reason I did not understand. "And what would you have told me if I'd listened to you?"

"Not to get married."

"Just that?"

"Just that."

"Being a bachelor isn't everyone's idea of fun!"

"There's bachelors and bachelors," said Trevose. He glanced out to sea. There was a ship on the horizon, far away, scarcely moving, a little man-made toy floating on the vastness of the Atlantic Ocean. "There's fun to be had," he said, "if you know where to go. St. Ives can be fun in the summer. I go there now and then. I prefer it to Penzance. Penzance is an ordinary sort of place. Dull really."

"I didn't know you ever stirred out of St. Just!"

"I don't announce it to all and sundry." He was still watching the ship, his hands in his pockets. "I don't go often. Maybe one Saturday night once in a while."

"But how do you get there?"

"Thumb a lift. Or there's the bus."

"You stay overnight?"

"Usually have to. No way of getting home late at night. But I don't mind. There's usually a free bed somewhere." He rubbed his nose absent-mindedly. "Why don't we go together some time? We needn't get involved in anything if you didn't want to but there's a place I know. . . . Interested?"

"Not much," I said frankly. "I don't want to waste my Saturday nights picking up women."

"But I wasn't talking about women," said Trevose.

[2]

After all had been made clear between us I said, "I'm sorry, I'm not that kind of man. And even if I was I've no intention of laying myself open to blackmail. I've got more sense."

"True," he agreed, unembarrassed. "You've got more to lose than I have. All right, let's forget it."

"I'll tell you what," I said. "I'm not averse to driving into St. Ives one evening and having dinner at that little fish restaurant by the harbor. Why don't we do that instead?"

"Fine," he said. "Sounds like a good idea. When shall we go?"

We agreed on a date and drifted into a discussion of lobsters. Later he said to me, "Sorry I brought up that other business," and I said, "Don't be so bloody silly! There's no need to apologize. I'm not a prig and I don't care what you do for amusement. It doesn't matter to me."

But I found it did. We went to St. Ives a couple of times and had some grand hours dining together and wandering around the town afterward, but on our third visit we went drinking and visited a pub he knew.

I didn't like the people there and wanted to leave, but Trevose was busy talking to an old friend and there was no dragging him away. In the end I told him I'd meet him at the car and left him with his friend, but although I waited a long time he didn't come. Finally I fell asleep in the car and only awoke when he opened the passenger door and slipped into the seat beside me.

I opened my eyes. It was dawn. "What the bloody hell were you doing?" I said in a burst of fury and saw his eyes widen as he lit a cigarette.

We quarreled. I lost my temper but he kept calm and let me shout at him without making any attempt to interrupt me. When I had finished at last all he said was "What's the matter, sonny? Jealous?"

I stared at him dumbly, and as I stared he put his hand on my shoulder in the gesture of comradeship he had made so often at the mine and said with an odd, contrite honesty, "I'm sorry, it won't happen again. I just wanted to show you, that's all."

There was a silence but when I said, fumbling for my words, "Show me what?" he said, surprised, as if it were the most natural thing in the world, "The truth, of course. What else?"

And then I saw it all.

[3]

We had a year together. That was all. Just a year.

What Helena thought, I don't know. She must have realized that there were nights I never came home, but she said nothing to me and I said nothing to her. I hardly ever saw her. I saw more of my mother, whom I visited regularly every week, than I saw of Helena. Toward Christmas I began to drop in at the farm with Trevose from time to time, but my mother didn't like Trevose. She couldn't have had any inkling of the state of affairs which existed between us, but although she was very civil to him I could see she was glad when I came on my own.

Spring came, the spring of 1930. The end was very near now, although I didn't know it. The end was coming very soon. At the close of April it was only four months away. There wasn't much time left.

May passed. Then June and July. There was no warning, no hint of what was to come. We went to the mine every day and left the "dry" in the evening just as we always did. There were no premonitions, no portents, just our ordinary working life all through the summer until the very end of August.

And then, on the thirty-first of August 1930, my world came to an end.

It was a day just like any other. I went down the mine in the morning and later ate my sandwich lunch at "croust-time" with Trevose at the two-forty-fathom level beneath the sea. When we had finished I said, "I'd better go to the surface now, I suppose. Someone from the freight company is coming to see me about that damned timber problem and I have to have a meeting with him in my office. I'll see you later."

"All right," he agreed. "How about the pub tonight?"

"Seven o'clock?"

"I'll be there." He grinned. "Get me a glass of cider if you're there before I am, and don't you drink it before I can get there to drink it myself!"

I laughed, waved, turned my back on him, and the light from my helmet turned with me to point down the long gallery back to the main shaft.

I never saw him again.

At the surface I changed, left the "dry" and walked across the yard to my office hut which adjoined the count house. It was a cloudy day but clear and still. I can remember looking back over my shoulder toward Cape Cornwall and seeing the engine house of the Levant standing starkly against that gray summer sky. When I reached my office I went in, closed the door and turned to hang up the raincoat I had slung over my arm.

It was then that a strange thing happened. I reached out to hang up my raincoat and the wall seemed to lean back a fraction from my outstretched hand so that I missed the hook. The coat dropped to the floor. I was just muttering a curse when all the objects on my desk, pens, pencils, ashtrays, began to rattle and beneath my feet I could feel the floor vibrating.

My first thought was that there was about to be a land subsidence directly below the flimsy building which housed my office. I dashed out into the yard. To my amazement I found the ground beneath my feet was still vibrating and as I looked around me wildly I saw a loose brick topple off a wall nearby and hit the ground with a crack.

Before I had time to recover from my surprise, the vibrations stopped. I waited, tensed, but the ground was still, the scene motionless and nothing stirred as far as the eye could see.

The door of Walter Hubert's office burst open and Jan-Yves rushed out. Swinging around to the buildings behind me, I could see men pouring out into the open from the dressing floors and the engine house, their shouts echoing weirdly in that airless silence.

"What the hell was that?" demanded Jan-Yves. He was white. "What was it, for Christ's sake?"

"I don't know," I said, but I did. By that time I had guessed what it was. It was an earth tremor, a rare but far from unknown phenomenon in Cornwall and the south of England. The tremors seldom did any serious damage and never rated more than a small paragraph in the local newspapers.

My blood ran cold.

I began to run. I ran and went on running, dodging the men who tried to ask me what was happening, and as I ran I thought only of my mine. I wasn't worried about the lower levels. They were new, sturdily built and could withstand a tremor or two, but not all Sennen Garth was new. Suddenly, far away in the recesses of my memory I heard the mine captain of the Levant say to me when I was a child, "Have you ever heard of a cave-in? Do you know what happens when timber supports are so rotten that one finger-touch will send them crumbling into dust? If there was a cave-in in the western reaches of Sennen Garth, do you know what would happen?"

I knew now what would happen. Knowledge wrapped icy fingers around my heart and throttled the breath in my lungs.

When I reached the main shaft all I could gasp was "Where's the gig?"

"Down at the two-hundred-fathom level, sir. Shall I—"

I grabbed the telephone, wound the handle. The line wasn't dead but no one answered it. Men clustered around me, but I was scarcely aware of them. I was aware of nothing save the telephone, my last link with my friends below ground, and my own crawling fear.

"Answer me," my voice said to the telephone. "Answer me."

But it was the mine who answered me first. The noise came echoing crazily up the main shaft to meet us, a far-off rumbling roar from the very heart of the mine. It was a shocking noise, primitive and annihilating. It went on and on as if it would never end.

I flung down the phone and ran outside. I stumbled across the yard, scrambled over the slag-heaps and crawled toward the shaft I had explored as a child. All I could hear was the rasping of my breath and the ring of my shoes against the loose stones and far away in another world the distant droning nothingness of the sea.

I reached the shaft. I fell on my stomach and hauled myself to the edge, and when I looked over the rim the blast of stale air rose up to meet me, the smell of air trapped long below ground.

I looked down into my mine.

I saw water. Swift-flowing, evil-smelling black water from the mighty water tank of the flooded mine next door. The tremor had ruptured the dividing wall, the two mines which had stood shoulder to shoulder since time out of mind were now as one, and the water was rushing in from King Walloe.

[4]

All my friends died; everyone on that shift died, and we weren't even able to bring the bodies to the surface. Later there was a memorial service and journalists descended on St. Just from all over the world and sympathetic gifts began to pour in to alleviate the lot of the widows and orphans. People were very kind.

I bought Trevose his glass of cider and watched it stand untasted at the bar as I drank my shot of whisky. I buy cider for him every year on the thirty-first of August. If anyone ever thinks me hard and unsentimental they ought to see me buy that annual glass of cider. It's odd how a trivial gesture like that can come to mean so much.

It would have taken a fortune to drain the mine and begin again, and anyway there was no more money. As it was I had already spent too much of Helena's capital, and even if I had spent the rest it would have proved to be a mere drop in the ocean of expenditure required. Sennen Garth was dead, and no power on earth would ever bring it back to life again.

Yet in dying the mine fulfilled the last of my childhood ambitions, for after the thirty-first of August 1930 there wasn't a tinner alive who hadn't heard of the famous Sennen Garth mine. Seven thousand miles from Cornwall in the heart of the Canadian Rockies I was to hear men say to me, amazed, "You worked in Sennen Garth? Jesus, how did you ever get out of that hole alive? That must have been the hell of a mine. . . ."

So I had everything I ever wanted for my mine, Sennen Garth, the last working mine west of St. Just. That was fair enough, after all. No man ever worked harder for getting what he wanted than I did, and no man ever made more sacrifices or devoted himself so wholly to his cause and his life's work. Yet when the fighting was all over and the battles had all been won, the only thing left for me to regret was that I was still alive to enjoy my mine's fame. For of course I should have died too, died in my own mine with all my friends about me, but that was the biggest part of the tragedy. I didn't die. My mine spared my life, just as I had always known it would, and I was left to live on alone with the estranged wife, the mighty mansion and the bleak unending web of lies which were left behind.

V

JAN-YVES: 1930-1945

Justice and Injustice

*Though John grew up to be an exceptionally wicked man
. . . he showed in later life a curious interest in religion—
which was not allowed to affect his conduct.*
　　　　　　　　　　　　　　—The Devil's Brood,
　　　　　　　　　　　　　　ALFRED DUGGAN

*A malign tradition has done much less than justice to the
character of King John. . . . It was not purely formality
that chaplains at Chichester said masses for the soul of King
John "of blessed memory" . . . [He] had a genuine and
even a conscientious interest in the administration of justice.*
　　　　　　　　　　　—Oxford History of England:
　　　　　　　　　　　　From Domesday Book to Magna Carta,
　　　　　　　　　　　　A. L. POOLE

*Whatever else one may say about John, there is no doubt
that his royal duty of providing justice was discharged
with a zeal and tirelessness to which the English common
law is greatly indebted.*

*He was industrious, clever and ingenious. At the same time
he was hot-tempered, wilful and capricious. He was generous to those who could not harm him, and merciless to
anyone who could. Above and behind all he was secretive
and suspicious, over-sensitive to the merest flicker of opposition, relentless in revenge. . . . Is it any wonder that men
delighted to tell stories of his wickedness without bothering
to establish their authenticity?*
　　　　　　　　　　　　　　—King John,
　　　　　　　　　　　　　　W. L. WARREN

1

It is possible that he saw little of his mother, for soon after his birth his parents became estranged, and Eleanor retired to Poitou, there to plot mischief for Henry with her older sons.

Perhaps the only one of the greater barons with whom John was on terms of back-slapping intimacy was his half-brother, William Longsword, earl of Salisbury, a bastard son of Henry II.

—King John,
W. L. WARREN

[1]

I was twenty-five at the time of the Sennen Garth disaster.

Twenty-five was a splendid age to be in my family. My father, for example, had been the master of a large estate, the husband of a beautiful woman and the father of a shoal of promising infants by the time he was twenty-five. He also had a reputation, soon to increase tenfold, as a historian. My father was a successful man. At twenty-five he had already made his mark in the world.

My three elder brothers (the legitimate ones) didn't do too badly either. Marcus never reached the age of twenty-five, but he certainly made full use of his time in the world before succumbing to dysentery at the age of twenty-three. It would be too unkind to call him a rake simply because he spent money like water to retain his place in the society columns, but there was no doubt he did have an extraordinary talent for making friends, charming birds from bushes, wasting my father's money and doing nothing which could remotely be described as work. My brother Hugh also had a talent for avoiding work, but he did at least have enough brain to know not only how to hang onto his money but how to make it grow as well. Hugh was clever. At twenty-five he had a wife, a daughter, his own home, his own income and all the time in the world to enjoy them in—and how many men of twenty-five can boast that, I'd like to know? Precious few, would be my guess. Finally, my brother Philip . . .

Well, I won't talk about Philip just yet. At the age of twenty-five Philip had a reputation so sacred in our part of Cornwall that he stood in danger of being unofficially canonized.

So there they all were, handsome heroes basking in golden success by their mid-twenties, and there was I, many years their junior, watching enviously from the wings. However, since it seemed to be taken for granted that one would have the world fawning at one's feet when one was twenty-five, I prepared myself for the inevitable and when my twenty-fifth birthday dawned at last on one wet August morning in 1930 I sat back and looked around and pricked up my ears to listen to the cheers.

There was a most unpleasant silence.

For I was nothing, no one. The family circle, completed before I was born, had remained closed to me, and even now twenty-five years after being born I was still scrabbling on the outside of the circle trying to get in, still tacked onto the family like some ill-fitting appendage, still wondering what I could do to become like my father, like my golden brothers—like anyone except myself.

I didn't want to be myself. I was the last person on earth I ever wanted to be.

"Good gracious me!" exclaimed my beautiful sister Mariana when she first saw me. "Did you ever see such an ugly child?"

I never forgave her for that. Years later when she wrote to ask my help, I turned her down. I had a long memory, stretching right back to the earliest days of my childhood, and I never forgot an insult or an injustice.

"That's a very naughty child, Mrs. Barlow," said the housekeeper I later hounded into handing in her notice. "I can't help thinking you're too lax in your discipline."

"He's a good child," said my old nanny whom I loved, "and I'll thank you to mind your own business, Mrs. Hollingdale."

I came to know early in life who my friends were; in fact I came to know several matters of importance early in life. The first fact I learned was that most people were against me. The second was that it was a fallacy to assume that there was any natural justice in the world at all. The only justice that existed one hammered out for oneself in the most expedient way possible, because in this world it was every man for himself and no one was going to raise a finger to help anyone else if it conflicted with his own interests. The third fact of life, a corollary of the second, was that all those nursery clichés such as "the good get their own reward," "a truthful boy is a happy boy" and "an honorable man has a satisfied mind" were a pack of lies. All the reward the good received were the jeers of the bad, a truthful boy usually ended up with a spanking and a satisfied mind was of little use if there were no material comforts to accompany it.

I was a realist. High-minded idealism and nobility of soul were all very well for some people, but they wouldn't do for me, because I was going to get on in the world and I was going to get what I deserved in spite of everyone who tried to stop me. If I had put my faith in the existence of natural justice I could have sat back and been high-minded and waited for what I wanted to fall into my lap, but at an early age I became convinced that the only hope anyone can have for obtaining their just rewards in this life is to possess a quick brain, a lack of scruples and an abiding resolve to trust no one and be forever prepared for those who smile upon you to turn and stab you in the back.

[2]

Having said all this it will be obvious why I felt motivated to put pen to paper to outline a few pertinent facts about myself. This is my insurance that I shall have a just judgment passed upon me by my children in case I should die before they're old enough to see the truth for themselves. If I were a high-minded idealist I would maintain a dignified silence and trust that natural justice would provide my children with a true perspective on their father's checkered career, but I know all too well that the famous Latin cliché *nil nisi bonum* . . . is as dead as a dodo, and since I do have certain influential enemies I think it would be a gesture of foresight if I set down the facts for my children before it's too late.

However, I must make one stipulation. No child of mine under twenty-one reads this manuscript, and I would prefer that none of my daughters read it until they were married. Yes, I know times are changing and I'm an old-fashioned hypocrite, but after all one must have certain standards, mustn't one? I don't think I'm being unreasonable.

First of all let me start by saying that I have no intention of dwelling at length on the events of my life before the Sennen Garth disaster in 1930, a few days after my twenty-fifth birthday. A veil is best drawn over my life before 1930, although I suppose if I'm to present a just picture of my life I shall have to refer now and then to the events of my misspent youth. Let me dispose of this painful subject as painlessly as possible by explaining exactly where I stood in relation to my family and my surroundings by the time I reached my twenty-fifth birthday.

My father had died in 1926, but my mother was still alive—two facts which meant very little to me since I had never cared for either of them. After they had become permanently estranged about ten seconds after my conception (a most remarkable accomplishment, I've always thought) the very idea of my existence was so repulsive to both of them that I was brought up by my large and comfortable nanny at Penmarric while my father removed himself to Oxfordshire to live with his mistress and his eight other children and my mother escaped to her farmhouse in Zillan parish. I saw neither of my parents till I was six. Then they repented and started pestering me for my attention, but by that time it was too late. I always thought it was odd the way they expected me to prostrate myself at their feet with filial devotion when they at last decided to take some notice of me.

However, long before 1930 I had decided that it would be politic for me to be on friendly terms with my mother and even before my father's death I had won my way into her good books without much difficulty. Naturally I had an ulterior motive: By chance I had discovered that my father had made my brother Philip his heir, and since there was a possibility that I might be Philip's heir when he chose to exercise his testamentary power of appointment I wanted to be sure that Philip regarded me in a favorable light. But there was only one road to my brother Philip's heart, and that one road was my mother.

I did not simply dislike Philip. I loathed him. I loathed him because he had all he wanted, because he was popular and successful, because he was my mother's favorite and the son my father favored in his will. I loathed him for his arrogance and for his attitude of contempt toward me, and I loathed him because I knew I was just as good a man as he was and deserved that golden popularity just as much as he did. Jealousy tore me apart. Even to look at him made my muscles knot themselves until they ached. I could hardly speak to him without making an immense effort.

My hatred was so intense that I often wanted to unleash it in a fight, but fighting was out of the question. I had to continue to woo him, win his favor, capture his confidence. Yet when I asked myself why I didn't throw in the sponge, catch the first tramp steamer to America and seek my fortune in another world, I couldn't at first give myself an answer. I wanted justice, of course. That went without saying. Penmarric should have been mine, not Philip's. He was my senior, it was true, and thus theoretically the heir by right of primogeniture, but my father was entitled to leave his fortune to a younger son if he preferred. Before I had had the bad luck to get sent down from Oxford (for being discovered in a compromising position during a light-hearted nocturnal raid on one of the women's colleges) I had definitely managed to become my father's favorite, and besides, he had been at loggerheads with Philip even after my fall from grace. The will, that masterpiece of illogical injustice, was unfair to me no matter how grievous my disgrace at Oxford.

So I wanted justice. But that wasn't all. I wanted Penmarric. It took me a long time before I realized how much my home meant to me, but I realized it when I was obliged to leave it and live in Penzance. I knew what I wanted then, when I woke each morning to stare at the tranquil waters of the south Cornish coast and the placid sands of Mount's Bay. I wanted the North Coast, the vital ugliness of the Cornish Tin Coast with its hideous cliffs and vicious flying spray, the roar of the breakers, the swoop of the gulls, the cruel empty moors sunning themselves beneath those restless changing skies. I didn't want the tame esplanade of Penzance or the stunted palm trees in the formal gardens near the Metropole! I wanted that other land, seven miles away across the hills, and most of all, even more than I wanted the land, I wanted the house, the ugliest old mausoleum in the whole of Cornwall, because for me it was home and I loved it and love somehow made it beautiful to me. Gradually as the months passed after my father's death and the years brought me closer to my twenty-fifth birthday and the Sennen Garth disaster, I came to realize that what I wanted most of all was to be master of Penmarric—not because of the money or because of the social prestige or because possession would symbolize success, but because I loved the house, each ugly gray stone, each square foot of the Cornish earth on which it was built, and because its very ugliness struck a spark of sympathy in my soul.

[3]

There were only two things Philip cared about, our mother and the Sennen Garth mine. By the time he became master of Penmarric I already had my mother eating out of my hand, so it was only logical that I should decide to turn my attention to the mine by offering to work there. I was penniless and had to earn my living somehow; and I thought it would be a wise move to learn as much as I could about the family business so that I could later win Philip's favor by proving my usefulness to him in the field of administration. Besides, I was already bored with helping my brother William with his duties as bailiff and felt a hankering for a new challenge in order to stave off my ennui.

The mine was exactly the challenge I thought I needed.

I soon realized I had bitten off more than I could chew. I loathed the place. The dark eerie galleries beneath the sea terrified me, and if it hadn't been for Philip's friend, the kingpin of the mining community, Alun Trevose, I would have abandoned my self-imposed apprenticeship before the end of my first week below ground. But Trevose made magic out of that mine. So great was his ability to inspire confidence in me that my fears dissolved as soon as he was within arm's reach and soon I found myself liking him as much as I trusted him. I liked his cynicism and his irreverent contempt for established institutions, and I liked the way he treated me as a man instead of following Philip's example and treating me as a schoolboy. For three months I trailed after him as he initiated me briefly into the mysteries of mining, but at last I was able to retire with my pride and dignity intact to the surface to help old Walter Hubert with the paperwork, and this suited me much better. Before long I was at ease with all aspects of the administration, including the accounts, and at times I was tempted to alter a figure here and there to improve my weekly salary. Common sense, however, always stopped me. If Philip had ever caught me being dishonest I knew I would have to forget my ambition to own Penmarric one day, and my dream of being master of Penmarric meant far more to me than a chancy increase in my weekly wage now and then.

By this time I was convinced I was Philip's heir. Even if he did marry (a disaster which his indifference to women made highly unlikely) I suspected he would be unable to beget anything but a lump of tin, and the only other rival I had was my infant nephew Jonas, the son of my dead brother Hugh and . . .

The most important woman in my life at the time of the Sennen Garth disaster.

My sister-in-law Rebecca, the sexiest woman west of the Tamar.

I could barely remember a time when I had not wanted Rebecca. I first saw her at Zillan rectory during a tea-party with the rector. I was almost seven years old at the time and she was twice as old as I was. Seven years old was a little young for carnal desire, but I do remember admiring her white skin and the glossiness of her dark hair. She was attractive at fourteen, and when she married Hugh at the age of twenty-one she was ravishing. I myself was fourteen then, in the throes of the darkest of adolescent depressions because I was so small and plain, consumed with the most unbearable frustration and racked by the most violent of fraternal jealousies.

In the end it was William who helped me to cope with the trials and tribulations of adolescence. William was the hero of my childhood, the eldest and best of my eight brothers and sisters, the idol who had assumed the roles of father, guide, philosopher and friend to me since I was six years old. William was always the first person I turned to when I was in trouble, so when I eventually discovered that I had inherited the strong predilection for the opposite sex which runs erratically through our family, it was to William that I eventually turned. I was sixteen when, beside myself with furious misery, I poured out to him in morbid detail every aspect of my inferiority complex. Women would never look at me. I repulsed them. I wished I had been castrated before puberty so that I wouldn't have to suffer so now. Nobody would ever love me. I was horrible, vile and sexually unattractive.

"How right you are," said William, urbane as ever. "I can't imagine any woman being attracted to a hideous scowl and a shifty expression and a mouth that turns down at the corners. Try smiling. Or laughing. Or better still, talking. No matter how good-looking a man is he won't attract anyone if he behaves like a stuffed dummy. The most valuable asset a man can have is an easy manner, a pleasant voice and an amusing line of conversation. You've got all three—when you try. So why give up without trying? All a man needs is nerve, charm and a bit of dash."

I sighed gustily. I didn't know what to say to women, I told him. I didn't know how to be charming. Most of them probably wouldn't like me anyway.

"Nonsense!" said William. "Most women will pay attention to anything in trousers. Stop being so overcome with false modesty and get out and enjoy yourself!"

But I didn't know how to set about it. I didn't know how I could meet a girl who might be friendly.

"I'll ask Charity," said William kindly. "Perhaps she knows a suitable girl brave enough to tolerate you."

Charity was the mistress he kept in St. Just. Before she had retired to devote herself exclusively to William's welfare she had won herself the reputation for being the best whore between Land's End and St. Ives, and even now was remembered as much for her generosity and warmheartedness as for her bedroom prowess and carnal hospitality. At William's request she gave me the address of a woman at Madron, and after that as far as women were concerned I never looked back.

Yet always at the back of my mind was the thought of Rebecca.

She and Hugh were very happy together. She had eyes for no man but him, and he—Hugh the philanderer!—had eyes for no woman save her. Marital bliss emanated from them so strongly that I could hardly bear to be in the same room with them whenever they visited Penmarric, and although as I grew older other women were to ease my frustration I spent all my teens and part of my twenties in love with a woman I couldn't have.

As soon as Hugh died I made my feelings clear to her, but that was too soon, she was too full of grief, and even when she began to recover she found she was pregnant and after that she had no wish to see me. I still called occasionally, but she was resentful of any attention from me, and in fact it upset me to see her pregnant with Hugh's child. I knew then that it would be many months before I had the chance of furthering our relationship along the lines I wanted.

The child, Hugh's posthumous son, was born eight months after Hugh's death, and my mother immediately wrote to say that as this was my father's first grandson to bear the Castallack name Rebecca would of course call the child Mark—or else some other family name which was suitable.

"I'll be damned if I will!" said Rebecca furiously, ripping the letter to pieces. "Who does she think she is, dictating to me like that? All right, I'll call him by a family name—a Roslyn family name! She called you Jan-Yves after her father, didn't she? And who was her father anyway? An illiterate fisherman from St. Ives! Well, I'll call my boy after my father—he at least was a semi-literate farmer! I'll call him Jonas. That was my father's real name. Joss was just an abbreviation."

"But I thought you didn't even like your father!" I protested. "You always said how disagreeable he was!"

"He'd had a hard life. He'd suffered."

"But—"

"No, don't *you* start dictating to me! That baby's name is Jonas and it's going to stay Jonas and if your mother dares to object—"

She did object. The quarrels over the wretched infant's name resounded back and forth across the moors between Rebecca's house at Morvah and my mother's house at Zillan and I wasted a lot of time attempting to pour oil on the troubled waters. But at least it gave me a good excuse to start calling on her again.

However, calling didn't get me very far, and as Christmas approached I found myself considering the situation afresh to make sure that I had made no error in my approach to her. My reasoning seemed logical enough; I knew without doubt that Rebecca wasn't going to remain chaste for the rest of her life; therefore since it was evident that she would one day sleep with another man I saw no reason why that other man shouldn't be me. I was available, kind to her, fond of the little girl Deborah, and ready and willing to help alleviate the loneliness of widowhood. Even though I was only twenty-one at that time I had already had enough women to know that I could get my own way with them if I tried hard enough. In theory I should be able to seduce her.

But in practice I was trying hard enough to burst a blood vessel and getting nowhere at all.

In the end it was Philip—of all people—who made matters easier for me. On Christmas Eve that year he gave his first dinner party at Penmarric and among the guests who were invited were Rebecca and myself. I had a hard time persuading her to go since she disliked Philip and was too much of a social half-breed to feel at ease at such a formal gathering, but once she was there I knew my efforts at persuasion had been worthwhile. I remember she wore a marvelous dress, bright red, with a neckline which so fearlessly exposed a section of the most breath-taking part of her anatomy that the view alone would have stopped a marauding army dead in its tracks. My mother once remarked that Rebecca's bosom was indecently large; I almost but not quite replied, "Who the devil wants a decent bosom?" The sight of Rebecca in that dress with her breasts swelling lushly upward from the strained scarlet satin was enough to make me so weak—or rather so strong—that I could hardly stand without severe embarrassment.

No woman, I thought to myself, not even Rebecca, wore a dress like that unless she was after something more indelicate than a good meal and decorous conversation.

I became more unbearably excited than ever.

When the evening was over I borrowed the Penmarric car, drove Rebecca back to Morvah and invited myself into the farmhouse for a cup of tea before beginning my return journey.

"All right," she said without enthusiasm.

We went into the kitchen. The children were staying the night with their great-uncle Jared Roslyn in the farmhouse next door and there was no one in the house apart from ourselves.

"I do like that dress," I said pleasantly. "But I can't believe you wore it without some sort of motivation."

"What's that supposed to mean?" she said in anger. "I wore it because I thought it was smart and fashionable and I didn't want to look dowdy besides that snooty Miss Meredith."

"Hardly fashionable, is it? Bosoms aren't in vogue at the moment, I hear."

She gave me a disdainful look and adopted her haughtiest, most ladylike tone of voice. "Must you," she said, "be quite so vulgar?"

"I don't see anything vulgar about a good bosom."

She turned away in a fit of temper, opened the larder door,

looked inside and slammed the door shut again. "You can't take a hint, can you?" she blazed, swinging around to face me. "How many more times am I supposed to say no? Are you so conceited that you can't accept the fact that I find you repulsive? Not only do you nauseate me physically but you revolt me with your smugness as well! Get out of my house and leave me alone!"

"I'll bet I'm as good as Hugh was in the bedroom. He and I were much the same height and build. Once you turned out the light you could imagine—"

"Don't, don't, don't!" She spun away from me, her shoulders shaking with sobs, and clapped her hands over her ears.

I couldn't stop myself.

Taking a step forward, I unhooked the top fastening of her dress before she whirled around and started to fight.

"Let . . . me . . . go!"

She fought wildly, scratching, clawing and biting.

I kissed her. I went on kissing her until all the fight had gone out of her and then I slipped my hand between her breasts and bent to kiss the flesh I exposed.

"No!" she said wildly, wrenching herself away. Her voice was harsh with sobs. "Go away—don't touch me!"

She escaped, ran out of the room and raced down the hall. I hared after her. She was stumbling up the stairs, the boards protesting noisily beneath her feet, but although I leaped up the stairs two at a time in pursuit she had dived into her room before I reached the landing.

The door slammed.

I stood staring at it, the blood pounding in my ears, and wondered if I was going deaf. There had been no sound of a key turning in the lock. Almost expiring with anticipation, I reached out and tried the handle.

The door was unlocked. Taking a deep breath, I tiptoed into the room.

She was lying face down on the bed, her voluptuous body asking to be released from the taut satin, her shoulders shaking with a virtuous display of protest. From the silver-framed photograph on the bedside table Hugh's face smiled at me knowingly. I placed the frame face downward on the table and waited. Nothing happened. There were no paroxysms of rage, no screams for help, no hysteria, and presently her sobs became softer and more inviting as if she had at last resigned herself to the inevitable.

I was dazed. My shoes eased themselves from my feet, my jacket alighted on a nearby chair and my tie floated toward the floor. Still hardly daring to believe that triumph was at hand, I stooped and, trembling in every limb, began to kiss the white naked nape of her neck as I peeled away that sensuous scarlet satin.

[4]

For a woman who said that I repulsed her and who had implied that she would not under any circumstances stoop to fornication, she really didn't do too badly. Despite the fact that I couldn't get enough of her she didn't seem to be dismayed. Her protests became mere courtesies to Hugh's memory; her stiffness dissolved at a touch; her sobs were swiftly transformed into shivers of sexual pleasure. We spent a wild, wicked, wonderful night together in that wide, deep double bed, and although she woke at dawn from a brief doze and begged me to leave before anyone should see my car still outside the house, I took her again while it was light enough for her to see my face. I thought it might be judicious to remind her who I was in case she had been fancifully thinking of me as Hugh. When I was dressed later she came downstairs to see me off and I asked when it would be convenient for me to call again.

"I don't want this to happen again," she said, her beautiful eyes brilliant with tears. "I've sinned terribly. I'll feel guilty for weeks."

"Nonsense," I said roundly. "You've been listening too much to your Uncle Jared and all that chapel tarradiddle about hell-fire and damnation. God wouldn't have made you the way you are unless he intended you to go to bed with men."

"You're an atheist. You can't understand."

"I most certainly am not an atheist!" I said indignantly, for religion had always fascinated me and I had often wished I could have studied either philosophy or theology at Oxford instead of trying to please my father by reading history. I confess I had never had any calling to be either a parson or a priest or even a Buddhist monk, but theological issues intrigued me, just as a legal problem will captivate a lawyer, and I would have liked to have given religion a more thorough intellectual examination—if only to prove to myself that natural justice did not exist and that God only bothered to help those who helped themselves. Now, annoyed at being accused of atheism, I said sharply to Rebecca, "I believe in God, just as you do, but I don't go to chapel, that's all. I don't believe it's wrong to enjoy oneself."

"I didn't enjoy it."

"My dear," I said, exasperated by this time, "I don't know what you were taught when you were a little girl but when I was a little boy I was taught it was very naughty to tell stories. In fact I grew up to believe it was even naughtier to tell stories than to admit that sex could just possibly by a great stretch of the imagination be enjoyable. But obviously you had a different childhood upbringing from mine."

"Men take advantage of a woman who enjoys that sort of thing," she said doggedly, not looking at me. "Men are always ready to take advantage of a woman and if the woman gives in she has nothing but unhappiness."

"But didn't you 'give in,' as you put it, to Hugh?"

"Not until we were married. After we were married it was different."

"After you were married you found you enjoyed sex as much as any woman!"

"Hugh was my husband. I loved him." Her eyes filled with tears. "He was good and kind and unselfish," she said, trembling. "No one knew Hugh as I knew him. He said I was the only person in the world who truly loved him, and I knew he was the only person in the world who truly loved me. My parents didn't love me. My father was always grumbling because I wasn't a boy and my mother never forgave me for ruining her health and spoiling her figure. Both of them used to shout at me when they weren't shouting at each other. My mother used to go on and on at me. 'Men take advantage of a woman,' she used to say, 'and don't you forget it. I wouldn't be in this hovel now,' she used to say, 'I wouldn't be in this state if I hadn't let Joss take advantage of me.' She had an affair with my father before she married him. She told me. Then he said he wouldn't go on sinning and that if she wanted to keep him she'd better marry him, but even when she promised to marry him he wouldn't marry her until she'd signed over all her money to him. She was so infatuated with him, you see, she just wanted to do anything he wanted—she couldn't bear the thought of losing him. But if he hadn't forced her like that she wouldn't have married him because she was so much better than

557

he was, a real lady with this money of her own and everything, and he was nothing, just a penniless farmer." A tear eased its way down her cheek. She fumbled for her handkerchief. "And then after they were married he changed," she said. "He made Mother unhappy. But it was too late by that time. He had all her money and she couldn't go away because she had nowhere to go—all her friends had turned their backs on her when she married. 'I wouldn't have married him and given him my money if I hadn't been so infatuated with him,' she said to me, 'and I wouldn't have been so infatuated with him if I hadn't stooped to a love affair. I would have kept the situation in perspective, seen things in proportion.' I think she did love me in a way even though my birth spoiled her health and figure. She was so determined I shouldn't make her mistakes—that's why she went on and on and on about not letting anyone take advantage of me. I think she did care what happened to me. I think she really did care."

"There, there," I said soothingly while casting a surreptitious glance at my watch. "I'm sure she did."

"My father went on and on at me too. 'There's only room for one slut in this house,' he said, meaning my mother, 'and just you remember that. If I ever catch you misbehaving yourself with any man you leave my house that same day and never return,' he said. 'You bloody well stay chaste till you marry or you'll regret it all your life. No man respects a whore and God punishes sinners. Just you remember that.' He kept on and on and on at me —I think he held it against me that I was like my mother to look at and he didn't want me to be too like her. Poor Mother."

"Well, both your parents are dead now," I said reasonably, moving out of the front door into the cold air of early morning. It was high time I left before my car was noticed outside her house, and I had every intention of leaving. "That part of your past is safely behind you. Now you can do as you please and enjoy yourself, and you can be sure I won't take advantage of you unfairly or even think of you as a whore and lose my respect for you. I don't react in that way where women are concerned, and besides, I love you. If you knew how often in the past I've longed for a night like this—"

"But it mustn't happen again! It mustn't!" Her eyes were dilated in her agitation. "We'd have no future—no good could come of it—I could never, never marry again—"

I clung to the worn shreds of my patience. "We do have a

future," I said, enunciating each word with clarity to induce her to understand such an obvious truth. "If you don't wish to marry me I'll try to accept your decision for the time being in the hope that you'll change your mind soon, but even without marriage we do at least have a future as a man and woman who enjoy each other's company. Now be sensible, darling, please—no emotional scenes! Face the facts. You need me and I need you, so we might as well go ahead and make the most of our mutual needs."

"I—I can't—I mustn't—"

"Very well," I said, thoroughly angry by this time. "When you get the itch for a spot of fornication write me a note and if I'm not doing anything too important I might drop in and offer my services for half an hour or so."

She burst into tears.

"Rebecca darling—"

"No, don't touch me! I gave you so much yet now all you can do is talk to me as if I were a whore!"

What can one do with such a woman? I did the only thing possible in the circumstances. I took her back into the hall and made love to her then and there on the hall floor. After that I kissed her, told her I would call again soon and then beat a rapid retreat to my bachelor bedroom at Penmarric to recuperate from my exhaustion.

[5]

I would have married her if she had accepted my proposal in the beginning. Unlike many men who practice fornication consistently I had no deep-seated prejudice against marriage. In fact I wanted to get married, not only to ensure myself a ready source of sexual gratification but also because I was lonely and liked to have someone around who could share a joke with me or even merely share a grumble at a spell of wet weather. The older I grew the clearer I came to realize that sexual gratification was available anywhere if one took the trouble to seek it, but a worthwhile friendship was much more elusive—and much more valuable.

At the time when I began my affair with Rebecca at the end of 1926 I was approaching one of the loneliest phases of my life. My favorite sister Lizzie obviously preferred Cambridge to Cornwall; I saw little of her, and to make matters worse her letters to me were full of nothing but swooning admiration for one of the professors, an intellectual with the stuffy name of Edgar St. John Callendar. Apparently they spent their time tea-drinking together and conducting passionate discussions on the subject of the Greek theater. I began to feel depressed. Privately I had long hoped that Lizzie would remain unmarried so that she could come and keep house for me if I failed to find a suitable wife; I hadn't anticipated her infatuation with academic life to outlive her adolescence and had certainly never anticipated her catching the eye of a Cambridge professor.

As if Lizzie's unwitting estrangement from me wasn't misfortune enough, I was horrified to see Charity dragooning William to the registry office and blackmailing him into making her his wife. William had belonged to me just as much as he had belonged to her, but now she had cornered him all for herself. Since he had always professed himself to be a confirmed bachelor I could hardly believe he had been so fickle and vacillating.

"Don't let her marry you!" I shouted at him, enraged, during a crucial stage of the proceedings. "You don't have to!"

"Silly of me, isn't it?" William agreed, unruffled as ever. "I suppose I must really want to marry her after all."

He was hopeless. I almost wept with anger, yet there was nothing I could do to stop him. To make this grisly year of my life even grislier I was turned out of my home. Philip decided he should try to beget a future caretaker for his mine and astounded me by announcing his intention to marry Helena Meredith, a cool, crisp blonde with repellantly well-bred bones and a slender, rather sexless body. I was sunk in gloom. I reasoned that Philip, homosexual or not, must know himself to be capable of a normal relationship with a woman or he would never have contemplated matrimony at all; much as I detested Philip I didn't think even he would have been capable of deceiving Helena by pretending he could be a normal husband when he was impotent, so in that case it now seemed inevitable that between them they would soon produce an heir to Penmarric. My ambitions seemed poised for sudden death. To make matters worse Philip gave me both money and permission to build a house for myself on the estate and made it clear he was buying me off his conscience and out of any future will he intended to make in regard to his wealth and property.

Life had never before seemed so monstrously unjust. I had a hard time accepting his bounty with a smile and displaying as much humble gratitude as my hypocrisy could muster.

After that I stayed for a time with William and Charity at their house in St. Just. I had no interest in building a house of my own on the Penmarric estate, no wish to watch Philip being master of the lands which should have been mine, no wish to clap my hands in admiration every time Helena brought a son into the world. Presently I invested Philip's money on the stock exchange with the idea of having a small income independent of my salary at the mine, but I was inexperienced in playing the market and soon lost every penny he had given me.

By this time I was in despair. I had no home and no money apart from my salary, and although William and Charity asked me to stay on as their guest I knew I was abusing their hospitality. I proposed again to Rebecca, but she still turned me down, and although I then suggested we lived together for a time without the blessing of the church she wouldn't have it. I supposed I could understand her refusal. In such a small rural community she would quickly have been ostracized for her loose-living and her Uncle Jared would undoubtedly have washed his hands of her. Besides, she had the children to think of. Naturally she wanted them to grow up with a good opinion of her and not to be affected by the hostility of a community which disapproved of her private life. I could understand, yet even though I understood, her refusal still hurt me. I would have slept with her every night if I had had the chance, but she refused to see me more than once or twice a week. She never once told me she loved me. Each time I had to beg to get what I wanted. If she hadn't had something so obviously worth begging for I would have abandoned her in a fit of rage and told her to go to hell, but no matter how much we cursed and yelled at each other beforehand I always went back to her afterward and she always ended our stormy scenes by an act of capitulation.

It was a very exhausting affair.

Finally I came to the end of my tether. I forced myself to face the unwelcome fact that Rebecca would probably never consent to replacing her beloved Hugh with a second husband, and with reluctance I came to the conclusion I could no longer wait for her to change her views on the subject of matrimony; it was imperative for my peace of mind that I acquire without delay a home, a decent income and a friendly woman who could keep me company when I couldn't sleep with Rebecca. I looked around feverishly. Almost at once my glance rested on Felicity Carnforth, and then and there, without any further hesitation, I decided to get married.

[6]

Felicity was the last person of importance to enter my life before the Sennen Garth disaster.

Her two brothers had been killed in the war, so Felicity as Sir Justin Carnforth's only surviving child was a considerable heiress. She was too much in love with her stable of horses to be greatly interested in a mere man, but she was astute enough to see that it would be more advantageous to her socially to be a married woman and that her father had no wish for her to remain a spinster. As far as romance was concerned she hardly interested me any more than I interested her, for she was an angular girl with buck teeth, but I liked her and thought it not improbable that we could evolve some mutually beneficial arrangement. I had by this time no romantic dreams of marrying for love; the only woman I loved refused to marry me, so that made nonsense of the notion that romance and marriage should go hand in hand. Presently I laid all my cards on the table, explained the entire situation to Felicity and was rewarded when she repaid my frankness by being equally frank with me.

"Well, I would like to get married, of course," she said. "Every girl does really, although everyone has different reasons. I'm sick of Daddy being grumpy and saying I'm not as pretty as Mummy was—as if it was *my* fault I inherited *his* looks!—and I'm sick of everyone saying poor old Felicity, she's jolly nice and all that but talk about being on the shelf . . . *You* know, Jan! You know how people talk! I wouldn't mind marrying you just to have a bit of peace. Honestly! I'm not in love with you, of course, but I'm not such a ninny as to expect true love will appear one day on a white horse and sweep me off to the altar. I'm simply not the type. Things like that happen to your gorgeous sister Mariana but not to girls like me. I don't care if you want to marry me for my money—at least you're frank enough to admit it. I couldn't have stood it if you'd swooned at my feet, sworn you loved me and promised me my money meant nothing to you! I would have laughed till I was puce and then we would both have been most horribly embarrassed."

I began to like her even more than I had before. We settled down and began to discuss a suitable marital arrangement.

"I'll ostensibly do my duty, I promise you," I said. "I'll live in the same house, act as your escort and look after you. But I can't promise fidelity, I'm afraid." I had already told her about Rebecca.

"What a shame she won't marry you!" said Felicity sympathetically. There was nothing bitchy about Felicity. "She's awfully attractive. I felt so sorry for her being widowed like that."

We discussed the matter further. "I think it would be best if we were husband and wife in name only," I said in my most businesslike voice. I had no desire to make love to her. "Then if anything goes wrong we'll have no trouble getting the marriage annulled."

"All right, but we'd better not have separate bedrooms to begin with or Daddy might smell a rat. I don't see why we shouldn't have twin beds, though. Twin beds are frightfully chic these days, everyone says so. Would you mind twins?"

I said I wouldn't mind in the least and we fondly departed from each other to announce our engagement to our respective families.

Rebecca at once flew into a passionate rage and called me heartless, faithless and a dozen other more unpleasant words besides. I was startled to see how radically the news affected her. For someone who had always, even after her surrender, professed to care nothing for me, she became hysterically vocal in objecting when I put her indifference to the test. Finally after I had spent at least two hours mopping up her tears and offering my usual brand of comfort, she calmed down and became more rational.

"You're not to blame," she said, blowing her nose on my sodden handkerchief. "It was wrong of me to blame you. You only turned to another woman because I'd always refused to marry you—I'd led you to believe I would never marry again, but oh, Jan, perhaps I was wrong, perhaps I should have accepted, perhaps . . . Oh, Jan, let's get married! I'm sorry I always treated you so badly—I didn't mean it—I do love you, Jan, I do—"

I was so childishly thrilled to hear such words from her lips long after I had given up hope of hearing them that I followed her example and lapsed into melodrama. I kissed her passionately, swore I'd never love anyone else as long as I lived, told her she was the most beautiful woman in the whole world and that I was the luckiest man who had ever drawn breath to live.

"All the same, darling," I said at last, "it *is* rather a tricky situation. You see, I really do have to marry someone wealthy. It's not that I don't love you, but—well, I have debts and obligations and now that Felicity and I have announced our engagement I really can't draw back. Supposing she sued me for breach of promise? Damn it, I'd end up in prison with my whole life ruined! I have to marry her—there's no way out of it now." In fact, I reasoned to myself, it was now absolutely impossible to draw back. It wouldn't have been fair to Felicity, and besides I had reconciled myself to the thought of sharing Felicity's prospects at Carnforth Hall. If I were married to Felicity I could live in the style to which I had long been accustomed and still have Rebecca whenever I wanted her, but if I married Rebecca I'd be in perpetual difficulty trying to make ends meet, particularly if we had children, and I had no guarantee I would inherit either Penmarric or the Penmar fortune. "Listen, darling," I said quickly. "This needn't make any difference to us. I must marry for expediency's sake, and who is there more suitable for a marriage of convenience than Felicity Carnforth? Surely not even you could be jealous of jolly old Felicity! I've had a talk with her and we've already worked out a sensible arrangement, marriage in name only, no sex at all—even separate bedroom," I added, slipping in a little lie to make the case more convincing. "Now I ask you, darling, would you really think I'd be tempted to make love to Felicity? Of course not! You know you're the only woman in my life and always will be."

"Oh, Jan—" She burst into tears again.

"Besides," I said, maintaining a fast pace, "you say you'll marry me, but are you sure you're not just making wild promises in the heat of the moment? I'd hate you to marry me, regret it later and then accuse me of tricking you into marriage while you were emotionally upset. And would you ever be able to put Hugh's memory behind you? If we were married wouldn't his memory always come between us?"

She gulped and blew her nose again. "Perhaps . . ." She was confused. "Yes, perhaps you're right, Jan, and I'm being rash in saying I'd be willing to marry you . . ."

I stifled a sigh of relief. I did love her very much and was terrified of losing her. At the same time I now saw clearly that I must marry Felicity. I felt as if I were walking on skates along a tightrope.

"I would love to marry you in so many ways," I said gently, "but it wouldn't be for the best, darling. You know it wouldn't."

Her lovely eyes filled with tears again. She looked ravishing. "Yes," she said. "You're right. I know you're right. It's just that . . ." A tear paused on the lush curve of her cheek and glittered like a diamond against her white skin. "It's so lonely here . . . and the children need a father. You're so good with the children, Jan."

"I'll come over here as often as I can," I said, touched. I hadn't thought of myself being good with children before. In fact I hadn't cared much for children except for the little girl Deborah, whose shy femininity appealed to me. "Marriage won't make any difference, darling, I promise you," I said sincerely. "We'll go on afterward just as before."

That was exactly what happened, even though my marriage turned out to be a little different from the prior arrangements I had made with Felicity. We were married nine months after Philip in the spring of 1928 and had a smart wedding in London. Felicity was determined to marry in style and make the most of her unexpected trip to the altar. The food at the reception was delicious, the champagne naturally the very best that money could buy, and afterward we roared merrily away to Paris to celebrate the occasion for another couple of weeks. However, the honeymoon proved to be my undoing. Felicity had wrought miracles with her appearance before the wedding and had bought a quantity of clothes which flattered her figure in the right places. Not content with revolutionizing her wardrobe, she had had her hair professionally styled and, I suspected, had also had a barrage of beauty treatments to enhance her looks. The results were shattering. By the time we reached the privacy of our Parisian hotel I knew that twin beds were going to make little difference to certain physical sensations which I had been forced to ignore during the journey, and by the time she had finally arrayed herself in the sauciest black negligée I had ever set eyes on I knew any attempt at chastity would be hopeless. We had a most successful wedding night and enjoyed ourselves enormously.

"Delightful!" said Felicity the next morning. "I wouldn't like to think I'd missed out on something. Never mind about the annulment, Jan darling, there's always divorce. I'm sure we can rustle up a little adultery if we're hard-pressed for a legal separation later."

So we continued to enjoy ourselves in Paris and again later when we stopped for a further two weeks in London before returning home. Felicity proved to be tremendous fun. We wined and dined everywhere from Soho to Knightsbridge, and we danced every dance from the fox trot to the Charleston. We danced until we dropped. Long afterward when I look back on my honeymoon I have a series of blurred memories of a London blazing with modernity—cocktails, night clubs, jazz bands, flappers with short-cropped hair and scarlet mouths, and all the time dancing, dancing, dancing . . . But our energy was limitless. When we weren't dancing all night we were racing around London during the day; we rowed on the Serpentine, walked in the park and even visited the zoo. By the time our honeymoon came to an end we were still enjoying ourselves so much that neither of us wanted to go home. The most extraordinary part of the situation was that by this time I was genuinely glad I had married Felicity and foresaw an amusing married life ahead of us, but as soon as I returned to Cornwall I fell under Rebecca's spell again and nothing could keep me away from her, not even my respect and liking for my new wife. Of course I never told Rebecca that Felicity and I had had a normal honeymoon, never mentioned that I still slept with Felicity once a week even after the honeymoon was over. I considered I owed it to Felicity to make at least a weekly gesture of appreciation since she was, as the saying goes, such a "good sport" and made what might have been a dreary marriage into a cheerful good-natured relationship.

Felicity and I had a wing of Carnforth Hall to ourselves; however, two or three times a week we were obliged to dine with her father and stepmother in the main part of the house. I was careful to maintain cordial relations with Sir Justin, who was an awful old bore, and he was so grateful to me for providing him with the hope of grandchildren that he was prepared to treat me generously. He increased Felicity's income by a large margin; Felicity instantly arranged a joint account for us at her bank, and after that I didn't have to worry about money any more. I bought a splendidly extravagant car—a Hispano-Suiza—and several new suits. Felicity bought some new horses and extended the stables. The only fly in the otherwise unblemished ointment of our happiness proved to be Felicity's new stepmother, my father's former housekeeper, Alice Penmar.

Alice and I had always disliked each other; now, linked to each other indirectly by our marriages, we continued to cling to our mutual distaste. She was one of those capable women who love to manage everything they can get their hands on. No doubt she managed Carnforth Hall even more admirably than she had managed Penmarric and Sir Justin even better than she had managed my father (I could never make up my mind whether or not she and my father had been lovers, but it did seem likely that she had been his mistress for a time). Certainly Sir Justin doted on her. She was fond of him, I think, and always treated him kindly, but I'm sure her heart was more in fulfilling her role to the community as Lady Carnforth than fulfilling her role to her husband in the conventional marital manner. At the time of my marriage she was about thirty-seven years old, clever, bitchy and sharp as a needle.

"She warned me against marrying you," confided Felicity, who didn't like Alice either. "Isn't that a hoot? Of course I jolly well told her to M.Y.O.B.—'Mind Your Own Business,' I said, straight to her face! I'm sure she thought I was beastly rude, but I didn't care. Then she started to try to tell me about you and Rebecca, so I said airily, 'Alice darling, is that all the gossip you can rake up? Jan's told me the *whole* story already!' My dear, she went puce with rage. It was so funny."

I began to feel nervous. I wasn't ashamed of my affair with Rebecca, but for her sake and for the children I did try to be as discreet as possible. Besides I now had Felicity to consider; I didn't want Felicity to be embarrassed by unpleasant gossip, but if Alice Carnforth was going to go around being bitchy on the subject of my mistress at Morvah I was going to end up by being thoroughly unpopular with my father-in-law.

I was much annoyed. "I wonder how Alice knew about my relationship with Rebecca," I said to Felicity as we brooded over the problem together.

"Alice knows everything," said Felicity. "She's that sort of woman. She rakes in gossip as easily as other women collect hats, and she can smell an illicit affair when all the couple have ever done in public is smile at each other and say, 'Nice weather we're having.' She's absolutely amazing. In fact I think her talent for raking in gossip is second only to her talent for twisting elderly men around her little finger. I'll never forget what a shock it was when Daddy said he was going to marry her. I knew he'd rather fancied her for ages, but I never actually thought he'd go ahead and let her lure him to the altar. After all, he absolutely loathed her father for jilting poor old Aunt Judith donkeys years ago, but Alice, apparently, had no trouble at all in convincing him that her father was doing Aunt Judith a favor by running off with someone else! I honestly think she could make him believe black was white if she tried hard enough."

We continued to ponder glumly over Alice for some time.

"I shouldn't worry too much if I were you," Felicity said sensibly at last. "As long as I'm obviously in the seventh heaven of marital bliss Daddy isn't going to believe a word against you. All he's really concerned about is my happiness, and if I'm happy he'll willingly believe your visits to Morvah are made out of sheer Christian charity to your widowed sister-in-law and your poor fatherless little nephew and niece. So long as Rebecca doesn't ditch the children and pop off with you for a naughty weekend at Budleigh Salterton I'm sure he won't even raise an eyebrow of disapproval."

This was true, but I still felt uneasy about Alice and had a nagging suspicion that she was going to make my life difficult before too many years had passed.

However, apart from Alice I had no complaint to make about my new life as a married man. I still hankered abortively for Penmarric, but even in that direction my prospects were beginning to revive. Philip and Helena had no children and I learned that Helena spent most of her time with my sister Jeanne and her husband Gerald Meredith at Polzillan House. Finally in the spring of 1930 all my doubts about Philip's sexual inclinations were eliminated; during one Saturday evening in St. Ives with Rebecca I glimpsed Philip and Trevose emerging from one of the seamier pubs in the heart of the artists' quarter, and it took me only one look to see the whole story.

The odd part was that Philip's behavior was no surprise to me since I had long suspected him of homosexuality, but I was shocked to the core by Trevose.

I stopped dead to stare at them. They didn't see me. They didn't see anyone but each other. Philip was laughing. Marriage had made him somber, but he wasn't somber now. Trevose was laughing too. His habitual expression of surliness had vanished and his smile was as spontaneous as it was relaxed. They wandered away down the alley together, their hands in their pockets, their movements unhurried as if neither of them had a care in the world. They were at ease, at peace, perfectly attuned to each other.

"What are you looking at?" demanded Rebecca, suddenly aware that my attention had wandered from her, but although she swung around at once to glance about her Philip and Trevose had already vanished from sight.

After a moment I said, "It was nothing. Just a couple of odd artists," and presently we began to speak of something else.

But I knew then how matters stood between Philip and Helena. The marriage had failed; there would be no children. A few months later I was just reflecting yet again that my chances for inheriting Penmarric were now as good as they had ever been, when all our lives were disrupted without warning by the disaster at the Sennen Garth mine.

2

John had at last married Isabel de Clare, heiress of the great Honour of Gloucester; though his nickname of Lackland stuck to him for life . . . he was now one of the greatest landholders in the west.

—The Devil's Brood,
ALFRED DUGGAN

Richard tried a balancing act with possible rivals to the throne. . . . John and his nephew Arthur—Geoffrey of Brittany's son. The late 12th century had not made up its mind about rules of inheritance and both had a good claim. . . . The trouble with balancing acts is that they only work if everyone in the act does his share of preserving the balance.

—King John,
W. L. WARREN

[1]

Of course everyone felt so sorry for Philip.

Even I felt sorry for him. While all England and the journalists of the world lavished well-deserved sympathy on the widows and orphans of the disaster, everyone in the surrounding parishes thought also of Philip. The mine was the great cause for which he had fought all his life; every man who died could be counted as his friend, and among the men who had died was Alun Trevose.

Philip's grief must have been unendurable. I myself was so appalled by the tragedy and so stunned by the loss of so many men who were well-known to me that I was moved to offer him as much sympathy as I could put into words.

But he didn't want my sympathy. "There are others worse off

than I am," he said, not letting me finish, and immediately bent all his enormous reserves of energy toward fostering a national fund for the widows and orphans and calling on each bereaved family to make sure there was no needless want to aggravate their suffering.

I saw him then in a new light. I had thought him selfish and utterly egocentric, but now I saw him care only for others; the bereaved turned to him in their grief and somehow he had the strength to comfort them. Previously I had thought him so hard and cold that I had doubted whether he could ever be emotionally affected by a tragedy; I had never seen him weep, never seen him betray the slightest distress at a funeral. Now I saw that he did indeed suffer, and his suffering was the harder for him because of this same superhuman self-control on which I've no doubt he prided himself so pitifully.

Felicity very decently offered to come with me to the memorial service, and although there was no need for her to be present I accepted her offer with relief. A shared ordeal is always less harrowing than an ordeal faced alone, but even with Felicity at my side it was still a harrowing occasion. The famous English stiff upper lip has never been a virtue of mine, and I find grief so infectious that my emotional response to it never fails to embarrass me.

After that it was several days before I saw Philip again; evidently he had found some solitary spot where he could lick his wounds like some dignified golden lion after a savage battle for survival. I was just wondering if I ought to call at Penmarric to see if either he or Helena needed my help when I received a telephone call from none other than Philip himself.

He sounded as abrupt and offhand as he usually did, but to my surprise asked me to have a drink with him at Penmarric the following evening. Helena, he told me, would be spending the evening at Polzillan House; Felicity wasn't invited; we would be alone.

"There's something I want to discuss with you," he added curtly. "Come at six-thirty, will you?" And with a touch of characteristic arrogance he replaced the receiver before I could say a word in reply.

When I dutifully arrived at Penmarric at the appointed hour I was so nervous I nearly drove my car up the steps to the front door. Medlyn pursed his lips in disapproval as he watched from the threshold, but then gave his unctuous smile as he showed me into the library.

Philip was there waiting for me. He looked better. The lines of pain were still deeply etched about his mouth, but his eyes were less tired and his hands were steady. He was drinking orange juice.

"Sit down," he said. "What will you drink? Whisky?"

My nerves stretched a fraction tighter as I sat down and pretended to relax. "Fine," I said cheerfully. "Thanks."

"Forgive me for not drinking with you but I feel I've consumed enough alcohol in the past few days to last a lifetime."

We settled ourselves, facing each other across the hearth. There was a pause. By this time I was convinced that his brush with death had made him think about his will with the result that he had decided to discuss with me my position as his heir. However, despite my excitement and my nervous anticipation I assumed my most tranquil expression and forced myself to wait for him to begin.

He inhaled from his cigarette, shook out the match. He was in no hurry. He was master of Penmarric, master of the situation. He could do as he pleased.

I went on waiting, detesting him for keeping me in suspense, and at last he said idly as if the news were of no concern to me, "I've been making plans for the future."

There was a pause. "Oh?" I said politely.

"Yes, I don't intend to go on living here exactly as if nothing's happened. I've decided to go away. I'm leaving Penmarric."

"Leaving!"

"Yes, I've decided to go to the tin mines of the Rockies and work in Canada for a while."

"Canada!" I began to wonder if my hearing were in some way afflicted. I could hardly believe I had heard him correctly.

"Well, what do you expect me to do with myself each day if I stay in Cornwall? Walk along the cliffs past the dead mines of the Cornish Tin Coast? Go to the pub in St. Just in the evenings when I know none of my friends will be there to meet me? Later, perhaps, when my mind has fully accepted the disaster, but not now. Now all I want is to get away."

This time I was too dumfounded to speak. My fingers wound themselves tightly around my glass and interlocked with one another.

"I'll come back, of course," he said casually. "I'm going to give myself three years. If I dislike the life there I may come home before then, but three years is the target I set for myself."

"But my God, Philip!" I exclaimed, suddenly finding my tongue. "What the devil are you going to say to Mama? How on earth are you going to break the news to her?"

He raised his eyebrows. "My dear Jan-Yves," he said with an ironic drawl that reminded me instantly of our father, "if you think Mama is the type of woman to have hysterics simply because I intend to go abroad for three years, then it's obvious you don't know Mama. I shall break the news to her tonight and I've no doubt that when she understands why I'm going she'll make no attempt to stop me." And before I could think of anything to say in reply he added abruptly, "While we're on the subject of Mama, let me say that I shall be relying on you to call on her at least once a week while I'm away. Will you promise me you'll call every week and look after her properly?"

"Yes, of course—good heavens, Philip, I think you might at least trust me to look after my own mother! I'm sorry I haven't been calling on her lately, but I've been occupied with other matters."

"Yes," he said coldly. "I've noticed the time you spend at Morvah with our sister-in-law."

"I—"

"There's one other point that bothers me in regard to Mama and that's this business of Adrian replacing old Barnwell as rector of Zillan. Have you heard about that yet? I had a letter from Adrian this morning and assumed he wrote to William by the same post but perhaps you haven't spoken to William today. Apparently the appointment's still only tentative, but Adrian's angling for a transfer from his Oxford parish more for Barnwell's sake than for his own. Barnwell's so old now and anxious to retire, but he doesn't want to leave the rectory where he's lived for the last fifty years or the neighborhood where he's spent most of his life. Rather than share the house with a stranger he fancied the idea of sharing it with Adrian. He always did have a soft spot for Adrian, if you remember."

"Did Adrian agree to this? Won't it interfere with his career?"

"Adrian didn't agree to it. He suggested it himself as soon as he heard of Barnwell's predicament and wouldn't take no for an answer when Barnwell said he'd be better off at Oxford. You know how noble and high-minded Adrian is. He can never resist the opportunity to do a good deed, and besides I don't suppose he'll be at Zillan for long; Barnwell can't last forever, and he must be nearly ninety by now."

I was silent, thinking of my younger half-brother. I had always been somewhat jealous of him because he had such a large place in William's affections, but I admired his intellect and liked him for his human weaknesses if not for his inhuman virtues. Since the war he had started to smoke too much and had developed a passion for cars. Whenever he came to Cornwall for a visit he always had to have a joy ride in my Hispano, and part of the legacy my father had left him had been spent on a decorous little Ford. He pretended he needed a car on account of a leg wound suffered during the war, but I knew better. I knew a fellow car fiend when I met one. He was unmarried and quite inhuman enough not only to preach chastity but practice it also; however, I suspected he might have had a fling or two up at Oxford before he had decided to become a clergyman, for I could still remember him blushing on the rectory lawn when the two of us had first met Rebecca, and I knew that unlike Philip he did find women attractive.

"He wrote to me because he was worried about Mama being one of his future parishioners," Philip was saying idly. "He asked me if I would broach the subject with her and said he would understand if she·didn't want him to call and chose to go to church at St. Just after his appointment. I must say I thought it was good of him to consider her feelings."

"What's Mama's reaction?"

"I don't know yet. I wasn't able to go over to the farm today to discuss it with her. But if she wants to go to St. Just to church in the future I hope you'll take it upon yourself to drive her over in the car every Sunday."

"I'll certainly make some arrangements for her transportation," I said evasively. If Adrian was going to be rector of Zillan I wanted to hear his sermons and see how he conducted a service. I enjoyed my weekly visits to church. I had a fondness for the ritual and tradition of a service apart from my intellectual curiosity relating to religion, and in my youth I believe I might have made a good convert to Roman Catholicism; however, no one had tried to convert me in my youth, and once I was past adolescence I found I had an ungodly aversion to confessing my sins to a celibate priest.

"It's tiresome about Adrian coming to Zillan," Philip was saying, "but it can't be helped. Of course Mama won't want him to call. If there's any awkwardness I trust you'll step in and act as mediator. . . . Now let me tell you about the other arrangements I've been making for the future. First of all, I've made up my mind that none of my family—except Mama—is to have any part in running Penmarric while I'm away. It's much safer and much easier for all concerned and avoids all risks of unpleasantness in the event of anything going wrong. I'd already made up my mind anyway to fire William, so—"

"Fire William! But—"

"Yes, I've thought for some time that he doesn't run the estate efficiently enough, and I was hoping that perhaps your father-in-law might employ him at Carnforth Hall—I remember you told me that the bailiff there is so old he can hardly mount his horse. As for Penmarric, I'm putting it in the hands of a trained professional—you know Smithson, who's been bailiff at Menherion Castle? Well, now that Francis St. Enedoc's selling the castle to that hotel company Smithson will be out of a job, so I thought I'd offer him the position here. Francis says he's loyal, hard-working, honest, efficient and all the rest of it, so I think that should turn out to be the best solution. Now, I—"

"Just a minute," I said. The shock that William was to be fired was bad enough; the news that Smithson was to replace him was even worse. "I know Smithson. He's a drab little man with a face like a weasel and a north-country accent you could cut with a knife. I can't imagine anyone less likely to be popular with a bunch of Cornish tenant farmers. Look, Philip, if you want someone to run the estate for you I'm sure I could do a more than efficient job—"

"I dare say you could," said Philip, very bland, "but as I've just told you, I don't want any of my family at Penmarric while I'm away. I think it much safer for all concerned to leave the estate in the hands of a hired professional."

"Are you trying to tell me I'm not even to set foot in Penmarric while you're away?"

"It's for your own protection. Then if anything goes wrong I can't possibly blame you."

"But surely someone should call to see that Smithson isn't stepping out of line—someone should inspect the accounts! You surely can't expect Helena to cope with that!"

"Helena's returning to Polzillan House," said Philip coolly, "since if I go off to Canada alone we can hardly pretend our marriage is anything but a failure. However, I'm retaining the housekeeper and a skeleton staff, and Mama and Michael Vincent will have a power of attorney and keep an eye on all the accounts. I've asked Michael to send Simon Peter Roslyn over once a month to look into estate matters."

"Simon Peter Roslyn!" I was stupefied.

"Yes, he said he knew you at Oxford. I didn't realize he was a friend of yours."

"Hardly a friend," I said. "I saw him once or twice and had a drink with him, but he was one of those hard-working grammar-school boys up on scholarships—all work and no play. Besides, he's older than I am. He was in his third year when I was a freshman." Simon Peter Roslyn was Rebecca's first cousin, the only son of her father's brother Jared. He was a pale, intense young man, very boring, who had an immense capacity for hard work, a fanatical devotion to left-wing politics and no interest in the more lighthearted pursuits of the majority of under-graduates. "He got a good degree in law, I believe," I said, "but of course only the grammar-school boys go up to Oxford with the idea that all one does there is to study *ad infinitum*. However, I believe he did well."

"He's doing well in Michael's firm," said Philip casually. "I believe Michael might make him a partner one day. He's been an assistant solicitor for two years now and has made quite a name for himself."

"Really?" I said. I wasn't interested in the commendable attempts of a farmer's son to make a success of a middle-class profession. "I'm surprised Michael took him into the firm since Michael's one of the biggest snobs left over from the nineteenth century. But perhaps he thought he was keeping abreast of the times and being democratic."

"I like Simon Peter," said Philip, pouring himself some more orange juice. "He's clever and agreeable and always has something to say for himself. I think he'll do a good job here."

"I see," I said, finishing my own drink and setting down my glass. I looked around the room at the elegant furniture, the oil paintings on the walls, and suddenly I thought of Simon Peter Roslyn lunching at Penmarric once a month when he came to inspect the accounts, Simon Peter Roslyn with his phony BBC accent, his china-blue eyes humorless behind his rimless spectacles, his soft white hands flicking the legal strings which would manipulate his entry into my house, my grounds, my home . . .

"I must say," I heard my voice observing in a studiously casual tone of voice, "I do find it rather unfair that Simon Peter Roslyn is to be allowed to come here whenever he pleases while I'm not even allowed to set foot in the place for three years."

"Unfair?" said Philip, giving me one of his hard, cool stares. "I see nothing unfair about it. It's merely a practical solution to a tricky problem—how to avoid family squabbles when I'm seven thousand miles away on the other side of the world. Frankly, I'm surprised you should be so upset about it. What's Penmarric to you anyway? I know you'll be looking for work now that Sennen Garth's closed, but I'm sure William would always welcome a hand with the Carnforth Hall estate—assuming your father-in-law gives him the job. In fact there's no need for you to work at all now that you're so well provided for financially. Your wife's an heiress and when old Carnforth dies you'll be master of Carnforth Hall. You've got all the money and property you need, and to be honest I think the Hall is a damned sight pleasanter place to live than this rambling old tomb of a mansion. You're well off! While I've been arranging my legal affairs with Michael and Simon Peter recently, I've been guided throughout by the knowledge that you're well provided for and that you don't need either Penmarric or my money should I happen to die before you do."

My heart gave a great thud. When it began to beat again a moment later I felt as if all the breath had been knocked out of my body by a violent blow below the belt. "I don't quite understand," said my voice precisely from somewhere a long way away. "Are you trying to tell me—"

"I've just signed my will," he said. "I've left everything to Jonas."

I stared at him. At first I found it hard to grasp what he had said. The silence seemed to last an immense time but was probably no longer than five seconds, and then at last I managed to say politely, "I see. Rebecca will be very pleased."

"I thought it was the just thing to do," he said. "After all, as I've said, you'll get Carnforth Hall and all the Carnforth money, and the boy has nothing except the name Castallack. I intend to make him my heir, pay for his education, see he knows all about the estate and so on. When I come back from Canada he'll be seven years old and I'll be able to get to know him better. He can come and spend weekends at Penmarric."

I said nothing. Speech was beyond me.

"I thought I'd tell you before I told anyone else," he said, "since after Jonas you're the person most concerned."

"Thank you so much."

"I intend to see Rebecca tomorrow and tell her my decision. I also want to have a look at the boy—I've hardly seen him. To be honest I'd prefer to name Esmond as my heir, but of course Esmond is excluded from the inheritance under the terms of Father's will."

I was seized by an ungovernable urge to hurt him and have some sort of revenge however futile for the injury I had suffered at his hands. "So you've given up hope of a son of your own?" I inquired pleasantly. "I'm sorry to hear that."

He didn't flinch. He held up his head and looked me straight in the eyes and said without hesitation, "I've already admitted my marriage is a failure, and since my wife and I don't live together it's hardly likely I'll have a son."

"Couldn't you get a divorce and try again?"

"I have absolutely no grounds for divorce and neither has Helena. Even if we were divorced the very last thing I'd do would be to remarry solely to get a son." He moved restlessly over to the sideboard and toyed with the whisky decanter. "Do you want another drink?"

"No thanks. I'd better be going."

Somehow I got out of the house without losing my self-control, but by the time I slid into the driving seat of my car I was conscious of nothing save my rage; I was so angry that I hardly trusted myself to drive. I managed to take the car to the gates of the grounds and then I stopped, got out and began to pace about in an attempt to calm myself, but calmness eluded me. All I was aware of was that I had been banished from Penmarric for three years and deprived of my just inheritance in favor of a four-year-old child who didn't even know Penmarric from Buckingham Palace.

My rage was painful; I felt as if my heart were bursting. I found it hard to believe my fortunes could be so persistently dogged by injustice. As if I could ever have been content with Carnforth Hall! As if the Hall would ever mean as much to me as Penmarric! I was beside myself with resentment, consumed with an impotent longing for revenge.

"He'll regret this," I said aloud to the gray walls which bounded the grounds. "I'll make him sorry. I'll make him pay." An owl hooted, a tree sighed in the darkness, the sea breeze blew cool against my cheek. "I'll not give up," I said to them all. "I'll get what I want in the end no matter how many people try to stand in my way."

I went on pacing up and down, planning a way of obtaining justice for myself and reversing the wrongs which had been inflicted on me. I lit a cigarette, smoked it, ground the butt to dust beneath my heel. Finally I got into the car and began the drive to Morvah, but I had barely reached Pendeen before I realized I had no desire to see Rebecca. As soon as she realized I was upset she would want to know why, and as soon as she knew why she would be in the seventh heaven of delight on account of her darling little boy's good fortune.

"To hell with Rebecca," I said to the steering wheel as I swung the car up into the hills toward Penzance. "To hell with Jonas. To hell with everyone."

I had one of my bleakest moods of loneliness then, a desolation of the spirit so vast that it was as if I stood alone in a barren landscape which stretched as far as the eye could see. When I arrived at Carnforth Hall it took me a long time to recover my equilibrium, but eventually I pulled myself together and began to think more coherently about the situation into which Philip had so casually jettisoned me.

The first thing I realized was that I was determined to live at Penmarric. I had been content to live at Carnforth Hall while I had been secure in the knowledge that I was Philip's heir and that the Hall was a mere temporary residence, but now I rebelled against living there for the rest of my days; having been formally deprived of Penmarric, I found I wanted it more than I had ever wanted it in my life. I was resolved to show Philip he had misunderstood the situation and reached the wrong decision in regard to his inheritance, and since action spoke louder than words I felt the best way of showing him his error was to maneuver myself into a position where I was living at Penmarric and running the estate. In that way I would prove to him that Penmarric, not Carnforth Hall, was my primary concern, and at the same time prove to him how capable I was in the administration of his affairs. Once I had convinced Philip that I thoroughly deserved to be his heir I felt sure he wouldn't bother himself with Jonas. Esmond was his favorite nephew, not Jonas, and anyway Jonas was growing up in a working-class atmosphere surrounded by his Roslyn relatives and would no doubt turn out to be unsuitable for such an inheritance as Philip proposed to hand him.

Philip had forbidden me to visit Penmarric on any occasion, but Philip had to be persuaded to change his mind before he left the country.

The next morning I rose early, cut a large bunch of exotic flowers from the greenhouses of Carnforth Hall and drove over to Zillan to see my mother.

[2]

My mother greeted me with great enthusiasm, exclaimed in delight at the flowers and invited me to have a cup of tea with her in the farm kitchen. She looked well; her movements were far from being those of an old woman, and as we sat down together at the table there seemed something uncanny about her gracefulness and poise. Certainly I found it easy to compliment her about how young she looked. Soon the conversation was flowing easily enough and presently—inevitably—we spoke of Philip and his plans.

"You'll miss him very much," I said sympathetically. "It's hard for you."

"I'd rather he were happy in Canada than miserable in Cornwall," she said staunchly, "and that's the truth. I can't bear to see him so unhappy. Of course it was a great shock when he first told me, but as soon as I saw it was what he wanted I made every effort to adjust to the idea. I've never tried to stand in Philip's way. I've always wanted the best for him, and if it's best he should go abroad for three years, then it would be very wrong of me to beg him to stay here. Besides, I shan't be completely alone. I have Annie and the Turner girls for everyday company, and then I have you and Jeanne only a few miles away. I really can't complain." She paused to sip her tea and I was just about to make some comforting promise to call often when she said, "Mr. Barnwell will visit me now and then, I dare say, although he's so old he can't get about much now. Mr. Barnwell has always been such a good friend to me ever since I first came to Zillan. I was sad to hear he's officially stepping down from his duties soon, but I'm glad that he'll still be living at the rectory."

"Yes, that's most fortunate for you," I murmured neutrally, and thought at once of the new rector, my father's son by my mother's rival Rose Parrish. I decided it would be more tactful to steer the conversation away from the subject of the rector of Zillan. "With regard to Philip's plans—" I began, but was interrupted.

"I hear Adrian Parrish has come to Mr. Barnwell's rescue," she said. "Philip told me about it yesterday evening."

"Yes," I said uneasily. "He told me too." I wasn't sure what to say.

"Philip said I can go to church at St. Just and that Adrian won't call here at the farm."

"Of course, Mama," I said briskly. "I'll arrange for the Penmarric car to call for you and take you over to St. Just each Sunday morning."

"Oh," she said, "but I don't want to go to St. Just. Zillan is much my favorite church and I don't want to worship anywhere else." She sipped her tea. "Don't tell Philip," she said. "It upsets him to think of me having to attend a service conducted by Adrian, so I shan't tell him I'm not leaving Zillan church to go to St. Just. I don't think I shall mind attending Adrian's services. After all, a clergyman is a clergyman, is he not, no matter who he is and where he comes from. One mustn't be unreasonably prejudiced, and besides if Mr. Barnwell is so fond of him he must have something to commend him, mustn't he?"

"Certainly . . ." I was so surprised by her decision that I could think of nothing else to say.

But my mother was already changing the subject. "I wish Helena was staying at Penmarric," she said, a shadow crossing her face. "I've promised Philip to keep an eye on household matters in his absence, but it seems sad to think that Helena won't be there to attend to such matters herself."

I decided to skirt the delicate subject of Philip's marriage. "I'm glad you at least will be there from time to time to keep the household in order," I said quickly. "I wish I felt as confident about Simon Peter Roslyn's ability to check on the affairs of the estate."

"Simon Peter Roslyn!" said my mother and her lip curled in scorn. "I must say, I don't know what Michael Vincent's doing employing a farmer's son in his office, but of course the war changed so many things and now nothing is the same as it used to be in the old days. I'm sure it must be very nice for Jared to know that his son's doing so well in life and working in a gentleman's profession—"

"—which entitles him to visit Penmarric once a month as a privileged guest," I added smoothly. "By the way, how often do you yourself intend to visit Penmarric, Mama?"

"About once a fortnight, I dare say."

"I'd offer to drive you over there, of course," I said regretfully, "but I'm sure Philip wouldn't permit it. I'm to be in the strictest exile from Penmarric while he's away."

"Oh, fiddle-de-dee!" said my mother at once. "Of course it would make things easier for me if you drove me to Penmarric in your car, and I'm sure Philip wouldn't object to you escorting me there now and then! I'll explain it to him and I'm sure he'll understand. . . . More tea, darling?"

I accepted more tea. I felt better, aglow with the satisfaction which arises after a tricky task has been successfully accomplished.

I had a foot in the door.

[3]

A week after that I gritted my teeth, scraped the barrel of my current stock of hypocrisy and called on Rebecca to congratulate her on her son's good fortune. She was cross with me since I hadn't been near her after my ill-fated visit to Penmarric, but I was used to her being cross and presently I had ironed away her ill-humor and she was smiling. She even asked me to stay to lunch, but I had arranged to have lunch in St. Just with William and Charity, so I postponed the invitation until another day.

William was thinking of moving from St. Just. He had taken his dismissal from Penmarric surprisingly philosophically, and I realized then that he had disliked working for Philip and was welcoming the opportunity to begin his duties as bailiff at Carnforth Hall. Philip's policy of single-minded extortion to provide money to keep Sennen Garth alive had hardly coincided with William's traditional policy of maintaining good relations with the tenants and showing consideration of their financial affairs when they were in trouble. Philip had accused William of inefficiency and I had been too well acquainted with the muddled state of William's office to deny this charge on William's behalf, but there are worse sins in the world than inefficiency and I had had no hesitation in recommending William to my father-in-law once I knew William was to lose the job at Penmarric.

When I arrived at his house that afternoon Charity told me that Adrian had already arrived from Oxford and would be preaching his first sermon at Zillan the following Sunday. Having unburdened herself of this latest item of news, she then retired to the kitchen to attend to the lunch and I had the chance to be alone for a time with my two half-brothers.

They were standing by the hearth together as I entered the room, Adrian very tall and thin, William an inch or two shorter in height and many inches thicker around the waist. They did not look alike and yet there was a curious likeness between them. They had the same set of gestures, the same mannerisms, the same tricks of speech, and this elusive resemblance was never more noticeable than when they were side by side.

"Jan-Yves!" said Adrian warmly and held out his hand in greeting. He stepped forward, his spare frame blazing vitality, his handshake tight with a power that grabbed the attention. He had a useful personality for a clergyman. No one could question his integrity, and he had the masculinity which would make him respected by both sexes, not merely by the female portion of his flock. He had a strong mouth, receding brownish hair and blue eyes with sparks in them.

I often wondered why he had never married.

"Welcome home!" I said, shaking hands with him. "How does it feel to be back in this part of Cornwall? I'm looking forward to hearing your first sermon."

"I shall certainly need some moral support! I'm glad to hear you were thinking of coming."

"Nothing could keep me away," I said with a smile, "and nothing could keep my mother away either, you'll be surprised to hear. She told me privately some days ago that Zillan was much her favorite church and she had no intention of worshiping anywhere else. She daren't tell Philip, of course, but I think she's looking forward to your first appearance in the pulpit."

There was a silence. William had that neutral expression on his face, the expression he always wore when my mother was mentioned, but I saw his eyes widen in skeptical surprise. I glanced at Adrian. There was neither neutrality nor skepticism in his expression. For one brief second he looked as embarrassed as he was astonished, but then that was wiped off his face and succeeded by an expression of polite interest. "Really?" he said pleasantly. "That was a brave decision for her to make and I look forward to seeing her in the congregation. But all the same, I won't call on her until she invites me. It's one thing to face me in church where I lose my identity beneath my surplice and quite another to entertain me over a cup of tea in the farm parlor."

I knew then that he had no wish to call on her, and I didn't blame him. She would have been the last person I would have chosen to call on if I'd been in his shoes.

"I suppose you've heard Philip's made Jonas his heir," I said in an effort to change the subject. "And have you heard how Simon Peter Roslyn is flourishing these days? Philip seems to have taken the most extraordinary fancy to him."

"I don't think it's extraordinary at all," said William before Adrian could reply. William was much shrewder than many people supposed. "Philip fancies Simon Peter not in spite of who he is but because of it. If Simon Peter were a gentleman I doubt if Philip would have paid him any attention whatsoever; we all know Philip suffers from inverted snobbism and this is just one more example of his preference for the working classes."

We discussed Simon Peter further while William mixed the drinks and handed us our glasses. Adrian was of the opinion that it was very commendable that Simon Peter should be doing so well after such a humble start in life, but I pointed out that humble or not Simon Peter had at least had money behind him; Rebecca's father had left his only nephew a useful legacy some years before.

". . . and we all know Joss Roslyn got hold of his wife's money and then spent very little of it," I concluded. "Simon Peter must be comfortably off financially. In fact," I added, struck by the injustice of the situation, "he must be the hell of a lot better off than I am."

I thought about this unwelcome fact later when I was driving home to Carnforth Hall, but finally I pushed it to the back of my mind and resolved not to think of Simon Peter any more. I still felt he was beneath my notice, and although my instincts told me I should acknowledge his unwelcome presence in my life by an active dislike, my pride told me that the best way to treat small fry was to ignore them.

So I ignored Simon Peter Roslyn. It was to prove one of the most expensive mistakes I ever made.

3

In the arrangements which the king made for the government of the country during his absence, he showed little political wisdom or judgment of character.
— Oxford History of England:
From Domesday Book to Magna Carta,
A. L. POOLE

King Richard could refuse his mother nothing. When she asked [that] John might be allowed to keep her company in England he was released from his oath to keep away. Nevertheless, Arthur was Richard's heir. . . . [Arthur] was only three years old and still in the keeping of his mother Duchess Constance . . . alleged to be the mistress of John Lackland.
— The Devil's Brood,
ALFRED DUGGAN

[1]

Philip left Penmarric with a suitcase in either hand and a raincoat slung over his shoulder and caught the train from Penzance en route to Southampton. My mother wanted to go with him to the very docks and say goodbye to him only when he boarded the liner, but he wouldn't have it. He disliked protracted farewells. At his request I drove them both to the station in the Carnforth Hall Daimler and went onto the platform with my mother to see him off. He was casual about his departure, offhand.

"Take care of yourself, Mama," he said, kissing her and graciously permitting her to cling to him for a few seconds. "I don't want anything to happen to you while I'm away. And make sure

585

there's plenty of elderberry wine to celebrate my return in 1933."

My mother, understandably, began to cry.

"Please!" he said harshly. "Don't get upset! I'll come back. I came back from Allengate, didn't I, and that was seven years! I'll be back this time. You'll just have to be patient, that's all."

I was just thinking what a callous brute he was when he turned away from her and I saw the tears in his eyes.

"Goodbye, Philip," I said. "Good luck."

He didn't answer. I don't think he was capable of it. He got into the train as the guard blew the warning whistle, and within seconds the engine was dragging the coaches forward and pulling him toward his new life in another land. I wondered how he would like it, tried to imagine what was in his mind at that moment, but it was no use. I found it as always impossible to understand him.

"Come on, Mama," I said at last. "It's time we went home."

She was suddenly an old, old woman with shaky movements and an aged face. I gave her my arm, led her out of the station and helped her into the car. She cried all the way back to the farm.

"Don't go, Jan," she said when I drew the car up in the farmyard and prepared to help her out. "Please stay a little while. Please."

"Of course, Mama. I was going to suggest it myself." But I was beginning to be anxious. Naturally I was sorry for her, but I had my own life to live and my own business to attend to, and I had no wish to be saddled with her problems indefinitely. I had already resolved to make it clear to her that while I was prepared to visit the farm once a week I was not prepared to dance attendance on her whenever she felt like it. I thought that was reasonable. I would observe my filial duty toward her as befitted a practicing Christian, but I intended to spell out exactly where that duty began and ended. After all, one had to preserve some sort of independence and I disapproved of old people leaning too much on the young.

However, it proved harder to leave the farm than I had anticipated. I had lunch with her willingly enough, but when I saw she expected me to stay to tea as well I did my best to lighten my future burden by reminding her that I wasn't her only child.

"Why don't you ask Mariana to come down for a visit?" I suggested cunningly. My mother had been proud of Mariana's success in society and Mariana had gone through a phase of being the favorite daughter some years ago. "I'm sure she'd like you to see Esmond again."

But my mother shook her head. "She wouldn't want to come. It's too provincial for her here and she doesn't like to be reminded that her mother lives in a farmhouse."

This was undeniably true. I began to feel uncomfortable. It was no good suggesting that I should summon Lizzie instead because I knew that Lizzie wouldn't come; my mother had never regarded her with much favor and there was an antipathy between them. I saw clearly for the first time that once Philip was removed from her she was quite alone.

"I'll fetch Jeanne," I said at last in desperation, although I knew Jeanne was far too deeply involved with her invalid husband at that time to pay my mother more than a fleeting visit. "I'll drive over to Polzillan House now and bring her back here."

"I'd much rather have you than Jeanne," said my mother tremulously and tried to cling to my sleeve to delay me.

I felt lower than the lowliest worm. "Now, Mama," I said severely, "that's not very fair to Jeanne, is it? You know how kind and sympathetic and well-meaning Jeanne always is."

"I don't want her fluttering around me as if I were an invalid," said my mother. "I don't want Jeanne."

Old people were really most difficult sometimes. I felt myself becoming irritated by her. "I'll call tomorrow, Mama," I said, "but I really must go now." Taking my leave of her firmly, I tried not to see the tears in her eyes, her shaking hands, her mute expression pleading me to stay.

I drove off down the lane in the Carnforth Daimler and flicked the sweat from my forehead as I turned onto the road to Zillan. I felt exhausted. When I arrived at Polzillan House I almost asked the butler to bring me a shot of whisky but thought better of it. Half past two in the afternoon was the wrong time for drinking whisky and I hardly wanted the rumor that I was an alcoholic to buzz around Zillan parish.

My sister kept me waiting five minutes before entering the drawing room to join me. She looked tired and plain. I could remember a time long ago when she had been a pretty child, but now she was too tall, too thin, and her mouse-brown hair was straggly and unattractive. She had large patient blue eyes and an anxious long-suffering smile.

"I can spare you no more than five minutes," she said nervously after we'd exchanged greetings. "Don't be cross but Gerry's so ill and I don't like to leave him. Dr. McCrae is coming at any moment and as soon as he arrives I'll have to leave you."

I knew my brother-in-law had taken a turn for the worse, but I had had no idea matters had reached such a critical stage. I hesitated uneasily, not sure how to phrase my request, but by that time Jeanne had already guessed why I had come.

"I suppose Mama sent you," she said. "Well, I'm sorry, but I can't possibly leave Gerry—it's quite out of the question. I'm sure Mama will understand that my husband must come first."

"But if you could go to the farm just for an hour—she really does need you, Jeanne—"

"Oh no she doesn't!" said Jeanne fiercely, and with a shock I saw that the expression in her eyes, usually so gentle, was stony with anger. "She never needed me! I spent so much of my time at the farm trying to please her but the only ones she cared about were the boys—and now all the boys are gone she expects me to come running to her! Well, I won't! She never did anything for me, so why should I do anything for her? All she did was spend her time telling me I was on the shelf and would never get married, and when I did get married she thought me a fool and spent her whole time making contemptuous remarks about my husband! I despise her—and you can go back to Roslyn Farm and tell her so!" And before I could even begin to reply she burst into tears and rushed out of the room.

I was so astonished by her uncharacteristic behavior that for a moment I remained exactly where I was in the middle of the drawing-room carpet. Finally, having pulled myself together, I left the house and walked outside to my car.

Dr. McCrae had arrived from Penzance. As I moved out of the front door he was running up the steps of the porch toward me. I knew him slightly. After old Dr. Salter of St. Just had retired he had recommended McCrae to me and I had consulted him when I had fractured my wrist six months ago. He was a dark, stocky Scot with a pleasantly ugly face and a flawless English accent.

"Hullo, Castallack," he said in surprise as he saw me. "Been visiting the patient?"

"Just pausing for a word with my sister. How are you?"

"Busy. Worried. Otherwise fine." He glanced past me through the open door to the silent hall beyond. "How did you find your sister?"

"Well, since you mention it, very tired and overwrought. I suppose this must be an upsetting time for her."

"Very," said McCrae abruptly. He seemed to shun the use of complete sentences. "Tragic." He glanced past me again as if he were afraid of being overheard and muttered in a rush, "Wonderful woman, your sister. Woman in a million. You ought to be proud of her. Well . . ." He drew a deep breath, hustled past me and added over his shoulder, "Have to rush—sorry old chap—my regards to your wife."

"Thanks," I said, staring after him, and began to speculate how many more surprises were in store for me before I arrived safely home at Carnforth Hall that afternoon.

I wondered if Jeanne was aware of Dr. Donald McCrae's unstinted admiration. Whether she was or not, I was glad her merits were being appreciated at last. I had a suspicion her invalid husband had long been too self-pitying to realize his good fortune in having a saint to look after him in his ill health.

I slid into the driving seat of my car, lit a cigarette and paused to think. My watch told me it was three o'clock. I could drive back to the Hall, have an early tea, finish reading my detective novel and go for a ride before sunset. Perhaps after dinner I could take Felicity out to the talkies to compensate for my recent surliness toward her; Philip's will had made me bad-tempered, and since she was the one who had to live with me she was also the one to suffer most when I was in one of my bleaker moods.

I felt a glow of satisfaction at the prospect of a pleasant evening ahead of me after such a trying morning and afternoon. Starting the engine, I eased the car down the drive of Polzillan House, turned left at the gates onto the road to Penzance and drove jauntily along humming to myself beneath my breath.

After a quarter of a mile I stopped humming. After half a mile I felt my glow of satisfaction fade away. Finally, a mile from Polzillan House I drew up the car in a gateway, lit another cigarette and tried to pooh-pooh my ridiculous feeling of guilt which was threatening to ruin my peace of mind.

For five long minutes I thought of my mother, all alone at Roslyn Farm.

"Serve her right," I said to the cows grazing in the field nearby. "I was alone at Penmarric for six years. She never came to see me when I needed her."

I thought of her crying on the station platform, crying all the way home in the car, crying in the parlor of Roslyn Farm because without Philip she was alone and knew it and could do nothing to make the situation otherwise.

"So what?" I said to the cows. "She'll get used to being alone. Old people should expect loneliness. It's one of the penalties of old age."

I thought of her clinging to my sleeve, begging me to stay, watching me depart with tears in her eyes.

"Damn it!" I yelled at the cows. "I owe her nothing! Nothing! Of all her children I have the least obligation to go out of my way to help her! She left me alone and now I'm damned well going to leave her alone and she can see how she likes it!"

I backed the car onto the road once more and resumed my journey to Penzance, but it was no good. I could curse as much as I wished, but I knew I wouldn't be able to go home and forget all about her. Wrenching the gears into place, I reversed into another gateway, turned the car and drove back enraged to Zillan.

There was no need for me to go back, I told myself. I had done my duty and had lunch with her. She had no right to expect anything else. No right at all.

But I drove on to the farm.

I parked in the farmyard, scattering the hens, and slammed the door after me as I got out. I went into the kitchen. It was empty.

"Mama!" I shouted, in the worst of tempers by that time. "Where are you?"

There was a sound from the front of the house. "Jan-Yves?" I heard her call tremulously. "I'm in the parlor."

I walked over to the door but she opened it before I could reach her and stood before me with an odd, half-defensive, half-excited expression which I did not understand.

"The rector's here," she said, stumbling over her words. "He said he thought he would choose this day to call for the first time since he felt sure I would be feeling lonely and in need of company. He's been so very kind."

And beyond her in the parlor I saw the somber suit and clerical collar of my half-brother, Adrian Parrish.

[2]

I was stupefied.

I stood there, staring at him and staring at her, and as I stared I felt the color creep into my cheeks and suffuse my face and neck until I thought I must have turned the brightest, most unbecoming shade of crimson imaginable. Speech was beyond me. I was struck dumb.

"Oh, Jan darling, don't be angry," said my mother quickly, mistaking the cause of my all-too-visible emotion. "It's all right. Mr. Parrish saw Ethel first and asked her if I wanted to see him. He wouldn't have come in if I hadn't invited him. Don't be angry— please."

I swallowed and shook my head.

Adrian said awkwardly, "I think I must be on my way. I have one or two other calls to make." He turned to my mother. "No doubt you'd prefer to be alone with Jan-Yves, Mrs. Castallack. Please excuse me if I take my leave of you now."

"You'll call again," said my mother, "won't you?"

"If I may. Thank you." He edged his way past me as if he could barely wait to escape from my presence. I noticed how he avoided my eye as if he were afraid he had given me great offense.

My voice said stiffly, "Stay longer. Don't rush off. What's the hurry?" and when he looked at me with a start I managed to smile to indicate I was pleased to see him.

He hesitated. "Thank you," he said at last, "but I really must be on my way. Perhaps some other time. Thank you again, Mrs. Castallack," he added, taking her hand for a moment before opening the front door. "I look forward to seeing you at matins next Sunday."

"Thank you," she said simply. "Goodbye." She stood in the doorway and watched him as he walked swiftly down the garden path to the lane.

When he was out of sight she closed the door. We were alone. The hall was eerily quiet as if all the ghosts of the old house had gathered to listen to our conversation.

Presently I said, "I went to Polzillan House but Gerald is too ill for Jeanne to think of leaving him. So I thought I would come back and have tea with you after all."

"Yes," she said. "Yes. Thank you, darling, that was very kind of you."

"I didn't really mean to leave you alone. I just thought that if I could get Jeanne to come over—"

"Yes, that's all right. I understand."

"I suppose Adrian thought it was a very poor show, me leaving you like that."

"Adrian? Oh no, we didn't talk about you at all." She moved back into the parlor and stood for a moment looking around the room. She was very still. She had her back to the light and suddenly I had a glimpse of the woman she had been forty years ago, hypnotic in her stillness, graceful in her movements, effortlessly able to fascinate whomsoever she chose. For the first time in my life I wondered how my father had ever managed to leave her for another woman.

At last I said, "You didn't . . . mind?"

"When you get past seventy," she said, "you find that what seemed so intolerable at forty ceased to be intolerable a very long time ago." After a pause she added casually, "I remember so well the first time I saw Adrian because it was just before Mark and I had our final quarrel. . . . We were at Brighton at the time."

I said nothing. I knew perfectly well that I had been conceived there, but she didn't know that I knew. My father had once given me a careful account of the circumstances surrounding my conception in an attempt to explain my mother's initial aversion to me.

"Adrian was a nice-looking child," said my mother, "fair-haired and chubby like a little choirboy. I remember being surprised by the name Adrian because I hadn't heard of it before."

She said nothing else, but presently my silence seemed to draw her attention to me, for she took my hand and leaned forward to kiss me on the cheek. "I'm so pleased you came back, Jan-Yves," she said. "I confess I was feeling very miserable until Adrian arrived."

"I shouldn't have left you," I said at once, thinking that family affairs had reached a new rock-bottom low when my mother had to turn to her husband's bastard for comfort because all her own children had deserted her. I felt consumed with guilt and shame. I almost hated Adrian for his courage in visiting her when she was the last person on earth whom he was morally obliged to visit, and resolved on the spot to start behaving exactly as a model son should behave toward his elderly widowed mother.

Throughout the days that followed I think I surprised myself as well as everyone else by my meticulous attention to her welfare. I called every day at the farm, brought her flowers three times a week, took her for a drive every Saturday afternoon and escorted her to church on Sundays. It was true that the more my conscience was appeased the less meticulous I became, but for several weeks at least my behavior toward her was beyond reproach.

While attending church at Zillan I soon became impressed with

Adrian's well-constructed sermons; several times I managed to discuss them with him afterward and we fell into the habit of lunching together once a week and spending a good two hours in delightfully intricate discussions of dogma, doctrine and deity. In matters of religious taste he was by no means a High Churchman and had been opposed to the Anglo-Catholic overtones of the revised Prayer Book which had caused such a stir a year or two earlier; on the other hand he did not care for the revivalist methods of the "Oxford Group," and thought the Buchmanite movement was more suited to America than England. He set out to steer a middle course between Low and High Church attitudes, but his primary interest was in making the church attractive to the younger generation who seemed to be drawn in increasing numbers to the predominant new prophets of the Left; neither Marx nor Freud nor Einstein exactly encouraged religious faith, and agnosticism was gaining ground as fast as the fashionable literary cult of debunking established attitudes and outlooks.

Adrian was astonished by my unlikely interest in the subject of theology, but when he asked why I was so interested in it I found it hard to give him an answer.

"I want to find out what God can do for me," I said at last. "I know there's a God somewhere, but so far He hasn't shown much interest in seeing I get a square deal in life. Realism tells me there's no natural justice in the world, but hope—probably false—leads me to think that there might be if one only knew how to reach it. I want to know if God is so detached from the world as He appears to be or whether He does shoot off a few bolts of natural justice when He feels like it. I want to find out more about God. I think if I can find out more about God I can find out more about justice."

"Perhaps," said Adrian, "if you found out more about justice you would find out more about God."

I privately thought this remark was a little slick for a clergyman, but I supposed it was crafty enough if one liked that kind of thing. I smiled and said politely, "Perhaps" and dredged up another subject to discuss with him. Occasionally we discussed politics, but politics were so depressing at that time that I tried to avoid the subject whenever I could. I knew it was terrible that unemployment was rising, but frankly by this time I was a little tired of hearing about the far-flung results of that tedious Wall Street crash, and although I felt sorry for the unemployed I preferred not to think of them unless I was absolutely forced to. I supposed the current Labour Government meant well, but for me Labour symbolized the dreariness of the masses, the ugly ribbon developments around big towns, the cheap shacks of council houses which offended the eye, the cheap goods in multiple stores and the cheap news of the popular press. I knew it was splendid that the lot of the masses should be improved, but I regretted the vanishing elegance and glamor of a more select age and knew exactly why my mother often spoke longingly of the "good old days" when the "age of the masses" was just a phrase in a social philosopher's notebook.

"But the good old days weren't really good at all," said Adrian. "They only seem that way because we look back at them across the horror of war. But we look back through rose-tinted spectacles."

I personally didn't see why one should always scorn rose-tinted spectacles but I didn't argue with him. If he wanted to go through life gazing at everything with the naked eye there was no reason why he shouldn't, but I found this ceaseless quest to confront reality unflinchingly a little tiring, to say the least. However, no doubt it was inappropriate for a clergyman with a social conscience to cherish a useless illusion or two.

William attended Adrian's services sometimes, but he was not a regular churchgoer and only turned up once a month as a courtesy to his brother. I saw him daily, however; he and Charity had left their house in St. Just and moved to the bailiff's cottage on the Carnforth Hall estate, but although William liked his new job he admitted to me that never a day passed when he did not miss Penmarric and all the familiar faces on the Penmarric estate. Sometimes we used to discuss the Carnforth estate together, but the Hall had never been my main interest and my knowledge of its affairs was superficial.

1931 arrived. Philip was happily settled in a tin-mining district of British Columbia and writing letters in praise of the Canadian mines, Smithson the new bailiff at Penmarric was amusing himself by ruling his tenants with an iron hand, and Simon Peter Roslyn was no doubt savoring to the full his monthly visits to my home to inspect his cousin Jonas's inheritance.

Since they were all so plainly enjoying themselves I decided it was high time I joined in the fun; at the end of January I abandoned my practice of visiting Penmarric only while acting as my mother's escort and instead began very cautiously to appear there on my own.

I was welcomed with open arms. I would drive to Penmarric, borrow a horse from the stables and go out riding on the estate, ostensibly for pleasure, but my rides would take me all over the estate so that I could spend as much time as possible talking to the tenants and discussing their problems with them. Nobody liked Smithson. Everyone asked how long Philip would be away and how long they would have to wait to make their complaints.

"Make your complaints to me," I said, welcoming their discontent and encouraging their confidences. "I'm in touch with my brother. Tell me all about it."

They told me. Smithson was extortionate. He had raised the rent again. Everyone who lagged behind in his rent payments was threatened with eviction. He had refused to repair the roof of Granny Logan's cottage because he said she had been behind with the rent, and everyone knew how poor old Granny suffered miseries from rheumatism in wet weather. He was boldly stealing—requisitioning, he called it—an acre of Tom Towan's farm because he wanted to build himself a fine house overlooking the sea.

"Mr. Castallack said I could," he said when I raised the matter with him and showed me Philip's authorization to prove it.

I noted where he put the authorization and presently burned it. Then I went to Penzance to see Michael Vincent.

I did have some success; I managed to establish that Philip had granted the authorization in a hurry without consulting his trustees, but Michael said the position could be legalized and advised me as politely as possible to refrain from stirring up more trouble. However, by this time the tenants were enjoying stirring up trouble without assistance from me, and when Smithson began to build his house in the autumn of 1931 he found building materials disappearing, tools vanishing and men failing to turn up for work. Naturally he complained to Simon Peter and naturally Simon Peter ran straight to his superior and naturally Michael told the police. A couple of old constables were put on duty at the site at night, but materials still kept disappearing and in the end Smithson sank to desperate measures; despite his failings I have to admit he did have a certain resourcefulness. Now, in the face of this continued hostility, he hired a gang of unemployed young toughs from St. Ives, housed them in tents and told them to protect his property from malicious damage.

The situation could hardly have been more inflammable. Soon fights began and breaches of the peace, until finally in the spring of 1932 even Michael had to admit that retaining Smithson as bailiff of Penmarric was more trouble than it was worth.

"I'll take over the estate until Philip comes home," I said, confident that this was the best solution that could possibly be devised to cope with the problem. "The tenants know me and trust me and I've had experience at the job. I could get everything running smoothly again in no time at all."

But Michael, stony-faced and hostile, merely repeated that he would write to Philip.

I waited, convinced that Philip would agree to dismiss Smithson, positive that he, if not Michael, would see the advantages of letting me run the estate instead. But I was wrong. Philip agreed to dismiss Smithson, but he didn't appoint me to manage estate affairs in his stead. He had chosen old Walter Hubert, the former purser of Sennen Garth, to totter out of retirement and put the Penmarric administration on a stable footing; deputies were to be appointed to perform the physical tasks of rent-collecting and inspection for him, and if he refused to take up the appointment Michael was to select the most suitable substitute he could find.

Naturally the substitute wouldn't be me. Michael was quite shrewd enough to realize that I had engineered the trouble at Penmarric, and by this time there was no love lost between us. Feeling sick with disappointment at this latest injustice, I went to London for a week or two to cheer myself up, but the mood of London seemed to have changed subtly and the frenetic gaiety I remembered so well from my honeymoon was missing. The great financial crisis of the previous year which had led to the formation of the National Government seemed to have left the city limp. There was still gaiety, of course, and still plenty of amusement for anyone who had money to burn, but the vitality of the Twenties seemed to be drifting into a less spontaneous and less striking form of frivolity. After a while I began to wonder if the fault lay with me; I was on my own, since Rebecca had refused to accompany me for the sake of her reputation and Felicity had preferred to stay at home for the sake of her horses, and although in theory this should have given me a delicious amount of freedom I found I was too lonely to do more than go through the motions of having a good time.

Finally I cut short my holiday after a performance of Noel

Coward's *Cavalcade* had wedged me for an entire evening among a middle-aged audience sobbing with nostalgia, and returned to Cornwall. I reasoned that if I couldn't enjoy a Coward play—or indeed any other of the current joys of London life—there must be something very wrong with me, but fortunately as soon as I reached Carnforth Hall family affairs prevented me from wallowing in my depression. My brother-in-law Gerald Meredith died at last, and after the funeral Jeanne closed Polzillan House just as Philip had closed Penmarric and departed with Helena for an extended visit to the Continent. No sooner had we waved goodbye to them than news of a more cheerful kind reached us: Lizzie had married her professor. However, she had done so with such stealth that not one member of her family had been invited to the wedding and—adding insult to injury—her letter informing me that she was now Mrs. Edgar St. John Callendar did not reach Carnforth Hall until after she had departed with her husband for a honeymoon in Greece.

I don't know whether I was more hurt than my mother or whether my mother was more hurt than I was. We were both of us deeply offended by the news.

"She might have told me!" exclaimed my mother angrily. "She might have let me know! I would love to have gone to the wedding!" Her curiosity overcoming her injured pride, she added, "A professor! Fancy! Well, I suppose that's quite suitable. I always hoped Lizzie would marry despite her plainness, but to be honest I feared her personality would tell against her even more than her looks. She was so aggressive and unfeminine."

I did not voice my opinion of Lizzie's behavior to my mother, but as soon as I had the opportunity I wrote her a stiff letter of congratulations. "I can understand you not inviting Mama to the service," I said acidly, "but I think you might have invited me. Am I ever to be allowed to meet your husband one of these days or is he to remain as private as your wedding?"

"Dearest Jan," Lizzie wrote contritely as soon as she returned from her honeymoon in September. "The wedding was just a short church blessing by a clergyman in front of two witnesses! I hardly thought it was worth hauling you up from Cornwall to be present, but please forgive me if I've mortally offended you. Of course I wasn't going to invite Mother to take the wedding arrangements out of my hands and turn the event into a circus, and anyway I think if Eddy had known my mother was coming he would have taken fright and locked himself in his study. He's very shy and sensitive, poor darling, and after spending almost seven years luring him into matrimony I simply couldn't run the risk of any last-minute hitches! However, now we're safely married he actually seems anxious to meet my family and so I expect we'll be making the trek west before long. Have you any idea where we can stay? Since both Penmarric and Polzillan House are closed I'm at a loss to know where to go. I'd like to stay with you at Carnforth Hall but I don't think I could stand Alice for long and I know Eddy couldn't stand Felicity. No offense meant, of course, but horsey, hearty women make him extremely nervous, and I don't want him upset. Perhaps it would be easiest if we stayed at the Metropole. Any suggestions?"

I began to have grave reservations about this husband of hers. After considering the letter again I was just about to write to propose I visit her in Cambridge to save her the tedium of a visit to Cornwall, when I suddenly saw how the situation could be turned to my advantage. I went pale with excitement. The idea simmered in my mind for five delightful minutes, and then I picked up my pen and wrote a charming letter inviting Lizzie and her husband to visit Penmarric at the earliest opportunity which presented itself to them.

[4]

My mother thought it was an excellent idea that I should be host to the visitors at Penmarric, and since she was in favor of the scheme Michael could hardly do less than acquiesce. I asked Felicity if she minded my spending a few days at Penmarric, but she was just off to visit friends in Devon and didn't mind in the least.

Luck at last seemed to be on my side.

I was excited at the thought of seeing Lizzie again, for as I have already mentioned she was my favorite sister, sharp-witted, quick-tongued and good company. We were rather alike; we both took after our father in looks, so both of us were in the unfortunate position of being plain children among a host of handsome older brothers and beautiful older sisters; and both of us were aware of an antipathy existing between ourselves and our parents. Only two years separated us in age, and in childhood at least we had had several interests in common. However, as we grew up we grew less alike. Lizzie, like our father, was a born intellectual with a passion for learning, but learning for learning's sake held no appeal for me, and although I was well informed—particularly on my hobby, religion—and didn't consider myself a fool, I was certainly not an intellectual. Lizzie's long love affair with the academic life of Cambridge was something I had never been able to understand. However, my lack of comprehension had not lessened my affection, and even now, long after I had accepted the fact that I seldom saw her, I had only to see her once to regret our long periods apart.

I started regretting them again as soon as she stepped out of her husband's chauffeur-driven Bentley to meet me on that fine September evening. She looked well—and smart, smarter than I had ever seen her look before. Her luxuriant black hair was coiled sleekly upward and crowned by a glamorous hat. Her skin, over which she had shed so many frustrated tears in adolescence, was milkily smooth; her slanting eyes sparkled; her full-lipped mouth seemed sensual instead of out of shape. She wore a cream-colored suit that emphasised the generous curves of her figure, and her legs, always good, were encased in a pair of the sheerest silk stockings.

"How you improve with age!" It was she who spoke, not I. We hugged each other. "Whatever happened to that ugly little horror I had to share a nursery with?"

"I was asking myself exactly the same question!" I kissed her. "Marriage must suit you, Lizzie."

"You too evidently! Here's Eddy. Eddy darling, this is Jan-Yves."

I turned to inspect my brother-in-law. I had expected a desiccated elderly bore, but instead I was confronted with a tall good-looking man of about forty-five with gentle blue eyes and a sensitive mouth. Lizzie had understated his extreme shyness. I could hardly get a word out of him until we had finished dinner that evening, but at last the two whiskys before the meal, the three glasses of Hock with the food and the two brandies after the cloth had been drawn finally gave him the courage to open his mouth.

"Interesting place, Cornwall," he said, making his major speech of the evening. "Elizabeth's told me there's a fine example of an ancient hill fort near here."

"Yes indeed," I said. "Chûn Castle." After I had talked for a minute of the archaeological glories of Cornwall, he asked several questions which tested my knowledge to its skimpy limits, but I held my own and soon he was talking of Greece, his favorite subject, and I was able to leave him to carry the conversation. Presently we joined Lizzie in the drawing room. I was just wondering if I would ever have the chance to speak to her alone when he excused himself from us and said he needed an early night after the long journey. "And I'm sure you two would like a few words together," he said with a shy smile at his wife. "I know it's been a long time since you've seen Jan-Yves, Elizabeth."

After such an understanding gesture my last reservation about him fell away and I decided I approved of Lizzie's marriage after all.

"Why did he take such a long time to marry you?" I demanded of her as soon as we were alone. "He seems a decent sort of fellow. Why couldn't he make up his mind?"

Lizzie launched into some high-flown rigamarole about how they had both believed in the intellectual validity of free love and had been content for some time to avoid such a fundamentally bourgeois institution as marriage. What she was really saying was that Eddy, a confirmed bachelor, had been frightened that a wife might have impinged on his dedication to his work, and Lizzie had evolved her own way of proving to him that he worked better with her than without her.

"I hope you haven't betrayed your intellectual principles by your trip to the altar," I said with a straight face.

"Oh heavens," said Lizzie, "it's much more comfortable to be married and respectable."

"How fortunate you both came to the same conclusion!"

We laughed together.

"I suppose I *was* rather naughty," admitted Lizzie presently, "but I did love him and at the end I did desperately want to marry him, so I don't think I was being too low. Not nearly so low as Mariana. Honestly! Whoever will she sleep with next?"

Mariana was then living in Kensington after leaving her husband and child, running off with some undesirable roué and becoming enmeshed in a most unsavory divorce.

"Of course her husband refuses to let her see Esmond," said Lizzie. "How much does Mother know about it all, do you think? I suppose Philip would have kept the newspapers from her when Mariana was the 'other woman' in that horrible divorce, but she must have heard *something*. Didn't you hear any of the details? My dear, it was three-in-a-bed and everything. I knew someone who was actually at the hearing and she said . . ."

From Mariana's sex life the conversation gravitated to mine. "I'm surprised you're still infatuated with Rebecca," said Lizzie—cattily, I thought. "And I can't think why you're still married to Felicity. I'm not suggesting you should marry Rebecca—it's obvious you can get exactly what you want from her without a trip to the altar—but why don't you divorce Felicity and at least be free to marry again when you want to?"

"I don't think you have any understanding of my relationship with Rebecca, Lizzie," I said coldly. "And as for my marriage, that's my insurance for the future. After all, one must have some sort of security, and now that I shan't inherit Penmarric—"

"You could go to London, get a good job and earn a living. You'd probably make a lot of money in no time, and anyway aren't you bored with being a gentleman of leisure by this time? No, don't tell me how you help run Carnforth Hall and write detective stories in your spare time! That's not a good enough excuse! You'll be telling me next you can't go to London because you couldn't possibly leave Mother!"

I had no intention of arguing with her; I was too pleased to see her again. "Mama's not a bad old girl really, Lizzie," I said, subtly changing the subject. "We never knew her properly when we were children."

"I knew her quite well enough, thank you! I suppose she'll have to come over to Penmarric tomorrow to inspect Eddy. What a bore! Would Rebecca come too with the children, do you think? I'd like to see if Jonas is such an abominable child as you say he is, and anyway I think a tea party with Mother alone might be too much of a strain . . ."

However, I knew my mother wouldn't want to meet her new son-in-law for the first time in Rebecca's presence, so I managed to coax Lizzie into agreeing that my mother should first come to lunch on her own.

"How difficult things are sometimes!" said Lizzie grumpily afterward. She was never at her best when a meeting with our mother was pending.

"I'm looking forward to seeing them both," said my mother politely when I arrived at the farm the next day to collect her. "I'm so glad you asked me to lunch." But her fingers were trembling as she drew on her gloves and I realized with astonishment that she was even more nervous of the coming meeting than Lizzie was.

In fact the meeting did begin uneasily. There was the usual awkwardness of the introductions and the opening remarks, and afterward I put my mother in the best armchair with a glass of sherry before her while Lizzie scrabbled frantically for a cigarette and Eddy wandered off in search of a distant ashtray. I was just wondering what I could say if my mother made some disparaging remark about women smoking when my mother herself put everything right with one short simple sentence.

"How fetching you look, Lizzie," she said politely. "It's a pity Jeanne doesn't take as much trouble to look smart and attractive. She looks very dowdy nowadays."

"Hm," said Lizzie, pretending to be impervious to the long-delayed stamp of maternal approval, but after that the tension in the atmosphere eased and they were more friendly toward each other.

My brother-in-law gazed at my mother in admiration when he thought she wasn't looking and was sometimes coaxed by Lizzie into saying "yes" and "no" when the occasion demanded it.

"I've never been to Cambridge," said my mother to him at lunch. "Isn't that a terrible thing to have to admit? But I once visited Oxford."

"Oh?" he murmured, obviously at a loss for words. "And did you like Oxford, Mrs. Castallack?"

"Not in the least," she answered, giving him the perfect response, and after that he felt encouraged enough to speak for some time on the glories of his chosen city.

"You must come and stay with us," he said kindly, taking no notice of Lizzie's horrified expression, and my mother smiled and was gracious and said yes, perhaps one day, although she didn't care to travel much nowadays.

After lunch the three of them walked off around the garden to inspect the greenhouses, and I drove over to Morvah to collect Rebecca and the children.

By the time four o'clock came we were all having tea together in the drawing room at Penmarric. It was an ill-assorted gathering. Rebecca, behaving as she always did when the gathering was too grand for her, became colorless; she was studiously polite to my mother, who was studiously polite in return, but made an awkward effort to be friendly to the visitors. Poor Deborah was even shyer than her mother and painfully self-conscious as well; she could answer questions only in blushing monosyllables. I might have begun to feel shy myself amidst so much reserve had it not been for the presence in that formal tea party of my nephew Jonas.

He was six years old, solid, chunky and tough. "Please" and "thank you" were not words he had ever found necessary to add to his vocabulary, so he wandered from one plate of cakes to the next and threw the cake on the floor if it did not appeal to his palate. He refused to have milk, upset his cup of tea and became angry when his mother, much embarrassed, begged him to sit down.

My mother eyed him thoughtfully. I could almost feel her fingers itching to slap him. Presently she glanced across at me and as our glances met she raised an eyebrow in distaste.

"All right, Jonas," I said. "That's enough. Sit down and behave yourself or else you go straight upstairs to my room where you'll stay until it's time for your mother to leave."

He put out his tongue and waggled it daringly at me. His blue eyes were bright with impudence.

"Very well," I said calmly, setting down my plate. "If that's what you want." I prepared to rise to my feet.

"You can't touch me!" he yelled, suddenly becoming nervous. "You're not my father!"

"Fortunately," I said with a smile.

"You can't touch me because you're not my father!"

"Jan," began Rebecca unhappily. "Jan, I—"

"Don't worry, I won't hurt him." I crossed the room as gracefully as a dancer, lifted him by the scruff of his neck and propelled him swiftly out of the room as he roared with fury and humiliation.

Outside in the hall I closed the door and relaxed my grip. He started to flail his small fists at me, so I tucked him firmly under my arm and carried him, still kicking and screaming, upstairs to my room.

"You beast!" he shouted, scarlet with rage. "You wicked ugly old man! I hate you!"

I supposed that to a six-year-old mind even a man of twenty-seven would seem elderly.

I locked the door, pocketed the key and stood looking down at him.

"Let me out!" he cried, stamping his foot imperiously. "Let me out! I want my mother!"

"You want your father," I said, "but fortunately for him he never had the chance to know what a little monster he'd begotten."

He dimly understood that he was being insulted and rushed at me again with flailing fists. One of his puny blows happened to prod a sensitive part of my anatomy, and suddenly I lost my temper.

"That's enough of that!" I said, white with anger, and as he saw my expression change the pugnacity drained out of him and he stepped backward away from me. "I've had more than enough of your unruliness and bad manners! It's time you learned you can't go through life doing exactly as you please while your mother runs after you with the apologies. Come here!"

He backed away, very small, very quiet. I stooped to the floor beside my bed and picked up one of my slippers.

"Mummy!" he shouted, panicking. "Mummy!"

"This is one occasion," I said, "when 'Mummy' isn't going to rush in to stop you getting a little well-deserved punishment."

"Mummy!" He was frantic. He made a rush at the door without realizing it was locked, and I caught him, swung him around and pulled down the trousers of his little white sailor suit.

He screamed and screamed even before I had laid a finger on him. In the end I gave him six sharp taps with the slipper and let him go. I remembered from my own childhood that humiliation is a more effective punishment than physical pain, and it seemed unnecessary to make the taps hearty whacks of the type one received at school. The beating was symbolic, a demonstration of authority; it was the humiliation he would remember, not the half-dozen brisk taps on the bottom.

He picked himself up, his face awash with tears, and flung himself at the door again, scrabbling at the handle with his little pink hand and impotently battering the panels with the other.

"Mummy, Mummy, Mummy—"

"No," I said. "You'll stay here until your mother's ready to leave. You've caused enough trouble for one day."

It was then, from the corridor outside, that I heard Rebecca calling my name.

Oh my God, I thought.

"Mummy!" shrieked Jonas. "Help! Help! Mummy!"

"Jonas!" I could hear her running footsteps, then the rattle of the door handle. "Jan? What are you doing to Jonas? Let me in!"

"It's all right," I said in my calmest voice. "Just a moment. I'll unlock the door."

I unlocked the door. She burst in.

"Mummy!" bawled Jonas, sobbing wildly. "Mummy!"

"Jonas darling—"

He flew into her arms and stuck there, weeping stormily against her bosom.

"There, there, darling. Mummy's here . . ." She looked up at me fiercely. "What did you do to him?"

"I gave him six taps on the bottom which wouldn't even have harmed an hour-old flea. There's absolutely no need for you to get upset."

"How dare you!" she stormed. "How dare you lay a finger upon him without my permission! Just because of our relationship you think you can treat my children any way you like!"

"Come, Rebecca, stop talking such nonsense. Did you ever see a child behave more atrociously than he behaved in the drawing room just now? You can't go through life condoning his mistakes, you know! There are times when children need to be punished and in my opinion this was one of them."

"I don't give a damn for your opinion! Who are you to dictate to me about how I should bring up my child? How dare you try to tell me—"

"For Christ's sake! Haven't you any idea of how a mother should behave? I'm beginning to think you've got even less idea than I thought you had about how to bring up children!"

She slapped me across the mouth. The blow made me cry out before I could stop myself. I looked at her. I was too angry to speak. Glancing down, I saw the child, white-faced and round-eyed, looking up at us.

"You've never liked Jonas," Rebecca said, trembling. "Never. And don't think I don't know why! You're jealous of him because one day he'll have Penmarric and you'll never have it, never as long as you live! You're jealous!"

"Be quiet." I moved away from her into the corridor. "I'll drive you home."

"We'll walk! I never want to see you again—never, do you understand? I'm finished with you. Utterly finished. Forever."

"Oh?" I said, engulfed by bitter rage. "And who are you going to take up with next? Your pale cousin Simon Peter, perhaps? I'll bet you could show him a thing or two! Or Peter Waymark? I hear he has a roving eye these days. Or young Farmer Polmarth over the hills at Zillan—now he's an eligible bachelor! You might even marry him—if he ever bothered to ask you, which he probably wouldn't in view of your current reputation as my mistress."

She hit me again, a vicious side-swipe, and her rings clawed at my face and left a trail of pain in their wake.

"Dear me," I said. "How unladylike."

She burst into tears and ran off, dragging the child with her.

When she reached the end of the passage and turned the corner I went back into my room. The slipper was still lying where I had dropped it. I kicked it under the bed. After a while I went to the window and stared outside at the summer afternoon, but there was no message there for me, only the sea melting hazily into the sky and the black rocks of the bleak headland shimmering in the heat.

I thought: I'll get her back. Within a week she'll be begging me to visit the farm again. She always makes these reckless scenes and then regrets them later. She'll come back.

But I felt wretchedly depressed.

4

At the point we have now reached the young king of France entered upon his life-work—the break-up of the Angevin empire and its incorporation in the royal domain. Philip, known to history by the surname "Augustus" [was] possessed of great political sagacity . . . though not a great soldier he was a shrewd and unscrupulous diplomat.

—Oxford History of England:
From Domesday Book to Magna Carta,
A. L. Poole

The selfishness of Philip's intentions should have been obvious but John was ready to take a gambler's chance. . . . It was a critical situation. Richard alone remained undisturbed: "My brother John," he said, "is not a man to win land for himself by force if there is anyone to put up a mere show of resistance."

—King John,
W. L. Warren

[1]

I heard nothing from Rebecca during the remainder of Lizzie's visit and was too occupied in entertaining my guests to dwell much on her silence, but after Lizzie and her husband had returned to Cambridge I became acutely aware of our estrangement. Finally I wrote her a letter in which I apologized for the scene with Jonas and offered to take her out to dinner.

She did not reply.

After that I pulled myself together, determined not to spend time mooning over a difficult woman who was bent on ignoring me, and flung myself heart and soul into enjoying my extended stay at Penmarric. I rode on the estate every day, went for long walks, wrote a little when I felt like it, and began to read my way through my father's extensive library. However, when all his historical and biographical volumes had exhausted my intellectual stamina I imported some books of my own and spent happy hours enjoying the exploits of Lord Peter Wimsey, Hercule Poirot and Bulldog Drummond. I also tried, with varying degrees of success, to read some less frivolous modern works—Huxley's *Brave New World*, which had just been published, the turgid anguishings of D.H. Lawrence and the more readable stories of J.B. Priestley. But on the whole I thought the earlier works of Wells, Galsworthy and Walpole were more entertaining than the latest crop of literary masterpieces.

Apart from reading I also developed a new fondness for listening; there was a wireless set at Penmarric, but it was old-fashioned and presently I bought a new one, which gave me a better reception and enabled me to enjoy listening to the test matches with the maximum of comfort. Soon I had smuggled in my gramophone from Carnforth Hall as well as a selection of my favorite records. Contemporary serious music, such as the compositions of Vaughan Williams and Delius, bored me, but I played Rachmaninoff so much that even today I can't hear that second piano concerto without thinking at regular intervals, "That's where I turn over/change the record." I bought the best of the popular music too—which for me meant Noel Coward—but jazz became my first love and soon the strains of Rachmaninoff faded to be replaced by the trumpet of Louis Armstrong. At first it seemed odd to hear such music at Penmarric; Medlyn, I know, was enormously shocked and used to bring my whisky and soda to the library with a cold-eyed distaste, but presently we both became accustomed to my father's former sanctuary being violated by such undignified American sounds and accepted the change in tradition without further thought.

I was certainly content enough on my own in many ways, but presently as my estrangement from Rebecca persisted I began to feel too solitary for comfort; in the end I invited Felicity to join me, but she had had an invitation to stay somewhere in the Midlands and soon she departed from Cornwall for several weeks.

I continued to visit my mother regularly and often brought her over to Penmarric for lunch and tea.

"How long are you going to stay at Penmarric?" she asked at the end of October. "You've been on your own here for some time now and I know Michael doesn't approve."

"I can't think why not," I said. "I'm not interfering in any way with Walter Hubert's administration and never even show my face in his office. I'm not sure how long I'll stay here. Till Felicity comes back to Carnforth Hall, perhaps."

But Felicity returned two weeks later and I made no effort to join her. Instead I renewed my invitation to her to come to Penmarric, but she was reluctant to leave her horses and we agreed amicably to live apart for a while.

"Michael's very annoyed," said my mother. "Perhaps you shouldn't stay here much longer, Jan-Yves."

"I'm not doing any harm," I said truthfully, but I saw her purse her lips disapprovingly even though she made no adverse comment on my behavior.

The very next day I had a visit from Simon Peter Roslyn on behalf of Holmes, Holmes, Trebarvah and Holmes.

He was a slim man, not tall but neatly made and well-proportioned. Manual labor might have given him a wiry toughness, but books and study had instead bestowed on him an air of wan asceticism. He was supposed to have been delicate as a child. Even now he hardly looked robust, but I hadn't heard of him missing a day's work from ill health, so I supposed his constitution had improved with age. He had limpid eyes, a soft handshake and a clever, calculating mouth.

"Good morning, Jan," he said pleasantly. He was always very pleasant to clients, but I disliked his casual manner and did not think the coincidence that had made us contemporaries at Oxford gave him the right to call me by my Christian name. "I've brought you a letter from Mr. Vincent. He asked me to give it to you, then wait for your reply."

Of course Michael had been unable to resist committing to paper his disapproval of my behavior and reminding me stuffily of my "gentleman's agreement" with my brother.

"How kind of him to be so concerned about Penmarric!" I said cheerfully, stuffing the letter back into its envelope. "Tell him I'm equally concerned and that's why I've decided to stay here."

"I see." Simon Peter looked at me blandly before allowing himself a smile. "Well, I can't say I blame you," he said to my astonishment. "I dare say I'd do the same if I were in your shoes. Confidentially Jan-Yves—" he lowered his voice—"confidentially I think Philip's given you a raw deal over this business. You'd be a lot more useful to him than old Mr. Hubert, and if you managed the estate you could keep everyone happy, including yourself. Mr. Hubert still speaks highly of your administrative abilities, and if you offered him a helping hand now I'm sure he'd be the last person to refuse it. Certainly if you stay on at Penmarric no one's going to evict you by force. Too much scandal, too much difficulty and too much trouble. Besides, Philip may well decide to settle permanently in Canada, and if he does I think the best solution would be for you to take care of the estate in his absence—or at least till Jonas comes of age."

I was suspicious of his attitude, of course, but his words echoed my sentiments so exactly that I couldn't help saying, "That would certainly be more sensible than this present arrangement. . . . Do you think Philip may settle out there? Does he ever hint as much in his letters to Michael?"

"I think I can read between the lines now and then." He smiled at me again. "He seems to like it in Canada."

"Yes, doesn't he?" I was unable to resist a smile of delight. "It's nice that things have worked out well for him there. However—" suspicion still lurked at the back of my mind "—isn't this advice rather . . . unethical? Wouldn't Michael disapprove if he could hear you?"

"There's no witness to our conversation," said Simon Peter, very tranquil, "and I always like to help an old friend. Besides, who knows? Jonas is a tiresome little brat, don't you think, and Philip could easily change his mind about his will. Frankly I hope he does. Jonas is spoiled enough already without being the recipient of a large unearned income, and anyway I disapprove of the principle of inherited wealth. I haven't touched a penny of the money my uncle left me except to pay for my articles with Holmes, Holmes, but since I've been earning I've been able to repay every farthing of that sum back into the bank. . . . Well, I must be on my way. I hope we can continue to be friends in the future, Jan, despite your current difficulties with Mr. Vincent and Philip."

"I'm sure we can, Sim!" I heard myself say heartily, for by this time I could not help but believe him to be sincere. Everything he said made sense; Jonas *was* spoiled and tiresome, and Simon Peter's remarks about inherited wealth rang true enough when I recalled his fanatical devotion to socialism at Oxford. Bearing this in mind it was not unreasonable that he should be willing to be on my side and offer support now in return for my friendship in the years to come when I might well be master of Penmarric. Watching him go, I even began to think that I had judged him unfairly in the past, and as I shook my head in regret it never once occurred to me that I was dealing with a man who was just as anxious as I was to carve himself a slice of justice from life and who wished above all else to raise the Roslyns of Morvah to the level of the upper classes he despised.

[2]

I wasn't in the least surprised when soon after my interview with Simon Peter I received a steady stream of visitors all anxious to jog my moral conscience. Michael came, of course, and after him my father-in-law, no doubt egged on by Alice, puffed over the hills from Carnforth Hall to tell me I was creating a scandal by living apart from my wife. A week later my mother arrived unexpectedly for tea. Finally even Adrian roared up the drive in his tinny little Ford to ask me in suitably clerical language just what the hell I thought I was doing. I succeeded in infuriating all four of them, and shameful though it is to admit such a thing I have to confess that I enjoyed every minute of it. In fact I was enjoying myself so much that I didn't give a damn when Sir Justin said he would advise Felicity to divorce me and would take care that I never got a penny of his money after his death. I even laughed when Adrian told me not to call at Zillan rectory for theological discussions while I was coveting my brother's possessions, living apart from my wife and committing adultery whenever the fancy took me. Michael's impotent rage amused me as much as my mother's icily ladylike disapproval. I continued to regard them with amused indifference—until the letter came from Canada, and then suddenly I was angrier than all four of my adversaries put together.

"My dear Michael," Philip had written in response to Michael's letter of complaint. "What a devil of a fuss everyone seems to be making on my behalf! I'm grateful to know that my interests at home are in the hands of honest men and I appreciate your attempts to kick Jan-Yves out as he deserves, but please don't worry unduly. My little brother is hardly the man to steal an inheritance if he meets with any form of resistance, and if he wants to continue to play houses like any child barely out of the nursery, I think we should humor him and not worry ourselves too much about his infantile behavior. If he wants to help Walter with minor matters relating to the estate, let him give what little assistance he can so that he can feel he's not entirely useless. I'm sure Walter would soon notice any attempt he might make to be dishonest, and since he has no power of attorney he must be fairly harmless anyway. So let him be. He's not worth bothering about. I'm still enjoying life here very much, thanks, and hope to have a few days' holiday in Vancouver soon. Yours, etc., Philip."

It was a crippling disparagement. I wasted too much time seething with fury, but at last I pulled myself together and considered the letter more sensibly. At least I had secured Philip's permission to help Walter on estate matters, and at least I was still allowed to live at Penmarric. Wasn't that exactly what I had wanted? It was foolish to get upset about Philip's insults when I now had the chance to prove to him—and to everyone else— how ably I could step into his shoes.

The new year, 1933, came. In spite of myself I was lonely. I missed Rebecca, missed my weekly lunches with Adrian, missed even seeing my mother as often as I used to. I still saw her occasionally, but she would not visit me at Penmarric, and although we were outwardly civil to each other we were privately estranged. I hoped Lizzie would come down for another visit in the spring, but when I invited her she wrote back to say she was pregnant and had no wish to make the tiring journey to Cornwall. To stave off my loneliness I immersed myself in my work and toiled long hours in the estate office so that, much to Michael's annoyance, my tasks were completed in the most irreproachable manner possible.

Meanwhile Philip seemed more settled than ever in Canada. Every letter he wrote to my mother mentioned his friends and his work and how happy he was. He was a paying guest now in the home of a widow, and in the spring of 1933 when he bought a camera and sent my mother photographs of himself with the woman and her small son, we saw that he looked fit and handsome, a very different man from the hollow-eyed, grief-stricken miner who had left Penmarric more than two years before. The boy had a small but astonishing resemblance to Esmond if one overlooked the long trousers and the unparted hair, and the woman was young, not more than thirty, and most decidedly attractive.

"Do you think I dare ask him more about her?" said my mother, beside herself with curiosity. "I don't want to pry, though. I suppose if he were at all interested in her he would have mentioned her more often in his letters."

I began to wonder. I knew more about Philip's sexual inclinations than she did, but I knew too that it was not impossible for a homosexual to have a normal relationship with a woman. If he were to get a divorce from Helena, remarry, have a son . . . It was just as well he was so happy in Canada and had no desire to return home to interest himself in his inheritance. As matters stood now I guessed he had no pressing desire to provide an heir for the estate and so had no inclination to arrange a divorce and remarry. If the woman was willing and he was able I felt sure he would be content merely to live with her without complicating the affair with divorce and marriage.

I had met a young widow myself by this time, a presentable woman of about thirty-five who had recently moved to one of the best residential districts of Penzance. At first she was wary of having an affair although willing to act as hostess for me when I entertained my county neighbors at Penmarric. For the first time since my quarrel with Rebecca I found myself enjoying a woman's company outside the four walls of a bedroom, but naturally I wanted her company there as well, and finally in the spring I was rewarded for my patience when she allowed me to take her to London for a week. After our return I began to entertain more lavishly than ever; there was a stream of visitors to Penmarric and with them wafted an atmosphere of gaiety and fun. I began to run a little short of money, but I controlled enough of the estate business by this time to tell Walter I needed a few extra pounds, and since Philip had granted him a power of attorney over a limited fund established for estate-management purposes after Smithson's departure, he was able to give me some extra money without resorting either to Michael or to my mother for approval.

In the summer, a year after Gerald Meredith's death, Jeanne announced her engagement to Dr. Donald McCrae, and three months later in September they were married by Adrian at Zillan church. We were all pleased for Jeanne. Nobody deserved happiness and an able-bodied husband more than she did, and no one was better suited to make her happy than Donald McCrae. She had no wish for the reception to be held at Polzillan House, where she had lived with Gerald, so I held the reception for her at Penmarric and launched her as lavishly as possible along the road of her second marriage. She and Donald became near neighbors of my new mistress in Penzance, and since Helena was also planning to buy a small house in the same neighborhood there was talk of putting Polzillan House up for sale.

I enjoy weddings. I like the church ceremony and I like the party afterward and I like the excuse to get tight on vintage champagne. I found Jeanne's wedding thoroughly enjoyable even though I was still deprived of a visit from Lizzie and even though Rebecca had invented some excuse not to be present. Lizzie had just given birth to a daughter and was confined to Cambridge, but she sent an amusing telegram and later I telephoned her to give her an eyewitness account of the wedding. As for Rebecca it was clear her purpose in absenting herself from the celebrations was to snub me. I told myself her snubs didn't matter, particularly now that I had a new mistress, but the next day as I nursed my hang-over I became very maudlin thinking of happy times gone beyond recall.

The sensation of the wedding had without doubt been my sister Mariana. She was nearly forty now and beginning to look it; her figure was still good but she wore too much make-up and I suspected she dyed her black hair to keep the white hairs at bay. She came unescorted but soon gathered a crowd of men around her and kept them entertained by her sophisticated conversation. I noticed that she smoked continuously and drank champagne as fast as if it were lemonade, two little traits that caused a stir among the conservative wedding guests unaccustomed to such London modernity.

"Rather vulgar," said my mother. "She doesn't look at all respectable."

Which was my mother's way of saying what was patently obvious: that Mariana looked like the most expensive whore in town.

After the wedding I cast around for another excuse to entertain and toyed with the idea of a moonlight picnic in the cove with a few carefully selected guests, but as my new mistress said she would leave me instantly if I held anything resembling an orgy I decided to give an orthodox cocktail party instead. I liked Lucy well enough and didn't want to lose her just then. I kept telling myself how fortunate I was. I was young, only twenty-eight, and able to do exactly as I pleased. I no longer had cause to complain about life's unfairness; there were plenty of men who would have envied my position in the world. Why, then, did I have to keep repeating to myself how fortunate I was?

My uncertainty didn't make sense.

"I wish you'd take more interest in this cocktail party," grumbled Lucy. "You're leaving me to do all the work."

I tried to concentrate on my latest venture, and for a time I succeeded in ignoring the baffling discomfort lingering at the back of my mind. On the day of the party I was just checking my lists to make sure there was nothing I had forgotten to arrange when Medlyn knocked on the library door to tell me someone wanted to speak to me on the telephone.

It was Simon Peter Roslyn.

I had invited him to the cocktail party. I hadn't wanted to, despite the cordiality that existed between us nowadays, but it would have been an error not to have invited him. He had become friendly of late with the Trehearnes of Helston, and since he attended their parties I supposed that made him socially eligible to attend mine. I had invited all the Trehearnes and had no wish for them to think I was ostracising their protégé, but as I went out into the hall to the telephone I couldn't help hoping he was about to make some excuse not to attend.

"Hullo, Sim," I said pleasantly. "Don't tell me I'm not going to see you tonight!"

He hardly allowed me to finish the sentence. "I can't talk now," he said in a low voice. "I'll be able to talk to you more this evening, but we've just had news that I thought you'd like to know. It's in relation to a certain party overseas."

I felt the strength drain out of my legs as my heart thumped painfully against my ribs. "Philip . . ."

"You'd better watch out for yourself," said Simon Peter Roslyn. "He's coming home."

5

*[Philip Augustus] sent his ally an urgent message:
"Look to yourself for the devil is loosed," and John
fled. . . .*

—King John,
W. L. WARREN

*To some this might have appeared cryptic, but for
John there was only one Devil, his brother Richard.*
—The Devil's Brood,
ALFRED DUGGAN

[1]

Philip was coming home. My castle in the air had dissolved at a
touch because Philip was coming home. I had no money and no
home and no reputation, for Philip was coming home from
Canada after exactly three years of self-imposed exile.

I might have known that Philip would always keep his word
to my mother.

I panicked. I was an adventurer who had misjudged the odds
on a gamble, and no gambler is more despised than the man who
loses even the shirt upon his back. In a series of frantic moves to
recoup the barest fraction of my losses I swallowed my pride and
cast around among those closest to me to see if they would help
me in my time of need.

[2]

My mistress said she would love to have me to stay but didn't see how she could without causing the most impossible scandal. After all, she was a respectable woman living in a respectable neighborhood. Of course if there were a divorce and a question of marriage . . .

"There's no question of marriage," I said bitterly and left her never to return.

After that I suggested a friendly reconciliation with Felicity, but apparently Sir Justin had threatened to disinherit her if she allowed me to return to Carnforth Hall and so I abandoned that idea. Felicity had always treated me so well; I couldn't make her risk losing her inheritance.

"I feel frightfully badly about this," she said, worried. "If I can do anything to help—"

"Well, if we could carry on financially as before—"

"Yes, of course. Daddy can't find out about that anyway since bank accounts are confidential, and I'm sure he believed me when I said I'd stopped our joint account. And if you ever want any extra money just say so."

"You're a wonderful woman, Felicity," I said, kissing her, "but I've caused you enough trouble. I'll try not to ask for anything else. I feel guilty enough living on your money as it is."

"Why? Men lived on their wives' dowries in the old days and thought nothing of it! Anyway, I want you to have the money. If a woman can't do as she likes with her money what on earth *can* she do with it, I'd like to know? One might as well be a pauper if one can't help an old friend occasionally."

But despite her assurances I still felt uncomfortably guilty and ashamed.

I was just wondering where to turn next when all my financial juggling of the past few months began to catch up with me and I found myself in the unenviable position of having to produce over seven hundred and fifty pounds in less than a week. Felicity very decently pawned her pearls for me, but I still had to borrow a considerable sum from the king of the Penzance moneylenders and even then I was unable to prevent my past manipulation of the Penmarric accounts from being exposed to the light of day. Since Philip was returning the estate's affairs had to be investigated in order to ensure that they were in perfect order, and it didn't take Michael Vincent's suspicious mind long to discover exactly what had been going on.

"So what it really amounts to," he said grimly, "is that Walter Hubert, using his—fortunately—limited power of attorney and acting in good faith, foolishly granted you money on the understanding that you would employ it to cover certain current estate expenses, and some of the more trusting tenants enabled you to exercise your natural dishonest tendencies even more freely by paying their rent to you in person. In other words, more than seven hundred pounds has been—"

"Let me write you a check straight away to put matters right. I'm sorry you've been inconvenienced."

"If you think I'm not going to tell Philip about this, I'm afraid you're gravely mistaken. Men have been prosecuted for doing what you've been doing—and jailed."

"I'm sorry to hear that," I said blandly and wrote out a check for the amount in question.

It bounced. I had ten pounds less in the bank than I thought I had.

"You're in bad trouble, aren't you?" said Michael in contempt, and I couldn't deny it.

My troubles stretched ahead of me as far as the eye could see.

"Mama," I said, "I hate to mention such a sordid topic as money, but I had rather a heavy expense this month and I'm somewhat poor. Could I possibly borrow ten pounds from you?"

"You needn't bother," she said politely. "I've already·made good your bad check to Michael. Or do you want ten pounds for something else?"

"Well . . . no, but—"

"Where are you going to live now?"

"I'm not sure," I said. "I haven't made up my mind."

But she did not suggest I come to stay.

That same evening I telephoned Lizzie in the hope that I could escape to Cambridge for a time, but unfortunately she was about to leave for Scotland; her husband had been granted a leave of absence for some reason and they had already made arrangements to lend their house to friends. Lizzie was apologetic but there was nothing she could do to help.

That left William.

"Well, of course you can come and stay!" he said, surprised

only because I had waited so long before trying to impose myself on him. "You ought to know by now that you're always welcome in our house."

I wished I were a small boy again when he said that; I wished I could run into his arms, bury my face against his chest and feel safe and secure and protected from the world. There was a lump in my throat. Tears pricked behind my eyes.

"That's good of you, William," I said abruptly, turning aside before my lip could begin to tremble. "Thank you very much."

[3]

Philip came home on the twenty-fourth of October. They said he looked well and happy. I didn't know. I stayed in my room at William's cottage and read books from dawn till dusk. I saw no one and made William promise not to tell anyone where I was. As soon as I had money in the bank again on the first of the month, I was determined to leave for London, but in the end my resolution came to nothing; three days after Philip's return my mother arrived at the cottage and asked if she could speak to me. William was out on the estate, and Charity, overwhelmed by my mother's imperious manner, said she would see if I was in the house.

"Jan!" She stuck her head around the door of my room. "Your mum's outside. What shall I do? She knows you're here."

I was in a most disreputable state. I hadn't shaved for three days and I knew I must reek of whisky. To add to my unsightly appearance I was clad only in my underclothes and was lying on my unmade bed amidst ashtrays overflowing with cigarette butts.

"Ask her if she'll be so kind as to wait," I said, closing my book. "Say I haven't been well and that I'm just getting dressed."

"You can get dressed later," said my mother tartly in the passage outside. "I'll see you now."

And before I could open my mouth in protest she had walked into the room and closed the door in Charity's face.

She turned to look at me. As I swung my legs off the bed and reached for my dressing gown I saw her eyes flicker over me and take in the situation at a glance. Her nose wrinkled delicately. Presently she sat down on the chair by the tallboy and looked the other way as I scrambled into my dressing gown and rummaged under the bed for my slippers.

At last she said, "How long do you intend to remain here?"

"I plan to go to London at the beginning of November." I tried to look her in the eyes. "I thought I'd try and get a job there."

"How commendable," said my mother, "but a little rash, perhaps? Philip is anxious to see you."

I was speechless. I sat on the edge of the bed and stared at the carpet.

"He's in a good mood and not inclined to harbor any grudges against you for your foolishness. Besides, as I reminded him, you did repay in full the money you took as soon as you were asked. I didn't tell him the check wasn't honored and that I made up the difference. I didn't think it was necessary for him to know that."

"How . . . kind of you."

"Not at all. I also reminded him that you ran Penmarric well—apart from your little lapse at the end with the accounts—and that you were popular with the tenants. In short, I advised him to retain you to run the estate for him."

I was finding it hard to speak. "I don't want—I can't—now that Philip's there—"

"Don't be so silly! Please—don't throw away this last chance to be on good terms with Philip! I've smoothed over your bad behavior, so now it's up to you to make the best of the situation. If you run off to London now with your tail between your legs you'll have no chance to inherit Penmarric should Philip become disillusioned with that terrible little Jonas and want to alter his will in your favor. But if you stay here, work hard and do everything you can to help Philip I wouldn't be surprised if he changed his mind eventually and named you his heir."

I went on staring at the floor. Presently I leaned forward and put my face in my hands.

"Good heavens, Jan-Yves, what's the matter with you? Oh, I suppose you've heard about Helena. But that needn't affect your prospects. If you're sensible now—"

I looked up. She stopped. "You haven't heard?" she said sharply.

I stared at her. "Heard what?"

She looked taken aback but quickly recovered herself. "Philip and Helena are reconciled," she said crisply. "She's gone back to Penmarric to live with him."

I went on staring at her. I thought of the widow in Canada and the possibility of Philip having a normal relationship with a woman. I felt my cheeks begin to burn; my mouth was dry.

There was a long silence. We sat watching each other, my mother cool and composed, I with no composure, no words, only a dull amazement that life could ever treat anyone so unfairly as it had treated me.

At last I managed to say, "That makes it irrelevant whether or not Philip prefers me to Jonas. He'll have sons."

"No, he won't," said my mother in a quick, hard voice. "He told me. Helena can't have any children. There won't be any sons." She began to put on her gloves again with deft motions of her fingers. "The inheritance will lie between you and Jonas," she said, not looking at me, "and I think you should have it. Penmarric means nothing to Jonas and everything to you. You've made a great many foolish mistakes and nearly ruined your chances, but all isn't yet lost. If you're clever and sensible Penmarric can still be yours one day if you outlive Philip." She stood up and moved slowly over to the door. "Philip brought me here this morning to persuade you to join us for lunch at the Metropole," she said over her shoulder. "He's at Michael's office now, but I've arranged to meet him at the Metropole at one o'clock, so I suggest you drive us there in your car." She glanced at my disheveled appearance and added, "I'll wait in the drawing room while you change—and don't forget to shave! You look like an escaped convict."

She gave me no chance to refuse to accompany her, so after she had gone I shaved, cutting myself twice, put on some clothes and pushed a wet comb halfheartedly through my hair. I looked white and sick and subdued. Turning my back on the mirror, I went outside to fetch the car from the shed where I had hidden it and prepared myself for the drive to the Metropole.

All I said to her during the journey was "How did you know I was staying with William?"

"Adrian thought you would probably be there."

We said nothing else. When we arrived at the esplanade I parked the car outside the hotel and escorted my mother inside.

"We'll wait in the main drawing room," she said. "We're a little early."

"Would you mind if I had a drink?"

"Is it really necessary, dear? You look slightly the worse for whisky as it is, if you'll forgive me saying so. However, you must do as you wish, of course. I don't want to dictate to you."

I sighed and lit a cigarette without asking her permission. I wasn't going to let her stop me smoking.

We waited ten minutes and made desultory conversation while I became increasingly ill-at-ease. I was just wishing I had left for London before my mother had tracked me down when the swing doors of the hotel lounge were flung wide apart and Philip walked into the room as if he owned the earth.

I looked at him, my great golden handsome brother, the greatest, most golden and most handsome of all my great golden handsome brothers. I looked at his immense height and his broad-shouldered, powerful frame. I looked at his fair hair and his suntanned skin, his firm mouth and his strong jaw. I looked at him and I hated him and wished with all my strength that he were dead.

He was smiling. Of course he was smiling! He was rich, happy and secure. Of course he would smile! I would smile too if I were in his shoes. How pleasant to be Philip Castallack with a wife who would tolerate anything, a mother who wanted only his happiness and a bunch of servants who were falling over themselves to lick his boots at his mansion by the sea.

But I wasn't Philip. I stood up, conscious only of my lack of inches, my ill-proportioned figure, my insignificant appearance. I saw myself then as if for the first time, Jan-Yves Castallack, twenty-eight years old, sent down from Oxford, unofficially convicted of fraud, penniless with nothing behind me but misspent years which I had wasted in trying to outshine my brothers and failing in every enterprise I had undertaken. I saw myself then as Philip saw me, the irresponsible younger brother, harmless, worthless and infantile. I remembered his letter to Michael. "My little brother is hardly the man to steal an inheritance if he meets with any form of resistance . . ." It had been a humiliating judgment. "My little brother is hardly the man . . ."

"Hullo Jan!" said Philip lightly with a smile which didn't reach the corners of his eyes. "Nice to see you again. What's all this nonsense about the accounts? Never mind, I'm sure it's not serious and I don't want to spoil my homecoming by exaggerating any schoolboy pranks you may have got up to in my absence. . . . Shall we go in to lunch? I see they've got lobster on the menu and I'm starving."

I said nothing because there was nothing to say. I was twenty-eight and a failure, and the lunch I spent with Philip and my mother that day at the Metropole marked the rock bottom of a wretched, dismal, contemptible career.

[4]

Philip still had business to complete after lunch, so I drove my mother back to the farm myself. Just beyond the boundary of Zillan parish she asked me to halt the car in a field gateway, and, dully surprised by her request, I obeyed her.

"Are you feeling unwell, Mama?"

"No, but I think you are. You're driving atrociously."

"I'm sorry, I'm not feeling myself at all. I apologize if I alarmed you."

"I'm not alarmed, simply annoyed. Darling, you must try and pull yourself together! Please—for my sake! I know Philip doesn't think much of you now—how can he after all this?—but you can convince him. I'm sure you can convince him!"

"It's out of the question." I put my hands on the wheel and gripped it tightly. "He'll never forgive me for this and he'll never alter his will in my favor. It would be better if I went away and made a fresh start in London."

"Make a fresh start here! If you were to turn over a new leaf—"

"He'll live another fifty years anyway. What do I care about his will? He'll outlive me."

"I hope you both live for another fifty years and longer," said my mother, "but sometimes fate plays strange tricks, and Philip, as you know, has never exactly fought shy of living a dangerous life in dangerous conditions. Also he *is* ten years older than you are. You're hardly in the same generation."

"It's no good," I said, "I can't do it. Even if Philip does change his mind and make me his heir I can't go back to Penmarric now as a mere bailiff. Not after I've been living there as master of the house for all these months. I've got to go away to London."

"Rubbish!" My mother was getting annoyed. "How can you win your way back into Philip's good books when you're three hundred miles away in London? Now, if you were to stay here and turn over a new leaf—"

"I can't do it." I was gripping the wheel, unable to look at her. "I've humiliated myself before too many people and everyone thinks of me as a failure. I can't do it."

"You can," said my mother, "and you will." Her fine-boned old hand reached out and closed on mine. "You must face this, Jan-Yves, because you'll never forgive yourself afterward if you run away. Running away won't help, you see—it won't make you feel less guilty and ashamed about what's happened here; on the contrary it'll make you feel more ashamed of yourself than ever. You must stay. I know it's hard, but if you can overcome this, if you can accept what's happened and begin again from the beginning—"

"I wouldn't even know where to begin."

"Well, you can start by ceasing to be in such a hurry! No, I'm serious! You've always been in such a hurry to do everything; you act as if you were engaged in some terrible race against time. You were in a hurry to get rich, a hurry to get married, a hurry to get Penmarric. Why do you have to hurry so? You're always in such a hurry that you don't even have time to be yourself—you're forced to strike attitudes all the time, adopt poses. I've seen you as the Dutiful Son, the Rich Man-About-Town, the Dashing Young Husband, the Master of Penmarric—but how often have I seen you as yourself? Perhaps you enjoy always acting the part of someone else, but oh, Jan-Yves, you can't know how terrible it is to be trapped in a part and know that your real self can never be allowed to show. Don't get trapped in one of your parts, Jan-Yves. Take time to be yourself and stop rushing from part to part antagonizing everyone who gets in your way."

"But time's so short." I fumbled for my words. "I'm twenty-eight. If I'd had some luck . . . nothing ever goes right for me—sometimes it seems my life's never had a chance to begin—"

"Didn't you realize that my life hardly began until I was thirty-one? Why, you're young, Jan-Yves, young! You have all the time in the world!"

I was silent, still gripping the steering wheel.

"Do you know how I spent my twenties? Do you? Has anyone ever told you how I spent my twenties before I married my first husband?"

"You were in service at Menherion Castle."

"Not in my twenties. I left the Castle when I was eighteen. I worked in shops. I worked in a hotel. I even worked as a barmaid. There! I've never told any of my children that before. I had a series of horrible degrading posts until I thought I'd sunk so low that there was no hope of me rising above such degradation again. I know how it is to feel that life's unjust and unfair! I know how it feels to be frantic because one's youth is slipping through one's fingers! Don't think I don't understand. But within ten years of working in that tavern I was mistress of Penmarric, and if such a change of fortune can happen to me it can happen to you. No more double-dealing, though. No more deceit and fraud. You must be honest, reliable and loyal, because if you are I'm convinced you'll reap your reward. Philip's a generous man and if he thinks you deserve it there's no reason why you shouldn't ultimately benefit from his generosity. Besides, strange as it may seem, he really does need you. He knows so little of the estate that your experience and advice would be invaluable to him, and I can't believe it would be so difficult for you—even after all this—to win his friendship and respect if you set about it in the right way."

She paused. There was a silence, and then when she next spoke there was a note in her voice that I had never heard before.

"Don't think no one believes in you any more after all this," she said. "Don't think no one has faith in you any longer. I believe in you. And I have faith. I don't care how foolishly you've behaved. I still believe that if you pull yourself together and act in a sensible manner I can be prouder of you than of any of my other children. It was all so easy for the others, wasn't it? But it was never easy for you."

I turned to face her. I looked at her for a long time until finally she kissed me and stroked the back of my head.

"Don't cry, Jan-Yves. Please. I meant what I said. I have the fullest confidence in you."

And it was then, with the tears wet on my cheeks and my defenses in ruins around me, that I forgave her at last for her past wrongs and felt all my hatred of her dissolve among the ashes of my pride.

6

*Richard's patronising forgiveness was the culminating
humiliation for John. The "child," as Richard called
him, was 27 years old, but could show a record only
of failure and dishonour. . . . In his efforts to emulate
[his brothers] he had shown only caricatures of their
qualities: where the young Henry had been gay, he
was frivolous, where Geoffrey had been cunning he
was sly, where Richard was bold he was merely bom-
bastic. The expedition to Ireland had been a fiasco; his
assumption of authority in England during Richard's
absence had been a hollow mockery. He stood in 1194
as a traitor and a fool . . . but, in fact, the real John
had not yet emerged.*

—King John,
W. L. WARREN

[1]

The next few months were not pleasant but I survived them
as best I could. My mother persuaded Philip to grant me a nominal
lease of the house in St. Just which William had occupied before
his dismissal from Penmarric, and I lived there on my own, apart
from an old woman of sixty who agreed to keep house for me.
During the day I worked with Walter Hubert on estate matters;
everything I did had to be approved by him and I had no control over any money. Philip paid me an overgenerous wage
through his bankers, and occasionally I bumped into him by
chance, but since he could not be bothered to talk to me for more
than five minutes at a time our relationship was hardly a close
one. In the evenings I went to the pub or spent my time trying to

find a new mistress, but my bank balance, burdened by the task of repaying the moneylenders, was too poor and my position at Penmarric too servile to allow me to approach a woman of my own class and I was finding the effort of having casual nights with any other type of woman too depressing to sustain for long. I saw Felicity occasionally and had a drink with William once a week, but otherwise I met few people. I was too ashamed of my loss of face to keep in touch with the friends who had flocked around me when I had lived as master of Penmarric, and the only person I saw often was my mother; every Wednesday I would dine at the farm, every Saturday I would escort her to Penzance for lunch and every Sunday I went with her to Zillan church for matins.

Seeing that I was making an effort to mend my ways, Adrian did his best to be friendly and even invited me to lunch at the rectory to resume our weekly forum on theological topics, but none of the other people whom I had antagonized during my stay at Penmarric made any friendly moves in my direction. When I saw Simon Peter Roslyn by chance during one of his business visits to Penmarric I was surprised when he even bothered to say good morning to me; Michael still regarded me as a criminal and would never condescend to do more than nod his head in my direction if ever we had the misfortune to see each other.

I had not forgiven Simon Peter for leading me to suppose that Philip was thinking of settling permanently in Canada. I didn't suspect him of deliberately leading me astray, but my cordiality toward him had cooled since my humiliation and I took care to avoid him whenever possible. In fact I was so busy trying to avoid him that I didn't at first notice that he was equally busy trying to avoid me.

The thought first occurred to me when after that unexpected "good morning" tossed casually in my direction he tried to slip past me with a speed that could only be described as furtive.

"It's all right," I said to him ironically. "You can relax. I didn't tell Philip."

He stopped. His china-blue eyes stared at me blankly. After a moment he said, "Tell Philip what?"

"That you encouraged me to assert myself at Penmarric."

"Pardon me," said Simon Peter Roslyn, greatly shocked, "but I did nothing of the kind."

For a moment I was so startled that I merely gaped at him

speechlessly, but then anger spurred me to a quick recovery. "You bloody well did!" I said. "You told me he wasn't coming home!"

"I'm afraid you're quite mistaken," said Simon Peter primly, a model of sharp-witted self-righteousness. "I told you no such thing."

"You said—"

"You asked me if I thought Philip would stay in Canada and I said I could read between the lines of his letters. That's all. I didn't say what it was I could read. You just put the wrong interpretation on my statement. Certainly I never encouraged you to assert yourself at Penmarric! I merely acquiesced in your decision to live there. What else could I have done? I knew Philip wouldn't take formal action to evict you, and I told you that. It was the truth. I never told you anything but the truth."

"Well, I'll be . . ." It took me a moment to go on. I was thinking of how Philip was planning to send Jonas away to school in the autumn, how Philip wanted Jonas to spend weekends at Penmarric that summer, how he was more anxious than ever to treat the child as his heir. And suddenly I saw Simon Peter working stealthily for his young cousin's advancement, making sure that I ruined myself in Philip's eyes, doing all he could to foster Philip's dislike of me and willingness to take an interest in Jonas.

"You dirty little bastard," I said slowly at last. "You crooked, double-dealing little lawyer."

"I played a fair game," said Simon Peter, still scrupulously polite. "If I outmaneuvered you, you have only yourself to blame. Come, Jan! That's all over now and I've no wish to quarrel with you. Let's bury the hatchet since it's likely we'll be seeing a good bit of each other in future. Have you heard that I'm buying Polzillan House? I approached your sister Mrs. McCrae about it the other day and she says she's willing to sell. I hope to move there in the autumn shortly before my marriage."

"Marriage?"

"Didn't you see the announcement in today's *Times*? Rosemary Trehearne and I have just announced our engagement. You know Rosemary, of course. I believe she was at Roedean with your wife."

I was speechless again. He smiled at me. "Uncle Joss's money came in useful after all," he said. "I'm glad of the opportunity to buy Polzillan House and give my future wife the sort of home to which she's accustomed."

My tongue began to recover from its paralysis. "Well, well," I said, "congratulations. I hope you enjoy yourself acting the part of a country gentleman."

"Gentlemen are born, I believe, and not made. My father is the greatest gentleman I know and he's a mere farmer who left school at the age of twelve. The type of man I would never call a gentleman is the aristocratic parasite who idles his way through Eton and gets sent down from Oxford for wasting his own time and his father's money."

"What a charmingly sentimental theory! Unfortunately you know as well as I do that a phony BBC accent, a smattering of good manners and money in the bank doesn't transform anyone into a gentleman overnight. However, I admire your courage in thinking you can live among the upper classes and be accepted by them on account of your well-bred wife and your well-appointed country mansion. It's too bad you only have to open your mouth and everyone instantly knows what strata of society you come from. I've always thought there was nothing so unfair as the English class system."

I had expected him to turn pale with anger. I had even thought he might tremble with rage. With each calculated insult I had hoped to see him flinch, but when at last I stopped speaking and waited in triumph for his reaction I found he did what I least expected—and outmaneuvered me yet again.

He laughed.

Now it was my turn to go pale with anger. I think I even began to tremble with rage, and the more I trembled the louder he laughed.

"My dear Jan!" he said in mocking imitation of an Oxford drawl. "Haven't you realized yet that you—your class, your way of life—are all an anachronism? The past was yours, all yours, but the future belongs to me. Up till now you've been able to ignore that, but you see, you can't ignore it any more. I won't let you ignore it. I'm moving in your social circles, living in your kind of mansion—even proposing to and being accepted by your class of woman. Your class is crumbling away, Jan, caving in beneath your feet, and who knows? In twenty years' time I may be dining with Jonas at Penmarric while you're reduced to living on your only forseeable inheritance—your mother's paltry little farm at Zillan!"

That finished it. I lost my temper. "Get out!" I yelled at him. "Get out before I have you thrown out! Get out of my house!"

"It's not your house," said Simon Peter Roslyn, effortlessly courteous. "How sad! It's a nice old place, isn't it? Perhaps I might buy it off Jonas one day and live in it myself! You can be sure that if I do I'll remember to invite you to dinner. I won't forget you, Jan, I promise. You'd be much too difficult to forget."

"Go————yourself!"

"Ah," said Simon Peter, "the public-school patois, known to most of the population as the language of the gutter! What charming advice, Jan old chap! May I suggest you yourself go and attempt exactly the same thing?"

And even before I had the chance to drive my fist into his prim little mouth he had turned his back on me and slithered smoothly from the room.

[2]

After that I found myself severely tempted to try to discredit Jonas in Philip's eyes, but fortunately my mother made me see the foolishness of such a move and insisted that Philip would eventually become disenchanted with Jonas without any assistance from me. This was such obvious good advice that I would have been a fool to ignore it, so I waited, biding my time and making no attempt to interfere.

It had now been definitely arranged that Jonas should go to Philip's old prep school in Surrey that autumn, and Rebecca had also consented to Jonas spending the summer weekends at Penmarric so that he could become accustomed to such surroundings; he would arrive on Saturday mornings, stay Saturday night, go to church with Philip and Helena on Sunday morning and return home to Morvah after Sunday lunch. Yet from the beginning there were difficulties. First of all he seemed to prefer Helena's company to Philip's; he liked to play croquet with her on the lawn and would trail after her when she cut flowers in the conservatory or walked with the dogs through the grounds. Second, despite Philip's efforts to interest him in more masculine occupations, he refused to ride and had an aversion unusual in a child to swimming in the sea or even walking along the beach.

"That's his mother's fault in my opinion," said Helena to me as we met one day in the grounds. "She refused to let either of those children bathe in the sea and kept reminding them of how their father died."

In the end it was Jonas's aversion to the sea that brought matters to a head. It was July by that time, and, having spent eight weekends at Penmarric, he had apparently allowed himself to be convinced that it was safe for him to go for a walk with his uncle along the cliffs and down to the shore at Cape Cornwall.

But on the beach he panicked and ran away.

Exasperated and baffled by such irrational behavior, Philip returned to Penmarric expecting to find the child hiding behind Helena's skirts and discovered that Jonas had vanished into thin air. It was at this point that I became involved in the dilemma; Philip came to my office, asked me if I had seen Jonas, and, on learning that I hadn't, told me the whole story.

"He's probably bolted for home," I suggested practically.

"But it's Saturday!" Philip stared at me angrily. "Damn it, he's used to staying Saturday night with us by now! Why should he run off home? Did he think I was going to beat him? Silly little bastard! I've never laid a finger on him and I don't intend to, although God knows my fingers have itched for a riding crop on more than one occasion—"

"You'd better make sure he's not at home before you do anything further." A glow of comfort was welling inside me as I thought of Jonas's stupidity, and I thought what a pleasant evening it was with the sunlight streaming across the herbaceous border beyond the window.

"All right, but could you come with me to Morvah? If there's any trouble with Rebecca I want someone who knows her as well as you do to stop her having hysterics. She might think I'd forced him to go down to the cove against his will or something equally absurd."

My pulse quickened at the thought of seeing Rebecca. I wondered if Jonas would provide me with the excuse I needed to enter the farmhouse kitchen again and watch her brewing a pot of tea.

He certainly provided me with the excuse to confront her. When we arrived at the farm Philip left me in the car and went around the side of the house to the back door, but although I prepared myself for a wait of several minutes only thirty seconds elapsed before he rejoined me with a baffled, angry expression in his eyes.

"He's there," he said curtly, "but Rebecca called me a monster and slammed the door in my face. What the devil she meant by that I've no idea. Could you try and convince her that I've never harmed one hair of her silly child's head? Monster seems a strange word to use when I've always done my best to be kind to the boy."

"Let me talk to her," I said with alacrity and hurried to the back door before he could realize how excited I was at the prospect of seeing Rebecca again.

The door was locked, so I knocked on the panels and rattled the handle. "Rebecca?" I called. "Can I come in? It's Jan."

The door flew open. Before I could say another word Rebecca had flung her arms around me and was sobbing violently against my chest.

I was so overcome with delight by this abrupt end to our estrangement that I flung my arms around her too and kissed her so hard on the mouth that she was unable to speak; it was some seconds before she managed to twist her mouth away and start gasping my name.

"Oh, Jan, Jan—"

"There, there," I said soothingly, stroking her hair. "It's all right, I'm here. What's happened? Is Jonas hurt?"

She started sobbing again. I couldn't get a word of sense out of her. "Where is the child?" I said at last. "He's here, isn't he?"

"Yes, he—he's upstairs . . . hiding . . . He's frightened." She accepted the handkerchief I gave her and began a halfhearted attempt at mopping-up operations. Her fingers were shaking. "He won't say a word except that Philip took him to the beach and he—Jonas—was so frightened that he ran away. Oh God, what shall I do? I should never have trusted Philip, never! I should have remembered what Hugh always said about him. I shouldn't have been deceived by the fact that Helena was living with him again—I've read about people like that in the newspapers—just because they're married it doesn't mean they can be trusted—"

"My dear Rebecca," I said, hardly able to believe my ears, "are you seriously trying to tell me—"

"What else could have frightened Jonas so much?" Tears were streaming down her face again. "I'm not letting Jonas ever go back there again," she said fiercely. "And I'm not letting Philip dictate to me about which school to send him to. Everyone knows what goes on at boys' boarding schools. I wouldn't put it past Philip to choose one which was specially—"

"My dear, you must be out of your mind."

"I was out of my mind before in letting him go off alone with

Philip! I'm not letting my boy be brought up by a . . . a . . ."

"—a generous honest man?" I did not even stop to think that it would be to my advantage to foster her grotesque suspicions. All I was conscious of was indignation that she should repay Philip, who had acted with the best of intentions, with such an unjust and unwarranted distrust. "For Christ's sake, Rebecca, pull yourself together and stop being so ridiculous! Philip may not care much for women, but there's a world of difference between a preference for masculine company and the kind of behavior you're trying to impute to him. Let me talk to Jonas. He'll soon tell you that you've allowed your imagination to lead you astray. Where is he? Bring him in here and let me talk to him."

"No," she wept, "no, I'm not letting Jonas be cross-examined by you about anything. Jonas is upset and frightened and he doesn't like you anyway. He hasn't forgotten that time at Penmarric when you—"

"Oh, for God's sake!" My patience snapped. I turned on my heel and wrenched open the back door. "If you won't let me help you and won't accept my advice, what the devil do you expect me to do? I've had enough of your melodramatics! I had more than enough of them in the past and I'll be damned if I'll put up with any more of them either now or in the future. Have hysterics if you must, but don't expect me to offer you my shoulder to weep on. I've got better things to do with my time even if you haven't."

I didn't wait for her to reply. I walked out, slammed the door and strode off angrily around the side of the house to the car.

The fresh summer breeze blew softly against my cheek. I stopped but I was too late; I was already in sight of the car and could no longer pause to consider what I should say to Philip. Opening the car door, I slid reluctantly into the driving seat.

"Did you get any sense out of her?"

I frowned at the dashboard, fidgeted with the keys.

"Jesus Christ, Jan! What are you hesitating for? What did she say? I want to know!"

I made the decision. Leaning back in my seat, I drew a deep breath and told him the truth.

There was a silence.

We sat there in my car, looking at each other, and from somewhere nearby a cow bellowed restlessly while a dog barked far away in the village. We went on looking at each other.

Philip's face was so devoid of expression that I thought at first he had not understood me, but then I saw his mouth narrow into a hard line and his eyes turn slate-gray as he clenched his fists.

He looked away. I was still trying to think of something to say when he spoke.

"What a stupid woman," he said. His voice sounded flat and tired. "What a stupid, stupid woman."

I opened my mouth to agree with him, but before I could say a word he rounded on me in a fury and shouted, "But I suppose you believed her! Maybe you even put the idea into her head! I wouldn't put it past you to suggest to Rebecca that her son wasn't safe with me! You'd like me to be estranged from Jonas, wouldn't you? You'd do anything you can to enable his mother to drive a wedge between us!"

I kept my head. "That's not true Philip," I said strongly. "I don't blame you for not trusting me and I don't blame you for suspecting me of such a thing, but I gave Mama my word that I wouldn't meddle in your relationship with Jonas and I've kept my promise. If you doubt that, ask Mama. She'll back me up. She knows I've turned over a new leaf. Talk to her, if I can't convince you! If you want to know the truth I've hardly spoken to Rebecca for over a year. We're estranged. This is the first time in eighteen months that I've been near the farm."

He stared at me in distrustful silence. He did not speak. His eyes were bleak and cold.

"Don't be a fool, Philip," I said, still keeping my head. "Give me credit for a little sense. I'm not a hysterical woman like Rebecca. Of course I don't think you harmed that child. You no more go around assaulting eight-year-old boys than I go around ravishing eight-year-old girls. The whole idea's absurd."

His fists began to unclench themselves. I saw his shoulders slump. After a long moment he said "Oh God" and stared blindly across the fields to the sea.

I felt sorry for him. In a clumsy attempt to show him I wanted to be friendly I said, "I feel I need a drink. Why don't we drive over to the Tinner's Arms at Zennor for a beer?"

He nodded, not speaking, still staring out to sea, so I started the engine and guided the car down the lane to the road. Beyond Morvah to the east along the coast road to St. Ives stood Zennor and the old pub. It was a beautiful evening. The sun was sinking toward a golden sea and the summer air was scented with the aroma from a small garden of flowers nearby.

634

"Let's sit outside," I suggested as we left the car. I thought he would prefer the open air to the intimacy of the bar. "I'll get the drinks. What will you have?"

"Anything. It doesn't matter."

When I emerged with two pints of bitter I found him sitting stiffly on a bench, his head bent, his hands clasped before him as if in supplication. Sitting down at his side, I handed him his glass.

"Thanks," he said.

We were silent. I wondered whether to speak of Jonas again but decided it would be better to let the matter rest. However, Philip came to the opposite decision. As I stared into my tankard I heard him say quietly, "How did Rebecca know that I prefer men to women?" And when I started, never having dreamt that he would refer to the subject other than obliquely, he added with careful logic, "She must have known that or else she wouldn't have imagined such a thing as this."

I tried to match his casual offhand manner. "She knows nothing," I said at last. "I used to say to her often that you took no interest in women, and I wouldn't be surprised if Hugh cast a few aspersions on your moral character while he was alive, but the scene at the farm just now was entirely the result of her imagination. She was upset because the child came home unexpectedly, and once she was upset any simple explanation of Jonas's behavior wasn't good enough for her."

"But she must have known something."

"Why should she? No one else does."

"Except you," he said. "You know. If you knew why didn't you tell Rebecca about it? She was your mistress."

"I preferred to keep what I knew to myself."

"Why? Why should you have bothered? What prompted you to be so discreet?"

"Respect, perhaps."

"For me?" He was mocking. He was even smiling in incredulity.

"No," I said. "Not for you. For Trevose."

The smile was wiped off his face. He was silenced.

"I liked Trevose," I said. "He was good to me. He needn't have been good to me, but he was. I don't forget people who are good to me like that, and I don't speak ill of them after they're dead. That's all."

He still did not speak. His eyes had an inward look as if he were thinking of the past.

"Besides," I said, "what was there for me to tell? That I had seen you one night in St. Ives with Trevose? You were often seen with him—that was nothing new. Short of describing the expressions on your faces there was nothing I could tell anyone."

"We often went to St. Ives." He lit a cigarette, shook out the match. "Helena knew, of course," he said abruptly. "It was inevitable that she should guess, but I knew Helena had too much pride to do anything but keep the knowledge to herself. I always took great trouble to be discreet, because I didn't want a shred of gossip to get back to Mama."

"She doesn't know anything."

"And she never will." He ground the burned stub of the match into the rough wooden table before us. His face was without expression now, without trace of pain or grief or regret. "I didn't find a second Trevose," he said. "At first I thought I could, but I was wrong. He was unique. I know that now. I'll never have a better friend than he was to me." He took a drag on his cigarette. "I liked Canada," he said. "The mines were interesting and I made plenty of friends, but no friend ever matched up to Trevose and after a while I got tired of looking. Then I found this widow. It was a relief to start living in a woman's house again by that time, but eventually she wanted an affair and—well, that sort of thing doesn't interest me. However, by that time I was clearer in my own mind about what I wanted. I saw I liked to live with a woman but I had to have my separate bedroom and my independence. No sex. No emotional scenes. I began to think of Helena again, but I knew I had no right to ask her to come back to me after the way I'd treated her, so I hardly expected her to agree to a reconciliation, let alone a reconciliation on the terms I wanted. But she did. Apparently she had tried an affair while she and Jeanne were abroad after Gerald's death and discovered she didn't like sex any better than I did. Ironic, wasn't it? It turned out that we were much better suited to each other than either of us had ever suspected." He flicked ash onto the ground and watched the breeze scatter it across the earth. "I think we're happy," he said. "We're certainly happier now than we were before."

"Yes," I said. I could think of nothing else to say.

"I'm glad I'm back in Cornwall. I liked Canada but I missed Cornwall a lot. Sometimes the homesickness seemed more than I could bear, but I stuck it out for three years, just as I said I would, and in the end I was glad I did. Those three years helped to give me a perspective on the past and also helped me to know myself better. It's important to know oneself well."

"Yes."

"It's a pity about Jonas," he said. "Poor little devil, I don't think it's his fault he's so difficult. It's a combination of his father being dead and his mother being the woman she is and his environment making him nervous of big houses like Penmarric and the way of life we take for granted. I'll still give him what assistance I can —if Rebecca will accept it—but he's not the son I wanted and I was no doubt optimistic in hoping that he ever could be. It's a pity, but I feel there's nothing more I can do about it now. I've done what I can. If Rebecca wants to blame anyone for what happens next she can blame herself—God knows it's not the child's fault that I've decided he's not after all suited to inherit Penmarric one day."

"You mean—am I to understand—"

"What else can I do? After this incident I have little choice but to change my will." He tossed his cigarette away and ground the butt to ashes beneath his heel. "Penmarric can go to you if you outlive me, and I wish you joy of the whole bloody inheritance. God knows you're the only one who seems to have any use for the place nowadays."

I tried to speak. I tried to smile. But as I began to stammer a few inadequate words to express my gratitude, he got up and walked away in calculated rebuff before turning to smile right back bitterly into my eyes.

7

*It is possible that during the years that followed, Rich-
ard himself, and his immediate entourage, began to
acquire a respect for the reformed John that then
emerged, for he spent them serving his brother faithfully on the field of battle and in the council chamber.*

*Isabelle of Gloucester played no part in John's public
life, and it is doubtful if she played much part in his
private life either; certainly she bore him no children.
. . . John set about freeing himself.*

—King John,
W. L. WARREN

[1]

It would be untrue to say that after this incident Philip and I
became close friends, but we were on better terms with each other
than we had been before; I began to be invited to dinner parties
at Penmarric at last, and occasionally Philip and I would go
drinking at the local pub. My position began to improve. I was
more likely to be given responsible work. At last I felt I was beginning to leave the most disagreeable part of my life behind, and
as the months passed I became less conscious of the memory of my
humiliation and disgrace.

Shortly after the scene with Rebecca, Philip told me he had
signed a new will in my favor and had left it in the care of
another firm of solicitors, Pomeroy and Pomeroy of St. Ives. On

this particular matter he had avoided the offices of Holmes, Holmes, Trebarvah and Holmes in order that no word should reach Simon Peter that Jonas had ceased to be heir to Penmarric.

"I want no more scenes with Rebecca," Philip said to me bluntly. "I've told Mama I've changed my will, and Helena knows, but if the news travels back to the Roslyns I'll never hear the end of it. Someone's sure to accuse me of being unfair to the child, poor little devil."

Jonas had not, of course, reappeared at Penmarric since the disastrous weekend in July, and eventually Rebecca informed Philip by letter that she had changed her mind about sending the child away to school. This was a most foolish decision, since she was depriving Jonas of his chance to have a decent education, but I was determined not to interfere. I had what I wanted and Jonas no longer concerned me.

My reluctance to become involved with Jonas made me reluctant too to become involved with Rebecca. If she had suggested that I visit her I would have gone to Deveral Farm without a second thought, but she made no move toward me and soon when I heard that she had a lodger for the holidays, a schoolmaster from Middlesex, I foresaw that she would make no attempt to renew our affair. I think my reaction to her accusations against Philip had antagonized her; she had turned to me for support only to find me totally unsympathetic. As if in revenge she seemed determined to ignore me—and focus all her attention on the schoolmaster from Middlesex.

Since my estrangement from her she had formed the practice of taking in a lodger during the summer months, and I had often wondered what her relationship was with these men whom she beckoned to Deveral Farm to supplement her income. Her first lodger, a writer from London, had been well into his sixties and obviously beneath her notice, but this schoolmaster was not much more than forty and not even unattractive. I regarded him with suspicion. Nobody else seemed to share my suspicions, but then nobody else knew Rebecca as well as I did. I knew that despite her protestations to the contrary she had a healthy sexual appetite, and I found it hard to believe she could have been without a lover since our last episode in the bedroom over two years before. After the autumn of 1934 she also had more moral freedom; her Uncle Jared, who had always kept a stern eye on her private life, died in September and was buried with his ancestors in Zillan churchyard after a memorial service at the Wesleyan chapel which he had attended for nearly fifty years. We all went to his funeral. He had been a well-respected man in the parishes of Morvah, Zillan and St. Just and was mourned by people from all stratas of society. Simon Peter was the chief mourner, and with him was not only his new wife, whom he had just taken to live at Polzillan House, but also one or two of the Trehearnes of Helston. Among the humbler mourners were the eight surviving daughters, but although Charity sobbed louder than any of them as her father's coffin was lowered into the earth none of her family gave her any indication that she was no longer disowned by them.

"Whore!" snarled Miss Hope Roslyn, the eldest of the three spinster daughters.

"Slut!" sneered Miss Prudence.

"Bitch!" sneered Miss Grace.

"You wicked, un-Christian old virgins!" screamed Charity. "At least I got myself a husband and the finest gentleman who ever did breathe!" And she flung herself against William's breast and wept piteously against his shirt front.

William, behaving cunningly in an embarrassing situation, said with immense grandeur, "Come, my dear, let's not keep the chauffeur waiting. I think it's time we returned to Carnforth Hall." To the hostile Roslyns he merely added, "If I didn't believe grief was the cause of your bad manners and bad taste I wouldn't be so ready now to overlook your contemptible behavior toward my wife. Good day." And turning his back on them, he walked off slowly toward the lych-gate with his wife leaning heavily on his arm.

It was the first time I had heard him refer to Charity as his wife. Ever since she had dragooned him to the registry office eight years before he had fought shy of any reference to the fact that he was a married man, but after Jared Roslyn's funeral all that was changed. He had always been happily married; now he was no longer ashamed to admit it. As he left the churchyard that day with his wife I envied him his happiness and wished I had a wife who could care for me as much as Charity cared for him.

But I had no one. Felicity and I were still good friends, but I knew our marriage was finished and that I should get a divorce so that I would be free to remarry whenever I chose to do so. Yet the idea of divorce saddened me; I lingered, postponing it for as long as possible, but early in 1935 I discussed the situation with Felicity and agreed to commit adultery at a certain hotel in St.

Ives known to her private detective. Felicity behaved very sensibly about the whole business—"After all," she said, "now that Daddy's halved my allowance and I can't even afford to give you any money, what's the point of staying married?"—but I became so upset that when the time came for me to commit my adultery I couldn't take advantage of the privacy of the hotel room but merely sat chain-smoking on the edge of the bed. It was a most distressing and sordid experience.

"We'll still be friends, won't we?" I said unhappily to Felicity afterward. "We'll still see each other now and then?"

"Of course!" said Felicity. "Why not? No hard feelings."

"I feel I've treated you so badly in so many ways — "

"Bunk," said Felicity. "We had some jolly good times and I don't regret a moment of it. Just think—if you hadn't married me no one would have done! Be thankful for small mercies, that's what I say. Don't go all conscience-stricken and pile on the sob stuff, there's a good chap, or I shall start howling myself. I say, why don't we go to the Metropole and have dinner and a bottle of champagne? No sad regrets! No going weepy on each other's shoulders! Let's go out and get tight and have a marvelous time!"

We did. But at the end of the evening we became maudlin, much against our better judgment, and she cried a little and said she'd loved me all along but had thought the only way to keep me was to give me as much freedom as I wished.

"Perhaps it would have been different if I'd had a baby," she said. "I hoped I would have one but then I went to a gynecologist —no, I never told you. Why? Oh, I don't know. I expect you were having one of your Rebecca moods when you simply didn't notice me at all. . . . It doesn't matter now. We aren't suited to each other, I know that really, and it's much more sensible to be divorced."

However, even when Felicity was granted a decree *nisi* in August of 1935 I found there was no one I wanted to marry. My depression deepened. Filled with a desire to escape from it, I went to Cambridge for a fortnight and was welcomed by Lizzie with open arms. She was pregnant again but feeling well, and she and her husband entertained me so hospitably that I soon forgot my troubles and began to enjoy myself. She seemed very happy. Her little girl, my niece Theodosia, was by this time two years old and already learning the Greek alphabet.

"Poor child," I said, amused.

"Nonsense," said Lizzie. "She enjoys it. I wish someone had tried to teach *me* Greek when I was two instead of letting me languish in ignorance until I was sixteen."

"Maybe she doesn't want to be educated," I suggested, but this idea was dismissed as too frivolous to be taken seriously.

It was while I was staying with Lizzie that I became sufficiently diverted from my personal affairs to take some interest in national events. In fact it would have been impossible to stay with Lizzie and not be forced to take an interest in at least one of the current issues under discussion—in this case the intellectual pros and cons of pacifism and its effectiveness in coping with the rising Fascist tide.

"But isn't fascism just a fad?" I said vaguely, "a reaction to all that Bolshevik hysteria of the Twenties? You surely can't take people like Mosley seriously! Of course I know that Fascist rally at Olympia last year was a bit of a disgrace, but—"

"Mosley!" said Lizzie, eying me as if I were a very unintelligent schoolboy. "Olympia! What about Hitler and his purges—if you're going to talk about last year's Fascist excesses what about the Night of the Long Knives in Germany? And what about Abyssinia and Mussolini, and Hitler adopting conscription in direct contradiction to the Treaty of Versailles? And what about—"

"Well, that's all abroad," I said, assuming a placid, self-satisfied air to tease her for her impassioned harangue. "Here at home things are all right, aren't they? Unemployment down, the economy cheering up at last, the Silver Jubilee—"

"Sentimental absorption in an admirable royal family," said Lizzie severely, "is no excuse for ignoring the political realities of a menacing international situation. The only hope of avoiding international chaos is by the propagation of pacifism—unilateral disarmament and individual conscientious refusal to fight are the only morally tenable solutions to present European problems in my opinion."

"Well, Baldwin still seems to believe in the League system," I said comfortably. "Look how he's replaced Hoare with Eden as Foreign Secretary."

"Politicians!" snorted Lizzie. "They believe whatever they want to believe, depending on how soon the next election is! I'm tired of watching Baldwin flirt with the idea of rearmament!"

"I don't suppose it'll matter if we rearm or not," I said soothingly. "Nobody's going to indulge in full-scale war again, not even your favorite bogeymen in their black shirts and swastikas. There's a limit to everything, after all."

"You sound just like Baldwin," said Lizzie coldly, "in one of his 'I'm just a plain, pipe-smoking, country-loving Englishman' moods."

But I only laughed at her.

It was in September, just after my return from Cambridge, that I met Rebecca face to face in St. Just. I had not seen her for some months and had schooled myself not to think of her any more as soon as I had realized that she paid more attention to her lodgers than she would ever again pay to me. I now considered myself over the worst of my long infatuation with her; I could even tell myself—and believe it—that she was a trying woman who had been a trying mistress and would have been without doubt a trying wife if I had ever made the mistake of marrying her. I no longer even admired her looks as much as I had once admired them. During the past couple of years she had put on weight in the wrong places; there were silver threads in her black hair and unmistakable lines about her eyes and mouth. She was not old, still under forty, but I could not look at her now without remembering that she was seven years older than I was.

I remembered those years when I met her in St. Just early on that rainy September afternoon. I looked at her and she no longer attracted me. I was free, beyond her reach.

"Good afternoon, Rebecca," I murmured out of politeness, expecting her to sweep past me in her usual sullen fashion, but to my surprise she stopped and gave me a distant smile.

"How are you, Jan?"

"Well, I suppose. And you?"

She shrugged. "All right." She smiled faintly at me again and the breeze caught the facings of her open raincoat and revealed the black jersey and tight gray skirt beneath.

"I hear you're divorced now," she said.

"More or less. We have the decree *nisi*."

She seemed to have lost the excess weight I had noticed earlier. Her waist was still small, her hips still well-molded, her bosom still overgenerous.

"I suppose you plan to remarry," she said.

"I suppose so," I said. "Eventually."

"You've no one in mind?"

"No."

She pushed back a strand of dark hair which had blown into her eyes. I glanced at her face again for the telltale lines of age but saw only her white skin, her black lashes and her moist, full-lipped mouth.

"How are the children?"

"They're both well. Deborah goes into Penzance now to take a typing course with shorthand, but she doesn't like it much. Jonas is doing well at school."

"So you're alone during the day."

"Yes," she said. "I'm alone." She was coloring a little. She turned and stared down the street.

"No lodger?"

"Not at present." She was blushing. She adjusted her grip on her shopping basket and tried to move past me, but I blocked the pavement.

"May I drive you home?"

"I have more shopping to do yet."

"I'll get my car and wait for you in the square."

She did not object. Thirty minutes later I was driving her to Morvah, and within an hour we were in bed together at the farm-house.

Afterward I lit a cigarette and said to her, "Why the sudden truce after all these months of hostility?"

"I was lonely."

"Even with your lodgers?"

"I was just the landlady renting rooms, nothing more."

"Oh?"

I must have sounded skeptical. She smiled unexpectedly. "A fifteen-year-old daughter and a nine-year-old son make excellent chaperones! Besides, I had no desire to do wrong. They weren't attractive men." She kissed me, laid her head against my shoulder. "I never managed to forget you, Jan. I did try, but it was no use. When I heard you were getting a divorce I couldn't help wondering if you'd found some other woman—I felt I had to find out—"

"There's no one else."

"Then . . ." She broke off. "Jan, you do love me, don't you?"

"More than any other woman in the world," I said and meant it. I was still wondering how I had managed to deceive myself into thinking she was no longer attractive. "I've always loved you—you should know that by now. It was you, not I, don't forget, who decided we should be estranged from each other for all these months."

"Everyone told me I should give you up." Her eyes were brilliantly dark. Her voice shook a little. "They said you didn't love me and were just using me whenever you felt like it. They said if I had a grain of self-respect I should end the affair and never take you back again." Her lips trembled. "They said I should be ashamed of myself with a young girl like Deborah in the house—"

"My darling . . ." I held her tightly in my arms; I hated to think of her being made unhappy. "Don't think of that any more."

"I tried to tell myself I didn't love you. It was easier when you were unkind to Jonas, it was easier to tell myself then that I didn't care. In the end I truly believed I didn't love you and could tell myself I'd been foolish to expect a second love in my life after Hugh. But then . . . when I heard you were divorced . . . oh, Jan, all the love came rushing back—I wanted you so much—"

"And I wanted you. Always."

We did not speak after that for a long time. At last I lit another cigarette. Outside beyond the window rain was still falling from leaden skies and a mist was swirling in from the sea.

"Jonas will be back soon," said Rebecca, but she made no move to leave the bed.

I thought of Jonas. One day Rebecca would find out that Philip had changed his will in my favor, and when she found out there would be more trouble. Jonas would always come between us; I knew that now. The older he grew the worse the situation would get, and there was nothing whatsoever I could do about it.

Almost as if she had guessed my thoughts she whispered, "Jan . . . Jan, could we—perhaps if we . . . Jan, we could be married now, couldn't we? You have a good salary from Philip and the nice house in St. Just—or we could live here at Deveral Farm . . ."

There was a silence. I fingered the sheet and didn't look at her.

"But Jan, now that you're divorced what's to prevent us from marrying?"

"I think we would soon quarrel over Jonas."

"Jonas would be good with you if he saw we were happy together."

I didn't answer.

"He could go away to school," she said timidly. "I don't want him to go but perhaps I was being selfish and not considering his best interests by keeping him at home. He wouldn't be any trouble in the holidays. He's a good boy really, Jan. I know he's been difficult in the past, but I think he'd be different if there was a man in the house he could treat as a father."

I knew at once that Jonas would never regard me as a substitute father. In his mind I would always remain the wicked uncle.

"Hm," I said and scrambled out of bed to get dressed. "It's an awkward situation. I'll have to think about it."

"But we might—perhaps—be married soon?"

"I'll have to think about it." I began to button my shirt. "It's not that I don't love you," I said reasonably, "but marriage is a big step, isn't it, and since I've already got one divorce behind me I want to be sure that before I marry again there's no possible risk of anything going wrong. Perhaps at Christmas I'll have a clearer idea of how matters stand."

But Christmas came and went and still I couldn't make up my mind. Jonas did make some effort to conceal his dislike of me, but dissimulation is hard for a small boy and I saw through his sullen politeness all too clearly. I knew he didn't want me to marry his mother. As if in silent rebellion against her infidelity to Hugh's memory he made a scrapbook of all the photographs of his father he could lay his hands on and mounted them lovingly on the dark leaves of an expensive album. For some days whenever I came to the farmhouse he was busy painting white captions beneath the photographs and pointedly emphasizing the fact that although some people might have forgotten his father he certainly had no intention of doing so.

This was all very commendable, and I've no doubt Hugh would have been proud of his son, but it hardly encouraged me to assume the role of stepfather. I had to ask Rebecca to be patient with me, and at Easter I did vow to myself that I would make up my mind one way or the other by the end of the school summer holidays. I reasoned that after eight weeks of Jonas being at home all day I should know whether or not I could tolerate him as a stepson.

I wasn't living at the farm, of course, but I did spend a great deal of time there. My mother disapproved, I knew; both she and Lizzie would have been disappointed if I had married Rebecca, and although William never spoke a critical word to me on the subject of my private life I sensed he also thought Rebecca would be the wrong woman for me to choose to be my second wife.

It was all most difficult.

It might have been easier if I had been smitten with the urge to marry someone else, but that was out of the question. I did not even expect it to happen, because I knew perfectly well that I wouldn't have the slightest desire to look at another woman so long as I could drive along the coast road to Morvah and have Rebecca waiting for me in the bedroom at Deveral Farm.

[2]

Money was tight at Penmarric that year. The house was costly to run, the servants' wages had gone up, and all the tenants' cottages seemed suddenly to be in a bad state of repair. The barren economic climate of the early Thirties seemed to linger on in Cornwall, and although I heard matters were supposed to be improving elsewhere I saw little sign of improvement among the ruined mines of the Cornish Tin Coast. The Penmar fortune seemed to diminish before my eyes; Philip was not extravagant in comparison to many landowners I knew, but he couldn't be bothered with budgeting and spent exactly as he pleased. He made enough fuss about other people counting his pennies for him but he himself was supposed to be above it all. Fortunately Helena took a less Olympian attitude to money. I noticed how she kept a watchful eye on the household accounts, and I guessed she supplemented her husband's bank balance with her own private income more and more frequently. I myself had to work hard not only to make the estate accounts look respectable but also to balance my own small financial resources. Gone were the days when I had been a reckless spender; if anyone had told me when I was up at Oxford that one day I would know not only how much was in my bank account without referring to my bank statement but also how much was in my wallet without taking it out to examine the contents, I would have laughed in scorn, but now I found I had such a tight hold on my money that I could account for every penny I spent.

"How middle-class!" my brother Marcus would have cried in horror in those golden days before the war, but times had changed and social conditions had changed with them.

"I hear Simon Peter Roslyn is quite the country gentleman nowadays at Polzillan House," said my mother with distaste. "That would *never* have happened before the war! Why, a Roslyn couldn't even have married a Trehearne of Helston in those days —or if he had, they wouldn't have been received. I don't want to seem old-fashioned, but I can't help thinking all these changes are not necessarily for the best."

But times went on changing. Our new King was soon to give up his throne to marry an American divorcée; 1936 was the year of the Abdication, and as if that were not disaster enough we had to digest the news of Mussolini at Addis Ababa and the formation of the Rome–Berlin Axis.

"I suppose you've been following the international situation in your usual Baldwinesque fashion," wrote Lizzie crisply from Cambridge. "That man ought to be put out to pasture along with those pigs he keeps. How dare he blame pacifism for the current international debacle? How dare he damn pacifism on the one hand and yet refuse to lift one finger to help a worthy cause in Spain?"

Like many intellectuals who favored the Left, Lizzie was gradually abandoning her pacifist stance as the Spanish Civil War assumed the dimensions of an ideological conflict. Indeed as the Thirties entered their second half it was the Left, formerly devoted to pacifism, who became militant and the Right who retreated into the pacifist cause.

"Everyone gets so hysterical about this war in Spain," I complained to William. "Personally I'm sure both sides are as bad as each other and I'm damn glad Baldwin's decided on a neutralist policy. I simply don't see Lizzie's argument that we should all go and fight for the Communists. Of course, I believe fascism should be contained wherever possible, but nevertheless I don't think one should be unnecessarily hotheaded about it. The days are long since past when everyone picked up guns and rushed into war at the drop of a hat. If Lizzie wasn't so wrapped up in all her idealistic intellectual theorizing about this wretched civil war she'd have the common sense to see that any intervention on our part would be madness—as well as being inconsistent with our past foreign policy."

"Lizzie will soon forget about Spain when that new baby grows up a little and demands more of her attention," said William placidly, but I doubted it. I knew her better than he did.

Lizzie visited Penmarric soon after the birth of her second daughter Pamela and gave my mother the opportunity to see both her new grandchildren. Successful marriages seemed to be in vogue at that time; Jeanne was clearly happy with her second husband, and, not to be outdone by Lizzie's ventures into motherhood, announced in 1936 that she expected a baby in the autumn.

"Rather late in the day," grumbled my mother, who nowadays seemed determined to favor Lizzie over her other daughters. "She'll be thirty-seven next Christmas. That's too old to have one's first child, in my opinion."

My mother was now seventy-seven, in full command of every faculty and extremely spritely for her years. She was crafty enough to pretend to be frail when she wanted extra attention, but we all knew she was amazingly fit and well.

"She'll live forever," said Philip with pride, as if he himself was solely responsible. "She doesn't look a day over sixty-five."

Philip was restless, but as far as I could judge not actively discontented. He spent much of his time wandering around the Tin Coast with a couple of old mining comrades on weekends and making journeys below ground more out of nostalgia than out of hope of finding a lode worth working. Helena was deeply involved in charity work. They seemed to co-exist harmoniously enough, and although they did not entertain much at Penmarric Philip did make the effort to take his wife to London every year for a holiday.

Adrian also had a holiday in London that summer. His old friend Mr. Barnwell died at last, and soon after his funeral Adrian was promoted to the staff of Exeter Cathedral; before taking up his appointment he had spent a week in London seeing his publishers and various interested persons at the BBC, for his first full-length theological book had been published in the spring of 1936, just before Mr. Barnwell's death. Adrian had made full use of those six quiet years at Zillan parish, and now he was to reap his reward by earning a reputation for himself as a theologian and finding his name become well-known in clerical circles. I admired his book very much. It was an advanced modern approach to Christianity which seemed to me to blow a breath of fresh air through the cobwebbed sobriety of the Church of England. The book was reviewed in the national press, not merely noted in clerical publications, and during his visit to London Adrian was even interviewed on the wireless—much to the awe of the parishioners of Zillan, most of whom still regarded the wireless as hopelessly newfangled.

The new rector had a hard time following in such illustrious footsteps; he was a thin, earnest man called Forrest whom my mother instantly disliked. "Too Popish," she said fussily, although all the poor man did was swing a little incense now and then. "And common," said my mother. "I wish Adrian were still here."

I wrote and told Adrian that. He had always been so kind to my mother that I thought he should know his kindness had been appreciated.

Esmond came to stay that summer as usual. His father was still alive, but only just; I think Esmond found life depressing in Scotland at his father's enormous mansion and was glad to escape to Penmarric each year. Mariana was now in Monte Carlo with a rich American and Esmond was still not allowed to communicate with her, but Philip and Helena treated him as if he were their son, and any stranger seeing the three of them together would have at once assumed they were his parents. He was sixteen now, strong and athletic, and shared not only Philip's passion for Cornwall but also a hint of Philip's passion for the Cornish mines. That summer, much against Helena's wishes, the two of them fell into the habit of exploring the abandoned mines together.

"Supposing something happened to Esmond?" she confided to me in anxiety. "Philip is as much at home below ground as an aeroplane pilot is in the sky, but Esmond is hardly in the same position as Philip. I worry terribly about him."

"Philip will look after him," I said soothingly. "He won't take any chances where Esmond's concerned."

She looked somewhat less anxious at this, but I suspected she went on worrying just the same.

I didn't worry. I had no hint of what was to come, no premonition of disaster. I was enjoying myself, working at Penmarric in the mornings and afternoons, taking a long lunch hour with Rebecca and entertaining myself exactly as I pleased on weekends. Those were good days for me, and by this time I had fully recovered from my disgrace following Philip's return from Canada.

"Thee looks powerful well and vigorous, Mr. Jan," said old Mrs. Trewint as I went into her shop in St. Just one August morning to buy a packet of cigarettes. "And so do the Master. He passed here an hour ago with young Mr. Esmond, Lord Roane, I should say, begging his pardon. It's all very nice to see an uncle and nephew so attached to each other as the Master and his Lordship."

I smiled, paid for my cigarettes and pocketed the packet.

"Which mine were they off to visit today?" I said. "Or didn't they say?"

"The Master says they was riding over the moors toward Zillan and the shafts up by Ding Dong. A shame it is to go underground on such a beautiful morning! But that's a Cornish tinner for 'ee. Pisky-led by the thought of tin. All they tinners is the same. Why, I remember when the Levant was working . . ."

I listened patiently to her reminiscences before escaping to Morvah to lunch with Rebecca. Since it was August the children weren't at school, but Jonas had caught the bus to Penzance to spend his pocket money on a brace of goldfish, and Deborah had walked over to Zennor to visit a friend for the day. There was no lodger that summer; Rebecca had decided she didn't need the extra income now that Deborah had finished her year at the secretarial school and would soon be earning her living, and besides a lodger would undoubtedly have made a nuisance of himself by getting in our way.

When I arrived we went straight to the bedroom as usual, and after Rebecca had gone downstairs at last to dish up the lunch I lingered for a few minutes between the sheets. I felt drowsy; I was just about to drift into a doze when I heard the sound of horses' hoofs below the bedroom window.

Someone had ridden up to the back door at a gallop.

I sat up at once, listening. Perhaps someone had come to fetch me for some reason. But who knew I was at Morvah? Only old Walter Hubert with whom I worked in the little office at Penmarric, and Walter wouldn't have sent for me unless there was an emergency.

Perhaps it was an emergency.

I sprang out of bed, flung back the curtain and leaned out of the window that overlooked the yard.

I saw him then, saw the sun burnish his hair to gold and glow upon his sunburned skin. He was slipping from his horse, running to the back door. The expression on his face made my blood freeze.

I turned, grabbed my shirt, pulled on my trousers and ran barefoot out onto the landing.

Rebecca was already calling me. "Jan!" She was at the foot of the stairs. Her eyes were dark with shock in her upturned face. "Jan . . ."

I raced down the stairs and pushed past her into the kitchen.

He was sitting slumped at the kitchen table, but as I burst into the room he started and twisted around to face me.

"Oh God." He was ashen. "Oh God."

"What happened?"

"He—he fell . . . Such a simple little shaft . . . We—we weren't even roped together—and he fell . . . The ladder came away from the wall. The ladder was rotten and he fell . . ."

I was dumb. I could only look at him without speaking.

"I went down," he said. "I went down by the rope. His back was broken. He died. In my arms. He died." Tears streaked his face. His eyes were blind. "He died," he said. "There was nothing I could do. And all he said was—"

"Yes?"

"He—he said, 'Perhaps this was what I really wanted,'" said Esmond, and began to cry as if his heart would break.

8

In a poor state of repair and ill-defended, it presented only a minor problem to Richard's talents. He was indeed too contemptuous of it, and without bothering to don his armour he went reconnoitring round it. . . . He was struck in the shoulder by a bolt from a crossbow. . . . He died bequeathing his jewels to his nephew Otto of Saxony, and his inheritance to his brother John.

—King John,
W. L. WARREN

It would be pleasant if it could be reported that Berengaria's life flowed in easy courses after Richard's death, but unfortunately she [lost] the friend who had stood by her in all her trials, the King's sister Joanna . . . after her brother's death the shock caused [Joanna] to give birth prematurely to a son, and she died herself the following day.

—The Conquering Family,
THOMAS COSTAIN

[1]

He was forty-one. At first I could not believe he was dead. "He was only forty-one," I said. "He was in his prime of life." I thought of his vitality, his restlessness, his immense reserves of physical strength, and I saw it all laid on the altar of the Cornish mines he loved so well, a gigantic sacrifice to futility, darkness and decay.

"He was only forty-one," I said. "That's young to die."

But he had lived longer than either Marcus or Hugh.

"There's a curse on your family," said Rebecca. "You spend your lives fighting each other and then you die young. There's a curse."

I remembered all those years when I had hated him and grudged him his good fortune. I remembered our quarrels and hostility. I remembered my jealousy, my resentment that he should always be so fortunate, and as I remembered I looked back into the past and saw not the good fortune I had envied, not the glitter of success, not the coruscation of a mighty popularity, but the emptiness, the disappointment, the wasted years of bitterness and frustration.

"We were friends at the end," I said. "I liked him once I no longer envied him. I admired him."

So because of this I grieved for him, for my great golden older brother, dead in his prime of life, and as I grieved I thought how others too would grieve at his loss and mourn the tragedy which had brought him to an early grave. I thought for three brief seconds of Helena and my sisters, and then in a flash of panic I remembered my mother, all alone at Roslyn Farm.

[2]

Somebody would have to tell my mother.

"I can't," said Helena, her calm face ravaged with grief. "I can't."

"Jeanne can't possibly," said my brother-in-law Donald McCrae over the phone. "The news itself was such a shock to her that she fainted and now it looks as though the baby's going to come two months early. I'm just about to take her to the hospital."

"Somebody will have to tell your mother," said Walter in my office. "Poor woman. It'll be a terrible blow for her."

"Lizzie," I said, clasping the telephone receiver with sweating fingers, "Lizzie, someone has to tell Mama, but I simply can't face it. What on earth can I do?"

"Have an outsider tell her," said Lizzie, very crisp and practical far away in Cambridge. "How about the new rector?"

"She doesn't like him. He hardly knows her."

"Donald, then—"

"Jeanne's in the midst of a miscarriage."

"Good heavens, what a frightful chain of misfortune! Is Jeanne very ill?"

"Donald just said he was taking her to the hospital."

"Oh God, I do hope she doesn't lose the baby—she wanted it so much."

"But Lizzie, who am I going to get to tell Mama? Who can I ask?"

"Perhaps old Dr. Salter—"

"He died two years ago. And Mr. Barnwell's dead too. If only Adrian were here—"

"Adrian will know what to do. Ring up Adrian. Listen, Jan, you will let me know as soon as you get word about Jeanne, won't you? I'm terribly worried about her. Did Donald mention anything about a Caesarian?"

"No, he didn't. Lizzie, isn't there anyone you can think of who might just possibly tell Mama about Philip?"

"Ask Adrian," said Lizzie. "Adrian will know." And before I could begin to say anything else the operator interrupted us and our conversation came to an end.

"What am I to do?" I said to Adrian five minutes later. "I know I'm weak and a coward and all the rest of it, but I simply can't nerve myself to do it. Can you think of anyone—*anyone*, Adrian—who might possibly—"

"Don't be afraid," he said. "Your mother must often have faced the possibility that Philip might die in a mining accident. Tell her clearly and slowly and be as simple as possible. Say you have bad news, that Philip's had an accident while exploring one of the old mines. She'll guess the rest."

"I can't," I said. I don't mind admitting I was crying myself by this time. My un-English upper lip was betraying me again and my eyes were blurred with tears. "I can't."

"Yes, you can," he said. "I know you can. Don't be afraid. Old people are more familiar with death than people of our age and more accustomed to thinking about what it means. Your mother's a believer; she's also a strong woman who's lived through many tragedies. She'll survive. But you must tell her. It wouldn't be right to send a stranger. You're her only surviving son and so you're the best person to tell her that even with Philip gone she's still not alone in the world. Now go out, get into that car of yours and drive over to Zillan to see her before she hears the news accidentally from a complete stranger."

I went. I drove away, still sniffling, along the coast road and then took the road which led over the moors to Zillan. On the crest of the ridge I paused, blew my nose and mopped myself up. After that I lit a cigarette and smoked it. Finally when I was composed once more I started the engine again and drove the last long mile downhill to the farmhouse.

I saw her as I drove up the lane. She was snipping busily with her shears at the wild roses which grew up the wall by the porch.

When she saw me she waved.

I halted the car and got out. The summer air was warm and quiet and infinitely peaceful. A bird sang, a bee hummed and a cricket whirred in the long grass nearby.

"Jan-Yves!" She was smiling. The faint breeze ruffled her white hair. She looked young for her years, happy and light-hearted. "What a nice surprise!"

Tears pricked behind my eyes. My throat ached, throttling my power of speech.

"Have you come to tea?" she said sociably. "Do stay!"

I shook my head.

"Is something wrong?"

I swallowed, cleared my throat. I still couldn't speak. To gain time for myself I opened the car door again as if I had forgotten something and fumbled at the dashboard.

"What is it?" She was beside me in a moment. It was amazing how quickly she moved still. "It's not bad news, is it, darling?"

I nodded, shut the door, fidgeted with the handle. I still couldn't look her in the face, but I felt her stillness suddenly, her tension, her mute expression of dread.

"It's Philip, isn't it?" she said.

I looked at her. She never flinched. She held her head erect and her eyes were steady and her back was straight and stiff and proud. We stood there together before that mellow old farmhouse on that quiet August afternoon, and at last after a long silence she said in a clear, cool voice, "I suppose it was in a mine."

I tried to speak then, but she wouldn't listen. I tried to tell her that he had died quickly with little suffering, but she didn't want to hear. She looked past me across the moors toward the tower of Zillan church and her eyes were empty of all emotion.

"It was really a miracle that he lived so long," she said in the tone of voice in which people discuss the weather. "I never expected him to. Sometimes, you know, I even thought it might have been better for him if he had died in the Sennen Garth disaster. With Trevose."

And as I stared at her, too appalled by her knowledge to reply, her unnatural calm disintegrated and her frail old body began to shudder beneath the terrible burden of her grief.

[3]

Later I said, "So you knew."

"Wasn't I supposed to?" Her mouth twisted a little but she could not even smile in irony. Her face was drawn with grief. Tears scarred ugly furrows down her withered cheeks. "How could I not know? I knew Philip better than anyone else in the world. Do you think I didn't know all his faults as well as all his virtues? Do you think I was so stupid as to believe him to be perfect? Do you think I never noticed that he preferred to be with that coarse, rude, unspeakably vulgar little miner? How blind you must have thought me! How fatuous and besotted! Of course I noticed! I noticed everything. But it didn't matter to me." Tears overcame her for a moment, but she brushed them aside. "I didn't care," she said. "It didn't make any difference. How could it? He was still Philip. All I wanted was for him to be happy, and if he was happy with Trevose, then that was what I wanted for him."

Her cheeks were wet with tears again. She sat hunched in her chair, an old, old woman who had lived too long and seen too much.

"I never said anything to him about Trevose," she said. "I didn't once reproach him. It would have been wrong for me to interfere, wouldn't it? I always tried not to interfere. I didn't want to antagonize him and I was afraid that if I made him angry he wouldn't realize that all I ever wanted was the best for him. How can it be wrong to want the best for your children? How can it be wrong to want them to be happy? I wanted Philip to be happy . . . but he wasn't. He was restless and becoming more so each day. He was already dissatisfied with his life at Penmarric—if it hadn't been for Esmond he would have left again by now. He was longing for the mines again. He talked of Australia, South Africa. No, he wasn't happy here. I knew he wasn't happy.

"Maybe it would have been different if he had loved Helena a little—if there could have been children—but their marriage was nothing. I spent such a long time hoping he would marry her. I was so convinced she would make him happy, but of course in fact I couldn't have been more wrong. I realized—too late—that poor Helena was the worst type of woman whom a man of his inclinations could possibly have married. She was too cold, too self-contained, too withdrawn—poor girl! No doubt her misfortunes

657

accentuated her worst attributes, but what kind of woman accepts her husband back under such impossible conditions? Certainly not a woman with normal passionate emotions.

"Yes, it was a pity they ever married. If I had known . . . But I didn't know. And then one day I saw Philip just looking—looking—looking . . . I thought he was looking at Helena. I went into the parlor saying, 'Oh, Philip, how nice of you to bring Helena to see me!' But it wasn't Helena at all. It was that surly, repulsive little man. I suppose you could never imagine how it feels for a mother to know what I knew then. For a moment I thought I would faint, which was silly of me because I never faint, I'm not one of these women who swoon at every slight jolt to their nerves. So I didn't faint. I believe I was quite composed. I said good afternoon politely and asked them if they would take tea and told them to sit down and make themselves at home. I didn't want Philip to know, you see. I don't know why. I suppose I didn't want him to feel ashamed—or obliged to make some sort of apology or worse still an explanation. Anyway I didn't want to interfere, and once I had lived with the knowledge for a while I found I could accept it and not mind. I tried so hard not to mind. You see, if it made Philip happy . . . You do understand, don't you, Jan-Yves? I only wanted Philip to be happy."

"Yes, Mama," my voice said. "I understand."

She went on looking at me, her eyes bewildered, her cheeks still wet with tears. "Then what went wrong?" she said. "I did all I could—no one wanted him to be happy more than I did, so why couldn't I get what I wanted for him? Where did I go wrong?"

But there was no answer I could give her. She looked at me for five silent seconds with those bewildered eyes full of grief, and then as if guessing the answer which I could never have voiced aloud, she put her hands over her face again and began to cry softly to herself in that cold, empty room.

[4]

I could not leave her. I remained with her till dusk and then suggested she come with me to St. Just and stay the night at my house.

"I would like to see him," she said, her hands twisting themselves together restlessly. "Will he be at Penmarric?"

"By now, yes, I expect so. A group of his old mining friends went off to the shaft to bring him to the surface, and the ambulance was driving up as far as Ding Dong mine to take the body to Penmarric. But you can see him tomorrow, Mama. Come home with me now and rest. My housekeeper will make you comfortable."

"I can't leave Annie," she said, referring to her simple old servant. "She wouldn't understand if I went away."

"Then I shall stay the night here with you, but first I must make some telephone calls. Where's the nearest phone? At the rectory, I suppose."

"Or Polzillan House," she said, but I had no wish to go calling on Simon Peter Roslyn.

"Will you be all right if I leave you for about half an hour to make these telephone calls?"

"Oh yes," she said blankly. "Yes, of course. Whom are you going to telephone?"

"William, to see what's happening at Penmarric. He left Carnforth Hall as soon as he heard the news and went over to Penmarric to be with Helena and help her make the arrangements. I also want to try to speak to Donald in Penzance. The news was such a shock to Jeanne that it brought on a miscarriage. Donald was just about to take her to the hospital when I last spoke to him."

But she did not take it in. Her mind was filled with Philip's loss and could not absorb news of a second tragedy in the family.

"No doubt Jeanne will be all right," I said uneasily, "but the baby will be two months early and might be in danger. I must phone Donald and find out what's happening."

"Yes," said my mother. "Yes, of course."

"When I see the rector shall I ask him to call?"

"Not tonight."

"Very well. I'll try and be as quick as possible." I stooped, kissed her and went outside into the twilight.

Five minutes later I was halting my car outside the rectory and asking Forrest if I could use his telephone. I phoned Penmarric first. Medlyn, sounding very subdued, answered as usual and on hearing my voice said he would fetch William at once.

"Jan?" said William a minute afterward. "Thank God you've phoned. I was just wondering if I should go over to your mother's house to fetch you. Where are you now?"

"Zillan rectory," I said, feeling my scalp prickle at the tone of his voice. "Why? What's happened? Surely not—there's not more bad news, is there? Is Jeanne all right?"

"She's very gravely ill. Helena left half an hour ago to join Donald at the hospital in Penzance."

"And the baby?"

"Born dead," said William, "and I'm afraid I have to tell you that Jeanne's not expected to live either."

[5]

After a long moment I said blankly to William, "What shall I do?" My mind was blurred; sweating palms made the receiver slip in my hands; my head ached and I felt dizzy with fatigue. "Shall I go to the hospital?"

"No, I think you should stay with your mother. Helena and Donald both realize you have to be with her—I discussed it with Helena before she left. But don't tell your mother yet about Jeanne or the baby."

"No . . . no, of course not."

"I've spoken to Adrian on the phone and he's coming down to Cornwall tomorrow. Lizzie telephoned for news of Jeanne, but that was before we knew anything definite, so there was nothing I could tell her."

"And Philip—the body . . . Is it—"

"Yes, they brought him back here. That's all been attended to. Esmond's here with me and he and I are keeping each other company."

I guessed from his tone of voice that Esmond was nearby.

"I'm glad you're with him," I said. "I'm glad he's not all alone at Penmarric."

"Yes . . . Is there anything else I can do while I'm here? I assume you'll be staying overnight at Roslyn Farm."

"Yes, I'll be staying there tonight and tomorrow I shall be driving my mother over to Penmarric to see Philip. You'll still be there then, won't you?"

"Probably."

"If there's any definite news about Jeanne—"

"I'll drive over to the farm to tell you."

He arrived at two o'clock in the morning. I awoke with a

start to find my mother stooping over me with a candle in her hand.

"Jan . . ." She was shaking my shoulder tremulously. "Jan, someone's knocking on the front door and there's a car outside with its headlights on. Who can it be?"

I was awake in an instant. I flung back the covers and scrambled out of bed. "I expect it's William," I said, pulling on my trousers. "He said he might call."

"But it's two o'clock," said my mother, a bent old woman huddling into her shawl. "It's two o'clock, Jan."

"Yes, I know. Now you go back to bed, Mama. I'll deal with this."

"I can't sleep. Why is William calling?"

"I think it might be about Jeanne."

"Jeanne?"

"She lost the baby, Mama. The shock of Philip's death—"

"Yes, it was a shock, a terrible shock. Poor Philip. Poor Jeanne . . . she lost the baby, you say?"

"I'm afraid so, Mama." I slipped on my jacket. "Now you go back to your room and after I've seen William I'll make some tea and bring it to you."

"Jeanne's too old to have a baby for the first time," said my mother. "Thirty-six is too old. I was thirty-six when Philip was born, but he was my fourth child."

"I won't be a minute, Mama. I'd go back to bed if I were you."

But she lingered in my room. I left her sitting on the bed and ran downstairs lightly, barefoot. When I opened the front door I found William waiting in the porch.

"Is Jeanne—"

"I'm afraid so. Helena has just arrived home from Penzance."

There was a long silence. The old house creaked and sighed as old houses do, and the wind moaned far away in the eaves.

"Come in," I said at last. "Mama always keeps brandy in the store cupboard. Let's have a drink."

"I'd better not come in."

"It's all right. She's upstairs."

He stepped reluctantly over the threshold and looked around him. He had not been to the farmhouse before.

"This way," I said abruptly and led him down the passage to the kitchens.

When we were seated at the table with our brandy glasses

before us he said, "Poor Helena looked as if she was walking in her sleep. I felt so sorry for her. Naturally I felt more than sorry for Donald too, poor fellow, but Helena's lost her husband and her best friend all within the space of twenty-four hours and that's too much to expect any person to bear, in my opinion. I don't know how you manage to believe in God, Jan, when such appalling and unwarranted misfortunes fall upon as blameless a woman as Helena and as decent a fellow as Donald McCrae. Where's the justice in that? There's no justice in the world and no God, that's all I can say."

"Say that to Adrian," I said, drinking the brandy. "He's the clergyman. I'm sure he knows all the answers."

"Adrian doesn't see death as I see it. He believes in the Resurrection."

"So do I."

"Do you, Jan? Do you really? How can you? It's beyond me. I'm afraid the older I get the more of an atheist I become."

"I'm too much of a coward to be an atheist," I said. "I couldn't bear not to believe in anything. I have to believe there's God, but don't ask me what Donald's done to deserve Jeanne's death and don't ask me what Helena's done to deserve a double bereavement, because I don't know. I'm not God and I'm not a clergyman and I don't have all the answers at my fingertips."

We were silent for a while. William helped himself to more brandy. "I suppose," he said as he swirled the brandy in his glass, "I suppose Jeanne at least had a taste of a happy, normal married life. She did at least have some sort of reward for all those years when she nursed that poor devil Gerald Meredith at Polzillan House. Also I suppose all Philip's dreams died with Sennen Garth and he had nothing much to look forward to. But I still don't see why Donald and Helena—"

The floorboards of the stairs creaked; from far away at the front of the house my mother called my name.

"Coming!" I shouted and added to William, "Wait here."

"All right. Don't tell her about—"

"No, of course not."

I left the kitchen and hurried up the passage to find my mother waiting uncertainly in the hall.

"Was it William?" she said.

"Yes, it's all right, Mama. I'm just giving him a drink in the kitchen. Shall I make you some tea?"

"No," she said. "No, I don't want tea. Jan dear, I'm so worried about the funeral. I can't sleep for worrying about it. I don't want that new rector burying Philip. I don't like him and he never knew Philip anyway. Do you suppose Adrian—but Adrian's very important now, isn't he? He's at Exeter Cathedral. Do you think it would be right to ask him to bury Philip?"

"I'll telephone Adrian tomorrow and talk to him about it," I said. "You mustn't worry about that now, Mama. We'll talk about it tomorrow."

"Perhaps he wouldn't want to bury him," she said. "His own brother. It would be too sad."

"Leave it all to me, Mama. I'll talk to Adrian tomorrow, I promise you. Now let me help you back to bed."

"No, don't bother to come upstairs. I can manage. But do you think Adrian would—"

"Yes, Mama, yes, I expect so. Try not to worry about it any more." In spite of her protests I helped her upstairs to her room and saw her safely into bed before I returned to the kitchen.

"I'm sure Adrian will conduct the funeral service if your mother wishes it," said William when I told him what had been said. "I don't think it would be too much to ask at all. I've no doubt Adrian's sorry that Philip's dead, but they weren't close friends and anyway Adrian isn't so affected by death as I am and he's accustomed to funeral services. I'm sure he would conduct the service if he was asked to do so."

"I'll ask him when he arrives tomorrow. Good God, what's going to happen about Jeanne? We can't have a double ceremony! That would be too much for everyone. Perhaps Donald wants her to be buried at their church in Penzance anyway."

"Let's hope so. Poor Jeanne, I'll miss her very much. She was always very kind to Charity, you know, and used to call often at our cottage after she married Donald and came to live in Penzance."

"Hm." I was trying not to think too deeply about Jeanne, trying to turn my thoughts instead to the organization of Philip's funeral. "Lizzie will come down, of course," I said carefully, "and perhaps her husband too as it's the long vacation at present. God, how are we going to get in touch with Mariana? I've no idea whereabouts she's living in Monte Carlo."

"Won't Esmond know?"

"He's not allowed to communicate with her."

"Get in touch with her husband's lawyers. They probably send her the maintenance allowance each quarter. They'll know where she's living."

"I don't suppose she'll come home anyway."

"Probably not." He finished his brandy and stared for a moment at his empty glass. "Talking of lawyers," he said slowly, "who has Philip's will? Didn't you tell me he went to another firm of solicitors when he decided to disinherit Jonas?"

It was then—for the first time since the news of Philip's death had reached me more than twelve hours before—that I allowed the knowledge of my future to rise out of my subconscious and stare me full in the face.

I was master of Penmarric. All I had to do now was to go to Pomeroy and Pomeroy in St. Ives for Philip's last will and testament and show the world that at long last against long odds Penmarric had fallen into the hands of the one person who loved it better than any other place on earth.

Justice, twisted and bizarre but still recognizable, raised a bloody and battered head to stare me starkly in the eye.

[6]

To my surprise I found that Philip had left specific instructions about his funeral in his will. He wanted to be buried at Zillan by his father's side, or, if there was no room, at his father's feet. Considering that Phillip and my father had spent their lives quarreling with each other I couldn't help but think this stipulation exceedingly odd, but it was stated in black and white and he had put his signature to the document, so there was certainly no ambiguity relating to the request. The rest of his will was simple. By the power of appointment granted to him under the terms of our father's will he had left his money and property to me; all his personal possessions, items outside the power of appointment, he bequeathed to Esmond.

"So he made another will," said old Michael Vincent, sitting in his office like a tired old spider clinging to his thick-woven web. "I thought perhaps he had. I knew it was awkward that Simon Peter and Jonas were cousins, although I drew up the previous will and Simon Peter had no hand in it. . . . Poor little Jonas. This will be a great blow to Rebecca. I'm sure she still believed Jonas was Philip's heir."

But I did not want to think of Rebecca. I knew she would fly into a rage as soon as she realized that I had ousted Jonas from his inheritance, and I had enough on my hands at that time without worrying about my future relationship with her.

"I've decided to consult Pomeroy and Pomeroy on all legal matters in the future," I said politely to Michael. "Perhaps you could arrange for transfer of all the relevant papers to them? I hesitate to dispense with your services when you've served my family for so long—" I saw him flush as I addressed him as if he were my social inferior— "but you've never trusted me and I certainly don't trust Simon Peter, so I hardly feel we can continue to do business together. I must thank you for all you've done for Penmarric in the past and assure you that I'm extremely grateful to you and your firm. . . ."

It seemed a fair enough revenge for all the years he had disliked me and tried to stand in my way.

I left his office and returned to Penmarric. Lizzie and her husband were expected that same evening and Adrian was to board their train when it stopped at Exeter. There was so much to do, so many arrangements to be made. My preoccupation with Philip's funeral left me little time to think of Jeanne, but that afternoon I managed to call on Donald and express a few words, however useless, of sympathy. Jeanne's funeral was to be in Penzance the day after Philip's funeral at Zillan. I offered to do what I could to help, but he said he realized I had enough to handle already and added that Jeanne's many friends were all being even kinder than he had anticipated.

On returning to Penmarric I found the car at the door and Helena dressed to go out. She wore black, of course, and the mourning clothes were unbecoming so that she seemed elderly and plain. Her fair skin had a transparent look which hinted at her extreme exhaustion, but she was completely composed. All through those appalling days I never saw Helena look other than faultlessly self-possessed.

"I was just going over to the farm to see your mother," she said. "I intend to tell her the news about Jeanne. I let you carry the burden of telling her about Philip, but I shall tell her about Jeanne. I don't think it will be too much for her. In fact she may well not grasp what I'm saying. There's a limit to everyone's grief, after all."

I knew she was referring to herself, trying to explain why her manner seemed so cold and unnatural. In an effort to sympathize I said awkwardly, "You needn't visit my mother yet, Helena. You've got more than enough to endure as it is. I'll tell her about Jeanne."

"No, I want to tell her. Thank you, Jan, but it's all right. I want to visit her."

After a moment I said, "When all this is over—"

"Oh yes," she said flatly, "I shall go abroad again, just as I did after Gerry died. It does help to go away. After I come back I think I shall go home to Warwickshire. I was happy there, and I still have several friends in and around the village where I used to live. I don't want to stay in Cornwall any more. Cornwall brought me little except unhappiness and tragedy. I shall go back to Henley-in-Arden and start all over again from the beginning."

We said no more. She was just about to leave when a messenger rode up the drive with a telegram and she paused as I opened the little envelope and unfolded the message inside.

"Devastated by news of Philip and Jeanne," we read silently. "So sorry I cannot come home for funerals but circumstances extremely awkward stop Will write in detail explaining stop Poor Mama how ghastly for her stop Deepest sympathy Helena and Donald stop Give darling Esmond my best love stop Mariana."

"Deepest sympathy!" said Helena contemptuously, turning aside in disdain. "Neither of them meant anything to her. I'm glad she's got the sense to stay away, although I suppose your mother will be hurt by her absence." She swept into the waiting car without another word. I remained where I was, the telegram still fluttering gently between my fingers, but when the car had disappeared from sight I went slowly indoors to show the telegram to Esmond.

He was disappointed to learn his mother wouldn't be coming to Cornwall. "I was so looking forward to seeing her again," he said wistfully. "That was the one bright spot on the horizon." He had not been allowed to see her for several years, but he hadn't forgotten her. "Of course Mama did wrong," I had heard him say once to Philip. "She shouldn't have left Papa and run off with someone else even though Papa was old and frail and couldn't entertain her as much as she would have liked him to. But she's still my mother, no matter what she does. Nothing can alter that."

He didn't refer to the fact that in abandoning her husband

Mariana had also abandoned her only child. I didn't once hear him reproach her for that. He was a far better son than Mariana deserved.

Lizzie and her husband arrived with Adrian that evening and the next morning Adrian and I drove over to Zillan together, he to see the rector about the funeral arrangements and I to call on my mother.

My mother, attended by Annie and the two Turner "girls," was in bed. She looked at her most elderly and frail, but when I tried to advise her against attending the funeral she refused to listen to me.

"I want to go."

"But, Mama—"

"I shall go."

"It would be too much for you—"

"I'm going, Jan-Yves."

She was as stubborn as a mule. Presently Adrian called but she could not bring herself to see him face to face at that time. "Tell him how grateful I am to him for coming," she said, suddenly tearful again. "Tell him how glad I am that he's going to conduct the service. Ask him to forgive me for not seeing him now, but say I'm so tired I don't want to see anyone but you, Jan-Yves."

"Yes, of course, Mama. Don't worry, I know he'll understand."

"It's just that four of my five boys being dead and both of *her* boys being alive . . . I know it's wicked of me to think that, but I can't help thinking it just the same."

"I understand," said Adrian when I told him, and I saw the compassion in his eyes. "But tell her I'll visit her whenever she wants to see me."

We returned to Penmarric. Finding myself at last in a position where all arrangements had been made and there was nothing else for me to do, I decided it was time to drive to Morvah, face Rebecca and find out if she intended to come with the children to the funeral.

But when I arrived at Deveral Farm it was Deborah who answered the door. "Mummy's not in, Uncle Jan," she said nervously, blushing a little. Poor Deborah wasn't a good liar. "Is there a message?"

"I was wondering if I would see all of you at the funeral on Friday."

"I—yes, I . . . think so . . . at least, I'm not sure. I would like to attend very much. I was fond of Uncle Philip and had such respect for him."

"Has Rebecca seen Simon Peter recently?"

"Yes. At least, that's to say, I'm not sure. I — "

"But she knows what's in Philip's will?"

"Yes—oh yes, because we thought Jonas—and then we heard—"

"Quite. Well, tell your mother that I'll send a car over to the farm on Friday to take her to Zillan church unless I hear from her to the contrary before then. Would you tell her that?"

"Yes, I will. Thank you, Uncle Jan."

As I departed I resolved to make no further effort to see Rebecca before the funeral since her fury evidently needed more time to cool. In spite of this I half wondered if I would see her at the inquest the next day, but I did not; the inquest itself was a mere formality, the verdict of accidental death a necessary prelude to the inevitability of the burial, and within twenty-four hours we were all preparing ourselves for the ordeal of the funeral service.

The time came at last. A light mist blew damply across the cliffs, an eerie half-light wreathed the ruins of the Sennen Garth mine, and five miles away across the moors there was a ghostly air in Zillan churchyard as Philip's body was consigned at last to the Cornish earth he had loved so well.

[7]

I went to that funeral expecting to be moved and I was moved. What else can I say? Adrian conducted the service faultlessly, the church was packed with people, the graveyard overflowed with mourners. Those are mere facts, but there are some things which are beyond the power of mere facts to describe. I went to the funeral of my brother who had died in an accident at the age of forty-one, but that wasn't the only funeral I went to on that cold morning in Zillan village. I went to the funeral of all my past jealousies and past hatreds which had so dominated my early life; I went to the funeral of past futility, past discontent and past mistakes. That morning at Zillan I buried a whole past world, a world in which I was forever unjustly doomed to the role of underdog and forced to struggle for my rights against a host of people so much more fortunate than I was. I had stared at the blank incomprehensible mirror of justice all my life in an effort to understand how I might glimpse my own reflection there, but now I had passed through the looking-glass and my whole world had been turned back to front. The people I had envied so uselessly for so long were all dead, all corpses in the earth beneath my feet, and the good fortune for which I had envied them had been a vast illusion masking frustrated, disappointing, even shallow lives. I saw my brother Marcus now not as the gay young man-about-town but as an incurably overgrown schoolboy without purpose or ambition; I saw my brother Hugh not as the glamorous adventurer with a talent for making money but as a shifty idler content to rely on his good luck until it deserted him one day on an isolated Cornish beach. And at last I saw Philip, not the golden hero of a thousand and one mining adventure stories, but an emotional cripple living in his own private twilight world which had collapsed into darkness after the disaster of the Sennen Garth mine.

So I stepped through the looking-glass, and when I turned to look back at my past world I saw how my attempts to carve some justice for myself had in fact been efforts to wreak injustice on my brothers. It seemed justice was a two-headed monster, a double-sided coin; I had been so concerned about the injustice of my situation that it hadn't occurred to me that what was unjust for me was just for other people and what was unjust for other people might bring me the justice I had sought all my life.

But it occurred to me when I saw Philip's coffin lowered into the fresh grave at my father's feet. I saw it and I wept, and as I wept I wept not only for Philip but for the unjust justice which I had misunderstood so thoroughly for so many wasted years in the past.

[8]

After the funeral I stayed overnight with my mother at the farm and the next morning as we breakfasted in her room I tried to persuade her to leave Cornwall for a few days to take the edge off her grief. But she refused to hear of it. She stayed in bed all day, since the doctor had strictly forbidden her to attend Jeanne's funeral that morning, and I left her with the Turner girls as I drove into Penzance for the service. Jeanne was buried quietly at her husband's Presbyterian church in an admirably plain, simple ceremony, but I'd be lying if I wrote I wasn't immensely relieved when it was all over. Afterward Lizzie and her husband took Esmond and myself to the Metropole for lunch, and later when we had all recovered a little from the ordeal of the second family funeral in two days, Lizzie volunteered to come with me when I called at Roslyn Farm for tea.

"I must show Mother I mean well," she said, "although to be frank I don't believe in lavishing sympathy on the bereaved."

However, she was so much taken aback by my mother's bed-ridden state that the next morning she cut some flowers from the garden at Penmarric and asked me to drive her back to the farm for a second visit.

"Now, Mother," she said briskly, sweeping into my mother's room with an armful of exotic blooms, "I don't think it's good for you to lie here and mope. Why don't you come to stay with us in Cambridge for a few days? You wouldn't even have to face a train journey since Eddy has ordered a car and chauffeur to drive us home, and we could arrange for you to return to Cornwall by car when it's time for you to leave."

"No," said my mother.

"Mother, I really do think—"

"It's kind of you, Lizzie, but no."

There was nothing to be done. She was adamant that nothing would induce her to leave her home.

"Old people are so stubborn," said Lizzie, exasperated, annoyed that her generous gesture had been rejected so peremptorily. "What can we do with her? Anyway, how long can she go on living in this house on her own with only that simple-minded old servant who's half blind and practically dumb? Supposing she had an accident?"

"I shall have a telephone installed," I said, "and I expect I shall visit her nearly every day. She'll be all right."

"She ought to move to Penmarric where she can be properly looked after."

"My dear Lizzie," I said, amused, "you obviously don't know Mama! No one tells *her* what to do. Wild horses wouldn't drag her to Penmarric."

"Well," said Lizzie with a quick shrug, "she's your worry, not mine. I suppose Eddy and I must be thinking about returning to Cambridge. The girls will be missing us. . . . By the way, what's happening to Esmond? Perhaps I ought to have the poor boy to stay. I don't suppose he wants to remain in Cornwall after all this."

"He's already made arrangements to return to Scotland, I think. But perhaps during the next school holidays—"

"Yes, I must invite him to Cambridge. By the way, I suppose there's no further word from Mariana?"

"None."

But a letter arrived three days later. Esmond had by that time left for Scotland, Lizzie and her husband had returned to Cambridge and Helena had gone on a visit to her Warwickshire friends before making arrangements to go abroad. The letter with its French stamp and Riviera postmark, was addressed to me in Mariana's elegant handwriting.

"My dear Jan-Yves," she had written. "I do hope all went well at the funerals and that they weren't too ghastly. Of course I thought of everyone constantly and wished I could have been there, but life has been extremely trying just lately and when I received your telegram with the news I was slightly embarrassed financially and could not have afforded the fare home. It really is so dreary not to have quite enough to do as one pleases on such occasions, and since I would like to come home and feel it's my duty to see Mama, I was wondering if you could be terribly sweet and wire me a hundred pounds? I simply hate to ask you, darling, but really I've had one misfortune after another this year and everything is frightfully difficult. I would so much love to see darling Esmond—is he still at Penmarric? I do hope he hasn't gone back yet to that dreary house in Scotland. Does Esmond talk of me much? I think of him so often.

"Once again, darling, I can't tell you how devastated I feel and how sorry I am for that nice man Donald McCrae and for Helena. Of course Helena hardly had the ideal marriage, did she, since her husband went off and left her for three years, but I suppose any marriage is better than none at all, poor woman. I do feel so full of pity for her. My fondest love to Mama, and if Esmond is still with you tell him how much I miss him and how I'm so longing to see him again. Now that he's older perhaps he can begin to understand some of the difficulties which resulted in our separation from each other. Do tell him that I can explain everything and that I've always loved him just as much as I used to even though we've been apart for so many years.

"Please write soon, Jan darling, all my love, Mariana."

I sighed, reread the letter and sighed again. I had little in-clination to help Mariana, and since probate hadn't yet been granted I didn't have a hundred pounds to send her without bat-ting an eyelid. I sat down, took up my pen and tried to phrase a polite but firm reply.

"Dear Mariana," I wrote baldly at last, "do you really want to come to Penmarric? Helena is away, Mama hasn't asked for you, and Esmond has gone home to Scotland. If you still want to come back notwithstanding these facts, let me know and I'll send you the money for your fare. I'm sorry to hear things haven't been going well for you, but trust your luck will change again very soon. Yours, Jan-Yves."

She did not reply, although whether that was because her cir-cumstances improved or because she no longer wanted to come home, I could not tell. I informed my mother that Mariana had written but decided not to show her the letter.

"She didn't write to me," my mother said. "She never wrote to offer sympathy. She only wrote to you because she wanted money."

That was perfectly true, but I thought it was tactful not to comment, and after that we did not speak of Mariana for some time.

It was the day after I had answered Mariana's letter that I found time to drive to Morvah at last and confront Rebecca. She had not been present at Philip's funeral and neither had Jonas, although Deborah had turned up with Simon Peter and his wife. I had not been able to have a word in private with Deborah after the service, but the only conclusion I could reach on the subject of Rebecca's absence was that she was still too upset to face me. This made me angry; I wasn't surprised that she should have been upset and disappointed to learn that Philip had changed his mind about making Jonas his heir, but I did think she would be sensible enough to see reason after a few days and admit to herself that I wasn't to blame for the situation. If she did blame me, I told my-self, and if she was determined to make a big scene to me about something that wasn't my fault, she couldn't love me nearly as much as she'd sworn she did. It was she who had promised that Jonas shouldn't come between us in the future; if she went back on her word now I would know I had done the right thing in staying unmarried to her, and if I had any sense I should then see to it that the issue of marriage wasn't raised between us again.

I admit I was nervous when I arrived at Deveral Farm, but so strong was my desire to face her and find out what was going on in her mind that I didn't stay nervous for long. When I walked around the house to the back door I found her hanging out some washing in the yard; Jonas, chewing a currant bun, was seated on a nearby water butt, and beyond the open window I glimpsed Deborah rolling pastry in the kitchen. As I rounded the corner of the house and came upon them they all paused to stare at me in silence.

After a moment I said shortly, "Perhaps I can have a word with you alone, Rebecca."

There was another pause. Deborah began to roll the pastry in a furious rush of energy, and Jonas sank his teeth once more into his currant bun.

"I've nothing to say to you," said Rebecca stonily at last. "Nothing. And you know why."

"Why?"

"You tricked my boy out of his inheritance."

So it was just as I had feared. She was, as I had always known, utterly unreliable. Just because she had sworn she loved me too much to let Jonas come between us and I had been fool enough to believe she meant what she said, I had come within an ace of a disastrous second marriage. For disaster it would most certainly have been. It was no use her promising not to make scenes or have tantrums whenever she felt like it. When she felt like making life difficult for me she would make life difficult for me—because she didn't love me enough to know any better.

My patience snapped. My anger mounted. For ten long years she had called the tune and beckoned me back to her bedroom whenever it suited her to do so, but she had called the tune and beckoned me back for the last time. I turned aside. "There was no question of me tricking Jonas out of his inheritance," I said abruptly. "It was you who lost it for him, not I. If you hadn't made that ridiculous scene when Jonas ran away from the sea shore—"

The kitchen door banged. Deborah had dropped the rolling pin and fled to the front room to escape from the scene. I stopped speaking, and as I hesitated Jonas slid off the water butt, planted his two little feet firmly on the ground and parked his currant bun on the window sill.

"I didn't run away," he announced. "And she didn't make any scene. You leave my mother alone."

I ignored him. "Rebecca, let's get this straight once and for all. First, I didn't trick Jonas out of the inheritance. Philip changed his will after you'd rejected all the kindness and generosity he had shown the child. Secondly, I knew this and kept the knowledge from you simply because Philip asked me to do so and I promised him I would. Thirdly—"

"You deceived me. All through these last few months when we've been so close—"

"I didn't deceive you. I simply honored my promise to Philip."

"You leave my mother alone," said Jonas, very tough and pugnacious. "You get off our land or I'll fight you."

"I don't believe you," said Rebecca to me sullenly. "I don't want to see you any more."

"Very well," I said, losing my temper. "I shall never come here again. Never, do you understand? And this time 'never' means 'never' and not 'later,' so don't try and pick me up again in St. Just when you're feeling lonely. If you can't trust me as a woman should trust someone she loves, then your love can go to hell as far as I'm concerned and I want no part of it."

"How can I trust you?" she shouted at me. "I've never been able to trust you, never! You've never loved me as I loved you—there was always some other woman somewhere—"

"Only because I couldn't get what I wanted from you without having to go on my knees for it!"

Jonas chose that moment to dance up to me with his fists clenched. "You be quiet!" he yelled. "You be quiet or I'll punch you on the nose!"

I hardly heard him. I was still looking over his head at Rebecca. "Well, I'm not going on my knees for it any more," I said furiously. "You can keep what you've got. There are other women who have got more than you anyway—women with a little less weight in the wrong places and a hell of a lot more willingness to please."

I stopped. There was a silence. She was still looking at me, and her eyes were wide and dark and uncertain.

"Younger women," I said.

I saw her flinch, but I saw nothing else. Turning on my heel abruptly, I walked blindly around the side of the house to my car and drove out of her life with my foot pushed down against the accelerator as hard as it would go.

She wrote to me two weeks later. It was a stiff, formal little note saying she regretted the scene and would like to see me again.

I didn't reply.

Presently she wrote to me again. This time it was a long muddled letter full of passion and pleas to be forgiven. Would I please come to dinner at the farm on any evening I cared to name?

I tore the letter up and threw it away.

A few days later she telephoned from a public callbox in Penzance.

"Listen, Jan," she said, "I made a mistake. I know I did. Please believe me when I say I'm sorry. I'll never distrust you again, I promise. I'll never tell you not to call. It was all a mistake."

"It was one mistake too many, my dear," I said. "It was the straw that broke the camel's back. I'm sorry." And I hung up before I was driven by weakness to forgive her and go rushing back to Roslyn Farm.

"If my sister-in-law Mrs. Hugh telephones again," I said to Medlyn, "I don't wish to speak to her. You can tell her I'm out."

"Yes, sir," said my butler with respect.

Everyone had respect for me nowadays. Why not? Times had changed. I was no longer a penniless nobody with a disgraceful record who worked for a salary on his rich brother's estate. I was master of Penmarric, living in the house I loved with my lifelong ambition attained; I was one of the wealthiest young men in Cornwall, able to do exactly as I pleased and come and go exactly as I wished. The ugly ducking, playing true to form, had become a splendid swan, and no one was more pleased than I was by the fairy-tale transformation. I now had everything I wanted.

And yet . . .

It's really most remarkable how the human race is so seldom satisfied with what it's got. Give a man the world and he's still pining for the moon.

"Now's the time for you to get married again," said Lizzie busily when I telephoned her one evening to stave off my loneliness. "Why don't you come up to Cambridge for Christmas? I can line up a whole host of charming girls for you to meet and we can all have a marvelous time! Why don't you come?"

"I can't leave Mama alone at Christmas."

"I'll write and invite her to come to Cambridge too."

"She wouldn't come, Lizzie. You know she won't leave the farm."

"Well, that's her mistake, isn't it? I fail to see why you should be penalized for her selfishness."

"It's not a question of being penalized—"

"Oh yes it is! She's preying on you just as she preyed on Philip! Really, Jan, I can't think why you're so sentimental about her all of a sudden! Why *shouldn't* you leave her alone for once? She left you alone for six whole years when you were a child!"

"She was there when I needed her," I said. "I didn't need her when I was a child. Any kind stranger can bring up a baby until he's six years old, and I had my kind stranger. But when I needed my mother later she was there."

"Oh, fiddlesticks!" cried Lizzie in a temper and hung up in high dudgeon.

She phoned again the next day. Her manner was meek, contrite and cunningly persuasive. She was sorry she had lost her temper, she said; her anger had merely stemmed from disappointment; she had set her heart on having me to stay for Christmas, but perhaps after all I was right and it would be wrong for me to leave Cornwall then. However, if I wanted to make a visit early in the new year . . .

". . . there's one girl in particular I'd like you to meet. Honestly, she has everything—beauty, brains, talent, charm—"

"I have no intention of remarrying at the moment," I said perversely, and it was true. Although I was lonely at Penmarric the final break with Rebecca had left me more wary of marriage than ever and more cynical too in my attitude toward women. "I shall wait until I'm at least thirty-five before taking the matrimonial plunge again."

But I didn't wait until I was thirty-five. I hardly waited until my thirty-second birthday eight months later, because in the spring of the following year I fell in love. On the twentieth of May 1937 I first met Isabella, and after that no power on earth could have kept me from hurtling into marriage faster than all the bullets from a thousand guns.

9

He married, with her father's consent, Isabel of An-
goulême, the affianced bride of Hugh the Brown, on
30 August, 1200.

—Oxford History of England:
From Domesday Book to Magna Carta,
A. L. POOLE

It is possible that John did not stop to consider ques-
tions of policy. Rumour had it that Isabelle entranced
him.

—King John,
W. L. WARREN

[1]

Isabella!

"But you can't be called that!" I protested. "No one's called
Isabella nowadays!"

"Am I supposed to be just like everyone else?"

Her parents called her Isabel.

"Playing safe," she said. "Poor dears, they're desperately conventional."

She had no brothers and no sisters.

"That's why they made a splash and gave me a four-syllable
Christian name," she explained. "They guessed even then that to
produce an offspring was a feat they wouldn't succeed in repeating. Poor dears, the triumph must have quite gone to their heads."

Isabella! Ash-blond hair shimmering in a long fine-spun curtain of white-gold softness, extraordinary wide-set green eyes with brown flecks in the irises, high cheekbones and a mobile full-lipped, provocative mouth.

"Of course, I know I'm not one of the world's most immortal beauties," she said. "I know my limitations."

She was very young.

"No, I'm not going to tell you how old I am or you'll be put off. Anyway I plan to be ageless. I shall look exactly the same when I'm forty as I look now."

She spoke as if to be forty was to be verging on senility.

Isabella! Clever, nimble-witted Isabella with her flair for guileless conversation . . .

"Of course I'm an absolute fool really," she said. "My parents paid heaps of money to send me to a horrible private school so that I could have every advantage they never had—running up and down a hockey pitch in winter, ugh!—and what happened? I didn't even manage to get my school certificate. If you knew how simply hopeless I was at maths . . ."

It wasn't until later that I discovered that mathematics had been so badly taught at her school that no one there had been up to the standard of the examination.

I met her on my way home from London.

It was the year of the Coronation, and like thousands of others we all converged on London for the great event. William, Charity, Adrian and I came up from the West Country, Lizzie and her family traveled south from Cambridge, and Esmond, who had just succeeded his father as Marquess of Lochlyall, came up from Eton to be present among the other peers of the realm in Westminster Abbey and make his traditional vows of homage to the new Sovereign. Naturally we were all bursting with pride that he should have a role, however minute, in the ceremony, and no one was prouder of him than Mariana, who flew over from France especially for the occasion. It was the first time she had seen him for several years. As soon as her husband had died earlier that year she had been planning her visit, fortified by the fact that there was now no one who stood between her and her son, and when she was finally reunited with him in London I think Esmond was as much affected as she was by the dramatic scene which ensued. However, I've no doubt he soon became as embarrassed as everyone else did by her unmistakable fondness for dry martinis, and after the exhausting splendor of the Coronation I had a strong suspicion he was relieved to bid his mother goodbye and return to Eton. Mariana wept copiously at parting from him once more, and had it not been for the fact that she had someone paying her bills for her in Monte Carlo I believe she would have stayed on in England. As it was, she vowed she was going to sever her ties with Monte Carlo and go to live with Esmond in Edinburgh, but when I took her to the airport I soon realized she had come to no definite decision about the future. She was in a most maudlin and introspective state of mind.

"Darling Esmond," she kept saying morosely. "Darling Esmond. Just as wonderful as I always knew he would be. I cried when I saw him again, just cried, darling. Honestly. I wish I could be brave enough to leave Monte and go back to Scotland to live with him, but oh, that dreary climate, I couldn't stand it, and all those dreadful strait-laced people. . . . I love Monte Carlo and the sun and everyone so warm and friendly. You must come to Monte to see me, Jan—no, really, I insist! I could introduce you to such utterly fascinating people, such witty elegant women. You ought to marry again, darling. You know, you're really quite attractive—did anyone ever tell you that? What a funny thing sex appeal is. S.A.! Do you remember when S.A. used to be called It? Funny to think back to old times. . . . Lizzie's husband's rather good-looking, but oh so dull, never saying anything, but Lizzie talks so much she never gives him a chance to say a word, does she? I wonder if he's faithful to her. So few husbands are faithful to their wives. If you lived in Monte Carlo you'd know that, no one's faithful to anybody—anybody, darling, honestly. But I like French men. English men are either dull like Lizzie's Eddy or else . . . Well, I don't know, but no Englishman—or Scotsman —ever treated me very well except for Esmond's father and he was a poppet, but old, you know, so old and when he was ill it was so dreadfully depressing. . . . I can't bear people to be ill, you know, darling, I hate illness and waiting for death and I hate old age—do you ever think of old age, Jan? I dread being old—and ugly and alone—like Mama . . . And I dread a lingering death, like poor Aunt Rose. You didn't know Aunt Rose, did you? Adrian reminds me of her a little, but perhaps William's more like her than Adrian, so sweet and gentle and kind. I never met a man like that, except for Esmond's father, and I ran away and left him be-cause I couldn't bear it any longer. . . . Oh, nothing makes sense, nothing! Nothing at all!" And she began to weep.

"How many martinis have you had this morning?" I said as we approached the airport. "Two? Three? Four?"

"One tiny one. Honestly, darling. Just one."

"You drink too much, Mariana."

"No, not really. I never get drunk, you know. I'm always very careful about that. I never get drunk."

And you're never quite sober either, I thought, but I said nothing.

The strain of seeing her again made me glad when the time came to leave London and return to Cornwall. After Lizzie and her family had returned to Cambridge we all drove down to Exeter, where I left William and Charity to stay with Adrian for a few days before I set off to Penmarric on my own. I did not leave Exeter until late in the morning, and just before the Cornish border I decided to stop for lunch at a restaurant by the wayside.

I had noticed the restaurant before on other journeys from the east, for it stood on the main road which runs from London to Penzance. It was in fact a small hotel, an old house with a thatched roof and plenty of Devon quaintness to attract the passing tourists. I hadn't stopped there before because it had no license and I usually like beer with my lunch, but this time I stopped primarily because I was hungry but also because the place had been repainted and there was a small sign in the window saying "Under New Management."

I parked my car nearby and went in. The hall was full of brass knickknacks and well-polished furniture; the ceiling sagged with black oak beams. As I glanced around a woman came out to meet me and said, "One for lunch, sir? This way, please." She was a pleasant-looking woman with the careful accents of the lower-middle classes, the sort of woman who would chatter away in the most presentable tones for some time but would eventually spoil the presentable impression by letting slip an unfortunate word or phrase that she should have learned long since to eliminate from her conversation.

The dining room was light and airy and very small; there were no more than eight tables, and as I was late the other guests were finishing their meal. I sat down, inspected the menu and decided to order pea soup, steak and kidney pie and strawberries with cream.

"Are you ready to order, sir?" inquired a high sweet voice from nearby, and, turning abruptly, I looked up into Isabella's eyes.

I cannot even begin to describe the force of that first impression. All I can say is that love struck me so suddenly that I was speechless. Anything less likely to happen to me would have been hard to imagine. I was almost thirty-two years old, very experienced, very cynical, very sure of what I wanted in a woman and which feminine attributes attracted me most. I liked mature women, often a few years older than myself, voluptuous women with lush curves, smoldering eyes and long black hair. As for the possibility of love at first sight I had long ago regarded that idea as absurd; no self-respecting man, I told myself, could believe in such a myth.

Yet now here I was, confronted with this slim slip of a girl with her long white neck and pointed little chin and ash-blond hair scraped back demurely from her schoolgirl's face, and I knew straight away that I was irrevocably committed to her. Why it's hard to say. Perhaps the secret lay in her eyes. There was a light there that I knew and recognized, a light that at once reminded me of myself. Because she was like me, just like me, and I knew it from the beginning. It was the likeness which made the meeting electrifying, the likeness and that strange spark of recognition. It wasn't until that moment that I knew I had always been alone, even when I had believed myself to be in love; I had not realized until I saw myself so clearly mirrored in someone else that in fact I hadn't been in love before. I looked at Isabella and in looking at her I saw someone so like me in spirit that I knew we would always be united by the mysterious clasp of a shared identity. I wanted her at once—not as I had wanted women in the past, but because once I had seen the extent of my loneliness in this revelation I knew I couldn't live without her.

It was as simple as that. I had always thought that falling in love produced a multitude of bewildered feelings, an uncertainty that arose from the fact that one's judgment was impaired by emotion, but I wasn't confused at all. Falling in love didn't produce confusion. It merely made the world seem extraordinarily clear and logical.

My voice said after a long pause, "Pea soup. Please."

"Rolls and butter?" she said sweetly.

"Yes. And water. Please."

She moved away busily and disappeared behind the screen which hid the kitchen door. When she came back a moment later and laid the bowl of soup and basket of rolls in front of me I saw that a tiny diamond sparkled on her finger as it caught the light.

"You're engaged?" I said surprised, without stopping to think what I was saying.

"Yes, I'm getting married in August." She looked at me boldly, daring me to speak again, egging me on to break every social convention ever invented.

"Then I shan't bother to come here again," I said. "What a pity."

She laughed merrily. "Oh, I'll still be here! My fiancé has the market garden down the lane and I expect I'll still come back here to wait at table to help my parents."

"It's not a good idea to live too near one's parents when one's married, you know. You'd do better to marry a stranger and move away from the area."

"Really? Do you speak from experience?"

"As a matter of fact I do. My own marriage ended in divorce."

"Oh? You mean your wife divorced you because your home was too near your parents?"

A shadow hovered close at hand. "Isabel dear," said the pleasant-faced woman who had welcomed me to the house, "don't chatter to guests. The gentleman's waiting to eat his soup." She smiled at me nervously. "I'm afraid my daughter's a little forward sometimes. I do apologize."

"My dear Mrs.—"

"Clay."

"—Mrs. Clay, there's no need to apologize. Your daughter's charming."

She looked more nervous than ever and beat a hasty retreat to the kitchens. However since she re-emerged a moment later and stationed herself by the sideboard while she pretended to observe the swaying honeysuckle beyond the window, I was obliged to finish my meal in decorous silence. Isabella waited on me with downcast eyes and a demure expression. I was about to decide that Mrs. Clay was more conscientious than any Victorian chaperone when a large man with a military mustache poked his head around the dining-room door. "Phone for you, Hilda," he said to Mrs. Clay and vanished without waiting for her reply.

The other guests had all gone by this time. As Mrs. Clay withdrew reluctantly I was alone with Isabella.

"I must confess I can't see you as a market gardener's wife." I said. "Do you honestly want to spend the rest of your life pruning roses?"

"There are other more interesting things to prune?"

"Perhaps I could show you my conservatory sometime."

"Your conservatory? How grand! Do you have one of those marvelous mansions where the gas lights flicker and the heroine screams at intervals and the skeletons rattle in the cupboards as soon as the sun sets?"

"Come and see it," I said, "and find out."

"Oh dear, I hope that doesn't mean you throw it open to the public and charge sixpence admission every day except Sunday with children half price!"

"I haven't yet been reduced to that degree of penury!"

"Thank goodness! In that case—" the door opened as her mother re-entered the room— "would you care to have coffee in the lounge, sir?" said Isabella meekly.

"Thank you, I will."

But it was her mother who brought the coffee, and although I lingered over it for some time I did not see Isabella again until I went outside to my car.

She was sitting in the front seat. "Do forgive me," she said, "but I simply couldn't resist your invitation to view your conservatory. Do we have far to go?"

We did, so I compromised by driving across the Devon border and stopping for tea in Launceston. Halfway through the afternoon it occurred to me to ask her about her fiancé.

"How old is he?"

"Keith? Twenty-three. He's so sweet. Sort of placid and steady and reliable."

It was patently obvious that she was already bored with him and was marrying to escape from her parents' watchful supervision.

"Don't marry unless it's for love," I said. "I married for money and a roof over my head, lost them both and hurt my wife, who's a very decent woman, into the bargain. It was a fiasco. Don't you dare rush into marriage with your market gardener unless you can't live without him, and if you can't live without him what the devil are you doing having tea with me in Launceston? If you cared a straw for your fiancé—a real straw, not a pseudo straw—you wouldn't have looked at me twice."

She gazed at me with her great green eyes and was silent.

"Isn't that true?"

"Yes," she whispered. "You understand."

"Then let's have no more of this market gardener nonsense.

Don't marry him. Marry me instead. I'm not in the least saintly but I can at least promise you that you won't be bored. Don't maroon yourself in an obscure Devon village! You know damned well you'd hate it in no time at all. Come and be mistress of Penmarric."

There was a pause. We stared at each other. "You really do understand, don't you," she said, subdued, at last. "You don't know me but you understand."

"You'll marry me?"

"Yes, of course. How soon can we be married?"

[2]

That's a true story, which no doubt explains why it seems stranger than fiction. It makes a good after-dinner anecdote and all the women exclaim, "No! Really? How romantic!" and the men gape and say, "By George, that was quick work!" and then everyone looks at one another and wonders if we lived to regret our rapid dive into matrimony.

Of course we did not marry immediately by means of an elopement to Gretna Green—that would have been too rapid even for our precipitate courtship—but we did at least manage to arrange everything so that Isabella didn't have to alter her original wedding date in August. Only she did not marry her market gardener. She married me and became mistress of Penmarric.

When her parents first realized my interest in her, they were horrified. I think they regarded me as a fiend in human guise who had descended upon them out of the blue, wrecked their daughter's engagement to a respectable young man and enslaved her passions with a snap of his fingers. I had to work very hard to win them over, but I can work hard when I want to and I was determined that Isabella and I should be married openly and with her parents' approval in a normal registry office ceremony.

My divorce precluded me from marriage in church.

"You were the innocent party?" said Mrs. Clay doubtfully.

"No," I said. "I was divorced for adultery, but it was all arranged for our mutual convenience. You can write to my first wife, if you like—she'll speak highly of me. We parted on a very friendly basis."

It was hardly a surprise that they regarded me with such extreme suspicion.

"Come and visit Penmarric," I said and added craftily, "You must meet my mother. She loves to have visitors."

They liked this. It appealed to their sense of stability and reassured them that my proposal was in good faith. After they had consented to come and inspect their daughter's prospective home and mother-in-law, I rushed hotfoot to Zillan.

"Mama," I said as soon as I had explained the position to her. "This is very, very important to me. Could you come to Penmarric and receive them with me when they arrive for lunch? They don't approve of me because they think I'm too rich, they know I'm divorced and they correctly suspect I've had a checkered past, but as soon as they see you the scales will be tipped in my favor. You can play the grand lady and they're sure to think you were born a duchess. Mention how we go to church together every week and that I'm dead keen to marry again and settle down! They're bound to lap up every word you say."

"Hm," said my mother skeptically. "I suppose you do know what you're doing."

"Mama, wait till you meet this girl. She's unique. I can't wait to marry her."

"She sounds a most designing woman to me."

"No, no, no, Mama, you've got quite the wrong idea! She's just a young girl—fresh, innocent—"

"Well, if she's not," said my mother, "she certainly pulled the wool over your eyes."

"I'm sure you'll like her. In fact I'm convinced of it. Just wait till you meet her!"

"Is she a lady? In my young day, a girl whose parents kept an inn was considered very common."

"Mama, you know how those things have changed! Her parents are simply pleasant ordinary people, well-meaning . . ." I glibly dismissed Major Clay's suburban inflections and Mrs. Clay's little lapses into lower-middle-class gentility. "Isabella has been to a private boarding school and speaks faultlessly," I said with truth. "I could take her to a garden party at Buckingham Palace without a qualm."

"I don't think you ought to rush this, Jan-Yves. You're too impulsive."

"Mama, I'm almost thirty-two years old and if I don't know my mind by this time—"

"Are you having an affair with this girl?"

"Mama!" I was scandalized. My mother was always the soul of

propriety. "I don't think you quite understand. In fact I'm sure you don't understand at all."

"I've lived long enough to know that nothing makes a man lose his common sense more quickly than seeing something he wants but can't have. I presume you're anxious to have an affair with her and she's being virtuous enough to refuse."

"Mama, you couldn't be more wrong," I said, exasperated. "I've never asked her to be my mistress. I want her to be my wife, and since I'm determined to marry her I have no intention of insulting her by—"

"So you haven't asked her to be your mistress," said my mother, interested. "Fancy! I wonder what she would say if you did."

"Really, Mama, I can't help thinking this conversation is rather improper."

"Why? Aren't I supposed to know about such things? Do you think I've never received an improper advance from a man? Now don't get cross, darling, but it does strike me that Isabella's not a very reliable girl. You see, you may be marrying her for all the right reasons, but she may be marrying you for all the wrong ones. You have money, for one thing, and belong to a higher social stratum. You're very eligible."

"Mama, when I first met her—"

"—she didn't know who you were. But she saw the cut of your suit, didn't she, and heard your voice when you spoke, and no doubt she ran to the window and saw your nice new expensive car outside. And what happens? You fall in love with her very providentially, and she at once breaks her engagement without a second thought. A girl like that should be regarded with extreme suspicion. If she's done it once she can do it again—and next time you'll be the one she throws over when she goes off with someone else."

"We love each other!"

"Is that a magic incantation to ward off all evil? Love can die, Jan-Yves, and don't tell me it can't because it can. I know. Also, don't overlook the disparity in your ages. Everything in the garden may be beautiful now that you're a mere thirty-two and she's seventeen, but how is it going to be when she's a dazzling thirty-five and you're middle-aged and past your prime on the wrong side of fifty? And don't tell me I don't know what I'm talking about because I do—all too well. I've lived through every year of such a situation myself."

"It's different if the husband is the elder of the two," I said obstinately. "Husbands should be older than their wives. You can't cite your own marriage as a parallel to mine."

"Very well," said my mother acidly in resignation. "Since I see I can do nothing to dissuade you I may as well do all I can to help. However, I don't think I shall like her."

But she did. Much to my surprise she was very taken with Isabella and completely revised her opinion of my proposed plans.

"Marry her," she said as soon as the Clays had departed after their round-eyed inspection of Penmarric. "You'll probably regret it occasionally but most married couples go through difficult times now and again. She's extremely presentable. Unfortunately I can't say the same for her parents, but at least they won't be living on your doorstep and you won't have to bother with them too often. It's a pity she's not a little older, but that can't be helped. She's much too attractive, of course, but I suppose I could hardly expect you to marry anyone plain. At least she's not a fool."

I rushed pell-mell back to the Devon borders. "My mother approves of you!" I said, delighted. "Isn't that wonderful?"

"Gorgeous," said Isabella. "But I wish my parents would hurry up and approve of you instead of dithering all the time and worrying themselves into peptic ulcers. Of course they were frightfully impressed with Penmarric and utterly bowled over by your mother, but they're still balking at the quick wedding. They want us to wait till Christmas. How on earth can we make them realize that we're definitely getting married on August the thirtieth and that nothing's going to stand in our way?"

"We'll send the notice of the engagement to *The Times*," I said comfortably, "and the date of the wedding. They can't argue any more after that. No one ever argues with *The Times*."

No one did. Our engagement was duly announced to the world, and a few days later the letters of congratulation began to pour in.

"Everyone who knows you is thrilled!" exclaimed Isabella naïvely after sampling a selection of the letters I had received. "Everyone's so pleased!"

"Yes," I said. "Yes, aren't they?" And before I could stop myself I was thinking of Rebecca and the stony silence emanating from the farm at Morvah where I had spent so much of my time in the past.

[3]

I saw Rebecca soon afterward. We met in St. Just outside Mrs. Trewint's shop. She was wearing a coat that was too small for her, flat shoes and no make-up.

"Hullo," I said when I had found my tongue. "I haven't seen you for some time. How are you?"

"Quite well, thank you."

"Good."

We paused, ill-at-ease with each other. She shifted her shopping basket from one hand to the other, adjusted a strand of hair and looked down the street toward the square.

"I heard about your engagement," she said.

"Oh?"

"Yes." Her fingers clasped the handle of the basket as if her life depended on it. "I'm glad," she said. "I would have written but—"

"That's all right," I said. "Of course."

"I hope you'll be happy."

"Thank you."

"I don't think I can meet your fiancée," she said. "Maybe you could explain to her."

"I've told her about us. She'll understand."

She adjusted the strand of hair again. "I must go—excuse me . . . the bus . . ."

Yet still she hesitated as if she half hoped I might offer her a lift in my car. But I was silent. At last she said quickly, turning away from me, "Goodbye."

"Goodbye, Rebecca," I said and watched her walk off, stumbling a little, down the street. She was almost at the square when she looked back. We were some distance apart by that time but I could still see her face clearly. Her eyes were blank with pain, her face streaked with tears. We looked at each other for one long moment across the yards which separated us, and then I turned, lit a cigarette with care and walked fiercely down the street to my car.

[4]

"I wouldn't mind meeting her," said Isabella, wide-eyed with sincerity, "but perhaps it would be false if we treated each other like long-lost friends. Naturally she must hate me. I would if I were her."

"My darling Isabella!" I stroked her silky blond hair and tried to say something else but was overcome with emotion by her generous and understanding nature.

"Well, I would!" she said. "I'd be desperately jealous if I were her! In fact I think I'd die with jealously. Truthfully! I love you so much, Jan darling."

"My angel," I murmured, still too much affected to be coherent, and buried my face for a moment in her hair.

"Jan."

"Hm."

"I suppose Rebecca must be frightfully attractive and glamorous to fascinate you for all those years."

"Yes, I did find her attractive." I couldn't think of Rebecca properly. Rebecca was far away, remote, part of a buried past. I couldn't even picture Rebecca when I was with Isabella.

"When did you first meet her?"

"When? Oh, ages ago . . . when I was seven."

"Seven! How old was she? Just a baby, I suppose."

"Heavens no, she was fourteen. She's seven years older than I am."

"Seven years!"

"Yes, she was a year younger than Hugh, and Hugh was eight years my senior."

"You mean—why, she must be practically forty!"

"Yes, I suppose she'll be forty next year."

"Oh," said Isabella, and then: "Poor thing, I feel quite sorry for her," said Isabella, and smiled up at me adoringly as I kissed her on the nose.

[5]

We were married on the thirtieth of August at the registry office in Exeter with the unqualified blessing of everyone except a minister of the church, and that same afternoon we were on the train to London en route to our honeymoon in Venice. It was the happiest day of my life. I was so happy I was almost incoherent. I was thirty-two years old and married to the most beautiful, most charming and most delightful girl who was as much in love with me as I was with her. I doted on her. In fact I was so beside myself with ecstasy that I could hardly wait to get to London, where I had arranged for us to spend the wedding night before we embarked for the Continent the following day. We stayed at the Dorchester.

Looking back, I suppose I was too naïve in my estimation of Isabella. I don't mean for one moment that she disappointed me on our honeymoon, but I confess it did give me an unpleasant jolt to discover that she wasn't a virgin and an even more disagreeable surprise to find that she lied about it.

For she did lie.

"I haven't been with a man before," she said. "Ever."

But she couldn't fool me. She could act her heart out and make all the right sighs and moans, but I wasn't deceived. I had had too much experience with too many different types of women not to know when a girl was a virgin and when she wasn't.

We had our first quarrel on the first night of our honeymoon.

"All right," she said at last in tears. "I lied. But I only lied because I was frightened of what you'd say if you knew. I was rather naughty once and I didn't want you to know about it. That's all. I'm sorry—please don't be cross—"

"Listen to me," I said levelly. "Let's get this straight once and for all. I don't want you lying to me about anything. I certainly won't hold it against you that you're not a virgin—God knows I'm no saint myself, but I have at least tried to be honest with you about it. I've told you about Rebecca, who was the most important woman in my life before I met you, and I've told you about Felicity. And there were other women too, unimportant affairs that meant nothing. I admit it! It's much better to admit everything right from the beginning, can't you see that? You needn't be afraid I won't understand or won't make allowances for you if you're honest, but I'll be very angry if I catch you trying to deceive me like that again. I want no deceit between us either now or in the future, is that clear? I want you to be honest with me."

"Yes, Jan." She sniffed and wiped each eye delicately with the corner of her negligée.

"How did it happen anyway? Was it just once after a party or something? With Keith?"

She sniffed again. "Well, no. Actually it wasn't with Keith."

"But it was just once—just a mistake. Is that right?"

She looked up at me miserably with great tear-filled green eyes and said nothing.

"For God's sake, darling, I'm only repeating what you've just said!" I was beginning to feel nervous. "You said you were 'rather naughty'—*once*. Was that a lie too?"

"Sort of."

"Then tell me the truth and let's get it over. Did you have an affair?"

"No . . . not exactly . . . It happened about six or seven times . . ."

"With the same man?"

She choked. Two enormous tears rolled down her white little face. She looked as pathetic as a waif and stray. "No."

I stared at her. I was just thinking in panic that I really didn't want to hear the truth as much as I thought I did when she said in a rush, "They were just boys from the neighboring school. Three of them. I went out with one, then with the next, and then with the third. It was all terribly secret. If I'd been found out I'd have been expelled."

"I see," I said and thought woodenly: Just a few schoolgirl escapades.

"And then there was Keith . . . well, he was terribly honorable and moral and everything, but once or twice—well, we did have a little lapse now and then—"

"You just told me Keith wasn't your lover!"

"No . . . well, I didn't mean to . . . I got muddled—confused —I mean, we were talking of the *first* time it happened—"

"I see. So you had an affair with Keith."

. "Not an *affair*—just one or two little lapses—"

"Well, I suppose he was your fiancé," I said, trying hard to be fair and not to frighten her by a display of anger. "That was excusable."

"Oh, Jan . . ." She flung herself against my chest and clung there. She seemed so small and weak and defenseless. Her body shook with sobs. "Oh, Jan, you're so good and kind and understanding and I love you so much—I love you a million more times than anyone else in the entire world—"

I was deeply touched. I smoothed her hair, kissed her forehead and held her tightly against me.

"I know I've been naughty, I know it, but you see I was so *bored*, Jan, so *bored* in that horrible prissy school locked up with all those dreary girls day after day, and when my parents left Surrey and came down to Devon I was so *stifled* by the country and being so far from a cinema and from London and from everything that was gay and amusing—"

"My darling, of course . . . I understand."

The poor little thing. Nobody had ever tried to understand her before. My heart ached with love for her.

"If only you knew how wonderful it was for me when *you* came and sat down in our dining room! You were so glamorous and exciting in your beautiful suit and your old Etonian tie and your gorgeous car—just like a glimpse of the promised land! And you were so charming and attractive and—oh, I adored you right from the first! If you only knew how shallow the others seemed in contrast, how young and inexperienced and so hopelessly *provincial!* I know just how Cinderella felt when she met her Prince Charming."

What else could I do after that but forgive her? We made love passionately for the rest of the night and slept from dawn until noon before resuming our journey to Venice.

Of course I married for love and not on account of mere sexual desire, but I have to admit that even if I hadn't married her for the best possible reasons I might eventually have married her for sexual reasons alone. She was tremendously exciting. Her fine-boned, neat little body with its round, hard little breasts and soft milk-white flesh made other women seem gross and clumsy in contrast. Her movements fascinated me. Her limbs were so supple and smooth—and so young. It had not occurred to me before that a young girl could be as stimulating as a mature woman, but it was true. I wondered what she would be like when she was at the height of her beauty and maturity later on, and as my imagination quickened I felt dizzy with delight.

I was ecstatically happy.

"We don't want children straight away, do we?" I said, raising a subject we had somehow never had time to discuss in detail. We had agreed to have children ("Two boys and a girl," I said; "two boys and an optional girl," said Isabella) but the timing of each conception was an item we had left unresolved. Now I decided that I didn't want to see her fascinating little body misshapen by an early pregnancy. I had waited long enough for a son. Another two years would hardly make any difference.

"Oh, no!" agreed Isabella wholeheartedly. "We can have children later. Let's have some fun first."

So we had our fun. Until the end of the summer and all through the autumn and winter we enjoyed ourselves to the full in Venice, Paris, London and Cornwall, I never thinking of the past, never looking at any other woman, and then on one cold morning in the March of 1938 I received a letter from Rebecca.

[6]

It was very short. All it said was "Dear Jan, I'm in bad trouble and there's no one else I can turn to. Please help me. I'll be at the house all Friday morning if you can manage to call. Rebecca."

I showed the letter to Isabella across the breakfast table. "I suppose I'd better go," I said reluctantly.

"Yes, do," said Isabella. "I can't wait to know what it's all about. But why can't she ask Simon Peter Roslyn for help? Why does it have to be you?"

"I've no idea."

"Why don't you ring her up and speak to her on the phone?"

"Deveral Farm's not on the phone."

"Really? How inconvenient," said Isabella and began to flick rapidly through the pages of her favorite fashion magazine.

We said nothing more about it, but presently I left her, got out my car and drove to Morvah. Rebecca must have been watching out for me from the window, for as soon as I drew my car to a halt outside the farmhouse she opened the front door and came out to meet me.

"Come in," she said. "I'm so glad you've come. Thank you, Jan."

She looked ill. There were dark circles beneath her eyes and an odd drawn look about her mouth. I looked at her closely, aware of a vague indefinable sense of alarm.

"Where are the children?" I said sharply.

"Jonas is at school. Deborah's working as usual—her bank in Penzance."

"No lodger?" I said as I followed her into the drawing room. "In March?"

"Well, I heard how your summer lodger came back for Christmas last year."

She still had her back to me and I could not see her expression. "Yes," she said. "He came back."

"It was a schoolmaster again, wasn't it?"

"A new one. He hadn't been here before last summer." She hesitated by the fireplace. "Do you want tea?"

"Not now." I looked at her again. She seemed different. Normally I wouldn't have noticed, but I was suspicious now, on the alert for the "trouble" she had referred to in her letter, and my eyes saw more than they would have done otherwise. Her face was a fraction fuller; I noticed that her breasts, though not larger than usual, seemed oddly taut, and suddenly I heard myself say in a flat, disbelieving voice, "You're pregnant."

She looked at me in amazement but said nothing.

"Aren't you?"

"Yes." She lit a cigarette. I had never seen her smoke before. Her hand trembled as she held the match.

After a moment I said, "The schoolmaster?"

"Yes," she said. "The schoolmaster." And as I stared at her, my anger against that unknown man mingling with my pity for her, she said in a rush, "I was so sad all last summer, Jan. I tried not to be, but I couldn't help it. When someone tried to offer me a little happiness—"

"Where is he now?"

"I don't know. I can't trace him. I wrote to his address but his landlady in London said he had gone without leaving a forwarding address. I couldn't believe it at first. After all, we'd been very close—he'd come down and spent Christmas with us—I . . . I was quite pleased when I first found out about the baby because I thought then that he might—"

"Marry you?"

She did not deny it. All she said was "I've been a widow such a long time, Jan. It's hard to be widowed when you're only twenty-seven."

"But look here, Rebecca, if this man's left you and you can't trace him—"

"Yes," she said. "Yes, I know. I've thought it all out. Don't worry, I didn't ask you here to give me advice about what to do. I know what has to be done. I simply want you to help me do it."

Uneasiness made my scalp prickle. I said sharply, "Just what the devil do you mean by that?" All I could think was: I want no part of her troubles. Not now. Let Simon Peter help her. He's her cousin. Let her turn to him.

"Please, Jan!" Her eyes were dark, beseeching me for pity. "Please help me! If you could tell me where I can go to get an abortion—Hugh used to tell stories about places in the back streets of Penzance, and I thought that if you could find someone there for me, someone reliable . . ."

She stopped. There was a long silence. Finally I managed to say, "No."

"Jan—"

"No."

"All right," she said sullenly. "I'll go my own way. I'll find someone somehow."

"A back-street quack? Good God, don't you know what a risk you'd be taking? I've heard about that sort of abortion! Charity had one years ago—William told me about it once. She nearly died, and later when she wanted to have children she found out that the abortionist had made such a mess of her that any idea of children was out of the question. Also she knew girls who—but I won't talk about the ones who died. Listen, I'll tell you what you must do. Get Simon Peter to take you to London and bribe a gynecologist to do the job properly for you in a decent hospital where there'd be no danger of anything going wrong. I'm sure if one paid enough money—"

"But Simon Peter's a lawyer," she said, "and abortions are against the law. I couldn't ask Simon Peter—I couldn't ask any of my Roslyn relations for help! Think what they'd say! They'd never speak to me again, never! As it is I'm terrified of them finding out what's happened."

"But damn it, Rebecca, what am I supposed to do? Leave my wife and take you to London myself? What am I to say to my wife? How am I to explain to her?"

"I don't expect you to go to London," she said levelly, her eyes dark in her strained face. "I don't expect that. How could I go to London anyway? What could I say to the children? I couldn't even go to London on my own."

"You must. Look, I'll phone Donald—Donald McCrae. He's in London now. He'll meet you off the train and look after you and he'll know the name of a man who'll do the job safely in the proper surroundings—don't worry about the money. I'll pay. But you must go about this thing in the right way, do you understand? It's no good going to a back-street quack."

"I couldn't take your money," she said.

"Don't be absurd. I don't mind helping you out financially."

"But what could I say to the children?"

"Say you're not well. Say it's nothing for them to worry about but your doctor has advised you to consult a London specialist. Be open and above board and they won't even question it. Is that clear? Are you listening to me? Will you do as I say?"

"Yes," she said in a muffled voice. "Yes, Jan, I will."

But she did not.

Two nights later Deborah telephoned me in a panic from the nearest callbox and said that her mother was very ill but had forbidden her to send for a doctor.

"She asked for you," Deborah whispered, crying into the phone. "Oh, Uncle Jan, I'm so frightened . . . she's so white and there's this terrible bleeding—"

"I'll be there in ten minutes," I said. "Don't worry, Deborah. It'll be all right." But as soon as I had finished speaking to her I got hold of the operator and summoned the ambulance from Penzance.

[7]

"All right," said the doctor at the hospital to me an hour later. "You'd better tell me. Who was the butcher? Whoever performed this operation deserves a life sentence to prevent other women from falling into his hands."

"I don't know," I said blankly. "I don't know who it was." I felt cold with shock. "I refused to help her find a quack. I was going to send her to London—to a gynecologist. She didn't want to go because she was afraid her strait-laced relations might find out and she didn't know what to say to the children, but I thought when I last saw her that I'd persuaded her to see reason."

"Your child?"

"No."

"Then why—"

"I wanted to help. She's my sister-in-law."

"I see." He paused. "I'm sorry" was all he could say when he spoke again. "I'm very sorry."

"But isn't there anything you can do?"

"Everything possible will be done, I promise you. Meanwhile perhaps we'd better do something about the children. How old is the girl?"

"Seventeen."

"Better tell her the situation isn't too good and that it would be as well for her to stay at the hospital for a while. The boy would be better off away from it all probably. Are there any relations he could go to?"

"I'll telephone Simon Peter Roslyn."

"The solicitor?"

"Yes, he's their cousin."

"Good. Ask him if he'd be so kind as to come to the hospital straight away."

"Very well," I said dully and walked slowly away down the white sterile hospital corridor to the cupboard in the hall where they kept the public telephone.

[8]

She spoke only once. A plainclothes policeman was at the bedside on the chance that she would reveal the name of the abortionist, and the doctor and nurse were present, but otherwise the only people there were Simon Peter, Deborah and I. Simon Peter would not look at me; he had his arm around Deborah, who was crying soundlessly into her handkerchief, and his eyes watched Rebecca. No other member of the family was there; Jonas was in the waiting room with Simon Peter's wife, and so there were just the three of us, just Simon Peter and Deborah and I imprisoned by those four hospital walls, and before us on the bed Rebecca lay motionless, her eyes closed, her lips ashen, her lifeblood ebbing away before our eyes.

All I could think of was the past. I thought of fourteen-year-old Rebecca Roslyn in her gingham dress on the rectory lawn, of twenty-one-year-old Rebecca Castallack just married to my brother Hugh; I thought of her sudden widowhood, Jonas's birth, her tortuous recovery from her bereavement. I saw her in that scarlet satin dress again, her first capitulation, our long uneven relationship spread over ten long difficult years. But I didn't think of the quarrels, the stormy scenes, the words we always regretted later. I thought only of the happiness, the joy and the laughter; I remembered only my pride in her when I took her out for an evening, my comfort in lying close to her in the bedroom, the longing for her which drew me back time and again to that farmhouse even after our worst quarrels. For ten years she had been the most important woman in my life, the woman I loved better than all the other women in the world. I had not loved her as I now loved Isabella, but I had loved her nonetheless and she had loved me. Then why, since this was so, had we so often made each other unhappy?

It was her fault, I told myself as the tears blurred my eyes, all her fault. She never trusted me when I told her I loved her. She refused to marry me and then refused to forgive me when I wouldn't marry her later. She was selfish and hurtful and made no effort to understand.

She spoke.

Her lashes flickered and her lids opened but her eyes beneath were blind. She opened her mouth, said very clearly in a strange, quiet voice, "Hugh?" and then after that there was nothing except for the knowledge that it was not her fault but mine, that I had been a mere clumsy, insensitive substitute who had never understood her, and as I watched, too stricken with grief and guilt to speak, a small shallow sigh escaped from her lips and she died.

[9]

I went out into the night.

It was dark and windy and the rain lashed against my face and mingled with my tears. I crawled into my car and sat there, unable to drive, marooned on a street in Penzance early on one sightless, stormy March morning, but at last I managed to drive up onto the moors and halt the car for a while. Dawn came. The sun was rising in the east beyond Marazion, and the wet gray spear of St. Michael's Mount rose from the cold morning sea like a tarnished dream.

After a long while I went home.

"Yes," I said to Isabella. "Yes, I'm upset. I can't help it. I'm sorry but I can't help it. Please forgive me."

"Oh, Jan darling, as if there was anything to forgive!" She put her thin child's arms around me and pressed her soft young cheek to mine. After a moment she said, "I mean, there isn't anything to forgive, is there?"

I looked at her. "What do you mean?" I said dimly. My mind

was in a haze of shock still and I couldn't grasp what she was saying. "I don't understand."

"Nothing, darling."

"If I ever find that schoolmaster who got her into trouble in the first place, I'll—"

"Yes, darling. I know."

"And who could she have gone to for the abortion? I hope to God the police find out who did it."

"Yes, darling, yes. I expect they will."

"If only she'd done what I told her to do! Why did she have to panic like that? I could have organized her journey to London for her—she needn't have been afraid! But I suppose she was in an irrational state where she saw things out of proportion and the prospect of a visit to London seemed suddenly more than she could cope with. She must have made up her mind to save herself the trouble—save me the trouble—she must have convinced herself that a quick visit to Penzance was the best way—"

"Darling, don't think about it any more. Please! It's wrong to blame yourself like this. You did your best for her, but she didn't take your advice—and that's all there is to say. Try not to worry about it any more. The police will soon find out who did it, I'm sure. Try to get some rest."

She took me off to bed. It was only there, with my head pressed against her breast as she lay quietly beside me, that I fell at last into the dreamless sleep of exhaustion.

[10]

Rebecca was buried in Zillan churchyard beside Hugh on a cold blustery afternoon a few days later. Her children were both there and so were all the Roslyns and her friends in Morvah. Her cousin Alice Carnforth came over in Sir Justin's chauffeur-driven Daimler and William and I arrived in my new Lagonda. No one spoke to us. Simon Peter was white-faced, tight-lipped and hostile, and even Deborah, usually so affectionate toward me, hurried away afterward without pausing to look in my direction. It was a sad, somber, depressing experience, and the memory of it was to upset me for many months to come.

The spring came; I took Isabella to London, then up to Cambridge to stay with Lizzie and finally to Scotland to spend August with Esmond in his remote Highland castle which he used as a country house. The long holiday did me good; gradually the memory of Rebecca's death began to recede from the forefront of my mind, and soon I had picked up the threads of my old life and was once more enjoying myself as much as I had been before the disaster.

"We were having such fun!" said Isabella wistfully. "Remember?"

"And we'll have just as much fun again," I promised her and set out to entertain her as lavishly as possible for the remainder of 1938 and the beginning of the new year.

But time was running out for us both, just as it was running out for the rest of the world, and although we plunged ourselves with determination into a gay carefree existence as two of the gayest most carefree members of the West Country aristocracy, I knew already that our lighthearted days were numbered. Times had changed since the Spanish Civil War had turned Lizzie into a militant and me into a pacifist. A stalemate had developed in Spain, but by the time Franco's forces finally won in 1939 everyone's eyes were not on the triumph of facism in Spain but its triumph in Austria and Czechoslovakia. Chamberlain was Prime Minister now. During the spring and summer of 1938 "appeasement" was an honorable word implying calm and reason and patience, but that was all changed after the drama of Munich. Hysterical relief that war had been avoided gave way to shame and renewed fear, and when Hitler occupied Bohemia and Moravia in the March of 1939 appeasement was dead and with it all our blind and irrational hopes for peace.

"War is unthinkable," I had said so often to William. "It just can't happen." And what I had really meant was: I don't want to believe that war can happen again; I don't want to believe that my life could be disrupted so unjustly because the contestants who had fought themselves to a bloody standstill twenty years before could be insane enough to assemble for a second round.

But 1939 was the year of the unthinkable, and on the first of September German armored divisions and planes invaded Poland.

The party was over. All that remained was a dog-eared photograph album of champagne memories, an empty nursery upstairs and the prospect of a long and indefinite separation to come.

10

*Duchess Constance died in 1201. . . . Now Duke
Arthur was doubly orphaned, and had lost his last tie
with the house of Anjou. He was entirely in the hands
of French advisers appointed by King Philip.*
—The Devil's Brood,
ALFRED DUGGAN

*". . . we heard that the Lady our mother was closely
besieged at Mirebeau, and we hurried there as fast as
we could, arriving on the feast of St. Peter ad Vincula.
And there we captured our nephew Arthur . . ."*
—King John,
W. L. WARREN quoting King John

[1]

"What a bore these Germans are!" said Isabella, but she was frightened.

"Doesn't look too good, does it?" said William to me, worried, over a glass of beer at the pub. "So this is where we got with our appeasement policy! I suppose we ought to have guessed months ago that militant madmen like Hitler are simply unappeasable—or was it that we all guessed and yet couldn't face the implications of such a horrifying truth?"

"Darlings," Mariana wrote scratchily from Paris. "Isn't this news the *end*? I'm having terrible difficulty getting away from this country now and only wish I'd left after Munich. Can you possibly lend me fifty pounds? I've been trying to contact

Esmond but without success—he must be somewhere in the wilds of Scotland—because I thought I could come and live with him in Edinburgh at last, but now I suppose he'll have to go away to fight and we'll still be kept apart . . ."

"You won't have to go away to fight, Jan, will you?" said my mother tremulously. "You're well over thirty. They'll take the young men first, won't they?"

"Why volunteer?" said Isabella, green eyes burning in a white face. "Why not stay here as long as you can?"

"Because if everyone did that," I said, "we'd soon have Germans at Penmarric and our children would grow up to be Nazis."

"But we have no children! And Penmarric's only a house—"

"Be quiet!"

"But it's true!"

I shook her in a fit of rage; she clawed at me but then burst into tears. "Oh Jan, I'm sorry, I can't help it, I'm so frightened, I don't want you to go—I want a baby—"

"We'll have a baby."

But we didn't.

"Oh!" cried Isabella. "Why did we wait? Why did this have to happen to us? Why, why, why? It's not fair!"

"No," I said, "it's not fair." And once again the two-headed monster seemed to rise up before my eyes, but now the face of justice was hidden from me in a dark shroud and only the face of injustice was left exposed. My search for justice, hitherto un-flagging, was now about to begin a long process of erosion until in the end it had narrowed itself down to a handful of basic elementary aims which guided my life.

The most basic of these elementary aims was simple. I wanted to stay alive. I could not face the injustice of a premature death. My second aim was to keep Penmarric solvent. I could not face the injustice of debt, mortgage and foreclosure. Finally before I was parted from Isabella I wanted to leave her with the prospect of a child. I could not face the reality that my young wife became bored too easily unless she had constant diversions to keep her occupied. My marriage had stood the test of time well while the sun shone and we lived in our frivolous world among our rich contemporaries, but now I was frightened. There are many flowers which flourish in greenhouses but which wither away once they're exposed to the cold air of a winter's day.

I was afraid to leave her.

But I left. What else could I do? The phony war came to an end, France collapsed and the British Army was washed into the sea at Dunkirk. We were alone. The sun shone all the way through that beautiful summer and sometimes one could look at the splendor of the countryside and imagine that nothing was wrong, that life was just as it had always been, but of course that was an illusion, the longing to escape from a reality too terrible to face.

For this was 1940. All England lay at death's door.

[2]

"My sermon this morning," said Adrian from the pulpit, "is inspired by chapter seventeen of the first book of Samuel, by that passage which describes how . . ." He paused. There was an immense silence. Then: "How David slew Goliath," said Adrian, and his voice rang out like steel striking sparks against a sheet of shining stone.

I met Adrian in London. He was fresh from a conference of important clerics and had been invited to give a guest sermon at St. Clement Danes. I was always sorry that church was bombed later. All through the war I carried with me the memory of sitting on my own in the midst of that full congregation and listening to Adrian as he announced to that intense, yearning silence: "David slew Goliath . . ."

All through the war. I never thought I would come through it all alive.

"I'll come back, Mama," I said dryly to my mother. "Only the good die young Look after yourself and don't try to do too much. I'll write to you as often as I can."

I hardly thought I would see her again. She was eighty now and strong for her years, but when one leaves anybody over eighty one should not take it for granted that they'll live forever.

I hated to say goodbye.

Worst of all was to say goodbye to Isabella.

"I'll let you know as soon as I get some leave," I said. "With luck we won't have too long to wait."

She nodded, white-faced, white-lipped, her green eyes enormous in her small pinched face.

"I'm sorry there's no—" But she could not say it. She had wanted a baby too much for too long.

I touched her soft hair. "When we next meet . . ."

Then I was on a train and her face was a white blur on a station platform, and injustice, cold and harsh and merciless, settled down to control my life.

[3]

I had been a spectator through most of 1940, forced to stand helplessly on one side and watch as the fiasco in Norway led to Churchill replacing Chamberlain and the fiasco at Dunkirk led to the huge upsurge of national morale when the fiasco was transformed into a victory. However, at last the army began to notice that I had volunteered my services and I was in uniform though still waiting to be posted when the handful of pilots won the Battle of Britain and put an end to Hitler's immediate plans to invade British soil. It was not until the last part of 1940 that my training was completed and I was shipped off to North Africa, but by that time the tide of fiascos had temporarily receded and Mussolini was receiving the first of a series of reverses which were to continue until the May of the following year.

I found myself serving in the forces commanded by General Wavell, and almost before I knew what was happening I was helping to push the Italians west to Benghazi. The campaign was a success; we took about a hundred and thirty thousand prisoners before withdrawing to Egypt. I almost allowed myself to feel cheerful about the war's outcome and would have been appalled if I could have seen ahead to the dark months of 1941 when we were expelled from Greece and Crete and the Axis powers occupied the whole of the Balkan plains.

While I was waiting in Egypt for the next offensive to begin, my principal source of interest lay in the letters I received from home.

"Poor Isabella is quite lost without you," my mother wrote. "I have really become very fond of her. I hardly thought she would settle down at Penmarric nearly so well as she has done, but in retrospect I don't think you could have chosen a better wife. I'm sure you miss her as much as she misses you."

"Your mother is very down at the moment," wrote Isabella gaily. "Poor old dear, she misses you terribly. We have tea together every week and I try to cheer her up. Lizzie wrote from Cambridge and said she'd like to come down for a visit but didn't see how she could get here since the chauffeur had been called up and petrol's so tricky and awkward these days. I explained to her that there was a wonderful invention nowadays called a train which catered for all people not rich enough to have a car, and had she heard of it? I shall never cease to be amazed at how the other half lives even though I suppose I'm now part of the other half . . ."

"My dearest Jan," wrote Lizzie. "I have had rather an extraordinary letter from Isabella, really quite radical. Is she perhaps a secret Socialist? If so, do tell her that I've been one for years. I've been toying with the idea of spending a few months in Cornwall to take the girls away from any risk of bombing (although I hear even Penzance is far from safe from bombing these days) but Eddy doesn't want to leave Cambridge, and anyway I don't *really* think that Isabella and I would get on very well together if I stayed for longer than a few days. Don't take offense, my dear, but as you must know Isabella and I never quite hit it off. However, I feel sorry for her now with you away, so perhaps I will go down to Penmarric eventually to offer some sympathy. . . . I hope she isn't too lonely all by herself in that ghastly house. Still, she's fond of William, isn't she—what a good thing he left the Carnforth Hall estate and came back to look after Penmarric for you during your absence. It's a pity he and Charity don't live at Penmarric, but I remember you told me how Charity insisted on staying in Penzance, where she's become so respectable, and refused to go back to live in St. Just where people have such unfortunately long memories . . ."

"My dear Jan," wrote William laboriously. "As you know, the days are long past when I could write long letters, so don't expect marvels every time you see my handwriting on an envelope! Hope all's well with you. Everything's more or less all right here except that little Isabella's a bit depressed and I lent her my shoulder to cry on the other night. I thought you'd rather she cried on my shoulder than someone else's!! Only joking, of course. Just thought I'd mention it in case she wrote you a depressed letter and I thought it would reassure you to know I cheered her up a bit and that she's feeling better now . . ."

"My darling Jan," wrote Isabella. "William is such a poppet— how lucky you are to have such a nice brother. I can't think how he can stand to be married to that horrid blowsy old ex-barmaid! She doesn't like me at all—I can't think why. Fortunately your mother doesn't like her either and we have a moan about all the Roslyns from time to time. Jonas is now staying at Morvah with his Roslyn spinster aunts—no, cousins, isn't it—and Deborah (take a deep breath!) has just entered a convent!!! Can you believe it! She and I were hardly bosom friends, but she did call at Penmarric to say goodbye before she left for Padstow . . ."

". . . so I decided to enter the convent," wrote my niece Deborah to me a little later. "I know Mummy wouldn't have wanted it, but she was a person who enjoyed all the worldly pleasures of this life, and so perhaps it would have been hard for her to understand that I have never been happy in the World, where there is so much sin and suffering and evil. I shall be much happier here and already am aware of the most perfect spiritual satisfaction. After this letter I shall never again refer to any past sins, but I would like you to know that I forgive you for all the suffering you caused my mother and for leading her into the sinful path which eventually resulted in her death. I have repeatedly besought Jonas to forgive you also but regret that I have not yet had any success in persuading him; however, I hope that by the Grace of God he may be enlightened and may also find it in his heart to forgive you, as I have. I shall remember you every day in my prayers and hope that perhaps when you come home from the war you will come and see me. . . ."

"Sir," wrote a rude hand with bold thick strokes of a cheap pen. "As you may or may not know, Deborah has gone into a convent and can't earn any money any more, so I'm reduced to begging from my Roslyn relations who haven't the money to spare anyway except for Cousin Sim and his mean streak is so mean it's a joke. None of you Castallacks have done anything for me except push me and my mother around to suit your convenience and I think it's time I got my fair share of Grandfather Castallack's money which you cheated me out of when you sucked up to Uncle Philip like you did when I was a kid and spread that lie about him being a homo so that my mother took fright. Could you send me fifty pounds? I've grown out of all my clothes and I don't want to be the laughing-stock of the school. And in case you think I just sit on my arse begging from my relations all the time, let me tell you that I get a job every holidays *and* do a paper-round in the term-time and I don't think Grandfather Castallack would have liked it to know that his grandson was just a common paper-boy at a bloody grammar school. Send the money to me care of Miss Hope Roslyn at Morvah where I'm living at the moment. And if you don't send the money I'll bloody well go over to Granny and make *her* give it to me, so if you want to make sure your mother isn't bothered you'd better pay up. I'll give you till the end of the month. Jonas."

". . . so there he was," wrote my mother, "on my doorstep. He's fifteen now, and except for Hugh's eyes he's the living image of his grandfather Joss Roslyn, whom I knew as a boy. Of course, thanks to your warning letter I knew what to expect. I was kind to him but firm. I said he had set about getting the money in quite the wrong way, and that if he had written to you respectfully you would have been pleased to help him, but as it was the tone of his letter didn't encourage you to offer him any assistance whatsoever. He immediately flew into a towering rage. He shouted at me—in extremely vulgar language—that he had a moral right to the money, and when I told him that was nonsense he called me an old —— and said I had always been against him and his mother ever since he could remember. 'Absolute nonsense,' I said to him. 'You and your mother went through life ruining your own chances.' '*He* ruined them!' shouted Jonas (meaning *you*). '*He* killed my mother! *He* stole my inheritance! He's a murderer and a —— robber!' 'Kindly leave my house this instant,' I said, 'or I shall telephone Mr. Parrish and ask him to come over at once to remove you by force.' He went, still cursing, and I haven't seen him since. What was all this nonsense about you killing Rebecca? As far as I can remember you told me that she got into trouble with one of her lodgers and then, poor foolish woman, got into worse trouble trying to extricate herself from the situation. Wasn't this true? Incidentally, talking of women in trouble I had a most distressing letter from Mariana today . . ."

"My dear Uncle Jan," wrote Esmond from India. "I hate to bother you when I'm sure you have so much on your mind these days, but I'm extremely worried about my mother. As you can see, I'm a long way from home and as I see no prospect of getting back to England in the forseeable future I don't know what I should do. Perhaps you would be kind enough to advise me. To cut a long story short, it appears that for some time now my mother has been in and out of homes seeking a cure for alcoholism. I didn't know she was an alcoholic, although I did sometimes wonder how she managed to spend the money I sent her so rapidly. My father always refused to pay her a penny more than he was legally bound to pay, but I financed her in secret even before he died and have been financing her ever since. Before I went overseas she managed to get to Edinburgh to see me and it was then that I realized what was wrong. I had her put in an excellent nursing home there before I left, but now she has voluntarily discharged herself, and to be frank I have to admit she is now being a considerable source of embarrassment to the servants in my house there. Unfortunately she seems to have formed an association with an undesirable man who has been treating my house as if it were his own, so much so that in the end my butler felt compelled to sit down and write me a letter in which he said that all the servants were on the point of giving notice. I was then, as you can imagine, placed in a very difficult position. I did not want to disclose my source of information to my mother, but at the same time I had to suggest that it would be best if she left my house for a while and went somewhere else. In the end I told her that I had heard Edinburgh was not considered safe these days and I strongly advised her to go down to Cornwall for the summer out of range of all possible bombing. I did *not* suggest she went to Penmarric, as I hardly felt it was right to suggest she impose herself on your wife's hospitality, and told her that it would be best if she stayed at the Metropole where she could stay as long as she liked without any embarrassment, and I naturally would pay the bill. In spite of all this I have had a letter from her today to say she has decided to go to Penmarric. I deeply apologize for any embarrassment this is going to cause you and your wife, but I don't think I can stop her now. What shall I do? I didn't want to write to Granny because I didn't want her to know about my mother's condition. If only I could get home I could probably make the necessary arrangements for her, but I don't see how I can. Do you think I could get compassionate leave? I doubt it very much. Please forgive me for burdening you like this, but I'm simply at my wits' end with this problem and I have no one else I can turn to. Your affectionate nephew, Esmond."

"My dearest Jan," wrote my mother. "I'm glad you were

sensible enough to tell me the truth and not to worry about 'sparing my feelings.' Of course it was shocking to see Mariana in such a state, but at least, thanks to you, I was prepared for the worst. Her own letter, which preceded her arrival, gave me more than a hint that all was not well, so I was in a way prepared for your letter which arrived soon afterward. Poor Esmond, what a wretched burden for a boy of twenty-one! How mature and sensible and grownup he sounds. Such a contrast to Jonas. I told Mariana she must stay with me and not at Penmarric since Isabella had not been well (a lie) and was not up to entertaining guests, but as you know, Mariana has always despised the farm and refused to stay there. William, thank God, came to the rescue and took her to stay at Carnforth Hall after telling Felicity the whole story, so Felicity and Alice together are now keeping an eye on her. It really is most distressing. I can't tell you how it upsets me to see Mariana, who was always such a beautiful, fastidious girl—too fastidious, I often thought!—now taking so little trouble with her appearance and wearing clothes that are not as clean as they should be. I asked her why she drank so much and she said nothing had ever gone right for her, which I thought was a strange remark seeing she made two brilliant marriages, had all the money she wanted, a series of beautiful homes and such a handsome charming son. But I believe people who drink too much are inclined to self-pity. 'Nothing ever went right for me,' she said. 'Nobody ever loved me.'—which I thought was a very maudlin and untruthful thing to say. However, one cannot argue with a person like that, so I said nothing and let it pass. . . . What a nice man William Parrish is. Both those Parrish boys turned out so well. I hear Adrian had lunch with the Archbishop of Canterbury the other day. . . ."

". . . so in spite of the war, the future seems to be full of promise for me," wrote Adrian. "It certainly seems almost indecent that in the midst of so much appalling misery I should feel so happy and fortunate, but I'm afraid—or rather, I'm glad to say—that's exactly how I feel. . . . I have left it rather late in life to be married, since I'm now nearer fifty than forty, but I think I have spent a lot of time hoping to find 'True Love' and 'The Ideal Woman' and judging every woman I met by a set of false and utterly unrealistic standards. However, since meeting Anne I realized I had no desire at all to be married to an impossibly virtuous paragon and would much prefer someone human who shared at least some of my human failings! Besides, Anne is perfect for me in every way, and that's all that matters, isn't it? She is the widow of a dean, so is well acquainted with the clerical existence and has two grownup children by her first marriage. In a strange way she reminds me a little of my mother—although since it's nowadays so highly suspect to write such a thing I almost hesitate to commit it to paper!—but then I'm forgetting that you never met my mother and so will be unable to see any resemblance when you meet Anne. . . ."

"Adrian is marrying a saint," scrawled William in his large untidy handwriting. "A nice woman, but a bit too 'good,' if you know what I mean. One feels she instinctively rates you as a good/bad/indifferent parishioner and allots you an appropriately suitable task to perform for the next church fete. I found her very charming and kind, but I couldn't help feeling I'd been weighed in the ecclesiastical balance and found wanting! Curious, isn't it, that I married a sinner and now Adrian's marrying a saint, but I'm sure he'll be happy. He and I have always been on slightly different planes. . . ."

". . . she didn't approve of *me*," wrote Isabella. "I think I rated as a 'lost girl' with promiscuous tendencies! I could see she was itching to practice some social welfare on me. William and I discussed her for hours when they had gone and Charity got annoyed and tried to turn me out. . . . There's no other news. My parents keep asking me to go home for a visit, so I suppose I shall have to summon the energy to go before long. Your mother is well, except I think that horrid Jonas has been bothering her again. . . ."

". . . so I gave him ten pounds," wrote my mother. "I suppose I shouldn't have done because he's sure to be back for more, but I do feel sorry for him, and I am after all his grandmother. I know he's coarse and ill-mannered—as Joss always was—but there *is* a small resemblance to Hugh, and somehow I can't help thinking that if Hugh had lived Jonas would have been different and that now he's merely the victim of circumstance. I know that's silly, since we're all the victims of circumstance, but I am getting sentimental in my old age and think so much of the past. I think often too of Mariana when she was young. . . . She has been ill again, and Alice Carnforth has been trying to get her admitted to a very good home. . . ."

". . . I was very shocked to see Mariana," wrote Lizzie. "Eddy insisted that I should take the girls away for a month as it's been so long since I've had a holiday, so we all trundled off to Penmarric on the train. After a couple of days I thought I'd better face the current skeleton in the family cupboard, so I went over to Carnforth Hall to see Mariana. It was an extremely depressing experience. She herself is in a state of constant depression and looks simply terrible. In fact the whole visit home depressed me enormously. Mother is letting herself be victimized by that juvenile delinquent Jonas. I heard him threaten her the other day when he thought she was alone at the farm, and I stepped in and gave him a piece of my mind so that he scuttled off with his tail between his legs. I told Mother that the next time he tries to get money out of her she should call the police. It's ridiculous to be terrorized by your own grandson. . . . Isabella was well, I'm glad to say, although at times her attitude did strike me as being a trifle eccentric. I hardly think you need worry, I hasten to add, since her eccentricity is far from serious, but she asks the oddest people to dinner at Penmarric—one was a most intense young market gardener who declared his mission in life was to develop a new form of hydrangea—and she drives around very dangerously in that fast car of yours (and I'd like to know where she gets the petrol). Apparently these odd people are old friends, known to her parents, so no doubt they're all very respectable in their own way; besides, she says William always chaperones her. Charity describes it in a somewhat sourer way but I expect she's having the change of life and shouldn't be treated too seriously at the moment, poor woman. All in all, I was almost relieved to get back to Cambridge. . . ."

"YOUR WIFE IS RUNNING LOOSE," said the carefully printed anonymous letter, postmarked Penzance and written on the brand of stationery that William kept at his house. "ASK HER HOW MANY PASSES SHE HAS MADE AT YOUR BROTHER WILLIAM PARRISH AND HOW LONG HER DINNER GUEST FROM DEVON STAYED LAST WEEK. SHE IS WORSE THAN A BITCH ON HEAT."

"My darling Jan," wrote Isabella, bright as a spring morning. "We did so enjoy Lizzie's visit although she went green with jealousy at my black market petrol! We got on quite well. What a pity her two little girls are so plain, but perhaps they'll improve later. Absolutely *no* news here, darling—really, I feel I'm letting you down with so much newslessness—I'm *so* sorry I haven't been writing quite so often. That old bitch Charity is still looking daggers at me whenever we meet—I'm sure she thinks I have designs on William. Honestly! As if I could *look* at anything over fifty! My parents came down while Lizzie was here and brought Keith with them. I know I used to boast how marvelous it was that Keith and I were still on friendly terms in spite of everything, but to be absolutely honest, it *was* a bit embarrassing to see him again and I wrote to my parents afterward and told them I didn't want a second visit from Keith any time in the future. Poor Keith! He was classified unfit for service because of a punctured eardrum and the Government's making him grow vegetables instead of flowers, so he's miserable, apart from the fact that he has a curvaceous landgirl to help him. . . . Oh darling, when are you going to come home? I know one shouldn't write moaning letters but sometimes I lie awake at night and think that I just can't bear the separation any longer. . . ."

"Can you get compassionate leave," said the telegram from Cornwall. "Bad news concerning Mariana stop Took overdose sleeping pills stop Inquest Wednesday funeral Thursday please come if possible stop William."

[4]

I was at Tobruk at the time. It was 1942, and Wavell had been replaced by Auchinleck before Rommel had driven us out of Cyrenaica at the end of January. Our retreat, coming so soon after the catastrophic news of Singapore, had depressed me and the chance of a visit home, no matter how brief, at first seemed too miraculous ever to come to pass. But my request for compassionate leave was granted; Auchinleck was busy telling Churchill that his army was in no fit state to go on the offensive when Malta was out of action and supplies were pouring into Rommel, and matters for the moment were at a standstill.

All the Cornish flowers were beginning to bloom when I arrived home. Abroad bombs had blasted Lübeck, Rostock and Cologne and at home we were suffering the retaliation of the Baedecker raids, but at Penmarric the air was fresh with the scent of the early Cornish spring and the sea was an azure haze beneath a peaceful sky.

At first all I could see was Isabella. Beautiful, radiant Isabella, her long shimmering hair flying behind her as she ran down the platform into my arms, her huge green eyes bright with tears, her wide mouth soft and sweet and passionate against my own.

"Oh Jan, Jan, Jan . . ." She could hardly speak. She clung to me. "Oh Jan, how I've missed you—I've been so miserable and lost and alone . . ."

I knew then that she loved me and that she had not been unfaithful and that she had been waiting for me as longingly as I had been waiting for her.

"How long?" she said. "How long do we have?"

"Forty-eight hours."

"Eternity! Forty-eight whole hours! Oh Jan, we mustn't waste any of them, they're all so precious!"

But for most of the time we were apart. I had to go to Carnforth Hall, talk to Alice and Felicity, make funeral arrangements with Esmond, who had also been granted compassionate leave. There was the inquest to attend ("Suicide while the balance of mind was disturbed," pronounced the coroner sonorously) and the day after that was the funeral at Penzance. It was a cremation. "She hated burials," said Esmond. "I can remember her saying to me that she loathed church funerals so much that when she died she didn't want anyone to suffer what she had suffered when her relations had died. She would have wanted it to be this way."

He left directly after the funeral, a tall young man in uniform, his face tanned by a southern sun, his eyes sad and shadowed, and I did not see him again for many years.

Lizzie left on the same train. Her husband was ill and she did not want to linger in Cornwall. We were obliged to say a hurried distressing goodbye to each other, each of us wondering if it would have been less hard not to see each other at all instead of for those few tantalizing hours, and then she was gone and I was alone on the station platform as the train drew out of Penzance toward Marazion.

It was evening, and I had to leave on the early morning train, so time was very short. I decided I must make one last call on my mother to say goodbye, so I got back into the old ponytrap, which the petrol shortage had brought out of retirement, and drove out of Penzance and over the moors to Zillan.

She had stood the unpleasantness of Mariana's death well, but her movements were slower now and she was more bent when she walked. When I arrived I found her indulging in her favorite pastime, reading her journal and poring over events of long ago as if she could somehow travel backward in time and live once more in an age where no war was a world war and the Germans had only recently become more than a collection of Ruritanian princelings, poor relations of Queen Victoria.

"We were all so excited by the twentieth century," she said. "I remember it very well. Jeanne was born right at the end of 1899. What a pretty little girl she was! So sweet and manageable. Sometimes when she was a baby she reminded me of Stephen. How odd that I still remember Stephen so clearly when he's been dead more than fifty years! My first child . . . It was sad he died so young. But then came Marcus and everything was better again. Mariana arrived after that. Then Philip . . ."

"Do you ever hear from Helena?"

"Yes, she writes every month. She's doing a lot of Red Cross work—I'm sure she's most efficient. Dear Helena. I was very fond of her. I hope I shall see her again one day, but I don't suppose I shall. I feel very old and very tired and one can't expect to live forever."

"Now that's enough of that sort of talk, Mama! When this war's over and I come home for good I shall expect to see you alive and well, do you understand? And after that I shall expect you to be alive and well for my son's christening, whenever that will be. You can't die just yet! I won't have it."

She laughed. I relaxed with a smile. Presently she said, "Talking of grandchildren—"

"Yes, I was going to ask you about Jonas. Perhaps I ought to see him before I leave."

"No—no, you have so little time. Spend it with Isabella. I can handle Jonas, and if ever he gets too difficult I can always telephone William and ask for help."

"Lizzie said Jonas had been threatening you—"

"No, he only wants money and tries to justify himself by saying that it's rightfully his. The only threats he makes are foolish ones—threats that he'll go to the police and say you arranged the abortion for his mother and should be prosecuted as a criminal for your part in her death. Of course the police wouldn't believe him, but it would be unpleasant and—"

"But my God, Mama, that's blackmail!"

"No, dear, because I'm giving him the money because I feel sorry for him, not because I'm afraid of his silly little threats."

714

"But he'll think—"

"I don't care what he thinks. He's just a silly boy who's not old enough to know better."

"He's a dangerous young thug! Look, Mama, next time he comes here I want you to send for William as soon as you see him coming, is that clear? I don't want you to be involved in this any longer."

"Well . . ."

"Please, Mama! I insist."

"All right, darling. But—"

"Do you promise?"

"Yes, I suppose so. If you wish."

I made sure she meant what she said, and after that, still feeling angry at the thought of her paying money in response to Jonas's wild threats, I reluctantly took my leave of her and returned to Penmarric to spend the last precious hours of my freedom with Isabella.

The phone rang at eight. We had no butler now since Medlyn had retired to nurse his rheumatism, and I had dismissed the footmen at the beginning of the war as an economy, but we had an efficient head parlormaid who now answered the phone.

"It's your mother for you, sir," she said, putting her head around the drawing room door.

I thanked her and went out into the hall. I can remember thinking how much more convenient it would be, if less aristocratic, to have the telephone in the drawing room. Perhaps after the war . . .

I picked up the receiver. "Mama?"

"Jan-Yves, I'm keeping my promise to you. Jonas is outside. He's almost at the front door. Are you going to come over yourself, or can you telephone William for me?"

"I'll come myself," I said at once. "I'll take the car. Isabella has some petrol for emergencies fortunately, so it shouldn't be long before I reach you. I'm going to teach that little ruffian a lesson once and for all."

I hung up the receiver and moved quickly back across the hall to the drawing room. Isabella looked up nervously as I came back into the room. "What did your mother want?"

"Jonas is bothering her again. Look, my darling, I want to settle this Jonas business before I leave. I must go—I'm sorry, but I must. I've no alternative."

"Oh Jan!"

"I won't be long."

"But—"

"I'm sorry, my dear, but there's no choice. I have to go." I stooped to kiss her and tried to ignore the anger in her eyes. "Wait for me in the bedroom," I said. "I'll come straight upstairs to join you as soon as I get back." And leaving her still angry in the drawing room, I ran out to the converted section of the stables where we kept the car.

I drove fast. I thrust the car down the drive and out along the main road through St. Just. Soon I was swooping cross-country over the moors, and by the time I'd crossed the ridge into Zillan parish the sun had disappeared into a darkening sea and dusk was falling across that eerie landscape. Swinging off the road, I nosed the car down the lane which led to the farm.

For a moment I thought he must have already gone, but suddenly I saw his bicycle against the wall of the dairy and I knew he was still there. I halted the car in the yard, got out and walked swiftly into the kitchen.

He was there, sitting at the table where his father must have sat before him, lounging in a chair with his feet casually resting on the table's edge. I hardly recognized him, for I hadn't seen him for three years and there can be a world of difference between sixteen and thirteen. The solid chunkiness of childhood had vanished; he was still tough, but it was a slim, wiry toughness coupled with his usual hostile expression and sullen mouth. His hair, bright in childhood, was now a coarse brown and he wore it swept back without a parting in an uncouth style. He looked what he was, a working-class rebel with an unpromising future, and although I searched his face for some small trace of Rebecca I searched in vain.

"So it's you," he said, not getting up. "I wondered if you'd bother to see me while you were home. I suppose you wouldn't have done either if it hadn't been for the old girl."

Cornish mingled with Cockney in his voice, but both were dulled by the veneer of a grammar school education. It was an ugly accent.

"Leave us, would you, Mama?" I said casually, and she left without a word.

"All right, you young bastard," I said, suppressing my distaste as best as I could. "You've been causing trouble ever since you entered the world, so I'm not surprised you've been causing trouble while I've been away. I really did think that even you wouldn't stoop to victimizing your own grandmother, but I see I was sadly mistaken."

"She victimized me!" He stood up. He was taller than me by about two inches. His blue eyes sparkled with rage. "You've both victimized me! I should be living at Penmarric with as much money as I liked and going off to some posh school, and yet all I have is room and board with three bloody spinster cousins at Great-Uncle Jared's dirty old farmhouse, and no money except what I can lay my hands on and an education at the local grammar! You did me out of my inheritance, you and your—old mother! You worked on Uncle Philip and got him to change his will—"

"Face facts, my dear boy," I drawled, determined not to humiliate myself by losing my temper and doing anything foolish. He was too big to spank now, and if it came to a fight I was sure he was tough enough to give me an embarrassingly good match. "Face facts. My mother and I had nothing to do with Philip altering his will."

"Oh yes you did!" he shouted. "Simon Peter told me—"

"Simon Peter detests both me and my mother. You can hardly rely on him for an unbiased judgment."

"It's the truth!"

"It is not the truth," I said deliberately, stressing each syllable. "The truth is that your mother exasperated Philip so much that he lost patience both with her and with you and washed his hands of any idea of making you his heir. If it hadn't been for your mother—"

"Don't you dare talk to me of my mother!" He was trembling from head to toe. "I know what you did to her!"

"—and while we're on the subject of the truth, let me say that someone—Simon Peter, no doubt—has been telling you and Deborah a pack of lies. I had nothing to do with your mother's death, nothing at all."

"You killed her!"

"Nonsense!"

"You're nothing but a bloody murderer! I know how she died! I'm not a kid any more! She was going to have a baby—*your* baby—and you made her go to some bloody quack to get rid of it!"

"I did nothing of the kind. I was trying to persuade her to see a London gynecologist. Anyway, it wasn't my child."

"You liar!" shouted Jonas. "You liar! Every damned soul in Morvah parish knew how you did nothing but —— her whenever you came to our house! Every damned soul knew how she loved you and how badly you treated her! She didn't love anyone else but you! My mother was good and beautiful and she wouldn't just have slept with any man who asked her—"

Something in me snapped. Hot dangerous rage made my brain spin.

"My dear Jonas," I said, "it's obvious you have an idealized picture of your mother. In actual fact, she wasn't half so virtuous as you would like to believe she was. Quite apart from the fact that she chased after me just as much as I chased after her—she even picked me up on a street corner once when she wanted a little after-lunch diversion!—it's obvious she took more than a nominal interest in this last lodger who spent Christmas at Deveral Farm before she died. It's about time you realized that your mother—"

He moved so quickly that I was caught off balance. I saw the blow coming but although I tried to dodge it it still caught me on the jaw and flung me back with a jolt against the wall. The room tilted. I gasped, struggled for breath, but when I saw him closing in on me again my reflexes sprang to life in jerky self-defense.

He tried to hit me again but this time I was ready for him. I sidestepped the blow and caught him a clean upper-cut on the chin that sent him reeling backward so fast that he lost his balance and fell. His head struck the wooden table leg; he hit the floor with a crash and was still.

I stood there, staring at him, my chest heaving as I recovered my breath. The kitchen door opened. As I glanced over my shoulder I saw my mother peering into the room.

"Jan . . ."

"Just a minute, Mama."

"What happened?"

"He hit me and I hit him back. He'll be all right." I flicked the sweat off my forehead and walked over to Jonas, who was still lying on the floor. "All right," I said curtly to him, prodding him with my toe in case he was shamming. "You can get up now."

He did not move.

"Jonas!"

No answer.

I bent, turned him over, stared at him.

"Jan . . ."

"Keep back, Mama." I knelt, unfastened his collar and tried to find the heartbeat, but all I could hear was my own heart pumping the blood so fiercely to my head that my ears were ringing.

"Here," said my mother in a voice which shook. "Have this mirror. Put it in front of his mouth."

I did. There was nothing. No clouding, no misting, not even the most nebulous trace of moisture.

He was dead. Rebecca's son was dead. My own nephew was dead, and I—

I had struck the blow that killed him.

11

Fifty years later Matthew Paris was not at all sure what had happened, and could only hope that it was not true that John had murdered him. Arthur simply disappeared and rumours that he was dead began to circulate. . . . What [Philip Augustus] did do, as soon as he believed that Arthur was no longer alive, was to taunt John with his disappearance. . . .

—King John,
W. L. WARREN

[Arthur] was a sixteen-year-old knight, who had been captured in battle while attempting to sack the castle that sheltered his eighty-year-old grandmother. His death was untimely, but not wholly undeserved.

—The Devil's Brood,
ALFRED DUGGAN

[1]

"Oh my God," I said. I could say nothing else. I knelt there, staring down at him, my mind too numbed to know what to do. "Oh my God."

It was my mother, not I, who took charge of the situation then. Looking back long afterward, I find it amazing how well she kept her head after such an appalling shock, but she told me later that she did not allow the shock to catch up with her until the next day; after that she stayed in bed for a week and dragged herself up again only when the doctor threatened to take her to hospital for an examination. But now, a minute after the disaster, she was icily calm. I had always known my mother was a tough old woman; now she proved it to me. As I remained motionless on the floor beside Jonas's body, she found the brandy bottle and slopped the liquid clumsily into two glasses.

"Drink this, Jan-Yves."

We both drank. I stood up but my legs were so unsteady that I had to sit down.

"It wasn't your fault," said my mother. "You didn't mean to kill him, I know that. It was an accident."

But I was much too appalled to reply. Would Simon Peter believe it was an accident? If anyone knew that Jonas had apparently been blackmailing my mother and myself for my role in Rebecca's death, perhaps any story of an accident would be regarded with extreme suspicion.

"I'll say I was in the room," said my mother. "I'll say I saw it happen."

But she was a prejudiced party, a biased witness, a suspect who could have plotted the murder with me.

"If only I hadn't given him money!" said my mother. "He must have told someone that it looked as if you had something to hide where his mother's death was concerned—he wouldn't have kept quiet about the fact that I was giving him money! Yet I was only generous with him because he was my grandson, not because of those ridiculous threats. I wonder if anyone will believe that?"

After a long while I said, "I wonder if anyone knew he was coming here tonight."

"We should act on the assumption that someone did."

"I think we'll have to say . . ." I stopped.

My mother looked at me. "He came. I telephoned and asked you to come over because he had been annoying me with demands for money and making himself thoroughly unpleasant. He was a difficult boy, but he was my grandson and because I did want to help him I occasionally gave him money. We shall tell the whole truth, Jan-Yves, and nothing but the whole truth. Up to a certain point. Then no one can ever prove that what took place beyond that point was not exactly as we say it was."

"Yes," I said slowly. "Yes . . . He was rude and difficult, so I spoke severely to him and told him not to bother you again. We quarreled—yes, we even quarreled, and then—"

"And then," said my mother, "he told you to go to the devil and walked out of the house. We stayed here a long time discussing the incident but at last you left to return to Penmarric.

You left here at eleven o'clock. At nine o'clock—that's now—you telephoned your wife and told her that Jonas had just left but that I was upset and it might be a little while before you arrived home since you felt obligated to stay with me until I was better."

"Yes," I said again. "Yes, that was how it was." I poured us some more brandy and we thought a little longer.

"I'm glad you've got the car," said my mother. "That makes everything easier. But what can you do with the bicycle? Will it fit in the back?"

"I'll get rid of that, don't worry. . . . Where's Annie? Is she in bed?"

"Yes, she's always in bed by dusk. Never mind her. What are you going to do with the bicycle, Jan-Yves?"

"There's that wild road that goes all the way to Ding Dong mine—"

"Is the mine flooded?"

"I don't know. Yes, I see what you mean. If I could get to Sennen Garth . . . but I don't think I could ever carry either him or the bicycle all the way down to the cove."

"Why the cove?"

"The main adits come out on the beach. If I could get to the adits—"

"There's an old shaft near King Walloe, the shaft Philip used to go down when he was a boy. He said that once Sennen Garth was flooded you could look down the shaft and see the water far below."

"That's right. I know the shaft you mean—he pointed it out to me once. But if the mine is ever drained—no, how can it be? I shall own it for as long as I'm alive and after that it'll hardly matter. I'll see that the mine is never drained."

"No one will want to drain it," said my mother. "Draining is too expensive and there's not enough accessible tin left to justify the expense. The Cornish Tin Coast is finished. You're safe enough."

"Then if I can take the car down to Sennen Garth . . ."

We talked for a while longer, going over the story, making sure that nothing had been forgotten.

"You know," I said at last, "I'm inclined not to get rid of the bicycle. Anyone can stumble into an unfenced mine shaft in the dark, but nobody is going to ride into one full-tilt on a bicycle. If the bicycle disappears it may cause more suspicion than if it were found. Supposing I give the back tire a puncture and leave it by the wayside of the road to Morvah? The police may argue then that Jonas, walking cross-country to his cousins' farmhouse, encountered some mishap in the darkness."

"Would Jonas abandon his bicycle? Wouldn't he get off and push it?"

"He was tired and cross. Perhaps there was even someone in a car who stopped and offered him a lift."

"Yes, that's possible, I suppose."

"The point is that if they don't find the body they can't prove anything, and they'll never find the body."

"True."

"Do you have any gloves?"

"Yes . . . why?"

"I've read enough detective stories to know I mustn't touch the bicycle with my bare hands."

She went off to find an old pair of Philip's gloves and I walked outside to get some sacking which would serve as a shroud. By the time I returned she was waiting for me in the lighted doorway of the kitchen.

"Would it be more prudent to turn out the light?" she was saying. "I have the horrible feeling that at least a thousand people are watching us from the hillside in the darkness."

"Yes, turn it out."

"Wait—phone Isabella to say you've been delayed!"

"I'll get the body in the car first—and the bicycle in the boot."

We worked silently in the darkness. When the task was over at last I went back into the hall and picked up the receiver of the phone.

"St. Just two-one, please . . ." I waited, listening to the empty silence. "Hullo, may I speak to my wife? . . . Isabella? Darling, I'm sorry but we've had rather a scene with Jonas—he's gone now but my mother's upset, so I doubt if I'll be home for at least another hour. . . . Don't wait up for me, will you. . . . Sorry, darling. . . ."

My mother was right behind me as I replaced the receiver. "Was she cross?"

"Yes, I'm afraid she was." I felt cold and tired and drained of all energy and emotion.

"Poor child, I expect she grudges you spending time with me." She laid a hand on my arm. "Jan-Yves . . ."

I looked up. "Yes?"

"Don't tell her."

"I think I may have to. It doesn't matter—a wife can't give evidence against her husband."

"Don't tell *anyone*," said my mother. "*Anyone*." She sounded very fierce for an old woman over eighty. "Listen, Jan. You and I are the only people who know about this dreadful accident. I shall die soon, and after that you'll be the only one who knows. Keep it to yourself. You needn't feel guilt-ridden about it. You're innocent of murder. It was an accident, and I know that just as well as you do. Besides, he struck you first and you struck him in self-defense—any court of law would acquit you if we could only prove what happened, but we can't prove it, so we're behaving in this very practical but very dangerous way. Don't make it more dangerous than it already is! Don't tell a soul what's happened. Don't tell Lizzie or William, and whatever you do, don't tell Isabella. It's a fallacy to say there should be no secrets between husband and wife. Sometimes it's better to have secrets, and this is one of those times. She's too young, you see, and she hasn't seen much of the world although she likes to pretend she has. It would be too much for her, and no matter how much she loves you she might always half wonder if it really was an accident after all. You do understand, don't you?"

"Yes," I said painfully, "yes, I understand, but—oh God! When I get home tonight she'll be waiting, expecting me to make love to her—"

"Then make love to her," said my mother. "She mustn't suspect that anything is wrong."

"But if there's a child . . . I shall look at it and remember . . ."

"Oh no you won't!" said my mother, very acid-tongued suddenly. "Do you think that every time I look at you I remember how you were conceived forcibly, against my wishes, in that horrible hotel in Brighton? When you were first born, perhaps, but not now, not after all these years when you've been so dear to me for so long. . . . Time puts everything in perspective, Jan-Yves, please believe me. This incident is horrific to you now, but in five, ten, twenty years it'll be a mere memory which you can recall without distress. You must believe that! Because it's true."

I took her in my arms and held her for a long moment. Her withered old hand stroked the back of my neck, caressed my hair and was still.

"You must go."

"Mama—"

"No emotional farewells. That would be too much for both of us. I hope very much that I shall be alive when the war's over and you come home for good, but if I'm not, God bless you and never, never forget that you're an innocent man."

I had another shot of brandy before going out once more into the cool night air. It was a clouded night but every now and then the clouds would part and the moonlight would filter palely across the moors. It would be dark enough for secrecy yet light enough for me to see what I was doing.

I slid behind the wheel of the car.

"Goodbye, Mama."

"Goodbye, Jan-Yves."

I left her standing there, a fragile, bent old woman who stared after me as I drove off down the lane into the darkness.

I wondered if I would ever see her again.

[2]

I left the bicycle with its punctured tire by the wayside just within the boundary of Morvah parish and drove on downhill toward the north coast with Jonas's body wrapped in sacking on the back seat behind me. From Morvah I went through Pendeen to St. Just and outside St. Just I took the disused track to the Sennen Garth mine.

I had to walk the last part of the way and my progress was slow because the body seemed so heavy, but I found the shaft without difficulty and paused on the edge to get my breath. Moonlight filtered through the clouds again and cast an eerie light upon the ruins of the scarred cliffs I had known so well in the past. I felt as if I had wandered into an ancient civilization, as if I had taken a step sideways in time in my efforts to escape from the terrors of the present. I shuddered, stared at the sacking at my feet, and for one long despairing moment I closed my eyes in prayer.

I asked God to forgive me. I asked Him for a just punishment so that I wouldn't have to live for the rest of my life with such unendurable guilt. I asked Him for the chance to suffer so that I could expiate my guilt and feel better.

"To suffer," I said to God, "but not to die."

To die would have been unjust. I didn't want to die.

"Let me live," I said, trying not to think of the holocaust of war to which I was soon to return, and suddenly I was not pleading with God alone but also with that two-headed phantom that was justice and injustice, the monster which had mesmerized me all my life. "Give me justice," I said. "That's all I want. Give me justice. Whatever it is, give it to me."

I bent down over the body. I was trying not to think of Rebecca, of the past, yet I found myself asking her to forgive me, as if she were standing beside me and could hear every word I said. Tears streaked my face and my chest was hurting from the effort of stifling my sobs. Making an enormous effort, I dragged the body to the edge of the shaft and heaved it over into the blackness below.

After a seemingly interminable time there was a splash, then silence.

It was over.

When I got back to the car I sat in the driving seat for quarter of an hour while I tried to get a grip on myself. Sobs still shook me spasmodically, but eventually I controlled them and wiped my eyes with my handkerchief. Presently I struck a match and looked in the driving mirror to make sure I did not look as if I had been crying, but my eyes only seemed blacker than usual and bloodshot as if I were intolerably tired.

Leaning forward, I forced myself to switch on the engine and back the car down the track to a place where I could turn it around and drive back into the village. Now I had to face the hardest part of all. I had to soothe Isabella's anger, assure her that nothing was wrong and behave toward her exactly as any loving husband would behave during the last stage of a forty-eight-hour leave.

I was dreading it.

[3]

I left at dawn to catch the early train to London, and she came with me to the station. There was barely enough black market petrol left for the purpose, but we took the car and drove off alone.

"Poor Jan," she said, snuggling up to me as I steered the car over the cold, empty moorland road. "I know you're upset even though you try so hard to hide it. You mustn't worry because of last night being so brief—it was just so wonderful to lie afterward in your arms. . . . I really think there'll be a baby this time. My intuition says there will be. And when you next come home . . ."

But there was no baby. She wrote three weeks later, a sad short letter, and I wondered what she would have said if she had known how relieved her news made me feel. I wanted no living memory of those forty-eight hours of compassionate leave.

Such memories as I had were bad enough.

[4]

The letters began to arrive soon afterward.

"My darling Jan, would you believe it! It seems that Jonas has mysteriously disappeared . . ."

"My dear Jan, don't pass out to see a letter from your elderly semiliterate brother once again, but I thought I must just tell you that everyone is looking for Jonas . . ."

"My dearest Jan," wrote my mother blandly, "no doubt you have heard the news now that Jonas has disappeared. It really is very odd and I can't think what can have happened to him. They found his bicycle the day after he left us but there is no other sign of him at all. We're all afraid he's had some kind of mishap, but the police don't suspect foul play. A policeman, quite a nice man, came to see me this morning since we apparently were the last people to see the boy, but I'm afraid I couldn't help him much apart from telling him that Jonas stormed out of here in a rage and that you stayed with me for another couple of hours to cheer me up. Of course I had to go into a little family history to explain why you and Jonas quarreled, but the policeman was very kind and understanding, and there's no need for you to worry . . ."

". . . it's all very odd," wrote William. "The theory at the moment is that Jonas went cross-country and fell into an unfenced mine shaft, but I don't agree with that. For one thing Jonas was in Morvah parish when he abandoned his bicycle and if he did go cross-country to his cousins' farm I can't believe he would have had any trouble. Jonas knew Morvah parish like the back of his hand since he'd lived there all his life, and come to think of it, I doubt his course would have taken him past any old shafts. Do you suppose he accepted a lift from some fellow who was mad? I can't honestly swallow that either since Jonas was so tough that he would have probably knocked out even the maddest of mad murderers. What do you think?"

"My dear Jan-Yves," said a cold typewriter on the headed office notepaper of Holmes, Holmes, Trebarvah and Holmes. "I am sure you will have been informed by now of Jonas's disappearance. Mr. Vincent has asked me to write to assure you that everything possible is being done to trace him, and since the police have apparently satisfied themselves that there was no foul play we have engaged private detectives for a closer investigation. I am employing them at my expense since I think Jonas's disappearance is—shall we say—curious to say the least. The general opinion of the police is that he was in a temper when he left your mother's farm and when his bicycle developed a puncture he was so exasperated that he accepted a lift from the first car that came and ended up in Penzance to cool his heels. They then think he may have yielded to a common adolescent impulse and decided to run away from home. It was well-known that he was a moody, discontented and difficult boy.

"However, there are one or two aspects of the situation that I cannot but feel have a certain significance. The first is that I doubt if Jonas would have abandoned that bicycle, even temporarily. He had to earn the money to buy it and it was new and very precious to him. He would have pushed it to Morvah, not left it by the wayside. Secondly, your mother has been giving him money recently. I happen to know this, since he hasn't been pestering me for extra pocket money for some time, and when I asked him about it he admitted that his grandmother had felt reluctantly obliged to help him financially. His exact words were: 'She doesn't want to but she can't say no.' I made no comment on this at the time, but since your mother is not inclined to be generous toward that branch of the family at the best of times I thought it odd that she should choose to be generous to Jonas when she had no pressing reason to show any generosity at all. Finally, Jonas had recently learned the truth about his mother's death and had been trying to trace the 'doctor' who conducted the illegal operation. Of course I strongly advised him against this, since the police had already investigated the matter, but he was anxious to find the 'doctor,' and through the 'doctor' prove once and for all the identity of the man who had reduced Rebecca to the position of seeking illegal medical aid.

"Naturally you will want this mystery to be solved as much as I do. I trust, therefore, that we will be able to forgo our past animosity and join together in a common cause to discover how Jonas disappeared and why. Yours sincerely, Simon Peter."

"My dear Simon Peter," I wrote back, careful not to fall into any of his traps by deducing from his letter any more than he had actually written, "thank you for your letter and for hiring the private detectives to attempt to solve this puzzling and worrying mystery. I only wish I could offer constructive suggestions about the disappearance, but I don't think I can. I expect you have already heard from the police that Jonas left my mother's farm in a rage that night because I had told him in no uncertain terms not to bother her any more. He had been bullying her for money for some time on the grounds that he was morally entitled to a share of my father's fortune, and since she's old and frail and sentimental she's been giving in to his demands for no reason save that he's her grandson. He really is rather a young thug, isn't he? I notice you don't speak of him with any great sympathy, and was interested to hear that you too have been experiencing difficulties similar to my mother's where Jonas's financial situation is concerned.

"He did not mention to me that he was conducting a private search for the quack who killed his mother. Personally I think it's disgraceful that the police haven't managed to track down the culprit, but no doubt their files are still open on the subject. I'm surprised Jonas thought there was any mystery about who fathered the child. However, since the man was (as far as we know) nowhere near Cornwall at the time of Rebecca's death, he could hardly have been responsible for finding the abortionist for her. I forget his name, but no doubt Deborah would remember it. I think he was a schoolmaster from somewhere around London.

"Remember me to your wife. I hear the war is keeping you busy on army legal work, so I was surprised to see the Holmes, Holmes notepaper. I also hear you have a son now in addition to the two daughters, so perhaps the war isn't keeping you so busy as I had supposed! Yours sincerely, Jan-Yves. P.S. I see no reason why you should carry all the financial burden of hiring the private detectives, and I insist on paying half the bill. Please let me know what I owe you as soon as you have a statement of their fees."

His reply was slow in coming, but when it arrived it was satisfactory.

". . . so I've called the detectives off the case and left the matter in the hands of the Missing Persons Bureau," he wrote. "Thank you for offering to share my expenses, and, accepting the offer in the spirit in which it was made, I enclose a copy of the Detective Agency's bill. However, I would like you to know that I am not satisfied and that in my opinion there has been foul play. Whether anything further will ever be discovered remains to be seen, but I can tell you now that as far as I am concerned the matter will not be completely closed, and I am certain that you will join with me in regretting this unsatisfactory conclusion to a baffling and distressing affair.

"The army keeps me on the run from one court-martial to the next so that I have become something of an expert on military law. But when I last wrote I was home on leave and took the opportunity to call at the office and dictate a few semi-business letters. My son is called John Henry after my grandfather, and I have already put his name down for Harrow. My wife's brother always speaks well of the place, and I suppose one should continue to act as though there will be a Harrow—or indeed any English institution—alive thirteen years from now when it's time for John Henry to go to public school. Still, I confess it's most pleasing to have a son, and in fact it does inspire one with some degree of faith in the future. . . ."

"To hell with him!" I growled and tore the letter to shreds. Yet despite the fact that the letter left me with an unpleasant taste in my mouth I began to feel safer. Simon Peter suspected I had killed Jonas but we both knew he would never be able to prove it. Bearing that in mind, I could forgive him for that barbed last paragraph in which he had reminded me not only that he at least had a son to come after him but also that his son would end up as much a gentleman as any son of mine would be.

I began to long passionately for a son of my own. When I got back from the war . . .

But peace was far off. It was still only 1942 and I had another three years in which to try to remain alive.

[5]

On June the twentieth, 1942, Tobruk fell to the Germans.

Rommel's triumph was my disaster. I was one of the thirty-three thousand obliged to surrender to the enemy, and eventually after a series of journeys far too sordid to describe I arrived on the barbed-wire doorstep of an Italian prisoner-of-war camp. Why Italy I have no idea. The only reason I could think of was that it was nearer Tobruk than Germany and that the Italians were glad to accept English prisoners after their series of reverses in North Africa earlier in the war. However, so depressed was I by that time that I couldn't have given a damn whether I was in Italy, Germany or Timbuktu.

God, evidently in close collaboration with the two-headed monster, had cunningly devised for me a much more interesting punishment than mere death in order to avenge Jonas's accidental departure from the world. I was an active man who hated enforced idleness and appreciated an active sex life. To have no woman for three years and to be so bored with inactivity that I nearly went out of my mind was the perfect punishment for me.

I was there until the end of the war.

My intense restlessness channeled me unawares into leadership among the prisoners. I organized concerts, poetry recitals, gymnastic displays and a dozen other activities to keep everyone including myself occupied. For someone who had displayed nothing but rebellious non-conformity at school, I developed the most astonishing community zeal.

"Yer nuffin but a ruddy tornado," said our tame Cockney wit. "On the go all the ruddy time with all those smart ideas. Major Smart-aleck, you are, not Major Castallack. You was named wrong at yer christening."

I did not try to escape. I helped four men get away, including my best friend, and was just preparing to join them later when they were all brought back and shot. After that I stuck to my concerts and gymnastics.

I began to dream more, dreaming during the day as well as at night. When I was asleep I dreamed of Cornwall and Penmarric. I dreamed of Isabella. And I dreamed of other times long ago, of my old nanny slipping teaspoonfuls of gin into her tea and reading me stories about hobgoblins before I went to sleep. I dreamed of my father saying, "Nanny's gone away. You're going to have a new nanny now and share the nursery with Elizabeth." And there was Lizzie, plump and black-haired, with a lollipop in her hand. I saw Mariana too, radiantly beautiful, the belle of the ball, coming down the great staircase at Penmarric, and Marcus was behind her, gay, charming Marcus, so effortlessly aristocratic, and suddenly Jeanne was clutching me and saying, "Oh, Mariana's so pretty! If only I could be as pretty as that! What a lovely ball this is!" But then the ball merged into the Penmarric stables and Adrian was muttering unhappily to William, "Do you think everyone has guessed by now who we are?" And suddenly my father appeared, his hand on Adrian's shoulder, until the scene was changing and Philip was shouting something about the Sennen Garth mine and the next moment I was down at the two-hundred-and-forty-fathom level and Trevose was saying with a laugh, "One bloody glass of cider wouldn't turn an elephant bloody pink!" And after that came the funerals, so many funerals, and deaths, so many deaths, and death wanted me too but I was alive and I was going to stay alive, and I was sane and I was going to stay sane because Isabella was waiting for me, and one day I would be coming home.

I dreamt I was home, running up the long twisting drive of Penmarric, and the rhododendrons were in bloom. Isabella was waiting at the porch and she was wearing a long white wedding gown and she was smiling at me as I ran toward her. So I ran and ran and ran, and I could smell fresh-mown grass and the salt wind from the sea, and the sunshine was bright and warm, and at last I reached Isabella and she was a mere waxen image and when I pushed my way past her into the hall, the house was dusty and deserted and the roof had fallen in.

"Isabella!" I shouted. "Isabella!"

I was sweating, but when I opened my eyes Penmarric vanished and I found myself in my hard prison bunk.

"For Christ's sake!" complained someone from close at hand.

"Shhh. It's only Major Smart-aleck reciting the Queens of Spain. Nothing to get excited about. Happens every night."

I fell asleep again. I was dreaming of Simon Peter Roslyn now, Simon Peter in a chauffeur-driven Rolls-Royce while I stood by the roadside and took off my hat and bowed as he passed by, and as I returned to my plow I was thinking that nothing mattered, not even Penmarric crumbling into ruins, because I had Isabella and Isabella loved me and Isabella would be waiting for me when I came home . . .

I was at a station, a big station, Waterloo, I think, and I was coming home at last and there were huge crowds everywhere so that it was difficult to see her. When I did see her at last she had her back to me and I thought how odd it was that she should have her back to me when she should have been searching for me as eagerly as I had been searching for her. I ran the whole length of the platform, in and out among all the people, and when at last I reached her I saw she wasn't Isabella at all but a strange woman I had never seen before. So I pushed my way through the crowds, and as I fought my way through the maze of people I began to shout her name.

"Isabella! Isabella! Isabella!"

"Shut up, Johnny, there's a good chap. You're giving us all insomnia."

"Chrissakes—"

"Recital's lasting a long time tonight. More value for money."

Isabella was waiting for me. Isabella would be there when I came home. All I had to do was stay alive. All I had to do was to stay alive and stay sane because Isabella was waiting for me and one day I would be going home.

I dreamt of the purple heather and green bracken and gray walls of Chûn Castle, and I would smell the wild roses around my mother's front door, and the banks of the narrow country roads would be gay with pimpernels and harebells and buttercups, and the garden of Penmarric would be a blaze of exotic colors. Isabella was there, in the garden of Penmarric, and Isabella was smiling and walking toward me and Isabella was saying, "I'm so sorry, Jan, but you see I thought you wouldn't come home. I was so *bored*, Jan, and so stifled, and—well, I'm afraid I just didn't want to wait any longer. I know you'll understand. You're so understanding, darling, and I'm sure you've guessed by now that I really loved Keith all the time. It was your fault for coming along and sweeping me off my feet when I was too young to know better. But don't blame yourself, darling, don't reproach yourself for the way things have turned out. I forgive you utterly. In fact I pray for you every day and hope that when you have a free moment you'll come and see us in Devon."

But of course that was all a dream, and I knew it was a dream as soon as I opened my eyes, because Isabella loved me and she was waiting for me, and one day—

And one day, in 1945, I went home.

[6]

I was at a station, a big station, Waterloo. It was filled with people. Oddly enough I half wished I was back in my dreams but this time I wasn't dreaming. It was reality.

I was very frightened.

I got out of the train, stepped onto the platform, tried to see my way through the milling throngs. Husbands and wives were being reunited all around me. Everyone was shouting and laughing and crying all at once. The air was heavy with emotional excitement, and when an engine suddenly let off steam with a roar no one seemed to notice.

I walked down the platform. I was in uniform and carrying my bags. It was possible I might look just like any other soldier from a distance, so I told myself it was up to me to try to see her, not for her to try to see me. I reached the barrier, went through to the gigantic hall beyond but there was no sign of her.

Perhaps she hadn't got my telegram. I lingered by the barrier straining my eyes for a glimpse of her, but all I saw were faceless people, men and women flying into each other's arms while I waited stricken and alone by the station platform.

So there was no justice after all, no two-headed monster capable of a benign smile, no God who cared. I had deceived myself fancifully for years. All that existed was chance, blind, haphazard chance spinning meaninglessly in a dark vacuum, for Isabella hadn't come to meet me, Isabella didn't care any more and Isabella was lost to me for the rest of my life.

My eyes began to fill with foolish unwanted tears of grief.

I closed my eyes for a second to blot the pain from my mind, but when I opened them again she was there, smiling, coming toward me with that light airy grace I had seen so clearly in my dreams, but this was a different Isabella, a changed Isabella, an Isabella who was at once both familiar yet terrifyingly strange.

I caught my breath, unable to move or speak.

I saw a woman, twenty-five years old, very smart, with ash-blond hair beautifully dressed beneath an enormous sophisticated hat, a slender, dazzling woman with great green eyes brilliant with tears and luscious, slightly parted red lips.

"Jan!" she cried. "Oh Jan, I couldn't find you—it was horrible —worse than my worst nightmares—"

And then all nightmares ended for both of us as she ran forward headlong into my arms.

ATLANTIC OCEAN

CORNWALL

Scale 0   1   2   3   Miles

OCEAN

Gurnard's He

ATLANTIC

Morvah •

*Polzilla
House* •

Zillan ⊚

Pendeen •

Chûn Castle •

⊙ *Deveral
Farm*

⊙ *Roslyn Farm*

Carn Kenidjack

• Botallack

Cape
Cornwall

⚒ Levant Mine

St. Just

*Sennen Garth
Mine* ⚒

*King Walloe
Mine* ⚒

⊚ PENMARRIC

To Land's End

Real place names thus: St. Ives

Fictitious place names thus: *Zillan*